THE
SECRET LIFE
OF DEBBIE G.

For BNPMRS

First published in India in 2020 by HarperCollins Children's Books
An imprint of HarperCollins *Publishers*
A-75, Sector 57, Noida, Uttar Pradesh 201301, India
www.harpercollins.co.in

2 4 6 8 10 9 7 5 3 1
Text © Vibha Batra
Illustrations © HarperCollins *Publishers* India 2020

P-ISBN: 978-93-5357-465-9
E-ISBN: 978-93-5357-941-8

Vibha Batra asserts the moral right
to be identified as the author of this work.

Typeset in 11pt/12 by Kalyani Ganapathy

Printed and bound at Replika Press Pvt. Ltd.

THE SECRET LIFE OF DEBBIE G.

Vibha Batra and Kalyani Ganapathy

HarperCollins*Children's Books*

1

...And I'm back! Sorry, got disconnected. Power cut. Third since morning. Would you believe it? I mean, I literally had a stroke when I checked my phone. My battery was down to 11%! Can't tell you how powerless that made me feel. Okie, before you can say lolzapalooza. Hashtag NoMoreLameJokes. So, where were we? Yeah, the backstory.

So you know the movie *I Know What You Did Last Summer*? Well, everyone knows what I did last summer. And the summer before that. And the summer before that...actually, make that every damn summer of my life.

Most folk in my class explored different cultures, discovered exotic cuisines, made new friends and of course, rubbed our noses into it on Facebook and Instagram.

Me? I traded the blistering Delhi loo winds by taking refuge in Chennai's sweltering climes. Way to beat the heat.

Yeah, so, there I was in Chennai, visiting my grandparents, doing the same things I did year after year. I'm pre–tty sure I did stuff that didn't involve food, but I can't seem to remember any of it.

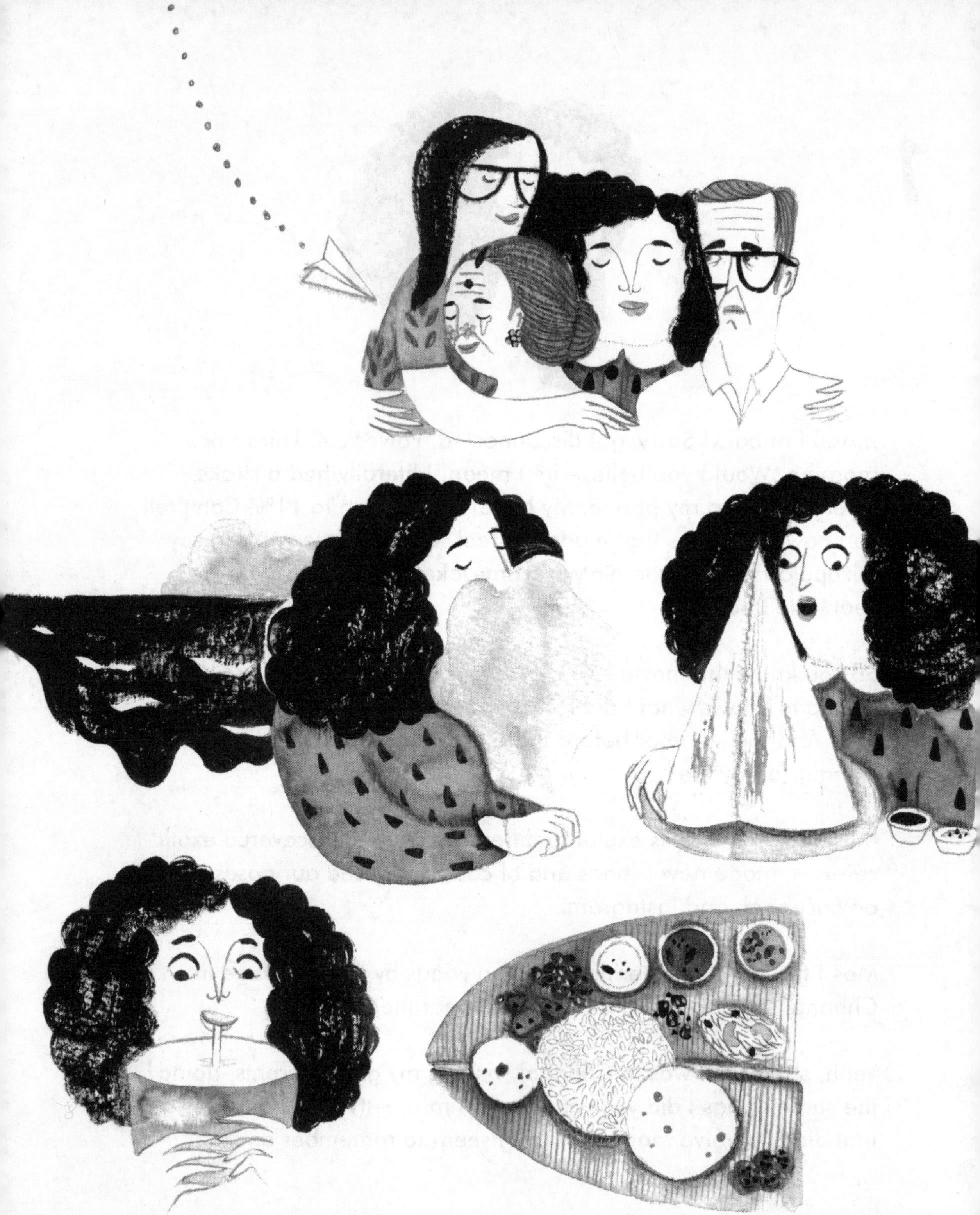

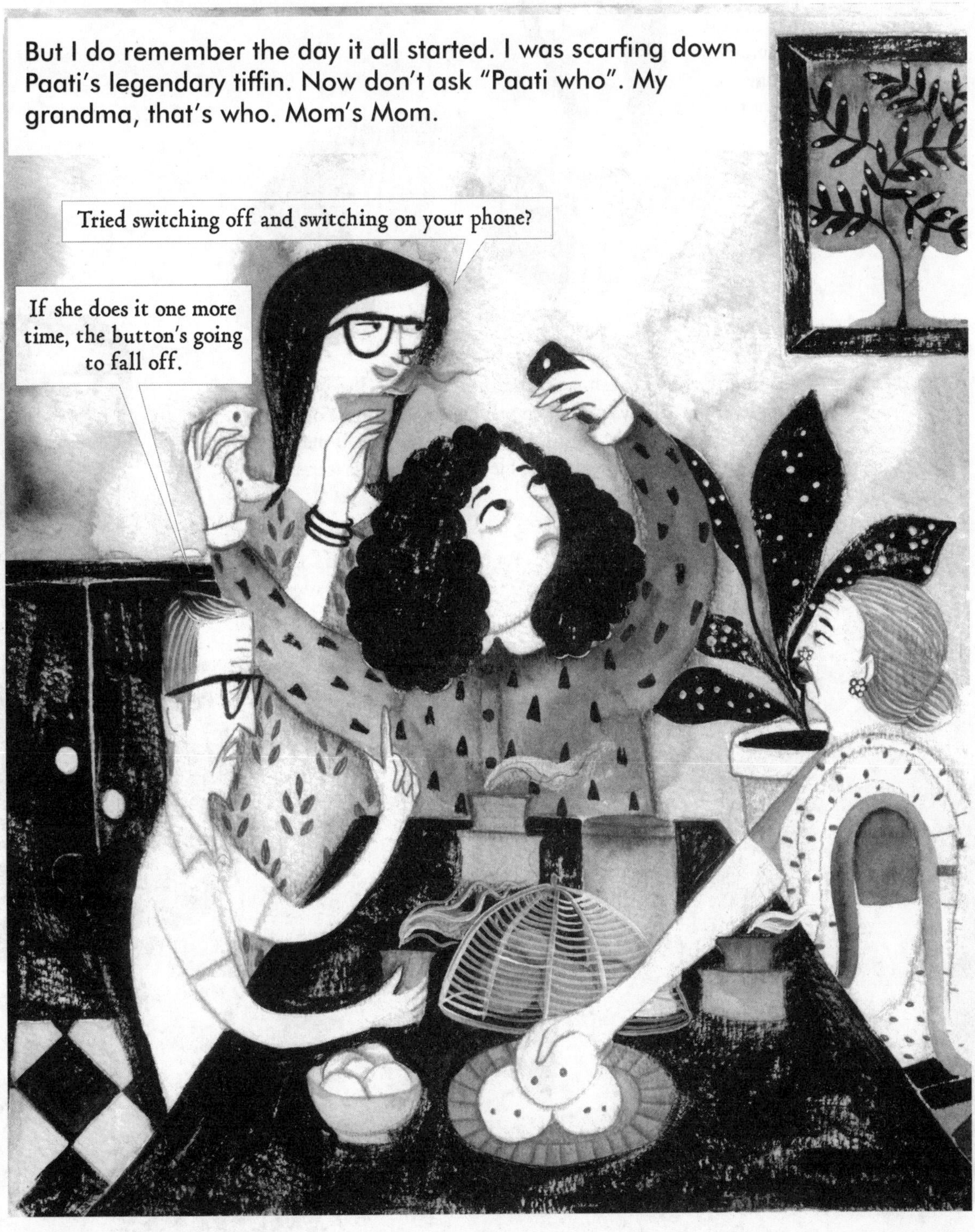
But I do remember the day it all started. I was scarfing down Paati's legendary tiffin. Now don't ask "Paati who". My grandma, that's who. Mom's Mom.
Tried switching off and switching on your phone?
If she does it one more time, the button's going to fall off.

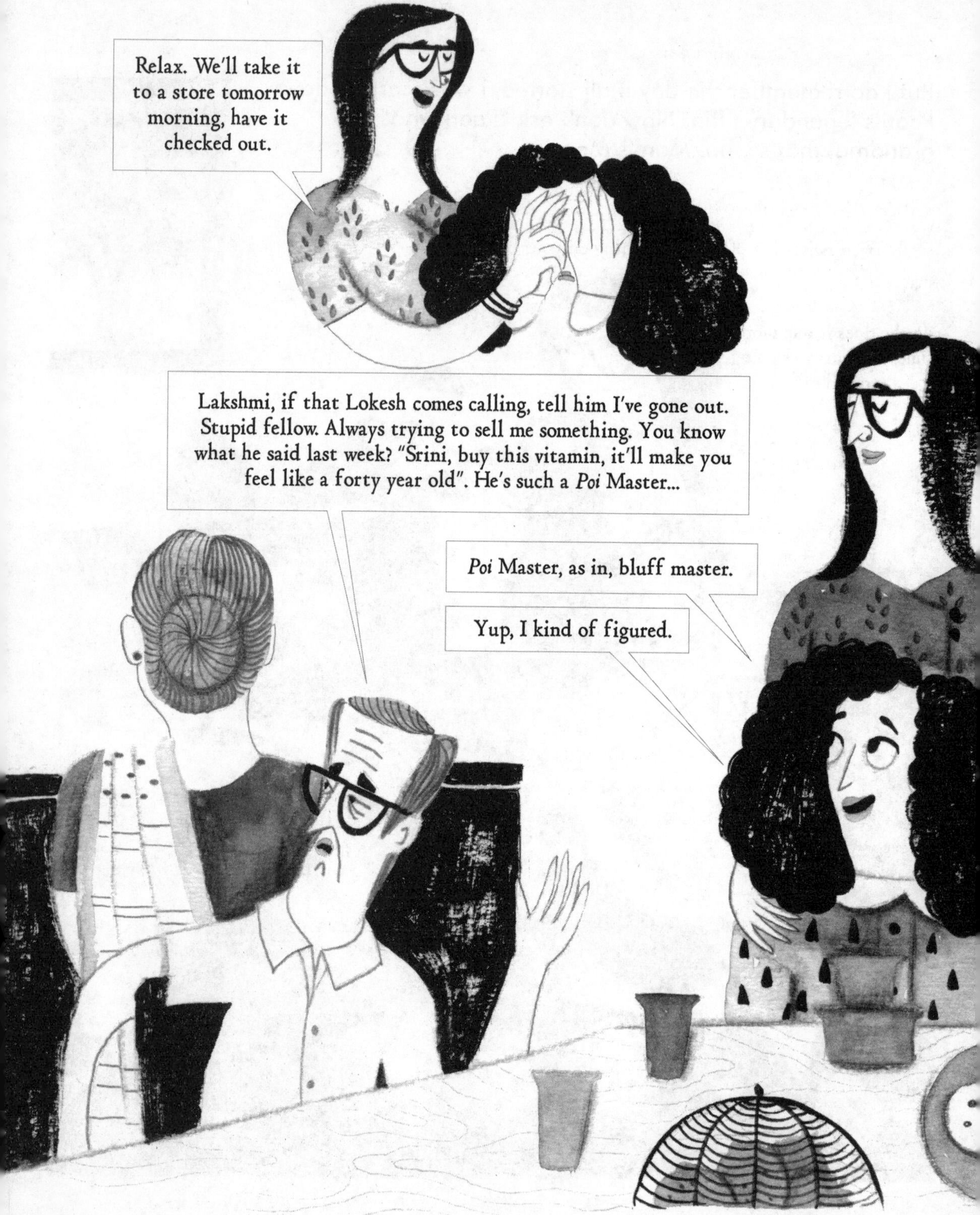
Relax. We'll take it to a store tomorrow morning, have it checked out.
Lakshmi, if that Lokesh comes calling, tell him I've gone out. Stupid fellow. Always trying to sell me something. You know what he said last week? "Srini, buy this vitamin, it'll make you feel like a forty year old". He's such a *Poi* Master...
Poi Master, as in, bluff master.
Yup, I kind of figured.

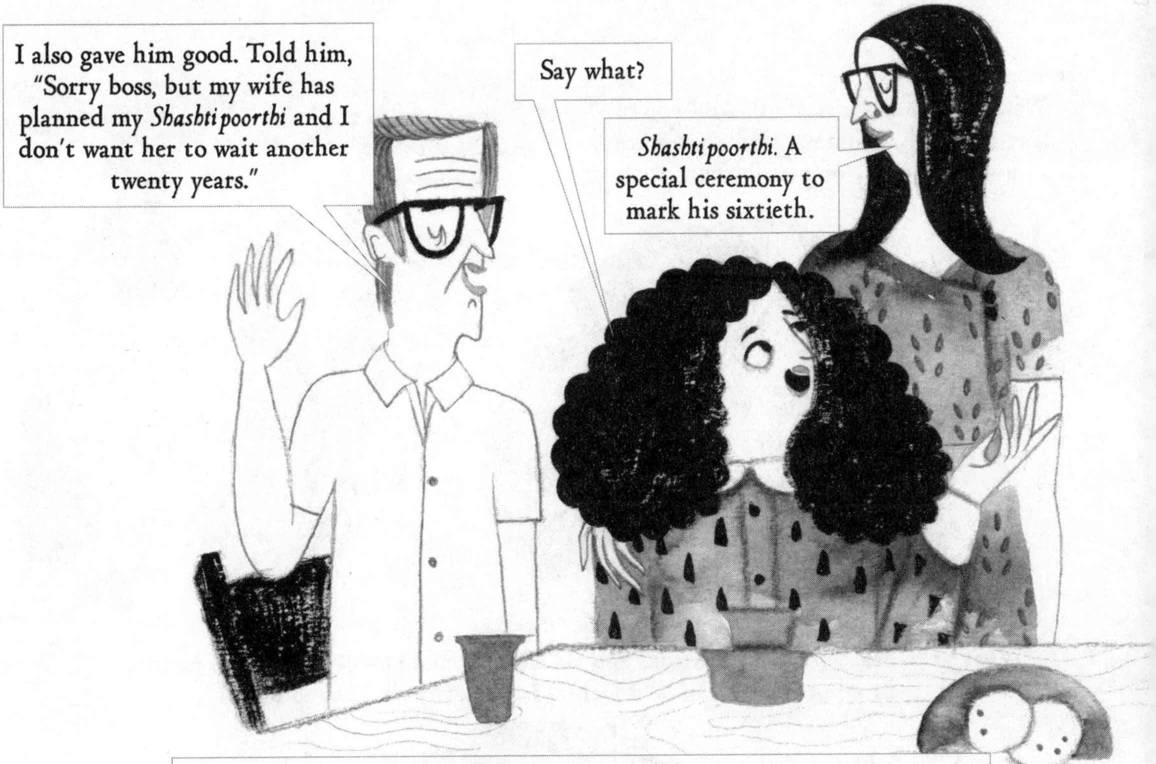
I also gave him good. Told him, "Sorry boss, but my wife has planned my *Shashti poorthi* and I don't want her to wait another twenty years."
Say what?
Shashti poorthi. A special ceremony to mark his sixtieth.

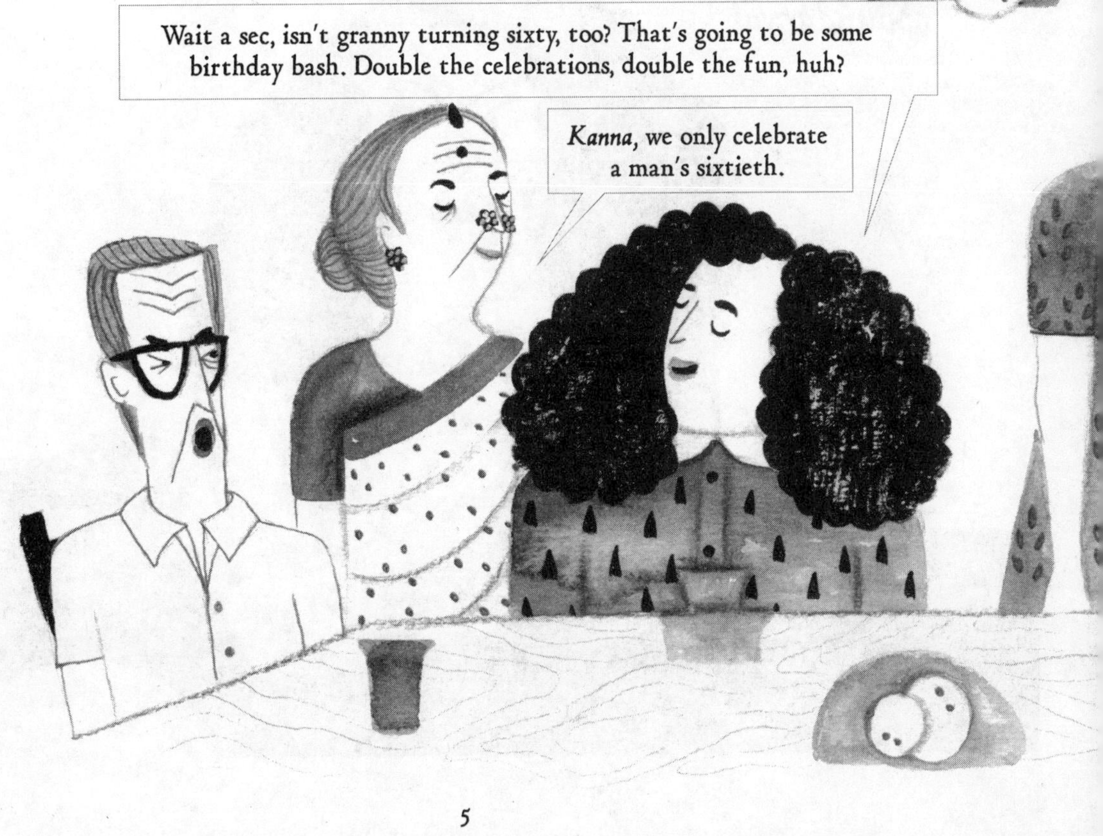
Wait a sec, isn't granny turning sixty, too? That's going to be some birthday bash. Double the celebrations, double the fun, huh?
Kanna, we only celebrate a man's sixtieth.

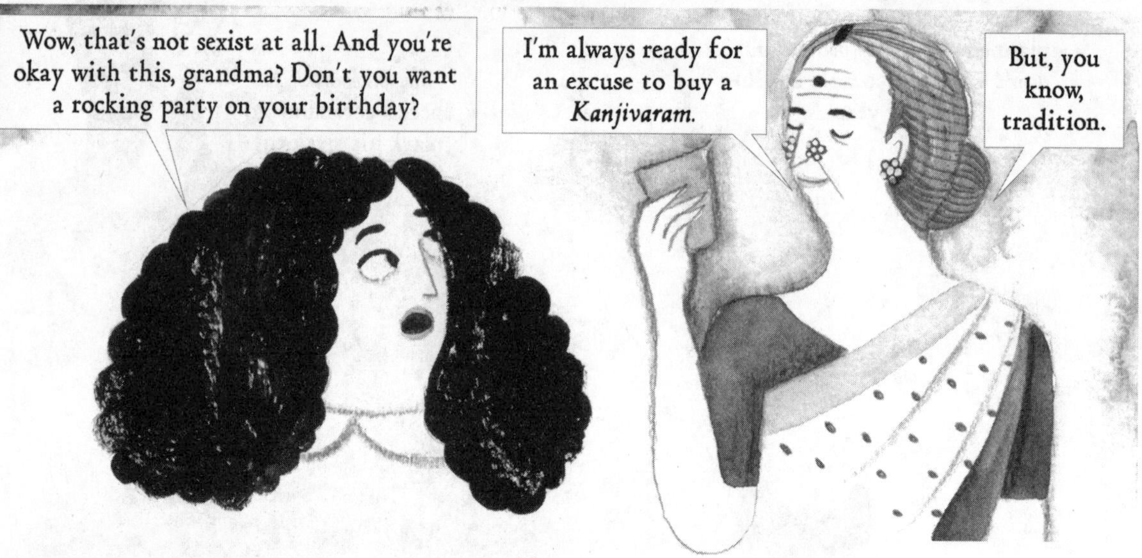
Wow, that's not sexist at all. And you're okay with this, grandma? Don't you want a rocking party on your birthday?
I'm always ready for an excuse to buy a *Kanjivaram*.
But, you know, tradition.

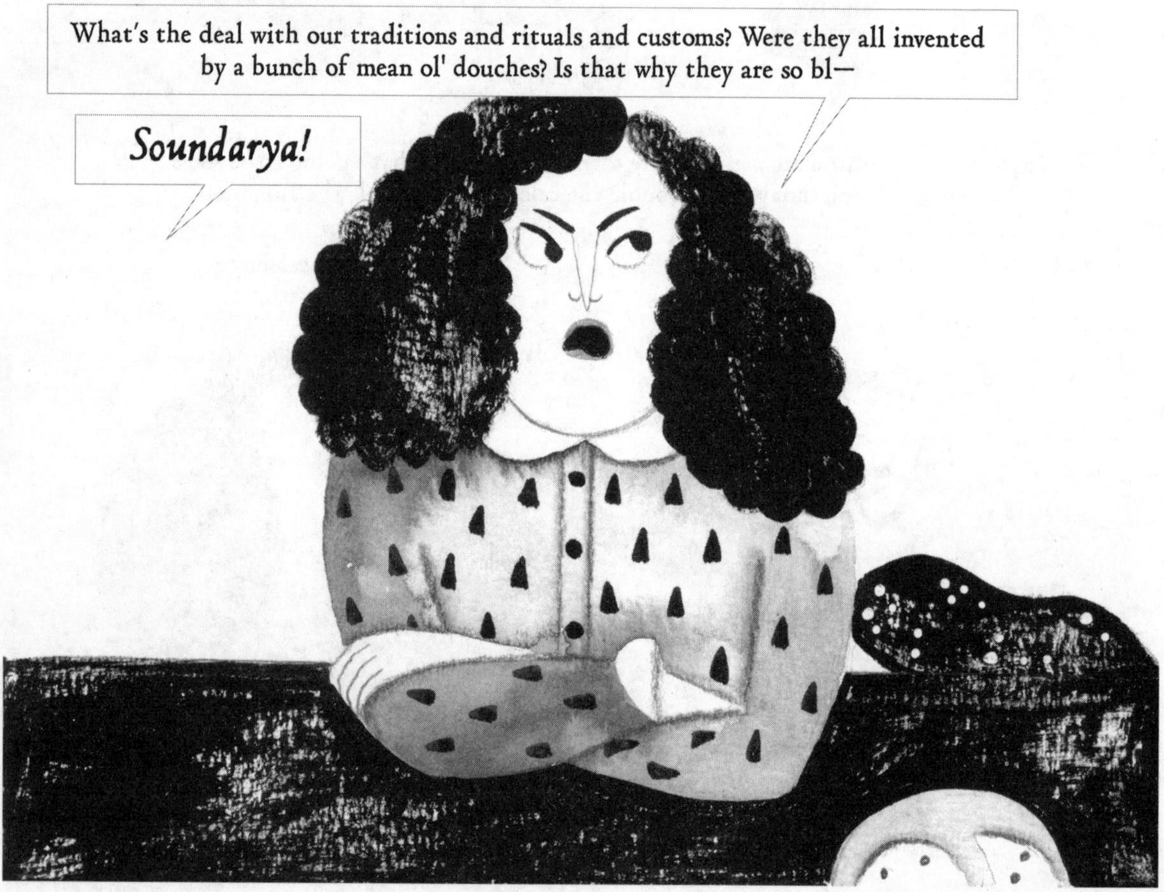
What's the deal with our traditions and rituals and customs? Were they all invented by a bunch of mean ol' douches? Is that why they are so bl—
Soundarya!

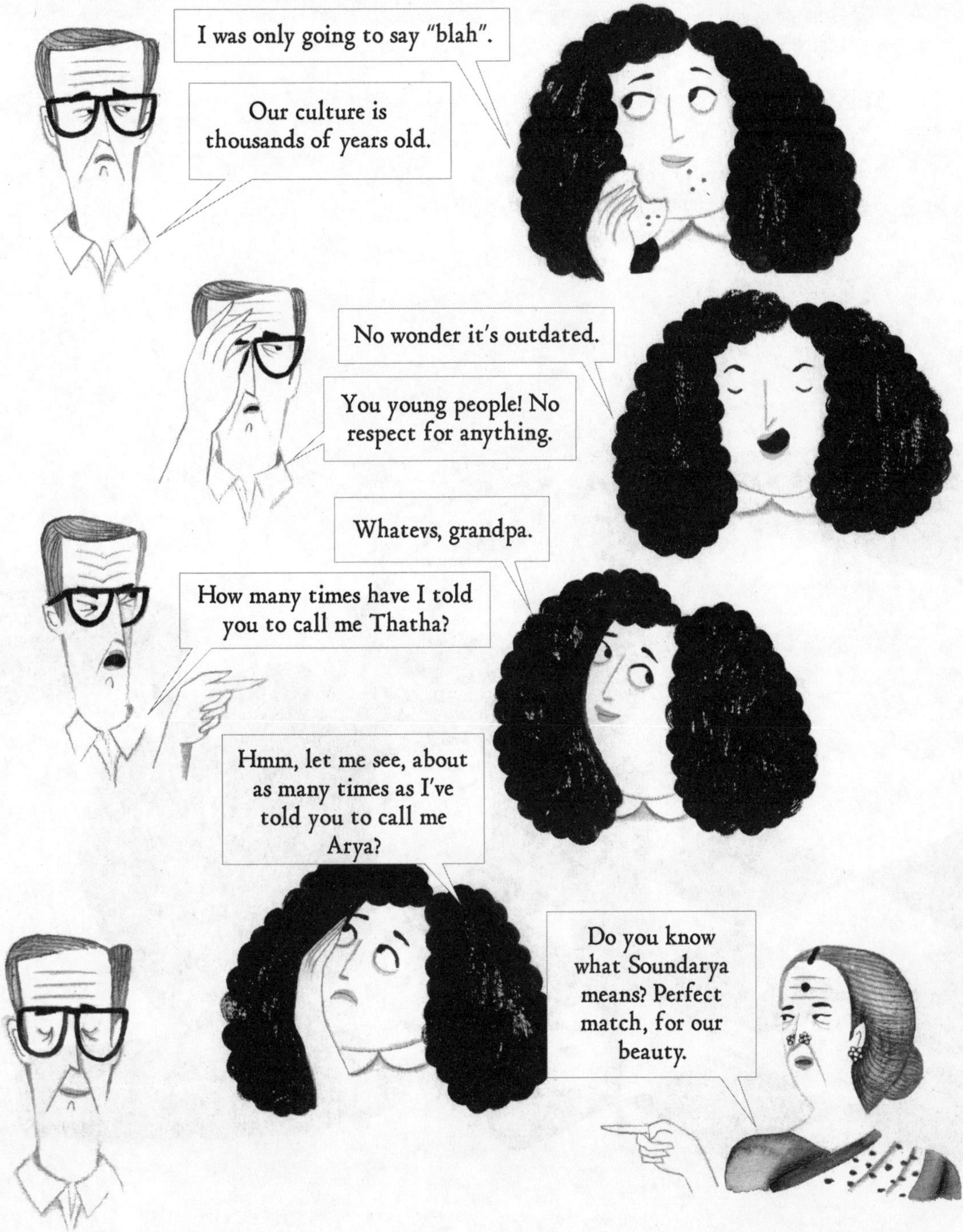
I was only going to say "blah".
Our culture is thousands of years old.
No wonder it's outdated.
You young people! No respect for anything.
Whatevs, grandpa.
How many times have I told you to call me Thatha?
Hmm, let me see, about as many times as I've told you to call me Arya?
Do you know what Soundarya means? Perfect match, for our beauty.

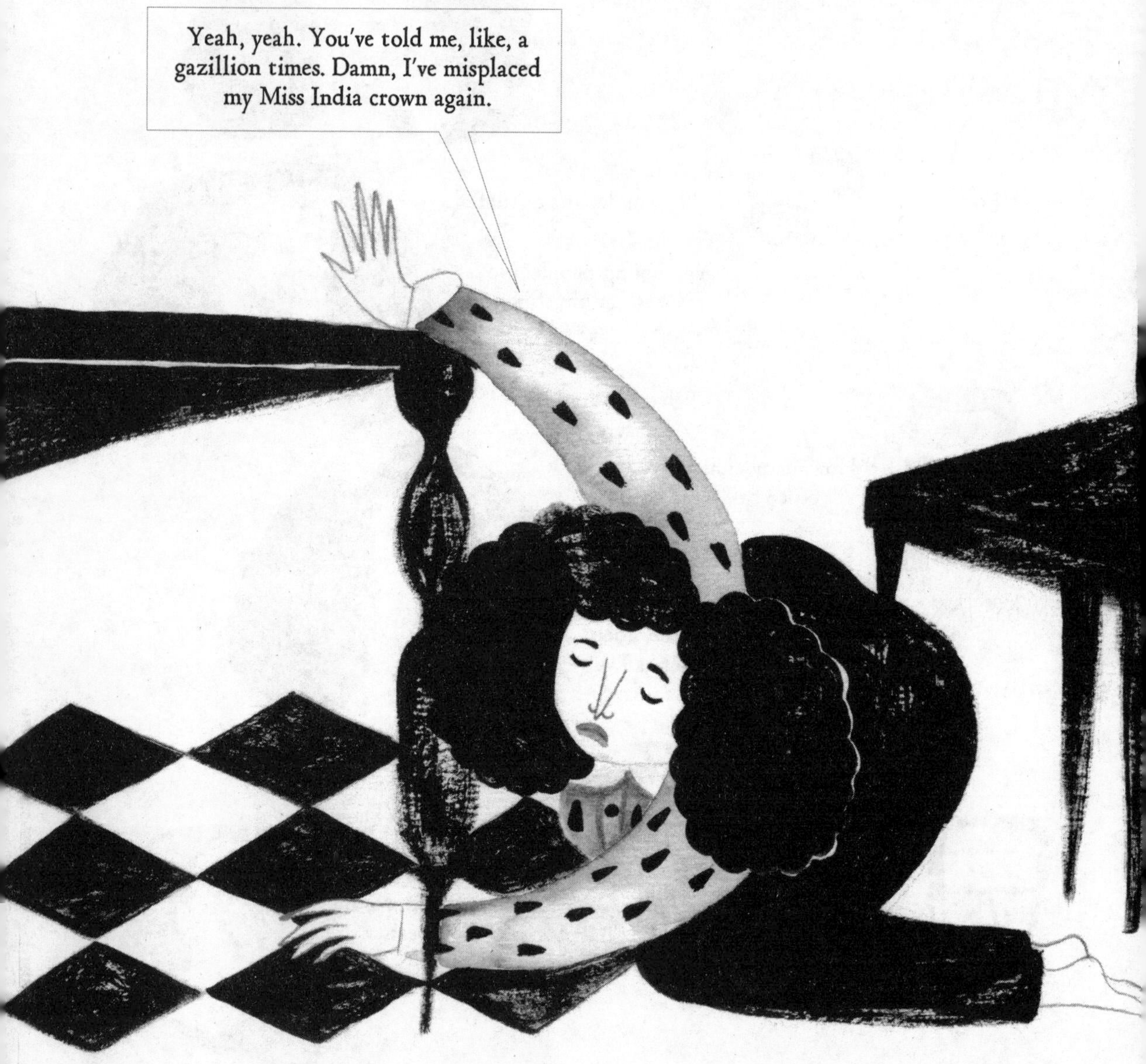
Yeah, yeah. You've told me, like, a gazillion times. Damn, I've misplaced my Miss India crown again.

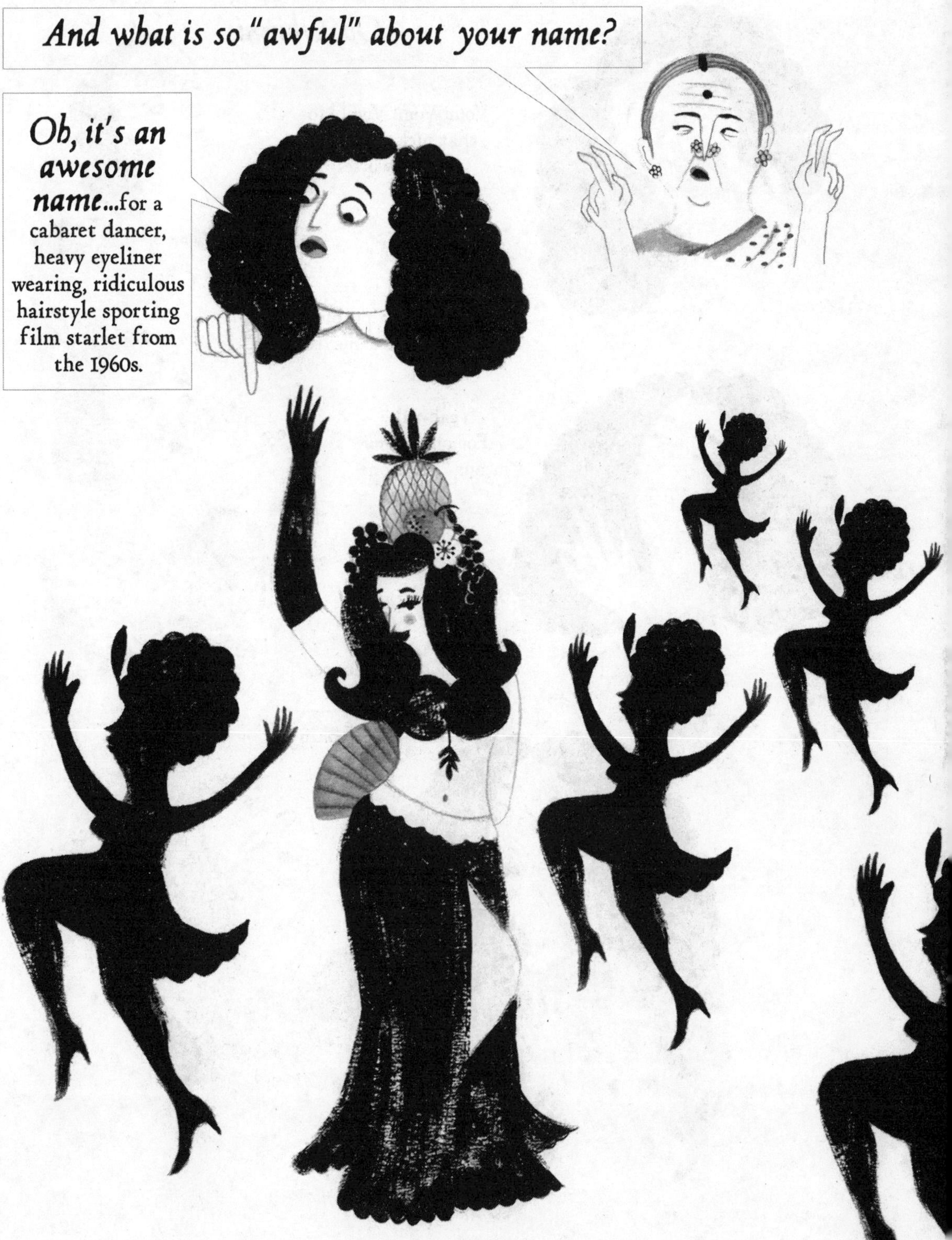
And what is so "awful" about your name?
Oh, it's an awesome name...for a cabaret dancer, heavy eyeliner wearing, ridiculous hairstyle sporting film starlet from the 1960s.

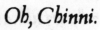

Oh, Chinni.

Vom! Vom! Vom! Not that nickname! It's waaay worse.

Now you've a problem with your pet name, too?

Yeah-aah! For one, *chinni* means "little one".

So?

I mean, just look at me.

I *am* looking at you.

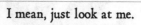

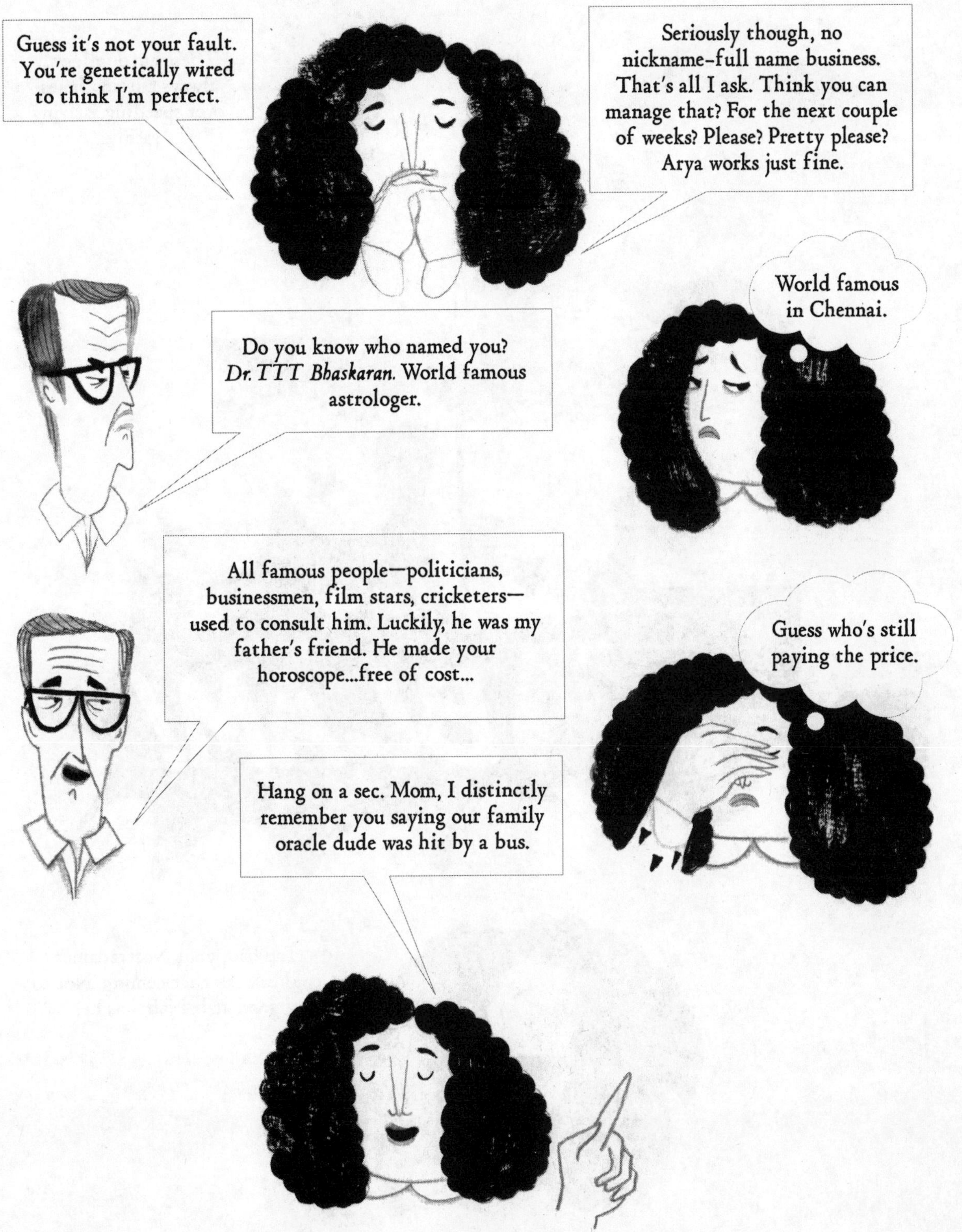

Guess it's not your fault. You're genetically wired to think I'm perfect.
Seriously though, no nickname-full name business. That's all I ask. Think you can manage that? For the next couple of weeks? Please? Pretty please? Arya works just fine.
Do you know who named you? *Dr. TTT Bhaskaran.* World famous astrologer.
World famous in Chennai.
All famous people—politicians, businessmen, film stars, cricketers—used to consult him. Luckily, he was my father's friend. He made your horoscope...free of cost...
Guess who's still paying the price.
Hang on a sec. Mom, I distinctly remember you saying our family oracle dude was hit by a bus.

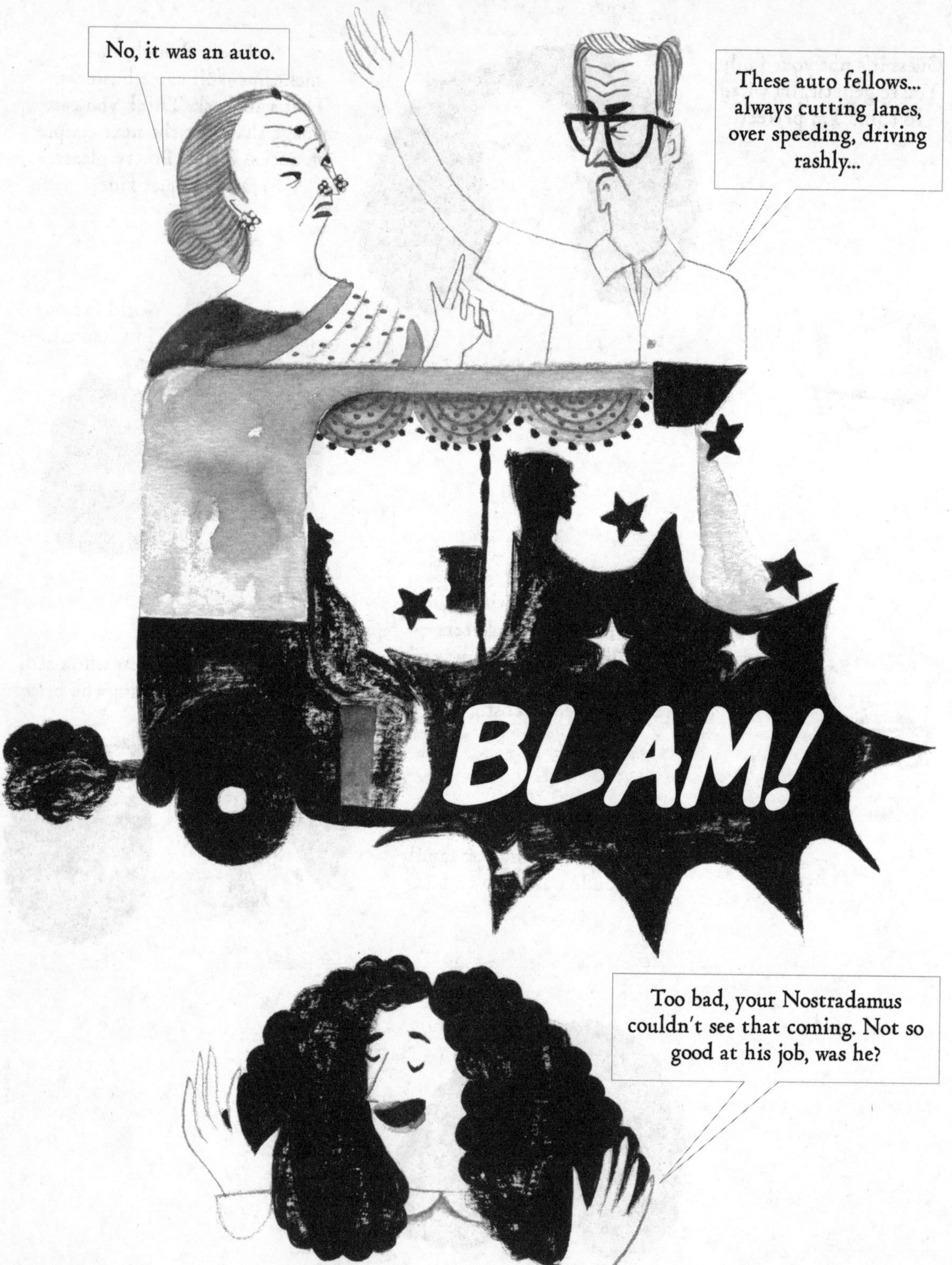
No, it was an auto.
These auto fellows... always cutting lanes, over speeding, driving rashly...
BLAM!
Too bad, your Nostradamus couldn't see that coming. Not so good at his job, was he?

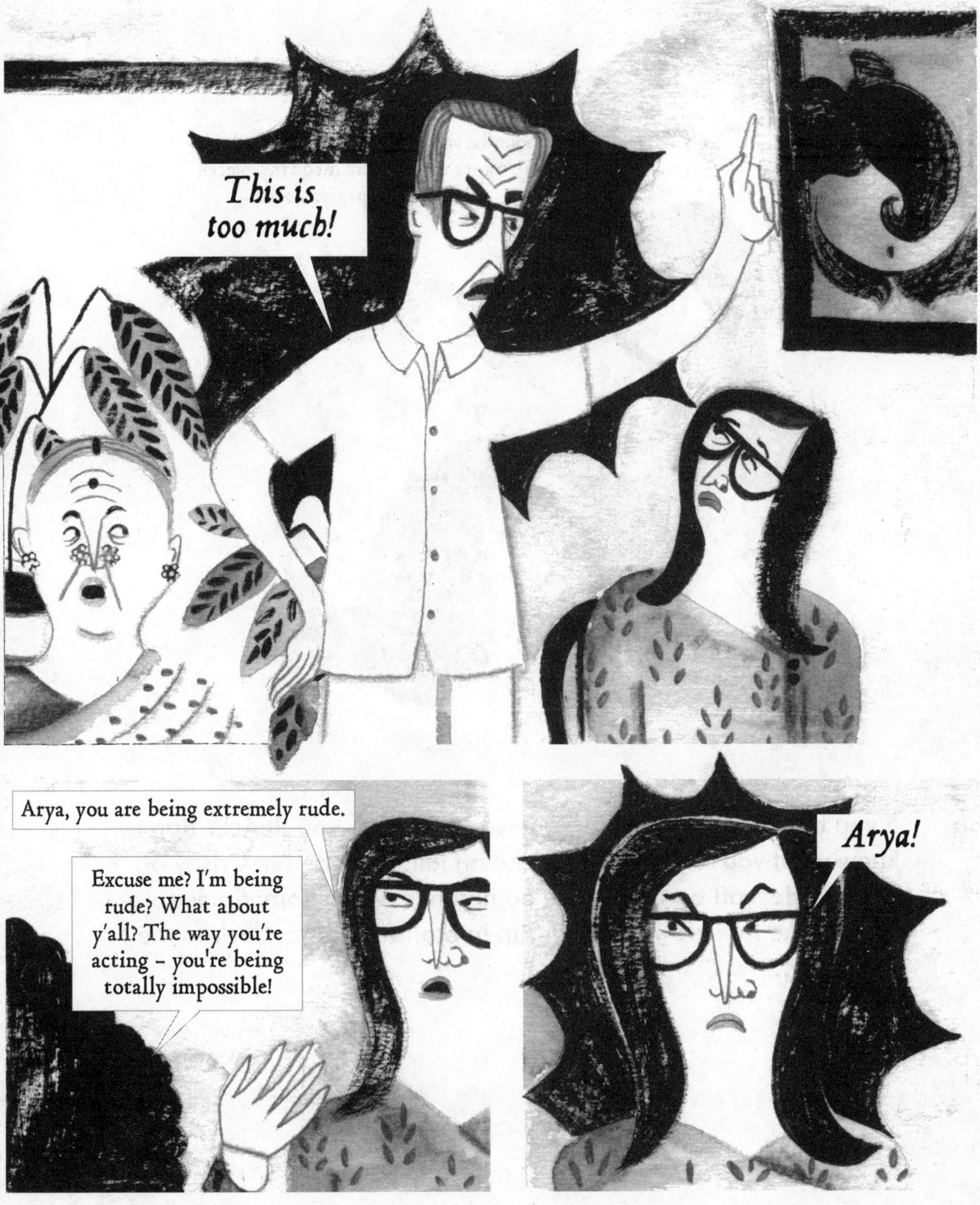
This is too much!
Arya, you are being extremely rude.
Excuse me? I'm being rude? What about y'all? The way you're acting – you're being totally impossible!
Arya!

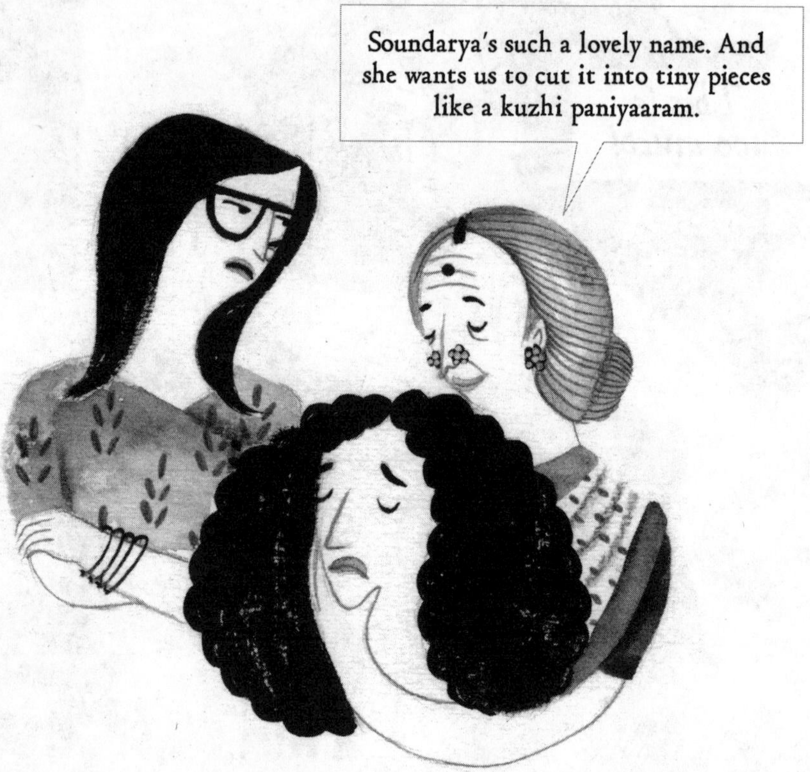
Soundarya's such a lovely name. And she wants us to cut it into tiny pieces like a kuzhi paniyaaram.

If you haven't tasted a kuzhi paniyaaram, god, you REALLY don't know what you're missing. It's like an idli. Only better. Crispy on the outside, soft on the inside. Sometimes sweet, sometimes spicy. Kind of like me. Now, before I slip into a food coma, back to the backstory...

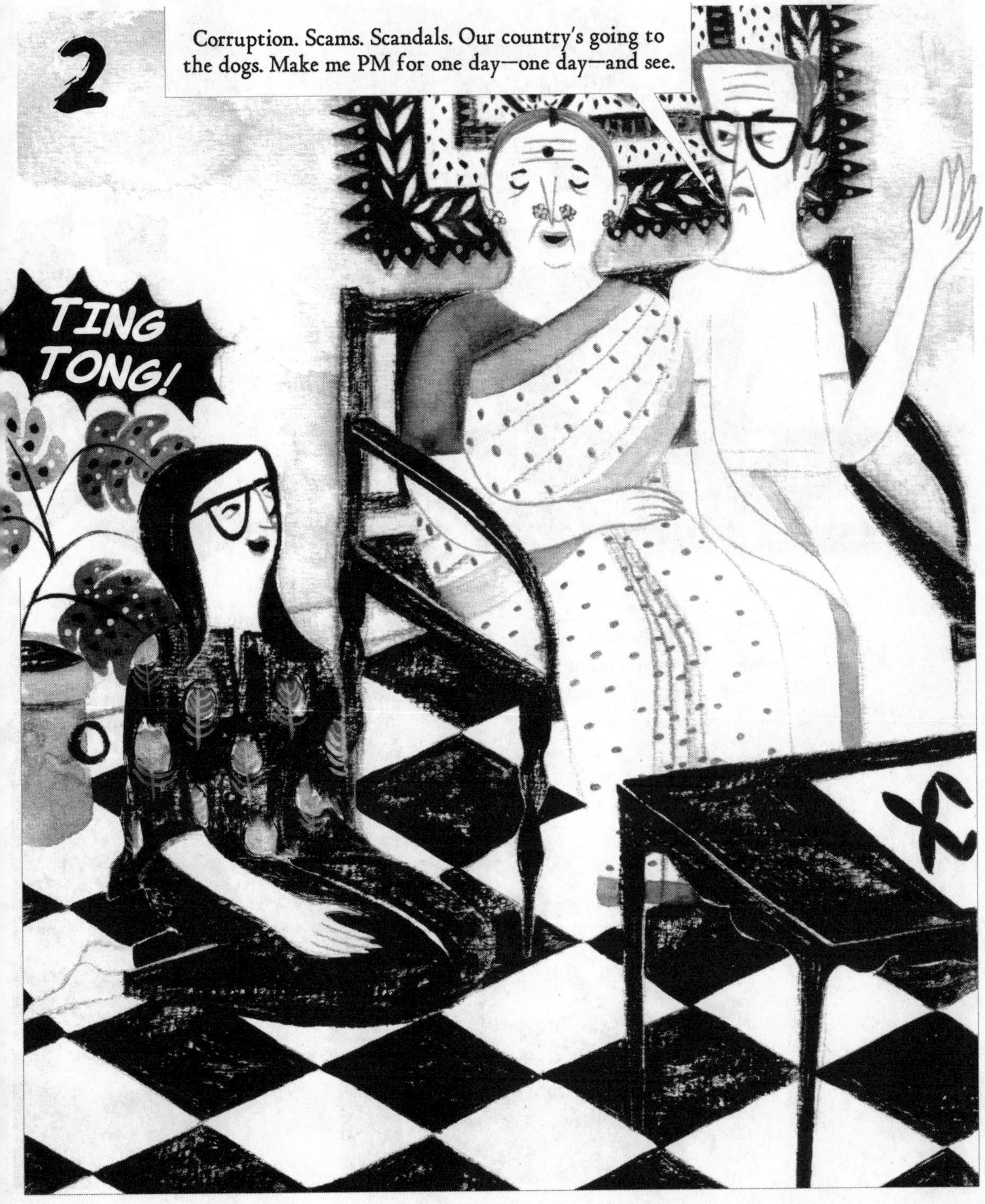
2
Corruption. Scams. Scandals. Our country's going to the dogs. Make me PM for one day—one day—and see.
TING TONG!

TING TONG!

I bet it's Lokesh Uncle – your best friend, grandpa.

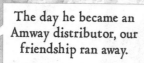

The day he became an Amway distributor, our friendship ran away.

Coming, coming...a little peace of mind is too much to ask.

TING TONG!

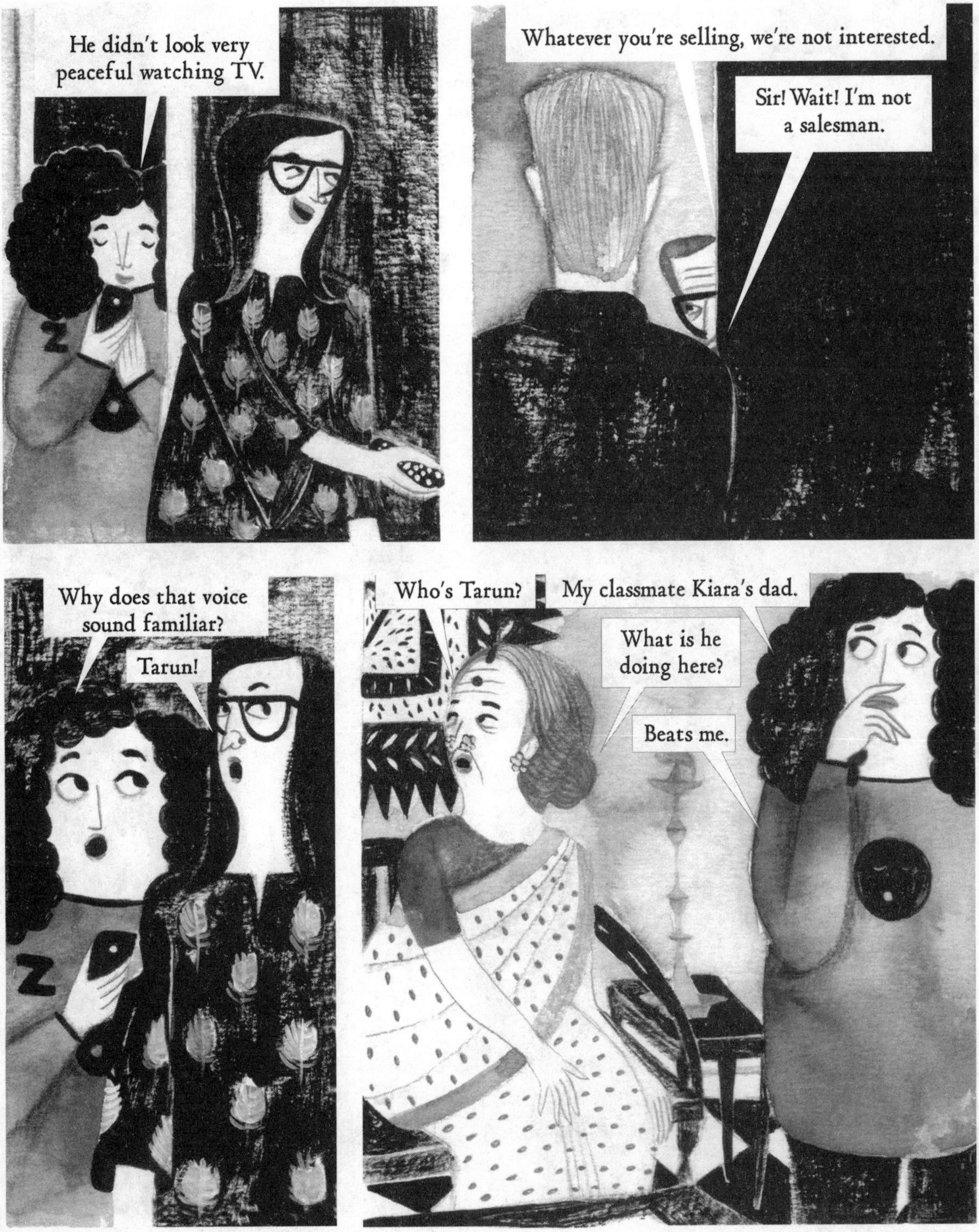
He didn't look very peaceful watching TV.
Whatever you're selling, we're not interested.
Sir! Wait! I'm not a salesman.
Why does that voice sound familiar?
Tarun!
Who's Tarun?
My classmate Kiara's dad.
What is he doing here?
Beats me.

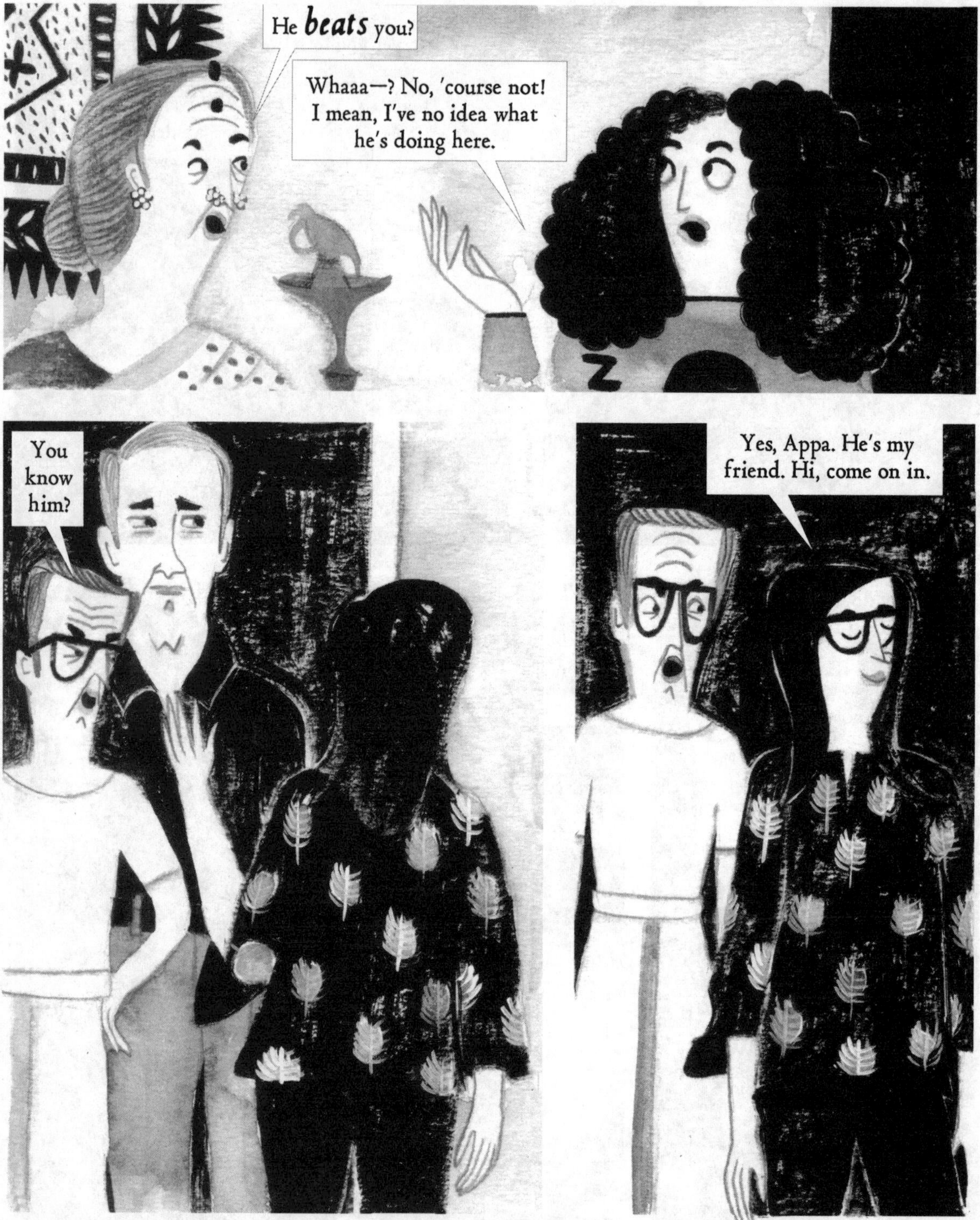
He *beats* you?
Whaaa—? No, 'course not! I mean, I've no idea what he's doing here.
You know him?
Yes, Appa. He's my friend. Hi, come on in.

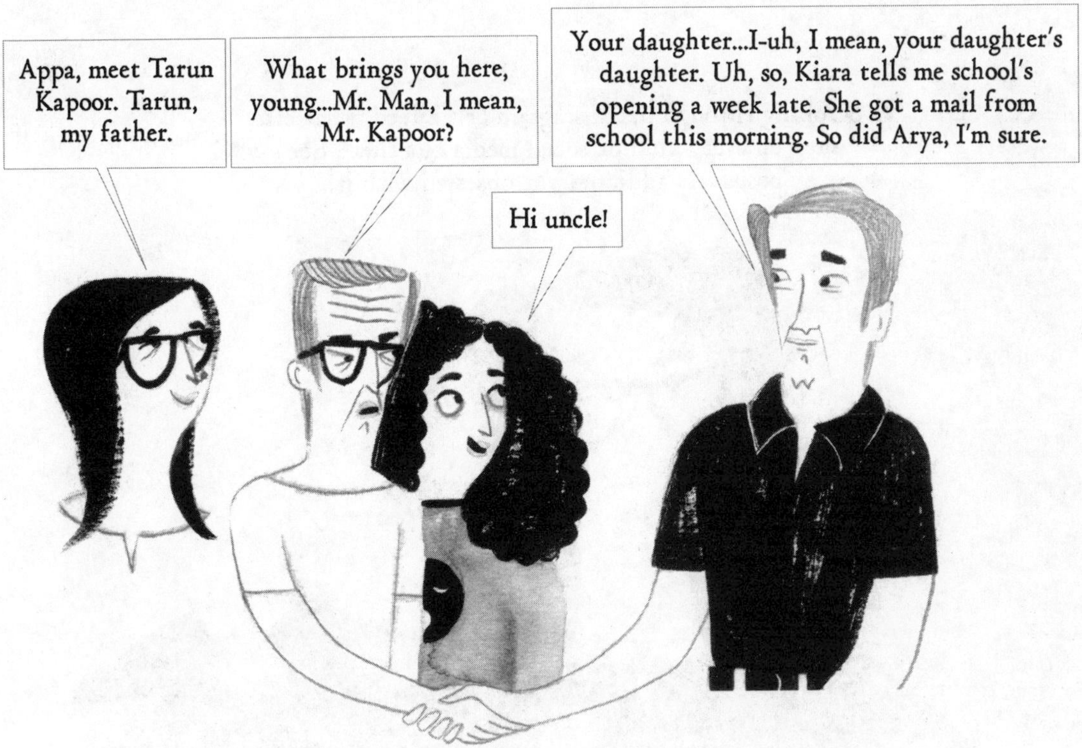
Appa, meet Tarun Kapoor. Tarun, my father.
What brings you here, young...Mr. Man, I mean, Mr. Kapoor?
Hi uncle!
Your daughter...I-uh, I mean, your daughter's daughter. Uh, so, Kiara tells me school's opening a week late. She got a mail from school this morning. So did Arya, I'm sure.

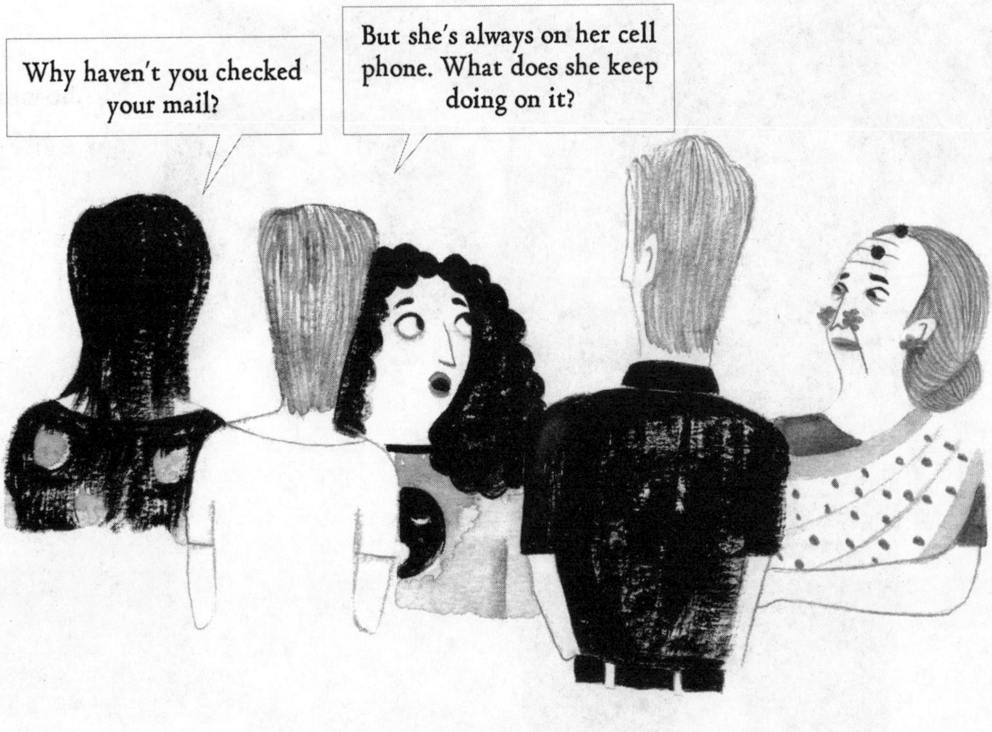
Why haven't you checked your mail?
But she's always on her cell phone. What does she keep doing on it?

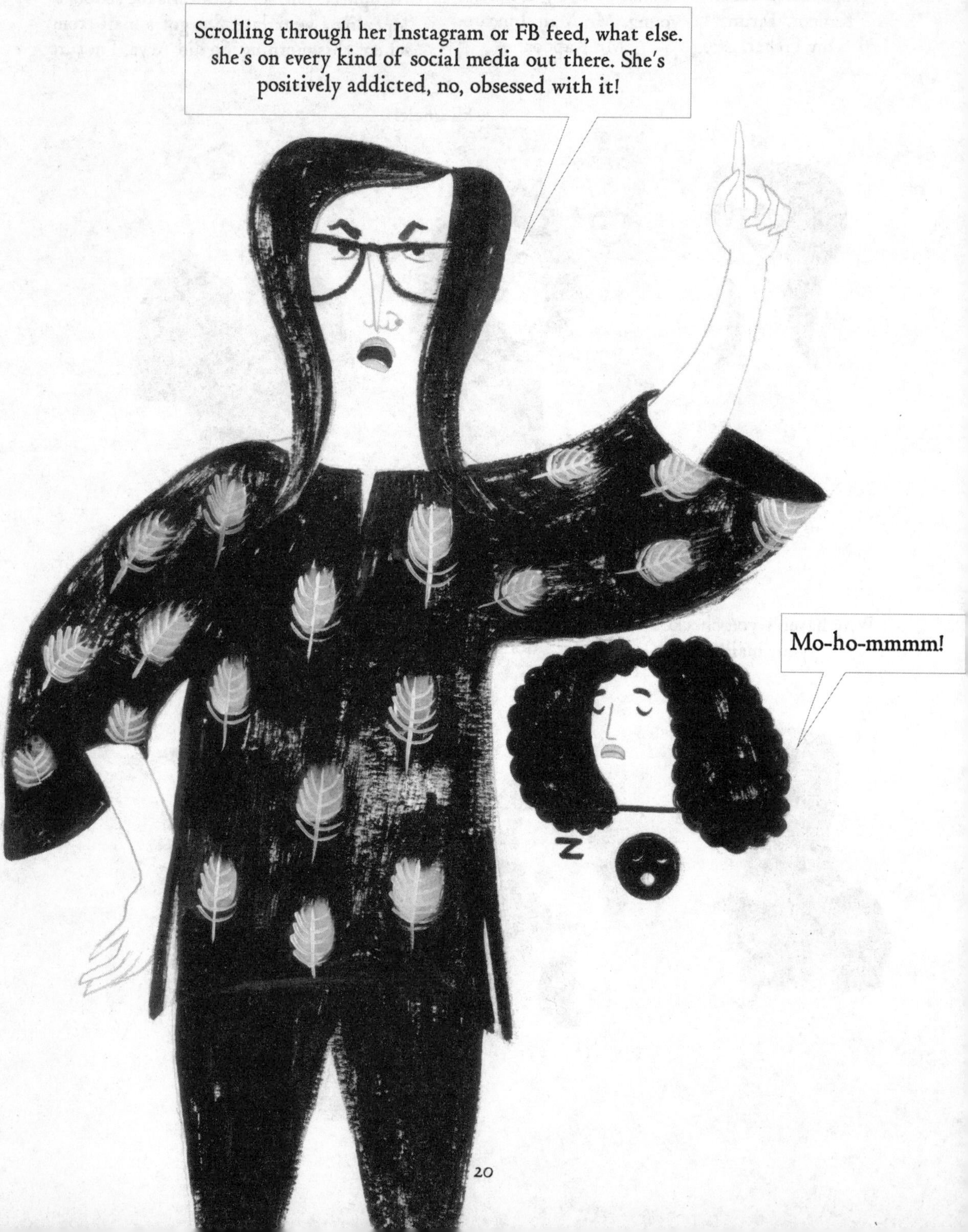
Scrolling through her Instagram or FB feed, what else. she's on every kind of social media out there. She's positively addicted, no, obsessed with it!
Mo-ho-mmmm!
Z

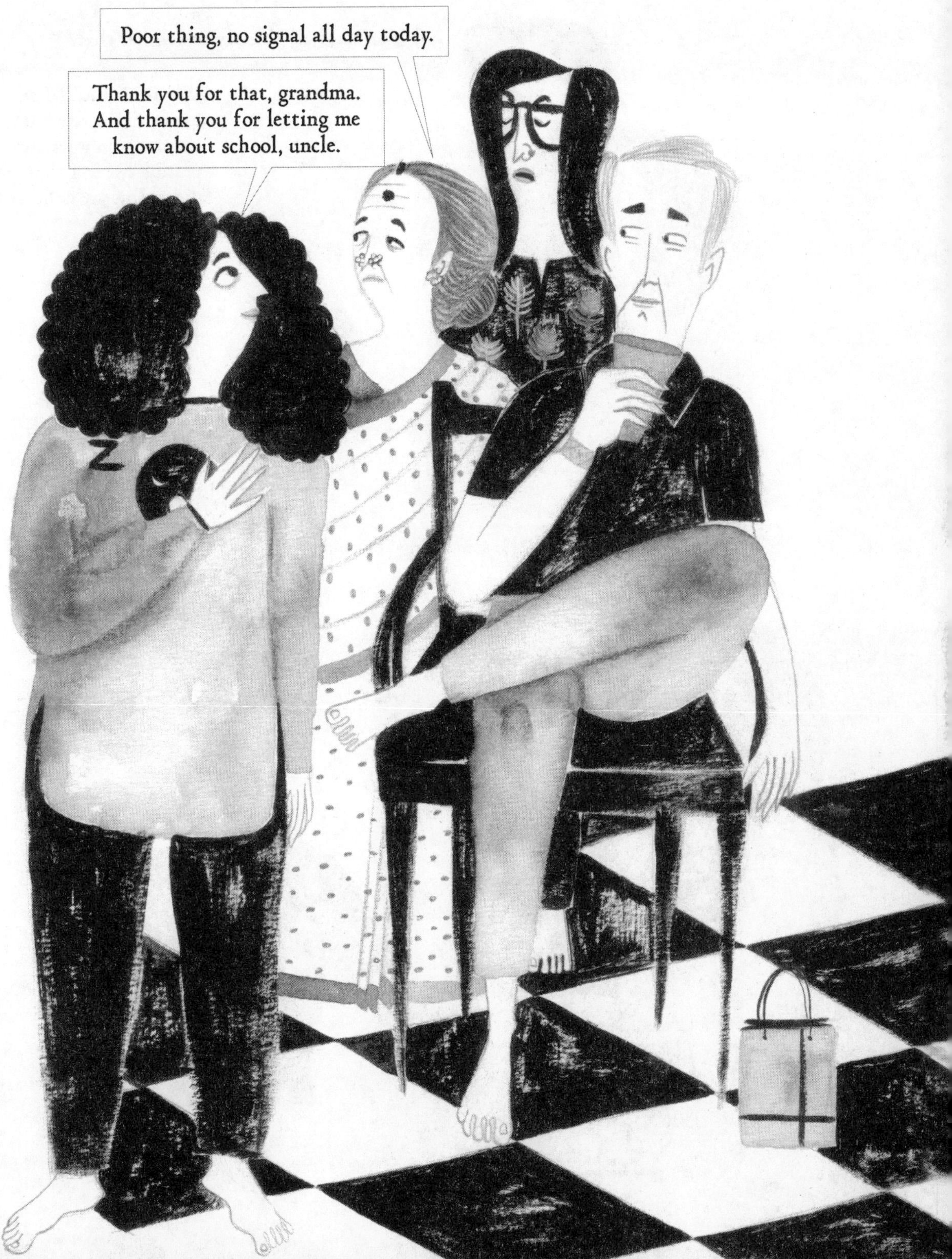
Thank you for that, grandma. And thank you for letting me know about school, uncle.
Poor thing, no signal all day today.

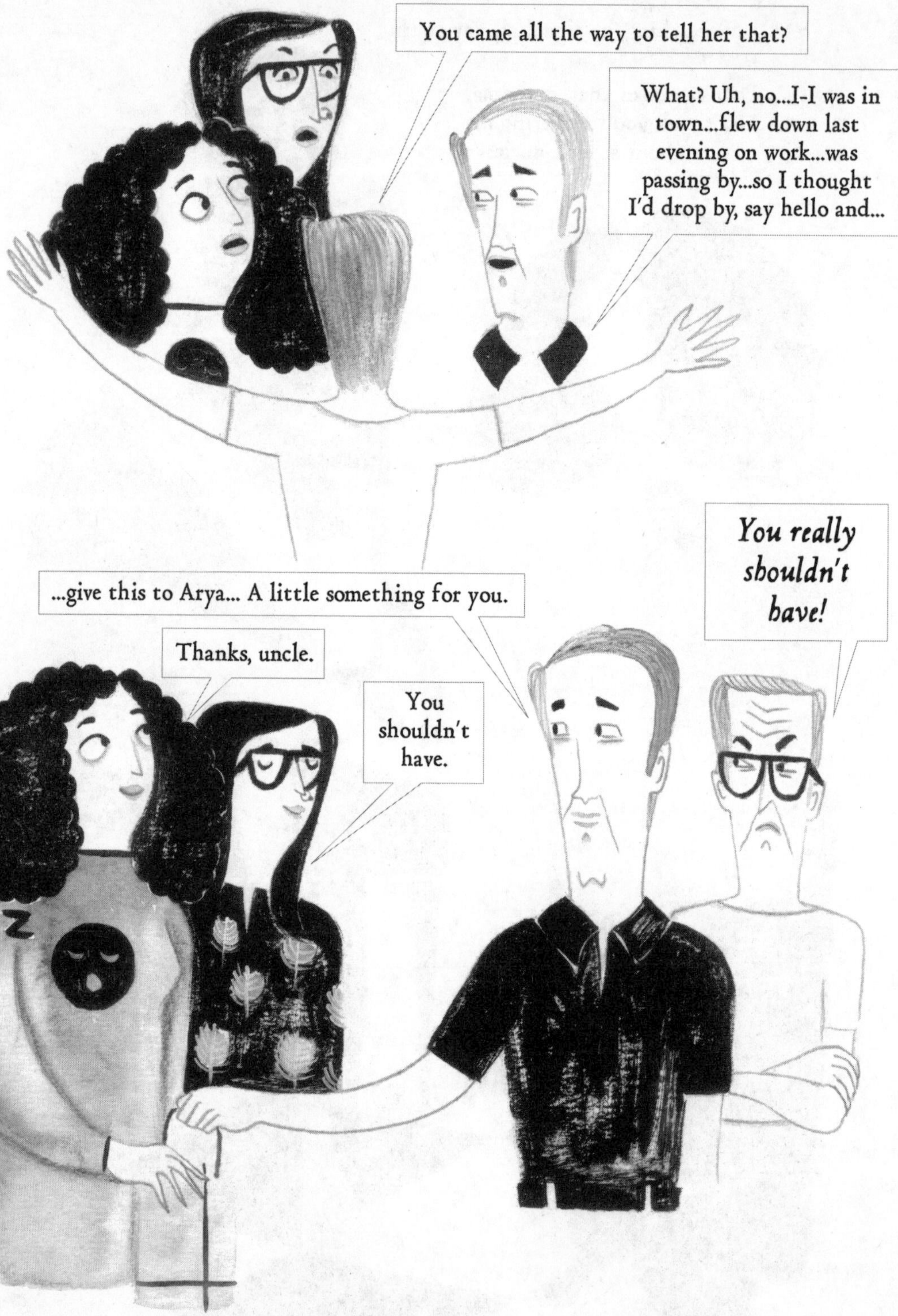
You came all the way to tell her that?
What? Uh, no...I-I was in town...flew down last evening on work...was passing by...so I thought I'd drop by, say hello and...
...give this to Arya... A little something for you.
Thanks, uncle.
You shouldn't have.
You really shouldn't have!

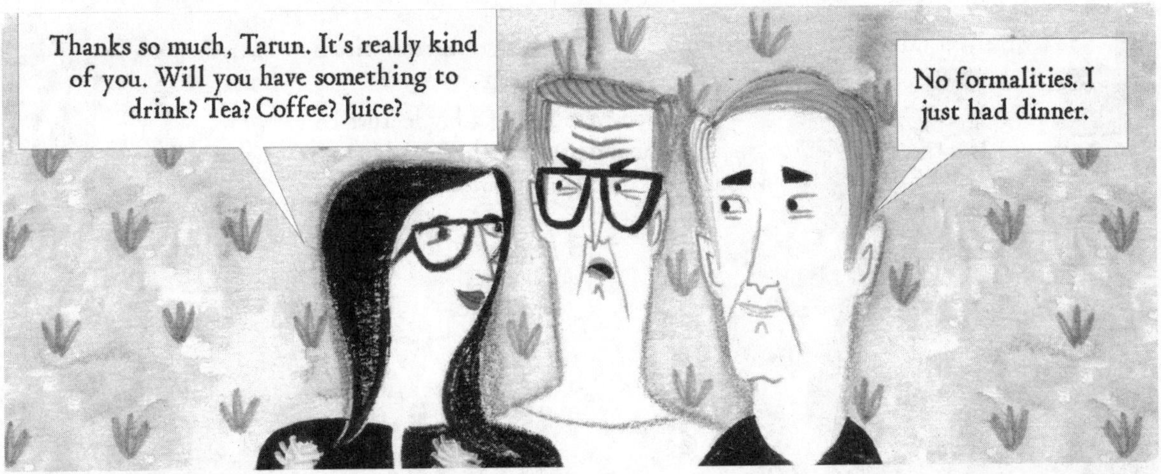
Thanks so much, Tarun. It's really kind of you. Will you have something to drink? Tea? Coffee? Juice?
No formalities. I just had dinner.

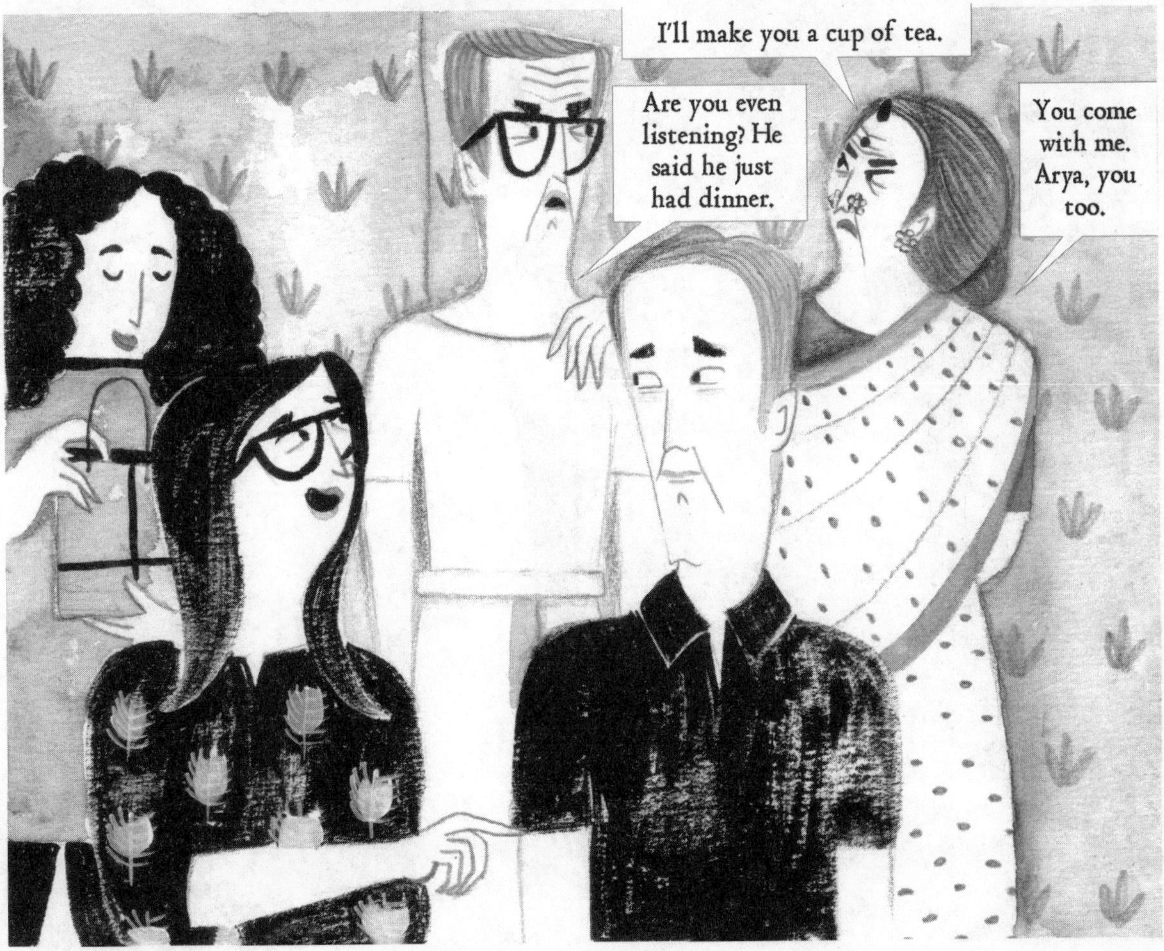
I'll make you a cup of tea.
Are you even listening? He said he just had dinner.
You come with me. Arya, you too.

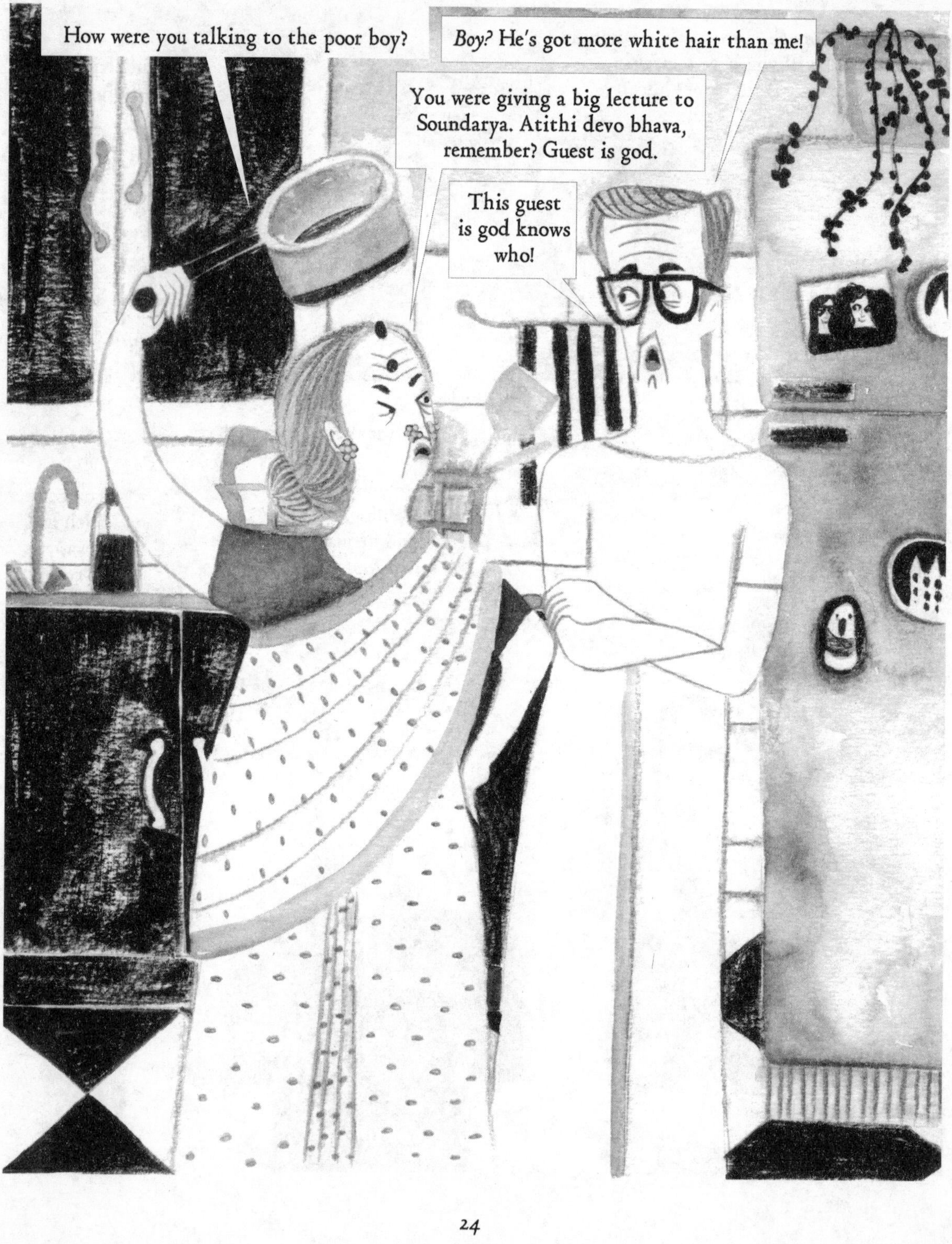
How were you talking to the poor boy?
Boy? He's got more white hair than me!
You were giving a big lecture to Soundarya. Atithi devo bhava, remember? Guest is god.
This guest is god knows who!

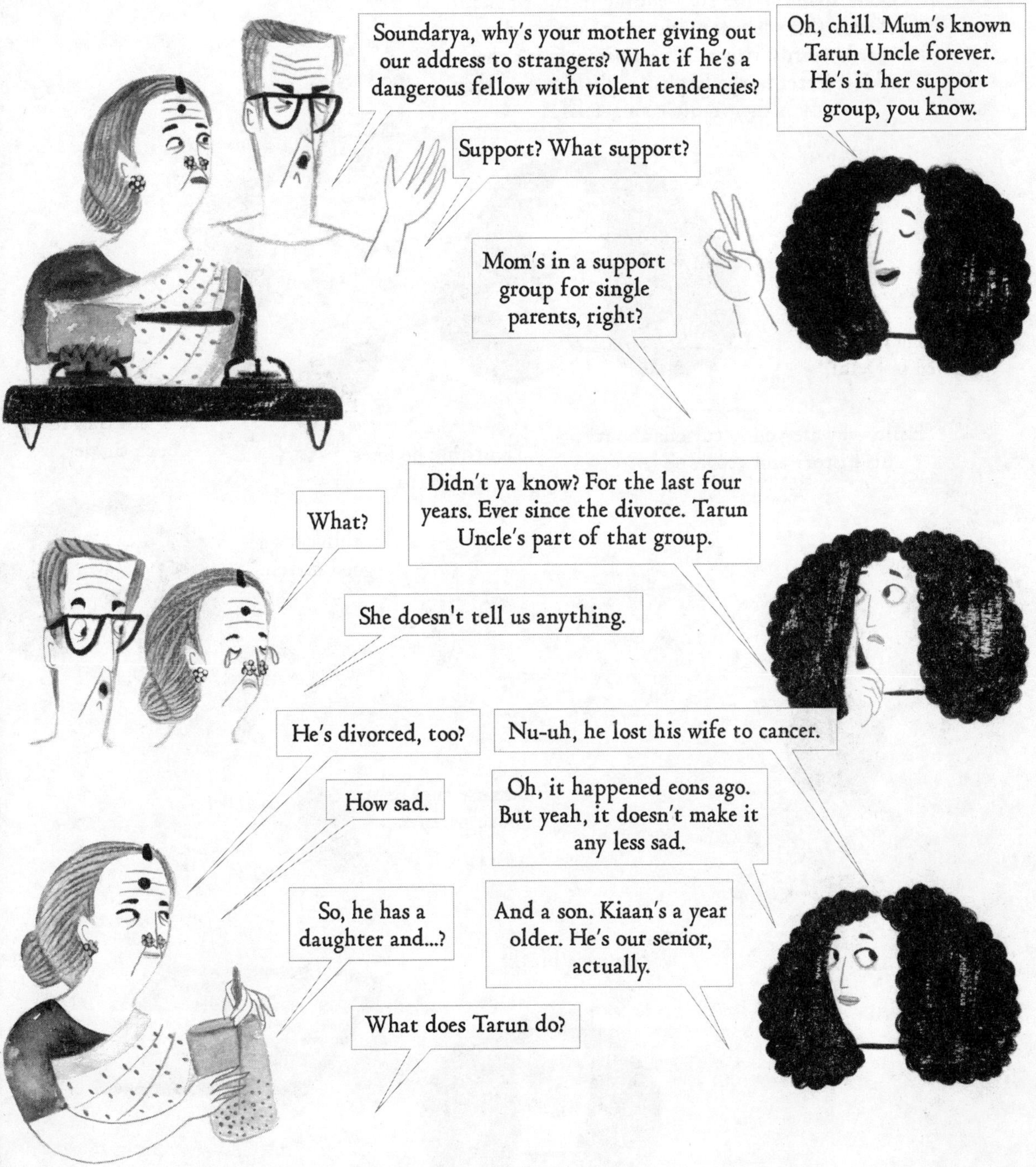
Soundarya, why's your mother giving out our address to strangers? What if he's a dangerous fellow with violent tendencies?
Oh, chill. Mum's known Tarun Uncle forever. He's in her support group, you know.
Support? What support?
Mom's in a support group for single parents, right?
What?
Didn't ya know? For the last four years. Ever since the divorce. Tarun Uncle's part of that group.
She doesn't tell us anything.
He's divorced, too?
Nu-uh, he lost his wife to cancer.
How sad.
Oh, it happened eons ago. But yeah, it doesn't make it any less sad.
So, he has a daughter and...?
And a son. Kiaan's a year older. He's our senior, actually.
What does Tarun do?

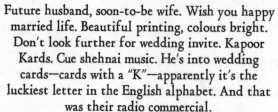

Future husband, soon-to-be wife. Wish you happy married life. Beautiful printing, colours bright. Don't look further for wedding invite. Kapoor Kards. Cue shehnai music. He's into wedding cards—cards with a "K"—apparently it's the luckiest letter in the English alphabet. And that was their radio commercial.

How long has Tarun lived in Delhi?

Hello, why are you so curious about his history and geography…

You think he likes Aishwarya?

I think it's a good match.

Gawd, grandma. Just 'cos they're both single?

Because they're both parents.

Gimme a break!

3

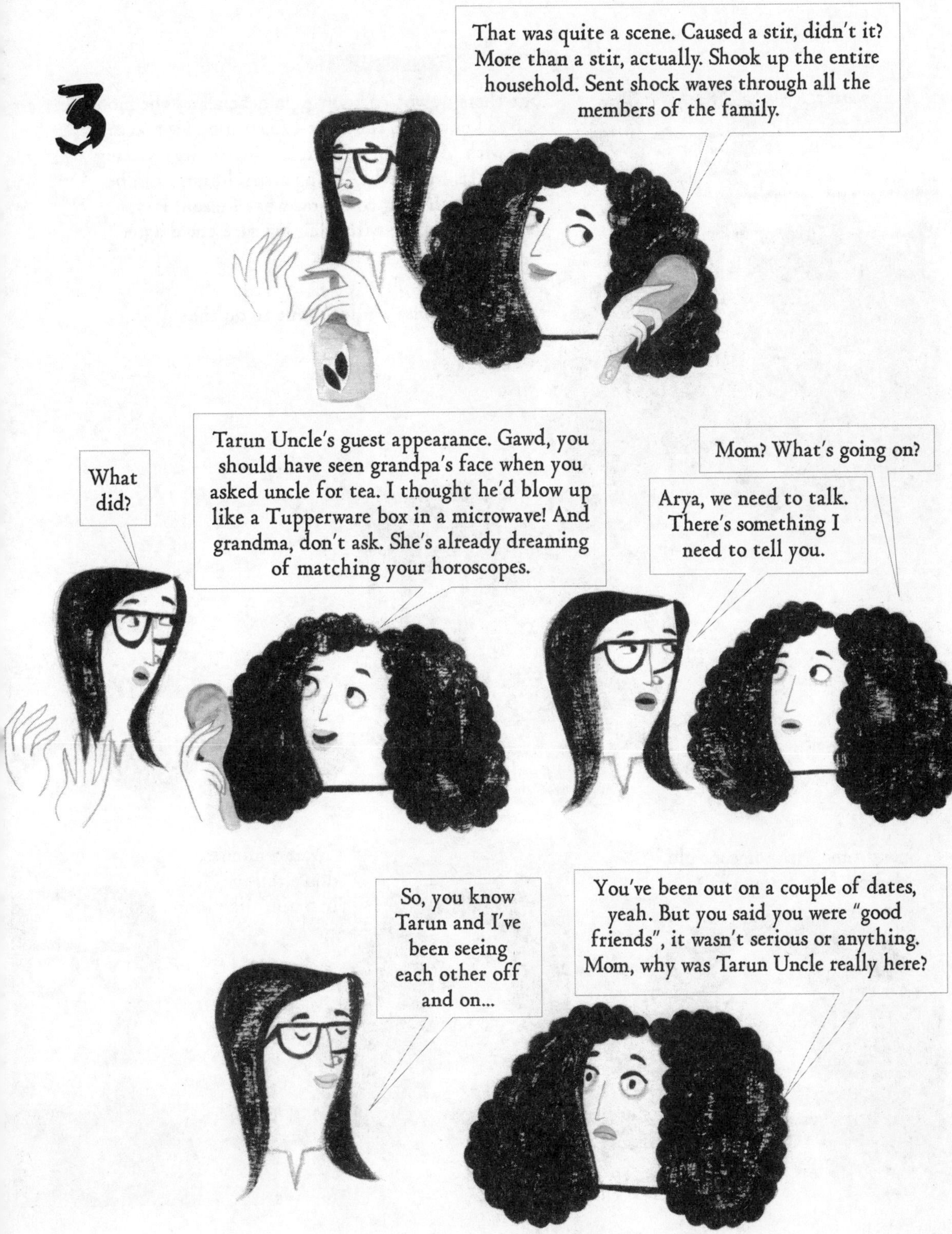
That was quite a scene. Caused a stir, didn't it? More than a stir, actually. Shook up the entire household. Sent shock waves through all the members of the family.
What did?
Tarun Uncle's guest appearance. Gawd, you should have seen grandpa's face when you asked uncle for tea. I thought he'd blow up like a Tupperware box in a microwave! And grandma, don't ask. She's already dreaming of matching your horoscopes.
Mom? What's going on?
Arya, we need to talk. There's something I need to tell you.
So, you know Tarun and I've been seeing each other off and on...
You've been out on a couple of dates, yeah. But you said you were "good friends", it wasn't serious or anything. Mom, why was Tarun Uncle really here?

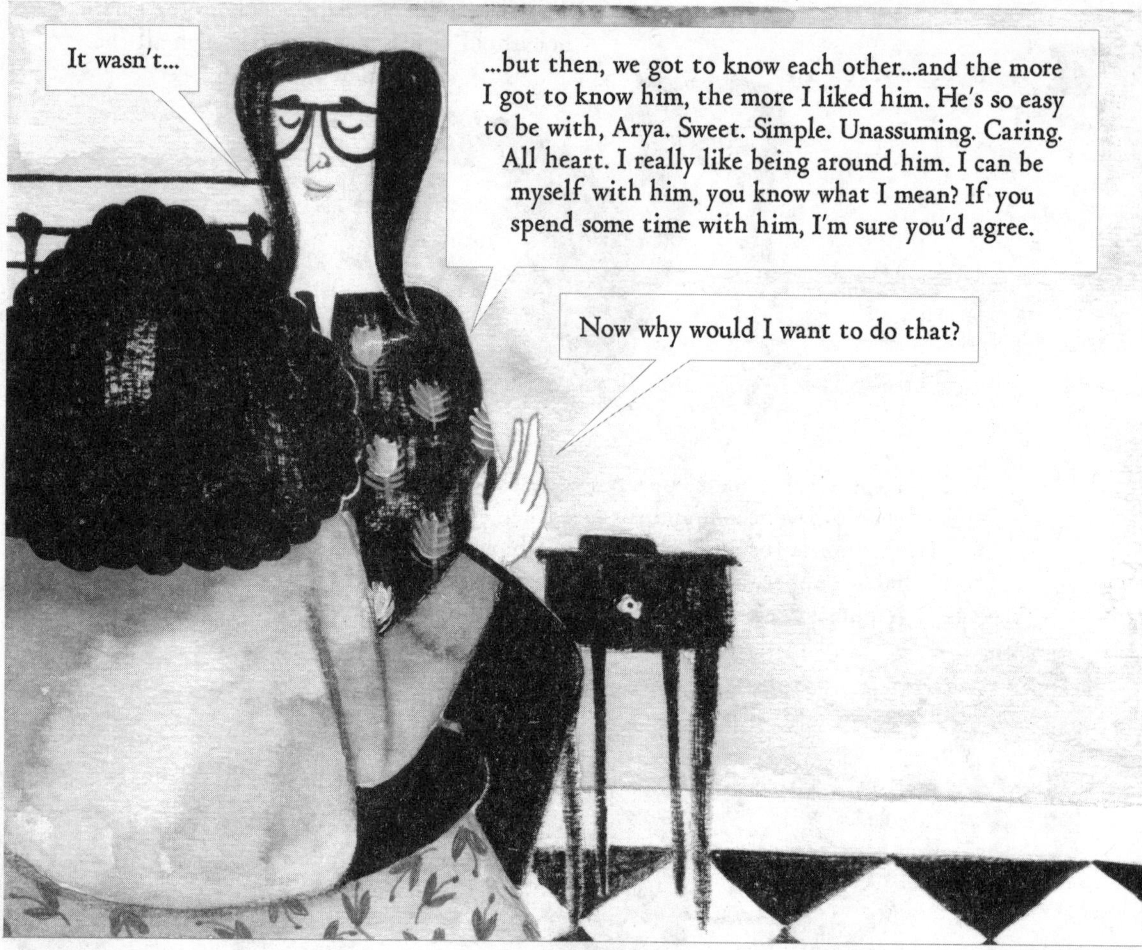
It wasn't...
...but then, we got to know each other...and the more I got to know him, the more I liked him. He's so easy to be with, Arya. Sweet. Simple. Unassuming. Caring. All heart. I really like being around him. I can be myself with him, you know what I mean? If you spend some time with him, I'm sure you'd agree.
Now why would I want to do that?

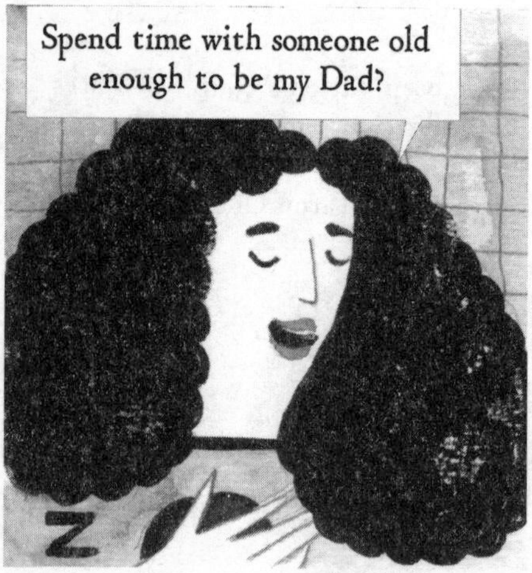
Spend time with someone old enough to be my Dad?

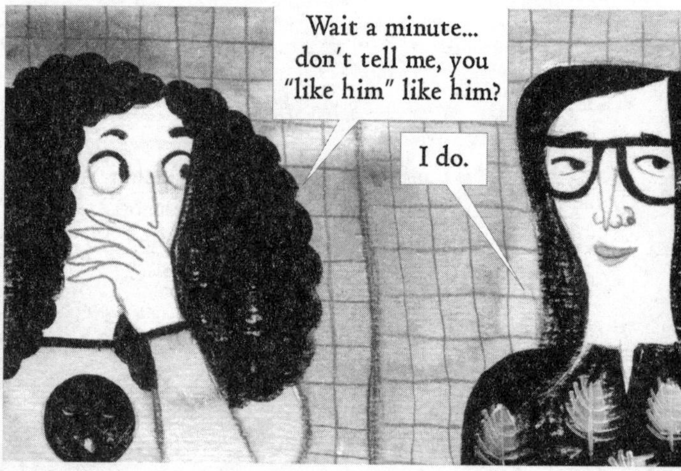
Wait a minute... don't tell me, you "like him" like him?
I do.

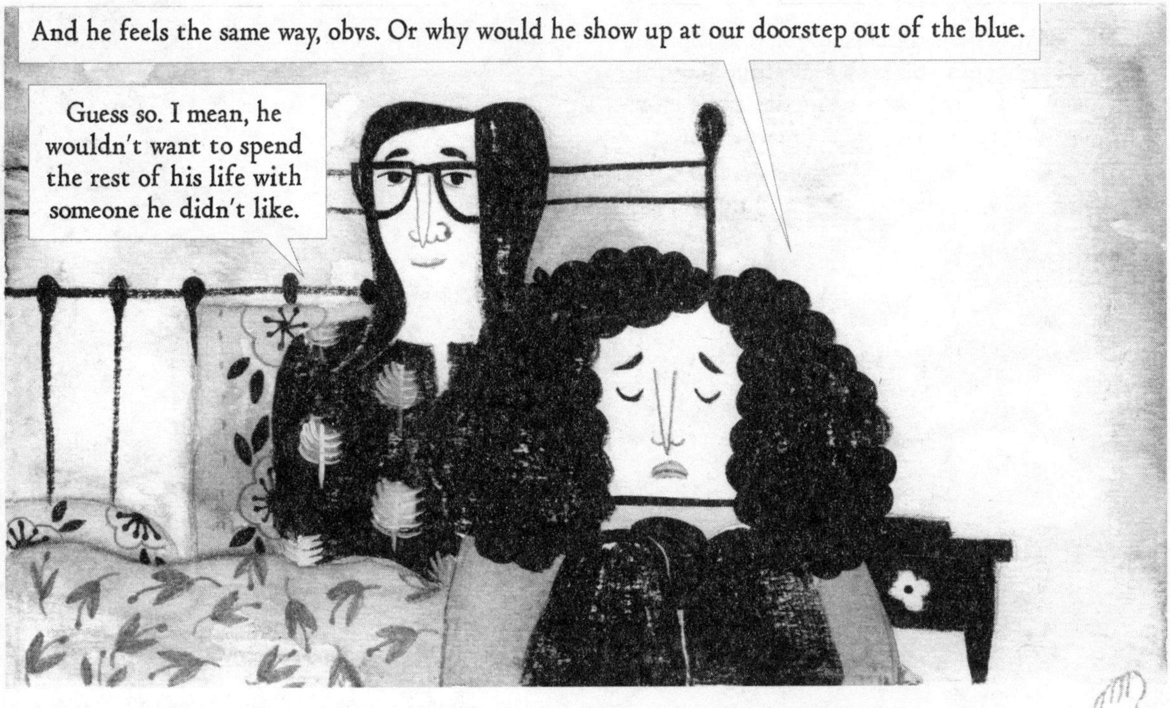
And he feels the same way, obvs. Or why would he show up at our doorstep out of the blue.
Guess so. I mean, he wouldn't want to spend the rest of his life with someone he didn't like.

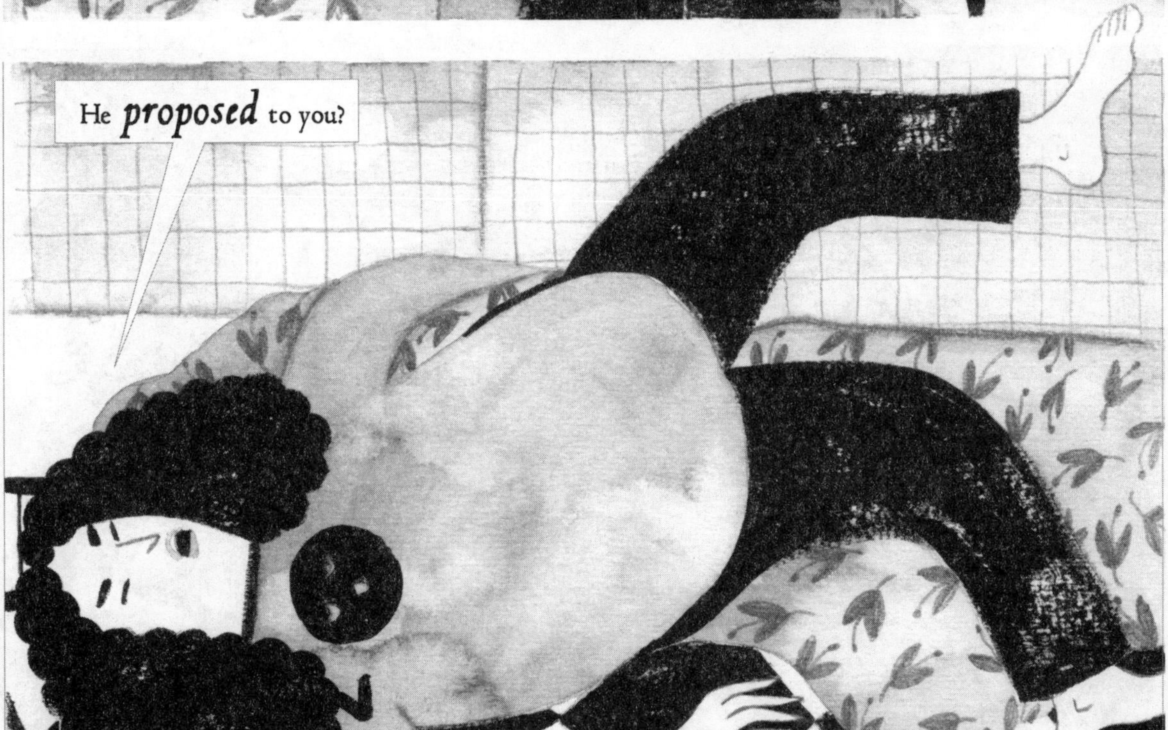
He *proposed* to you?

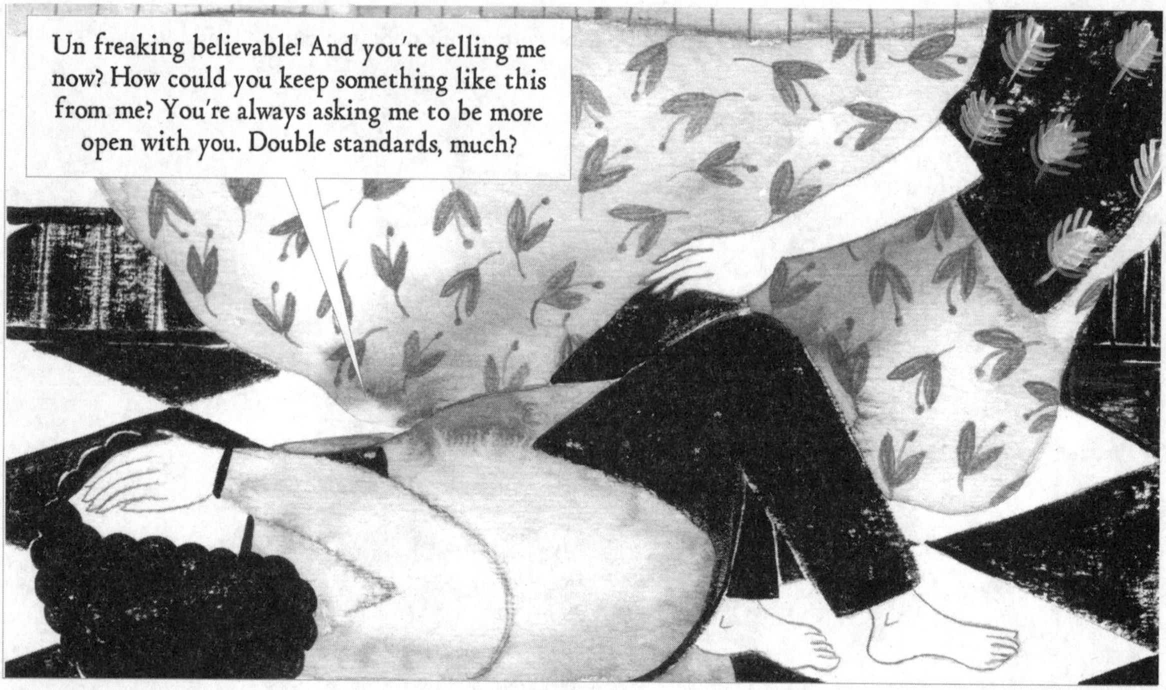
Un freaking believable! And you're telling me now? How could you keep something like this from me? You're always asking me to be more open with you. Double standards, much?

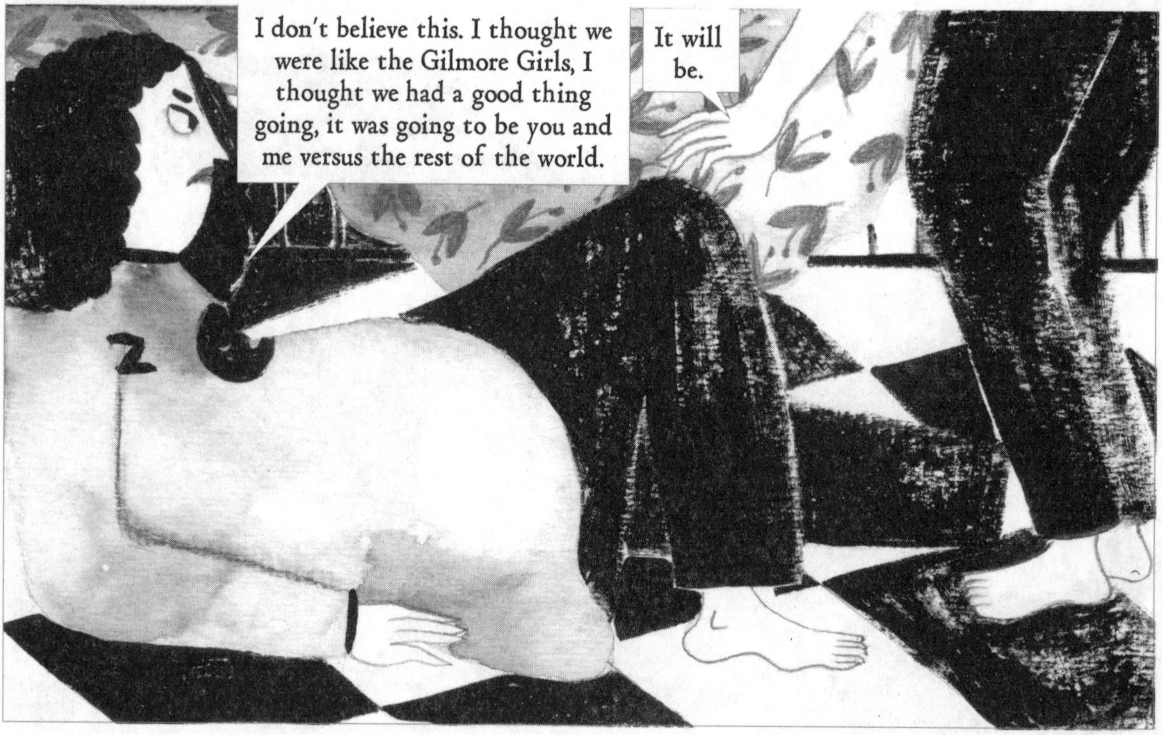
I don't believe this. I thought we were like the Gilmore Girls, I thought we had a good thing going, it was going to be you and me versus the rest of the world.
It will be.

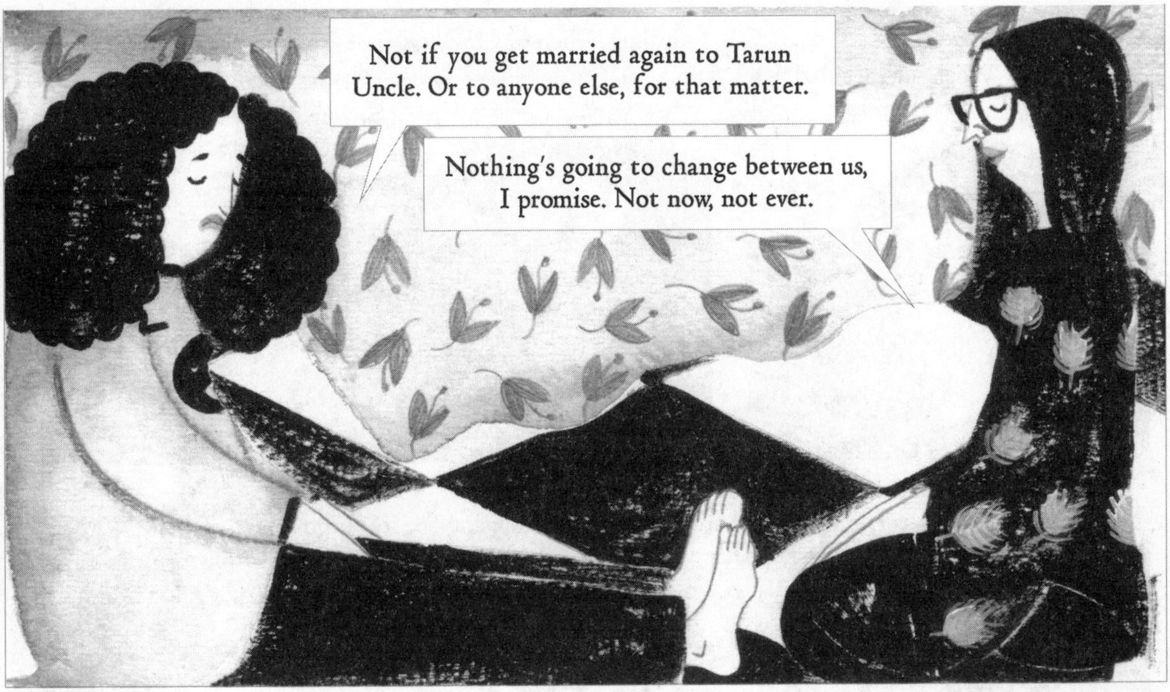
Not if you get married again to Tarun Uncle. Or to anyone else, for that matter.
Nothing's going to change between us, I promise. Not now, not ever.

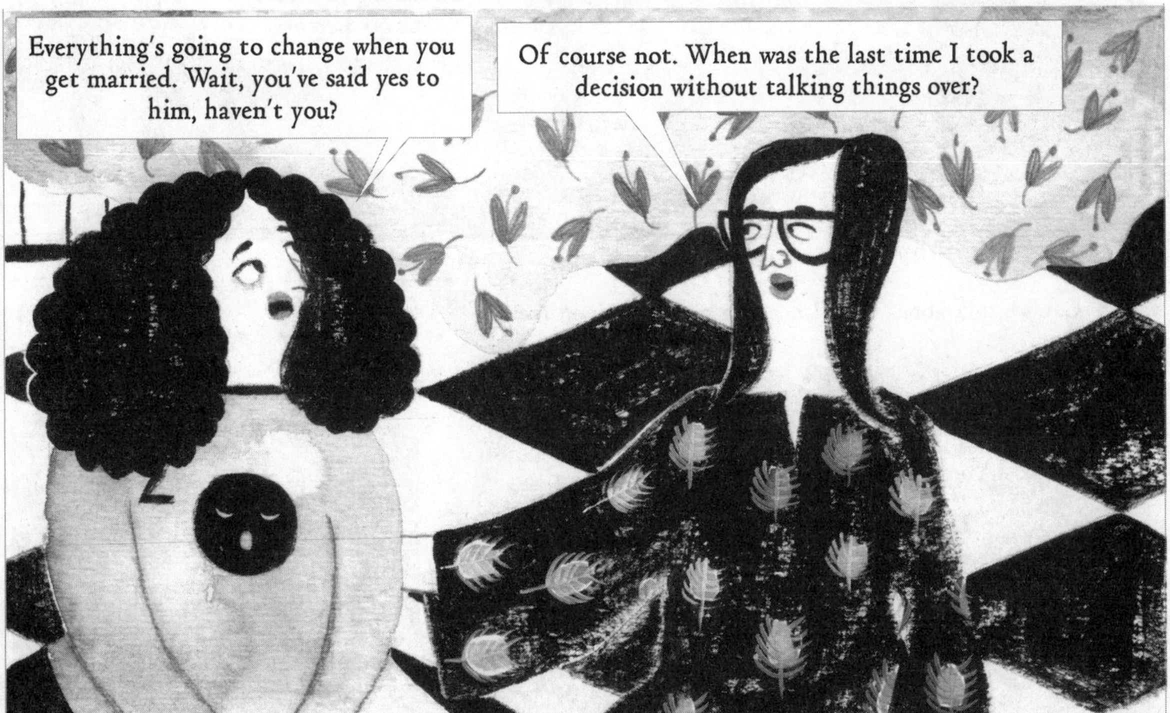
Everything's going to change when you get married. Wait, you've said yes to him, haven't you?
Of course not. When was the last time I took a decision without talking things over?

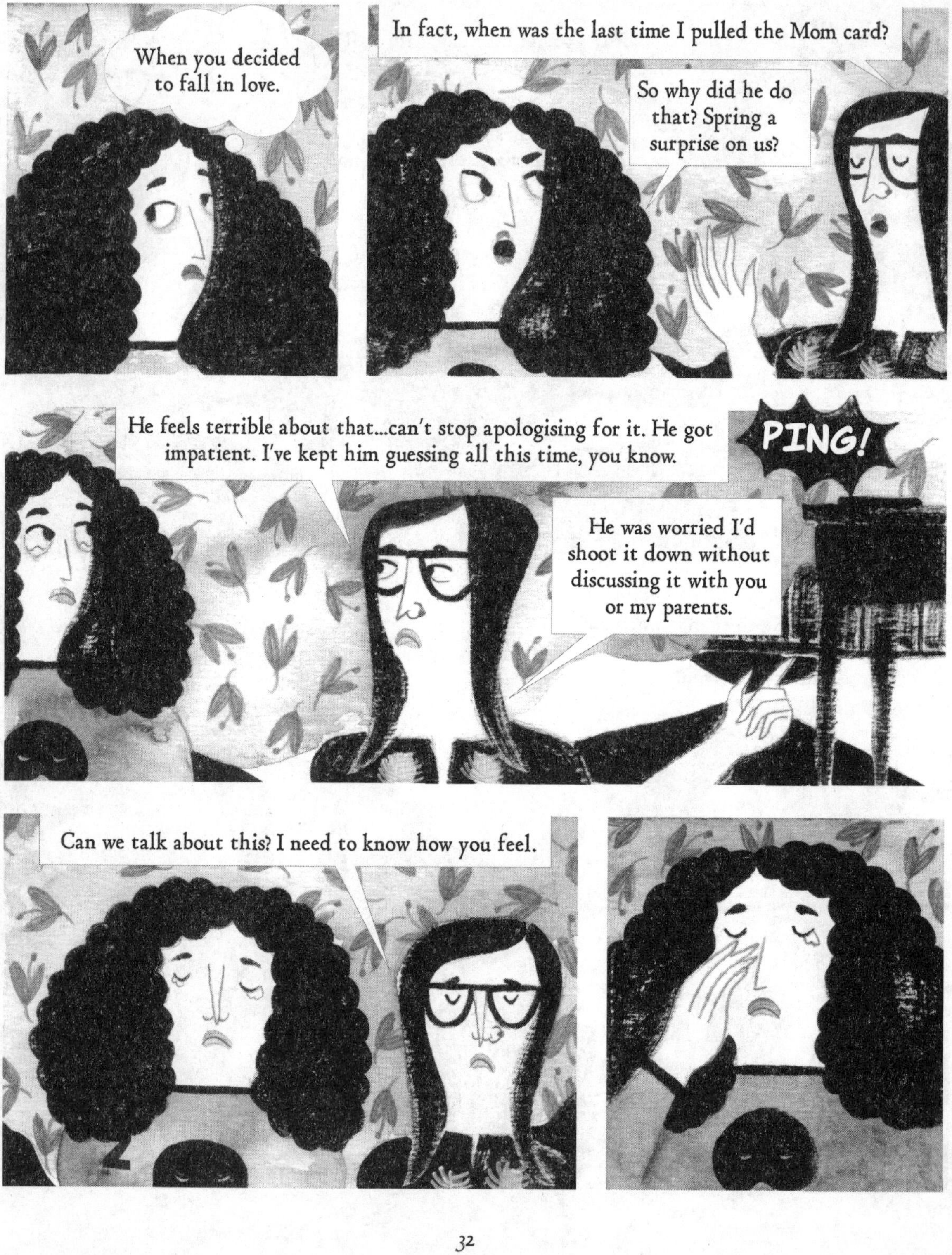
When you decided to fall in love.
In fact, when was the last time I pulled the Mom card?
So why did he do that? Spring a surprise on us?
He feels terrible about that...can't stop apologising for it. He got impatient. I've kept him guessing all this time, you know.
PING!
He was worried I'd shoot it down without discussing it with you or my parents.
Can we talk about this? I need to know how you feel.

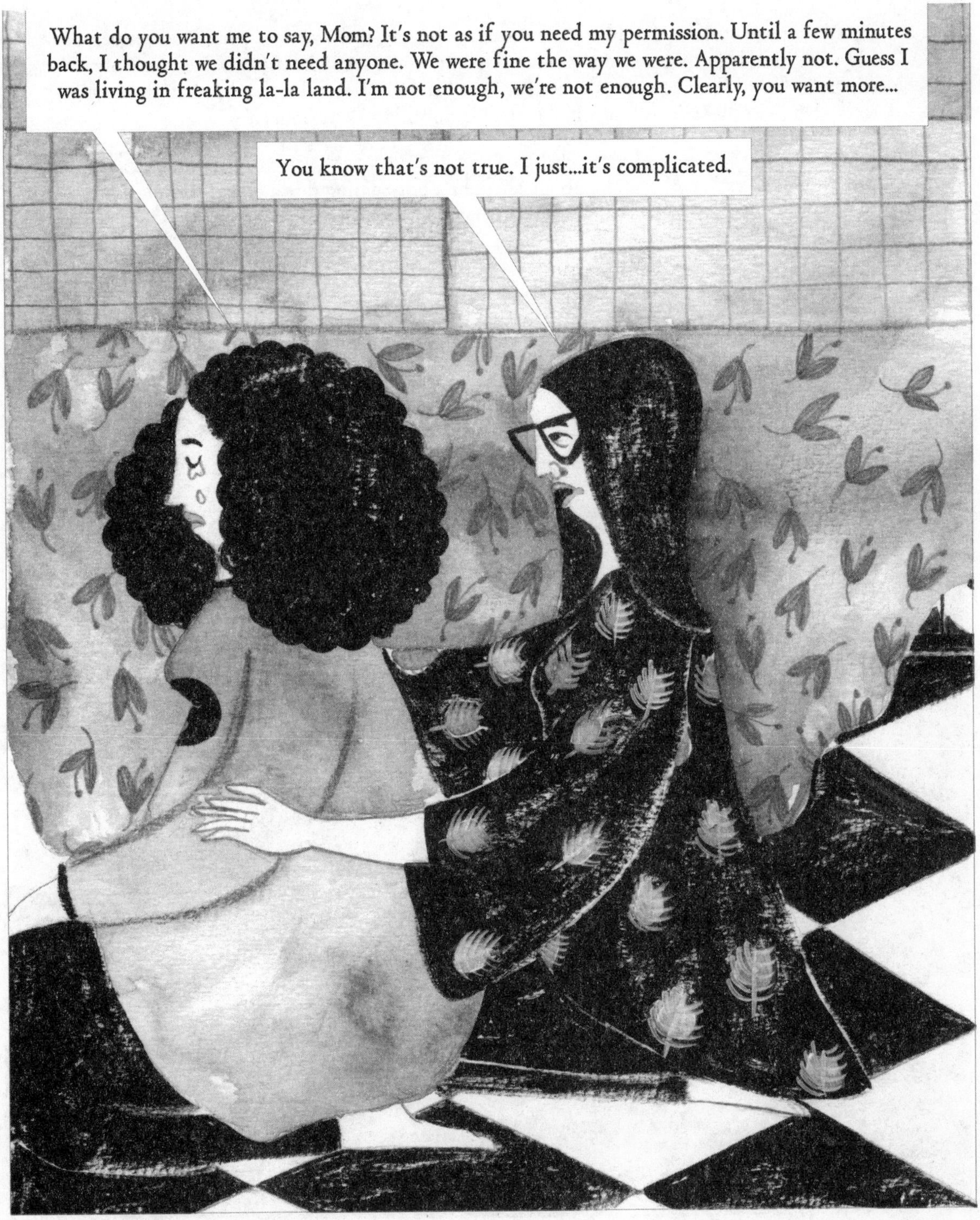
What do you want me to say, Mom? It's not as if you need my permission. Until a few minutes back, I thought we didn't need anyone. We were fine the way we were. Apparently not. Guess I was living in freaking la-la land. I'm not enough, we're not enough. Clearly, you want more...
You know that's not true. I just...it's complicated.

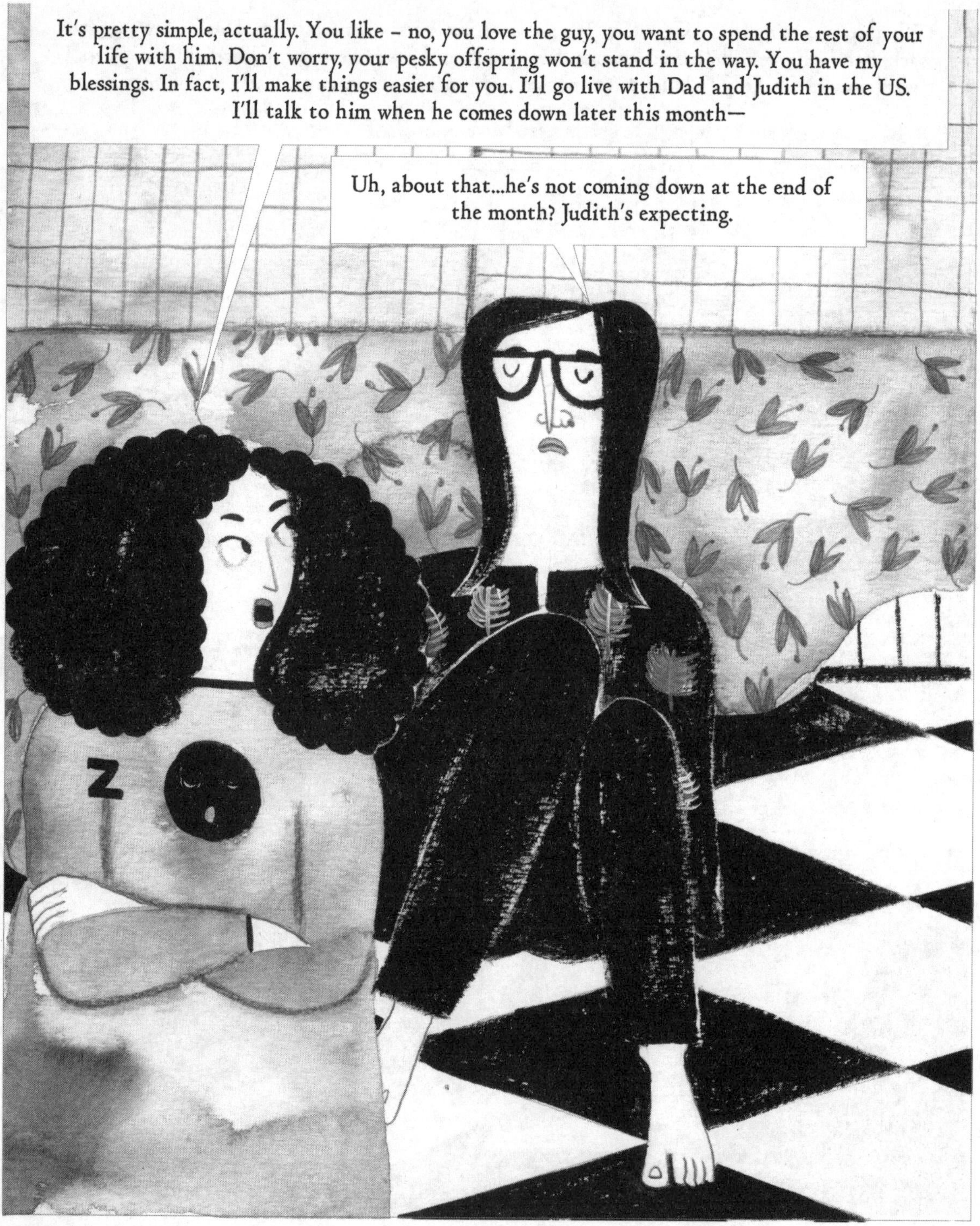
It's pretty simple, actually. You like – no, you love the guy, you want to spend the rest of your life with him. Don't worry, your pesky offspring won't stand in the way. You have my blessings. In fact, I'll make things easier for you. I'll go live with Dad and Judith in the US. I'll talk to him when he comes down later this month—
Uh, about that...he's not coming down at the end of the month? Judith's expecting.
Z

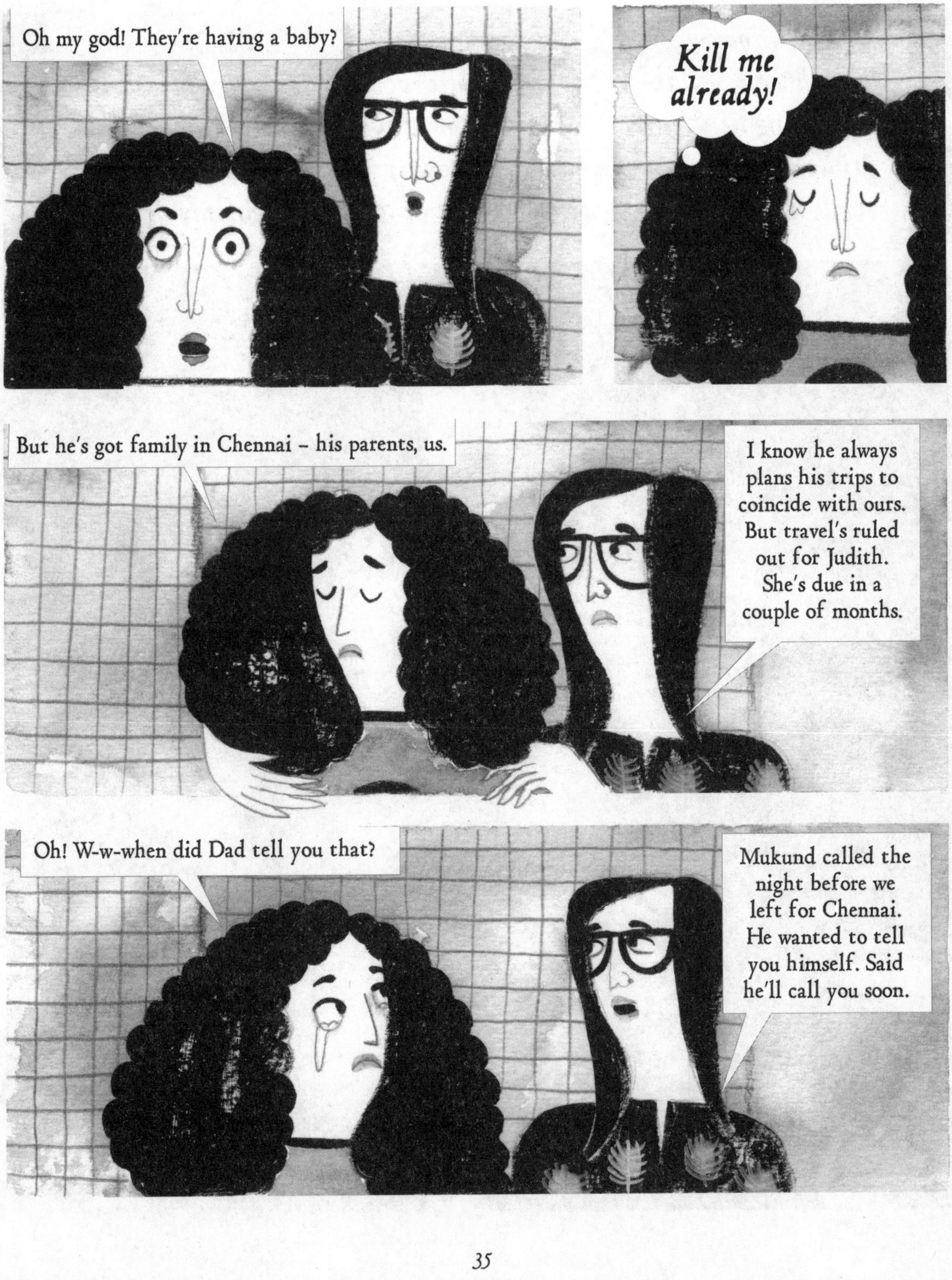
Oh my god! They're having a baby?
Kill me already!
But he's got family in Chennai – his parents, us.
I know he always plans his trips to coincide with ours. But travel's ruled out for Judith. She's due in a couple of months.
Oh! W-w-when did Dad tell you that?
Mukund called the night before we left for Chennai. He wanted to tell you himself. Said he'll call you soon.

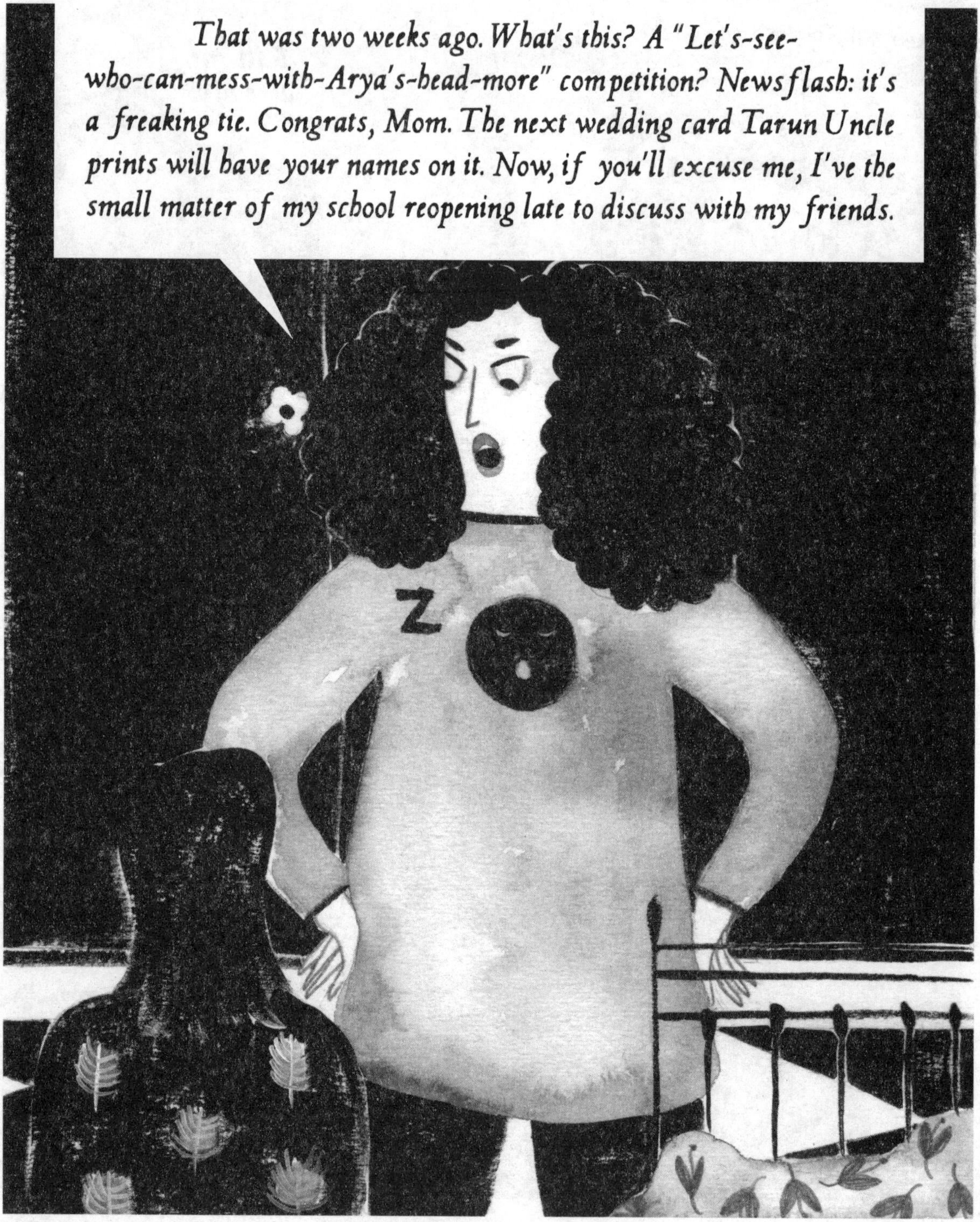
That was two weeks ago. What's this? A "Let's-see-who-can-mess-with-Arya's-head-more" competition? Newsflash: it's a freaking tie. Congrats, Mom. The next wedding card Tarun Uncle prints will have your names on it. Now, if you'll excuse me, I've the small matter of my school reopening late to discuss with my friends.
Z

4

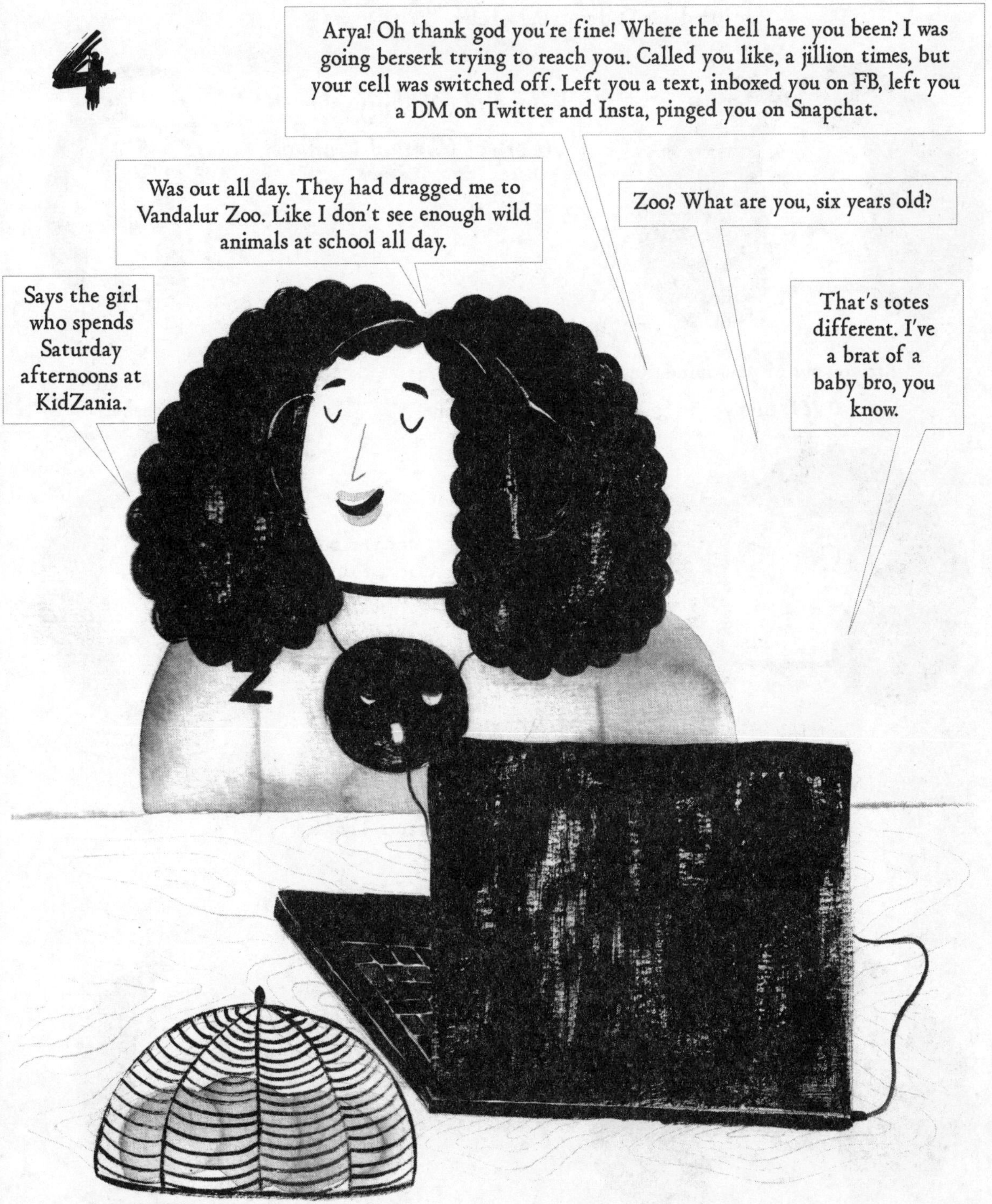
Arya! Oh thank god you're fine! Where the hell have you been? I was going berserk trying to reach you. Called you like, a jillion times, but your cell was switched off. Left you a text, inboxed you on FB, left you a DM on Twitter and Insta, pinged you on Snapchat.
Was out all day. They had dragged me to Vandalur Zoo. Like I don't see enough wild animals at school all day.
Zoo? What are you, six years old?
Says the girl who spends Saturday afternoons at KidZania.
That's totes different. I've a brat of a baby bro, you know.
Z

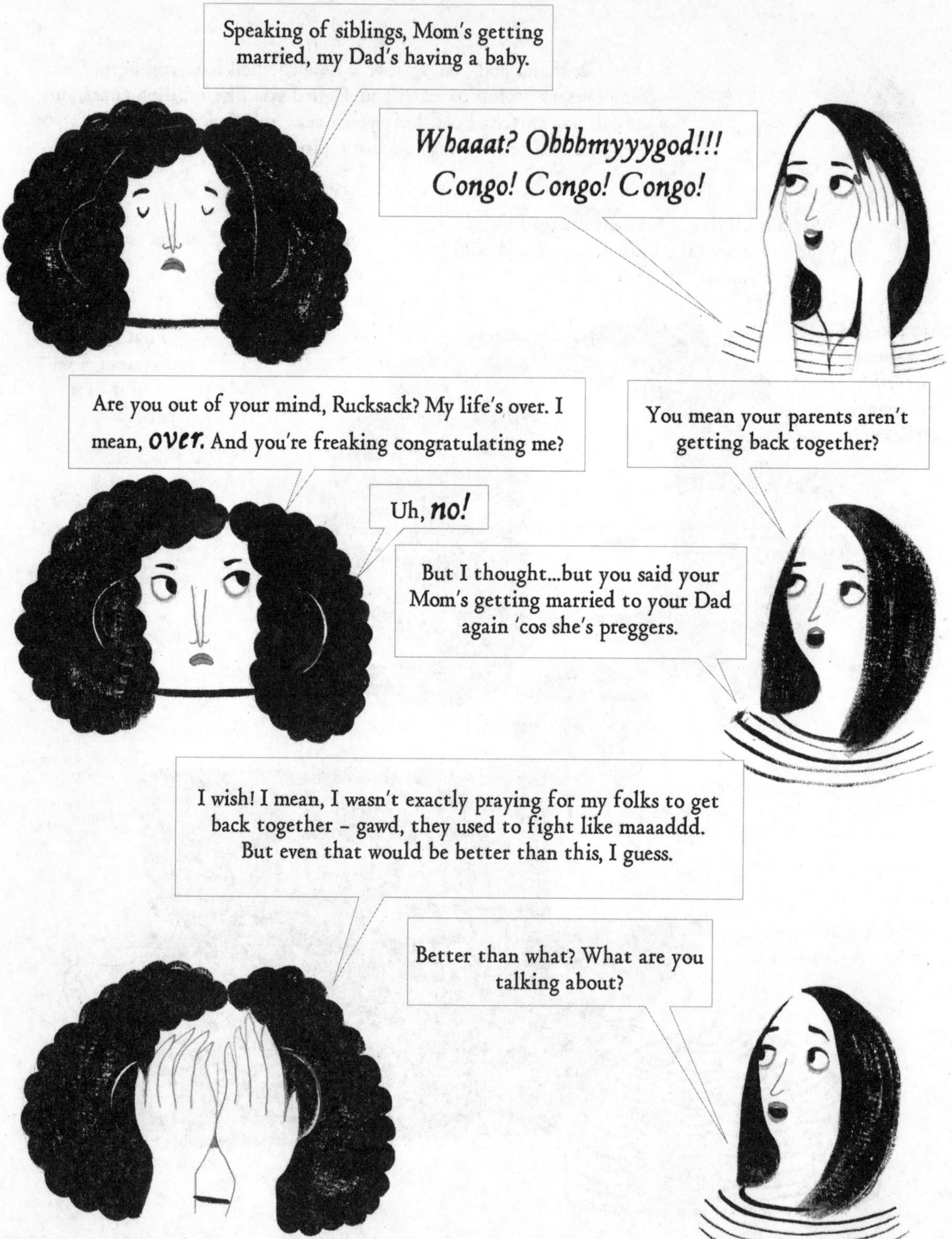
Speaking of siblings, Mom's getting married, my Dad's having a baby.
Whaaat? Ohhhmyyygod!!! Congo! Congo! Congo!
Are you out of your mind, Rucksack? My life's over. I mean, over. And you're freaking congratulating me?
You mean your parents aren't getting back together?
Uh, no!
But I thought...but you said your Mom's getting married to your Dad again 'cos she's preggers.
I wish! I mean, I wasn't exactly praying for my folks to get back together – gawd, they used to fight like maaaddd. But even that would be better than this, I guess.
Better than what? What are you talking about?

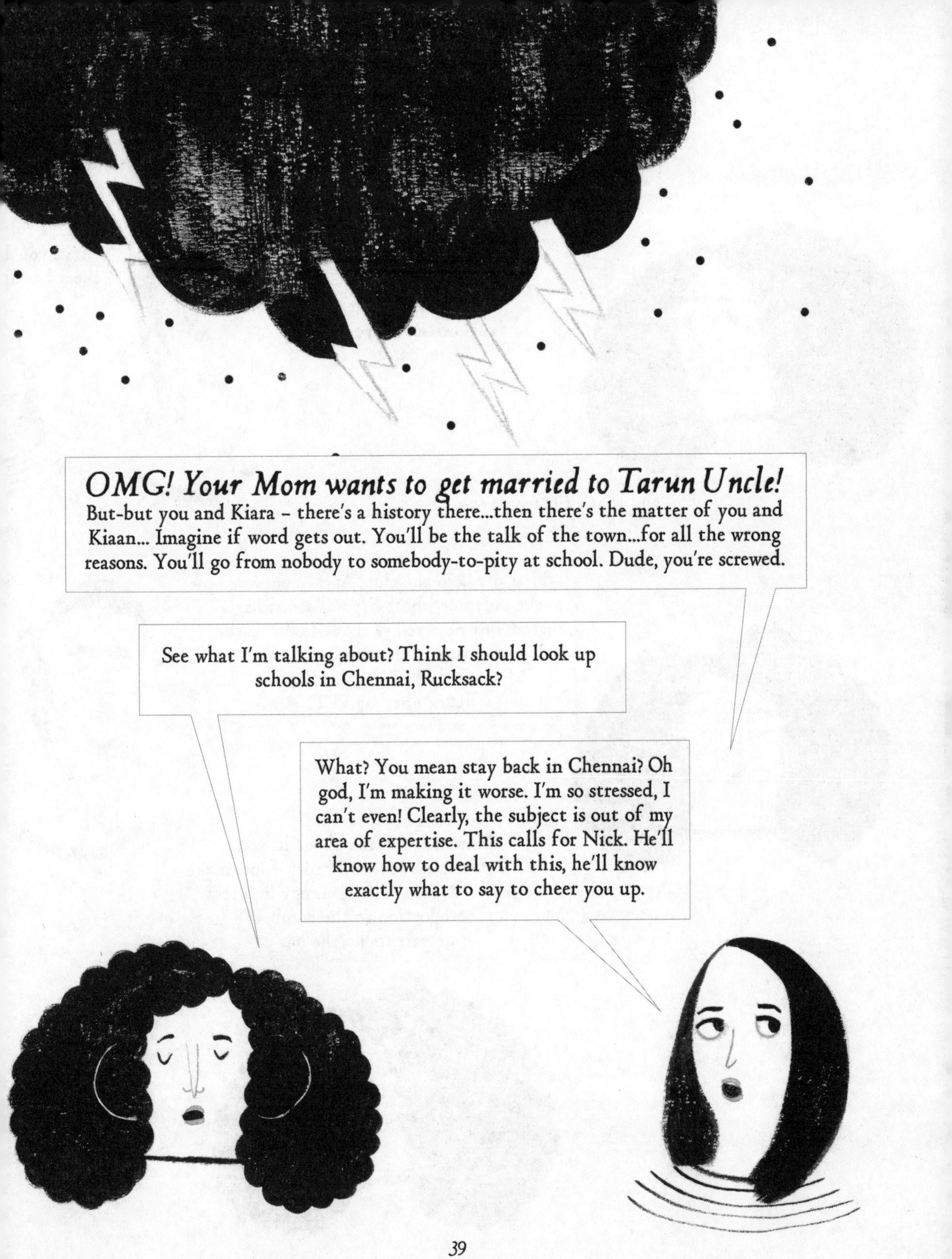
OMG! Your Mom wants to get married to Tarun Uncle!
But-but you and Kiara – there's a history there...then there's the matter of you and Kiaan... Imagine if word gets out. You'll be the talk of the town...for all the wrong reasons. You'll go from nobody to somebody-to-pity at school. Dude, you're screwed.
See what I'm talking about? Think I should look up schools in Chennai, Rucksack?
What? You mean stay back in Chennai? Oh god, I'm making it worse. I'm so stressed, I can't even! Clearly, the subject is out of my area of expertise. This calls for Nick. He'll know how to deal with this, he'll know exactly what to say to cheer you up.

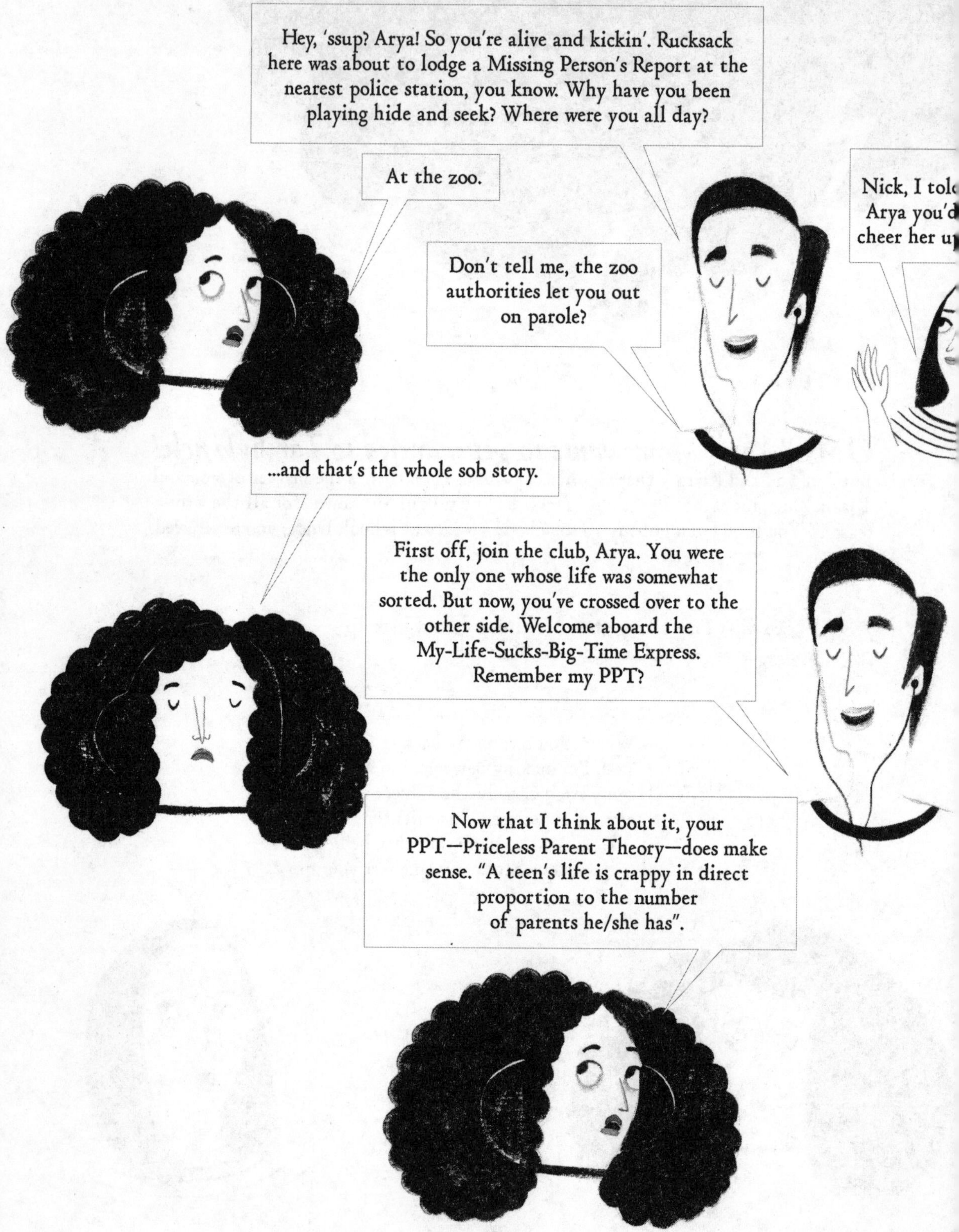
Hey, 'ssup? Arya! So you're alive and kickin'. Rucksack here was about to lodge a Missing Person's Report at the nearest police station, you know. Why have you been playing hide and seek? Where were you all day?
At the zoo.
Nick, I tol Arya you'd cheer her u
Don't tell me, the zoo authorities let you out on parole?
...and that's the whole sob story.
First off, join the club, Arya. You were the only one whose life was somewhat sorted. But now, you've crossed over to the other side. Welcome aboard the My-Life-Sucks-Big-Time Express. Remember my PPT?
Now that I think about it, your PPT—Priceless Parent Theory—does make sense. "A teen's life is crappy in direct proportion to the number of parents he/she has".

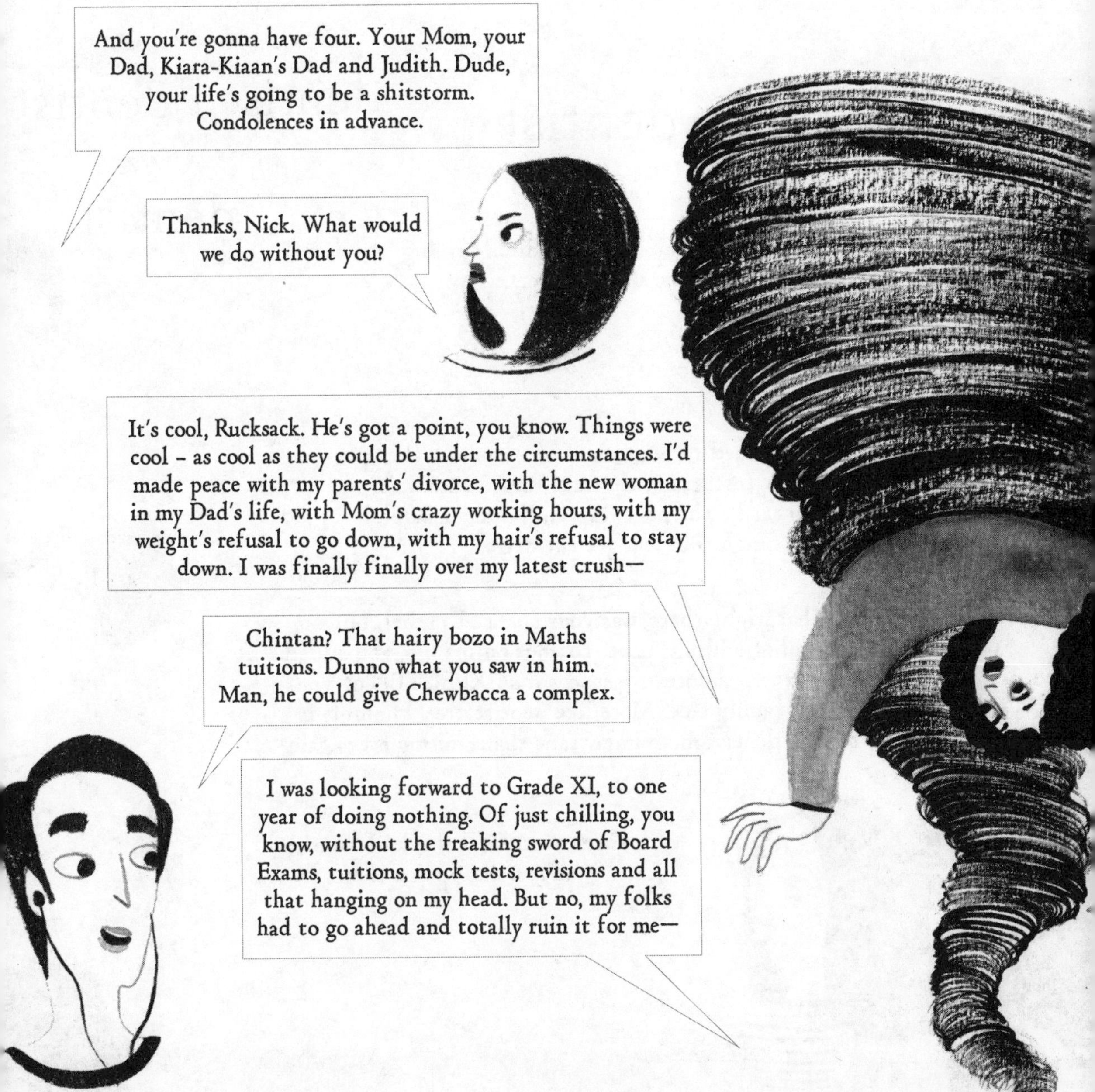
And you're gonna have four. Your Mom, your Dad, Kiara-Kiaan's Dad and Judith. Dude, your life's going to be a shitstorm. Condolences in advance.
Thanks, Nick. What would we do without you?
It's cool, Rucksack. He's got a point, you know. Things were cool – as cool as they could be under the circumstances. I'd made peace with my parents' divorce, with the new woman in my Dad's life, with Mom's crazy working hours, with my weight's refusal to go down, with my hair's refusal to stay down. I was finally finally over my latest crush—
Chintan? That hairy bozo in Maths tuitions. Dunno what you saw in him. Man, he could give Chewbacca a complex.
I was looking forward to Grade XI, to one year of doing nothing. Of just chilling, you know, without the freaking sword of Board Exams, tuitions, mock tests, revisions and all that hanging on my head. But no, my folks had to go ahead and totally ruin it for me—

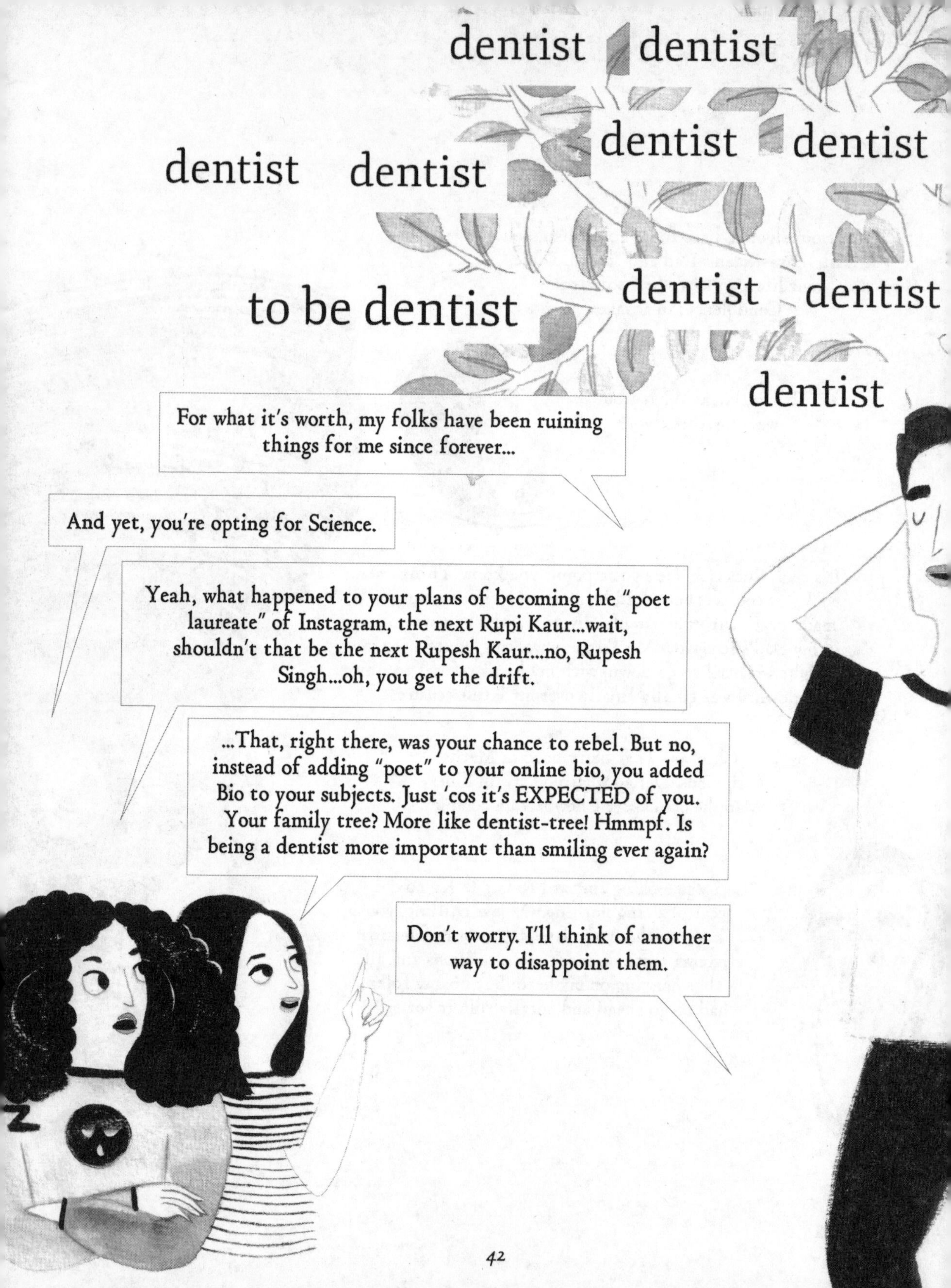
dentist dentist
dentist dentist
dentist dentist
to be dentist
dentist dentist
dentist
For what it's worth, my folks have been ruining things for me since forever...
And yet, you're opting for Science.
Yeah, what happened to your plans of becoming the "poet laureate" of Instagram, the next Rupi Kaur...wait, shouldn't that be the next Rupesh Kaur...no, Rupesh Singh...oh, you get the drift.
...That, right there, was your chance to rebel. But no, instead of adding "poet" to your online bio, you added Bio to your subjects. Just 'cos it's EXPECTED of you. Your family tree? More like dentist-tree! Hmmpf. Is being a dentist more important than smiling ever again?
Don't worry. I'll think of another way to disappoint them.

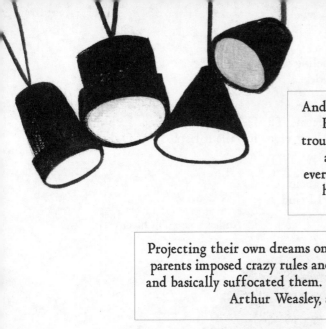

And don't even get me started on your folks, Rucksack. Coaxing you to join theatre troupes, making you audition for ads, movies, and even those godawful soaps, where everyone looks as though they are in fashion hell, hamming away to high heavens—

Projecting their own dreams on to you. Just 'cos their parents imposed crazy rules and restrictions on them and basically suffocated them. Not exactly Molly and Arthur Weasley, are they.

Oh god, you're right. My life's the pits. Now I'm depressed.

You speak for all of us, my child.

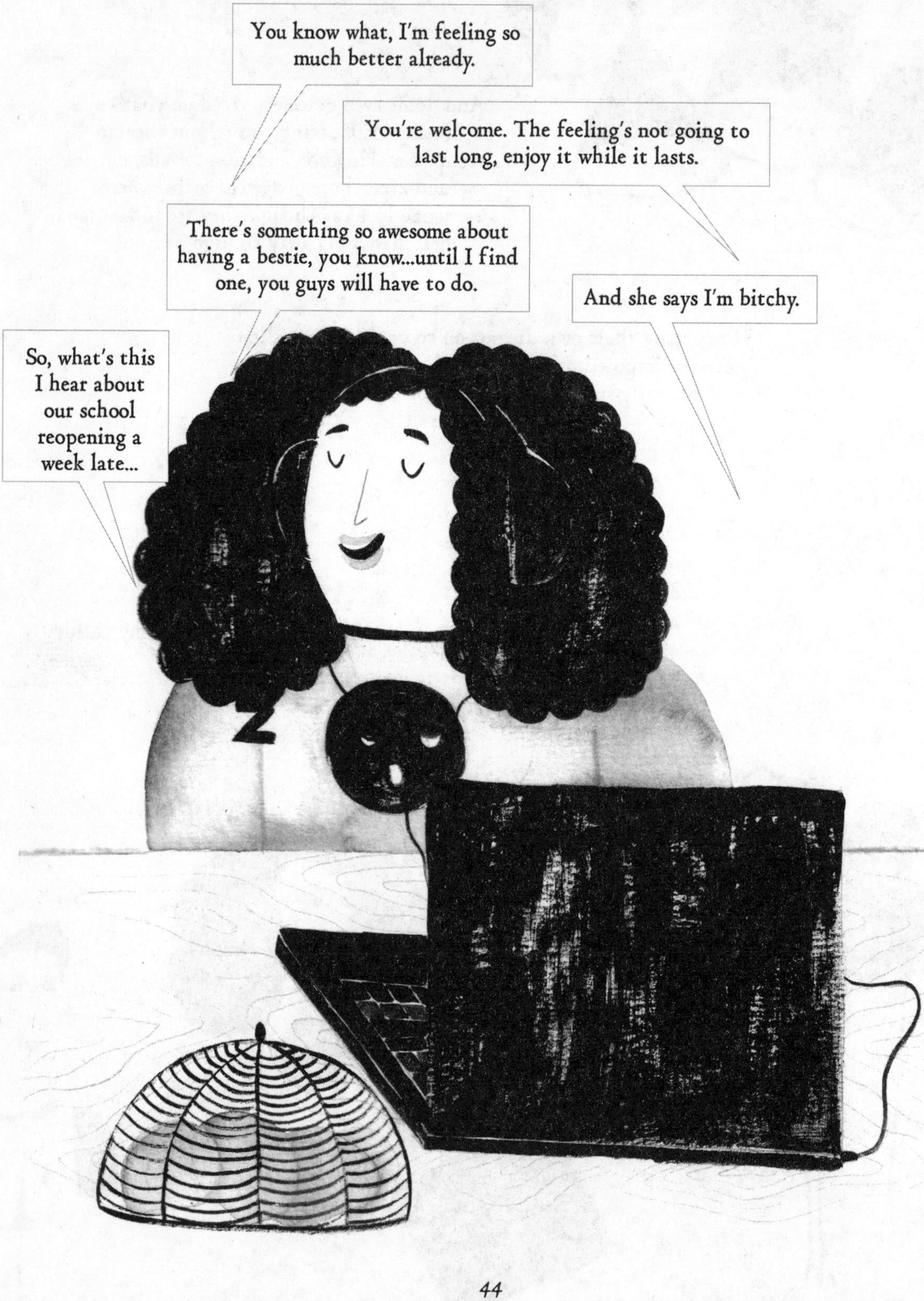
You know what, I'm feeling so much better already.
You're welcome. The feeling's not going to last long, enjoy it while it lasts.
There's something so awesome about having a bestie, you know...until I find one, you guys will have to do.
And she says I'm bitchy.
So, what's this I hear about our school reopening a week late...

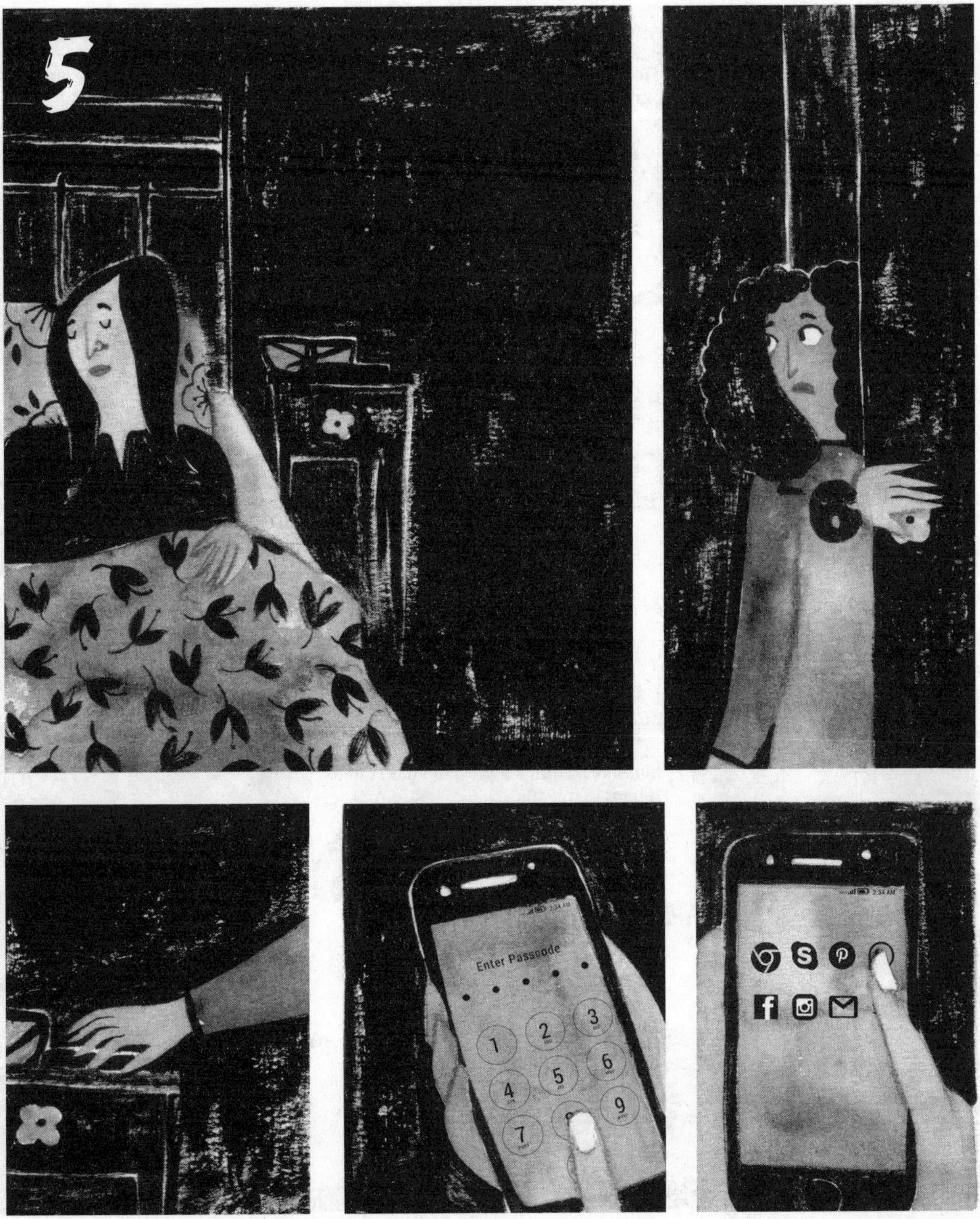
5
6
Enter Passcode
1
2
3
4
5
6
7
8
9

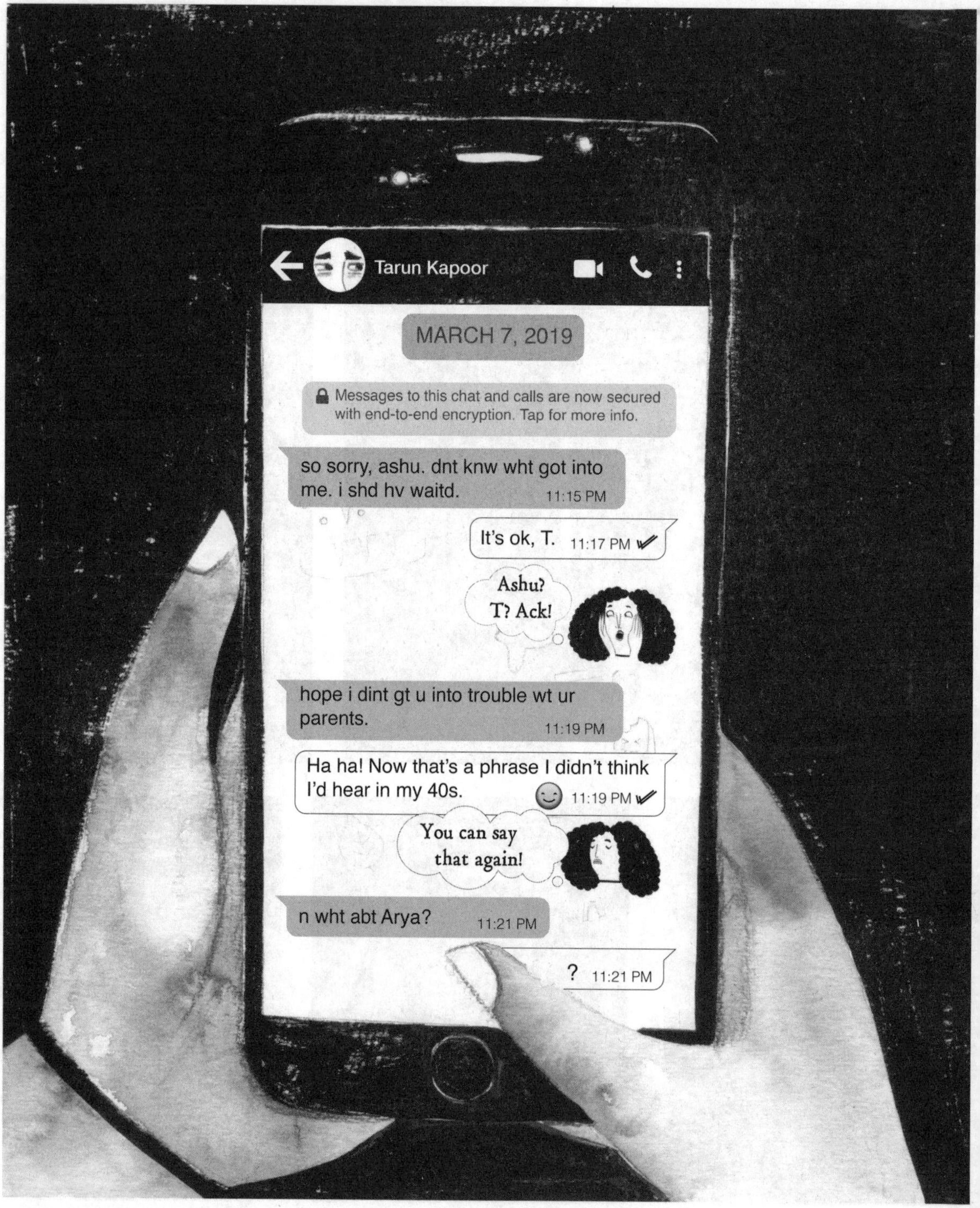
Tarun Kapoor
MARCH 7, 2019
Messages to this chat and calls are now secured with end-to-end encryption. Tap for more info.
so sorry, ashu. dnt knw wht got into me. i shd hv waitd. 11:15 PM
It's ok, T. 11:17 PM
Ashu? T? Ack!
hope i dint gt u into trouble wt ur parents. 11:19 PM
Ha ha! Now that's a phrase I didn't think I'd hear in my 40s. 11:19 PM
You can say that again!
n wht abt Arya? 11:21 PM
? 11:21 PM

hw did she react? was she shocked? angry? did she guess? oh god, I'm an idiot!!! 11:23 PM

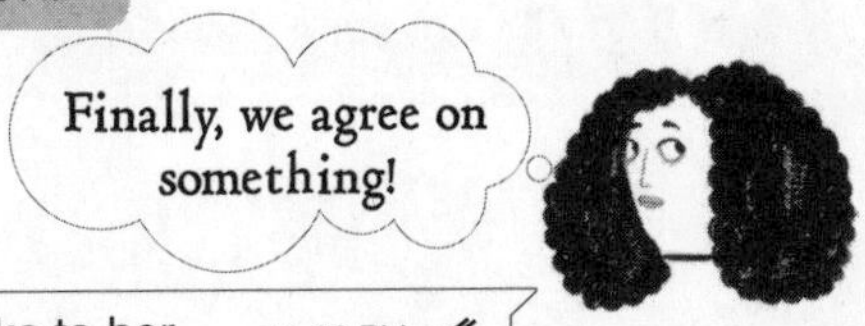
Finally, we agree on something!

Calm down, T. I spoke to her. 11:23 PM

you did? and? 11:25 PM

She was upset, shaken up. It was to be expected. 11:25 PM

bt u cn brng hr around, right??? u wl convince hr??? 11:27 PM

I don't know, T. She has a mind of her own. I wouldn't have it any other way. I've raised her to think independently. Encouraged her to question things. Given her the freedom to make her own decisions. I can't expect her to behave differently now. 11:27 PM

i dnt undrstnd, ash. wht r u sayin??? 11:30 PM

I'm just saying I need time, Arya needs time. I don't want to rush her into anything. I'm sure she'll come around. 11:30 PM

bt wht if sh doesn't??? wht if she's dead against the idea??? wht wl we do thn? 11:33 PM

We've been through this, T. My answer's the same. She's a great kid. She deserves the best. 11:33 PM

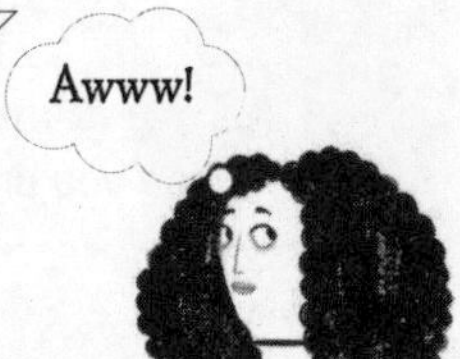
Awww!

i'll luv hr as much as my own kids, ashu. promise. 11:36 PM

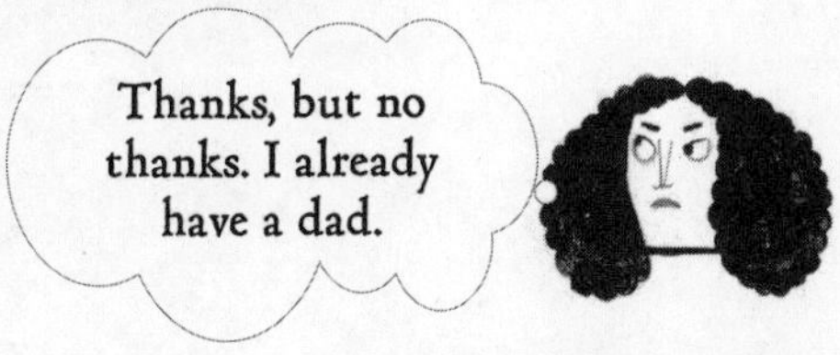
Thanks, but no thanks. I already have a dad.

I'm not a great mother, you know.   11:38 PM ✔

ash, u knw tht's nt true.   11:38 PM

Whatcha talkin' about. Mom? You're right up there.

I just haven't been able to give her time. You know how crazy hectic things are at work.   11:38 PM ✔

tht's bcos u startd a nw firm!!! thngs wl settle dwn.   11:40 PM

The divorce was hard on her. She's been through a lot. Doesn't help that Mukund's away and she gets to see him only once a year.   11:42 PM ✔

it's nt ur fault tht ur ex movd to America!!!   11:42 PM

Ummm, do they still say America?

I may not be able to give her the best of things or my complete undivided attention or be there for her all the time but I'll do everything in my power to make her happy.   11:44 PM ✔

evn if it means breaking up wt me???   11:44 PM

☹ ☹ ☹ I'm sorry, T. If Arya's not for it, then it's what it's got to be. I hope you understand.   11:47 PM ✔

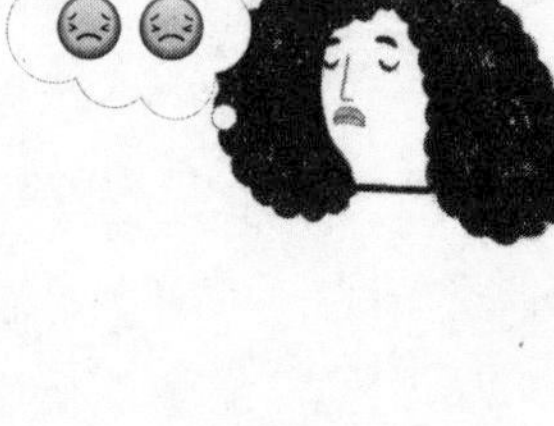

48

I know, I shouldn't have, but her phone was practically calling out to me. Yeah, it was "password protected". Took me like, two seconds to crack it. Parents, I tell you. Even middle graders don't put the month and year of birth as their passcode. After going through the convo, okay, okay, after snooping around, two things became pret–ty clear: 1. My habit of texting long freaking paragraphs? Could totally see where I got that from. 2. Tarun Uncle? He wasn't so bad. Pity, I couldn't say the same about his punctuation. But it wasn't as if I signed him on to play step daddy on the spot. That happened a couple of days later.

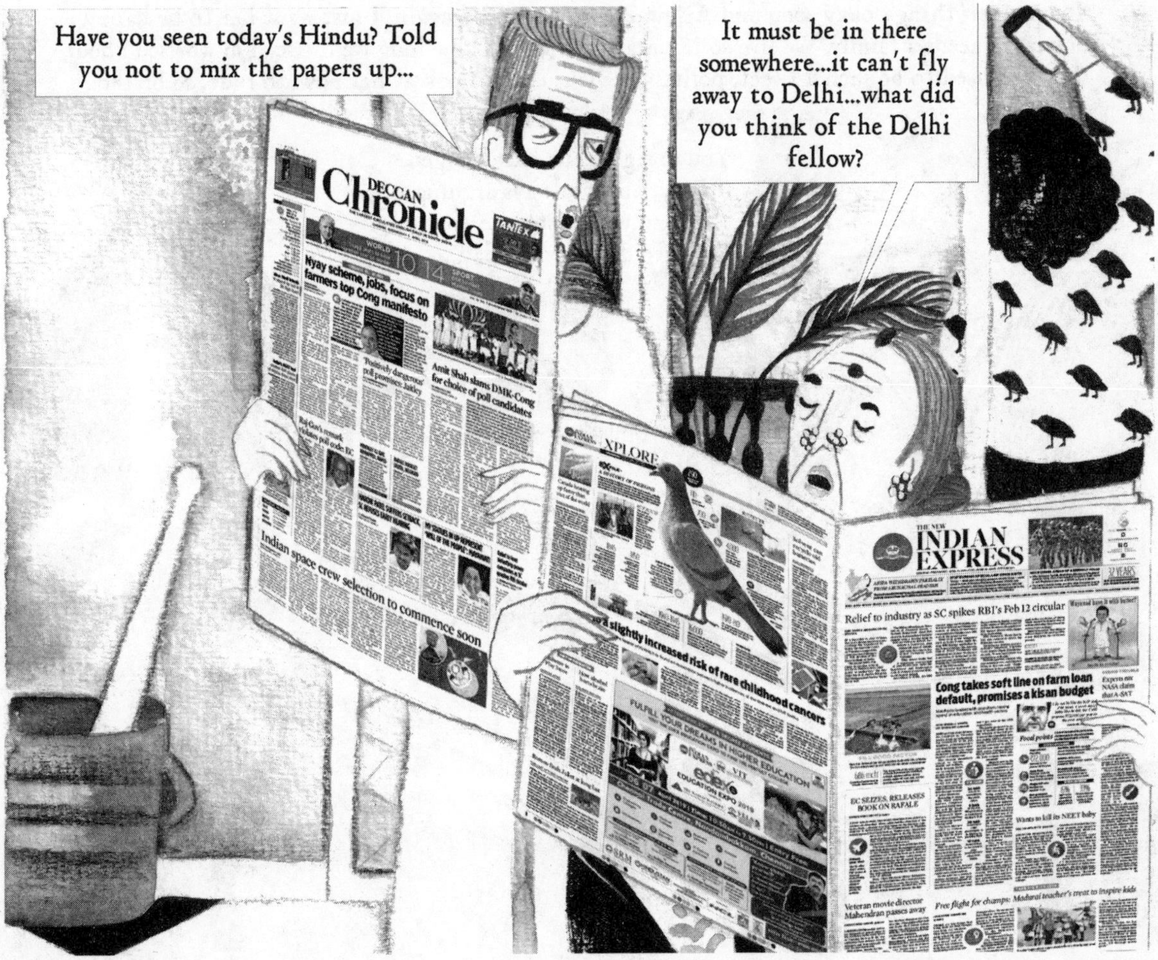
Have you seen today's Hindu? Told you not to mix the papers up...
It must be in there somewhere...it can't fly away to Delhi...what did you think of the Delhi fellow?
DECCAN Chronicle
Nyay scheme, jobs, focus on farmers top Cong manifesto
Indian space crew selection to commence soon
XPLORE
a slightly increased risk of rare childhood cancers
THE NEW INDIAN EXPRESS
Relief to industry as SC spikes RBI's Feb 12 circular
Cong takes soft line on farm loan default, promises a kisan budget

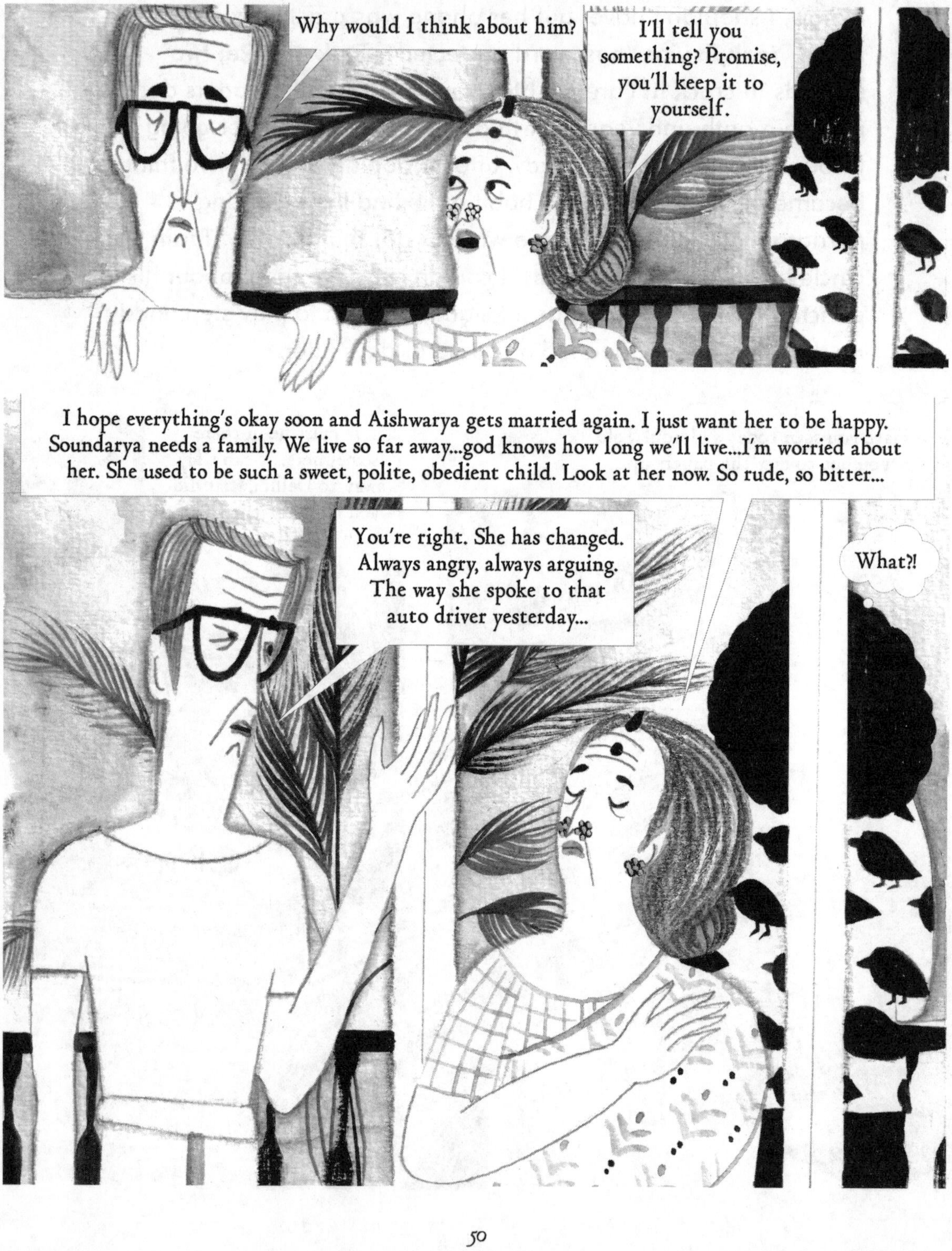
Why would I think about him?
I'll tell you something? Promise, you'll keep it to yourself.
I hope everything's okay soon and Aishwarya gets married again. I just want her to be happy. Soundarya needs a family. We live so far away...god knows how long we'll live...I'm worried about her. She used to be such a sweet, polite, obedient child. Look at her now. So rude, so bitter...
You're right. She has changed. Always angry, always arguing. The way she spoke to that auto driver yesterday...
What?!

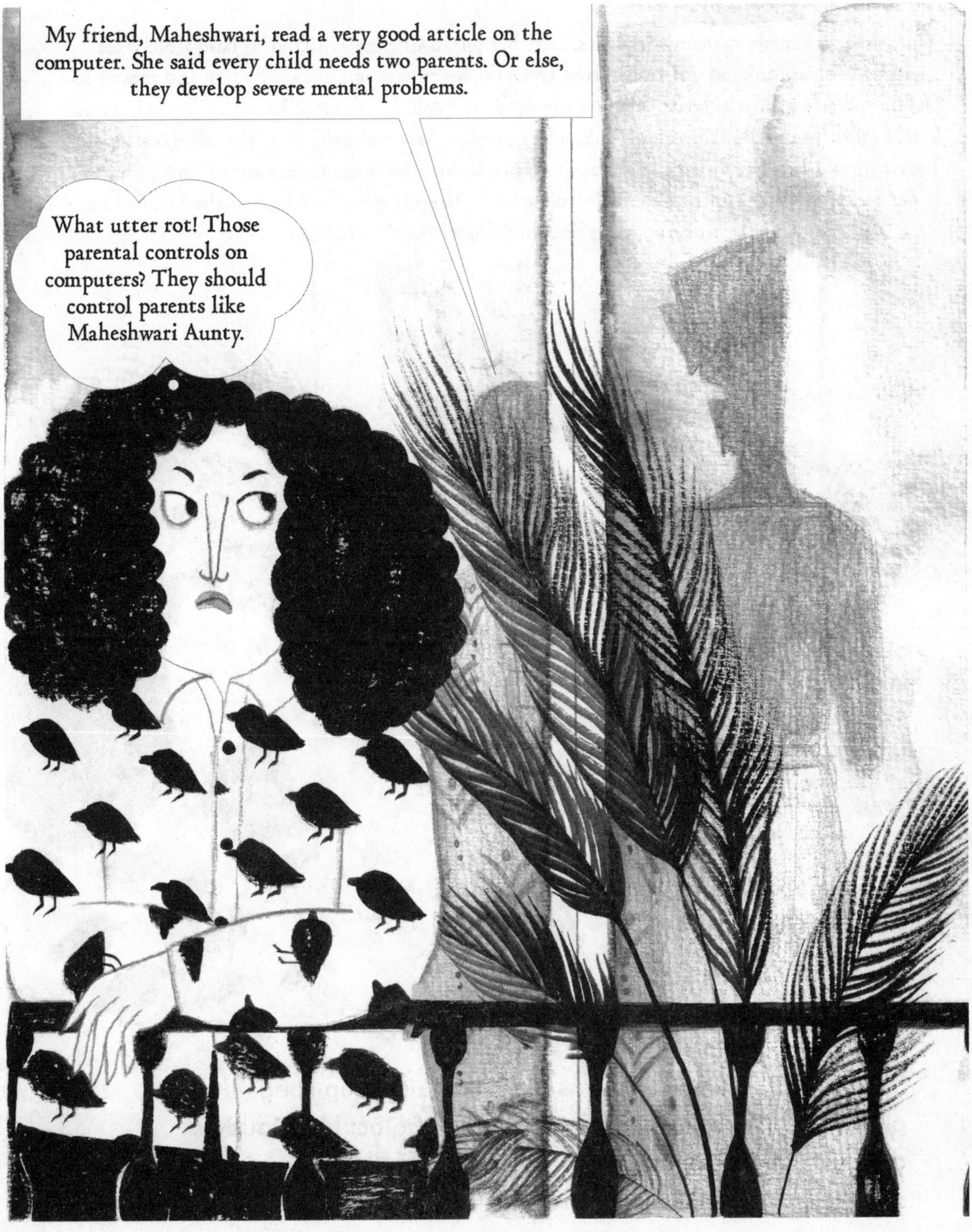
My friend, Maheshwari, read a very good article on the computer. She said every child needs two parents. Or else, they develop severe mental problems.
What utter rot! Those parental controls on computers? They should control parents like Maheshwari Aunty.

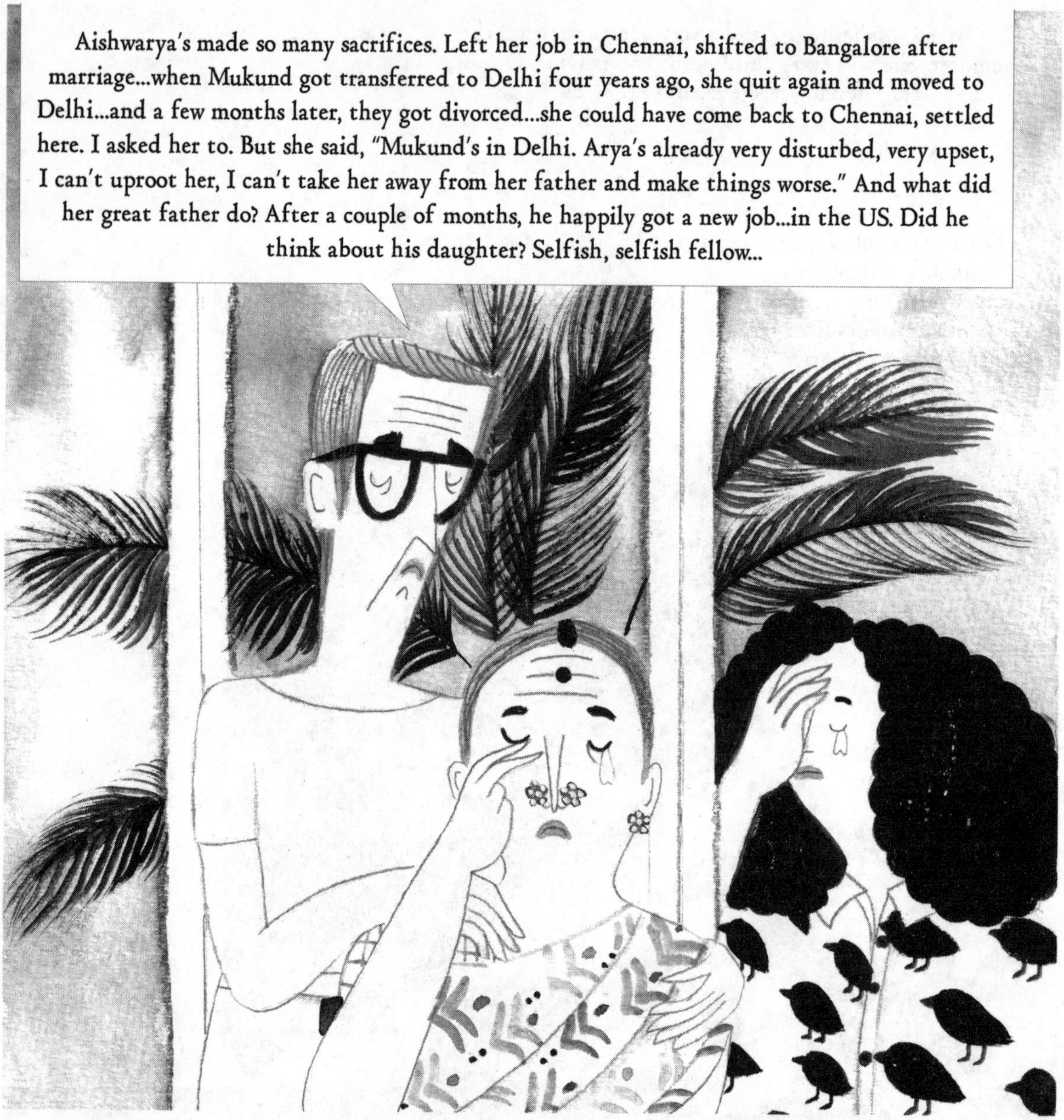
Aishwarya's made so many sacrifices. Left her job in Chennai, shifted to Bangalore after marriage...when Mukund got transferred to Delhi four years ago, she quit again and moved to Delhi...and a few months later, they got divorced...she could have come back to Chennai, settled here. I asked her to. But she said, "Mukund's in Delhi. Arya's already very disturbed, very upset, I can't uproot her, I can't take her away from her father and make things worse." And what did her great father do? After a couple of months, he happily got a new job...in the US. Did he think about his daughter? Selfish, selfish fellow...

Selfish. Selfish. The word was like a freaking pop song – it kept playing on loop in my head. Was I going to act like Daddy's daughter? After all that Mom had done for me? Or was I going to suck it up and put "we" before "me"? I knew what I had to do...

6

...I had to ping Manasi. She was a friend from Bangalore. Her Mom had remarried, they had moved to Mumbai, and we'd gone from being Society homies to social media buds. We weren't exactly Blair-Serena, Rory-Lane, but she was cool, in a Yoda sort of way. More importantly, she was the only one sailing in the same freaking boat.

Hey. Ages! How's it going?

Hey u. Same old, same old. U?

Been better. Heart the new DP, BTW. How's Mumbai?

TY. Flooded. Frustrating. Same as always.

Damn! Bet you miss B'lore.

Every. Single. Day. 😩😩

How's Del?

Unbearably hot. Unsafe. Same as always. Am in Chennai at the moment. No place like B'lore, though. It's amaze. Awesome weather, great food, safe-ish. How are things? School? Home?

Dunno what I hate more. Forget it, you don't wanna know.

Actually, I do. So, here's the thing. Mom's kind of seeing someone and I think it's serious.

That blows! Pray they don't get hitched.

I think they just might. What's it like? You know, having a new family?

It's like having an old family, but a jillion times worse. Imagine having to change cities, schools, apartments, basically your whole life. My life wasn't perfect — far from it. But still. You know what I'm saying, right? It's like you're used to a certain life. It's your life, and one fine day, it's not. And you didn't choose your new life. But there's nothing you can do about it.

😣😣😣😣😣😣😣

It's awful in the beginning. You know, like the first day of flu. You're just down and out. And then, you get used to ***that,*** and it gets better... and worse...

Not ***exactly*** like the flu, then.

...'cos there's always something worse.

Gawd! What am I gonna do? How the hell am I gonna deal? Any hot tips? You know, for Fellow Daughters of Divorce and Remarriage? You know, in case it happens?

Just pray. Hard. That it doesn't, I guess. And read this book...A Teen's Guide to Parents' Divorce... and also, Your Parents' Marriage Is Over, Your Life Isn't. Will send links...and watch Blended...Stuck in Love...Yours, Mine, & Ours. Would you believe it's based on a real life couple? They had—believe it or faint—18 kids between them. Hang in there. If you ever need to talk, you know where to find me. May the force be with you. 😚

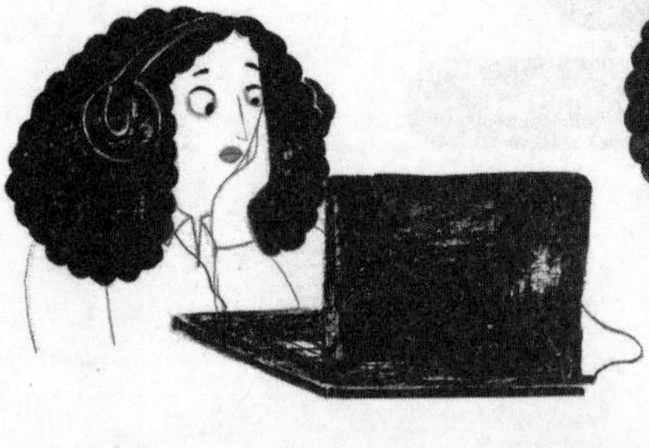

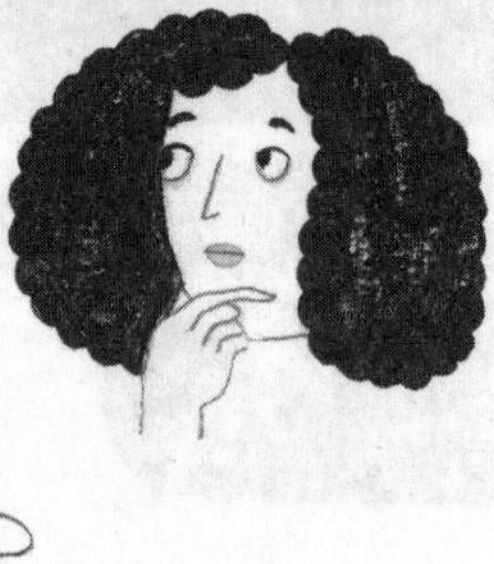

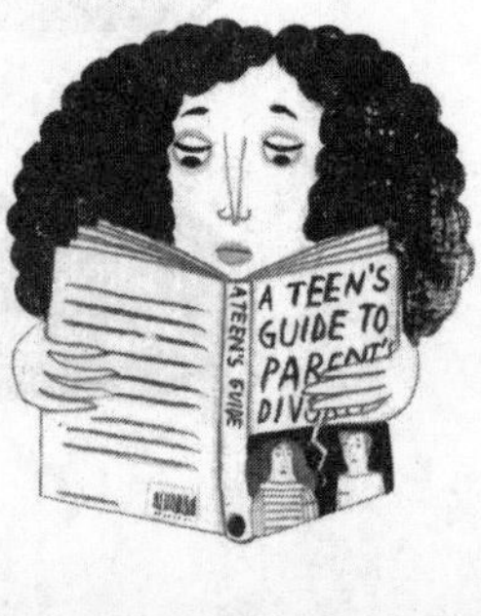
A TEEN'S GUIDE TO
A TEEN'S GUIDE

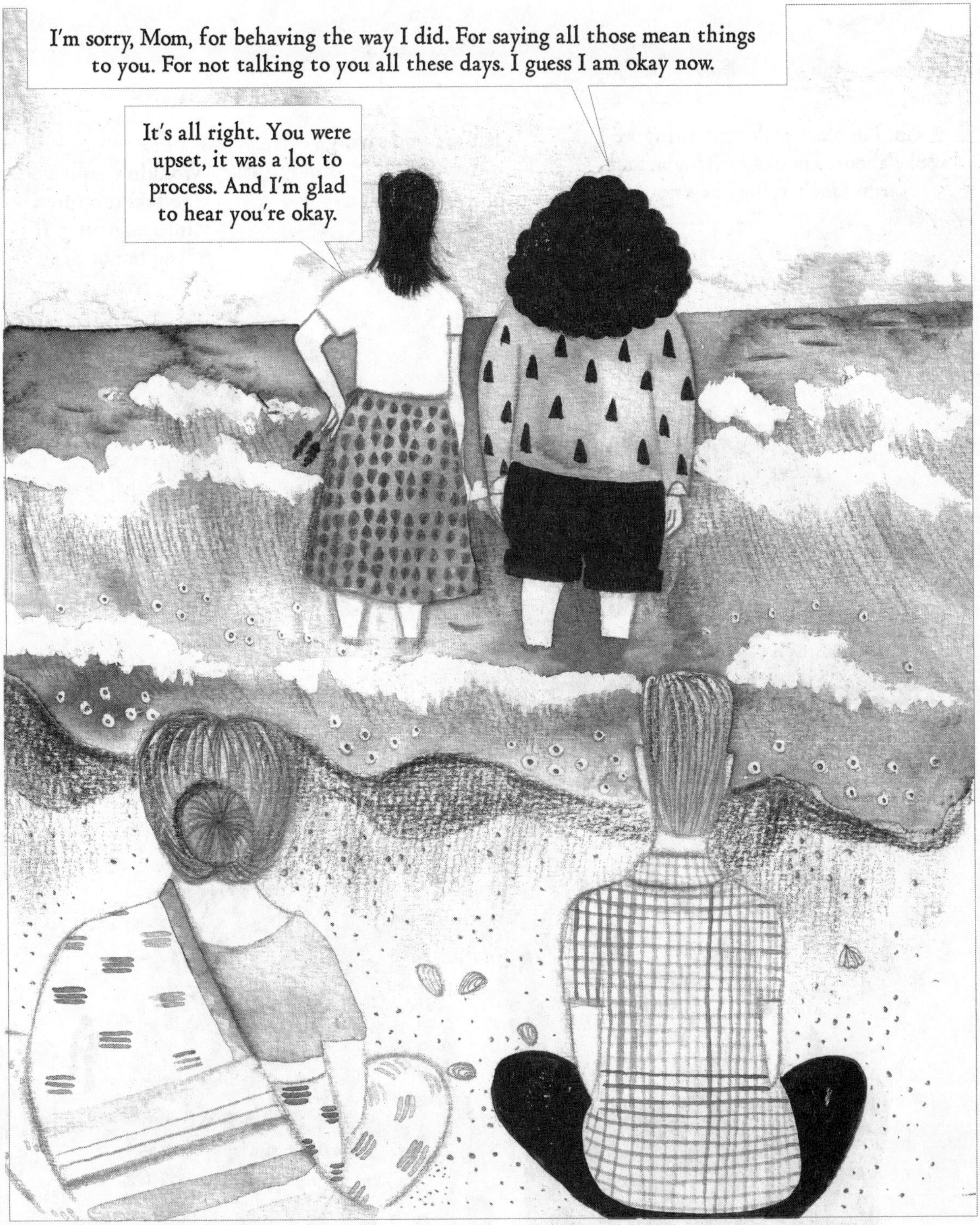
I'm sorry, Mom, for behaving the way I did. For saying all those mean things to you. For not talking to you all these days. I guess I am okay now.
It's all right. You were upset, it was a lot to process. And I'm glad to hear you're okay.

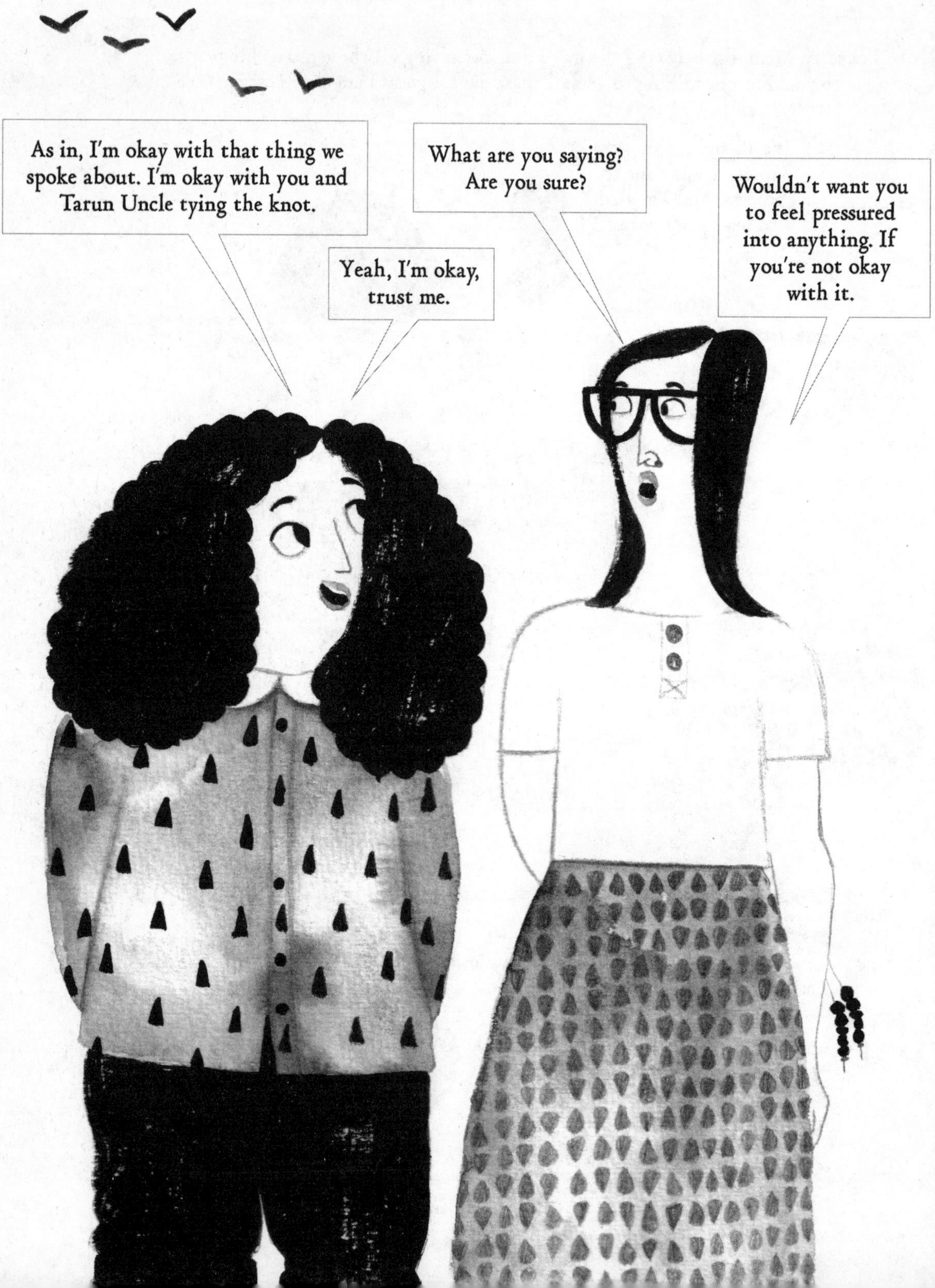
As in, I'm okay with that thing we spoke about. I'm okay with you and Tarun Uncle tying the knot.
What are you saying? Are you sure?
Wouldn't want you to feel pressured into anything. If you're not okay with it.
Yeah, I'm okay, trust me.

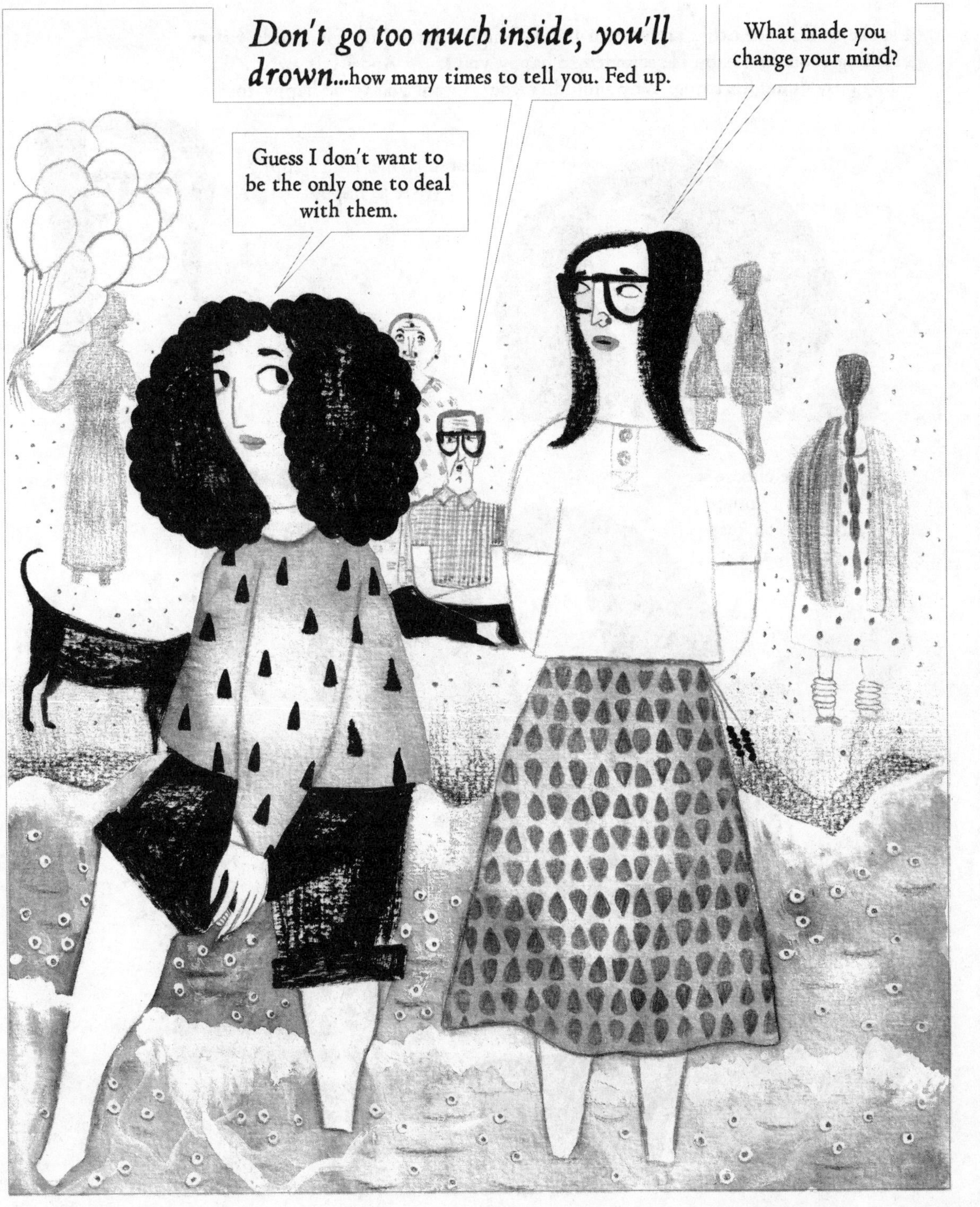
Guess I don't want to be the only one to deal with them.
Don't go too much inside, you'll drown...how many times to tell you. Fed up.
What made you change your mind?

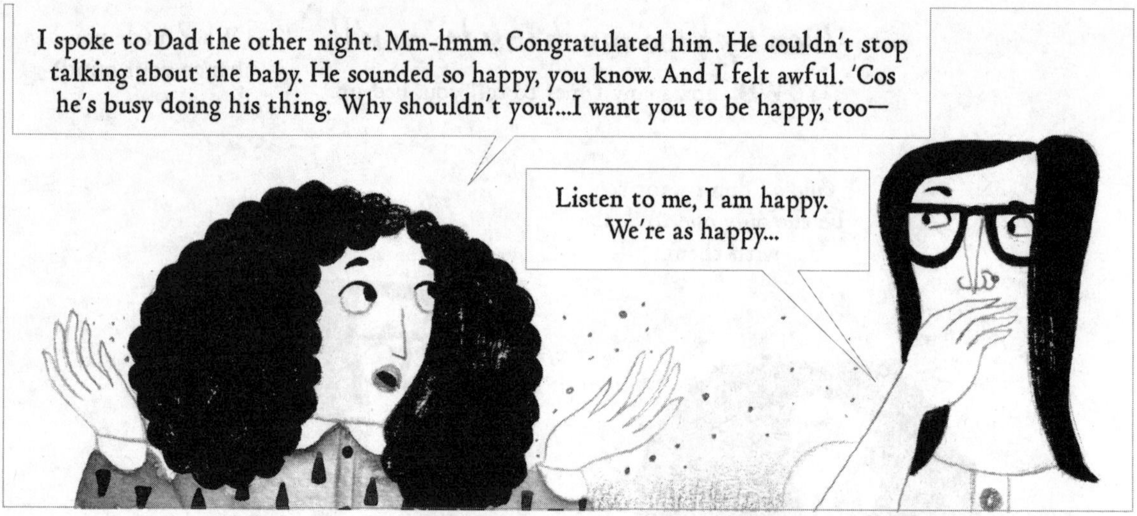
I spoke to Dad the other night. Mm-hmm. Congratulated him. He couldn't stop talking about the baby. He sounded so happy, you know. And I felt awful. 'Cos he's busy doing his thing. Why shouldn't you?...I want you to be happy, too—
Listen to me, I am happy. We're as happy...

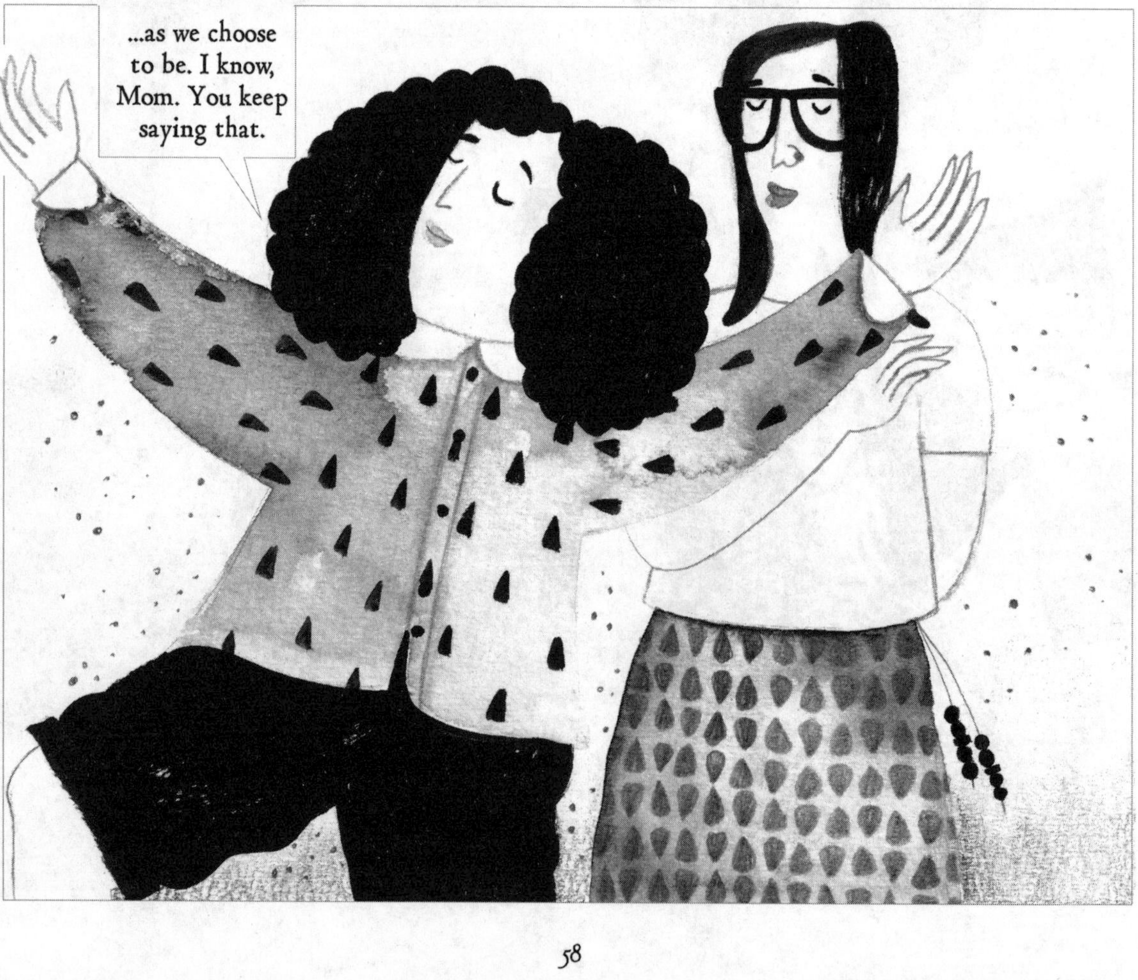
...as we choose to be. I know, Mom. You keep saying that.

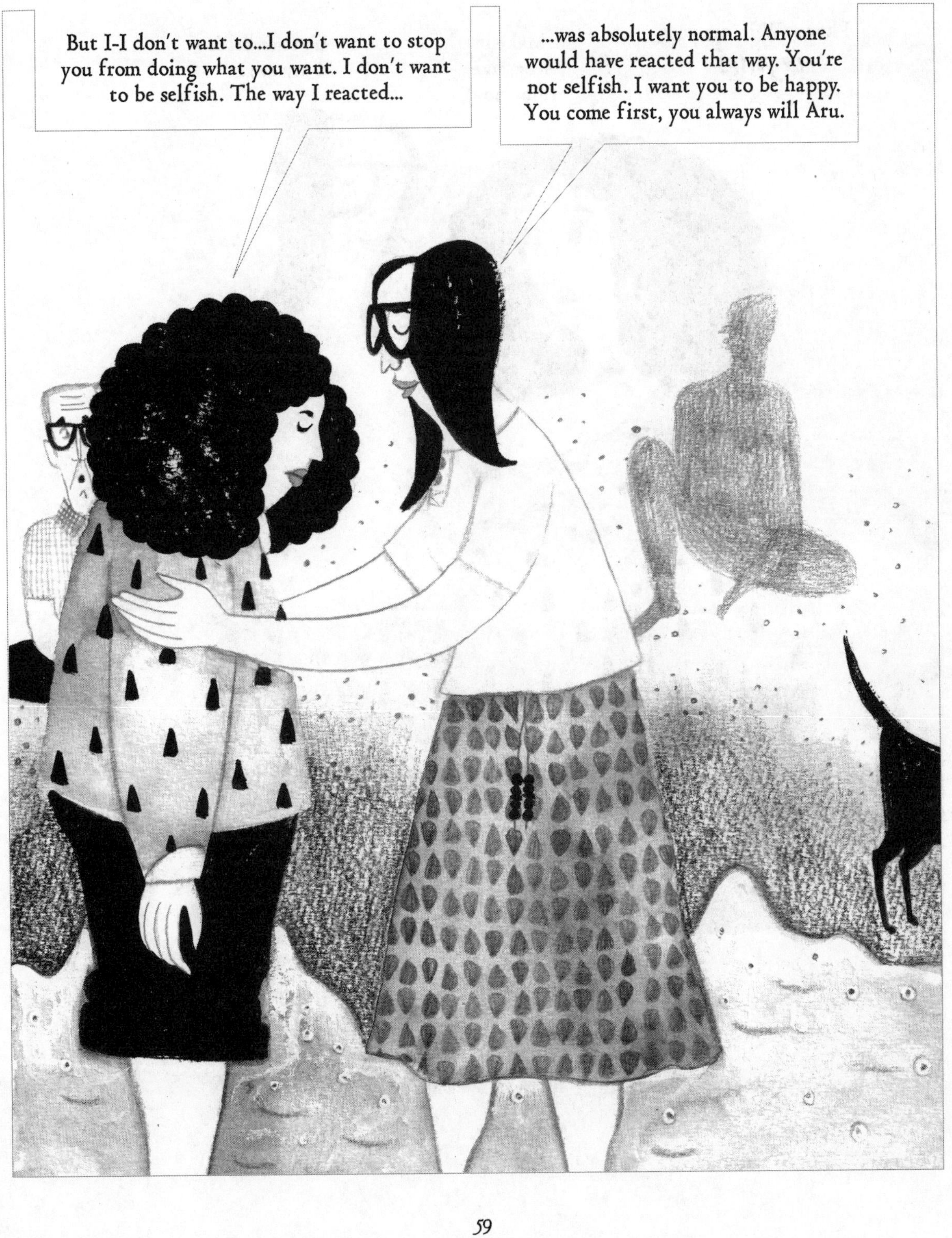
But I-I don't want to...I don't want to stop you from doing what you want. I don't want to be selfish. The way I reacted...
...was absolutely normal. Anyone would have reacted that way. You're not selfish. I want you to be happy. You come first, you always will Aru.

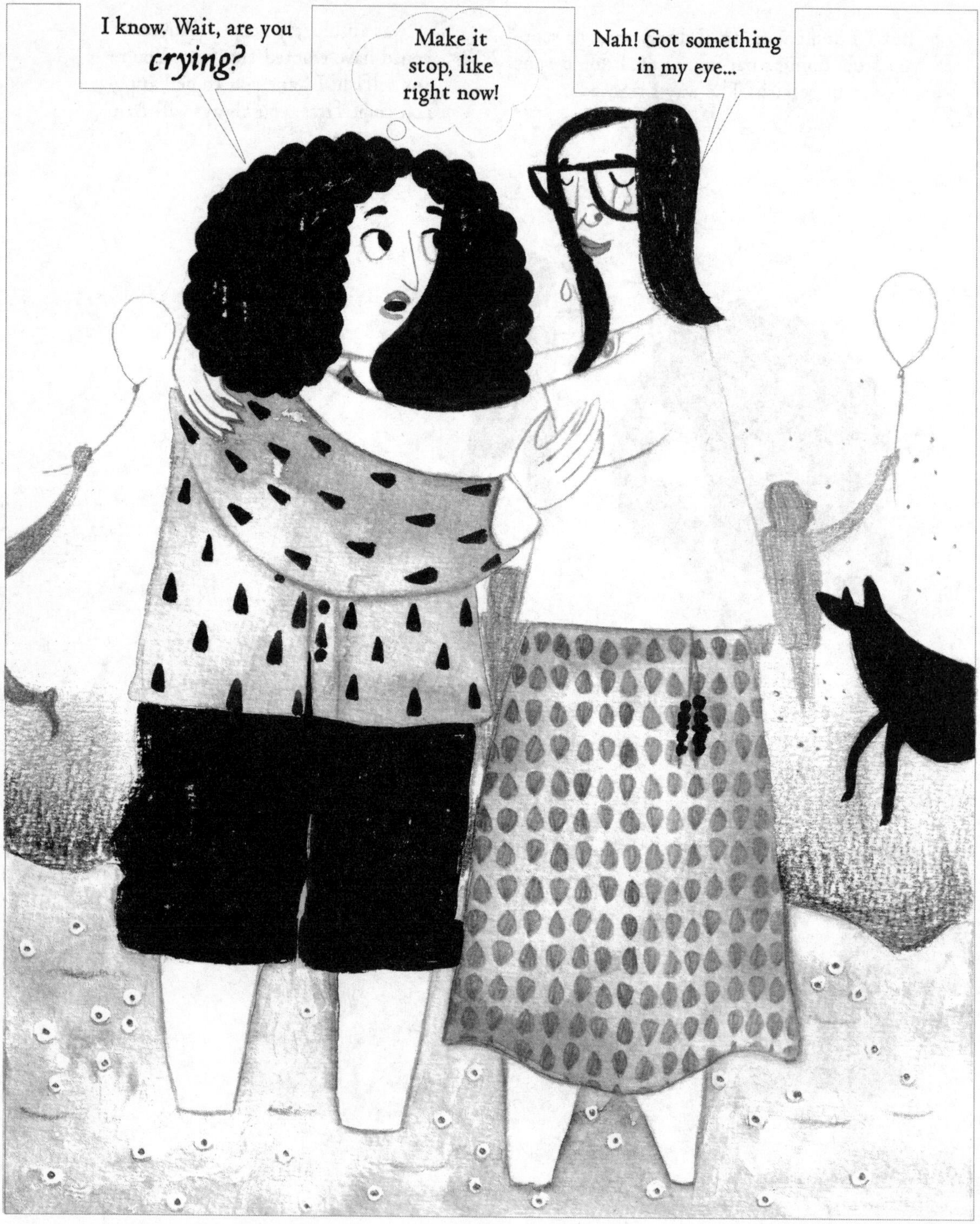
I know. Wait, are you *crying?*
Make it stop, like right now!
Nah! Got something in my eye...

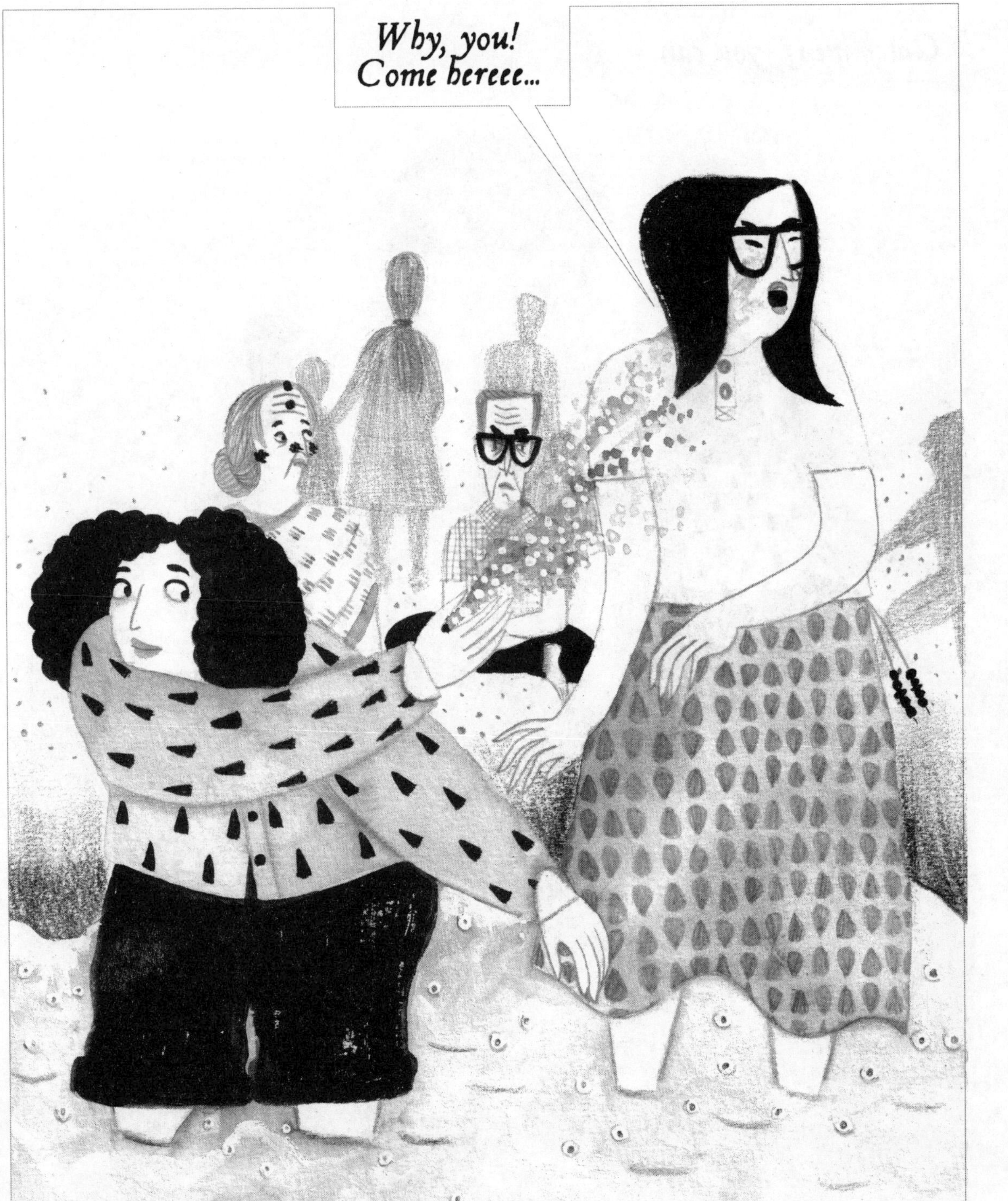
Why, you!
Come hereee...

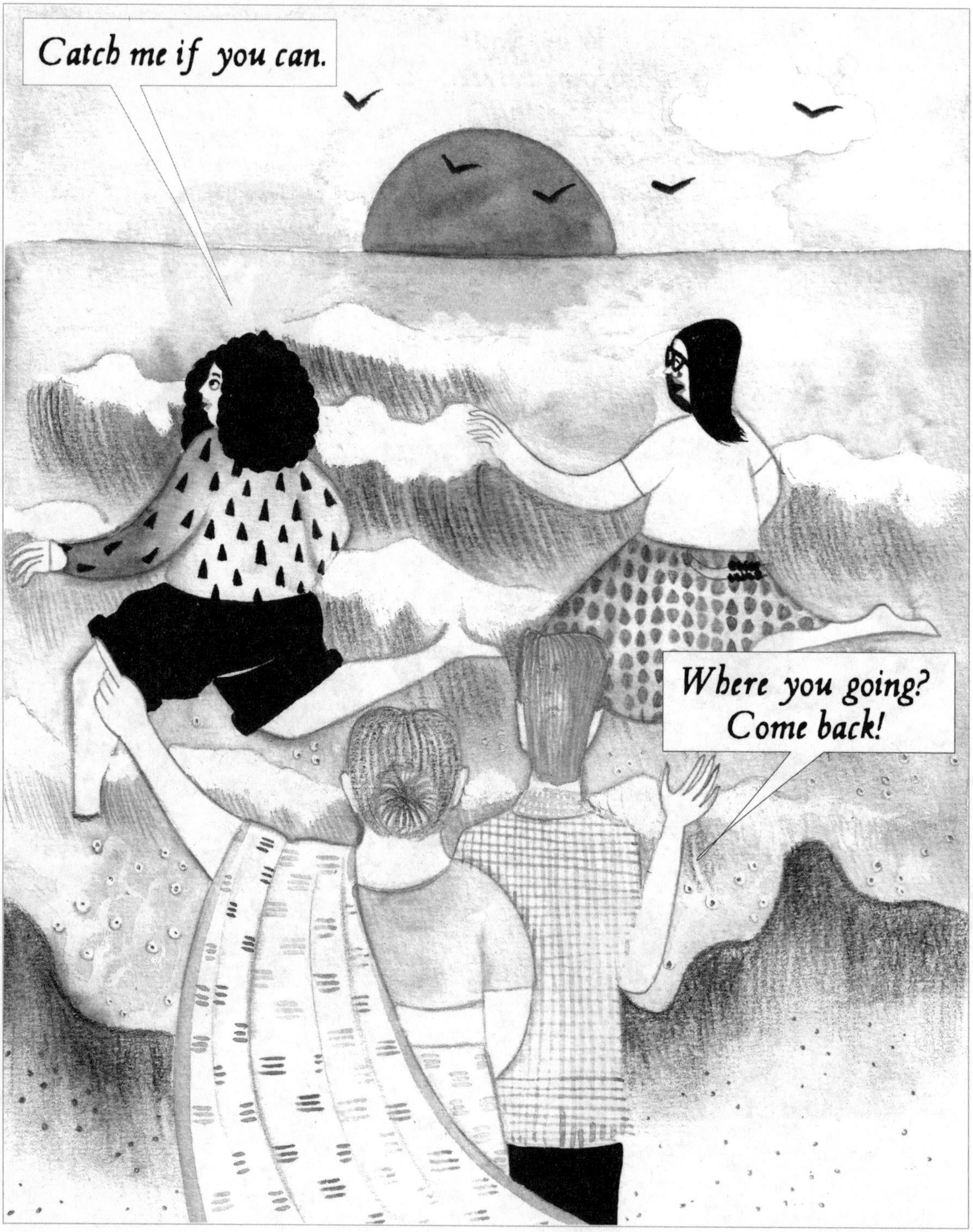
Catch me if you can.
Where you going? Come back!

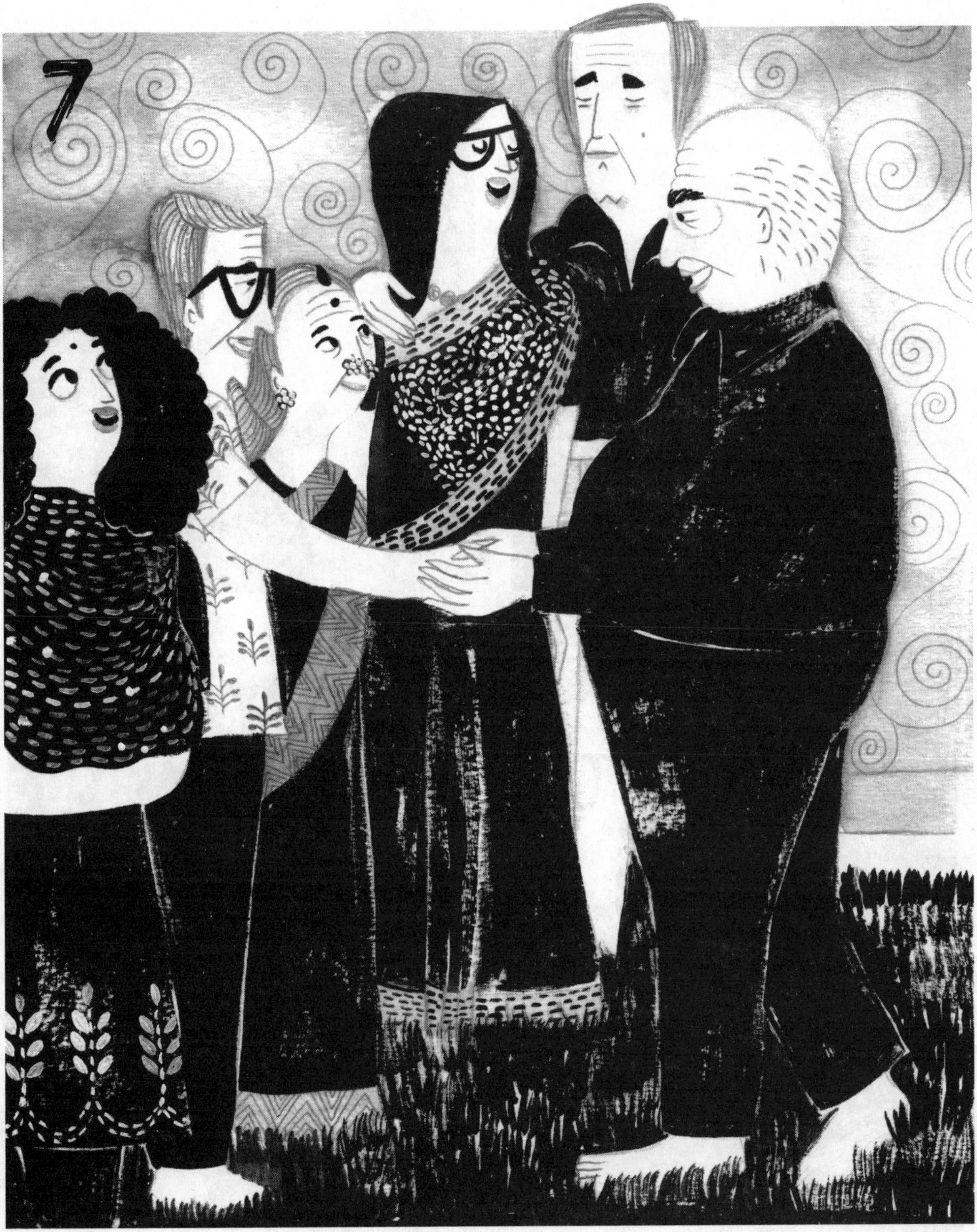
7

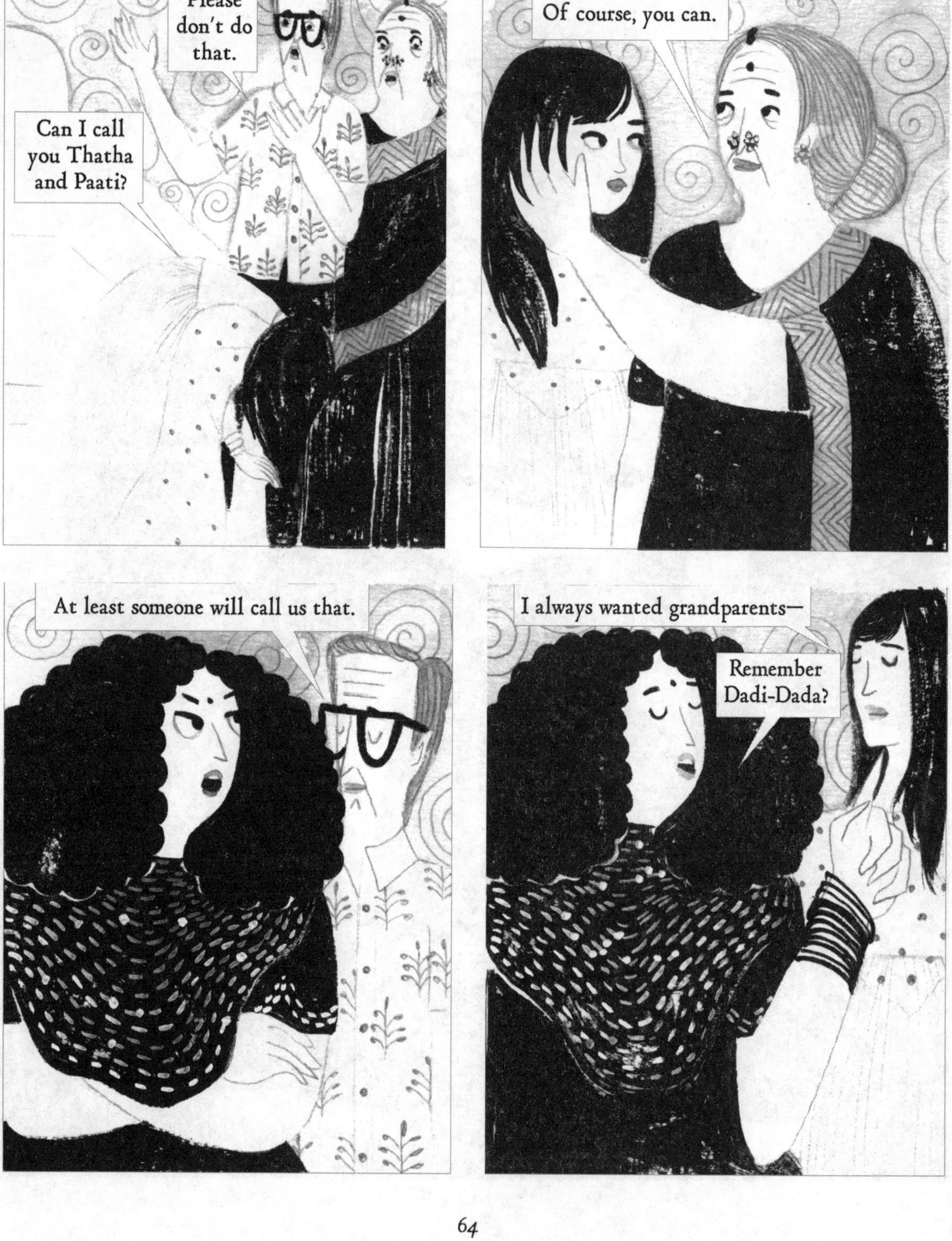
Please don't do that.
Can I call you Thatha and Paati?
Of course, you can.
At least someone will call us that.
I always wanted grandparents—
Remember Dadi-Dada?

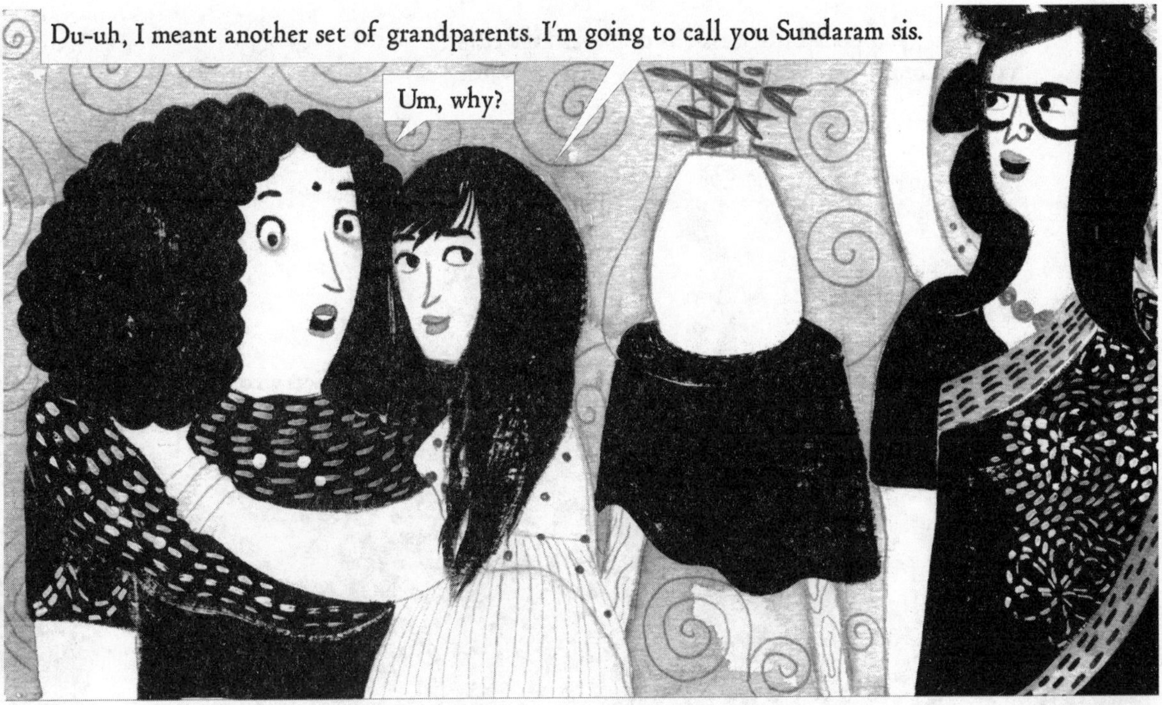
Du-uh, I meant another set of grandparents. I'm going to call you Sundaram sis.
Um, why?

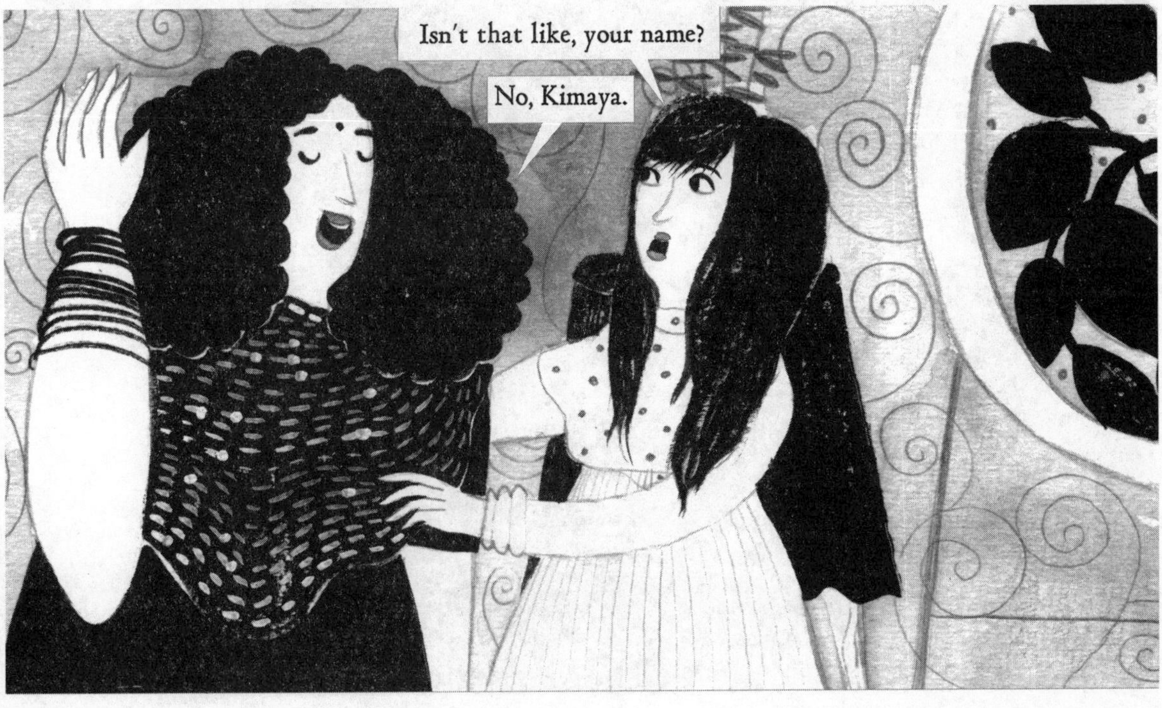
Isn't that like, your name?
No, Kimaya.

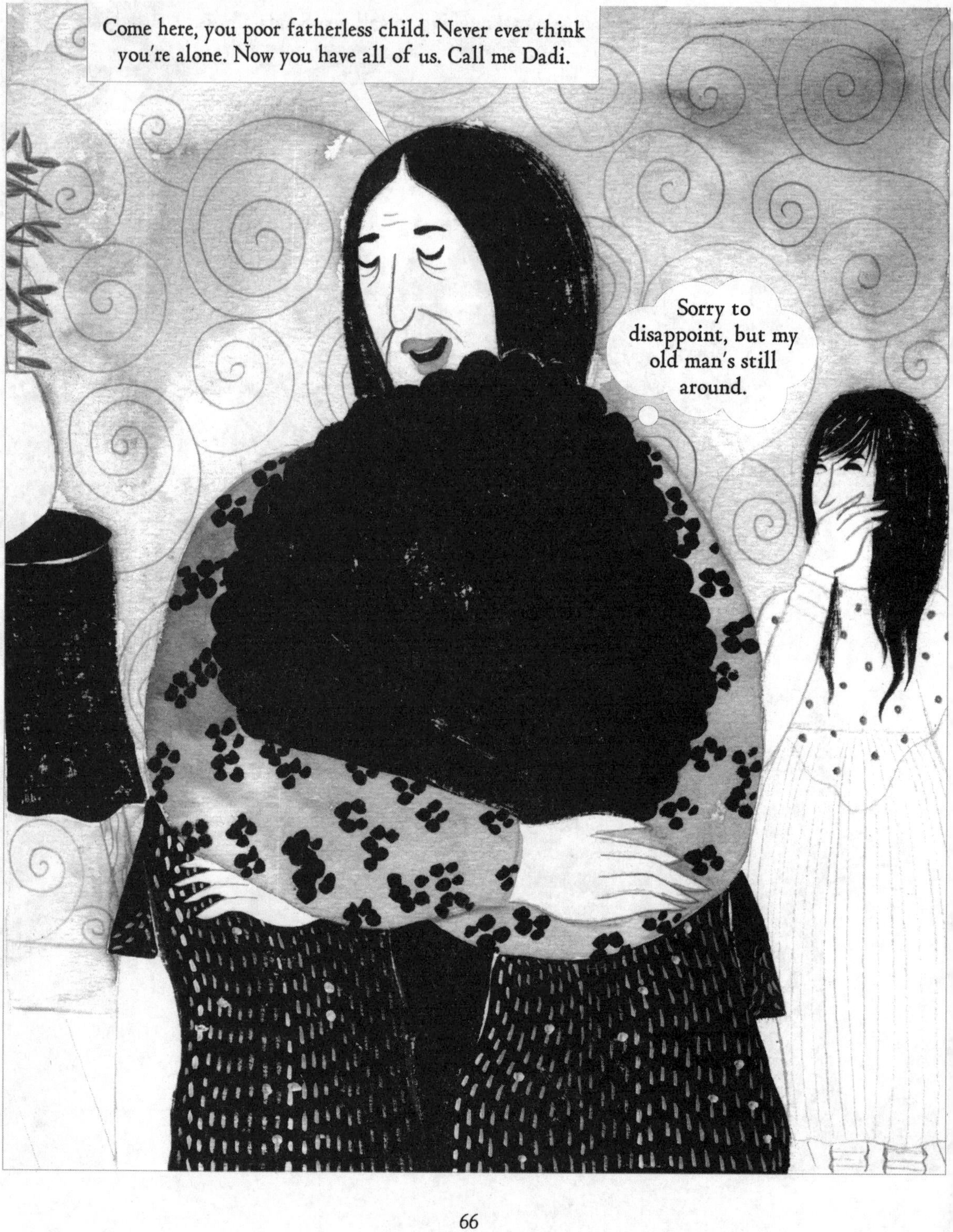
Come here, you poor fatherless child. Never ever think you're alone. Now you have all of us. Call me Dadi.
Sorry to disappoint, but my old man's still around.

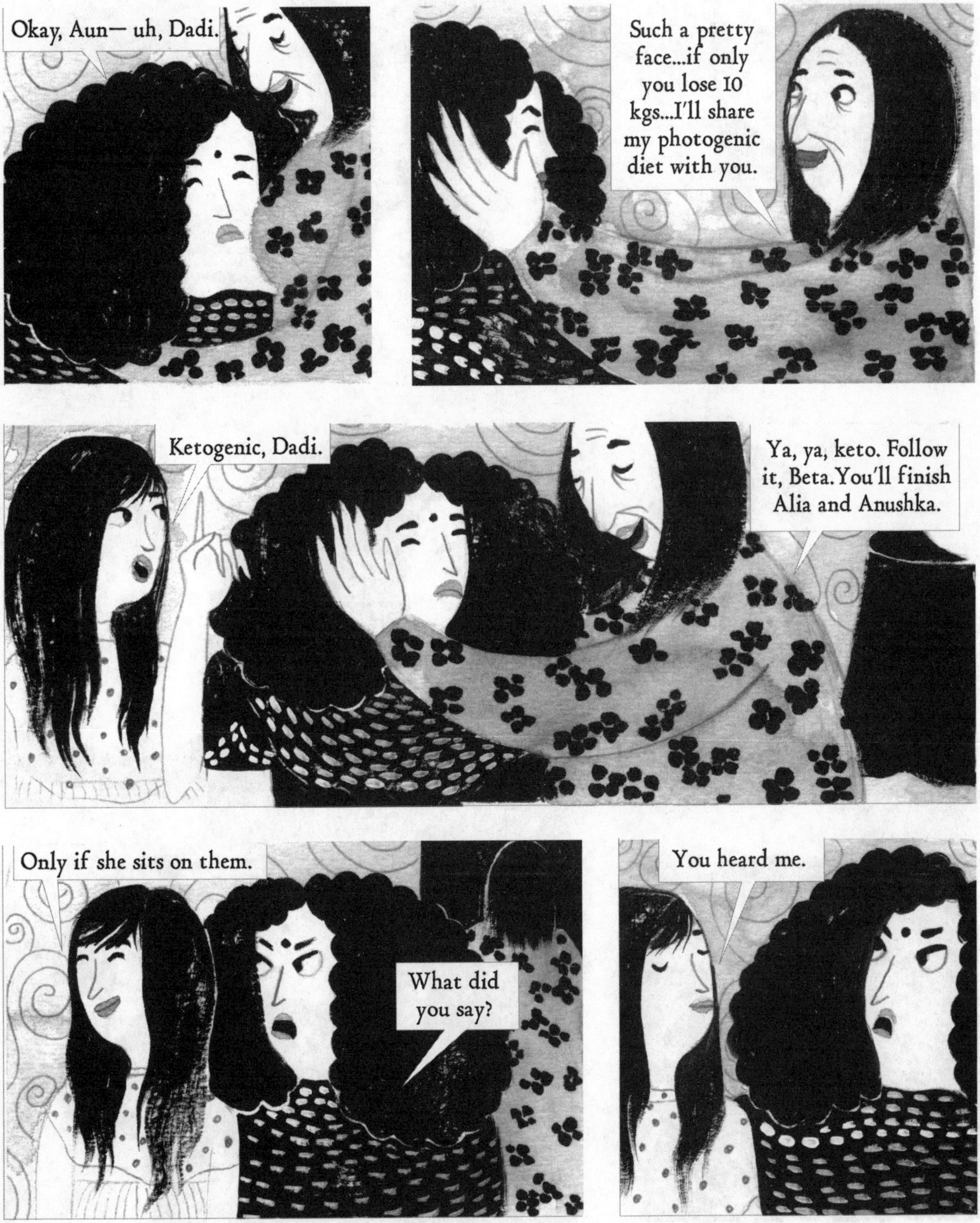
Okay, Aun— uh, Dadi.
Such a pretty face...if only you lose 10 kgs...I'll share my photogenic diet with you.
Ketogenic, Dadi.
Ya, ya, keto. Follow it, Beta. You'll finish Alia and Anushka.
Only if she sits on them.
What did you say?
You heard me.

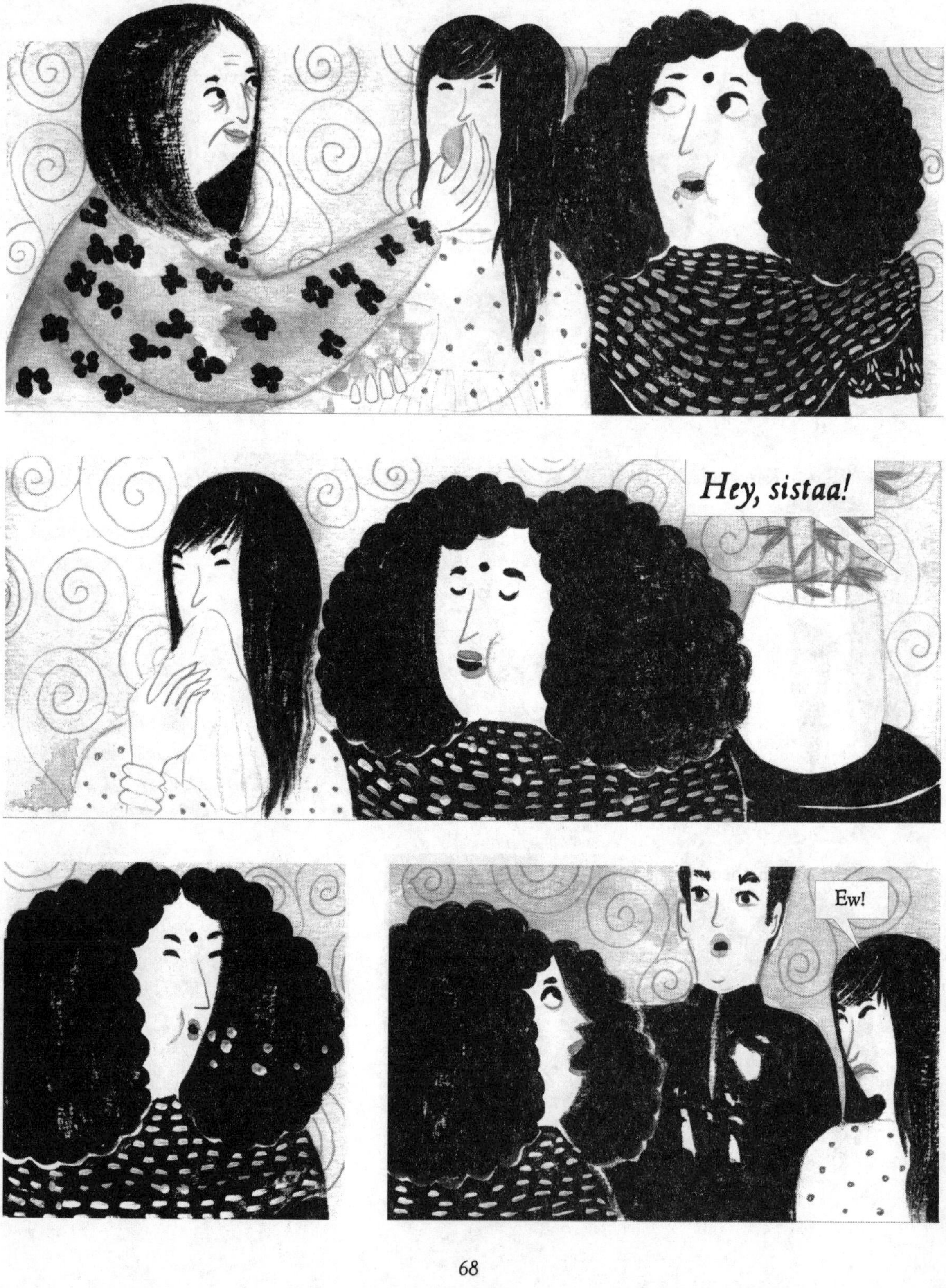
Hey, sistaa!
Ew!

Oh my god, sorryyy...

No worries. I was going to get it dry-cleaned anyway.

While you were still wearing it.

You know I'm the luckiest guy in the world. I always wanted two baby sisters.

You got more than you bargained for. 'Cos Arya's equal to two people.

Some people prefer curvy creatures to stick figures. Remember? Hey, your lips touched a gulab jamun. Shouldn't you go to the restroom and throw up, like, now?

I think you've got me mixed up with Natasha.

Your bestie Natasha?

Natasha has bulimia?

Please, she's not my bestie. We're in the same group. Anyway, a kickass body calls for sacrifices. Something you wouldn't know about.

Don't mind her, Arya. She's so retarded.

That's plain offensive. The word you used. Not cool. Inappropriate.

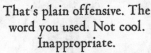

For real? Oops! My bad. I meant, she's a spaz.

I was crushing on this dude?

69

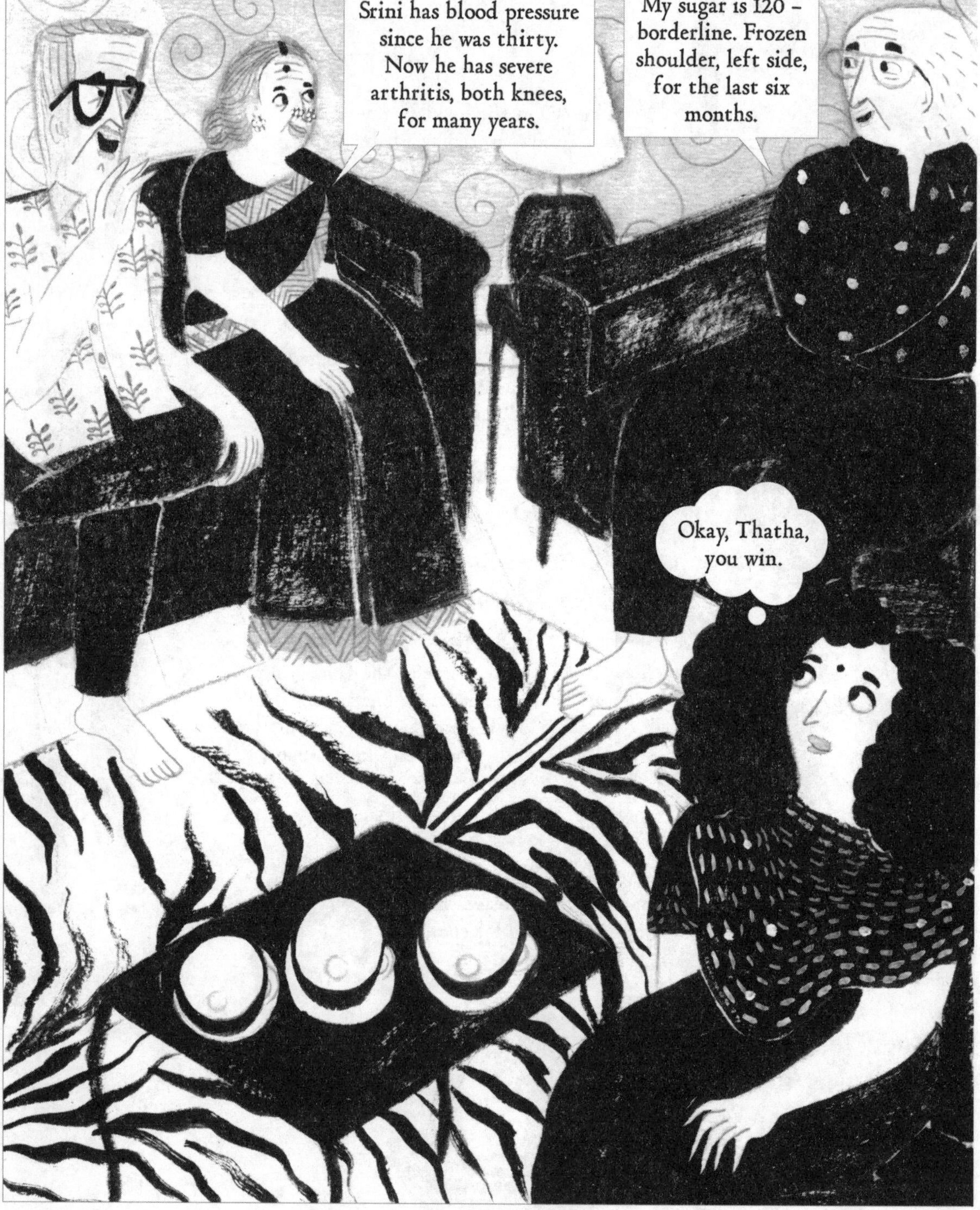
Srini has blood pressure since he was thirty. Now he has severe arthritis, both knees, for many years.
My sugar is 120 – borderline. Frozen shoulder, left side, for the last six months.
Okay, Thatha, you win.

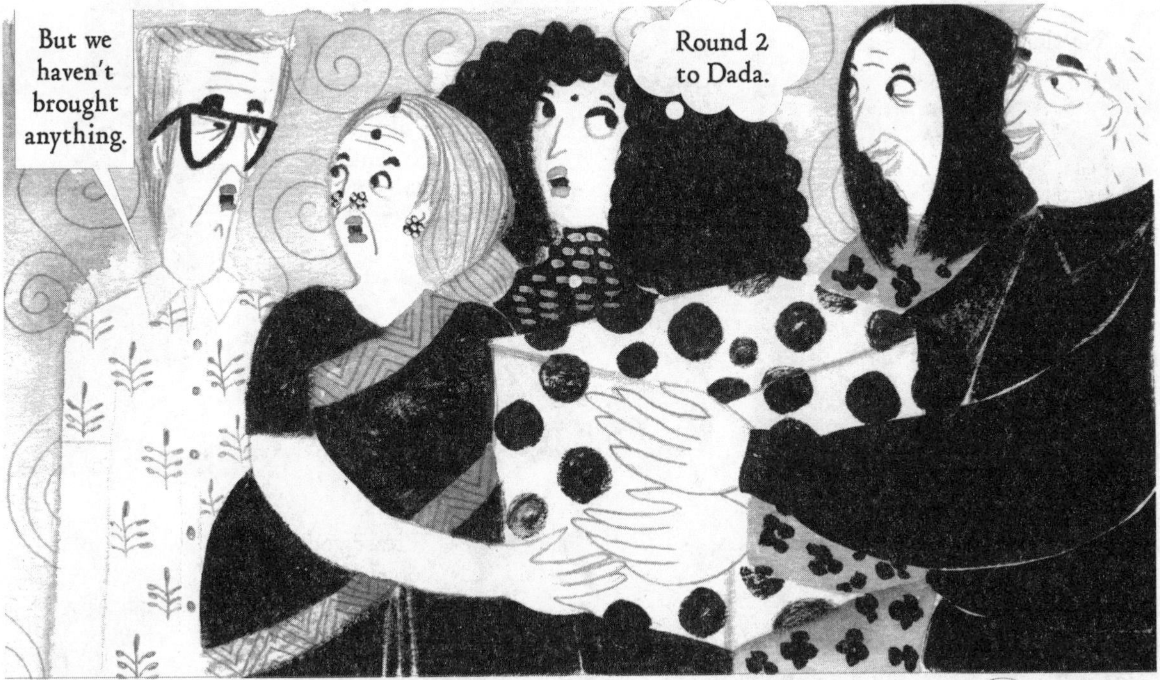
But we haven't brought anything.
Round 2 to Dada.

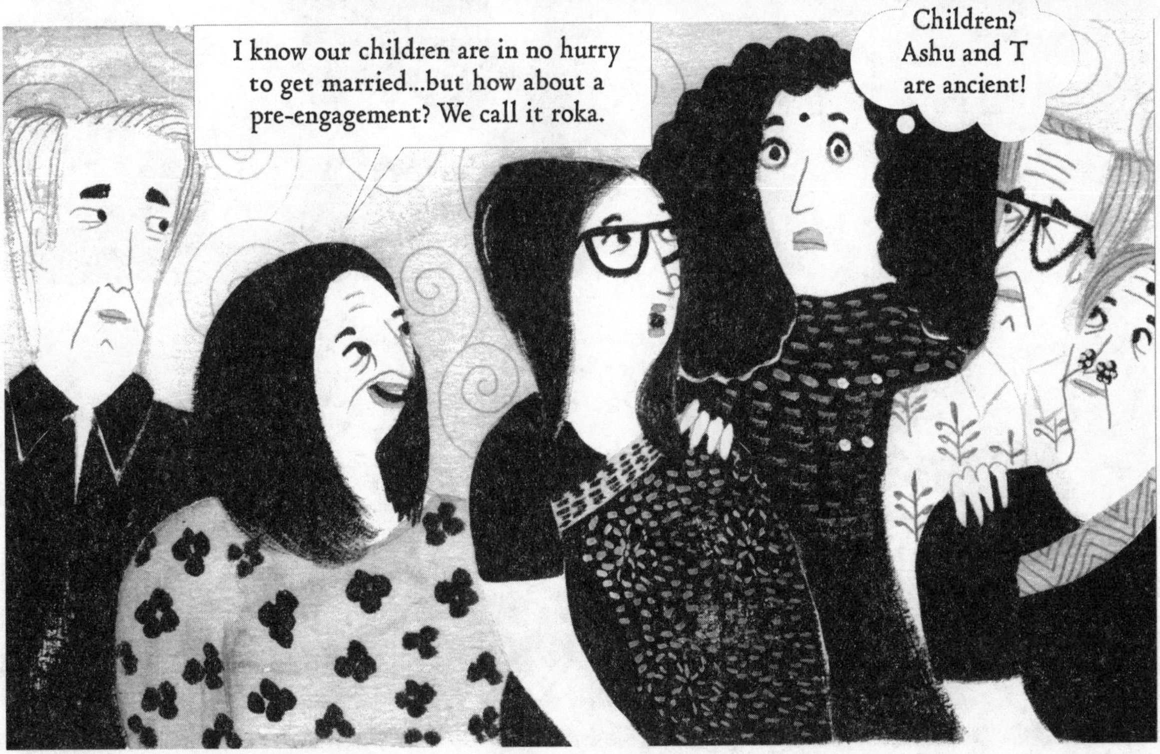
I know our children are in no hurry to get married...but how about a pre-engagement? We call it roka.
Children? Ashu and T are ancient!

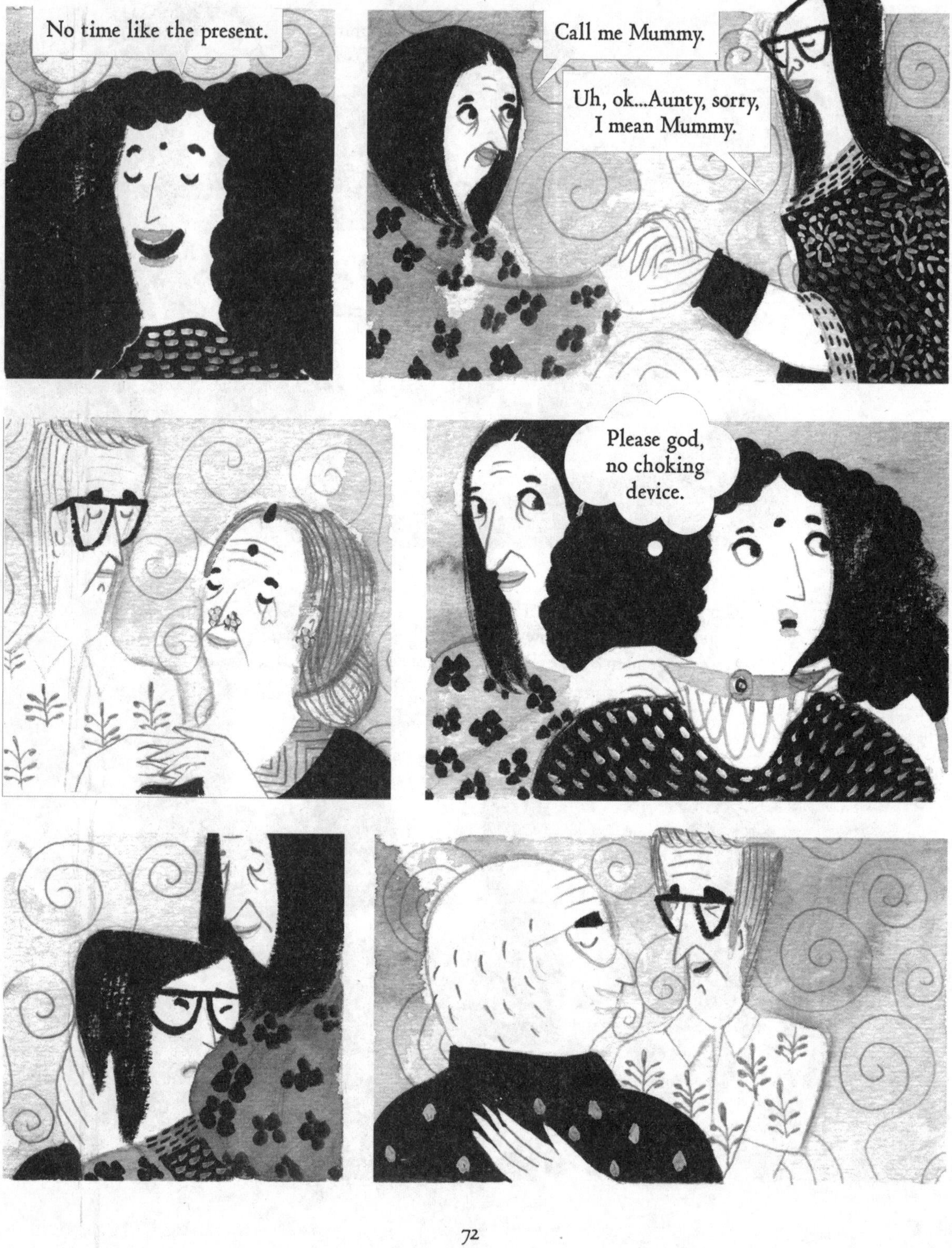
No time like the present.
Call me Mummy.
Uh, ok...Aunty, sorry, I mean Mummy.
Please god, no choking device.

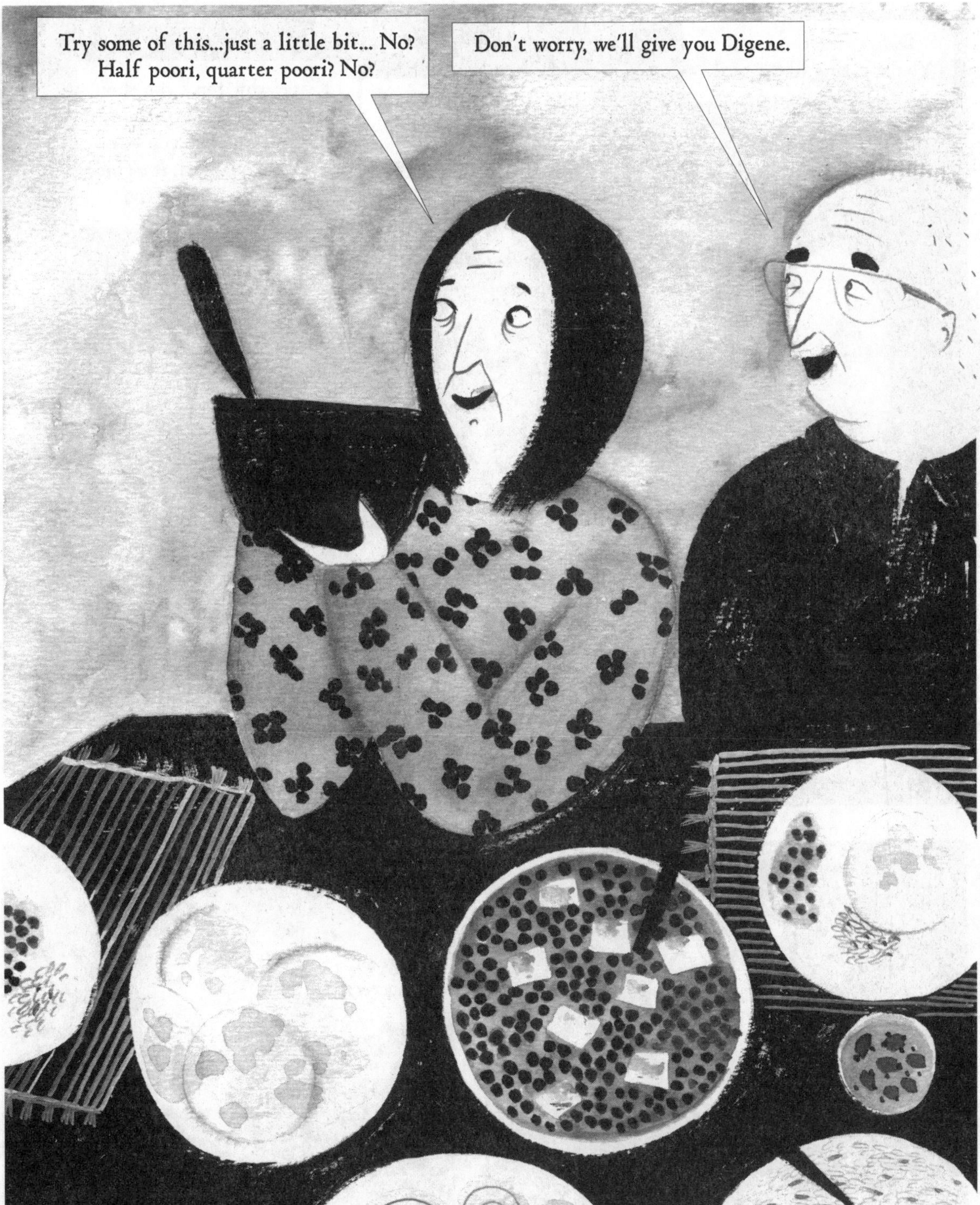
Try some of this...just a little bit... No? Half poori, quarter poori? No?
Don't worry, we'll give you Digene.

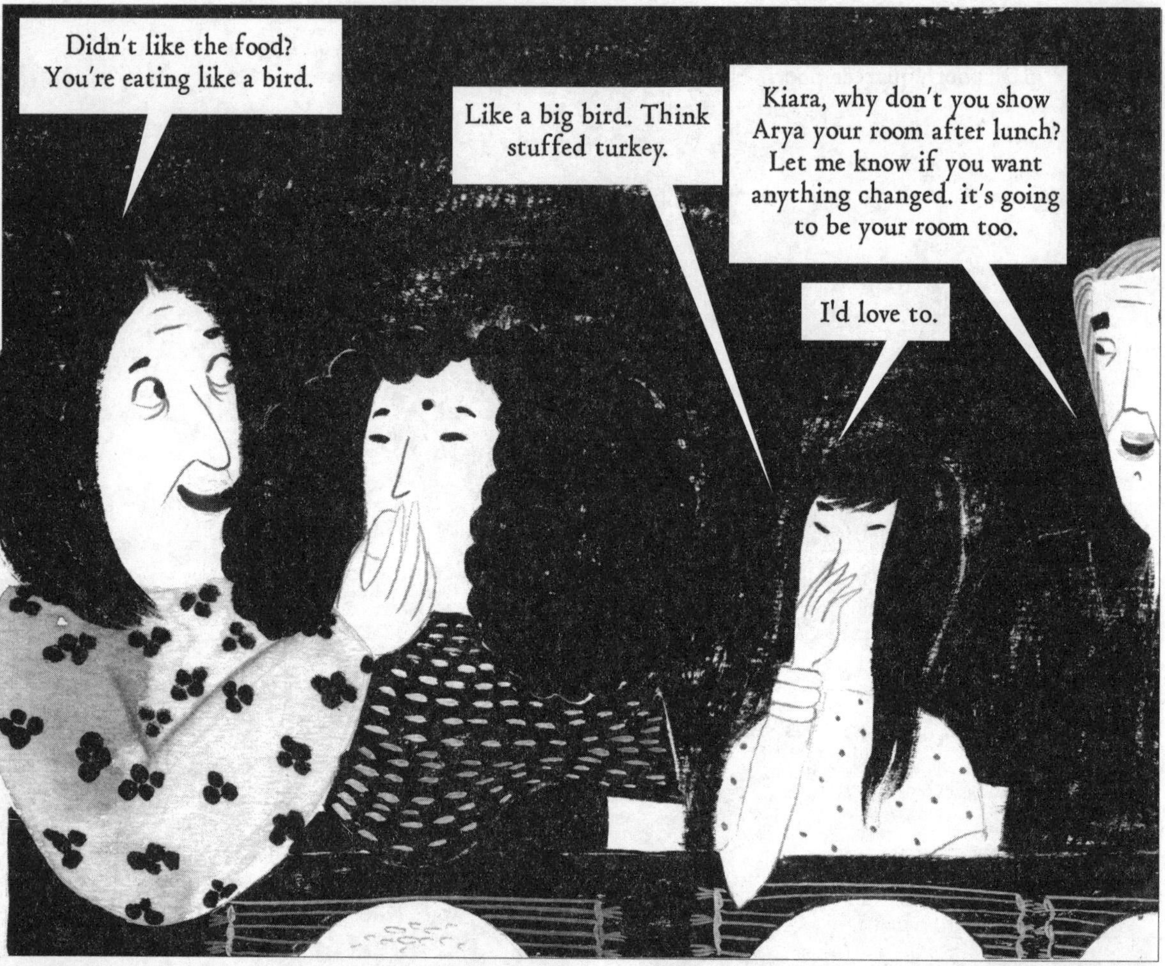
Didn't like the food? You're eating like a bird.
Like a big bird. Think stuffed turkey.
Kiara, why don't you show Arya your room after lunch? Let me know if you want anything changed. it's going to be your room too.
I'd love to.

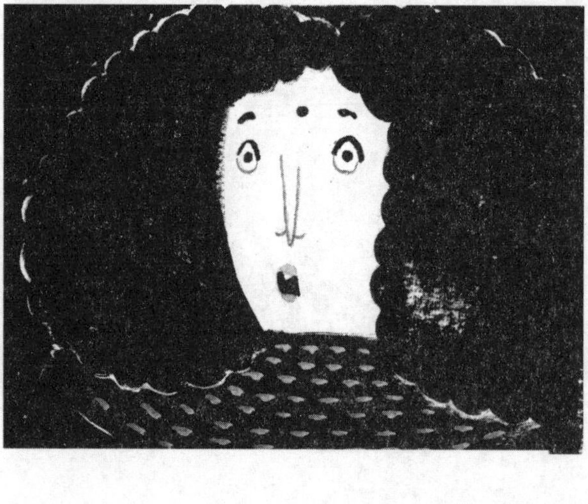

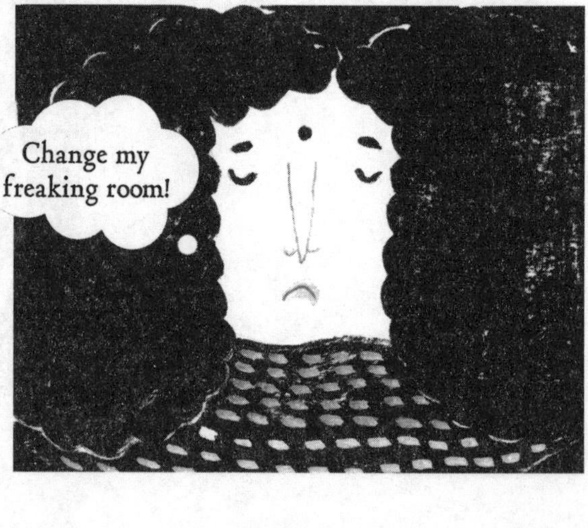
Change my freaking room!

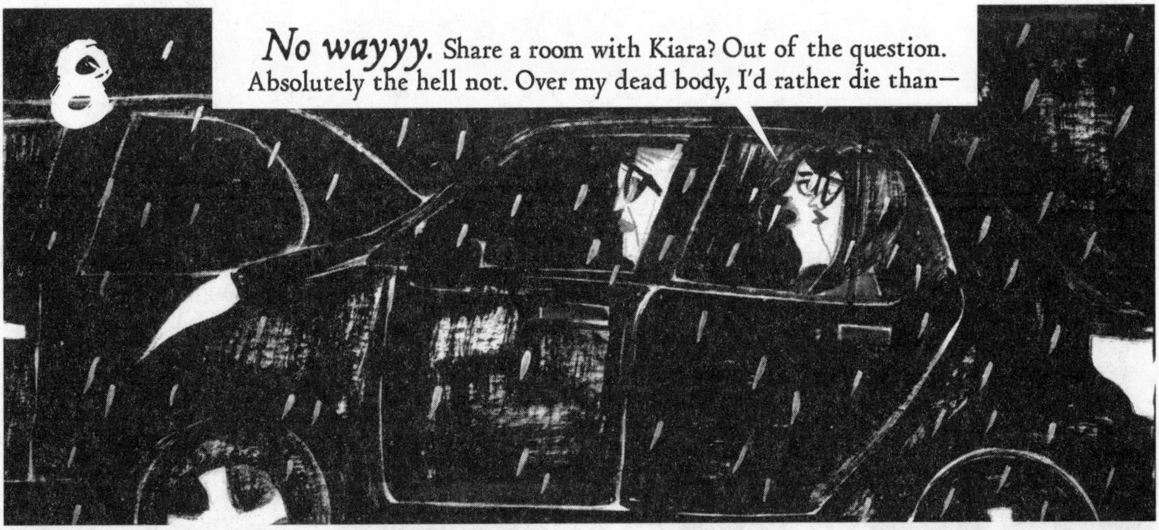
No wayyy. Share a room with Kiara? Out of the question. Absolutely the hell not. Over my dead body, I'd rather die than—

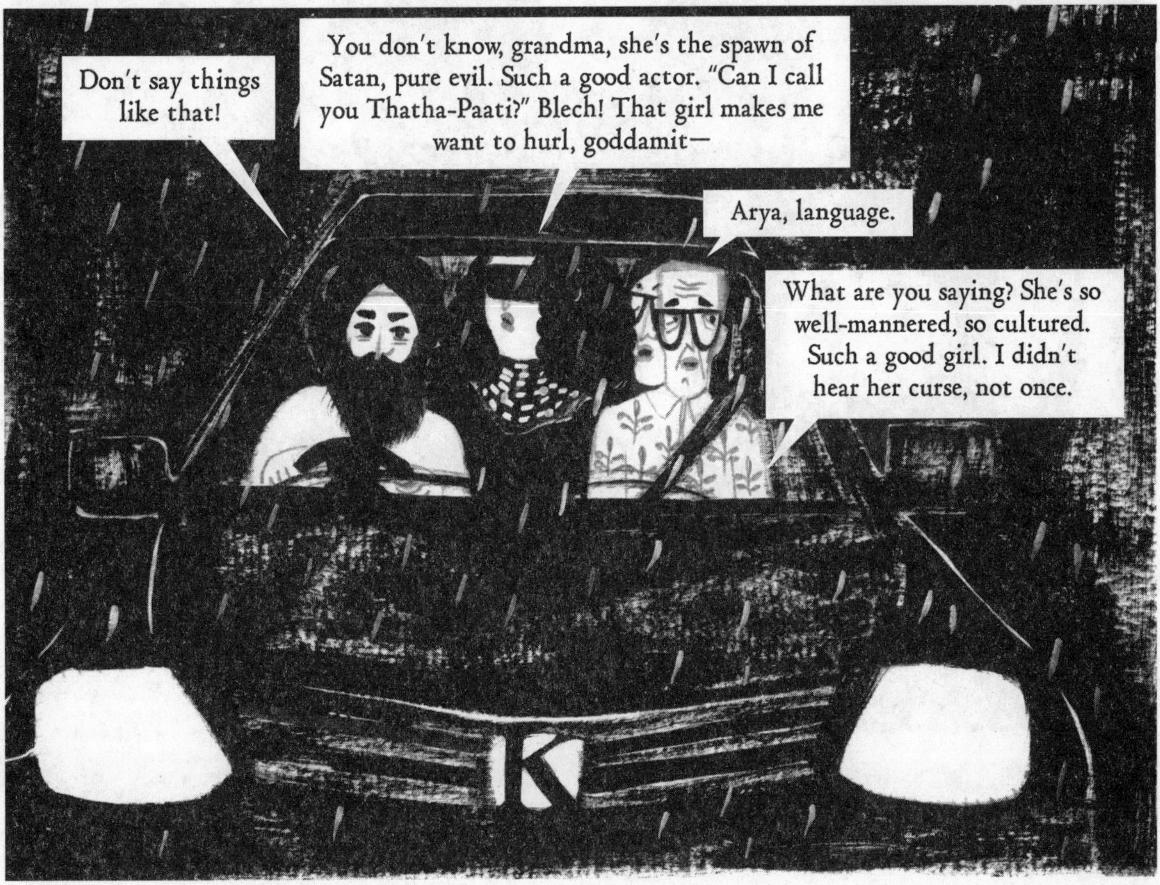
Don't say things like that!
You don't know, grandma, she's the spawn of Satan, pure evil. Such a good actor. "Can I call you Thatha-Paati?" Blech! That girl makes me want to hurl, goddamit—
Arya, language.
What are you saying? She's so well-mannered, so cultured. Such a good girl. I didn't hear her curse, not once.

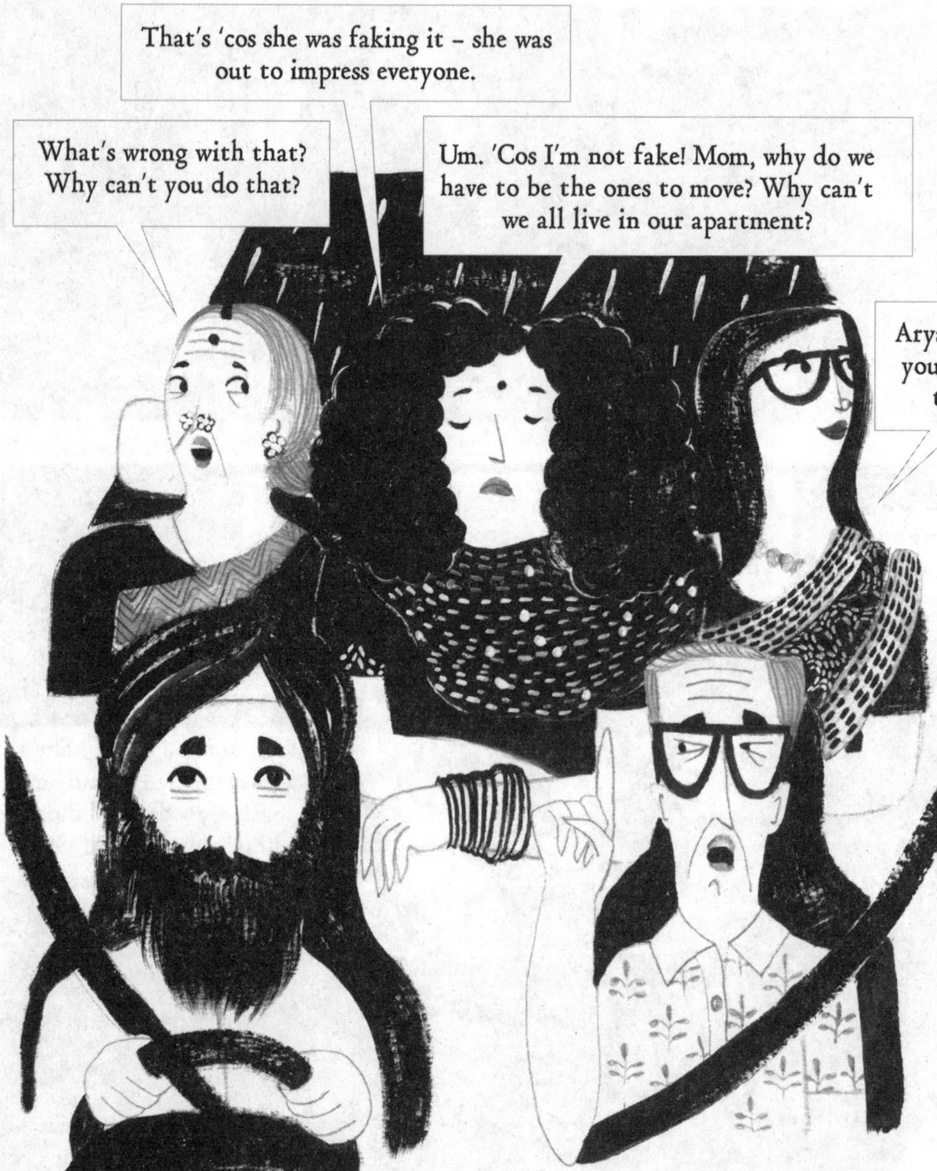
That's 'cos she was faking it – she was out to impress everyone.
What's wrong with that? Why can't you do that?
Um. 'Cos I'm not fake! Mom, why do we have to be the ones to move? Why can't we all live in our apartment?
Arya, you know your Dad pays the rent.

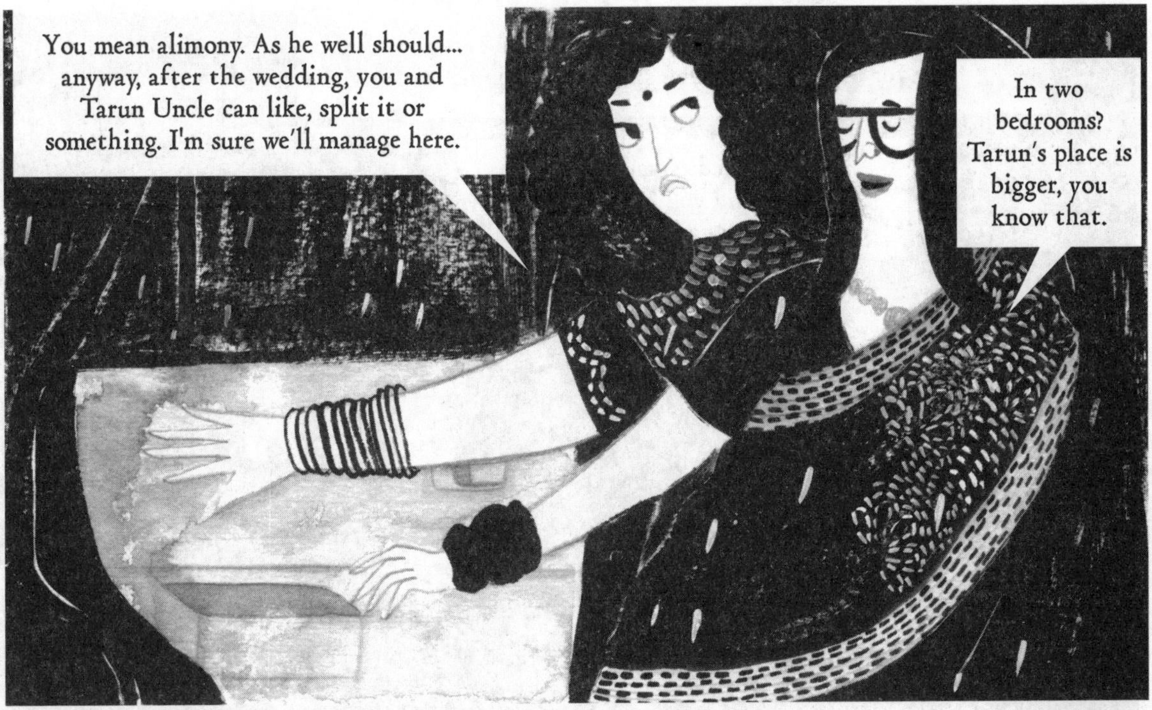
You mean alimony. As he well should... anyway, after the wedding, you and Tarun Uncle can like, split it or something. I'm sure we'll manage here.
In two bedrooms? Tarun's place is bigger, you know that.

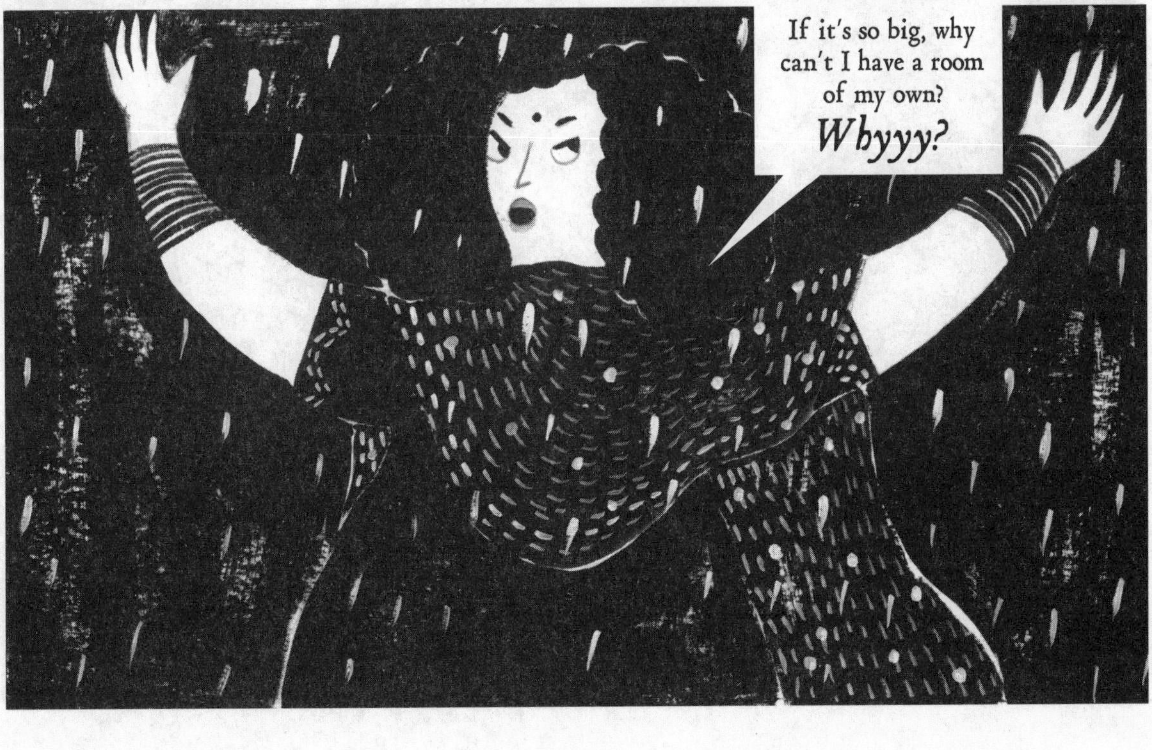
If it's so big, why can't I have a room of my own? *Whyyy?*

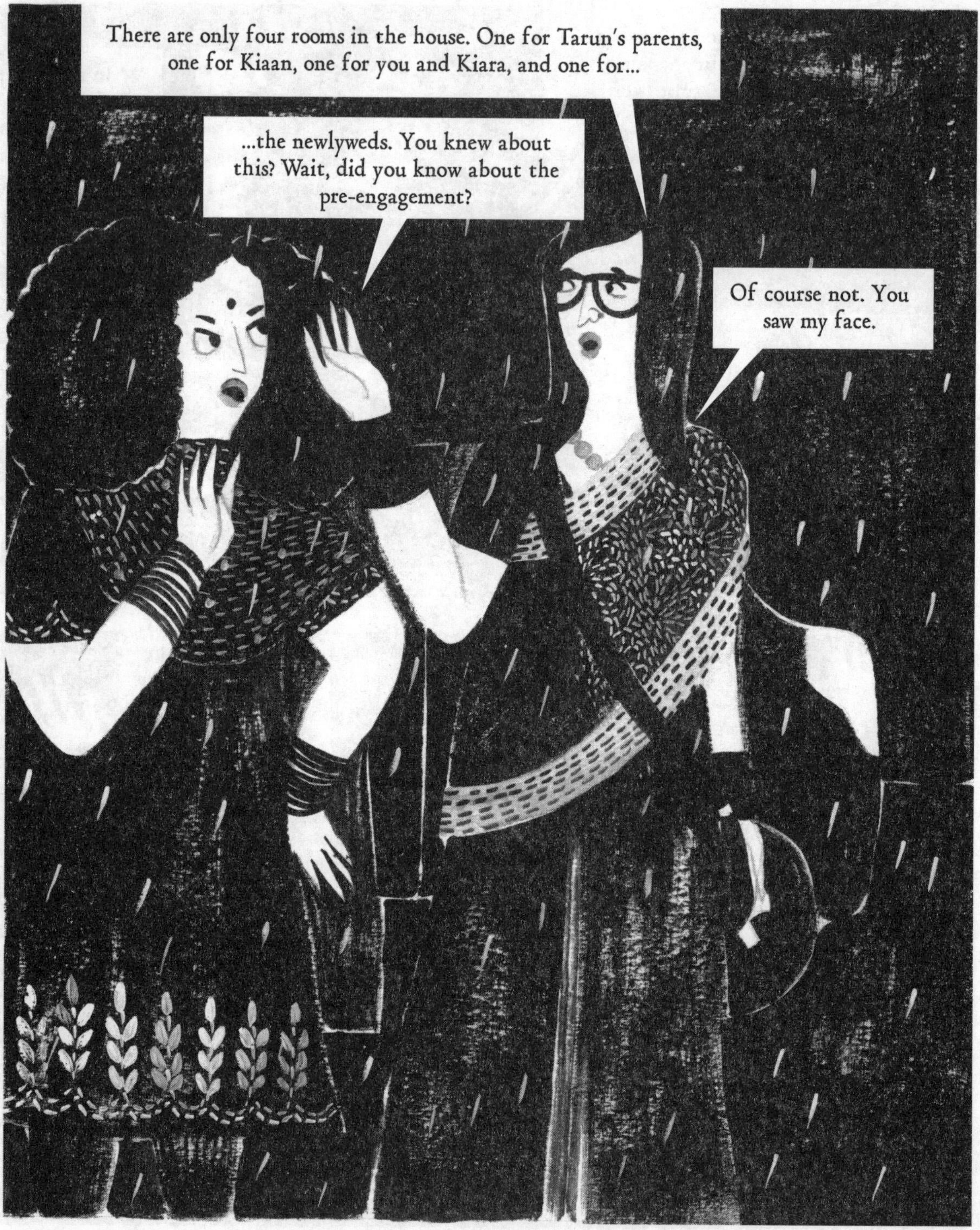
There are only four rooms in the house. One for Tarun's parents, one for Kiaan, one for you and Kiara, and one for...
...the newlyweds. You knew about this? Wait, did you know about the pre-engagement?
Of course not. You saw my face.

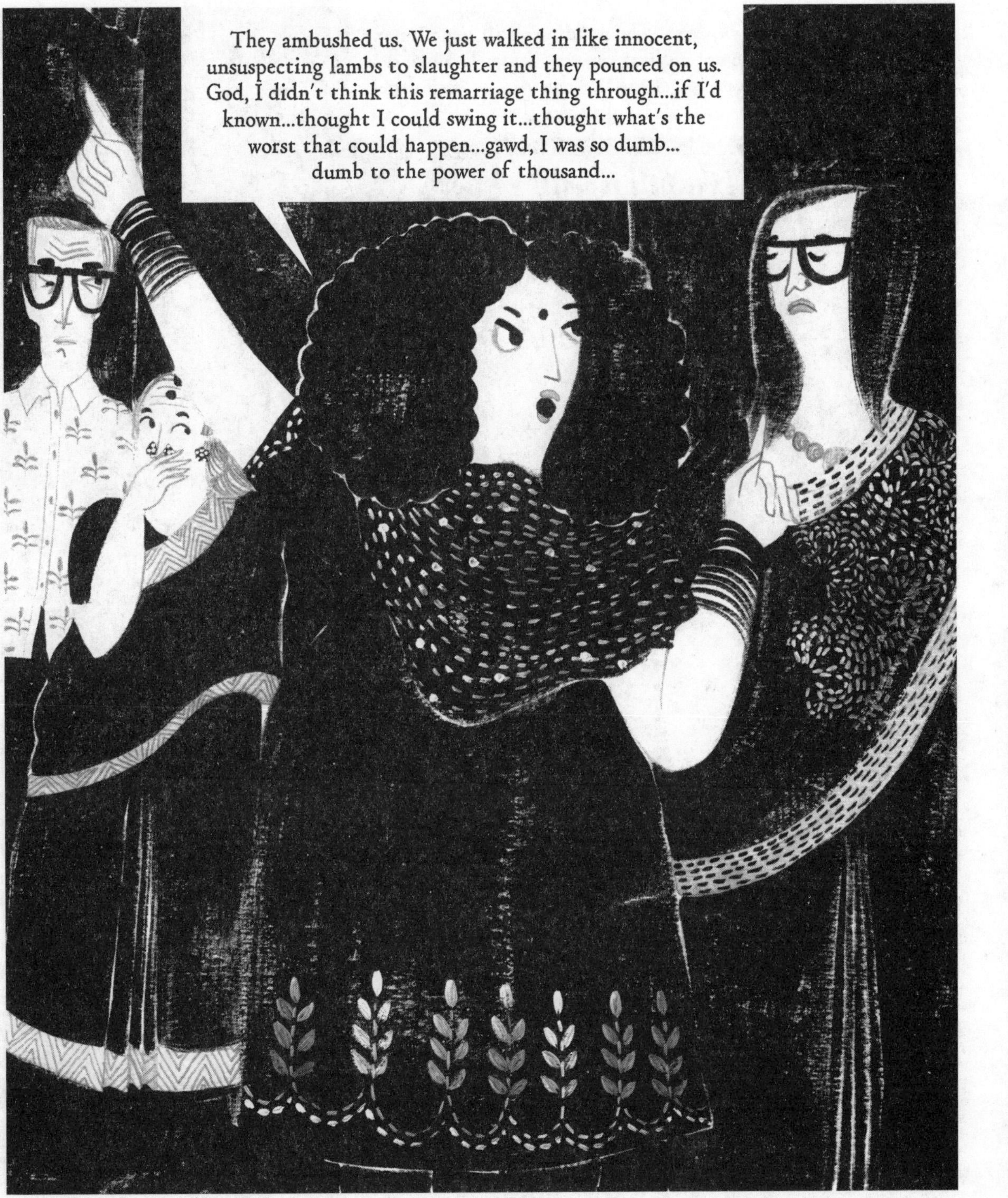
They ambushed us. We just walked in like innocent, unsuspecting lambs to slaughter and they pounced on us. God, I didn't think this remarriage thing through...if I'd known...thought I could swing it...thought what's the worst that could happen...gawd, I was so dumb... dumb to the power of thousand...

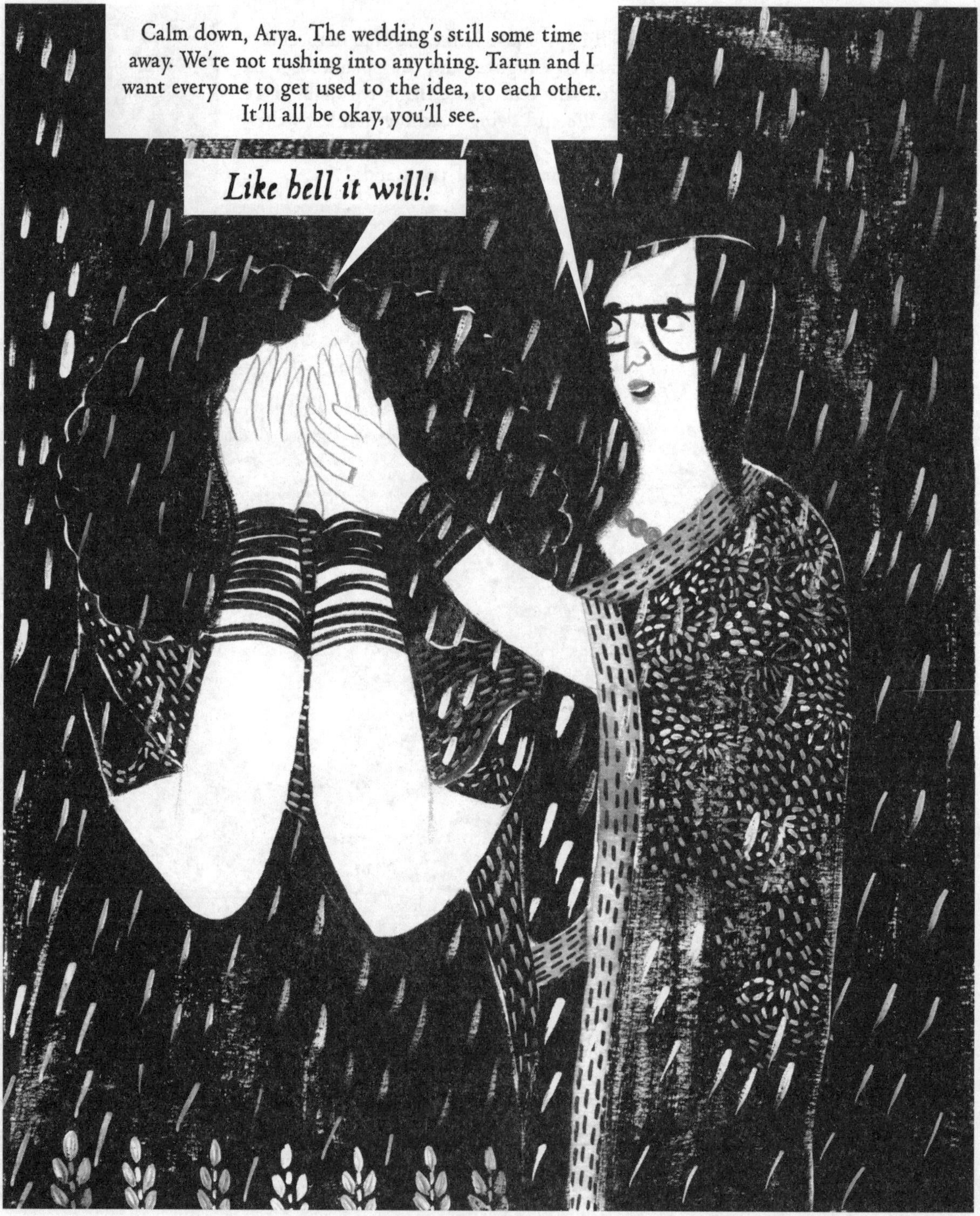
Calm down, Arya. The wedding's still some time away. We're not rushing into anything. Tarun and I want everyone to get used to the idea, to each other. It'll all be okay, you'll see.
Like hell it will!

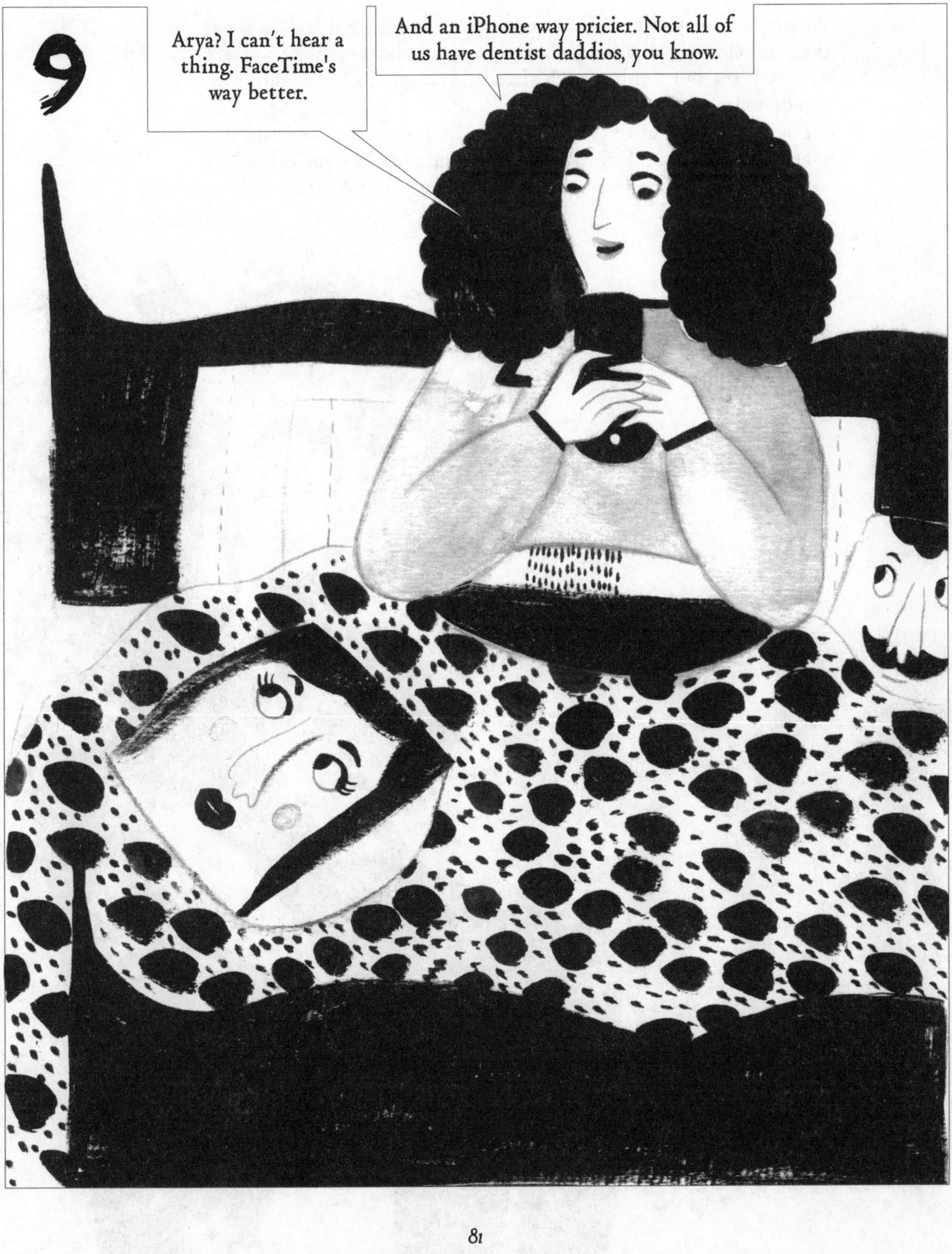
9
Arya? I can't hear a thing. FaceTime's way better.
And an iPhone way pricier. Not all of us have dentist daddios, you know.

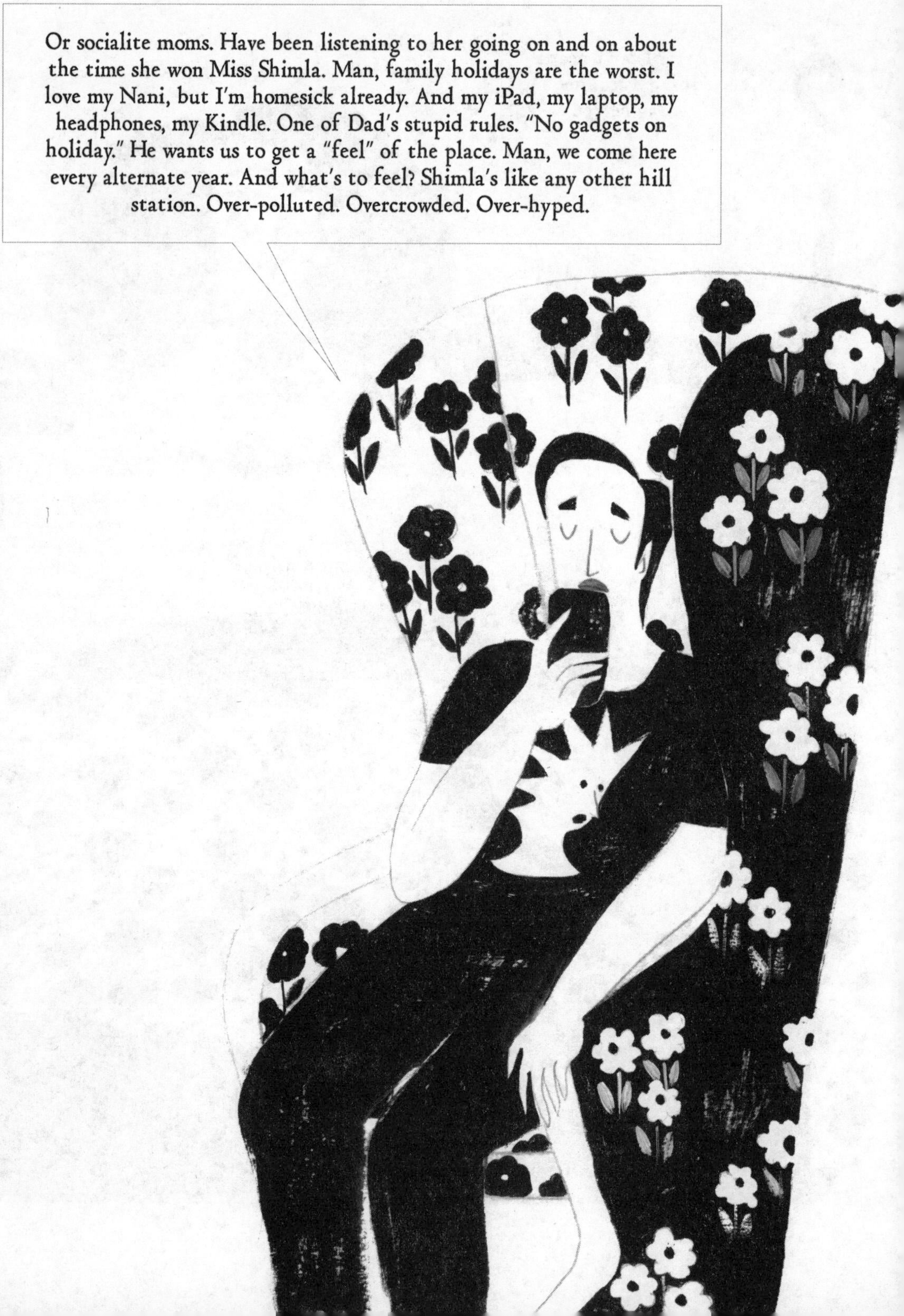
Or socialite moms. Have been listening to her going on and on about the time she won Miss Shimla. Man, family holidays are the worst. I love my Nani, but I'm homesick already. And my iPad, my laptop, my headphones, my Kindle. One of Dad's stupid rules. "No gadgets on holiday." He wants us to get a "feel" of the place. Man, we come here every alternate year. And what's to feel? Shimla's like any other hill station. Over-polluted. Overcrowded. Over-hyped.

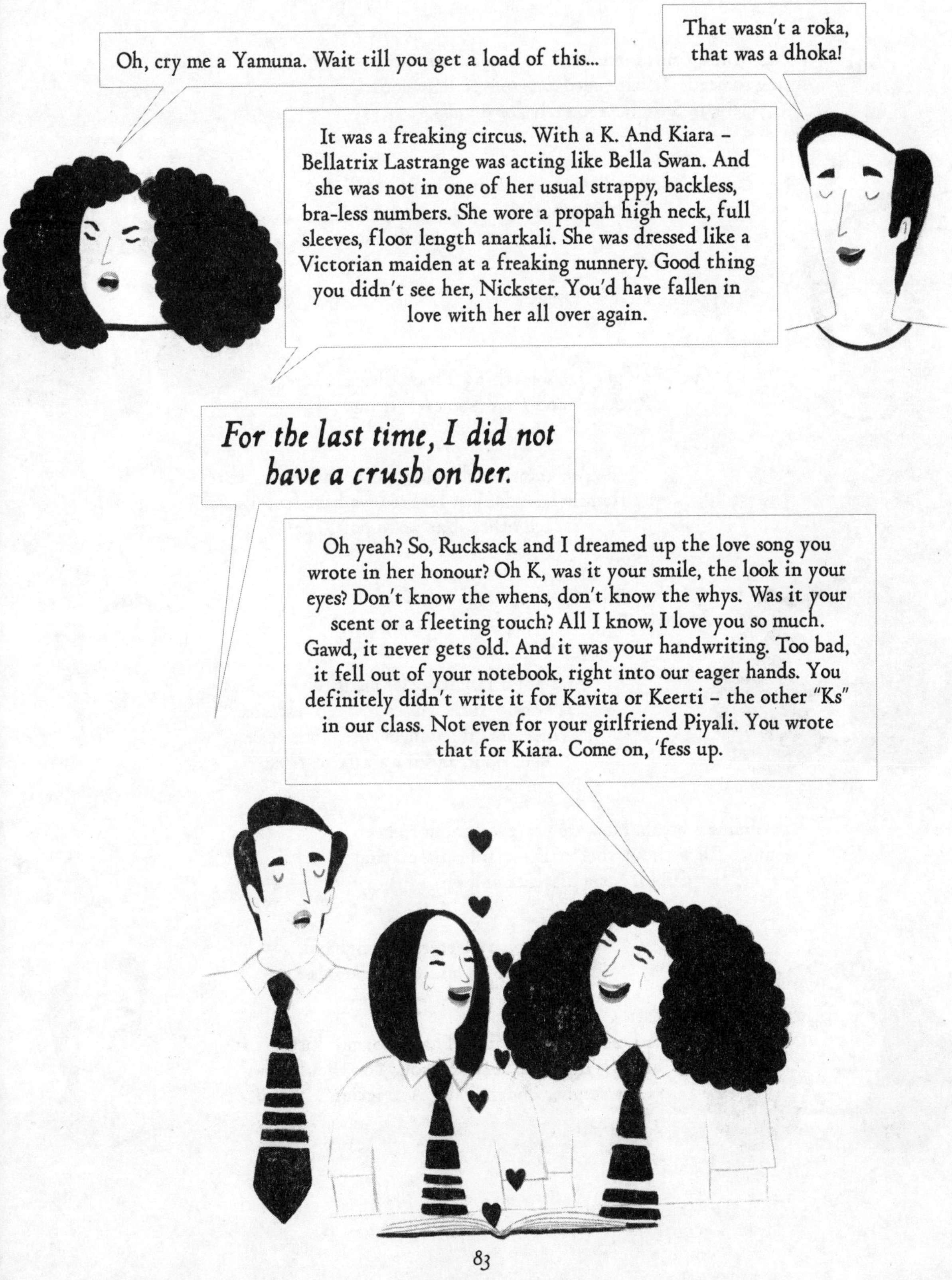
Oh, cry me a Yamuna. Wait till you get a load of this...
That wasn't a roka, that was a dhoka!
It was a freaking circus. With a K. And Kiara – Bellatrix Lastrange was acting like Bella Swan. And she was not in one of her usual strappy, backless, bra-less numbers. She wore a propah high neck, full sleeves, floor length anarkali. She was dressed like a Victorian maiden at a freaking nunnery. Good thing you didn't see her, Nickster. You'd have fallen in love with her all over again.
For the last time, I did not have a crush on her.
Oh yeah? So, Rucksack and I dreamed up the love song you wrote in her honour? Oh K, was it your smile, the look in your eyes? Don't know the whens, don't know the whys. Was it your scent or a fleeting touch? All I know, I love you so much. Gawd, it never gets old. And it was your handwriting. Too bad, it fell out of your notebook, right into our eager hands. You definitely didn't write it for Kavita or Keerti – the other "Ks" in our class. Not even for your girlfriend Piyali. You wrote that for Kiara. Come on, 'fess up.

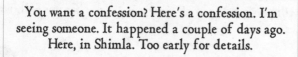

You want a confession? Here's a confession. I'm seeing someone. It happened a couple of days ago. Here, in Shimla. Too early for details.

You're shitting me. Wait, seriously? Oh. My. God. Someone's good enough for our Nickster! Wait, does Rucksack know?

You're the first to know.

Aw! Okay, give me something. Please please please. Rucksack and I tell you everything.

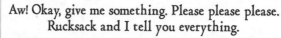

We've known each other for a while now...we're family friends...just realised we have feelings for each other...but we're poles apart—

No one said we've to fall only for our clones. So, she's not a fan of video games?

And not a fan of social media either. Says it's toxic, fake, causes low self-esteem, emotional disconnect, promotes rude behaviour, and is a waste of time.

Gimme a break. How are you even going to keep in touch without the "evil" social media playing Cupid? Long distance and all?

I'll write letters in longhand, drive up on long weekends.

Snail mail and landlines. That's not pre-historic at all. She'll be the death of you. You should save her number under "Fatal Attraction", Nick.

10

Dunno why you're making such a huge deal. Not as if she's your first girlfriend.

Maybe I don't want to jinx it.

Oh, come on. Give me something to go on.

I think I've already let on more than I intended to.

Wait till I get a boyfriend. I'll show ya.

So long as he's nothing like Kiaan, I'll be okie.

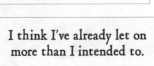

Ew! Why would you even say that? You were right about him, by the way. He kept saying all this politically incorrect stuff. Embarrassing, really.

Told ya. His shoe size is bigger than his IQ. Let him spend time with Aishwarya Aunty. She'll straighten him out. Look how you've turned out. You think twice before saying *black* board.

Can't wait to tell Rucksack about Fatal Attraction.

Yeah, you'll have to be the one to tell her. Got to go.

Ooh! You've to call Fatal Attraction, right?

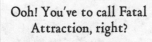

TTYL.

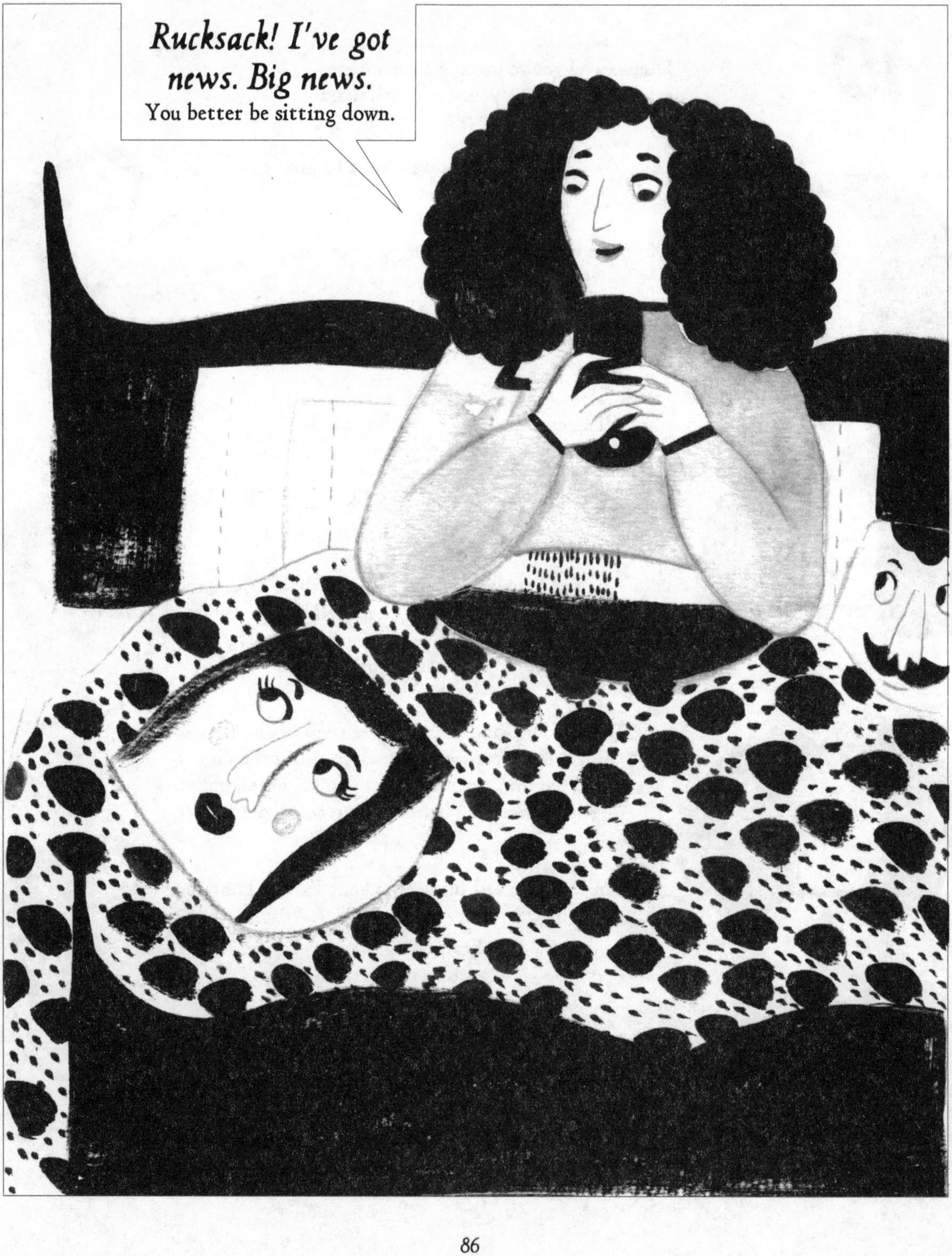
Rucksack! I've got news. Big news.
You better be sitting down.

Hey hey hey! What happened?

N-n-nothing. You were saying...

The audition...it didn't go well?

I don't want to talk about it.

That bad, huh?

It was awful! They gave me like, this never ending monologue and...and I tried my best, I did...but the whole time, they were just doing timepass...a girl outside told me they had already cast Aryan Khan's sister for the part...

Who the hell is Aryan Khan?

You don't know...

The only Aryan Khan I know calls SRK daddy.

...never mind...he's like, TV's Zayn Malik. Google him... If they had already made up their minds, why did they give us hope...

I didn't know Hindi soaps had hotties.

Why did they waste your freaking time. Gawd! And then they crib about mediocrity. What about talent? What about merit? Who cares about all that? Long live nepotism. These people make me sick.

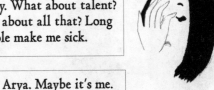

I don't know, Arya. Maybe it's me. Maybe I'm not talented.

What kind of talk is that? You're bloody good. Your impressions of Bollywood stars? You're a rockstar.

You're only saying that 'cos you're my friend...I haven't starred in any of the school plays...only played bit roles here and there...I haven't bagged a single movie or show or commercial and I've been auditioning for a year now...

These things take time, you know that. It will happen. Something will come along soon. Trust me.

I don't know, Arya. I can't take it anymore. I want out, I want to come back.

Then why don't you?

I can't. You know how it is. It'll break Mom's heart.

What about your own heart? Doesn't that count for something?

She's done a lot for me. And this means so much to her. She'll be crushed. I can't, I can't just up and leave. She spoke to Diggy Uncle—

This Diggy Uncle of yours, such a dodgy character, I tell you. Is his production house even legit? You sure he doesn't make pornos or something?

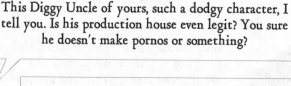

Eeeeks, no! He's small time, but he's on the level. Think Mom would let him suggest leads otherwise? Uncle's lined up something. Next week.

Whoa! That's cutting it too fine. I know you've got above 60% in the Board Exams and internal admission/online registration is a breeze and it's "only humanities" but still. We don't call our Princy "Prickles" for nothing, you know.

It's going to be so weird. Me in Humanities, you in Commerce, Nick in Science.

Rucksack, don't switch tracks. You sure you want to do this? Stay back? Try again?

We all do unpleasant things for the ones we love.

You're right.

And you're bursting with news. Spill it.

Oh my god, yeah...so check this out – when we go on a holiday, we come back with a souvenir. And our Nick? He comes back with a girlfriend.

Whattt?

I'm happy for Nick, just a little bummed though.

Because he told me first?

Na-ah! I know you guys are intellectuals and look down your noses on us plebs—

Wha—? We do not.

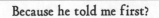

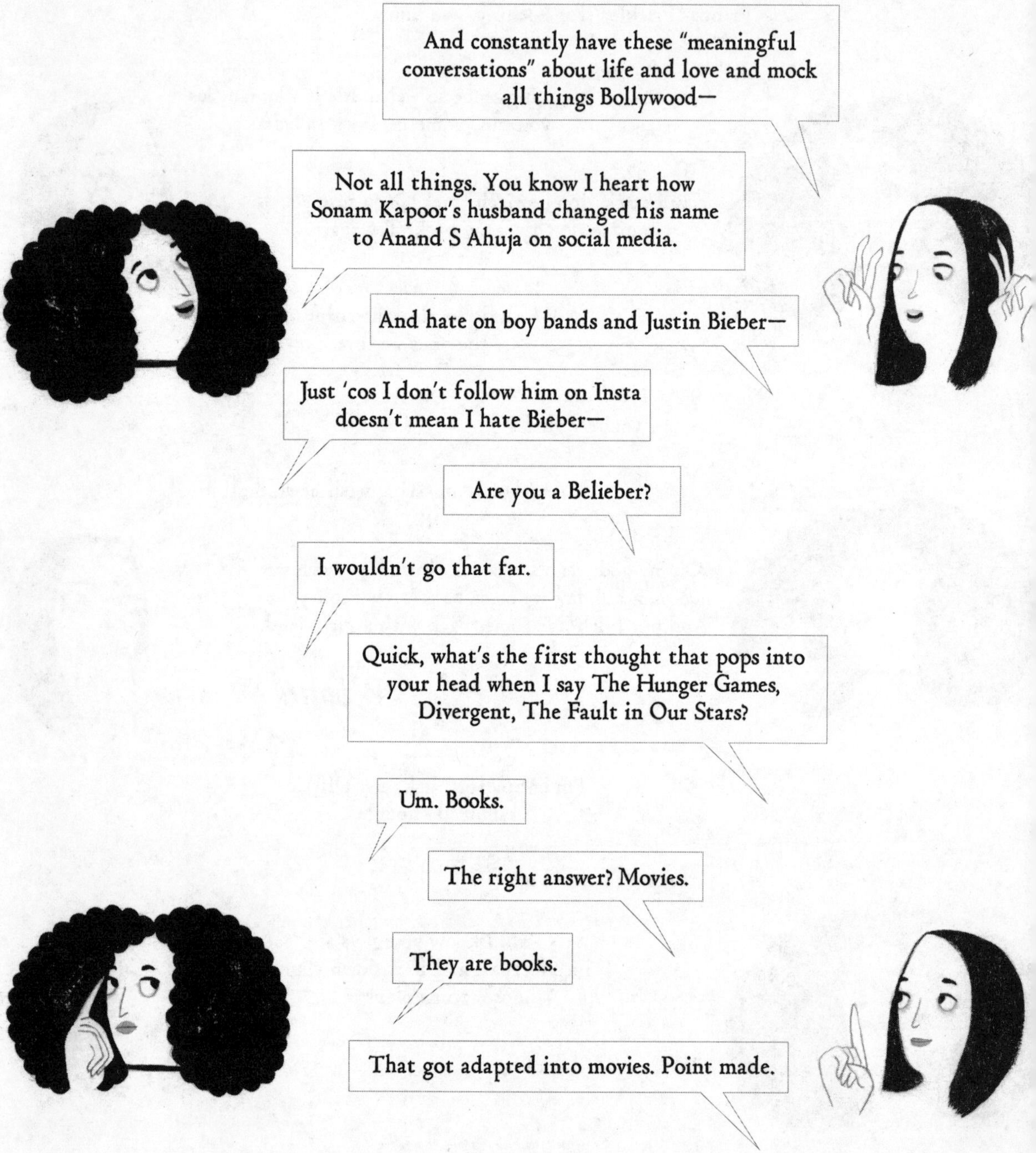
And constantly have these "meaningful conversations" about life and love and mock all things Bollywood—
Not all things. You know I heart how Sonam Kapoor's husband changed his name to Anand S Ahuja on social media.
And hate on boy bands and Justin Bieber—
Just 'cos I don't follow him on Insta doesn't mean I hate Bieber—
Are you a Belieber?
I wouldn't go that far.
Quick, what's the first thought that pops into your head when I say The Hunger Games, Divergent, The Fault in Our Stars?
Um. Books.
The right answer? Movies.
They are books.
That got adapted into movies. Point made.

So not. Do Nick and I ever leave you out of convos? Do we make plans that don't include you? Do we ever meet behind your back? Nope. In fact, you guys are much closer. You've known each other since kindergarten.

You know, Nick would probably say you and I are much closer.

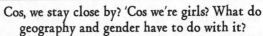

Cos, we stay close by? 'Cos we're girls? What do geography and gender have to do with it?

I know, I know. What I'm trying to say is we're all pretty close. But you and Nick have your own thing going. And it doesn't bother me. Not even a smidge. We all have our own equations. Hey, I just thought of something. Maybe we should come up with a cool name for us. The Awesome Threesome or something.

Threesome? Really? Nick's found someone, but we're still single. Is that the message you want to give out to the dudes at school? Threesome? Really now. Anyhoo, forget all that, why exactly are you bummed?

I'm just put out 'cos he's acting so secretive. Not fair. We tell him everything.

I know, right? Let's badger him till he gives in. Give him a hard time, will you please?

It'll have to wait. Got to get my beauty sleep. Bye!

11

I was so caught up with everything that was going on in their lives, something completely slipped my mind: The juicy titbit Kiara had blurted out. You know, about Natasha and her bulimia. I'd no idea it would come in handy later. Anyway, that wasn't the last piece of goss to came my way... It all happened at the "family" get-together. A ridiculous idea my Mom and Tarun Uncle came up with so we all get to know each other. As if it wasn't enough that we all go to the same school already...

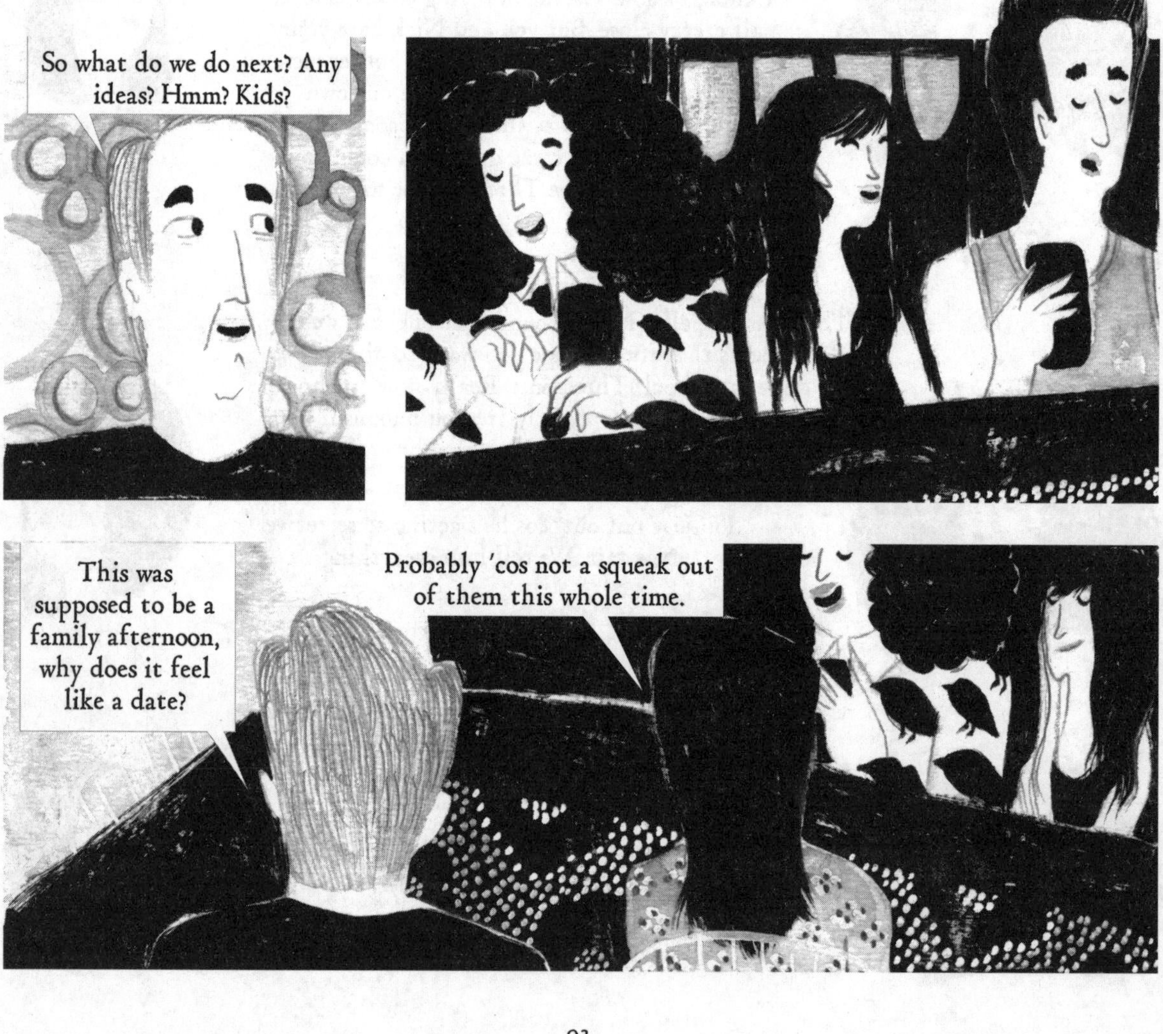
So what do we do next? Any ideas? Hmm? Kids?
This was supposed to be a family afternoon, why does it feel like a date?
Probably 'cos not a squeak out of them this whole time.

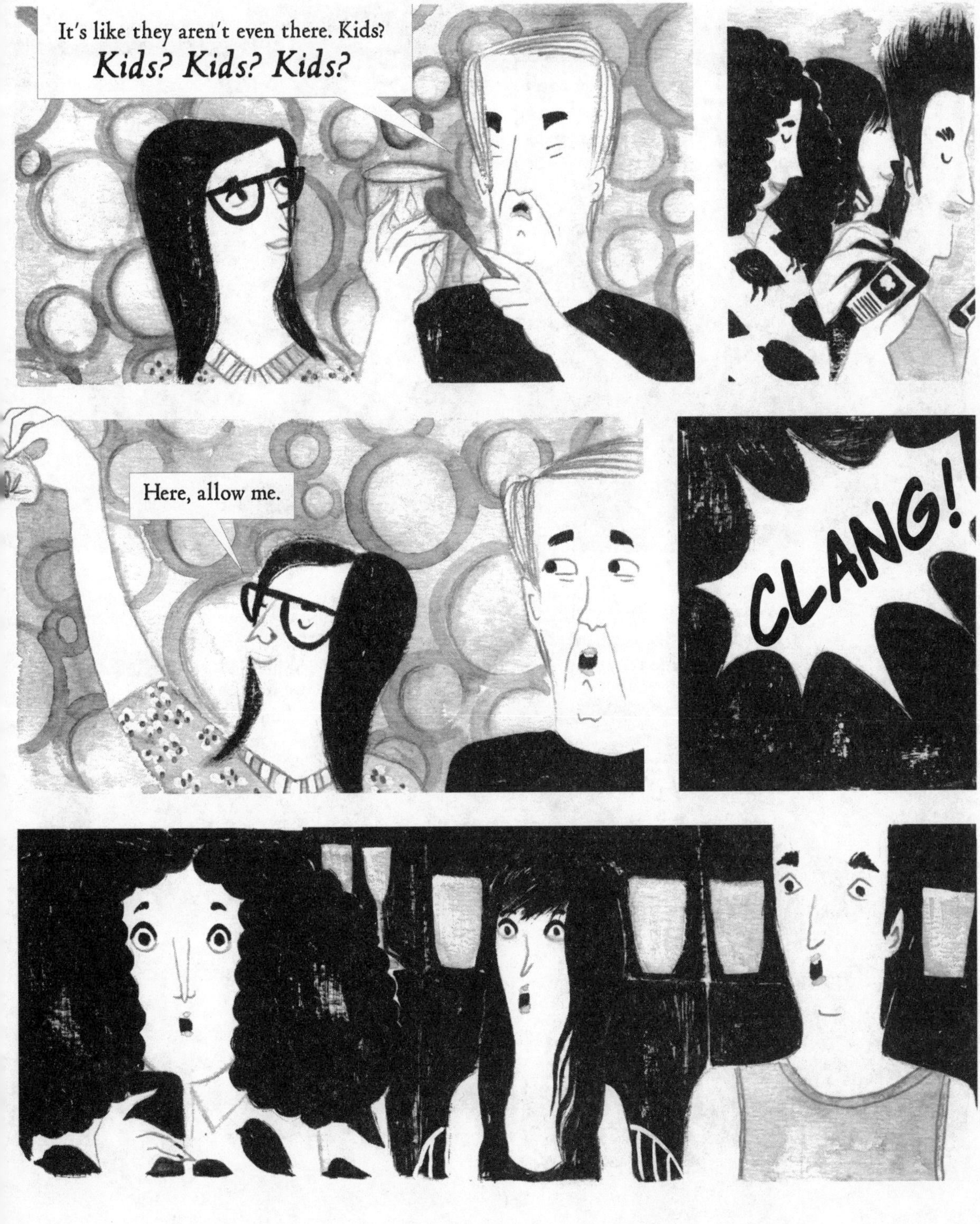
It's like they aren't even there. Kids?
Kids? Kids? Kids?
Here, allow me.
CLANG!

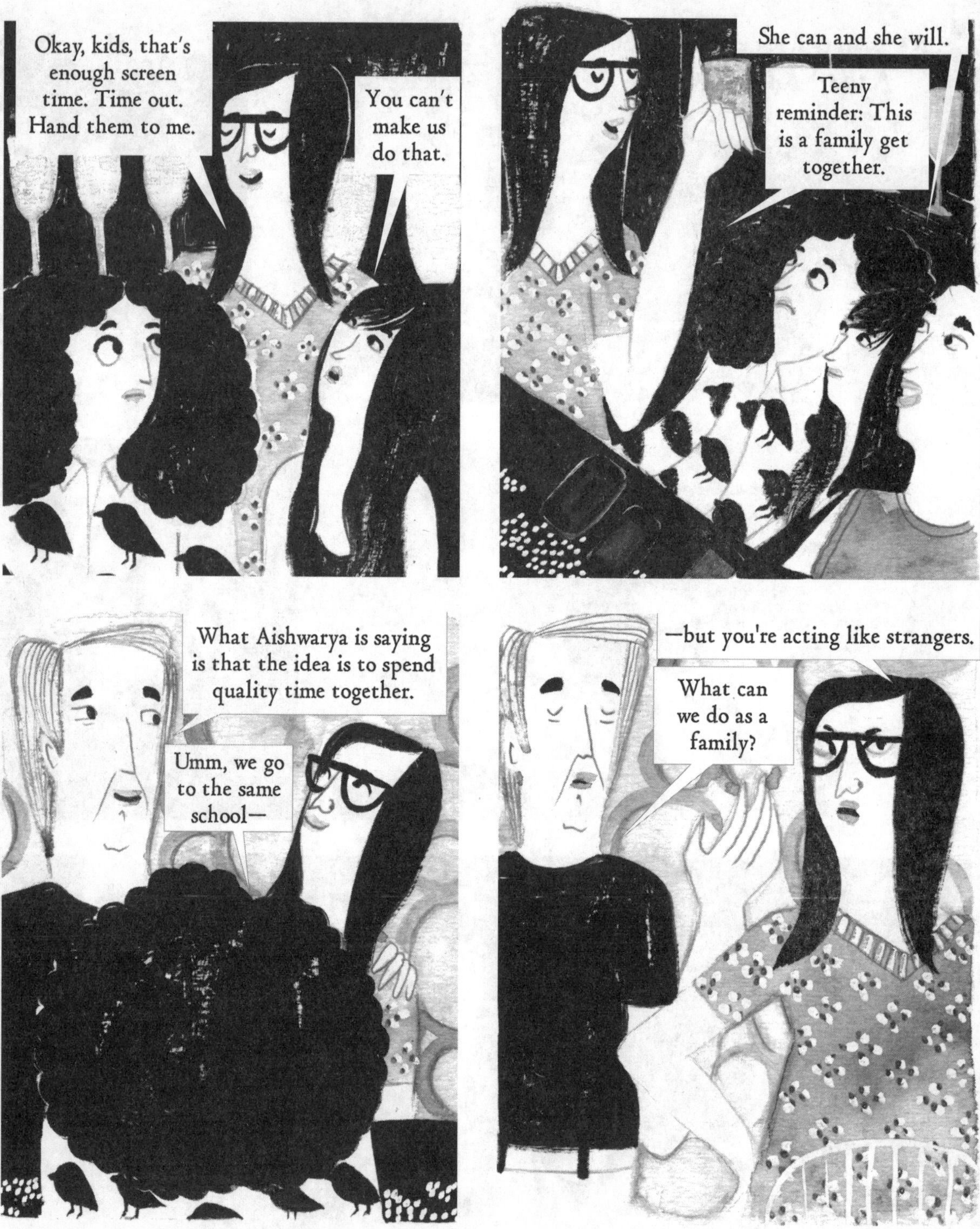
Okay, kids, that's enough screen time. Time out. Hand them to me.
You can't make us do that.
She can and she will.
Teeny reminder: This is a family get together.
What Aishwarya is saying is that the idea is to spend quality time together.
Umm, we go to the same school—
—but you're acting like strangers.
What can we do as a family?

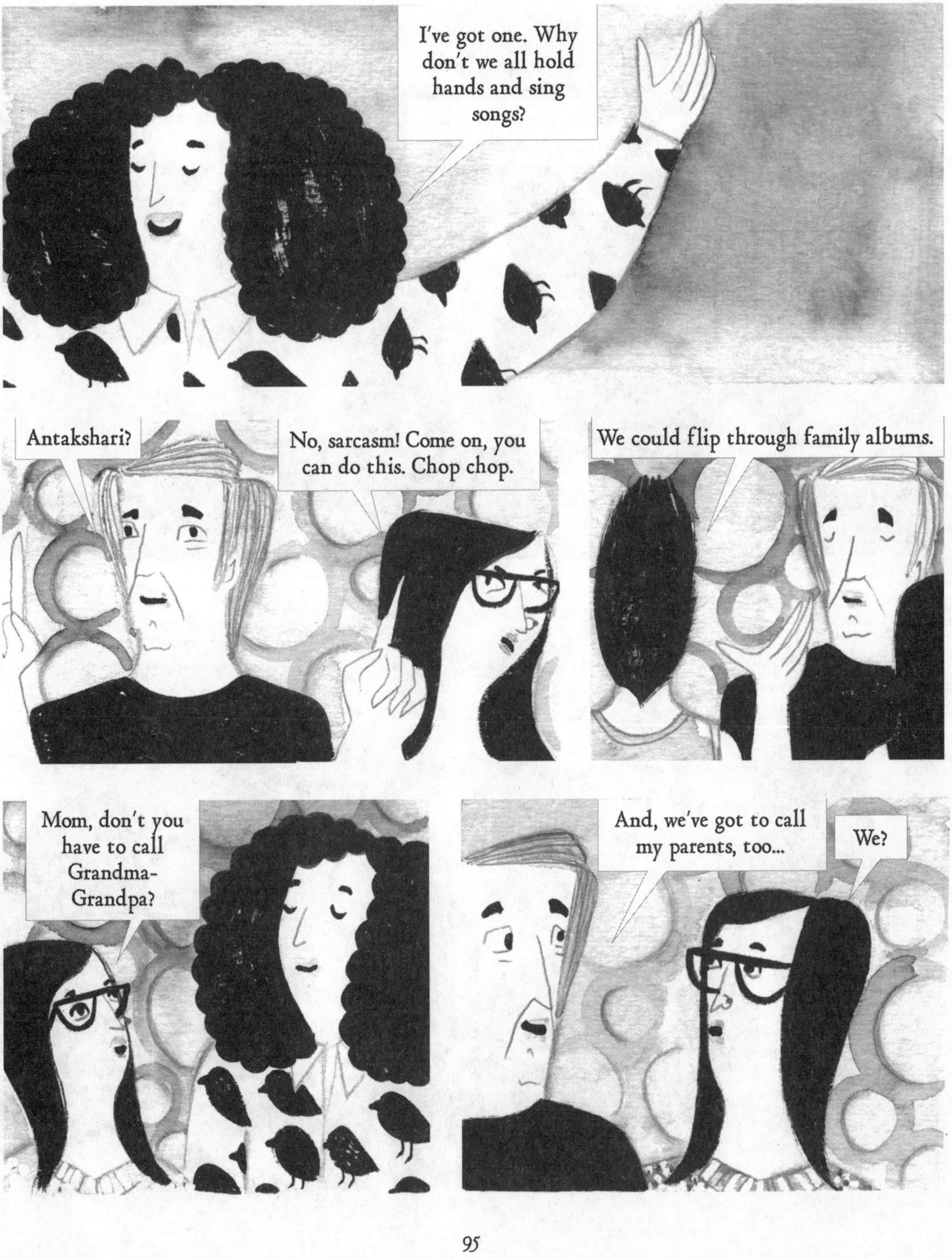
I've got one. Why don't we all hold hands and sing songs?
Antakshari?
No, sarcasm! Come on, you can do this. Chop chop.
We could flip through family albums.
Mom, don't you have to call Grandma-Grandpa?
And, we've got to call my parents, too...
We?

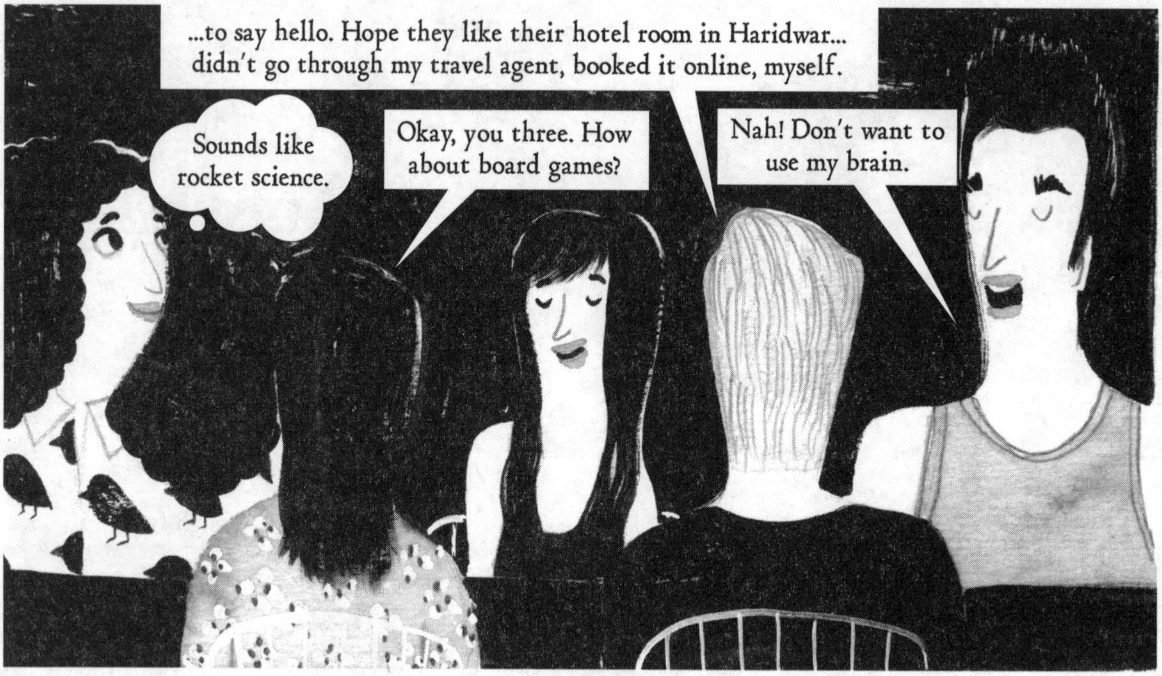
...to say hello. Hope they like their hotel room in Haridwar... didn't go through my travel agent, booked it online, myself.
Sounds like rocket science.
Okay, you three. How about board games?
Nah! Don't want to use my brain.

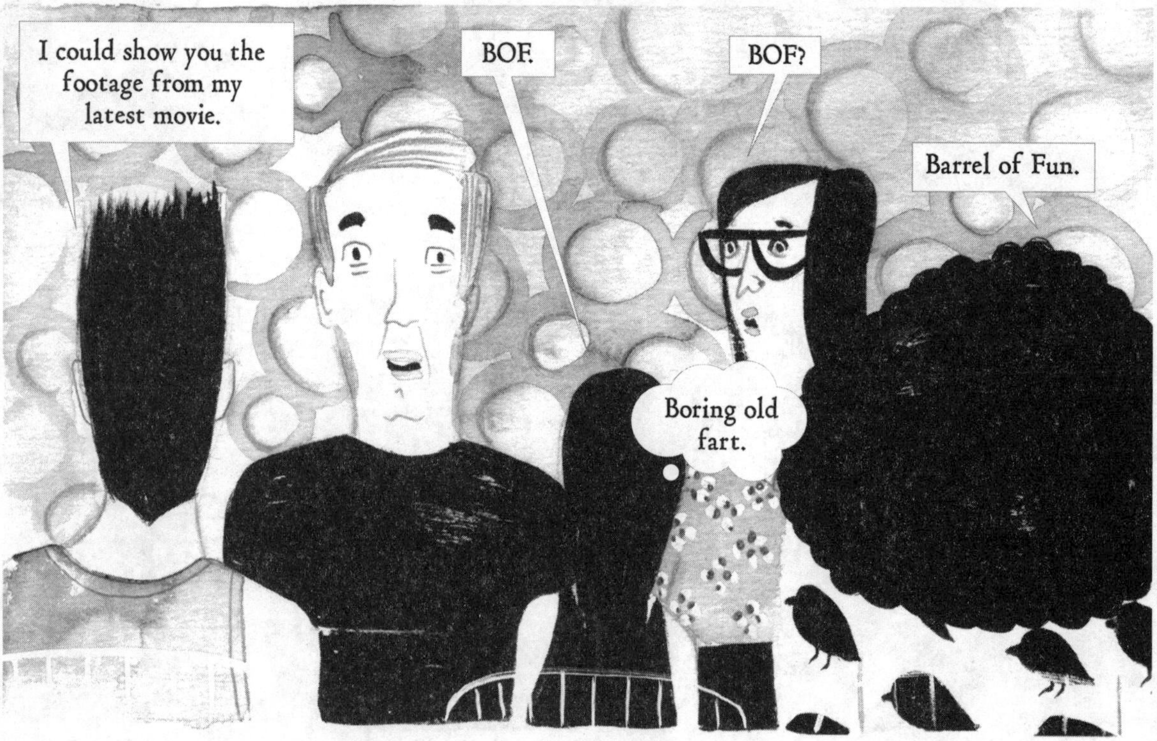
I could show you the footage from my latest movie.
BOF.
BOF?
Barrel of Fun.
Boring old fart.

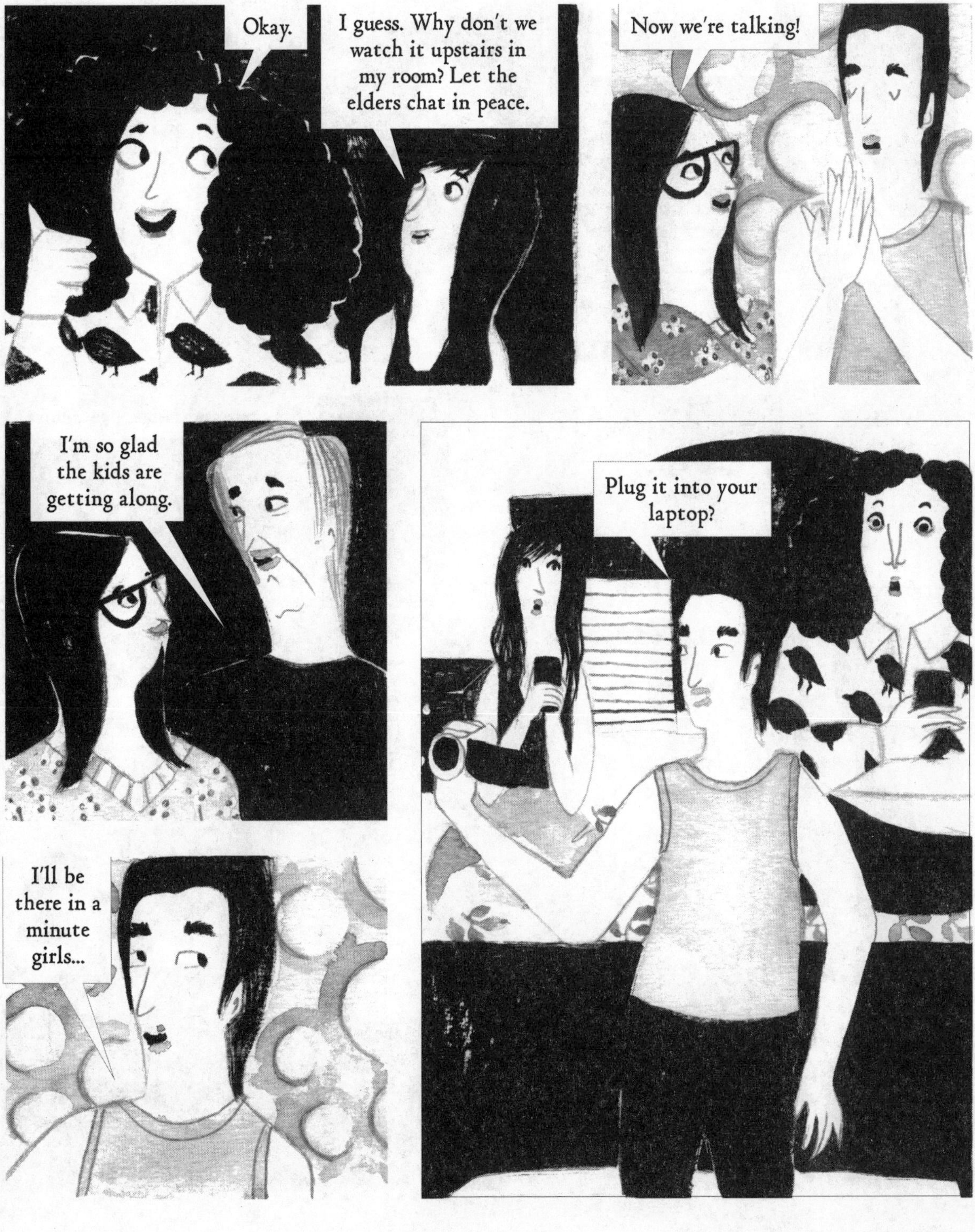
Okay.
I guess. Why don't we watch it upstairs in my room? Let the elders chat in peace.
Now we're talking!
I'm so glad the kids are getting along.
I'll be there in a minute girls...
Plug it into your laptop?

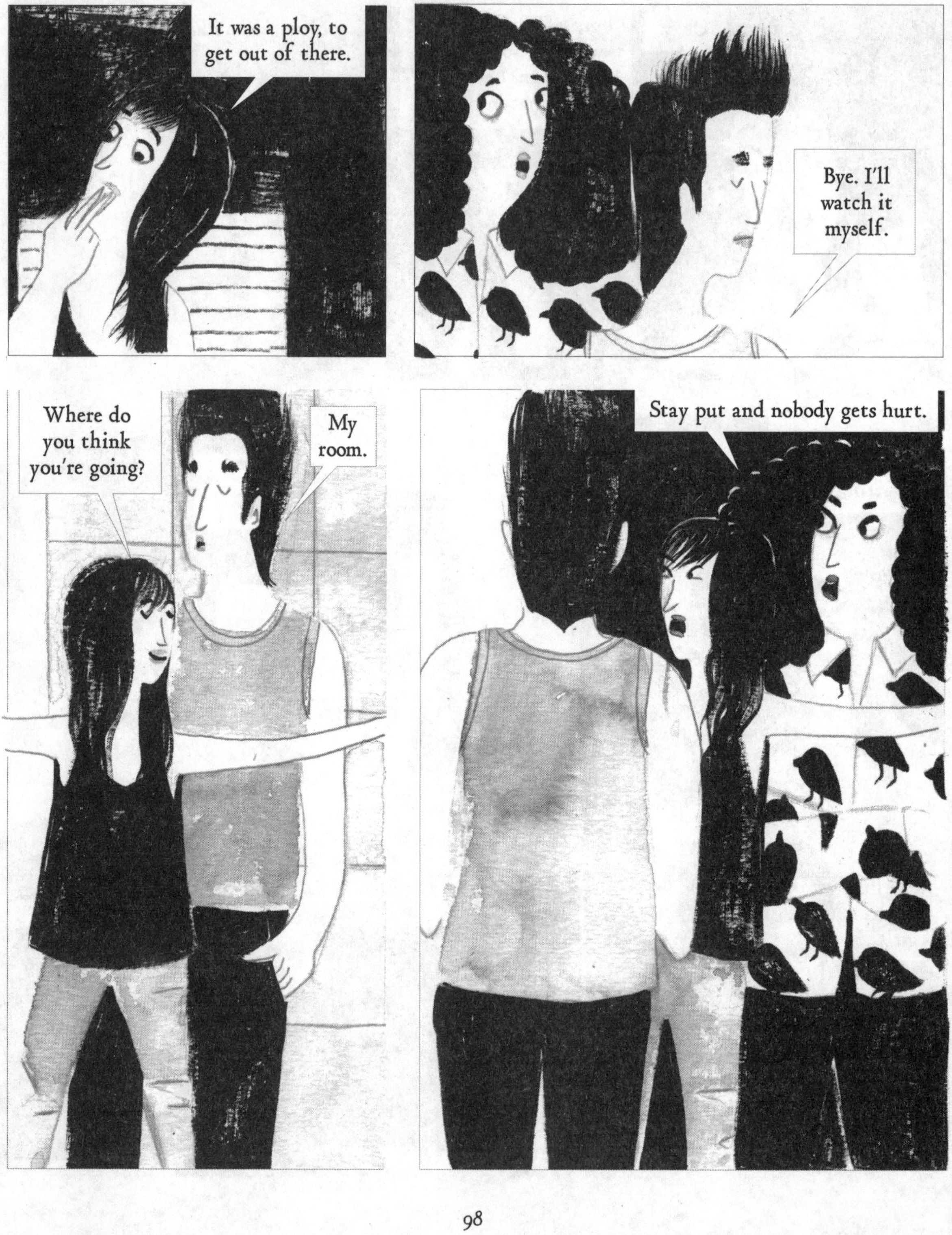

It was a ploy, to get out of there.
Bye. I'll watch it myself.
Where do you think you're going?
My room.
Stay put and nobody gets hurt.

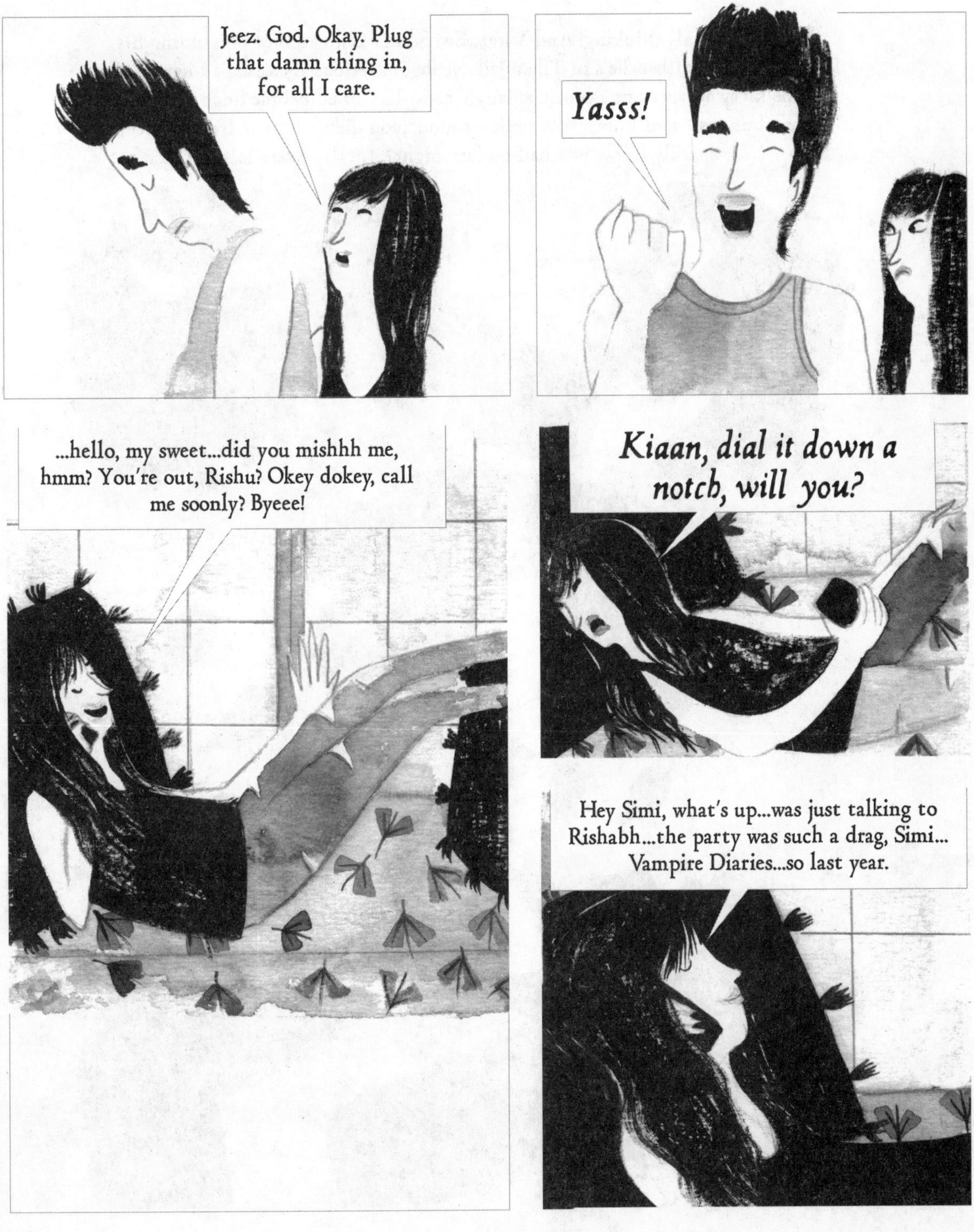
Jeez. God. Okay. Plug that damn thing in, for all I care.
Yasss!
...hello, my sweet...did you mishhh me, hmm? You're out, Rishu? Okey dokey, call me soonly? Byeee!
Kiaan, dial it down a notch, will you?
Hey Simi, what's up...was just talking to Rishabh...the party was such a drag, Simi... Vampire Diaries...so last year.

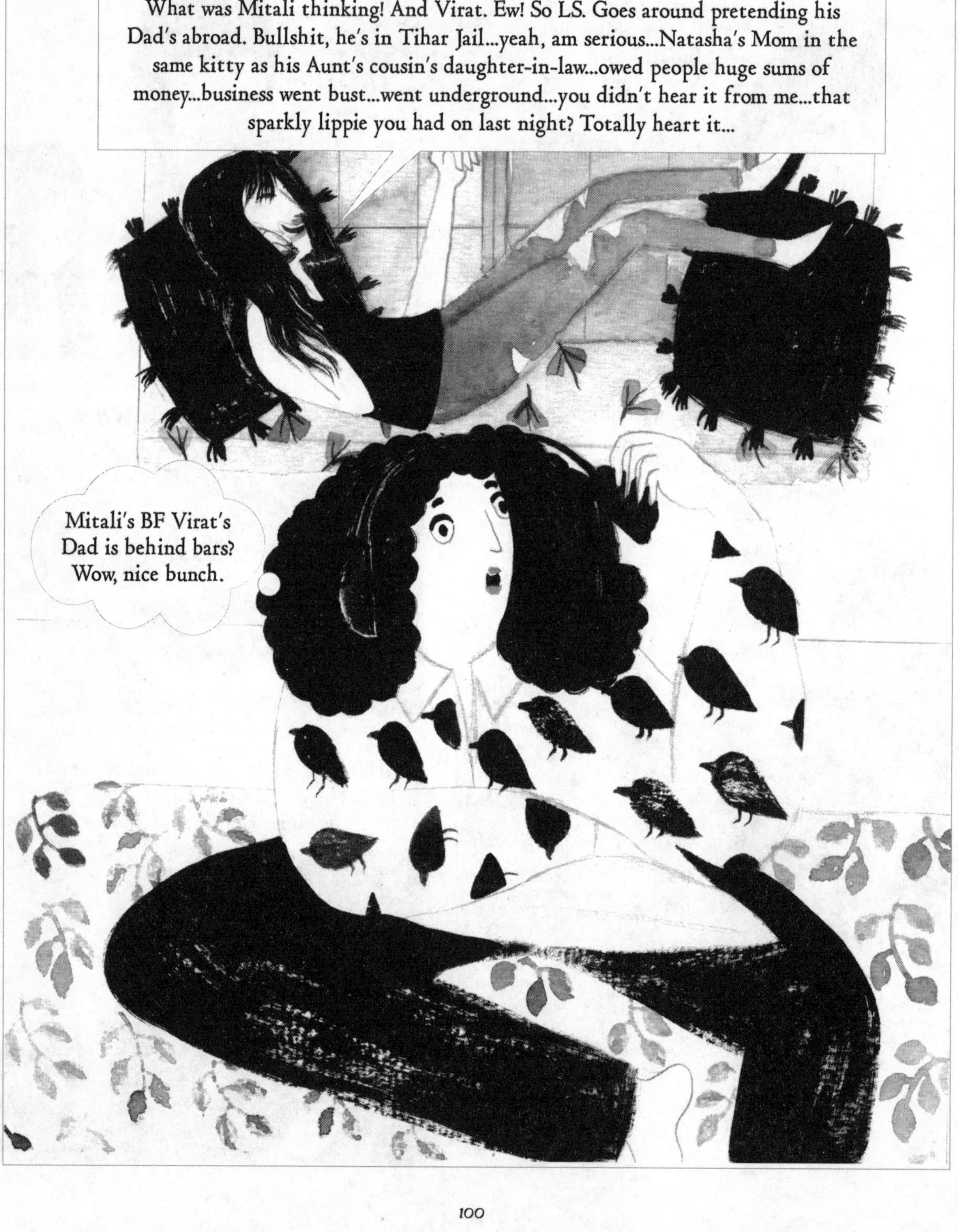
What was Mitali thinking! And Virat. Ew! So LS. Goes around pretending his Dad's abroad. Bullshit, he's in Tihar Jail...yeah, am serious...Natasha's Mom in the same kitty as his Aunt's cousin's daughter-in-law...owed people huge sums of money...business went bust...went underground...you didn't hear it from me...that sparkly lippie you had on last night? Totally heart it...
Mitali's BF Virat's Dad is behind bars? Wow, nice bunch.

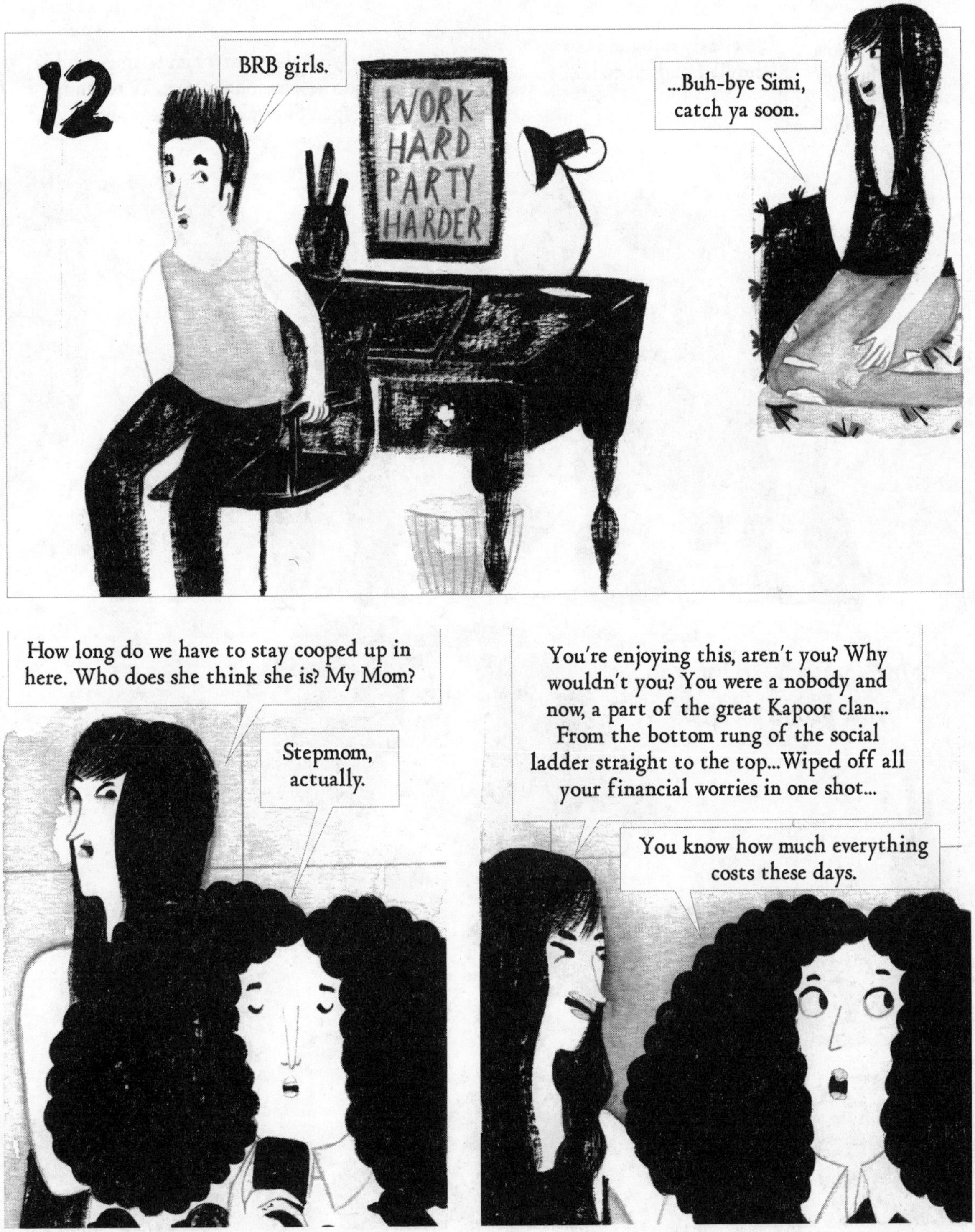
12
BRB girls.
WORK HARD PARTY HARDER
...Buh-bye Simi, catch ya soon.
How long do we have to stay cooped up in here. Who does she think she is? My Mom?
Stepmom, actually.
You're enjoying this, aren't you? Why wouldn't you? You were a nobody and now, a part of the great Kapoor clan... From the bottom rung of the social ladder straight to the top...Wiped off all your financial worries in one shot...
You know how much everything costs these days.

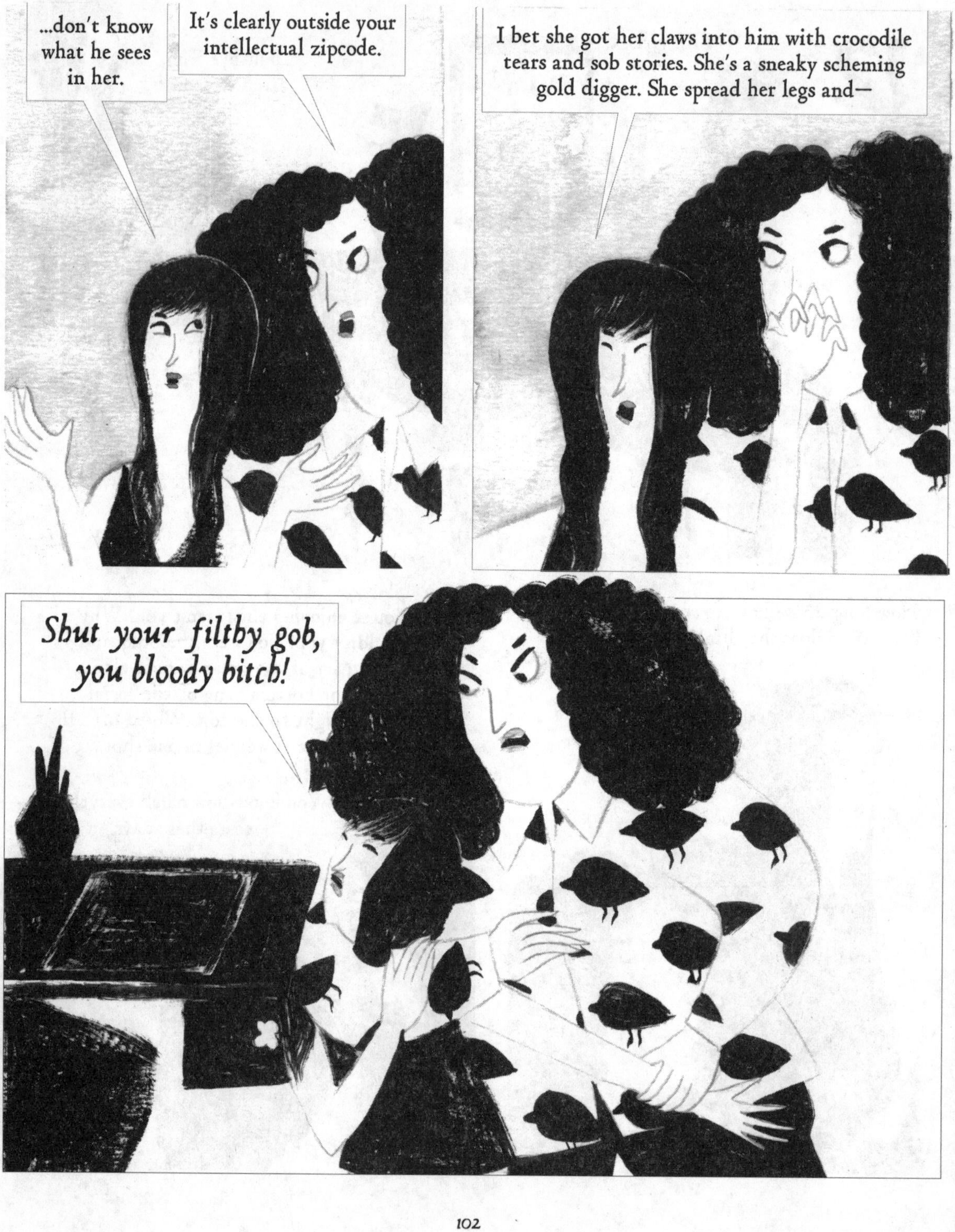
...don't know what he sees in her.
It's clearly outside your intellectual zipcode.
I bet she got her claws into him with crocodile tears and sob stories. She's a sneaky scheming gold digger. She spread her legs and—
Shut your filthy gob, you bloody bitch!

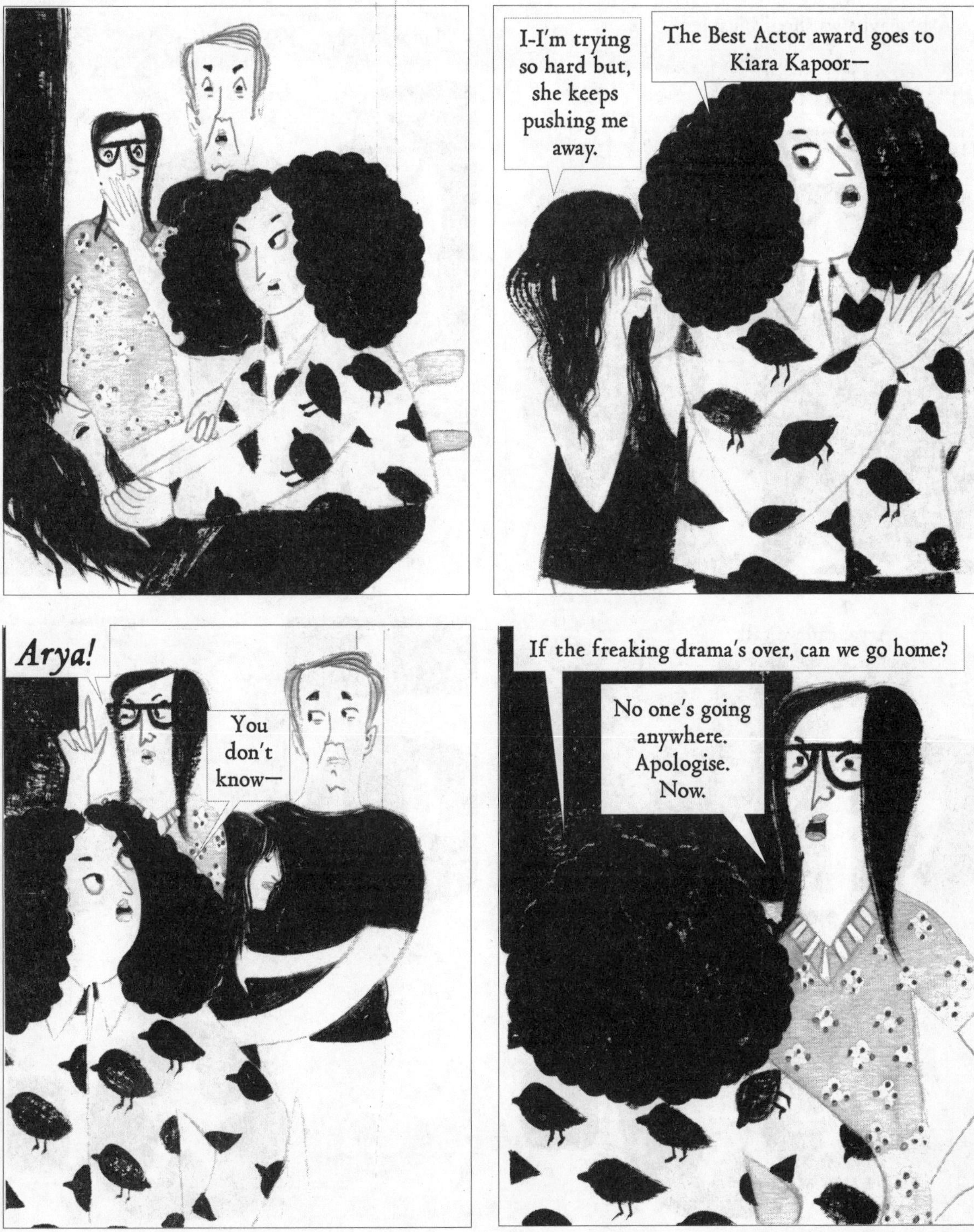
I-I'm trying so hard but, she keeps pushing me away.
The Best Actor award goes to Kiara Kapoor—
Arya!
You don't know—
If the freaking drama's over, can we go home?
No one's going anywhere. Apologise. Now.

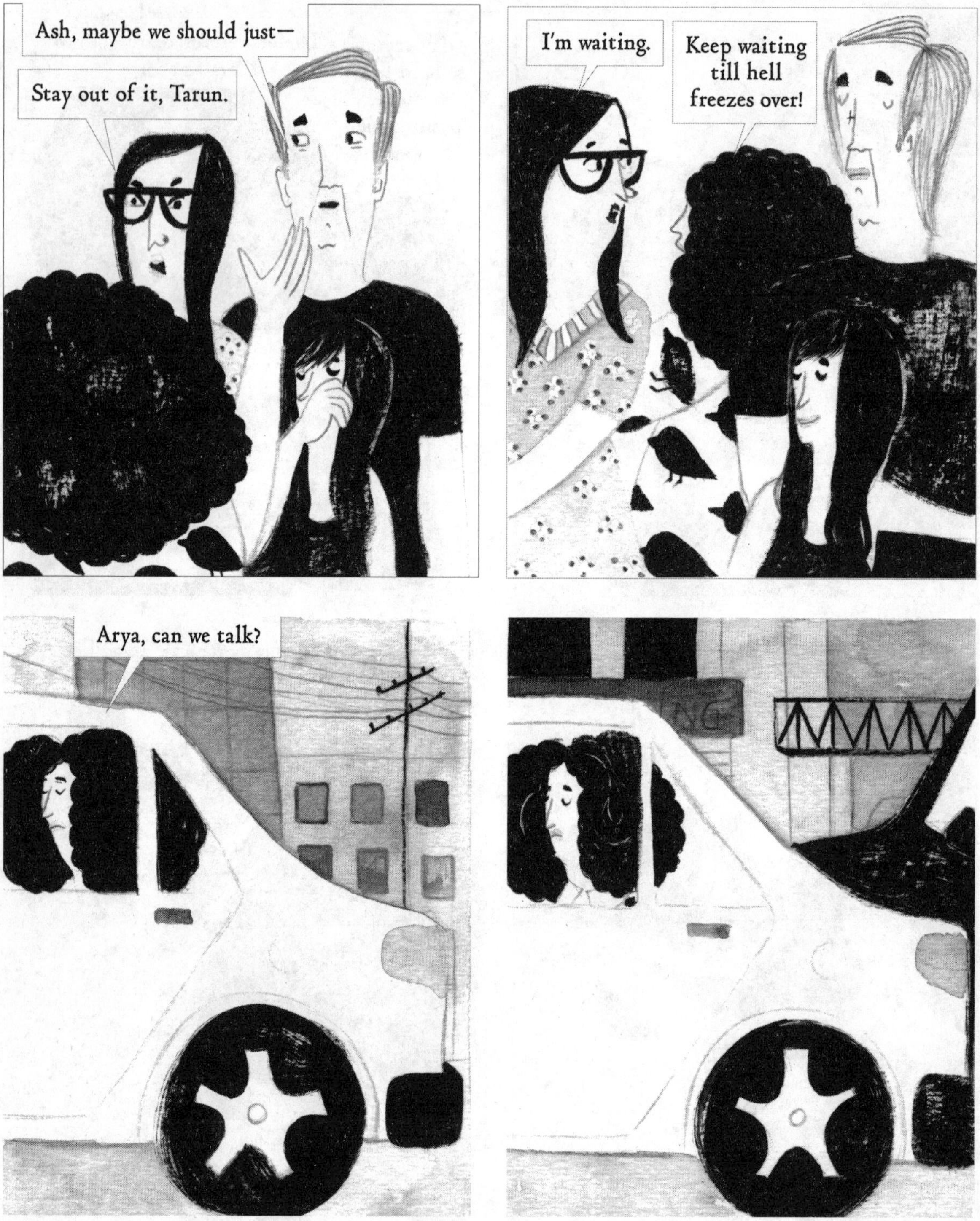
Ash, maybe we should just—
Stay out of it, Tarun.
I'm waiting.
Keep waiting till hell freezes over!
Arya, can we talk?

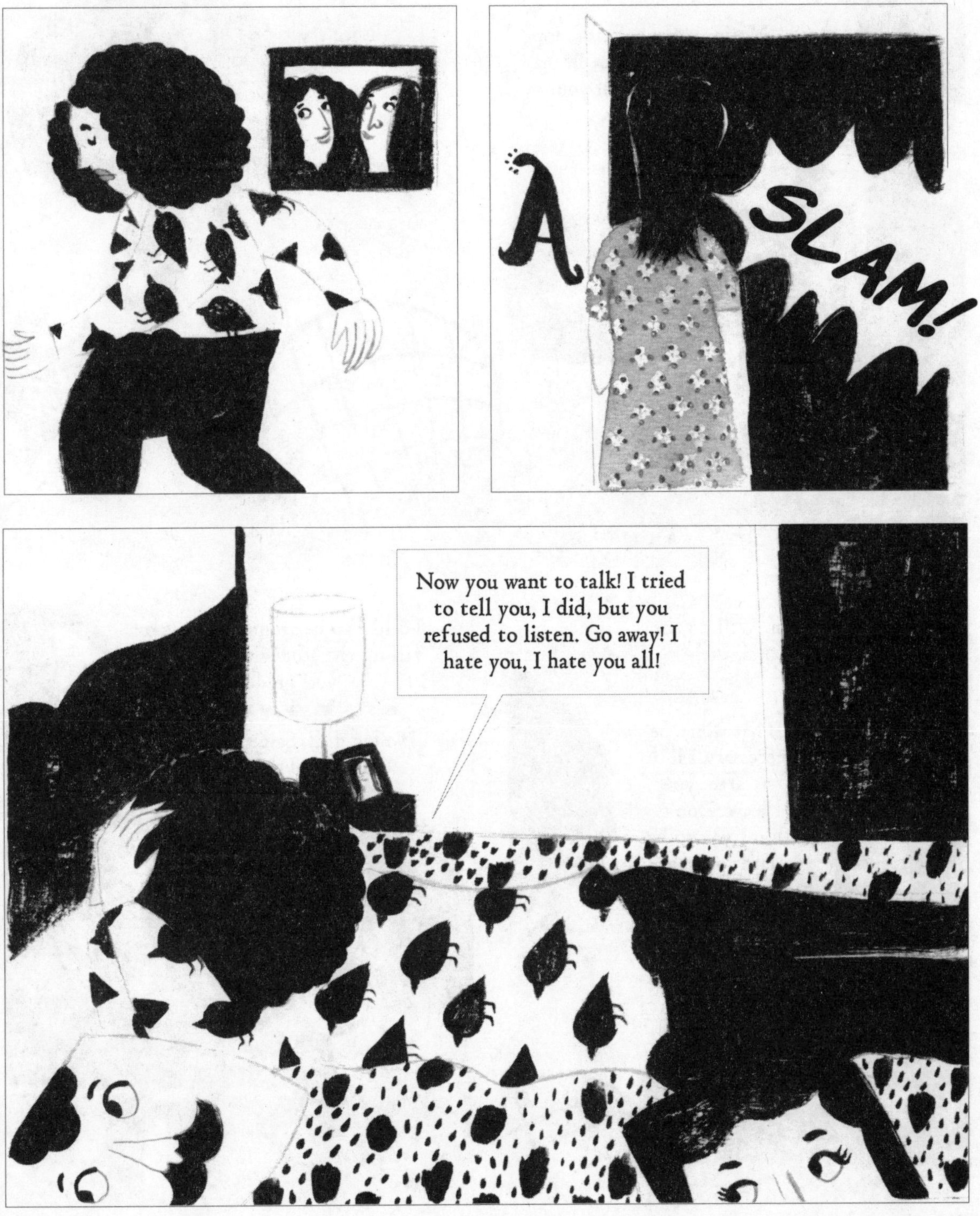
A
SLAM!
Now you want to talk! I tried to tell you, I did, but you refused to listen. Go away! I hate you, I hate you all!

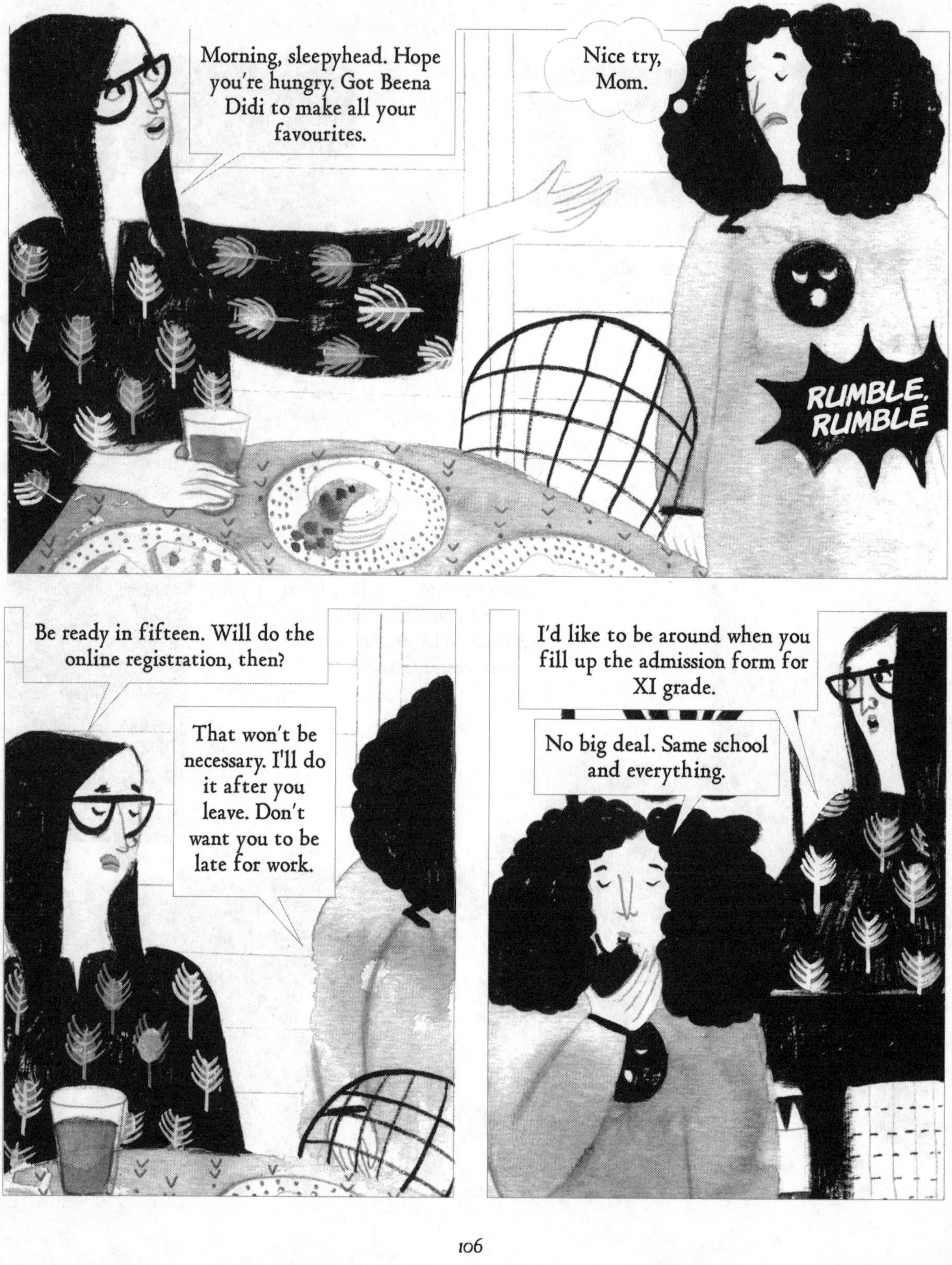
Morning, sleepyhead. Hope you're hungry. Got Beena Didi to make all your favourites.
Nice try, Mom.
RUMBLE, RUMBLE
Be ready in fifteen. Will do the online registration, then?
That won't be necessary. I'll do it after you leave. Don't want you to be late for work.
I'd like to be around when you fill up the admission form for XI grade.
No big deal. Same school and everything.

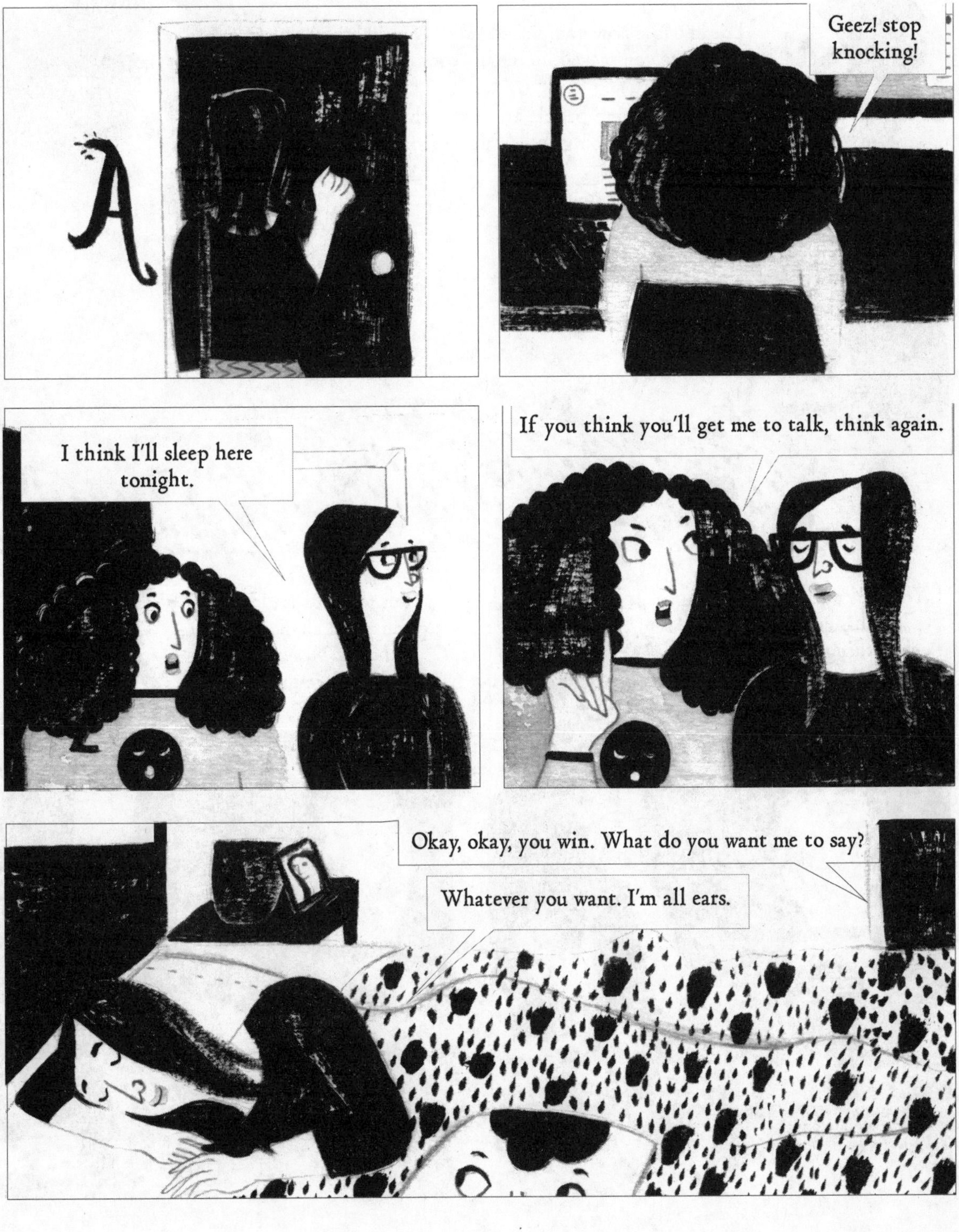
A
Geez! stop knocking!
I think I'll sleep here tonight.
If you think you'll get me to talk, think again.
Okay, okay, you win. What do you want me to say?
Whatever you want. I'm all ears.

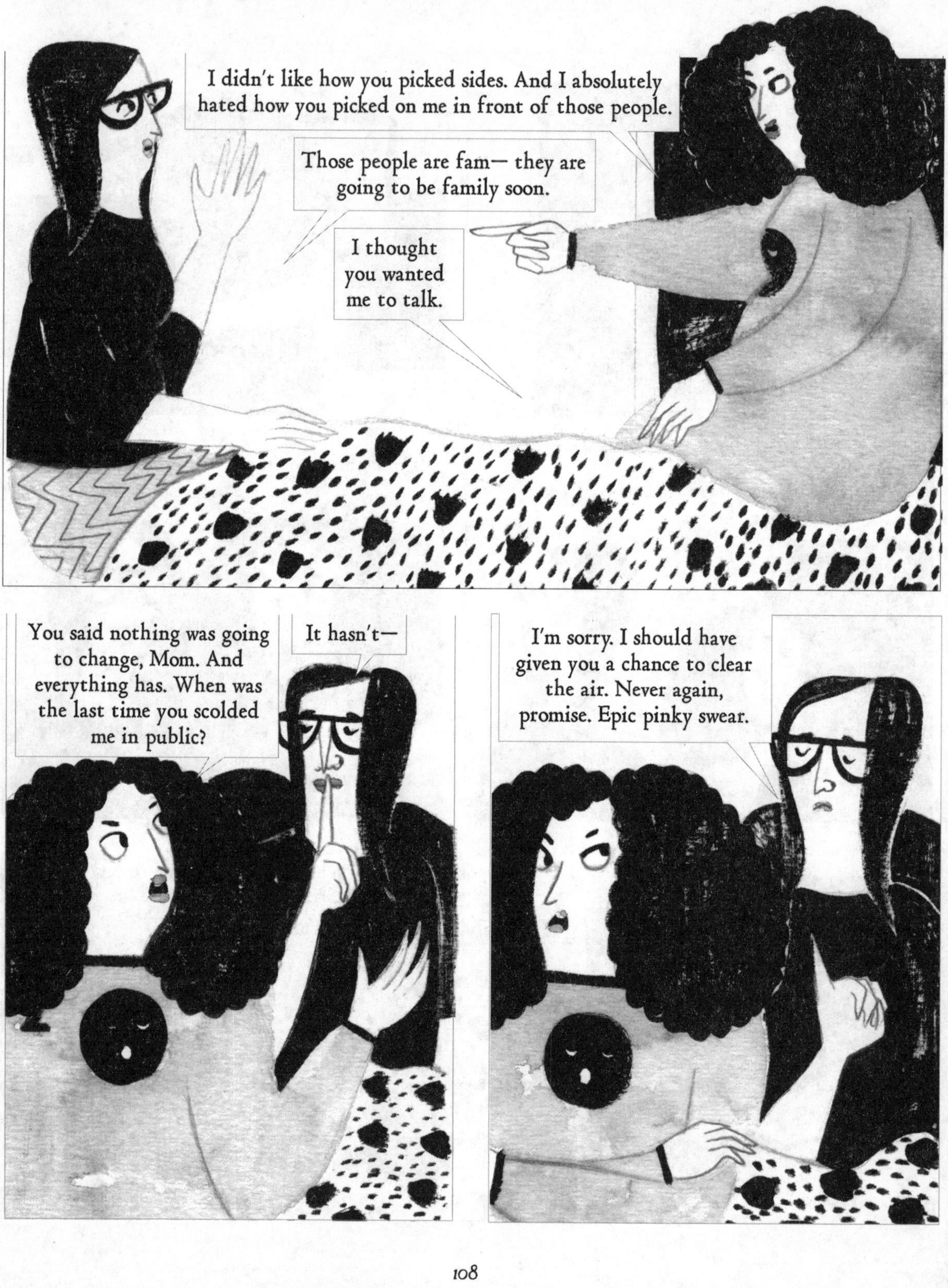
I didn't like how you picked sides. And I absolutely hated how you picked on me in front of those people.
Those people are fam— they are going to be family soon.
I thought you wanted me to talk.
You said nothing was going to change, Mom. And everything has. When was the last time you scolded me in public?
It hasn't—
I'm sorry. I should have given you a chance to clear the air. Never again, promise. Epic pinky swear.

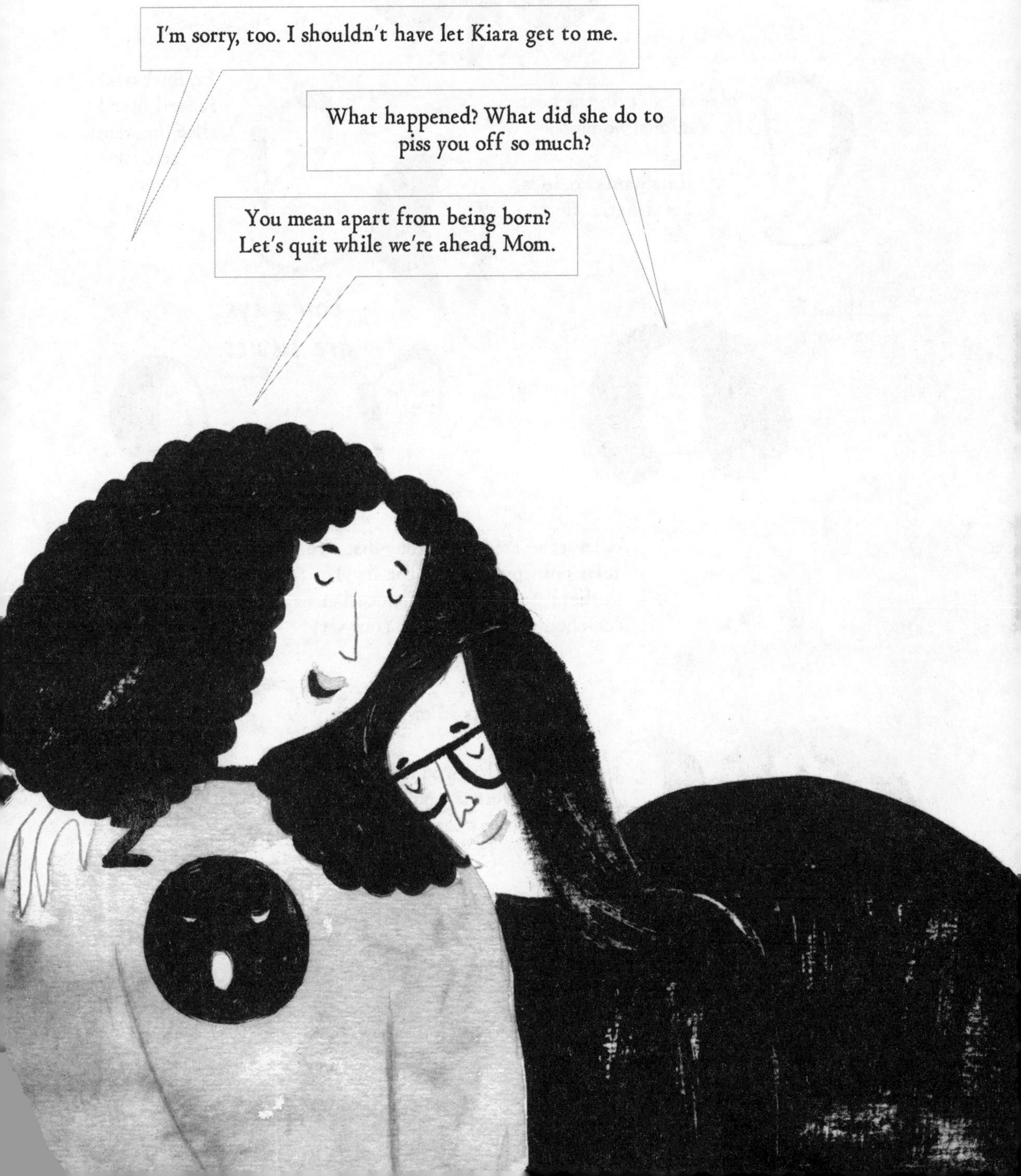
I'm sorry, too. I shouldn't have let Kiara get to me.
What happened? What did she do to piss you off so much?
You mean apart from being born? Let's quit while we're ahead, Mom.

13

Come back, you guys. Delhi's not the same without y'all.

Man, I can't do the heat and dust no more.

All he wants to do is Fatal Attraction.

Er, Rucksack? Russell Brand called, he wants his lame jokes back.

I think it was dope.

You guys are juvies.

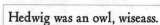

At least, we aren't in a long distance relationship that will soon involve medieval forms of communication. You should buy a pigeon. Your very own Hedwig.

If I wanted to listen to pathetic one liners, I'd have gone for the stand-up comedy open mic night.

Hedwig was an owl, wiseass.

Scratch that, you're so carnivorous, you'll probably eat the pigeon before you train it.

Why bother?

This is Rukhsar Omar bringing them to you live and exclusive.

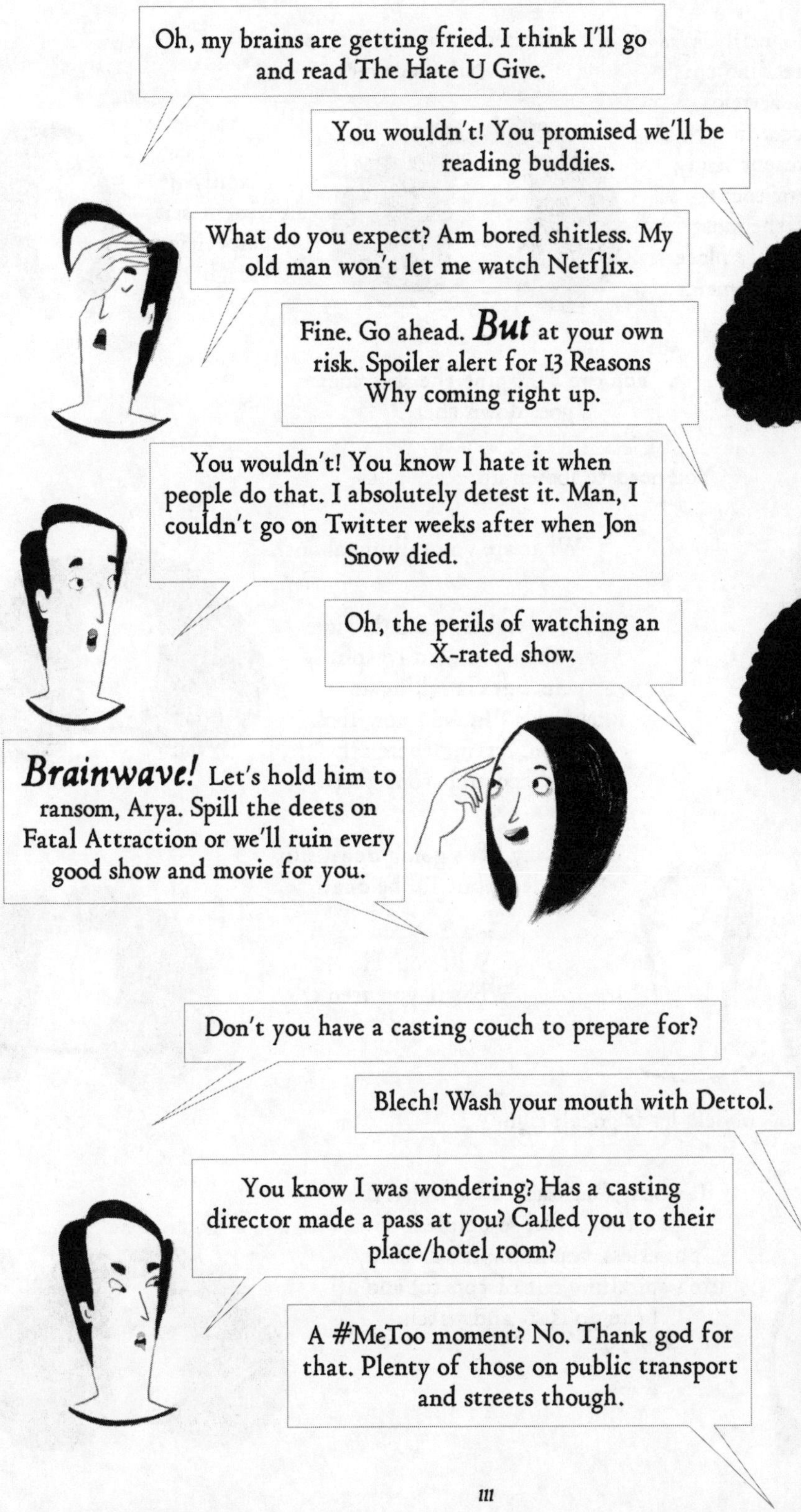
Oh, my brains are getting fried. I think I'll go and read The Hate U Give.
You wouldn't! You promised we'll be reading buddies.
What do you expect? Am bored shitless. My old man won't let me watch Netflix.
Fine. Go ahead. But at your own risk. Spoiler alert for 13 Reasons Why coming right up.
You wouldn't! You know I hate it when people do that. I absolutely detest it. Man, I couldn't go on Twitter weeks after when Jon Snow died.
Oh, the perils of watching an X-rated show.
Brainwave! Let's hold him to ransom, Arya. Spill the deets on Fatal Attraction or we'll ruin every good show and movie for you.
Don't you have a casting couch to prepare for?
Blech! Wash your mouth with Dettol.
You know I was wondering? Has a casting director made a pass at you? Called you to their place/hotel room?
A #MeToo moment? No. Thank god for that. Plenty of those on public transport and streets though.

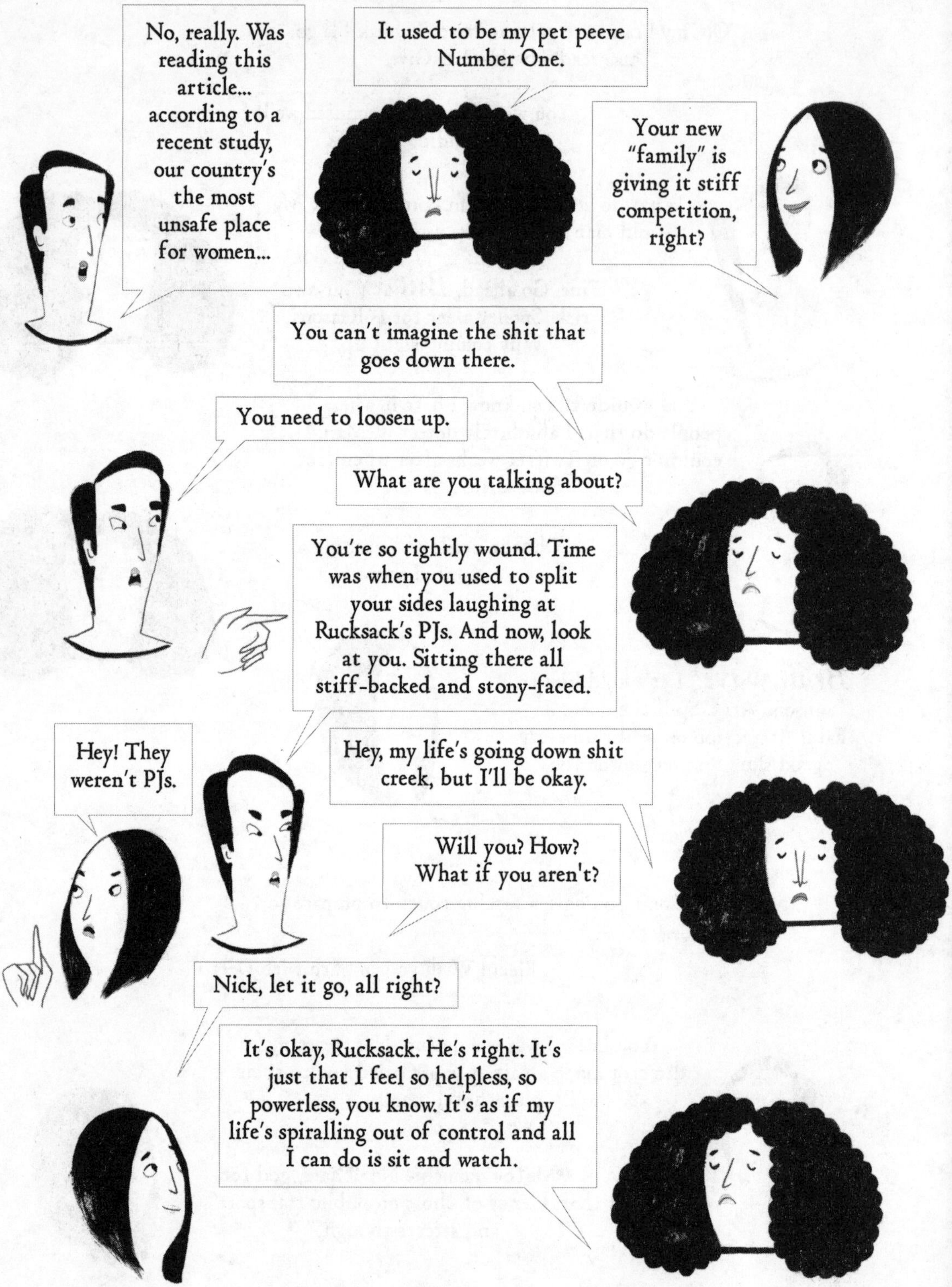
No, really. Was reading this article... according to a recent study, our country's the most unsafe place for women...
It used to be my pet peeve Number One.
Your new "family" is giving it stiff competition, right?
You can't imagine the shit that goes down there.
You need to loosen up.
What are you talking about?
You're so tightly wound. Time was when you used to split your sides laughing at Rucksack's PJs. And now, look at you. Sitting there all stiff-backed and stony-faced.
Hey! They weren't PJs.
Hey, my life's going down shit creek, but I'll be okay.
Will you? How? What if you aren't?
Nick, let it go, all right?
It's okay, Rucksack. He's right. It's just that I feel so helpless, so powerless, you know. It's as if my life's spiralling out of control and all I can do is sit and watch.

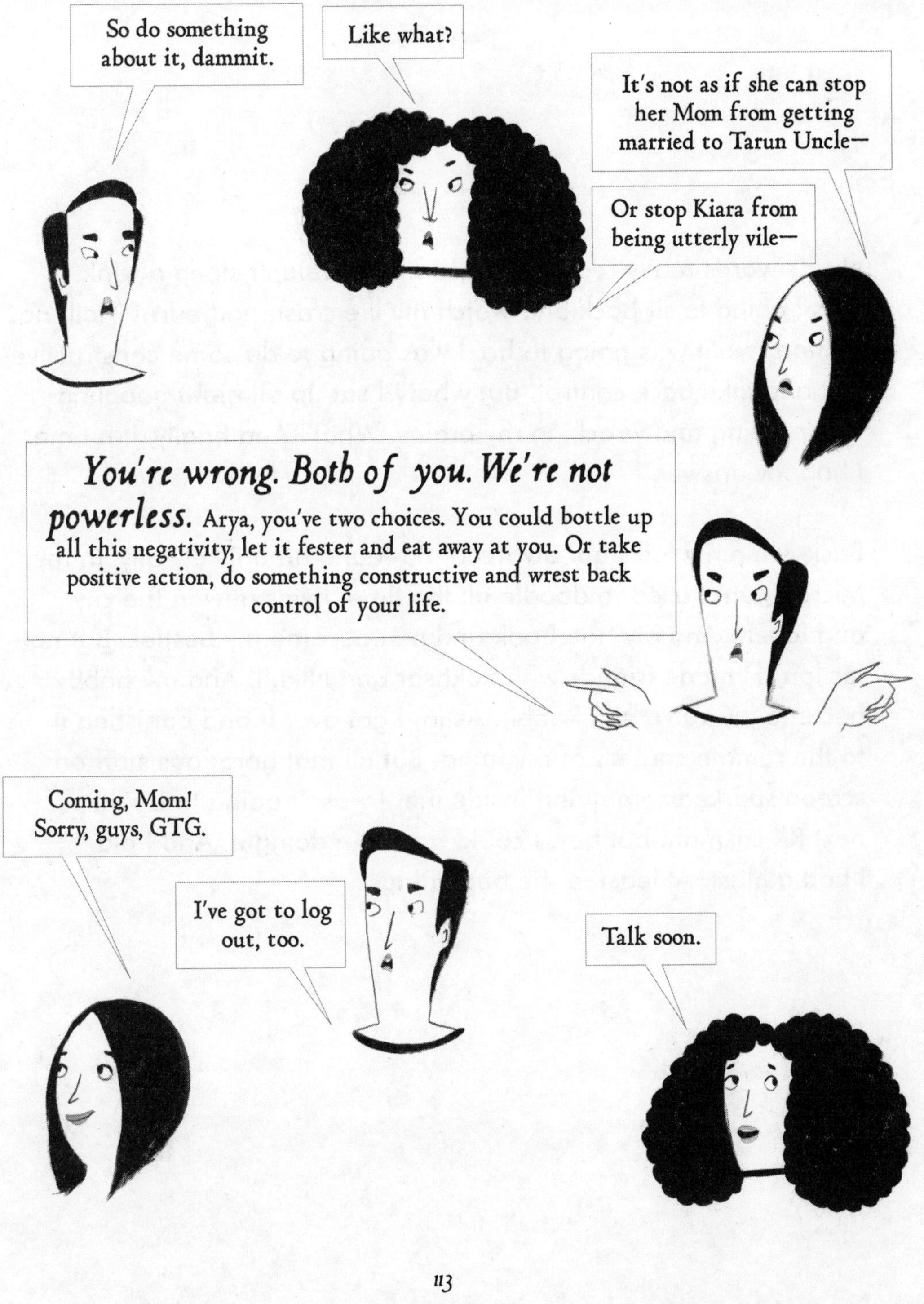
So do something about it, dammit.
Like what?
It's not as if she can stop her Mom from getting married to Tarun Uncle—
Or stop Kiara from being utterly vile—
You're wrong. Both of you. We're not powerless. Arya, you've two choices. You could bottle up all this negativity, let it fester and eat away at you. Or take positive action, do something constructive and wrest back control of your life.
Coming, Mom! Sorry, guys, GTG.
I've got to log out, too.
Talk soon.

Nick's words really really haunted me. I couldn't sleep a wink. Was I going to sit back and watch my life crash and burn? Hell, no. Option Two it was going to be. I was going to do some constructive shit and take back control. But what? I sat up all night googling and reading and wracking my brains. What? And finally, it hit me. I had my answer.

Back when my folks got divorced, I'd found an unlikely ally. In my Micron pen. I used to doodle all the time. I was new in the city and lonely. And my notebook and pen became my besties. But not for long. I made friends with Rukhsar and Nikhil. And my hobby became my Velveteen Rabbit. As in, I got over it and banished it to the remote corners of my mind. But all that gorgeous stuff on screen sparked something inside me. I wasn't going to be the next RK Laxman, but hey, I could have fun doing it. And I did. I had a blast. At least in the beginning...

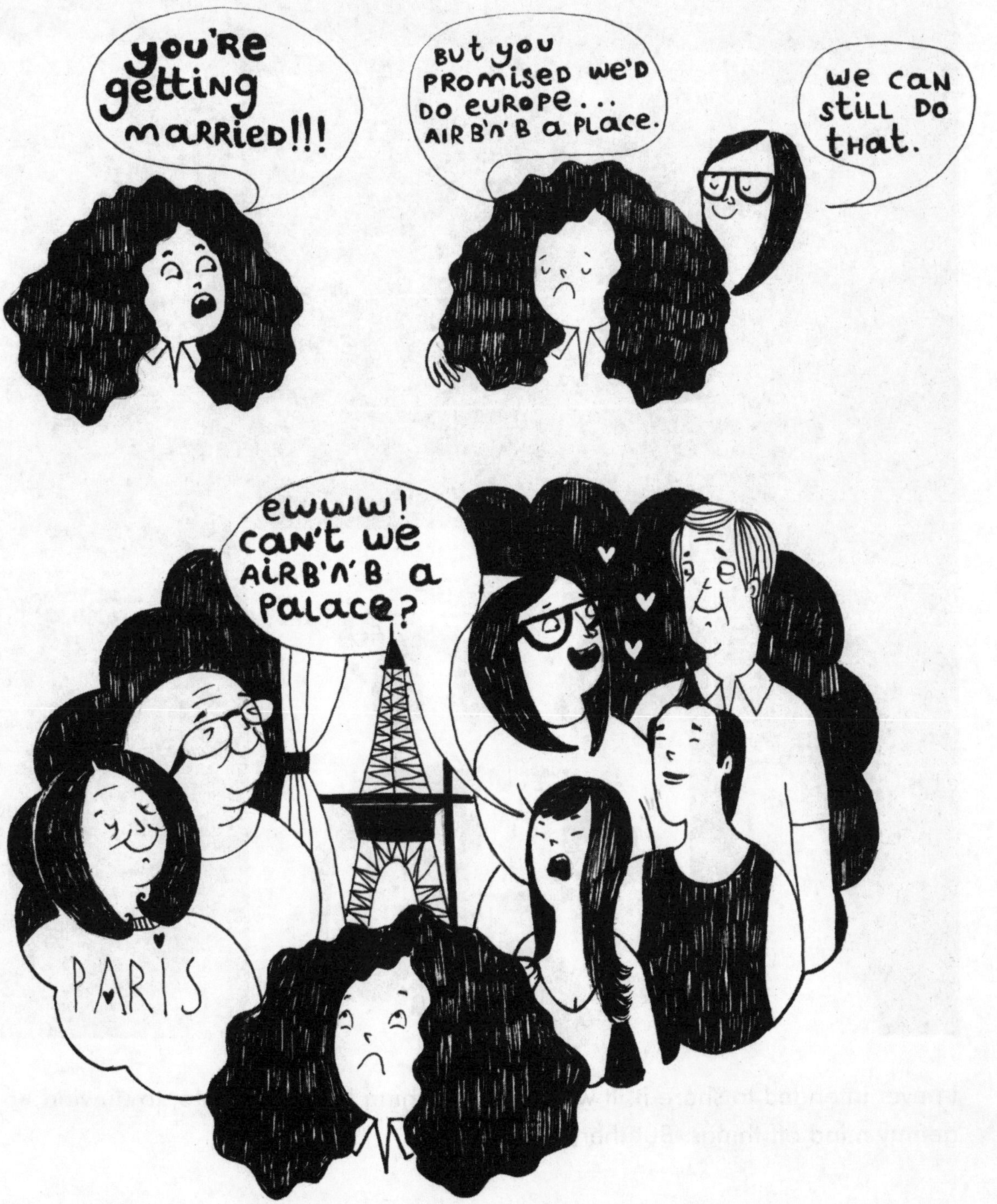
you're getting married!!!
But you promised we'd do europe... air b'n'b a place.
we can still do that.
ewww! can't we airb'n'b a palace?
PARIS

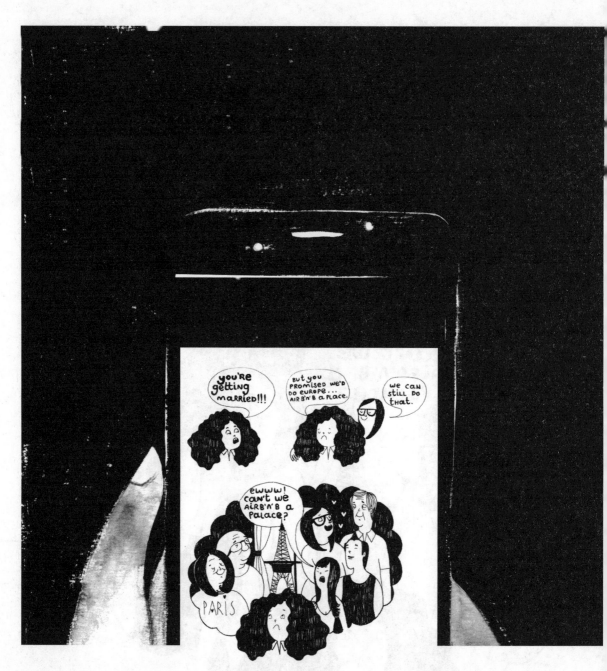

I never intended to share it. It was just something I needed to do, to unwind, to get my mind off things. But then...

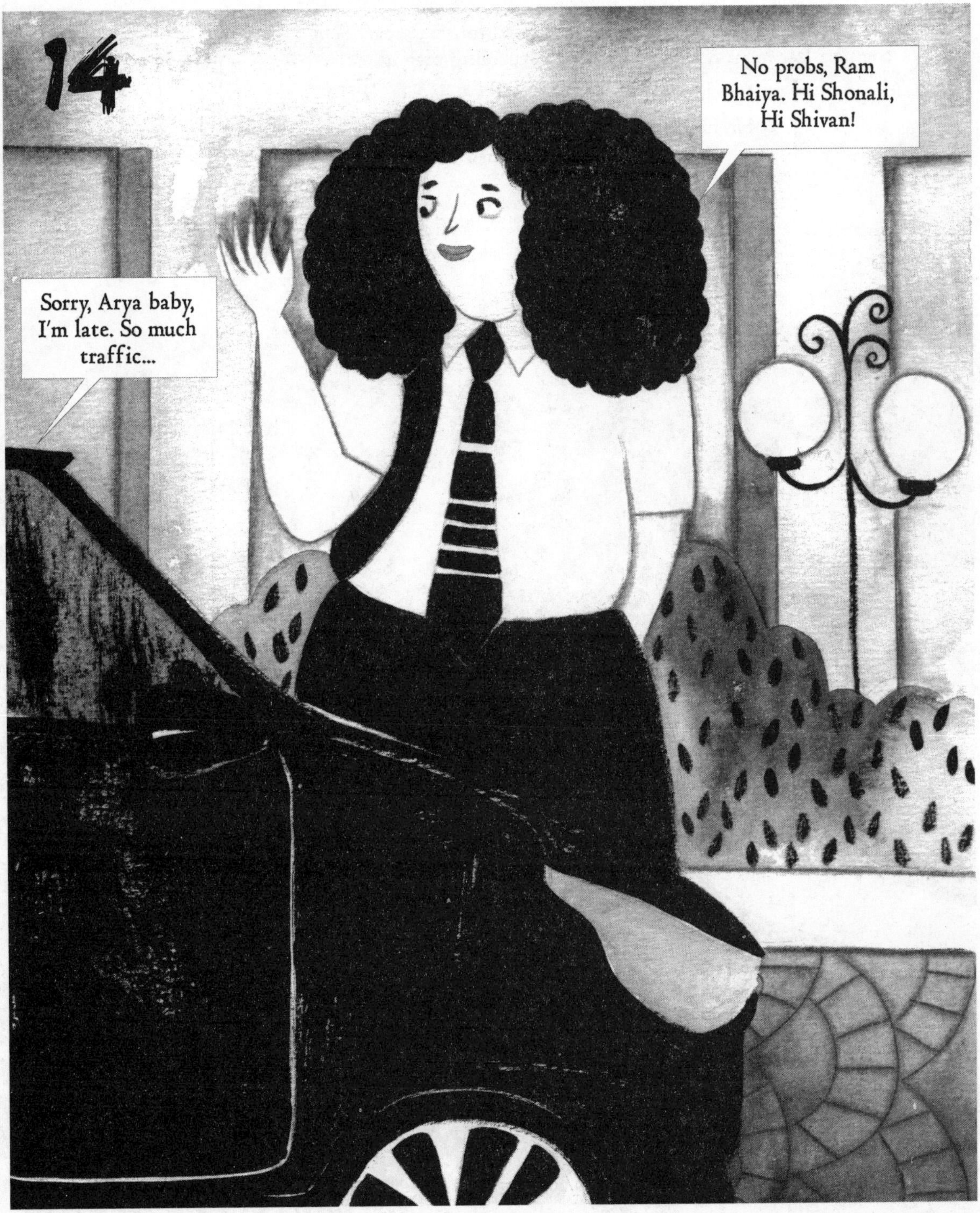
14
Sorry, Arya baby, I'm late. So much traffic...
No probs, Ram Bhaiya. Hi Shonali, Hi Shivan!

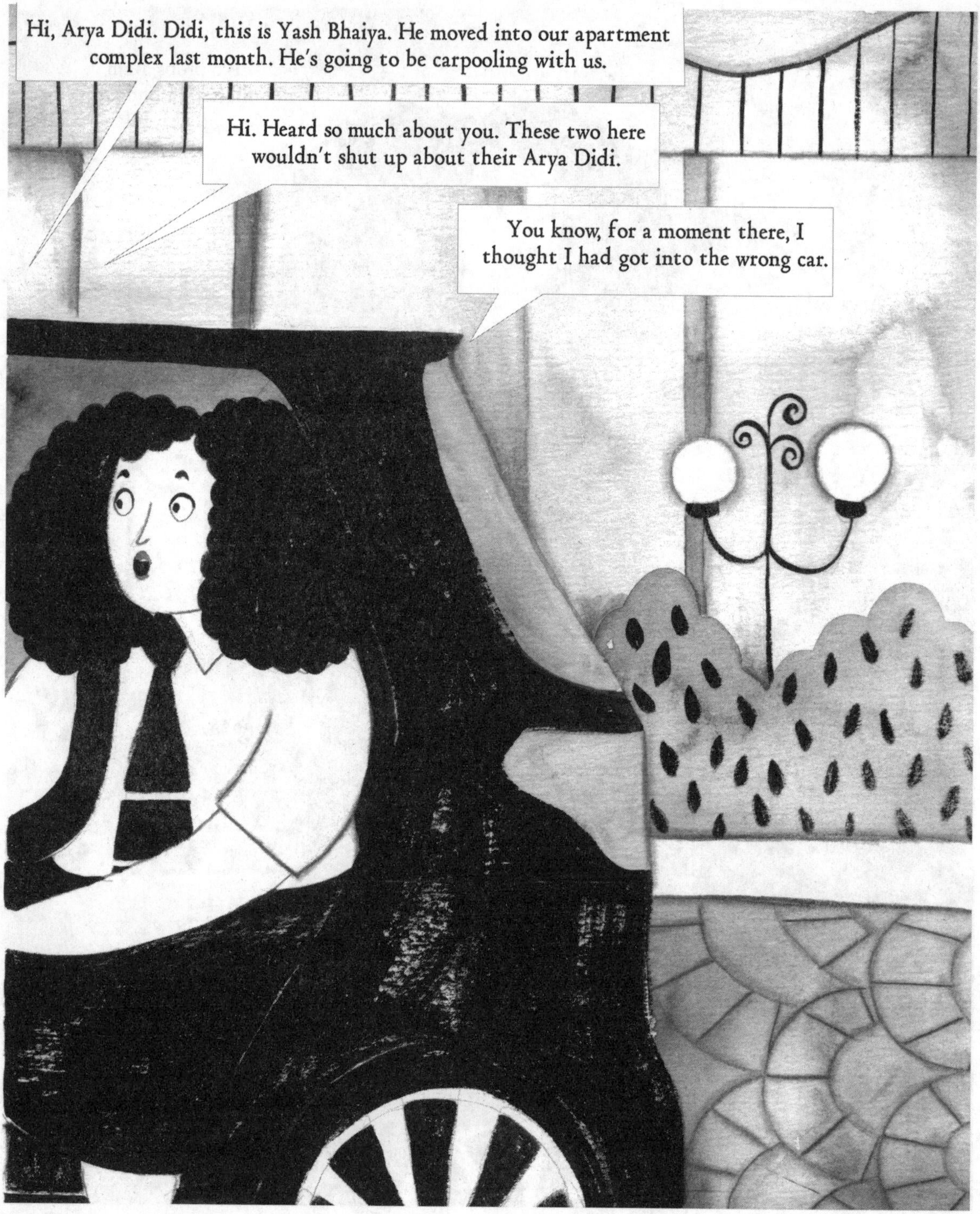
Hi, Arya Didi. Didi, this is Yash Bhaiya. He moved into our apartment complex last month. He's going to be carpooling with us.
Hi. Heard so much about you. These two here wouldn't shut up about their Arya Didi.
You know, for a moment there, I thought I had got into the wrong car.

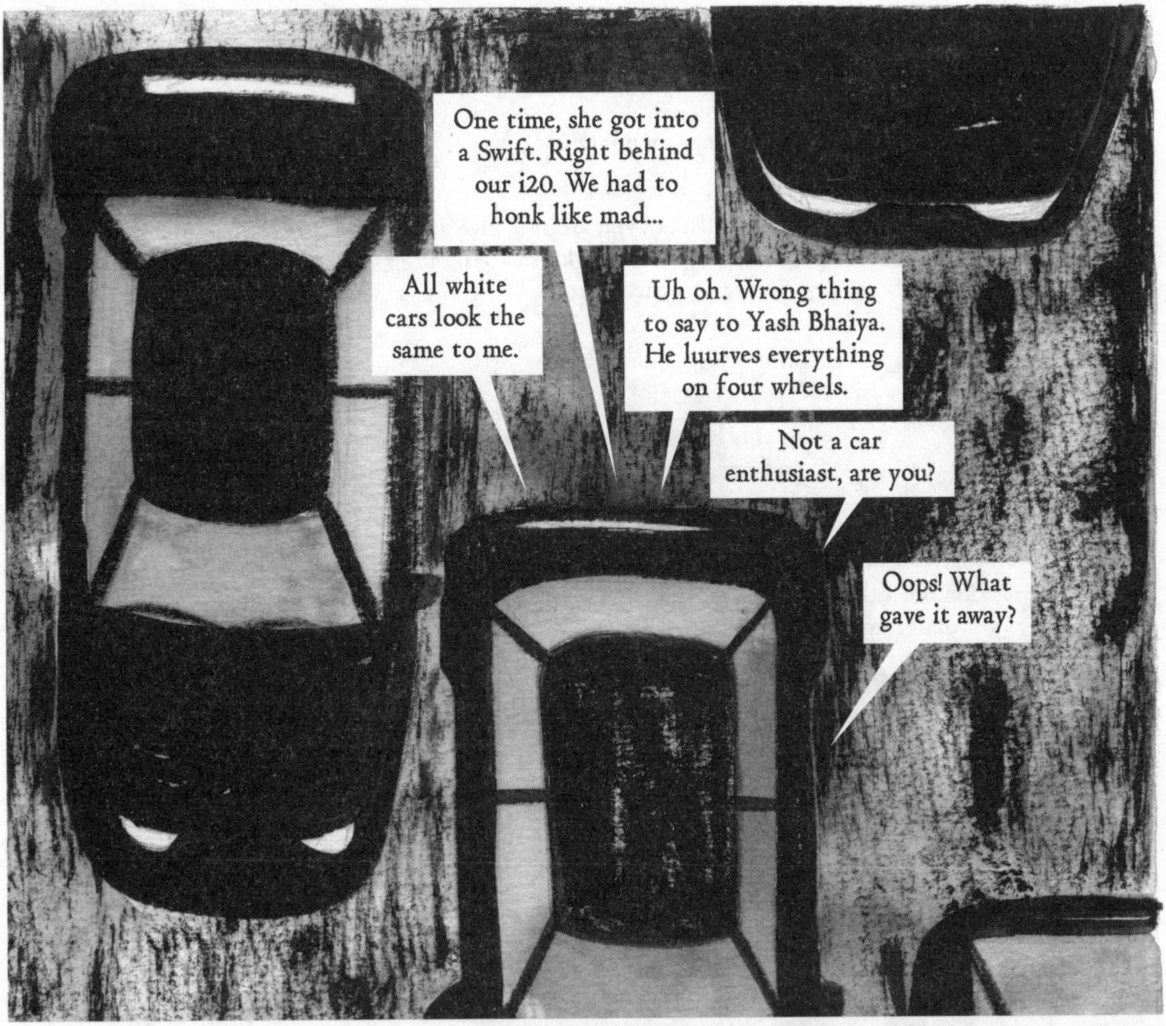
One time, she got into a Swift. Right behind our i20. We had to honk like mad...
All white cars look the same to me.
Uh oh. Wrong thing to say to Yash Bhaiya. He luurves everything on four wheels.
Not a car enthusiast, are you?
Oops! What gave it away?

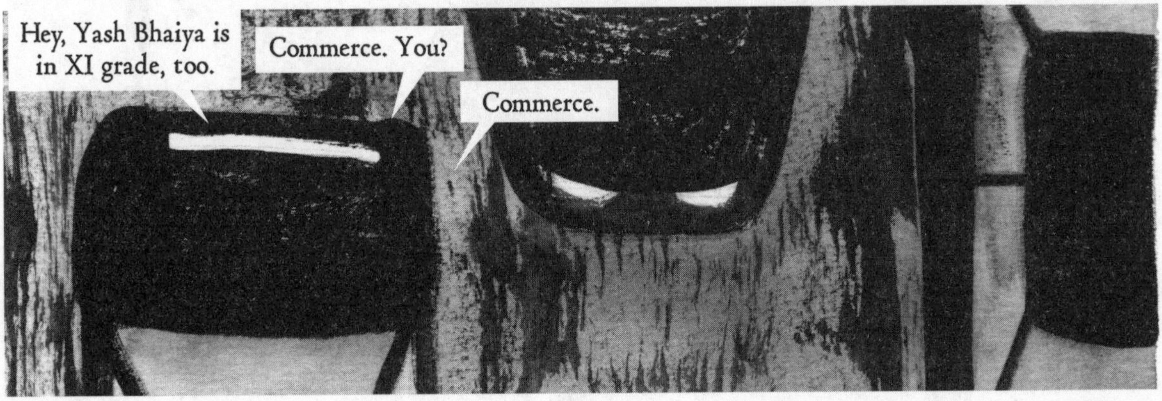
Hey, Yash Bhaiya is in XI grade, too.
Commerce. You?
Commerce.

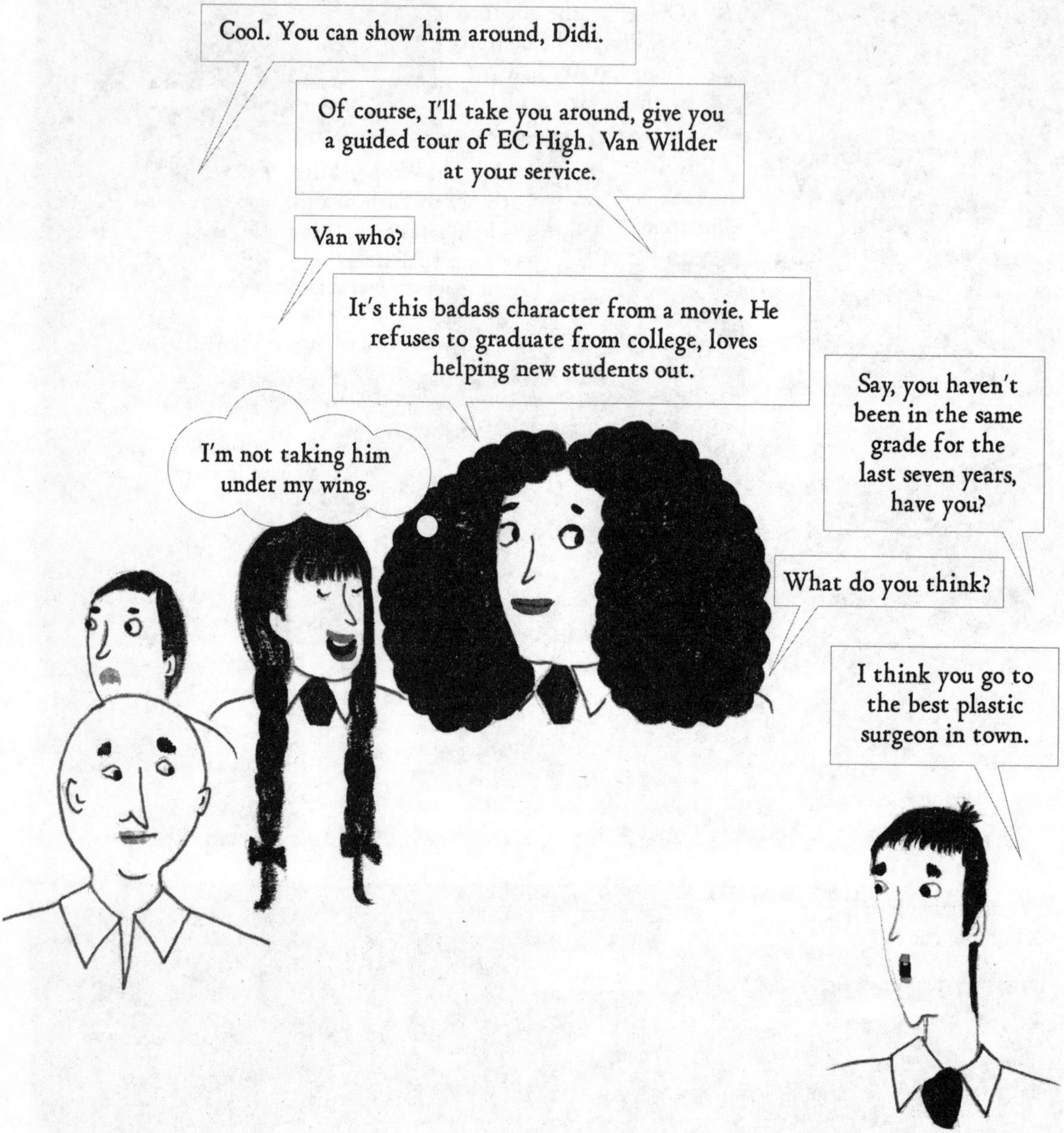
Cool. You can show him around, Didi.
Of course, I'll take you around, give you a guided tour of EC High. Van Wilder at your service.
Van who?
It's this badass character from a movie. He refuses to graduate from college, loves helping new students out.
I'm not taking him under my wing.
Say, you haven't been in the same grade for the last seven years, have you?
What do you think?
I think you go to the best plastic surgeon in town.

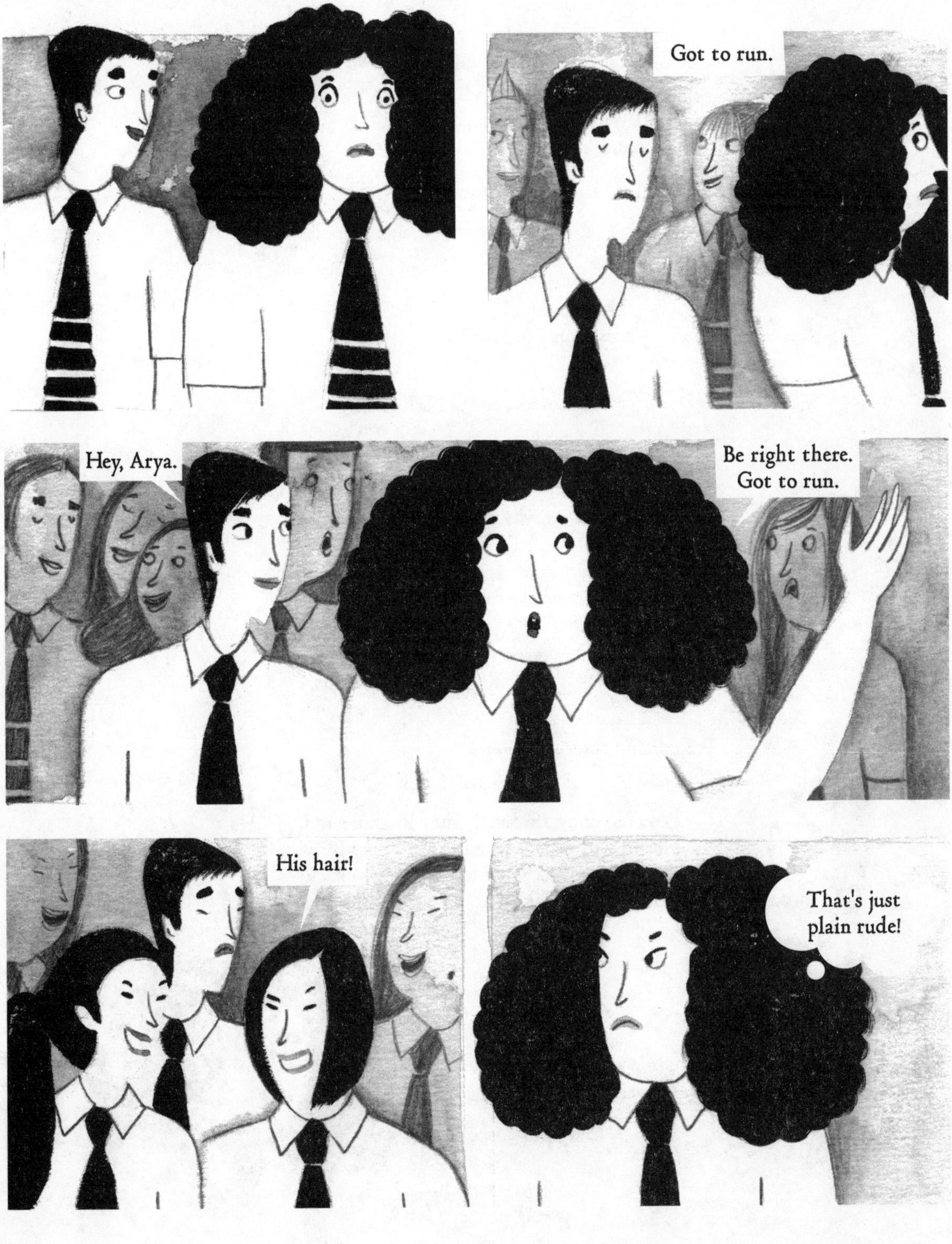
Got to run.
Hey, Arya.
Be right there.
Got to run.
His hair!
That's just
plain rude!

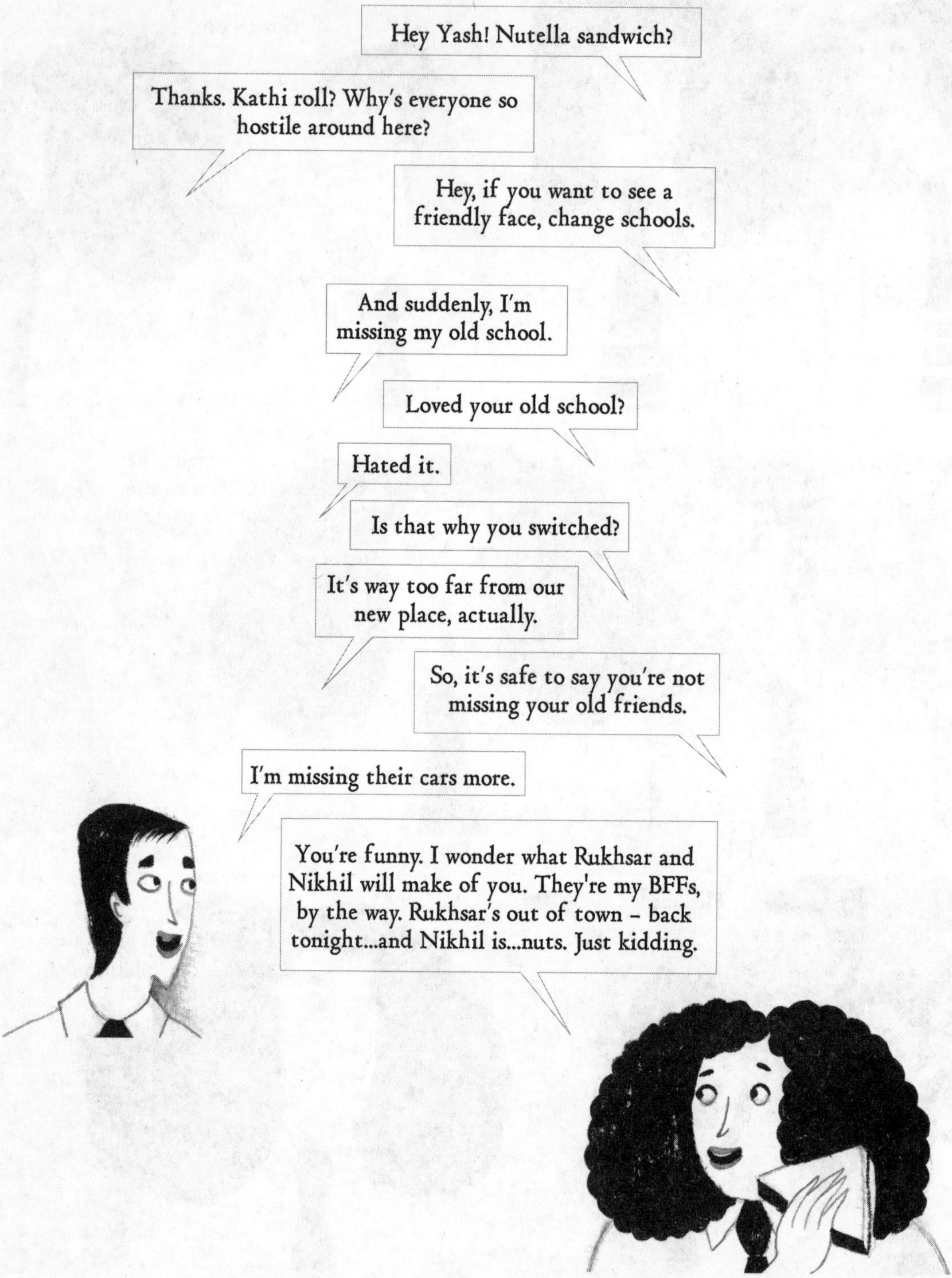
Hey Yash! Nutella sandwich?
Thanks. Kathi roll? Why's everyone so hostile around here?
Hey, if you want to see a friendly face, change schools.
And suddenly, I'm missing my old school.
Loved your old school?
Hated it.
Is that why you switched?
It's way too far from our new place, actually.
So, it's safe to say you're not missing your old friends.
I'm missing their cars more.
You're funny. I wonder what Rukhsar and Nikhil will make of you. They're my BFFs, by the way. Rukhsar's out of town – back tonight...and Nikhil is...nuts. Just kidding.

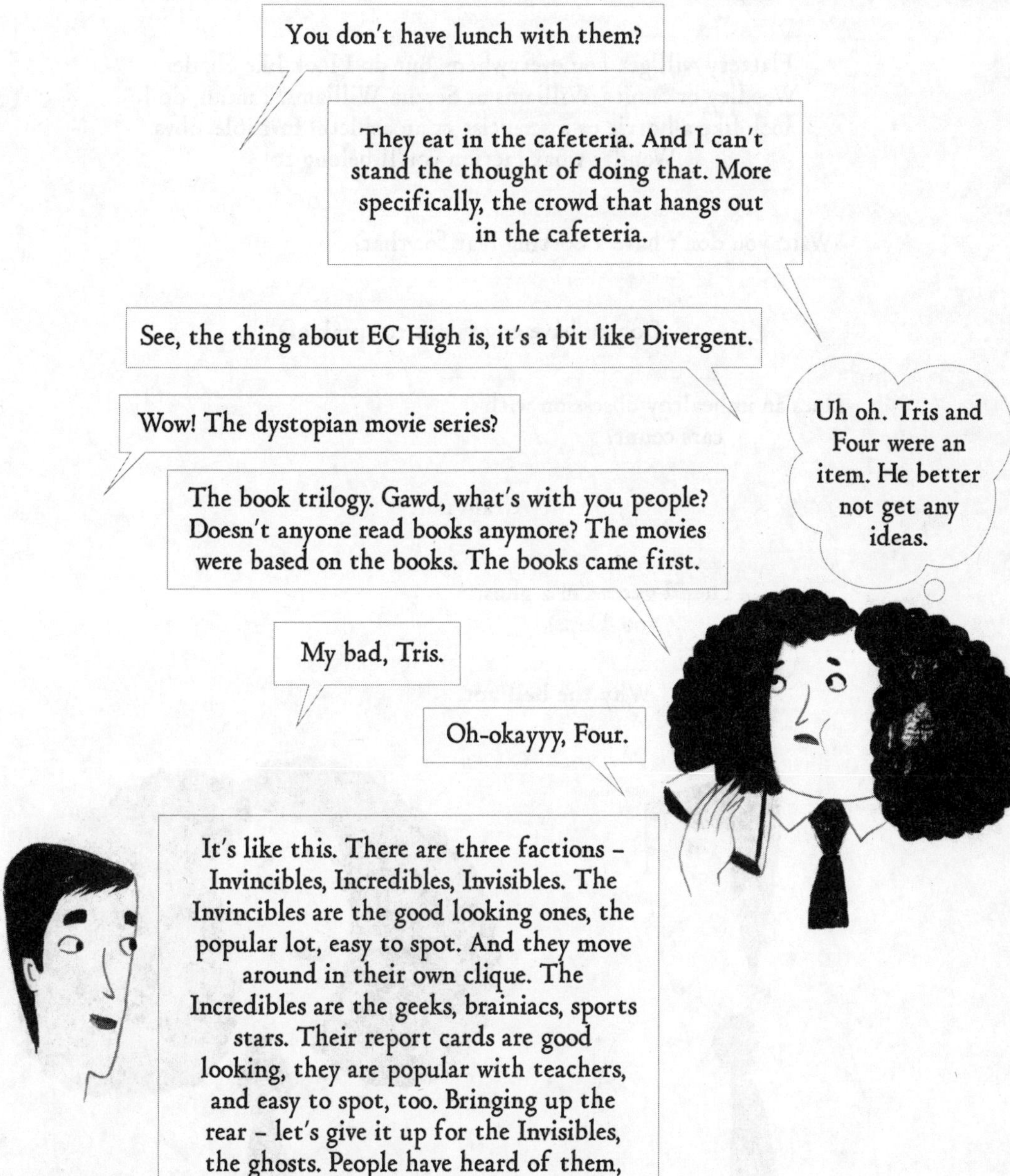
You don't have lunch with them?
They eat in the cafeteria. And I can't stand the thought of doing that. More specifically, the crowd that hangs out in the cafeteria.
See, the thing about EC High is, it's a bit like Divergent.
Uh oh. Tris and Four were an item. He better not get any ideas.
Wow! The dystopian movie series?
The book trilogy. Gawd, what's with you people? Doesn't anyone read books anymore? The movies were based on the books. The books came first.
My bad, Tris.
Oh-okayyy, Four.
It's like this. There are three factions – Invincibles, Incredibles, Invisibles. The Invincibles are the good looking ones, the popular lot, easy to spot. And they move around in their own clique. The Incredibles are the geeks, brainiacs, sports stars. Their report cards are good looking, they are popular with teachers, and easy to spot, too. Bringing up the rear – let's give it up for the Invisibles, the ghosts. People have heard of them, but there are no confirmed sightings. They roam the hallways undetected.

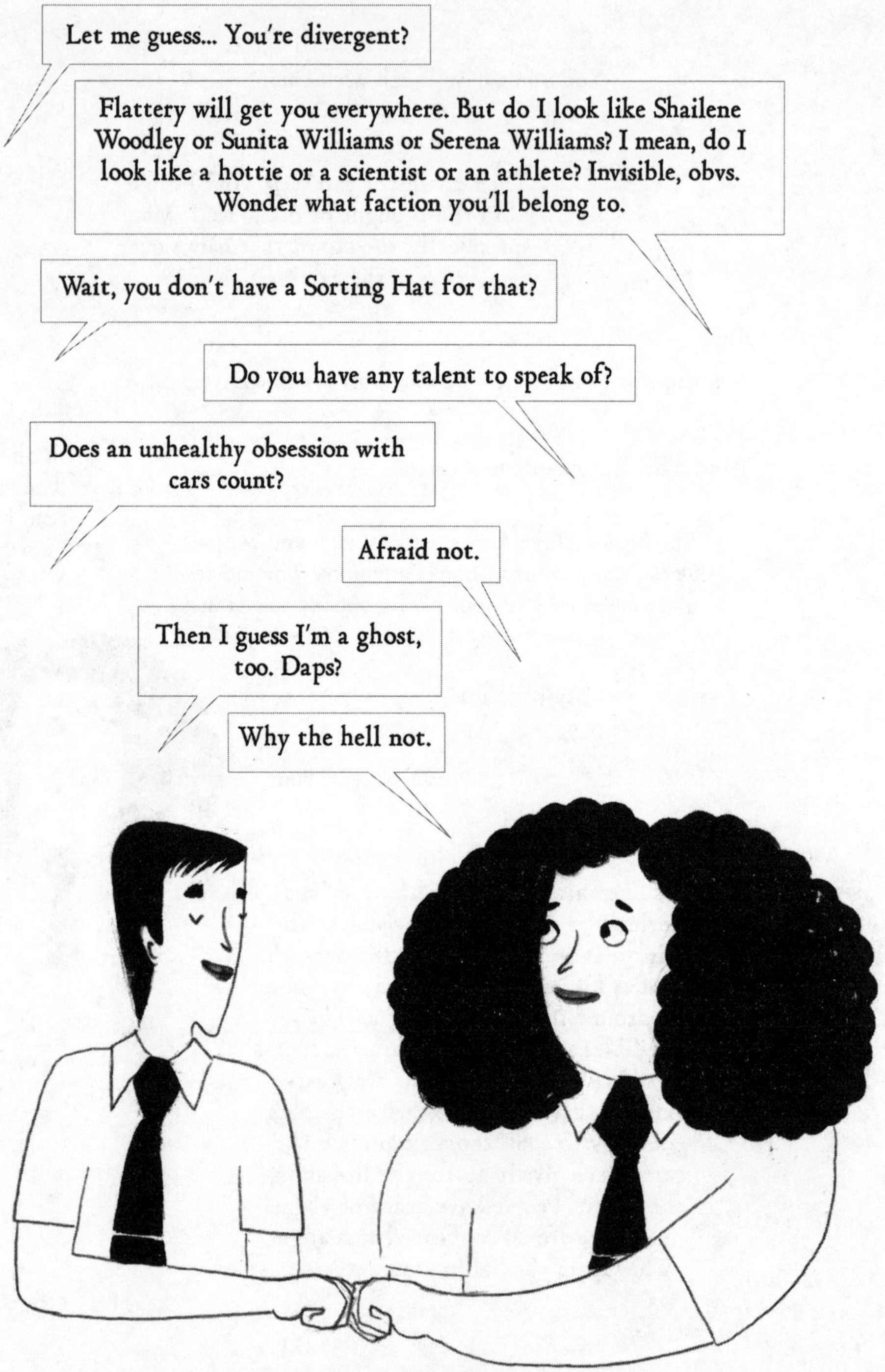
Let me guess... You're divergent?
Flattery will get you everywhere. But do I look like Shailene Woodley or Sunita Williams or Serena Williams? I mean, do I look like a hottie or a scientist or an athlete? Invisible, obvs. Wonder what faction you'll belong to.
Wait, you don't have a Sorting Hat for that?
Do you have any talent to speak of?
Does an unhealthy obsession with cars count?
Afraid not.
Then I guess I'm a ghost, too. Daps?
Why the hell not.

15

Chat in an hour, peeps? 4:30 PM ✓✓

Nikhil
Have Eco coaching. 4:30 PM

Okie. After that? 4:30 PM ✓✓

Nikhil
Have Physics tuition. 4:32 PM

Uh-Okaaaayy. After that? 4:32 PM ✓✓

Nikhil
Have Chemistry classes. 4:32 PM

FINE. Talk to you in 2...years. 4:33 PM ✓✓

Nikhil
Spoken like my main girl. (Rucksack, now please don't be like, "What does that make me?" A guy's allowed to have two main girls, all right?)
4:35 PM

Would ask you why you're doing this, why you're embarking on this absolute madness (tuitions for all subjects, really?) but guess you won't have the time to send out a reply, Nickster.
4:36 PM ✓✓

Nikhil
Not taking English tuitions, FYI. 4:37 PM

Thanks for that, Captain Obvious 4:37 PM ✓✓

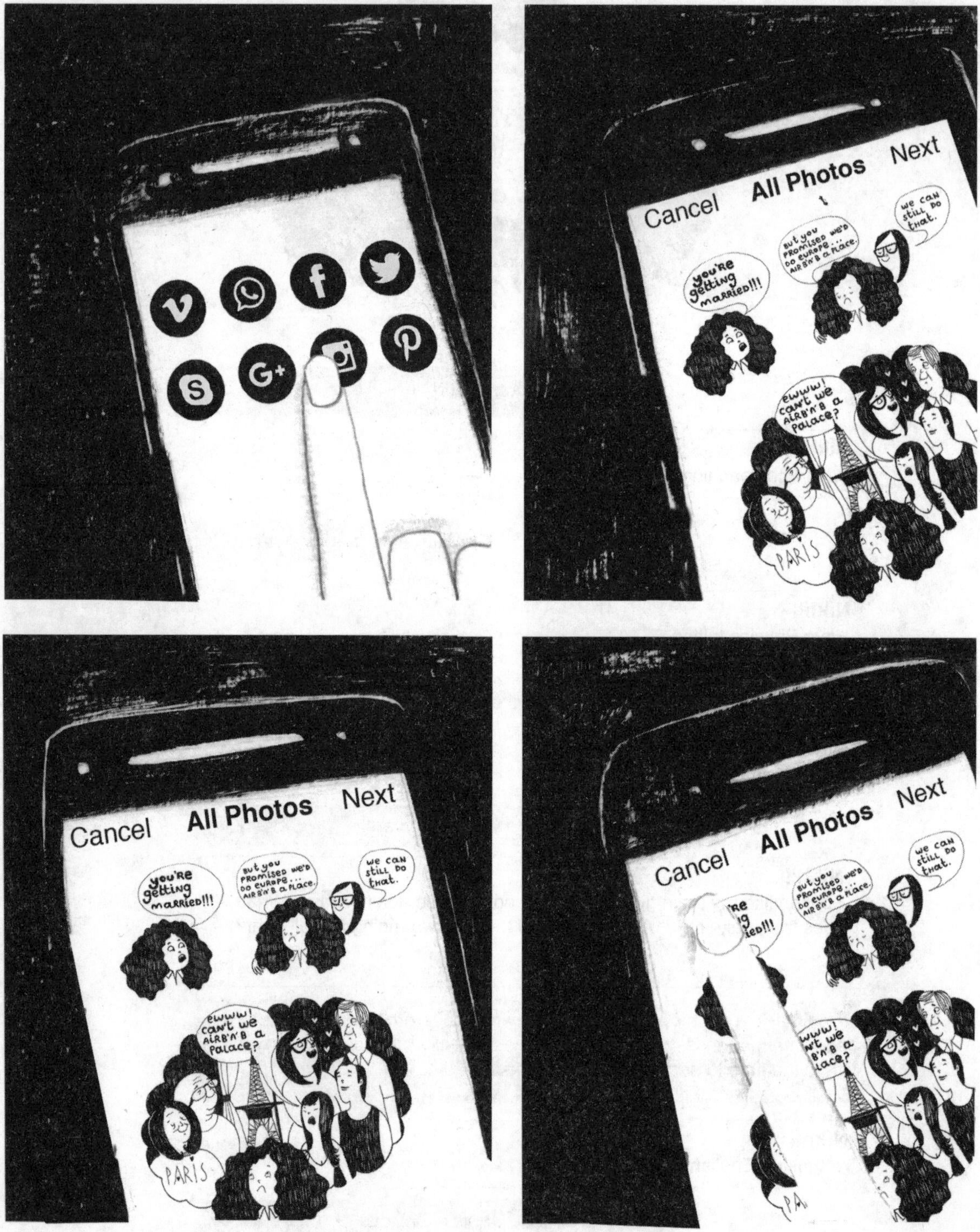
Cancel
All Photos
Next
you're getting married!!!
but you promised we'd do europe... air b'n'b a place.
we can still do that.
ewww! can't we airb'n'b a palace?
PARIS
Cancel
All Photos
Next
you're getting married!!!
but you promised we'd do europe... air b'n'b a place.
we can still do that.
ewww! can't we airb'n'b a palace?
PARIS
Cancel
All Photos
Next
but you promised we'd do europe... air b'n'b a place.
we can still do that.

Rukhsar
U thr   4:50 PM

Am I ever going to see you again? 4:50 PM ✓✓

Rukhsar
Sounds like someone's missing me   4:50 PM

Been two whole weeks since the term started and you're still cooped up in Mumbai.   4:51 PM ✓✓

Rukhsar
Uh oh. I better have a legit excuse AND a medical certificate.   4:52 PM

No shit, Sherlock. I'd hate to be you when Princy finds out about your little adventure...speaking of, how did the audition go last week...and why the hell have you been AWOL since... wait a freaking sec...   4:53 PM ✓✓

Are you doing that thing? You know, acting all dejected, when, in fact, you're bursting to share the good news?   4:53 PM ✓✓

Rukhsar
Yeah!!   4:54 PM

Sooo... You landed the part???   4:55 PM ✓✓

Rukhsar
YASSS!   4:55 PM

AAAAAAAA! OMG! I'm so psyched! You're gonna be on TV! You're gonna be a freaking CELEB! Woooot! Woooooot!!

4:56 PM

Rukhsar
I've got my mojo working! Take that, everyone who thought I couldn't do it! 🎉

4:56 PM

Yeah, baby! Told ya, it was going to work out!

4:57 PM

Rukhsar
I know, I know. I'd almost given up...was sure it wasn't going to happen for me...but you-you believed in me even when I didn't believe in myself. Dunno what I'd have done without you.

4:58 PM

You'd have done just fine. And you have. You've bagged a TV serial all on your own. It's all you. Gawd, am I proud of you. You're the BEST. 😍

4:59 PM

Rukhsar
Awwww! Dad's meeting the Princy this week. She's going to find out sooner or later. I'd much rather she heard it from us. It's just a matter of a few months... I don't have a very big role... I slip into a coma after the first few episodes...and then, they transplant my brain into this evil tantric.

5:01 PM

Jeez! I nearly slipped into a coma myself.

5:02 PM

Rukhsar
Seriously though it's not one of those long running shows. Will wrap up in a couple of months. Dad's going to assure the Princy I'll make up for lost time. Will take special classes and catch up with the syllabus. Think she'll be okay?

5:04 PM

I hope so. 5:04 PM ✓✓

Rukhsar
What am I gonna do if she isn't? Change schools? Stay back? 5:05 PM

Don't stress. It's going to be fine. I mean, she'd be crazy to lose such an average student like you. 5:06 PM ✓✓

Rukhsar
Gee, thanks. I thought you were going for star student. 5:07 PM

Hey, you're insanely talented. Not just academically. 5:08 PM ✓✓

When does the show go on air? 5:08 PM ✓✓

Rukhsar
Next month. They want to shoot a bank of episodes. 5:09 PM

Ooh! Look at you, spouting telly jargon. Next up, full-fledged Bolly blockbuster. Watch out, Hollywood. Okie, I'm rushing to the stationery store right now. To buy an autograph book. The next time you come down, am going to make you sign every page. Am gonna auction your autograph on Ebay when you win a Golden Globe. 🤓 5:10 PM ✓✓

Rukhsar
You mean an ITA - Indian Television Award. 5:11 PM

I'm so so SO happy for you. 🖤 5:12 PM ✓✓

Rukhsar
I know. Love ya too. 5:12 PM

Has that happened to you? Have you felt a teeny bit bummed when things worked out for a close bud? You know, when they fell in love or got a hot new gadget, went some place really exotic on holiday? I'm not talking about jealousy, no. We love our friends too much for that. I mean, how their accomplishment makes us feel about ourselves. How their suddenly cool life makes us feel about our lives. It's why, for a fraction of a nanosecond, our chest tightens, our stomach lurches, a sinking feeling comes over us, and we feel low.

Things were beginning to look up for Rukhsar, whereas my life was about to nosedive. Soon, she wouldn't have time to breathe, let alone keep in touch with friends back home. All I would be busy doing? Downloading books and music and movies and TV shows. Yeah, I'm a pirate, so sue me. Anyway, I should have remembered that when my life was smooth sailing, Rukhsar's was turbulent. But I didn't. When things are going good, we're too busy lapping them up to realise things are going good. I tried to give myself a pep talk. Tried to tell myself all those things I used to tell Rukhsar. "Hang in there", "You'll be okay", "Things will work out". But they sounded pretty damn hollow to my own ears. How the hell did Rukhsar buy them?

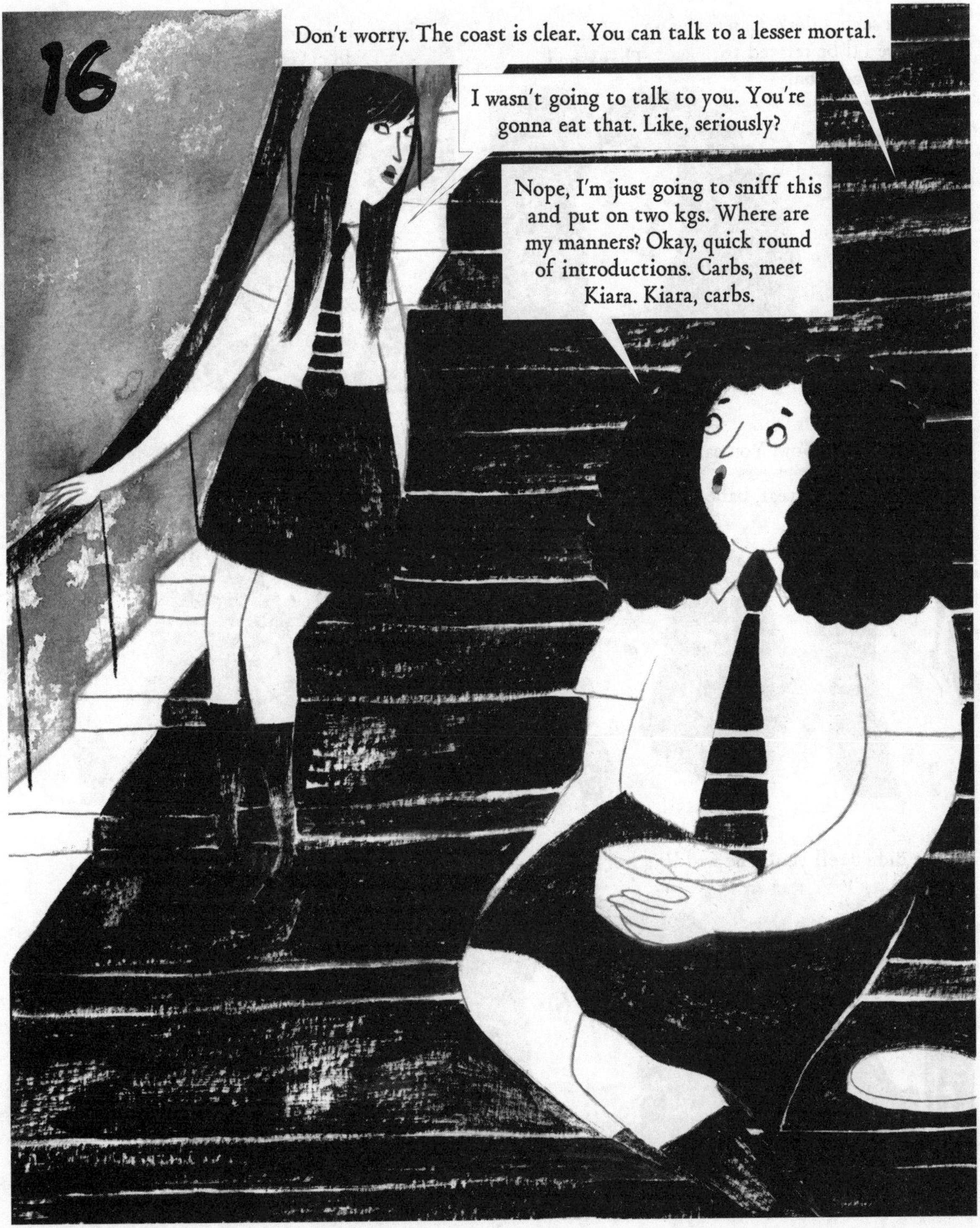
16
Don't worry. The coast is clear. You can talk to a lesser mortal.
I wasn't going to talk to you. You're gonna eat that. Like, seriously?
Nope, I'm just going to sniff this and put on two kgs. Where are my manners? Okay, quick round of introductions. Carbs, meet Kiara. Kiara, carbs.

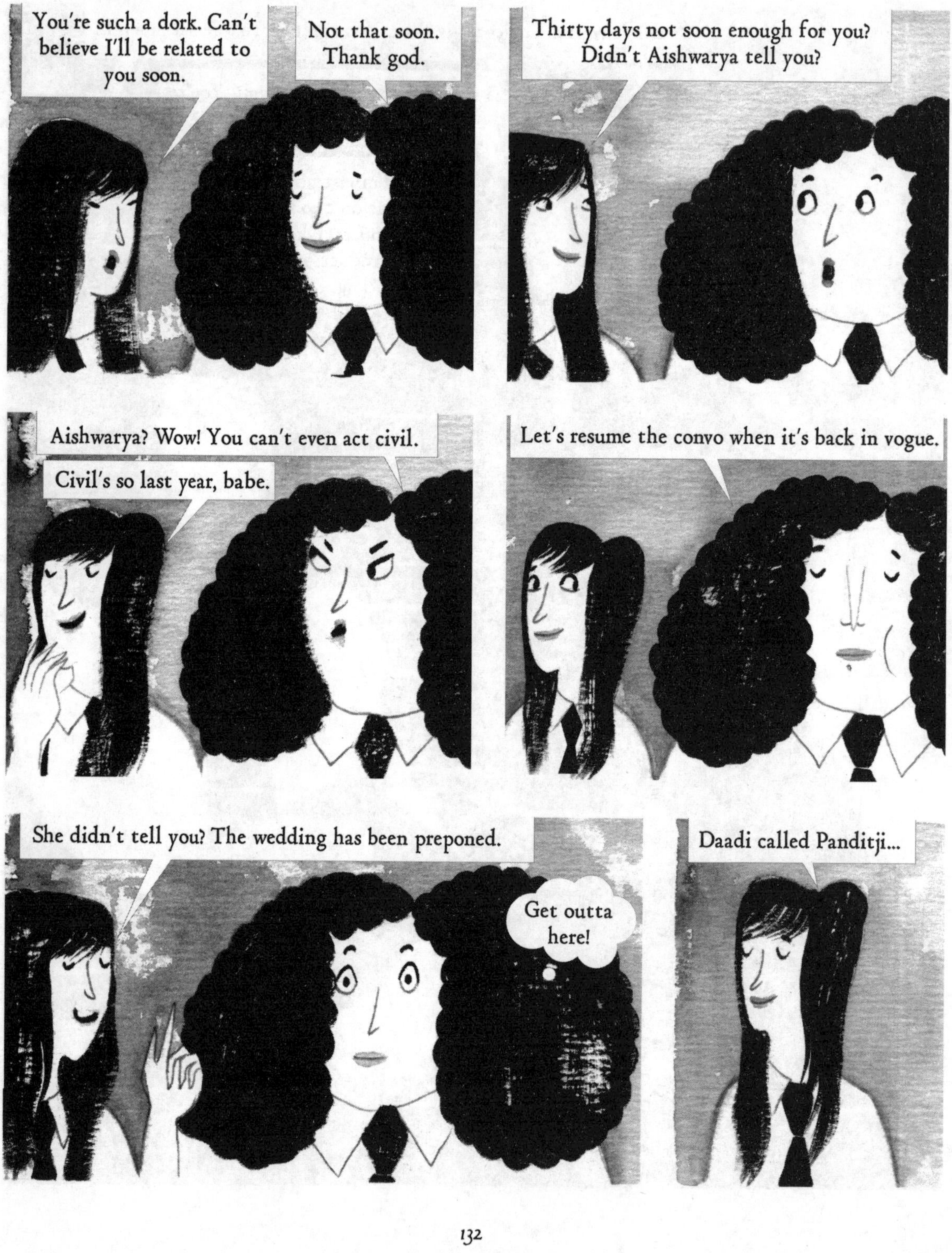
You're such a dork. Can't believe I'll be related to you soon.
Not that soon. Thank god.
Thirty days not soon enough for you? Didn't Aishwarya tell you?
Aishwarya? Wow! You can't even act civil.
Civil's so last year, babe.
Let's resume the convo when it's back in vogue.
She didn't tell you? The wedding has been preponed.
Get outta here!
Daadi called Panditji...

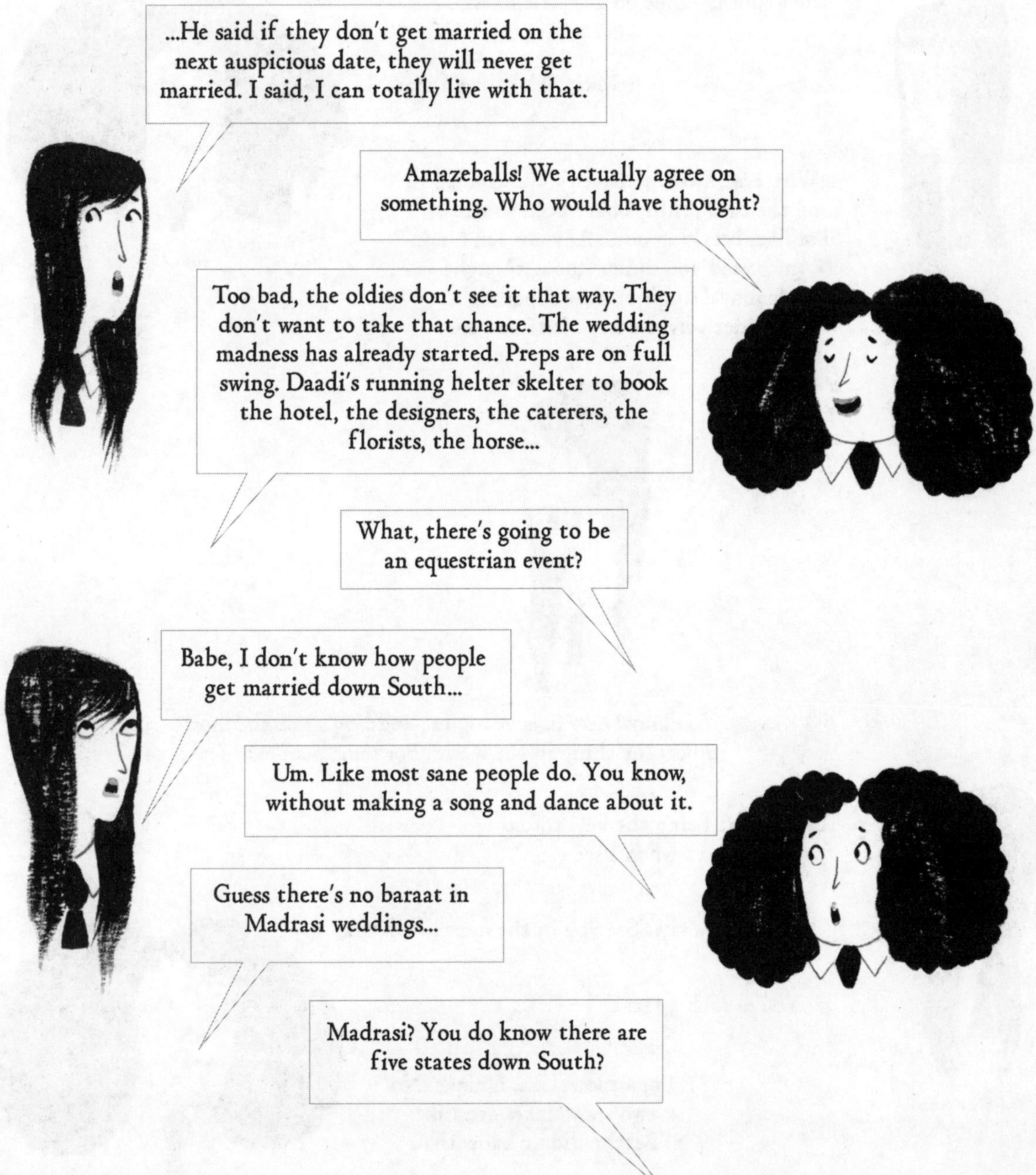
...He said if they don't get married on the next auspicious date, they will never get married. I said, I can totally live with that.
Amazeballs! We actually agree on something. Who would have thought?
Too bad, the oldies don't see it that way. They don't want to take that chance. The wedding madness has already started. Preps are on full swing. Daadi's running helter skelter to book the hotel, the designers, the caterers, the florists, the horse...
What, there's going to be an equestrian event?
Babe, I don't know how people get married down South...
Um. Like most sane people do. You know, without making a song and dance about it.
Guess there's no baraat in Madrasi weddings...
Madrasi? You do know there are five states down South?

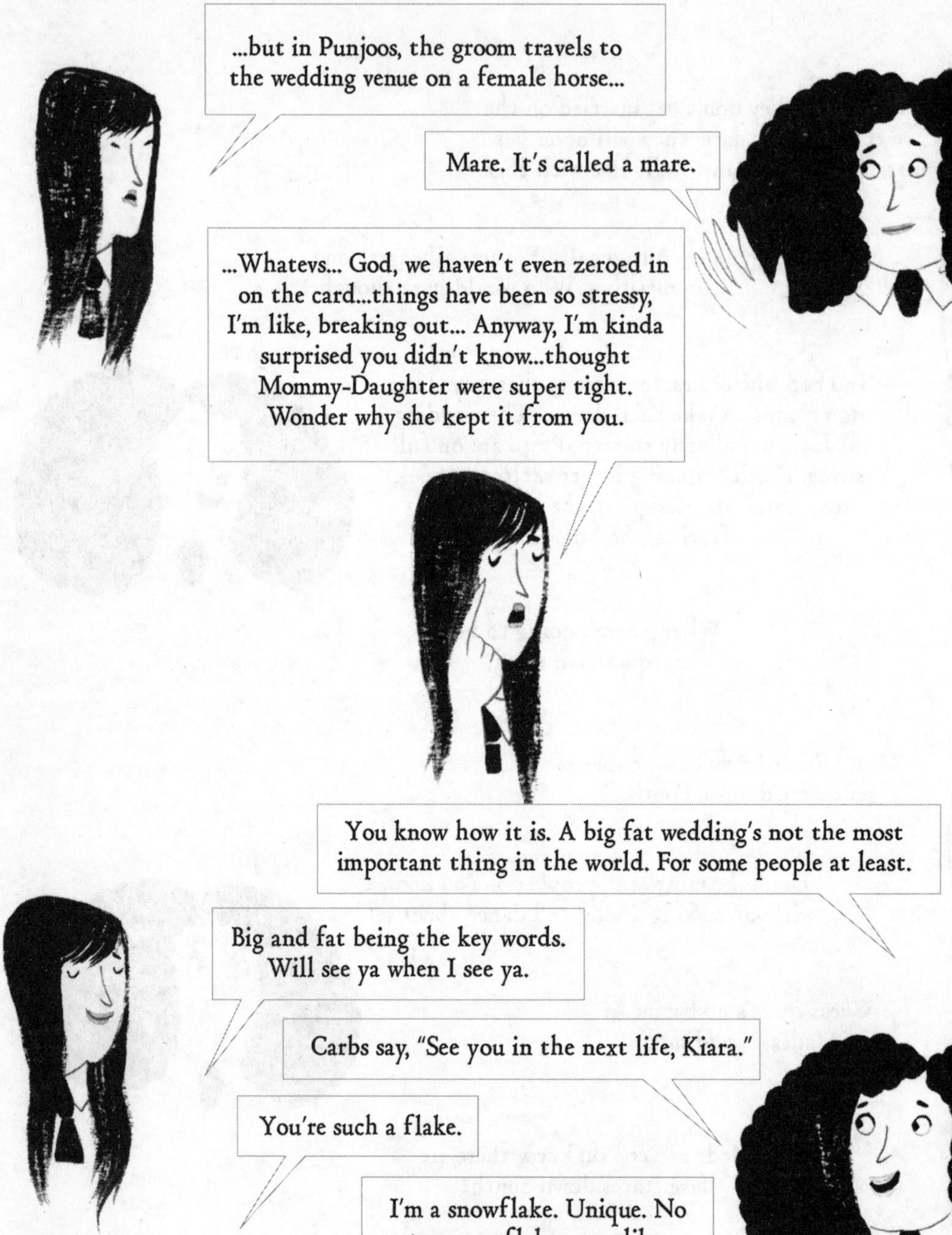

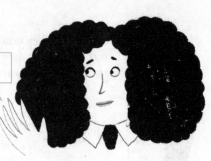

...but in Punjoos, the groom travels to the wedding venue on a female horse...
Mare. It's called a mare.
...Whatevs... God, we haven't even zeroed in on the card...things have been so stressy, I'm like, breaking out... Anyway, I'm kinda surprised you didn't know...thought Mommy-Daughter were super tight. Wonder why she kept it from you.
You know how it is. A big fat wedding's not the most important thing in the world. For some people at least.
Big and fat being the key words. Will see ya when I see ya.
Carbs say, "See you in the next life, Kiara."
You're such a flake.
I'm a snowflake. Unique. No two snowflakes are alike. Betcha didn't know that.

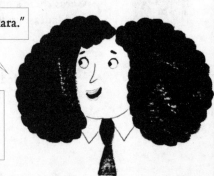

And just like that, *The End of the F****** World* wasn't just a show I was streaming. I mean, I was mentally prepared for the wedding. It was going to happen sometime in the near foreseeable future. You know, after I went to study abroad or got a job and moved to another city. But next freaking month? Mom had promised! Sworn she wouldn't rush into it. That she'd ease me into things. In what parallel universe did this qualify as "easing"? How could she just spring this on me? HOW? There was only one explanation: Mom had changed. She didn't care. All she wanted to do was please her new family, and to hell with her old family. Actually, she hadn't even "sprung" it on me. She'd kept me in the dark. Why? Why? WHY? Did she think I'd fly off the handle? Like the last time? Well, I'd prove her wrong. I'd play it so cool, so cool, I'd practically be a flake...er, I mean, a snowflake.

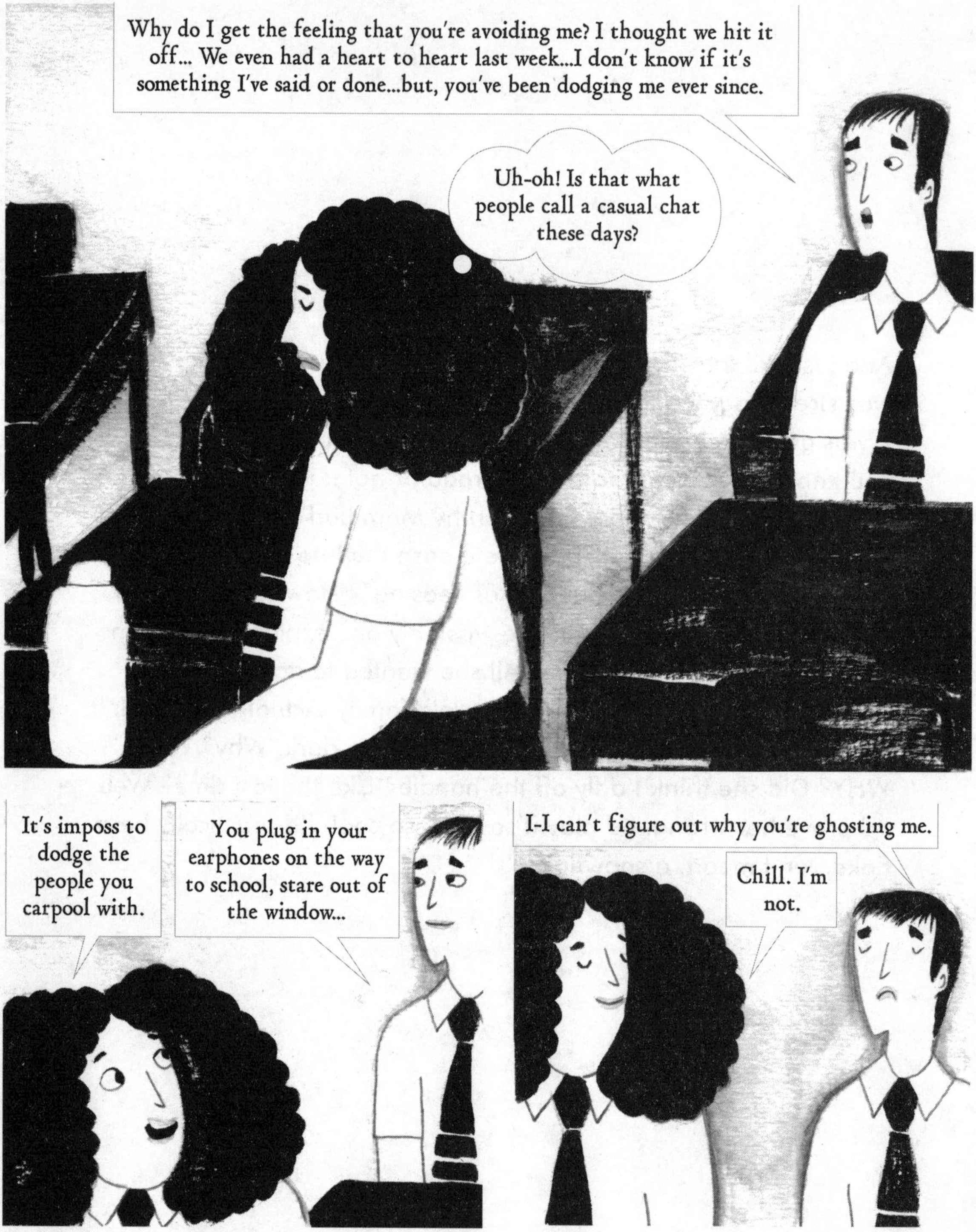
Why do I get the feeling that you're avoiding me? I thought we hit it off... We even had a heart to heart last week...I don't know if it's something I've said or done...but, you've been dodging me ever since.
Uh-oh! Is that what people call a casual chat these days?
It's imposs to dodge the people you carpool with.
You plug in your earphones on the way to school, stare out of the window...
I-I can't figure out why you're ghosting me.
Chill. I'm not.

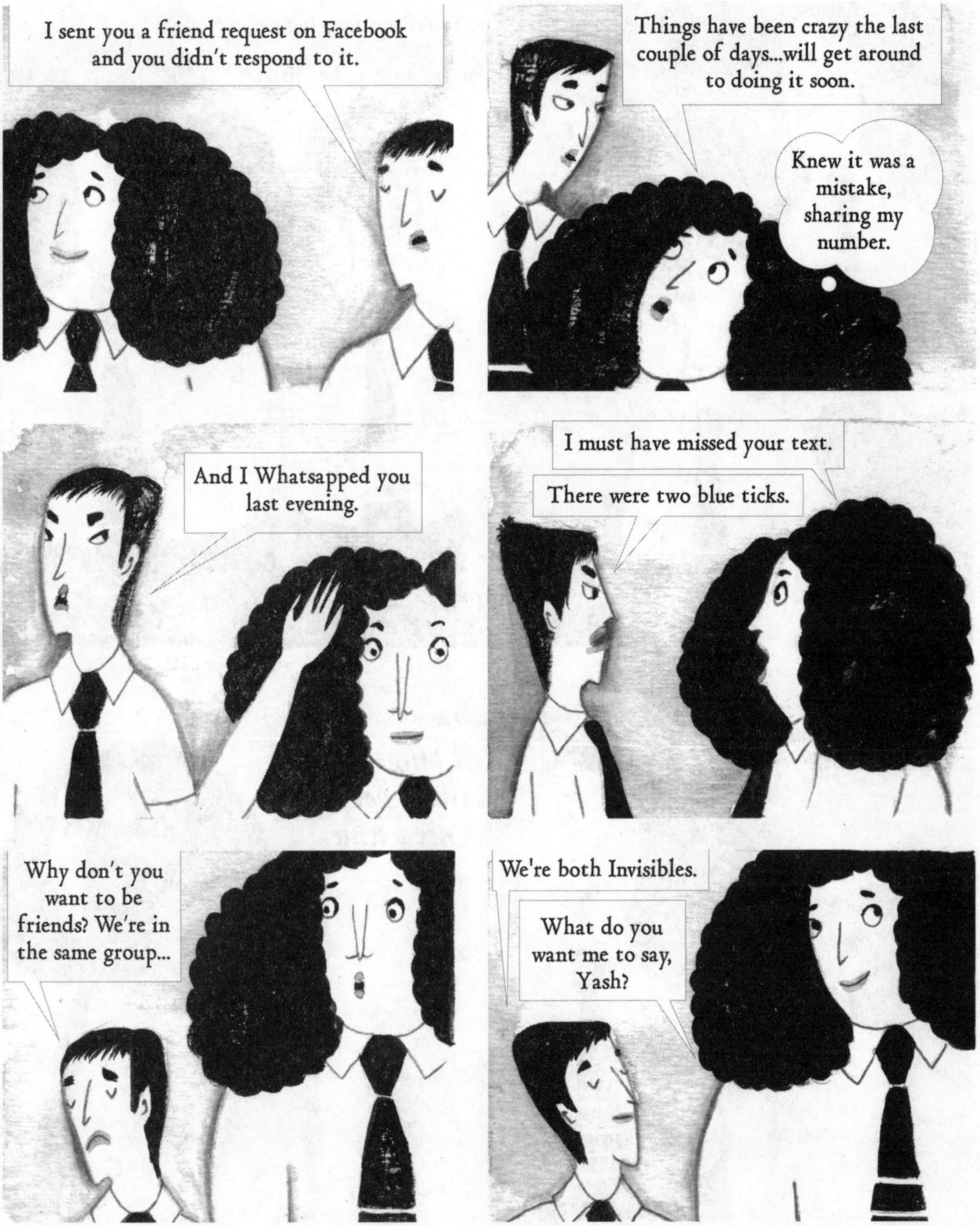
I sent you a friend request on Facebook and you didn't respond to it.
Things have been crazy the last couple of days...will get around to doing it soon.
Knew it was a mistake, sharing my number.
And I Whatsapped you last evening.
I must have missed your text.
There were two blue ticks.
Why don't you want to be friends? We're in the same group...
We're both Invisibles.
What do you want me to say, Yash?

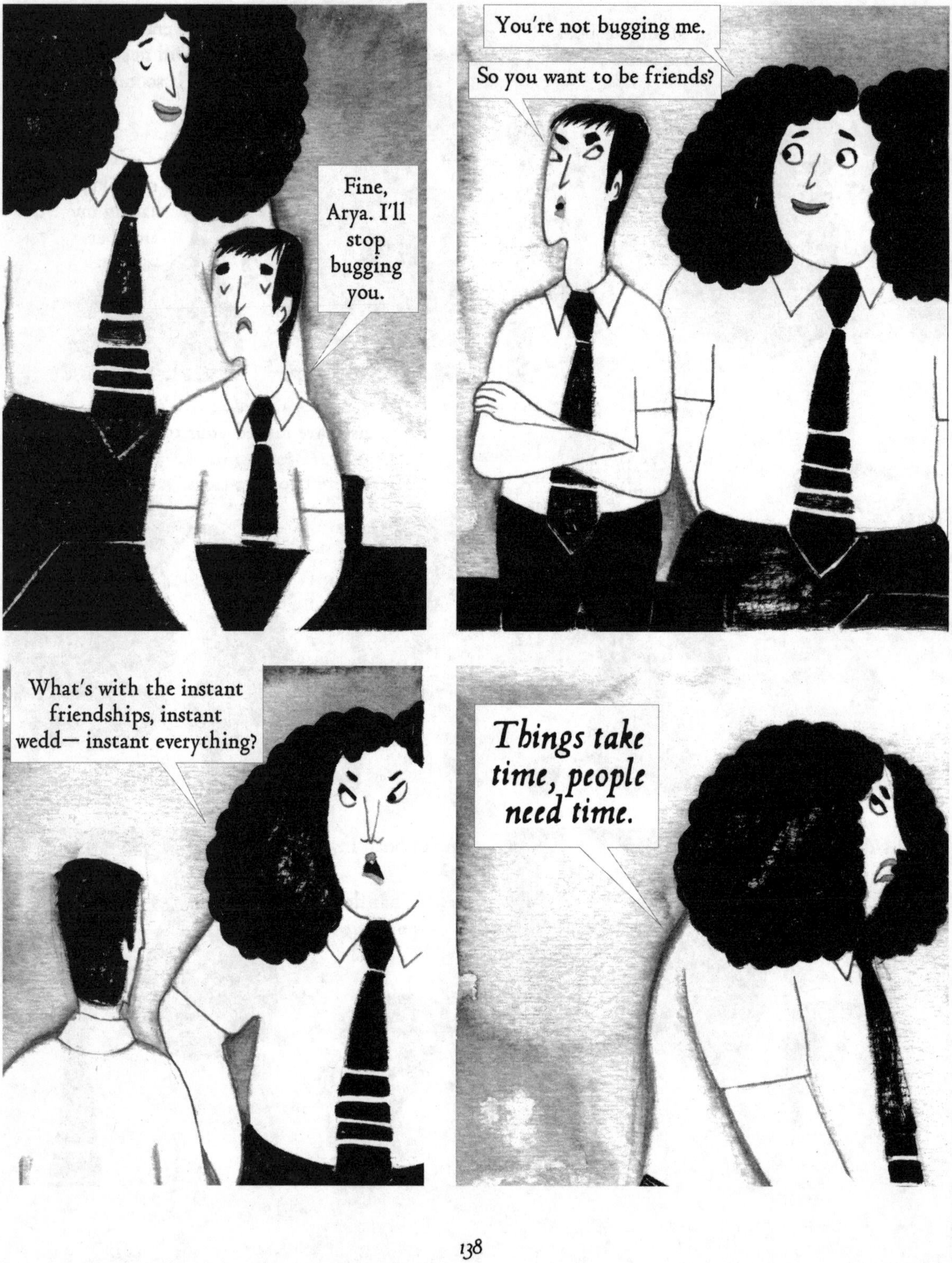
Fine, Arya. I'll stop bugging you.
You're not bugging me.
So you want to be friends?
What's with the instant friendships, instant wedd— instant everything?
Things take time, people need time.

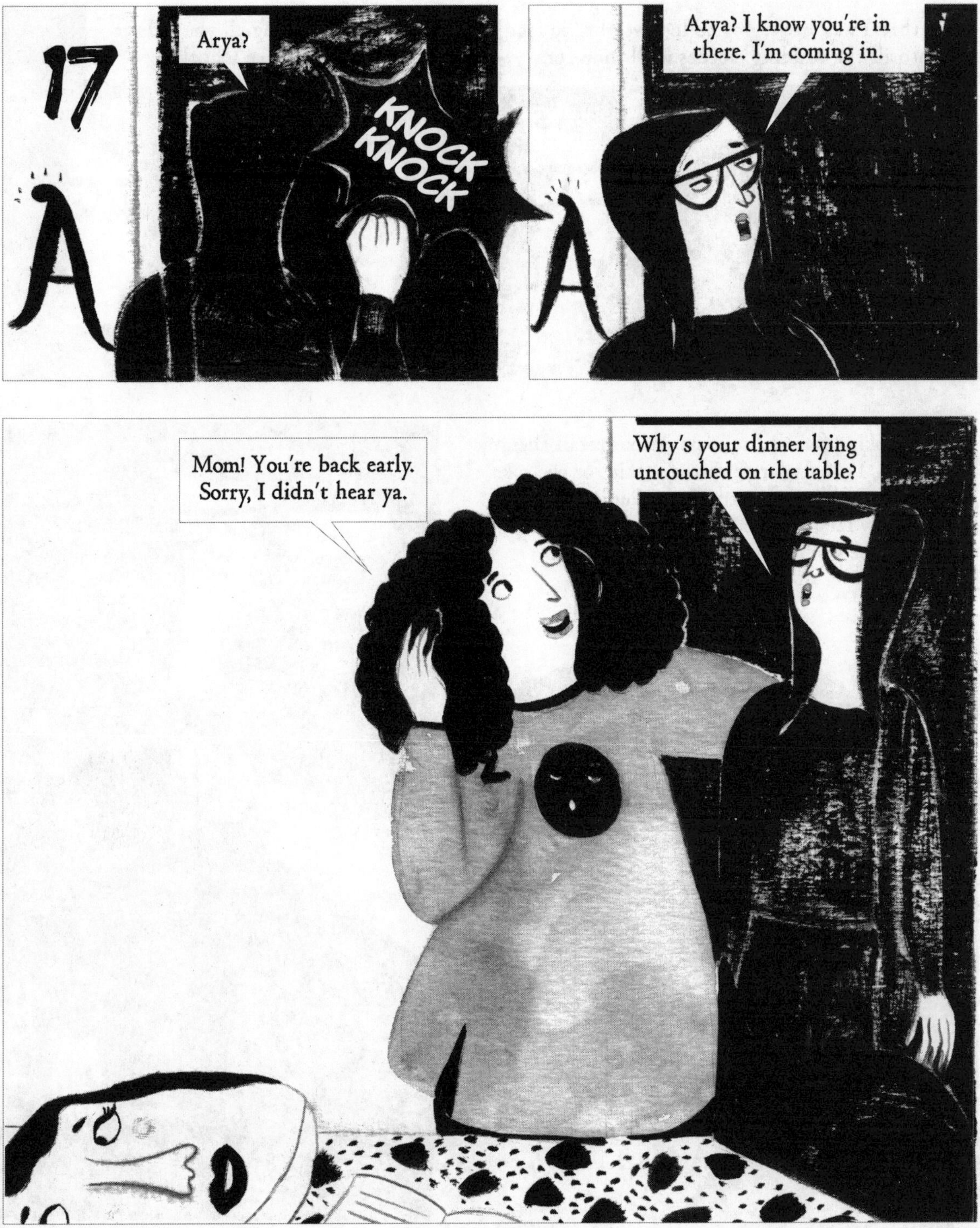
17
Arya?
KNOCK KNOCK
Arya? I know you're in there. I'm coming in.
Mom! You're back early. Sorry, I didn't hear ya.
Why's your dinner lying untouched on the table?

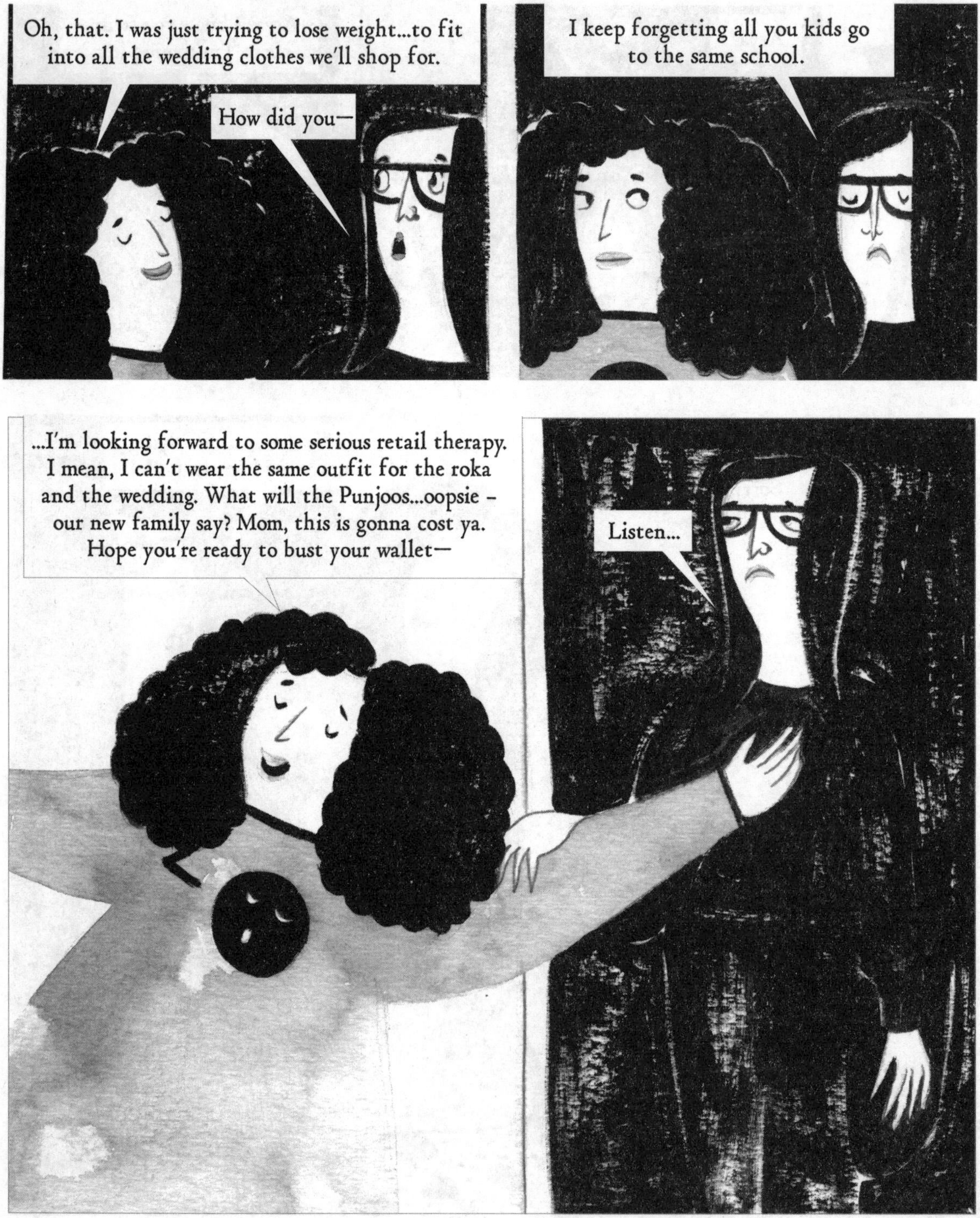
Oh, that. I was just trying to lose weight...to fit into all the wedding clothes we'll shop for.
How did you—
I keep forgetting all you kids go to the same school.
...I'm looking forward to some serious retail therapy. I mean, I can't wear the same outfit for the roka and the wedding. What will the Punjoos...oopsie – our new family say? Mom, this is gonna cost ya. Hope you're ready to bust your wallet—
Listen...

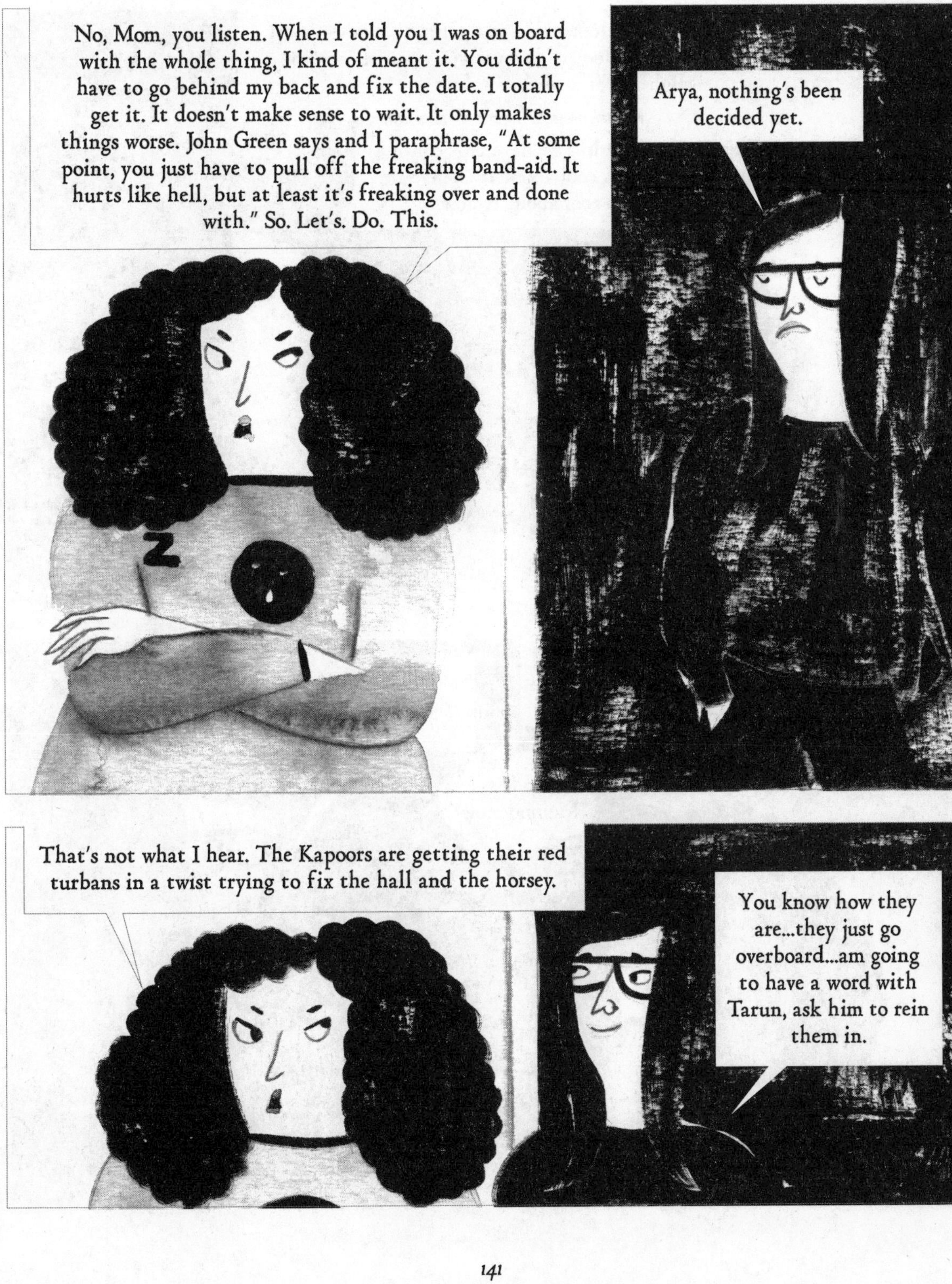
No, Mom, you listen. When I told you I was on board with the whole thing, I kind of meant it. You didn't have to go behind my back and fix the date. I totally get it. It doesn't make sense to wait. It only makes things worse. John Green says and I paraphrase, "At some point, you just have to pull off the freaking band-aid. It hurts like hell, but at least it's freaking over and done with." So. Let's. Do. This.
Arya, nothing's been decided yet.
That's not what I hear. The Kapoors are getting their red turbans in a twist trying to fix the hall and the horsey.
You know how they are...they just go overboard...am going to have a word with Tarun, ask him to rein them in.

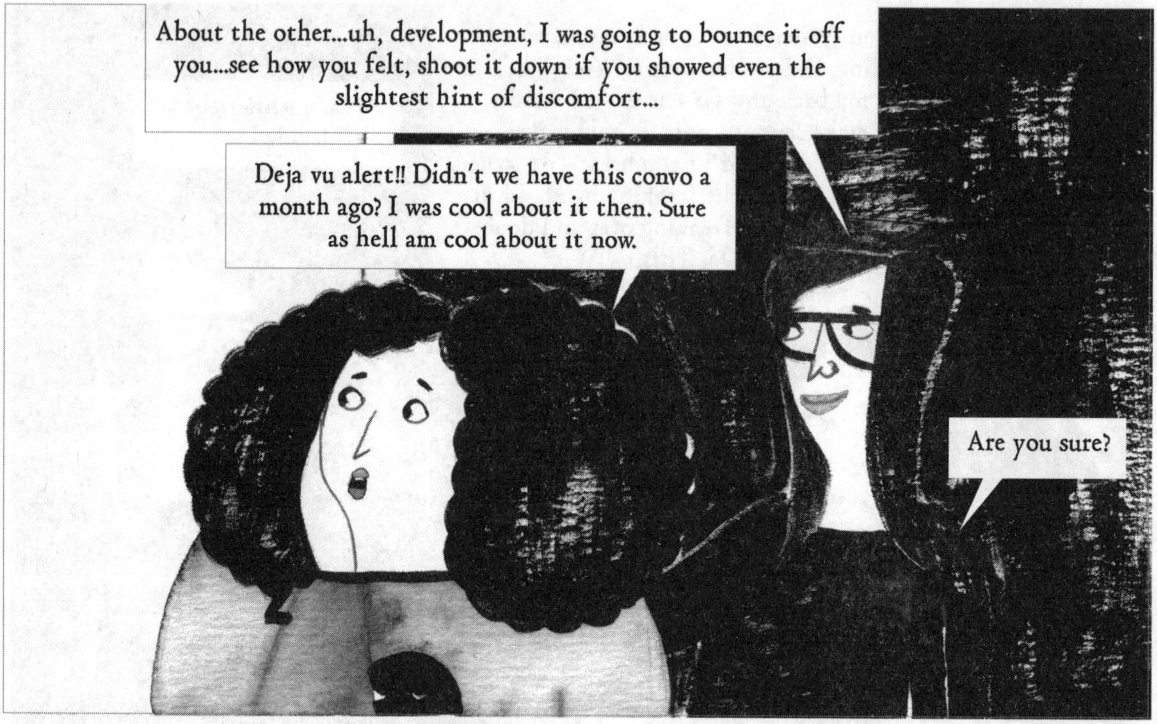
About the other...uh, development, I was going to bounce it off you...see how you felt, shoot it down if you showed even the slightest hint of discomfort...
Deja vu alert!! Didn't we have this convo a month ago? I was cool about it then. Sure as hell am cool about it now.
Are you sure?

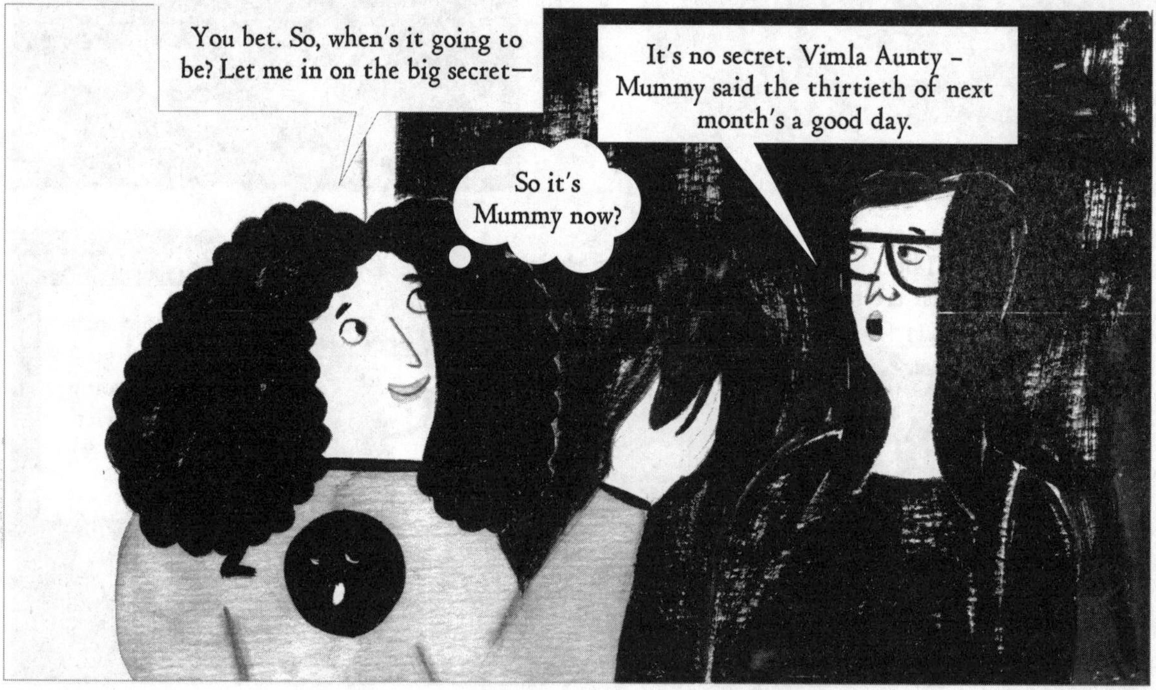
You bet. So, when's it going to be? Let me in on the big secret—
It's no secret. Vimla Aunty - Mummy said the thirtieth of next month's a good day.
So it's Mummy now?

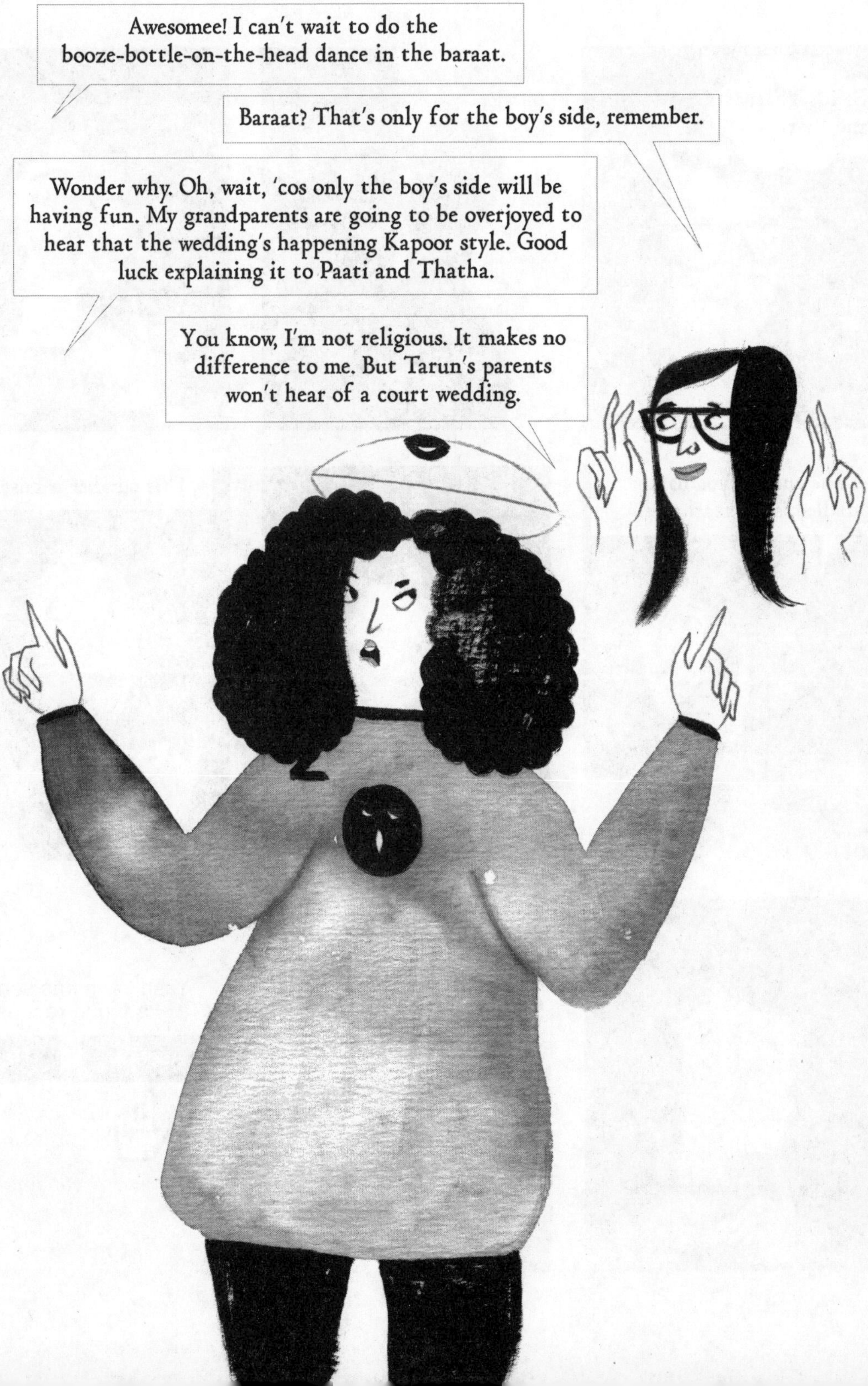
Awesomee! I can't wait to do the booze-bottle-on-the-head dance in the baraat.
Baraat? That's only for the boy's side, remember.
Wonder why. Oh, wait, 'cos only the boy's side will be having fun. My grandparents are going to be overjoyed to hear that the wedding's happening Kapoor style. Good luck explaining it to Paati and Thatha.
You know, I'm not religious. It makes no difference to me. But Tarun's parents won't hear of a court wedding.

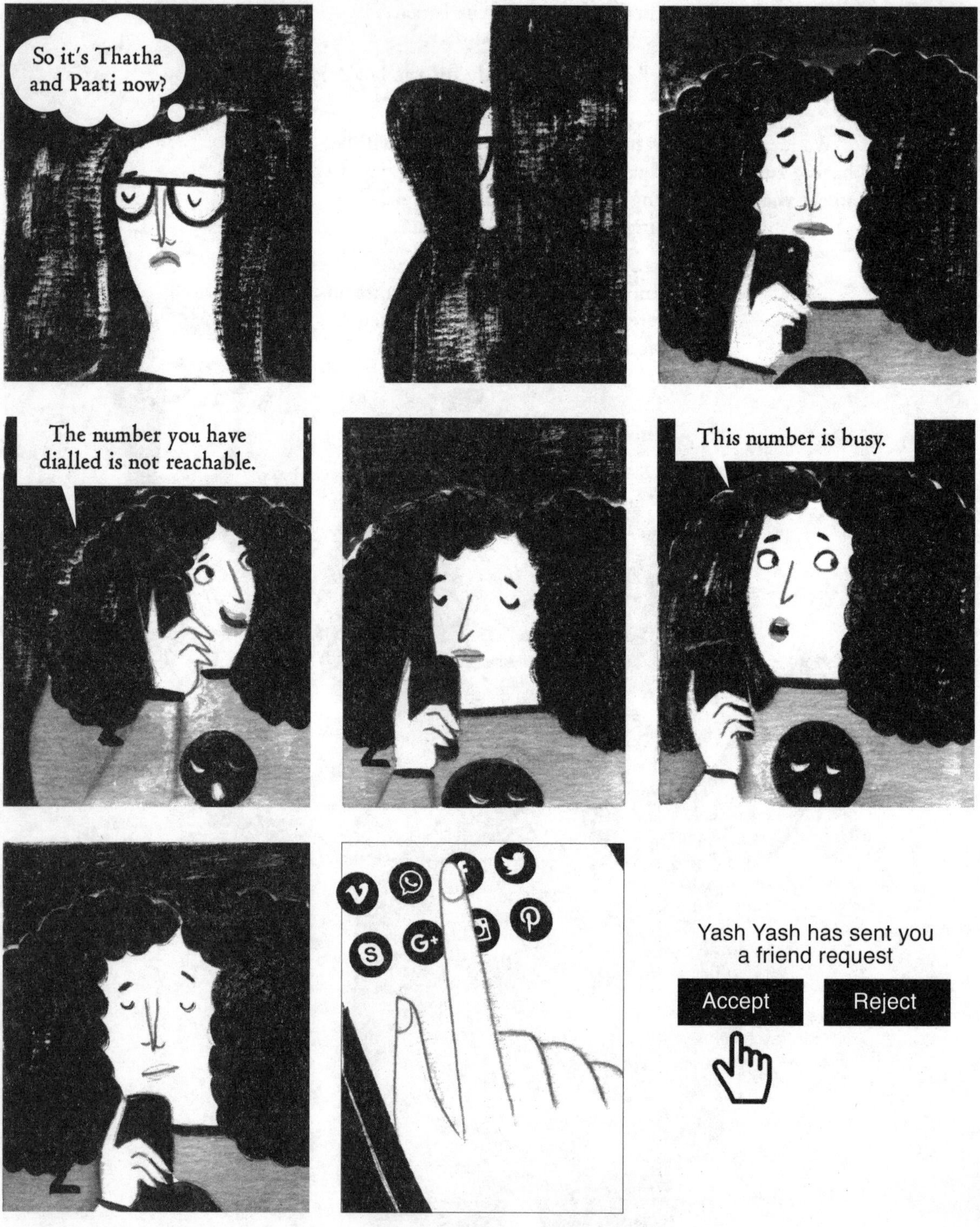
So it's Thatha and Paati now?
The number you have dialled is not reachable.
This number is busy.
Yash Yash has sent you a friend request
Accept
Reject

Good time to talk?

Yeah, sure. This is a surprise.

I just wanted to apologise.

For not accepting my friend request or for not replying to my text?

For being short with you earlier today. I'm sorry.

It's okay.

There's a lot of stuff going on in my life right now...I'm trying to deal with it...without much success obvs...

If you want to vent...

Offload all my probs on to you? What, you're a call centre for frustoo classmates?

I've been told I've a good ear...

Thanks. Can I take a raincheck?

Sure. Any time.

So, whatcha doing?

Reading the jumbo anniversary issue of Overdrive.

That's some heavy reading, dude. Guess you needed a b-r-a-k-e from it. 😊

Soowiiee, GTG. Grandpa calling.

Thatha! Hello! To what do I owe the pleasure?

How can Aishwarya do this to us...how can she get married like this...You know what she's saying? "Appa, don't consult your priest, no jatakam, no muhurtham, nothing"... This is too much...your Paati's been crying non-stop...we never expected this from her...Soundarya, only you can make her understand. You can do it. I told Lakshmi, "Soundarya's a sensible child. She'll talk to her mother, make her realise she's making a mistake."

So this is what it feels like to be the good kid. Gawd, I could get used to it.

Me?! I can't promise, Thatha. You know how Mom is...

You have to do something!

...But I'll see what I can do.

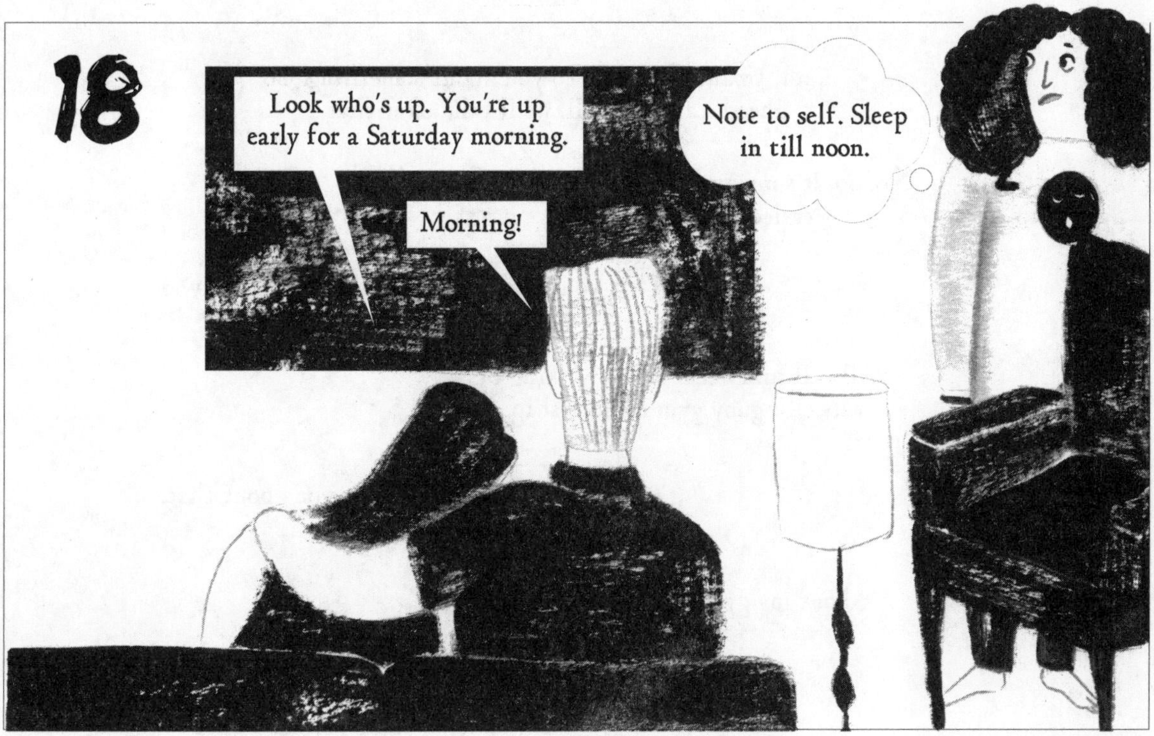
18
Look who's up. You're up early for a Saturday morning.
Morning!
Note to self. Sleep in till noon.

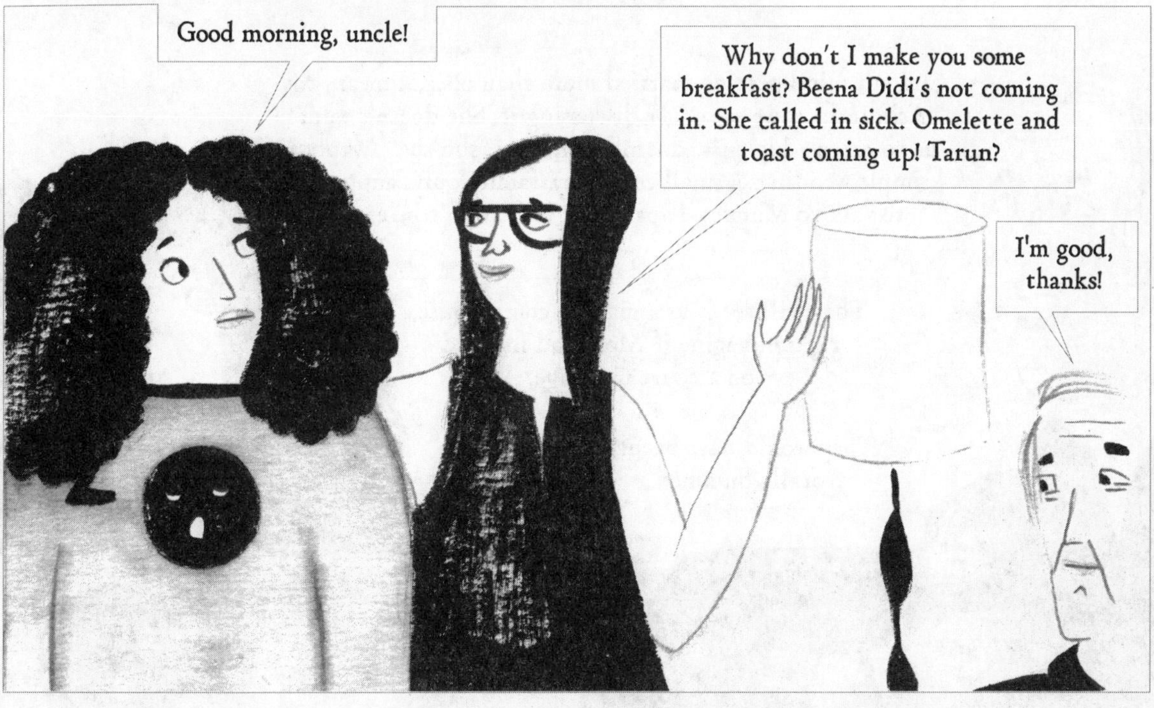
Good morning, uncle!
Why don't I make you some breakfast? Beena Didi's not coming in. She called in sick. Omelette and toast coming up! Tarun?
I'm good, thanks!

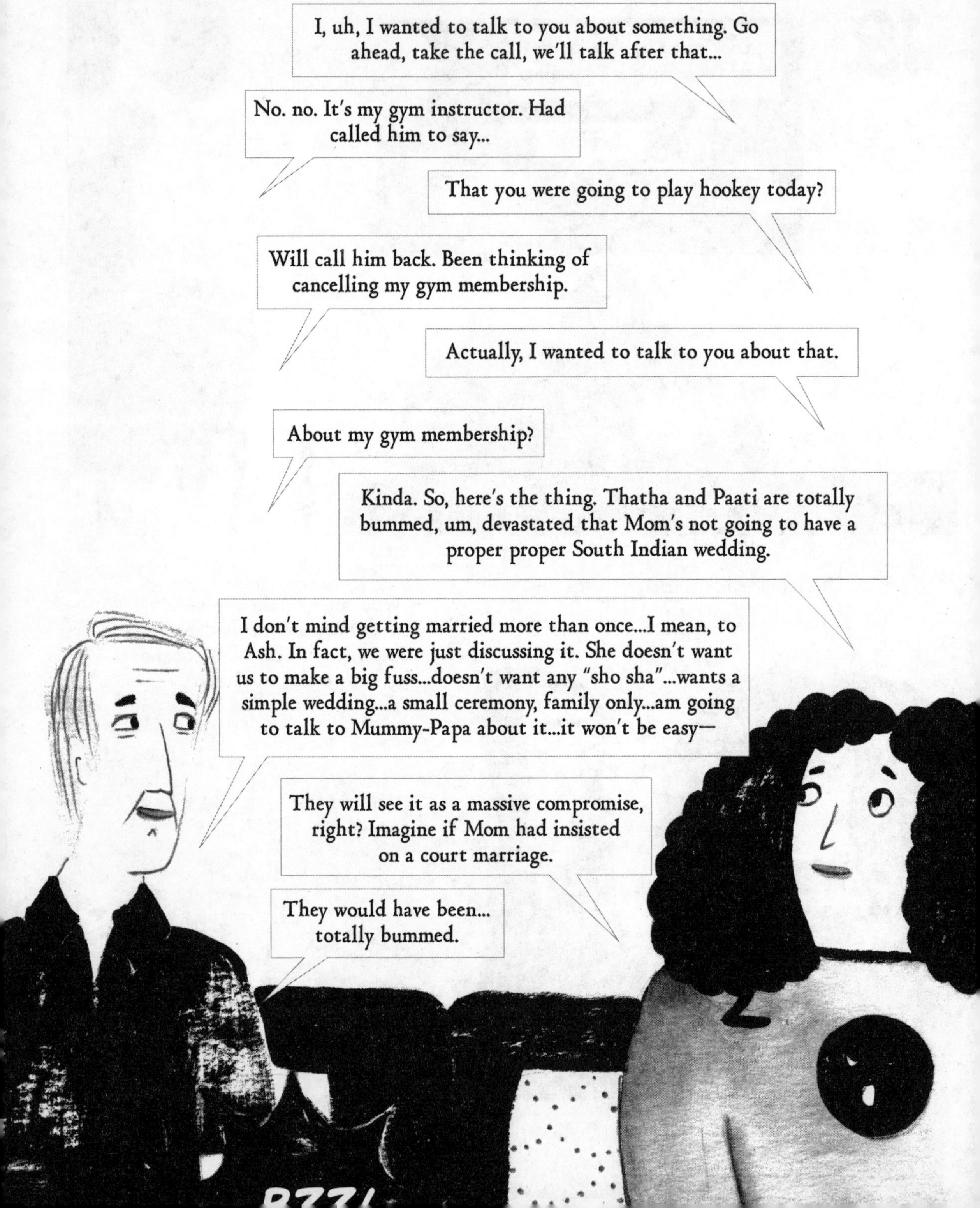
I, uh, I wanted to talk to you about something. Go ahead, take the call, we'll talk after that...
No. no. It's my gym instructor. Had called him to say...
That you were going to play hookey today?
Will call him back. Been thinking of cancelling my gym membership.
Actually, I wanted to talk to you about that.
About my gym membership?
Kinda. So, here's the thing. Thatha and Paati are totally bummed, um, devastated that Mom's not going to have a proper proper South Indian wedding.
I don't mind getting married more than once...I mean, to Ash. In fact, we were just discussing it. She doesn't want us to make a big fuss...doesn't want any "sho sha"...wants a simple wedding...a small ceremony, family only...am going to talk to Mummy-Papa about it...it won't be easy—
They will see it as a massive compromise, right? Imagine if Mom had insisted on a court marriage.
They would have been... totally bummed.

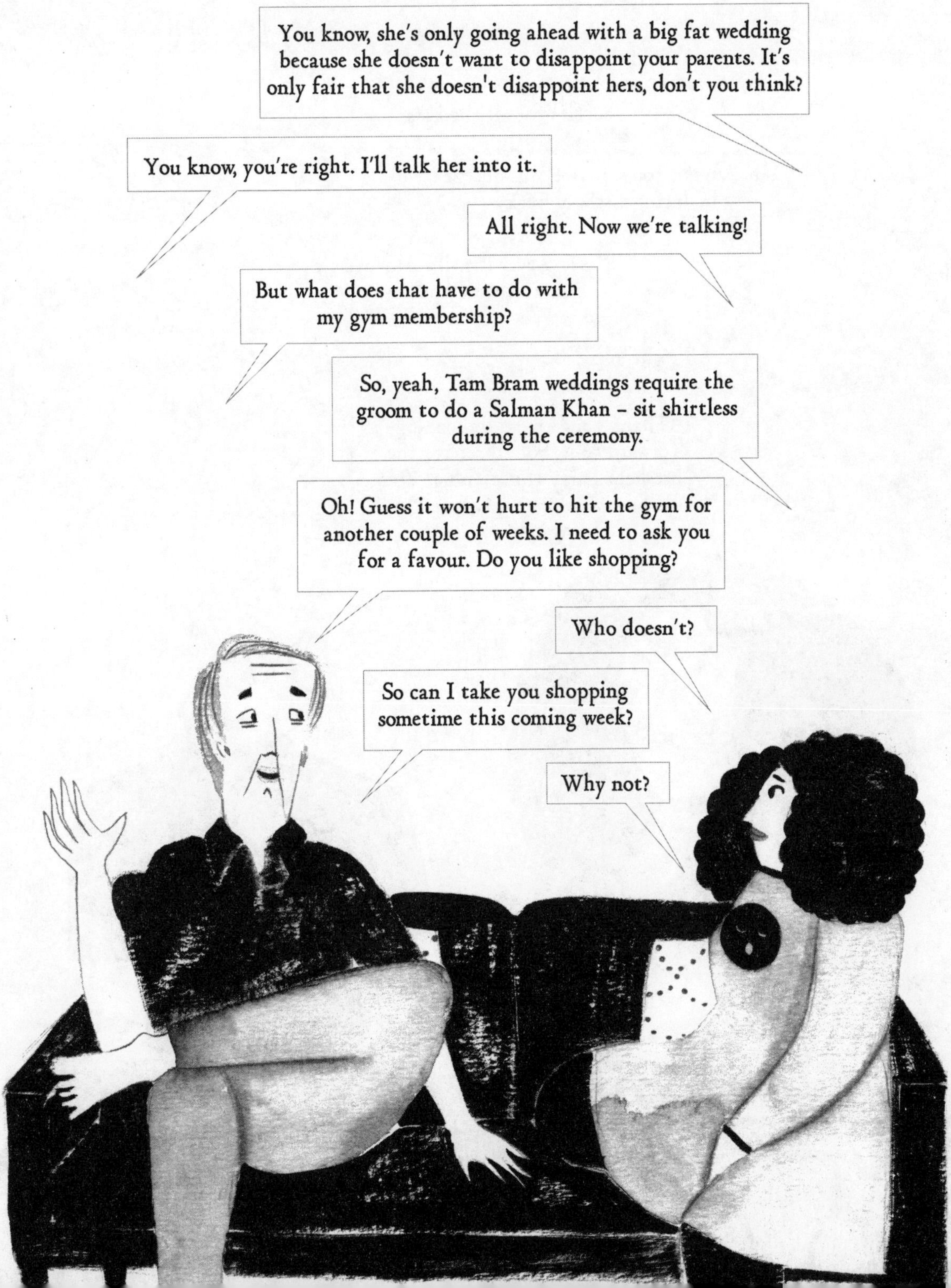
You know, she's only going ahead with a big fat wedding because she doesn't want to disappoint your parents. It's only fair that she doesn't disappoint hers, don't you think?
You know, you're right. I'll talk her into it.
All right. Now we're talking!
But what does that have to do with my gym membership?
So, yeah, Tam Bram weddings require the groom to do a Salman Khan – sit shirtless during the ceremony.
Oh! Guess it won't hurt to hit the gym for another couple of weeks. I need to ask you for a favour. Do you like shopping?
Who doesn't?
So can I take you shopping sometime this coming week?
Why not?

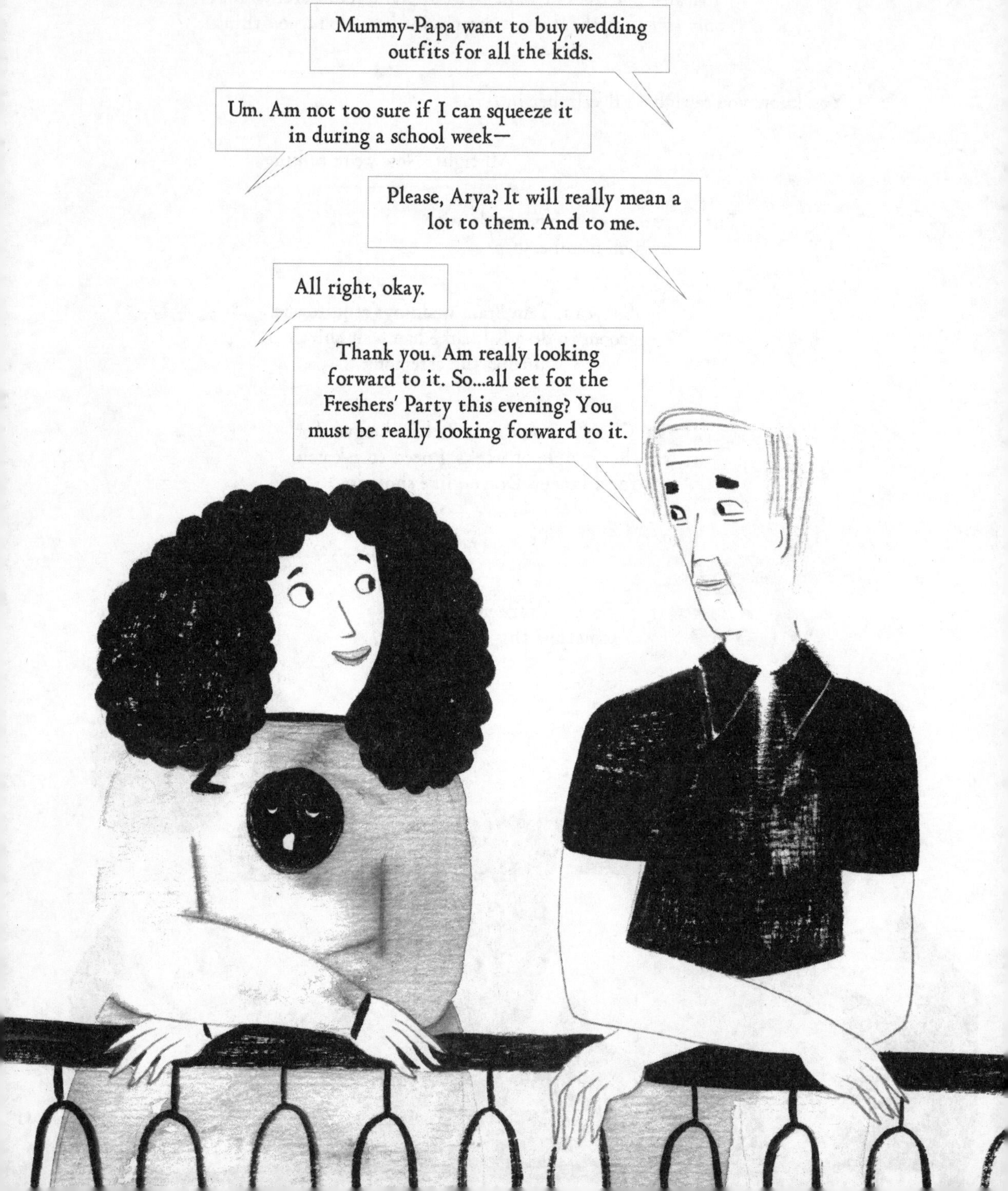
Mummy-Papa want to buy wedding outfits for all the kids.
Um. Am not too sure if I can squeeze it in during a school week—
Please, Arya? It will really mean a lot to them. And to me.
All right, okay.
Thank you. Am really looking forward to it. So...all set for the Freshers' Party this evening? You must be really looking forward to it.

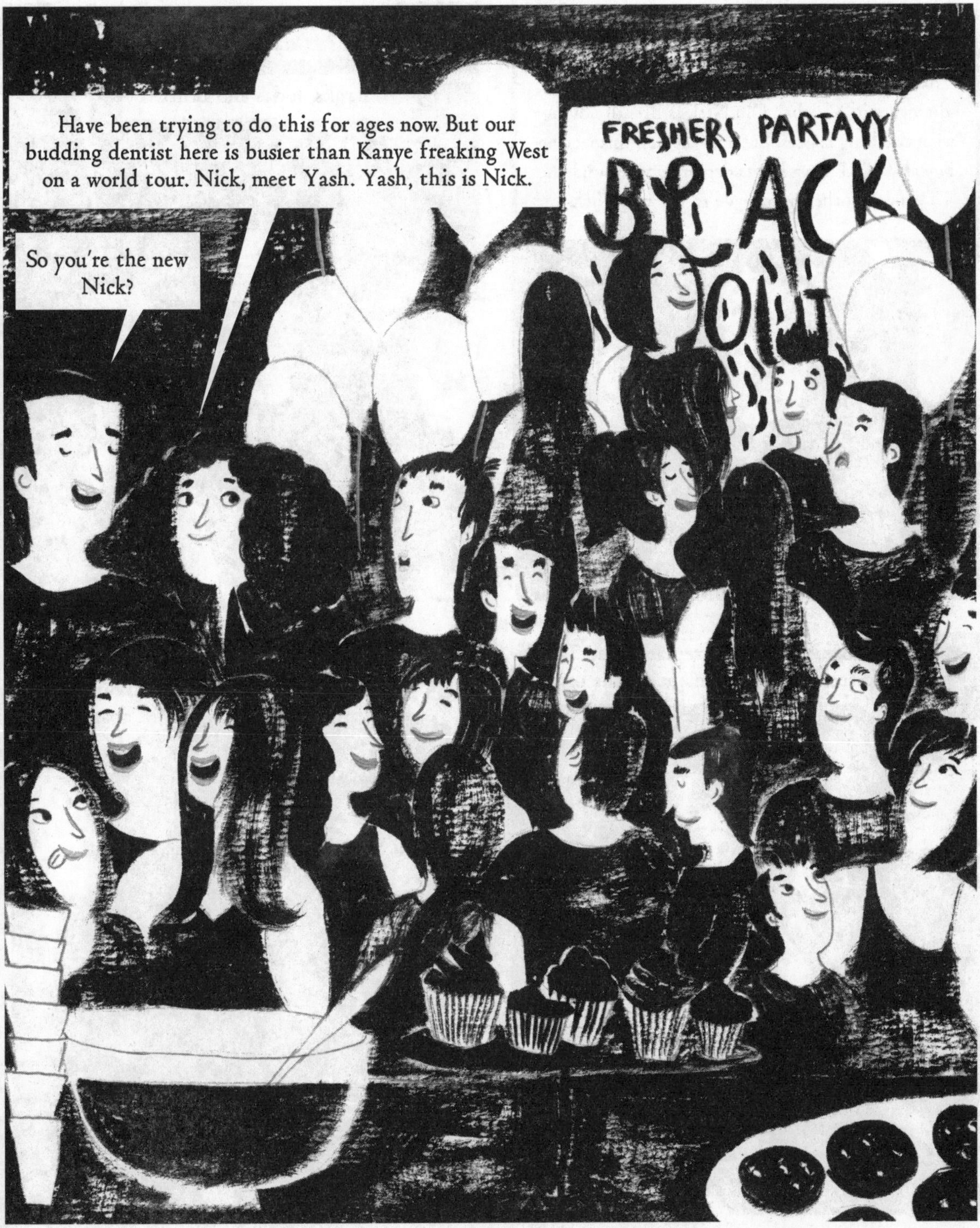
Have been trying to do this for ages now. But our budding dentist here is busier than Kanye freaking West on a world tour. Nick, meet Yash. Yash, this is Nick.
So you're the new Nick?
FRESHERS PARTAYY
BLACK OUT

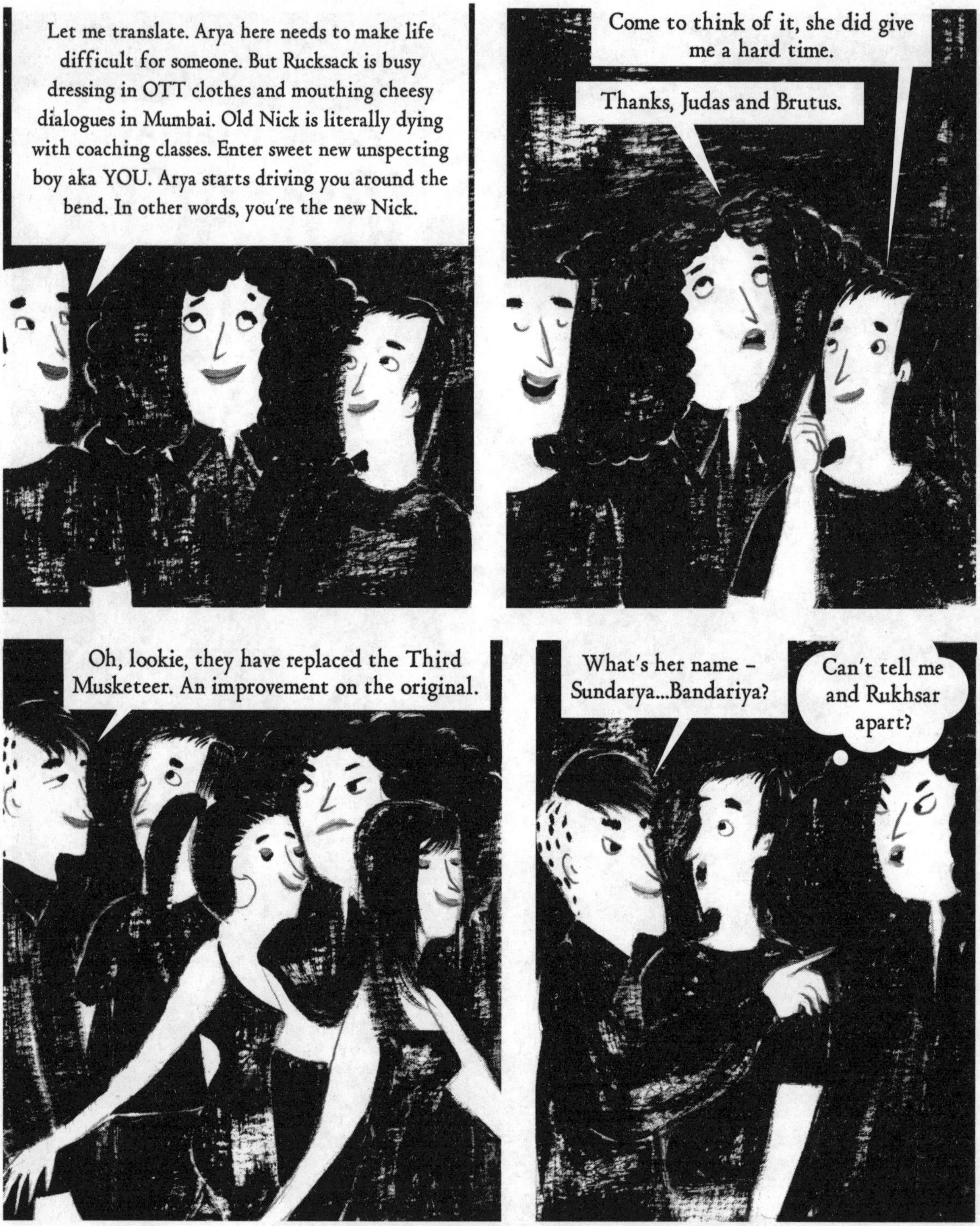
Let me translate. Arya here needs to make life difficult for someone. But Rucksack is busy dressing in OTT clothes and mouthing cheesy dialogues in Mumbai. Old Nick is literally dying with coaching classes. Enter sweet new unspecting boy aka YOU. Arya starts driving you around the bend. In other words, you're the new Nick.
Come to think of it, she did give me a hard time.
Thanks, Judas and Brutus.
Oh, lookie, they have replaced the Third Musketeer. An improvement on the original.
What's her name – Sundarya...Bandariya?
Can't tell me and Rukhsar apart?

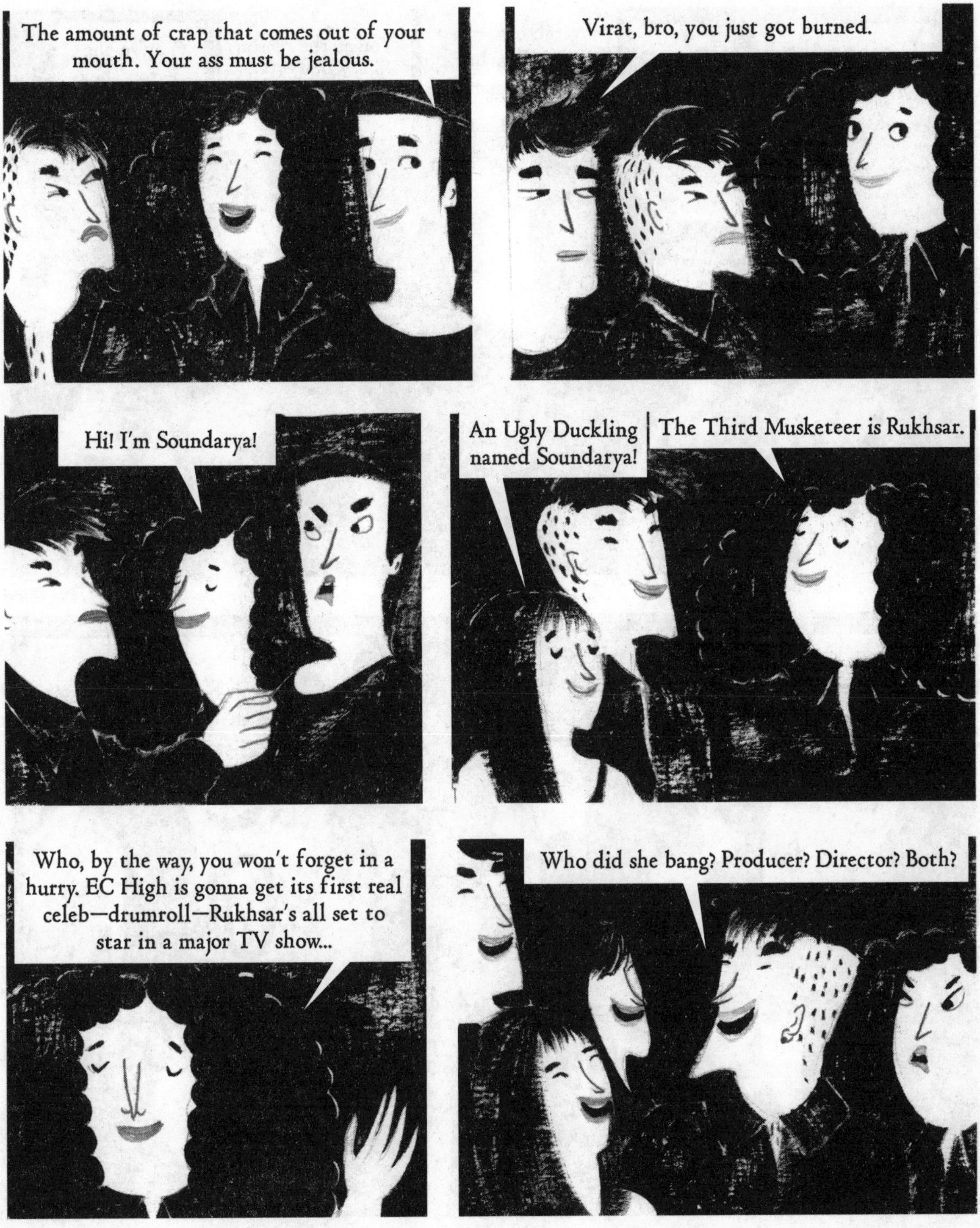

The amount of crap that comes out of your mouth. Your ass must be jealous.
Virat, bro, you just got burned.
Hi! I'm Soundarya!
The Third Musketeer is Rukhsar.
An Ugly Duckling named Soundarya!
Who, by the way, you won't forget in a hurry. EC High is gonna get its first real celeb—drumroll—Rukhsar's all set to star in a major TV show...
Who did she bang? Producer? Director? Both?

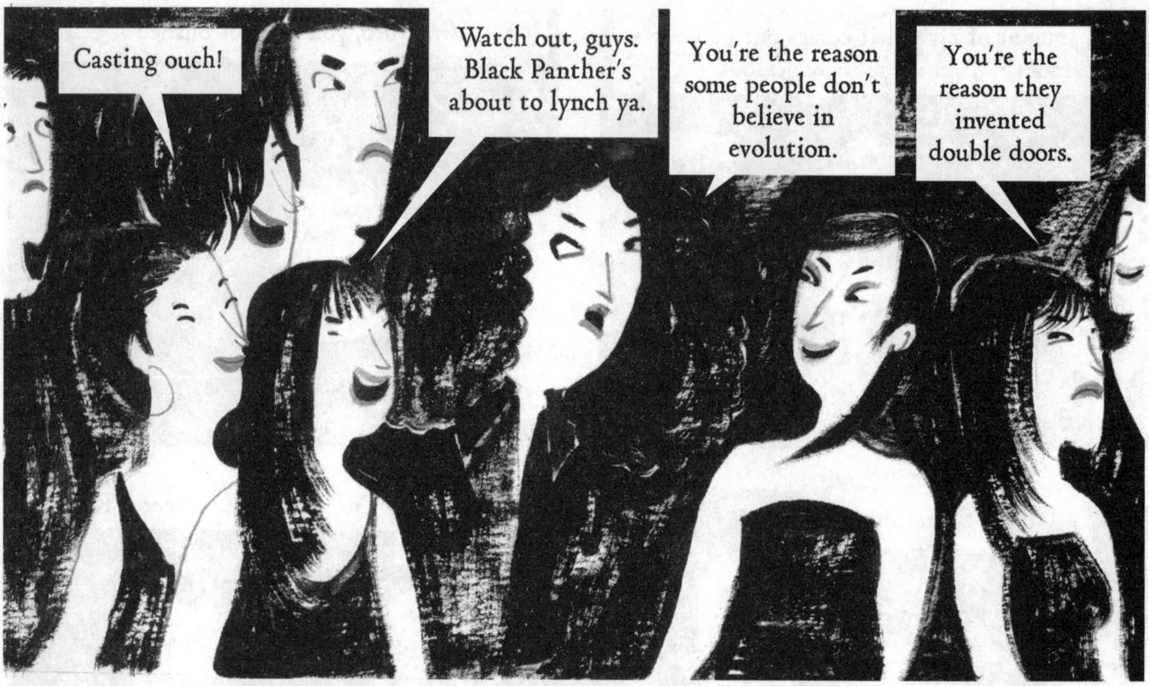
Casting ouch!
Watch out, guys. Black Panther's about to lynch ya.
You're the reason some people don't believe in evolution.
You're the reason they invented double doors.

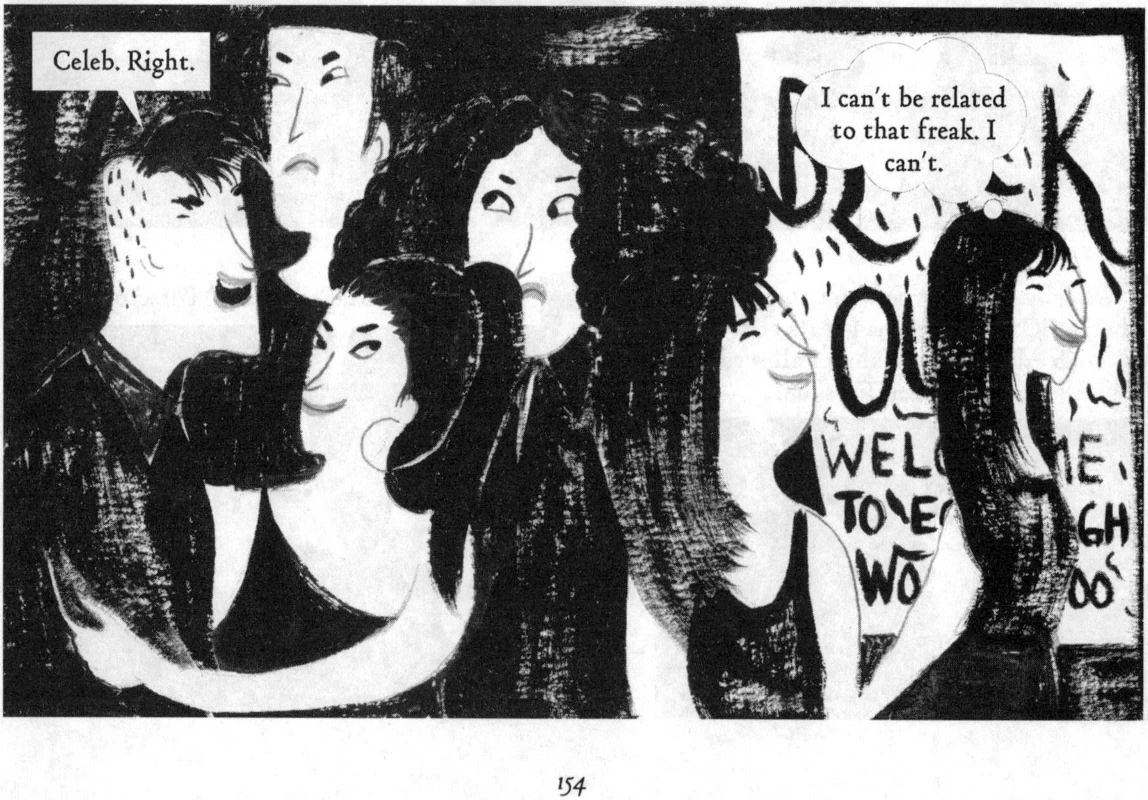
Celeb. Right.
I can't be related to that freak. I can't.

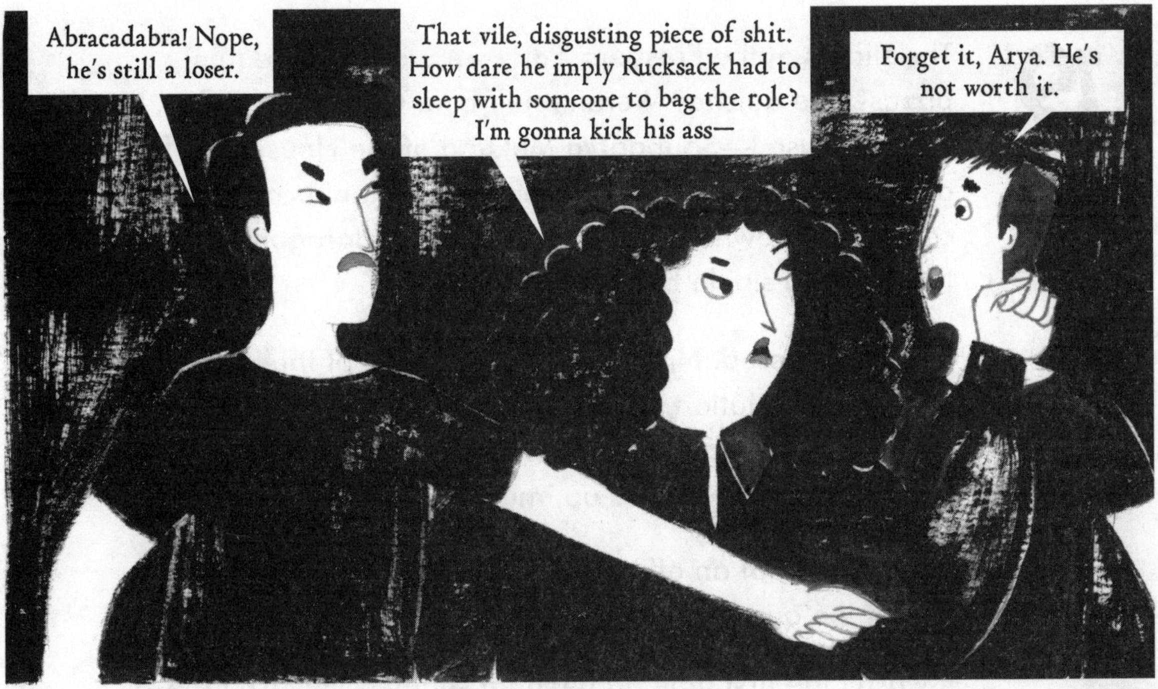
Abracadabra! Nope, he's still a loser.
That vile, disgusting piece of shit. How dare he imply Rucksack had to sleep with someone to bag the role? I'm gonna kick his ass—
Forget it, Arya. He's not worth it.

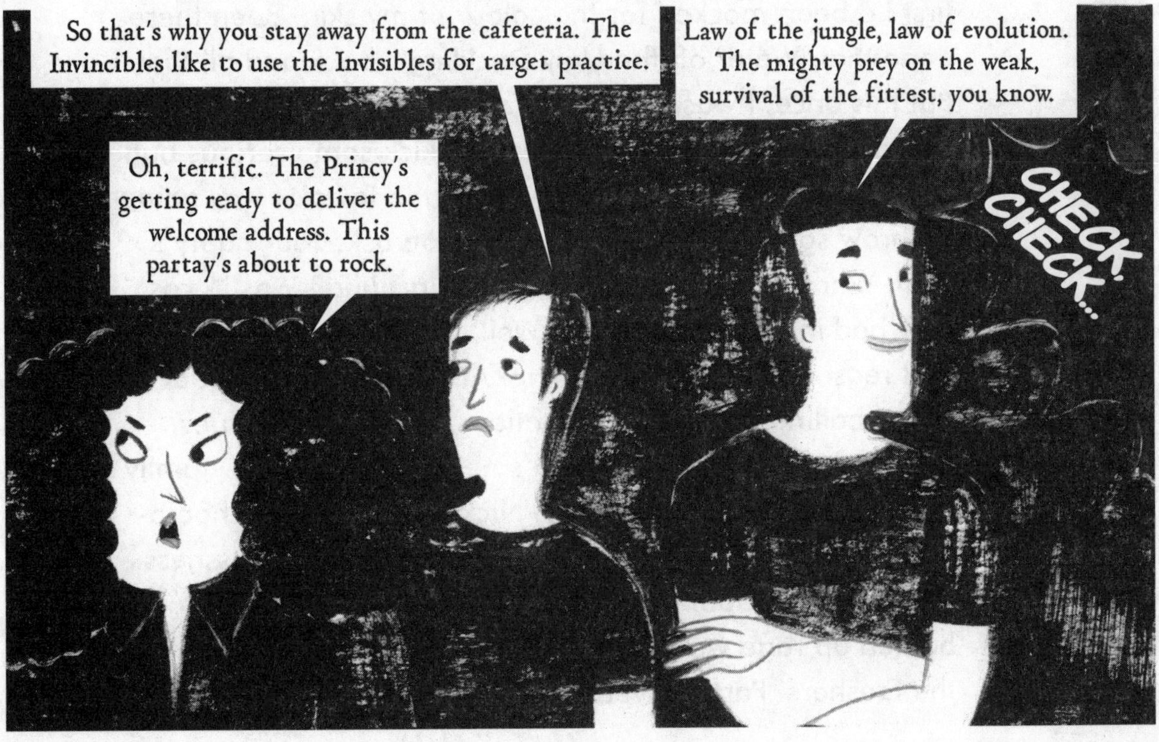
So that's why you stay away from the cafeteria. The Invincibles like to use the Invisibles for target practice.
Law of the jungle, law of evolution. The mighty prey on the weak, survival of the fittest, you know.
Oh, terrific. The Princy's getting ready to deliver the welcome address. This partay's about to rock.
CHECK. CHECK...

19

The sliders at the Freshers' Party were delish. The mini pizzas? The quiche? Weren't half bad. Or so I was told. Yup, because I—Soundarya Mukund of the House Iyer, first of her name, undisputed queen of Eatomania contests, certifiable chowhound and mother of fooddragons—did NOT have a single bite.

I was that pissed. Nick mentioned the law of the jungle and the law of evolution, but he kinda forgot about two other laws. Newton's. Every action has an equal and opposite reaction. Whatever goes up, must come down.

Suck it up? Not an effing chance. Deal with it? Out of the question. I was done.

It wasn't the first time I'd been fat shamed, it wasn't the first I'd been mocked for the colour of my skin. Been there done that. Water off the Ugly Duckling's back and all that. But this once, I wasn't going to roll over and play dead. I was going to roll up my sleeves and kick some serious butt. This once, I wasn't going to throw in the towel. I was going to throw some solid punches. Why, you ask. Your query's legit. What was so different this time around? Was it 'cos they had insulted my bestie? Well, that was part of it. The real reason though? The timing. At that point, my head was a boiling cauldron of emotions. I had major issues: Mom's shotgun wedding, Dad's new family, my new family, Rucksack's newfound success, Nick's new GF and choc-o-block schedule. All that frustration, all that powerlessness. Swirling and bubbling and threatening to spill over. My bottled up rage was seeking an outlet. And the incident at the Freshers' Party served as the trigger.

I got back home seething with anger. I wanted to make those aristocractic superbrats pay. I wanted to make those entitled snoots regret ever picking on us. I wanted to hurt those stuck-up sickos where it hurt most. But how? It was about a week later that it hit me...

...Fatal Attraction feels that social media is like an invisibility cloak for trolls...it accords them anonymity...emboldens them to take on the high and mighty, treat celebs as fair game...it motivates them to say mean, outrageous, disrespectful stuff...behave in an offensive manner – something they probably wouldn't do offline, in a face to face interaction.

Yeah, let's blame every evil known to mankind on social media. What about personal responsibility?

I mean, think about it, trolls have zero accountability...Which is why, Fatal Attraction isn't a fan of...sdfedd sfygege deekgt...

Uh, um, sorry I zoned out for a bit.

Really? I'm the one juggling school and multiple classes and a relationship and YOU are going to look all spacey?

I better crash. Talk soon.

And just like that, I knew exactly what I was going to do. The Invincibles had messed with the wrong girl. I was going to set some serious #TrollGoals. Oh yeah, they were probably going to give me a red tick—verified internet troll—on social media. Nikhil was wrong. The weak would inherit the earth. Oh yeah, they would. And cyberspace was a good place to start.

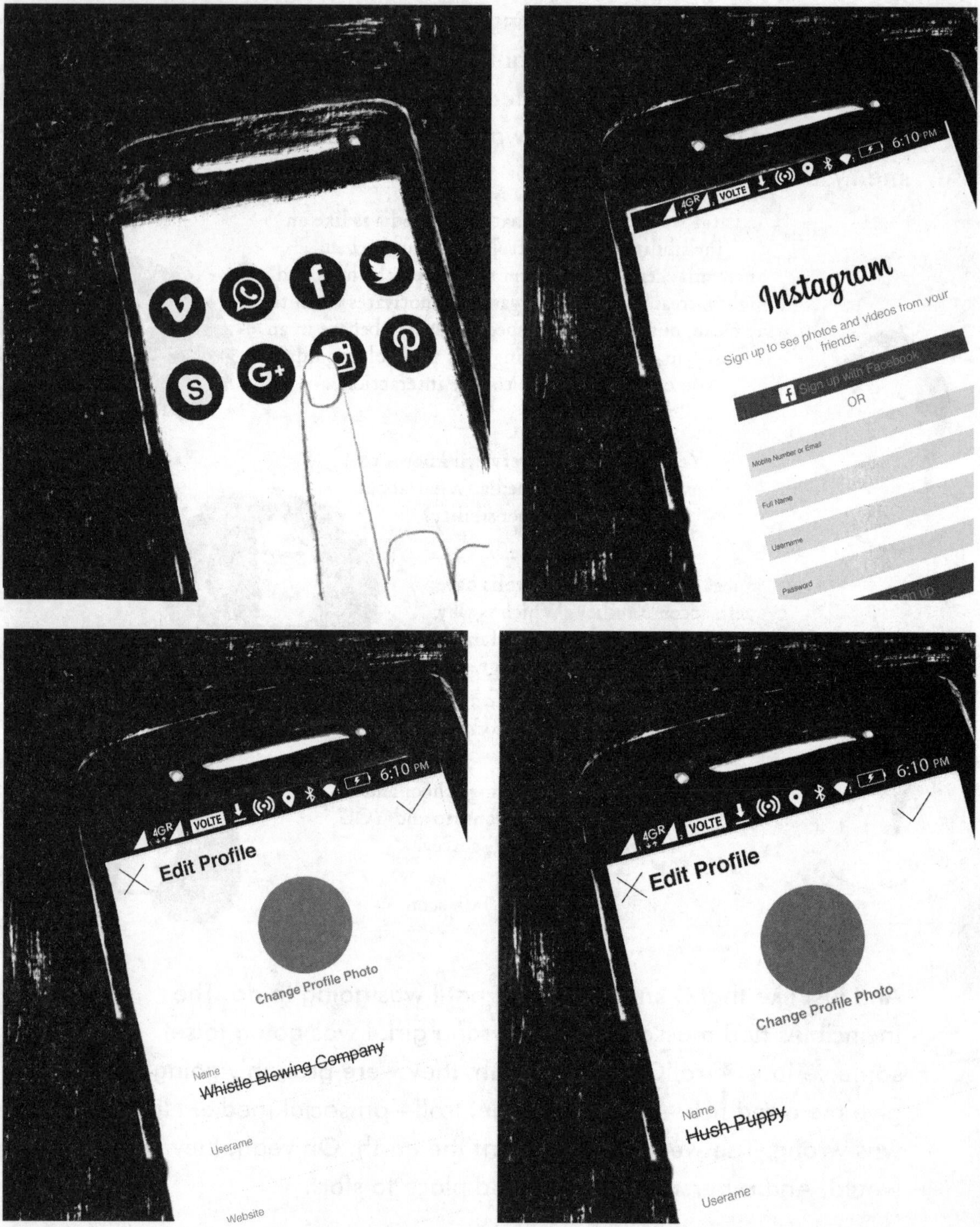
6:10 PM
VOLTE
Instagram
Sign up to see photos and videos from your friends.
Sign up with Facebook
OR
Mobile Number or Email
Full Name
Username
Password
Sign up
6:10 PM
VOLTE
Edit Profile
Change Profile Photo
Name
Whistle Blowing Company
Userame
Website
6:10 PM
VOLTE
Edit Profile
Change Profile Photo
Name
Hush Puppy
Userame

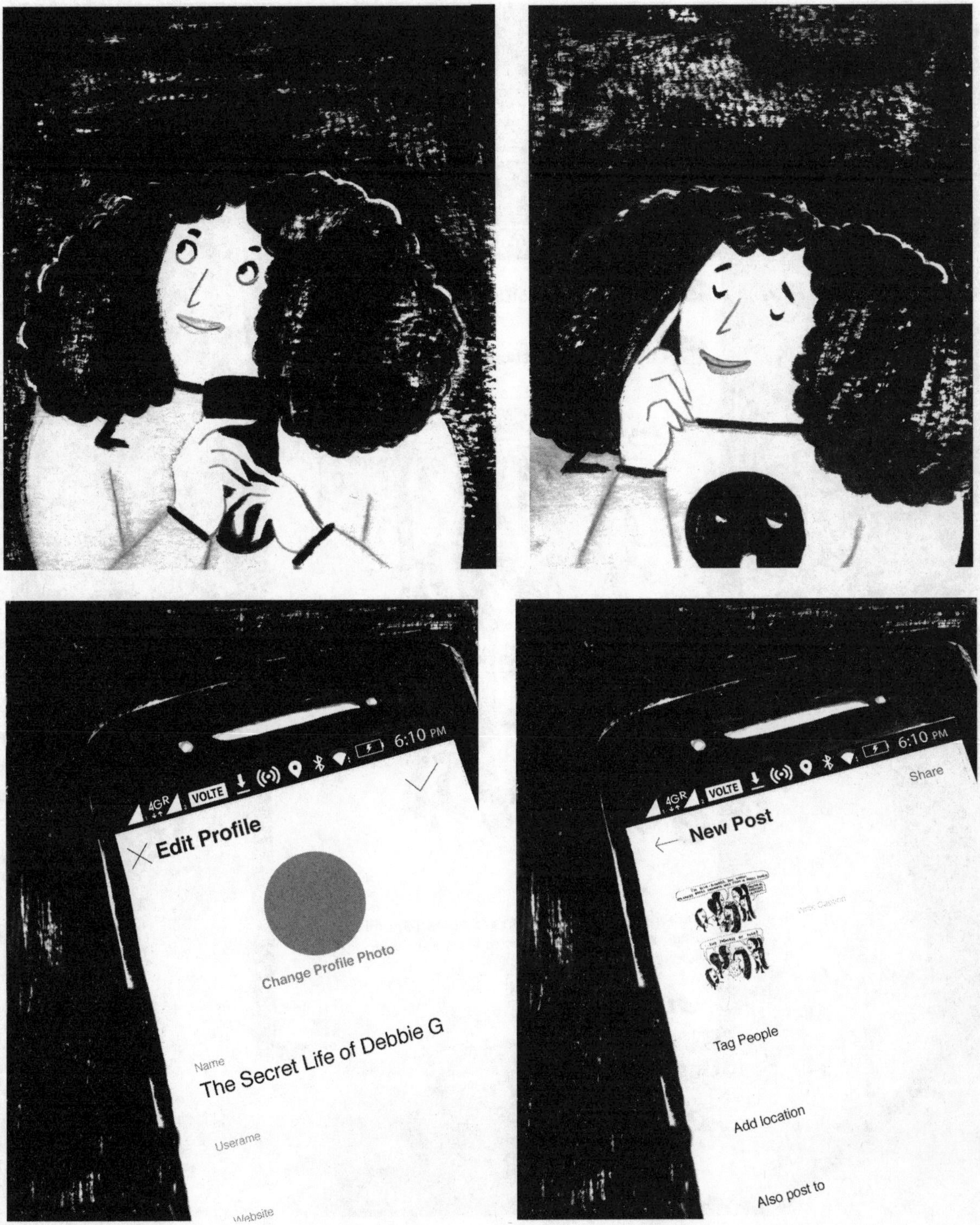
6:10 PM
VOLTE
Edit Profile
Change Profile Photo
Name
The Secret Life of Debbie G
Userame
Website
6:10 PM
VOLTE
Share
New Post
Tag People
Add location
Also post to

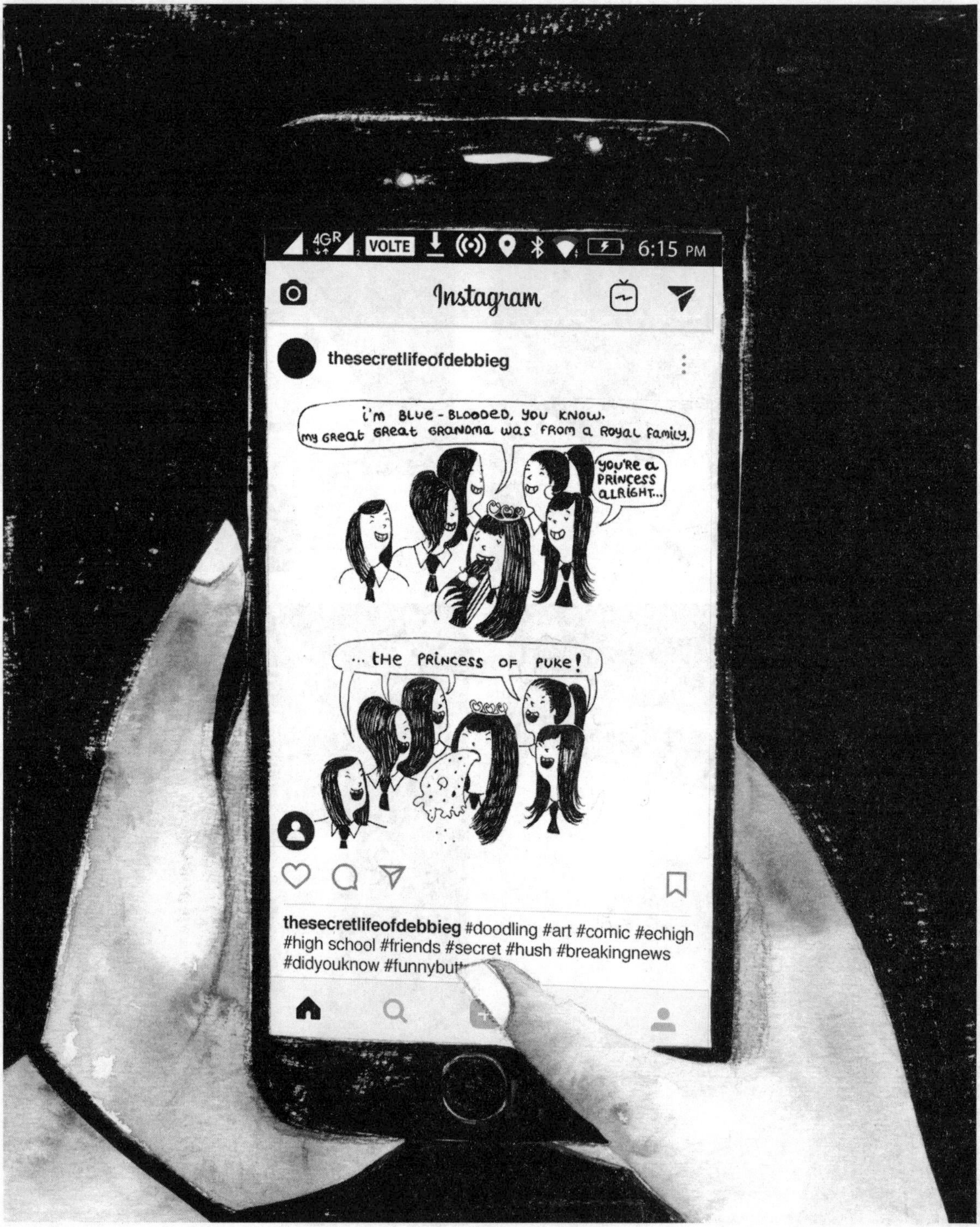
4GR
VOLTE
6:15 PM
Instagram
thesecretlifeofdebbieg
i'm BLUE-BLOODED, YOU KNOW. MY GREAT GREAT GRANDMA WAS FROM A ROYAL FAMILY.
YOU'RE A PRINCESS ALRIGHT...
... THE PRINCESS OF PUKE!
thesecretlifeofdebbieg #doodling #art #comic #echigh #high school #friends #secret #hush #breakingnews #didyouknow #funnybutt

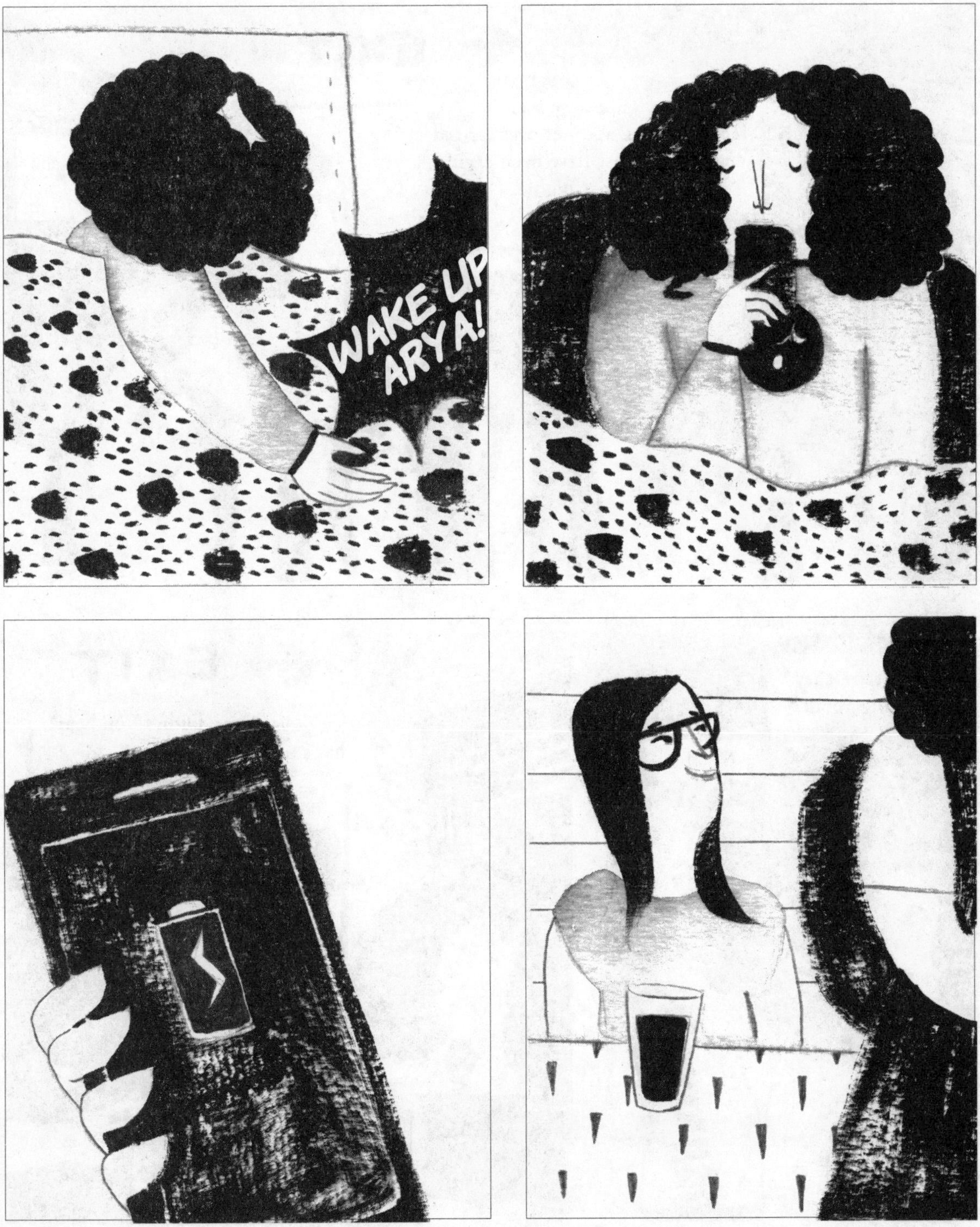
WAKE UP ARYA!

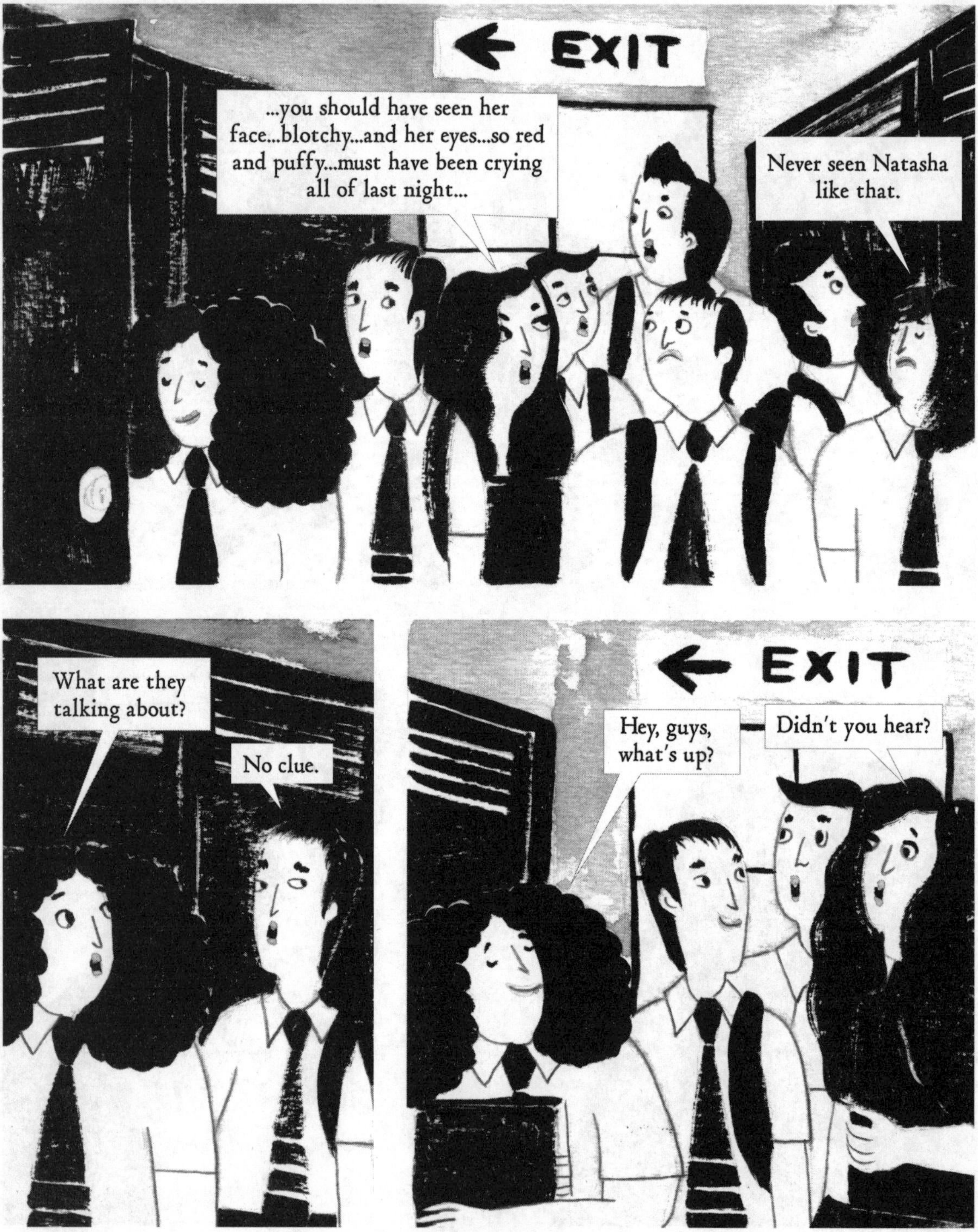
EXIT
...you should have seen her face...blotchy...and her eyes...so red and puffy...must have been crying all of last night...
Never seen Natasha like that.
What are they talking about?
No clue.
EXIT
Hey, guys, what's up?
Didn't you hear?

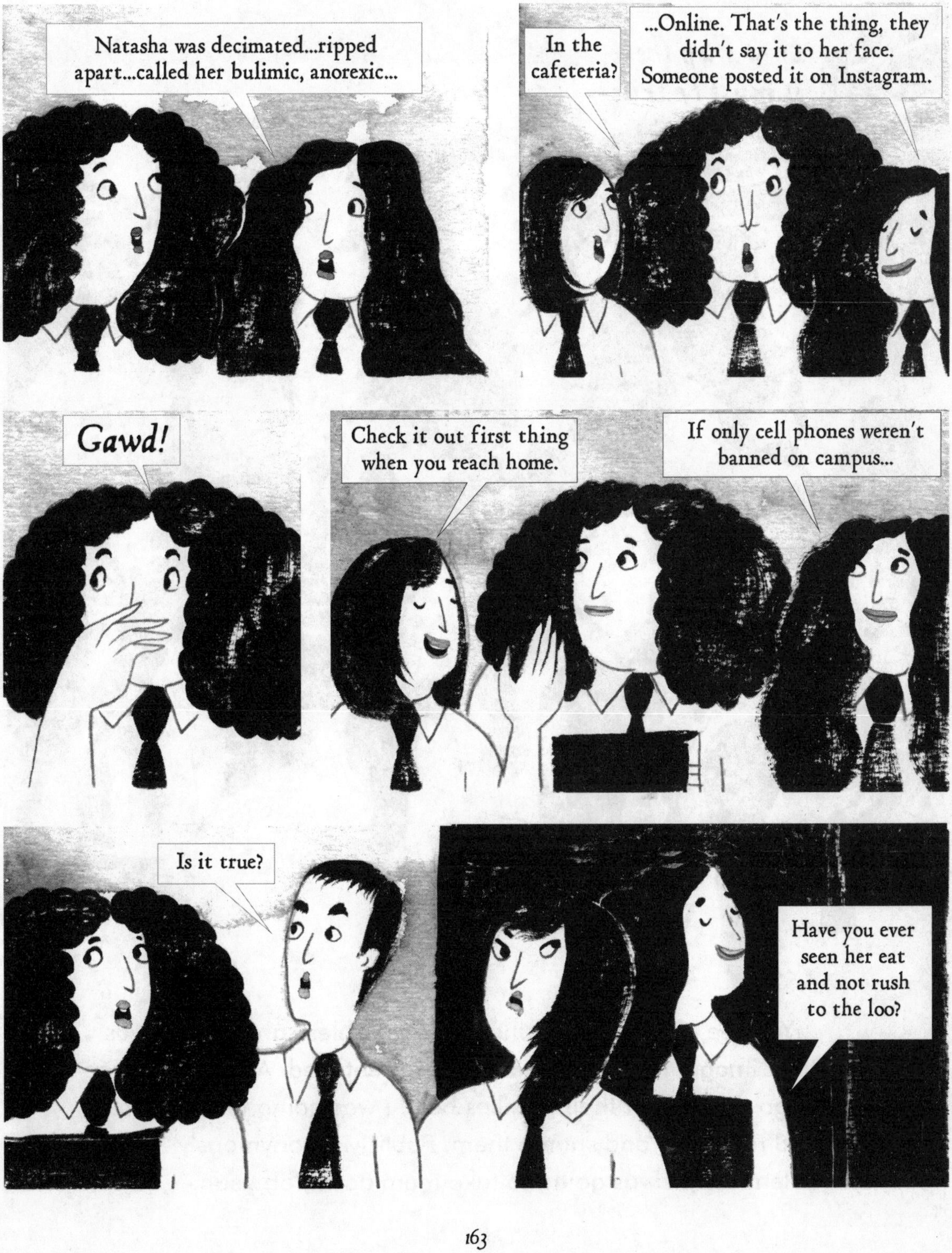
Natasha was decimated...ripped apart...called her bulimic, anorexic...
In the cafeteria?
...Online. That's the thing, they didn't say it to her face. Someone posted it on Instagram.
Gawd!
Check it out first thing when you reach home.
If only cell phones weren't banned on campus...
Is it true?
Have you ever seen her eat and not rush to the loo?

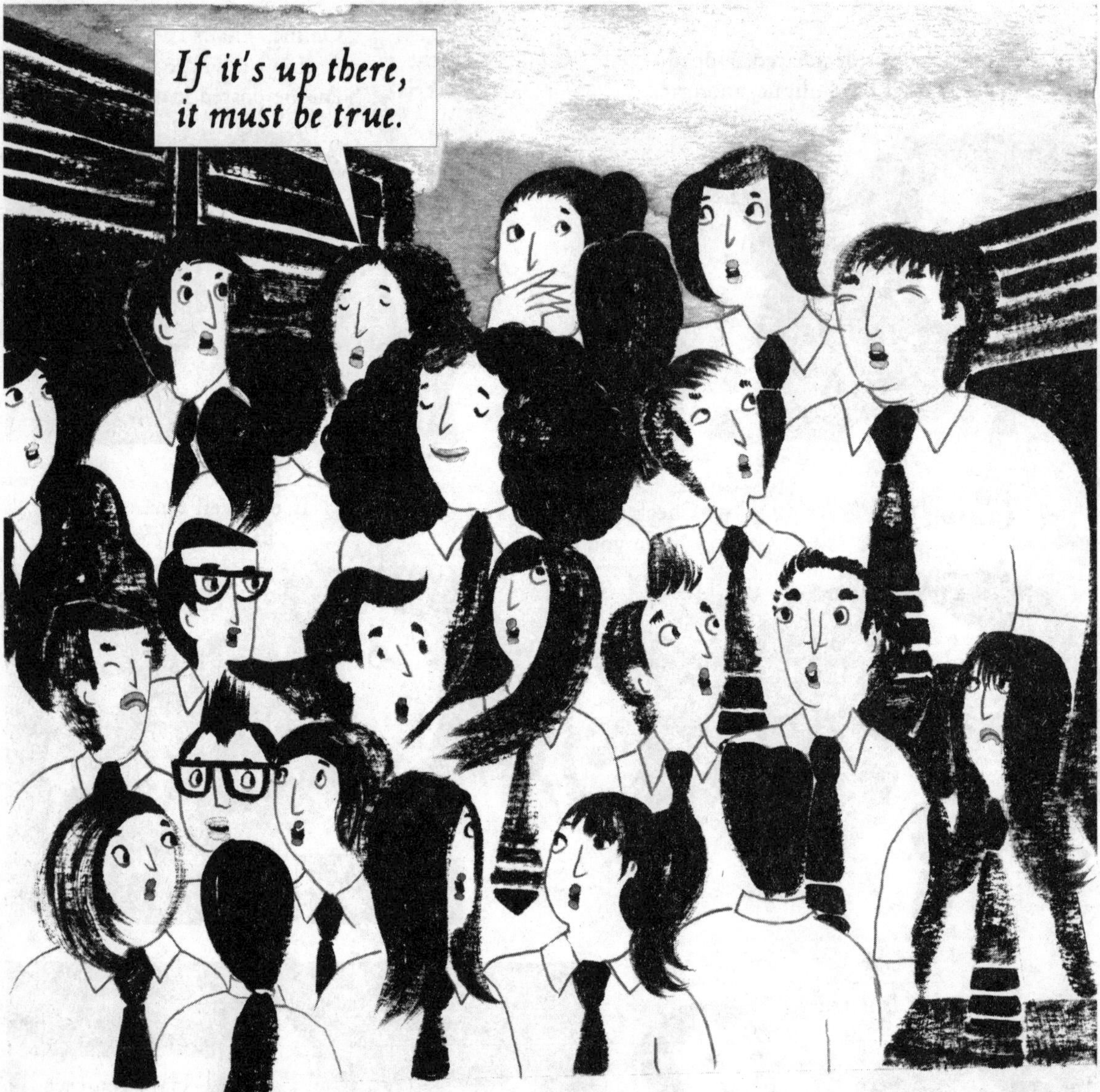
If it's up there, it must be true.

...You see, the one thing that the Invincibles cared about was their image, their reputation, their street cred. And I was going to go straight for their Achilles heel. I was going to embarrass and humiliate and shame them. Publicly. Anonymously. Relentlessly. I was going to take them down, oh yeah.

20

See? Precisely why the most dangerous things on earth are not guns, not bullets, not bombs. It's ideas. I mean, they are positively lethal. They can blow up reputations, assassinate characters, rip apart lives. You want to bring a person down? Easy peasy. Plant a seed of doubt in people's heads. Let gossip and imagination do the rest. And that's it, kaboom! I mean, it's dynamite. Don't try it at home. Actually, don't try it anywhere. At all. I wish I hadn't. But that's now. Back then, I was like a guided missile. Wreaking widespread havoc and mass destruction. And for a change, the Invincibles were at the receiving end. So much so, I actually started looking forward to meeting Kiara...

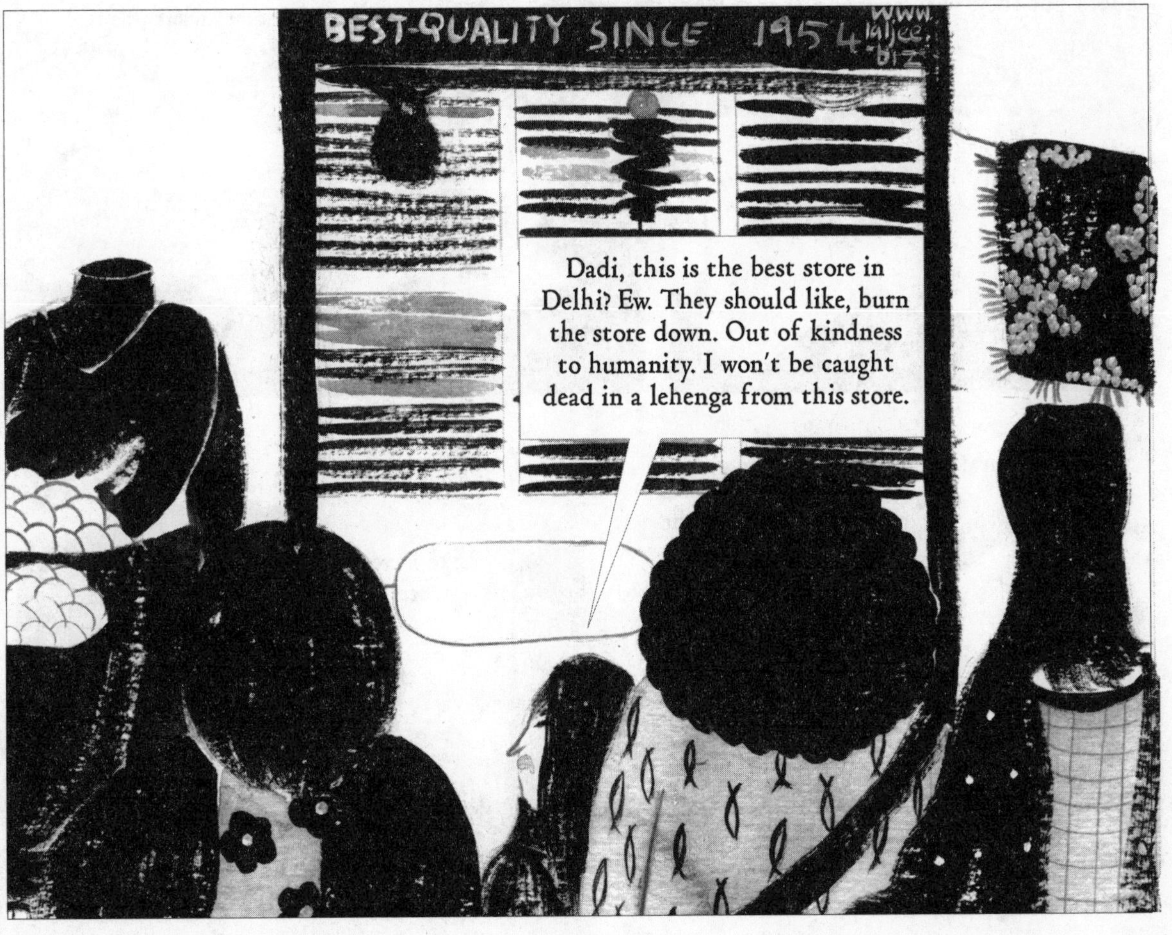
BEST-QUALITY SINCE 1954 www.laljee.biz
Dadi, this is the best store in Delhi? Ew. They should like, burn the store down. Out of kindness to humanity. I won't be caught dead in a lehenga from this store.

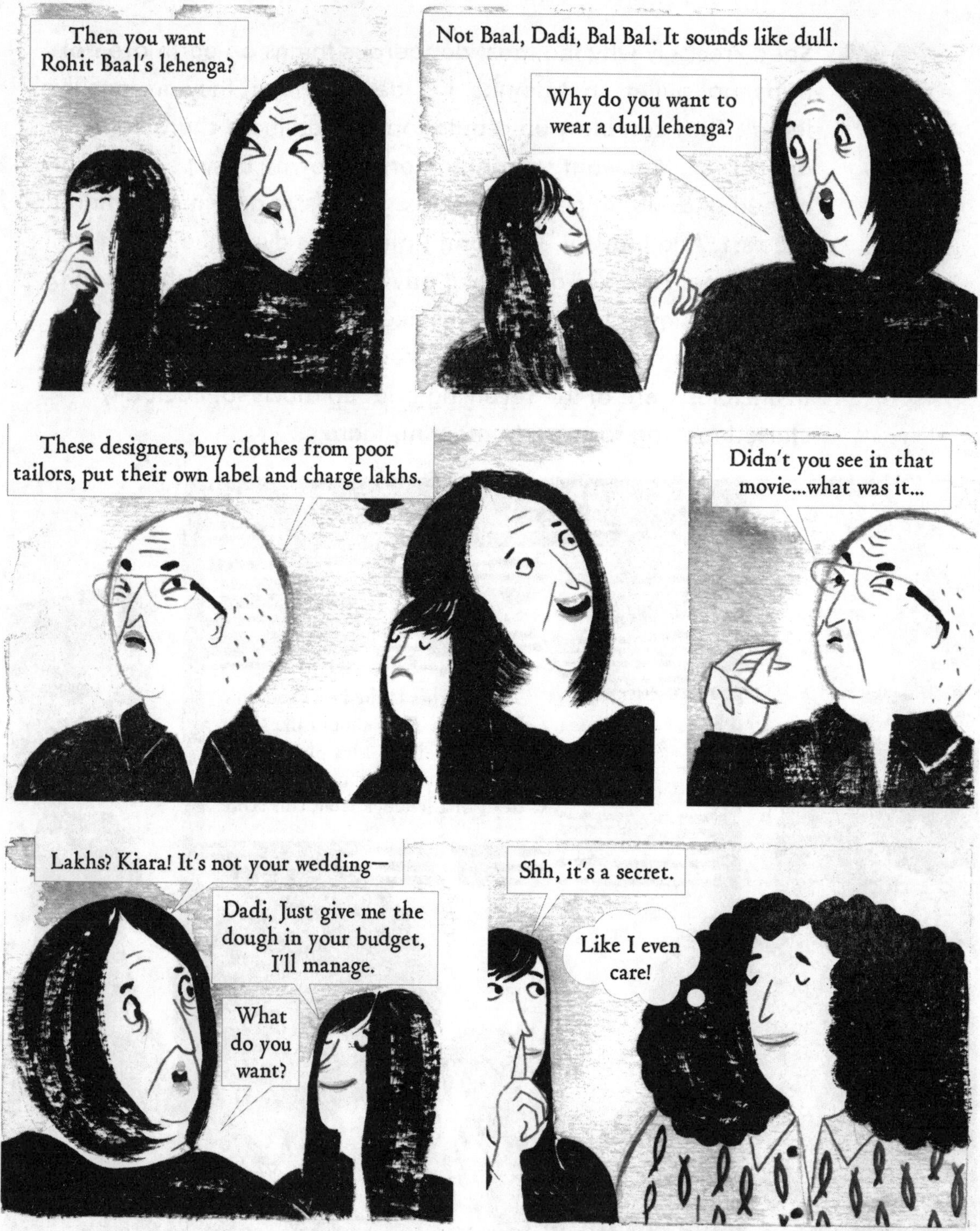
Then you want Rohit Baal's lehenga?
Not Baal, Dadi, Bal Bal. It sounds like dull.
Why do you want to wear a dull lehenga?
These designers, buy clothes from poor tailors, put their own label and charge lakhs.
Didn't you see in that movie...what was it...
Lakhs? Kiara! It's not your wedding—
Dadi, Just give me the dough in your budget, I'll manage.
What do you want?
Shh, it's a secret.
Like I even care!

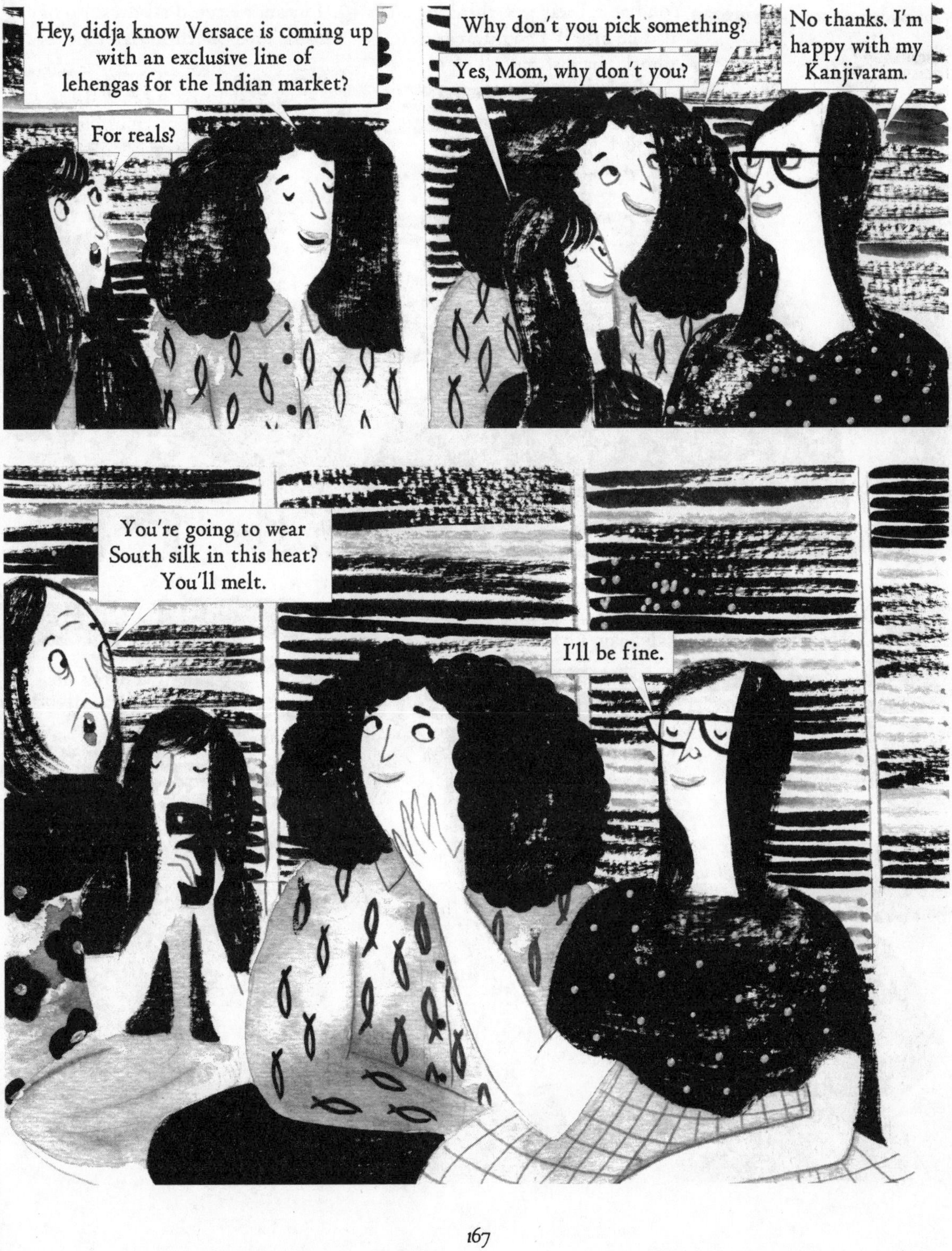
Hey, didja know Versace is coming up with an exclusive line of lehengas for the Indian market?
For reals?
Why don't you pick something?
Yes, Mom, why don't you?
No thanks. I'm happy with my Kanjivaram.
You're going to wear South silk in this heat? You'll melt.
I'll be fine.

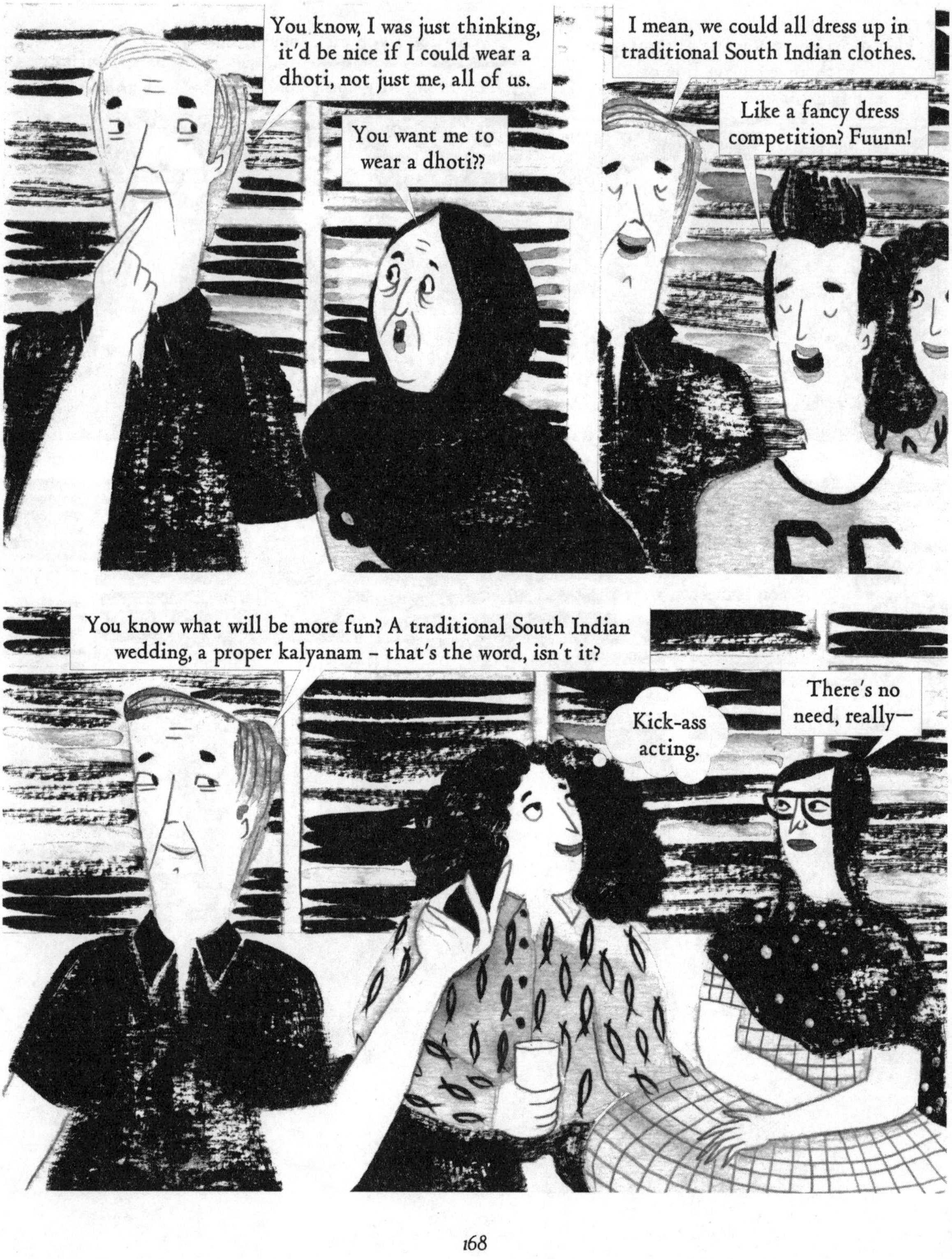
You know, I was just thinking, it'd be nice if I could wear a dhoti, not just me, all of us.
You want me to wear a dhoti??
I mean, we could all dress up in traditional South Indian clothes.
Like a fancy dress competition? Fuunn!
You know what will be more fun? A traditional South Indian wedding, a proper kalyanam – that's the word, isn't it?
Kick-ass acting.
There's no need, really—

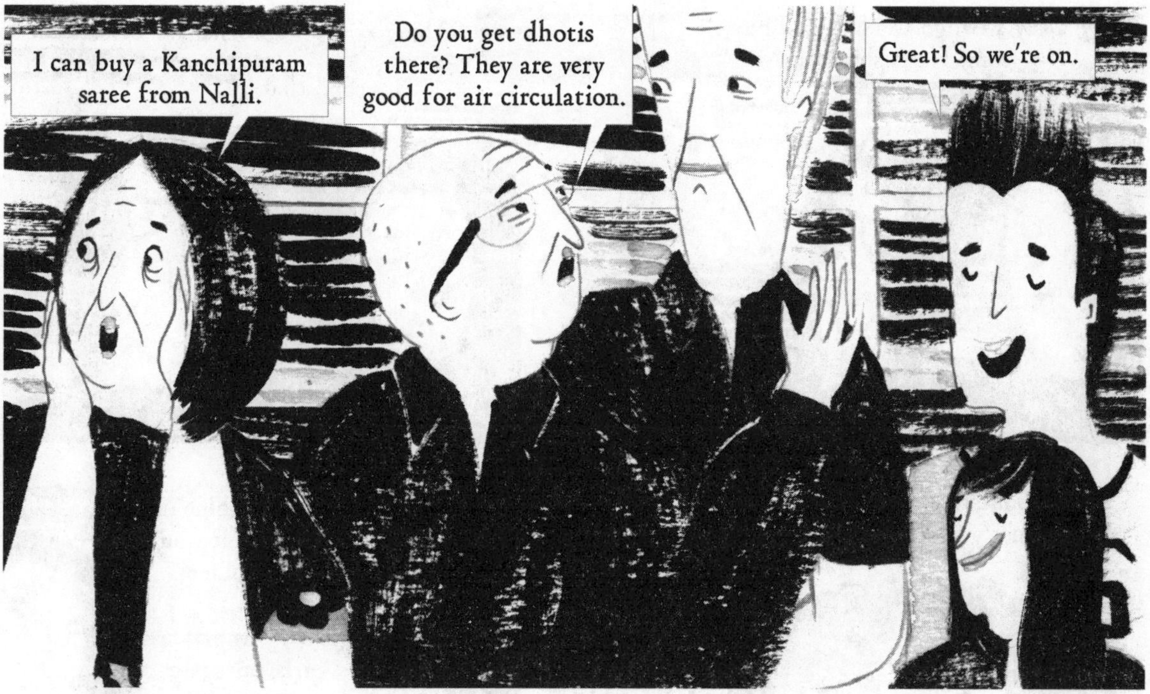
I can buy a Kanchipuram saree from Nalli.
Do you get dhotis there? They are very good for air circulation.
Great! So we're on.

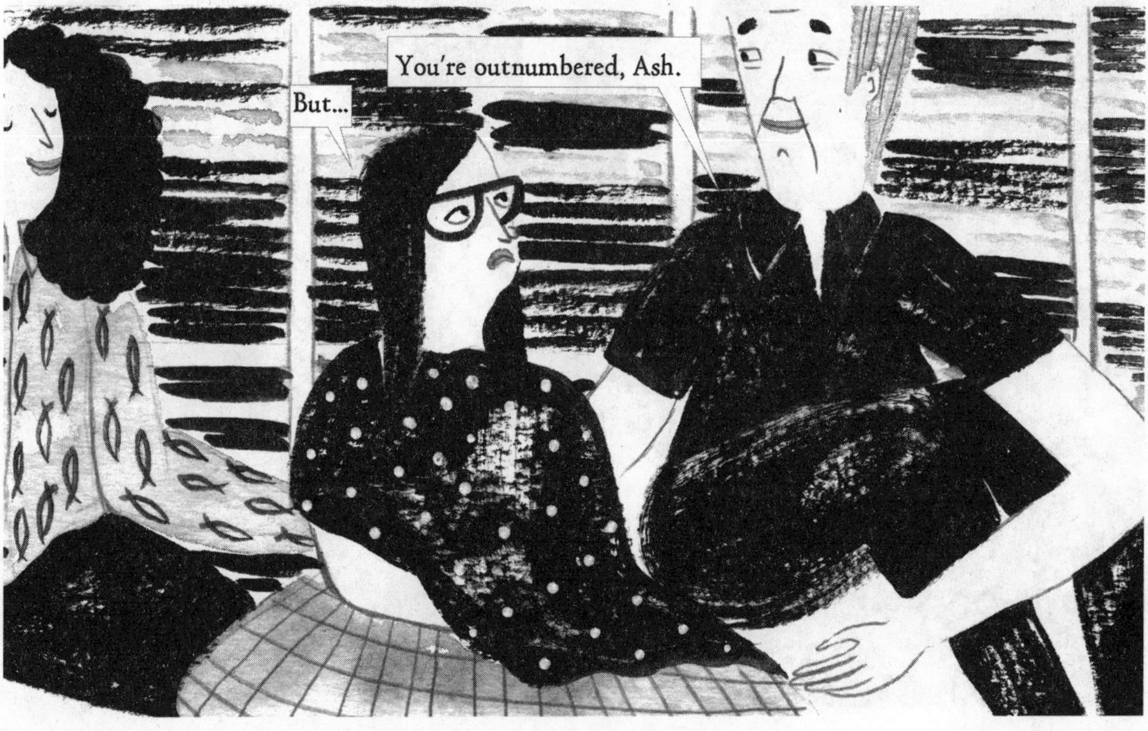
But...
You're outnumbered, Ash.

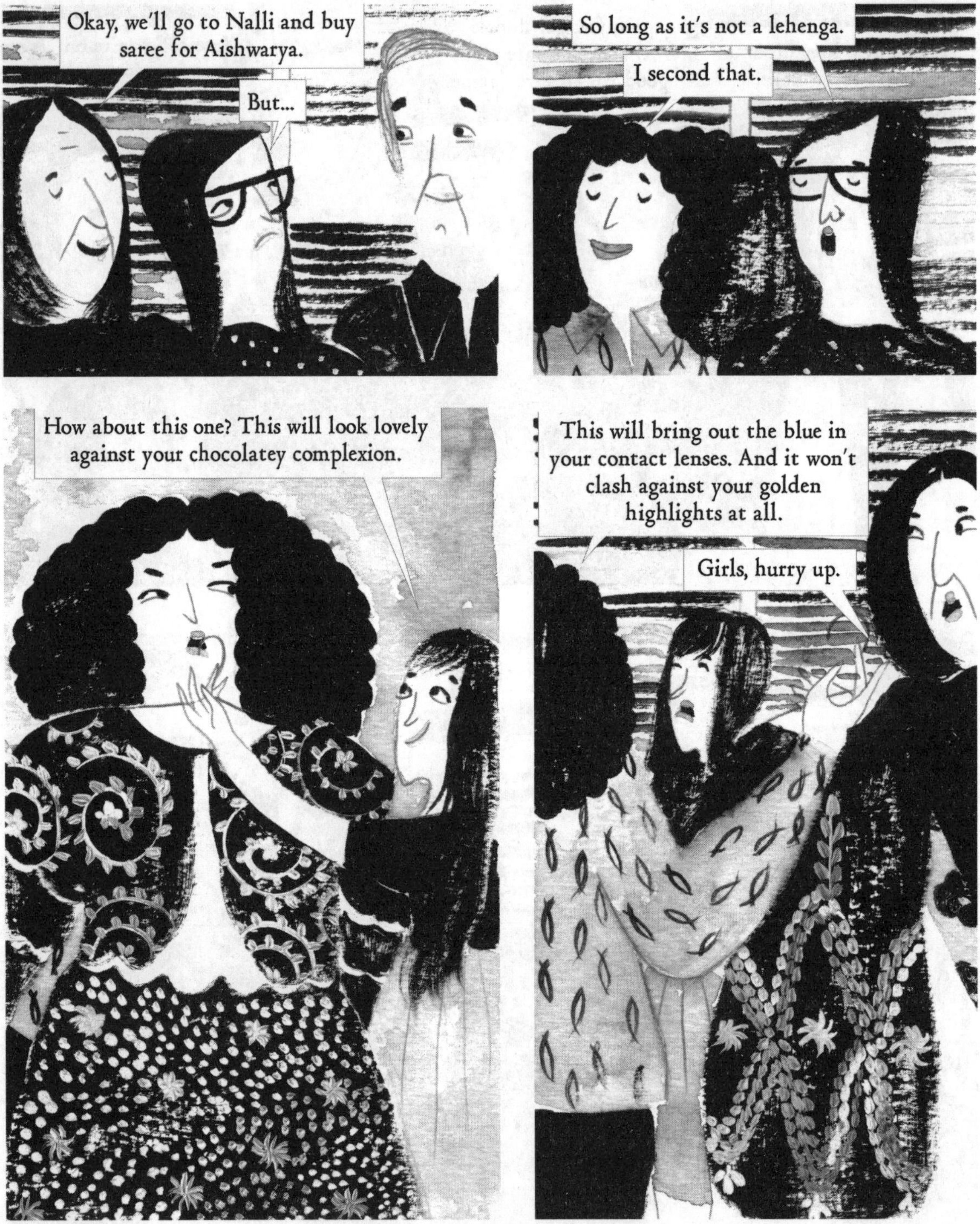
Okay, we'll go to Nalli and buy saree for Aishwarya.
But...
So long as it's not a lehenga.
I second that.
How about this one? This will look lovely against your chocolatey complexion.
This will bring out the blue in your contact lenses. And it won't clash against your golden highlights at all.
Girls, hurry up.

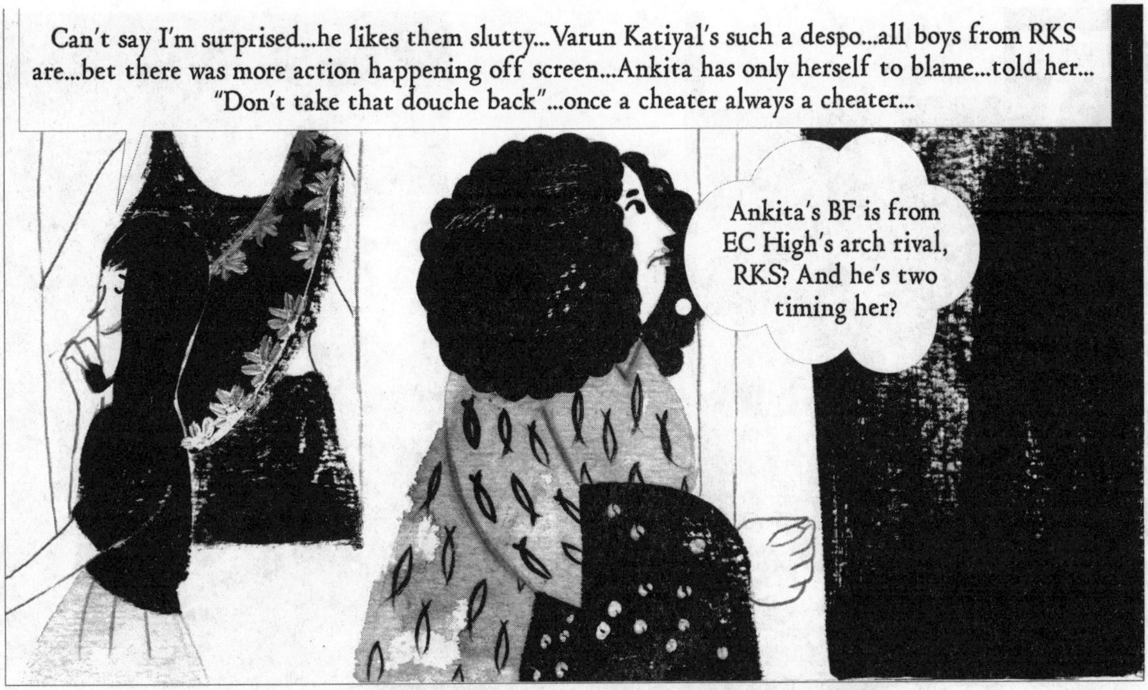
Can't say I'm surprised...he likes them slutty...Varun Katiyal's such a despo...all boys from RKS are...bet there was more action happening off screen...Ankita has only herself to blame...told her... "Don't take that douche back"...once a cheater always a cheater...
Ankita's BF is from EC High's arch rival, RKS? And he's two timing her?

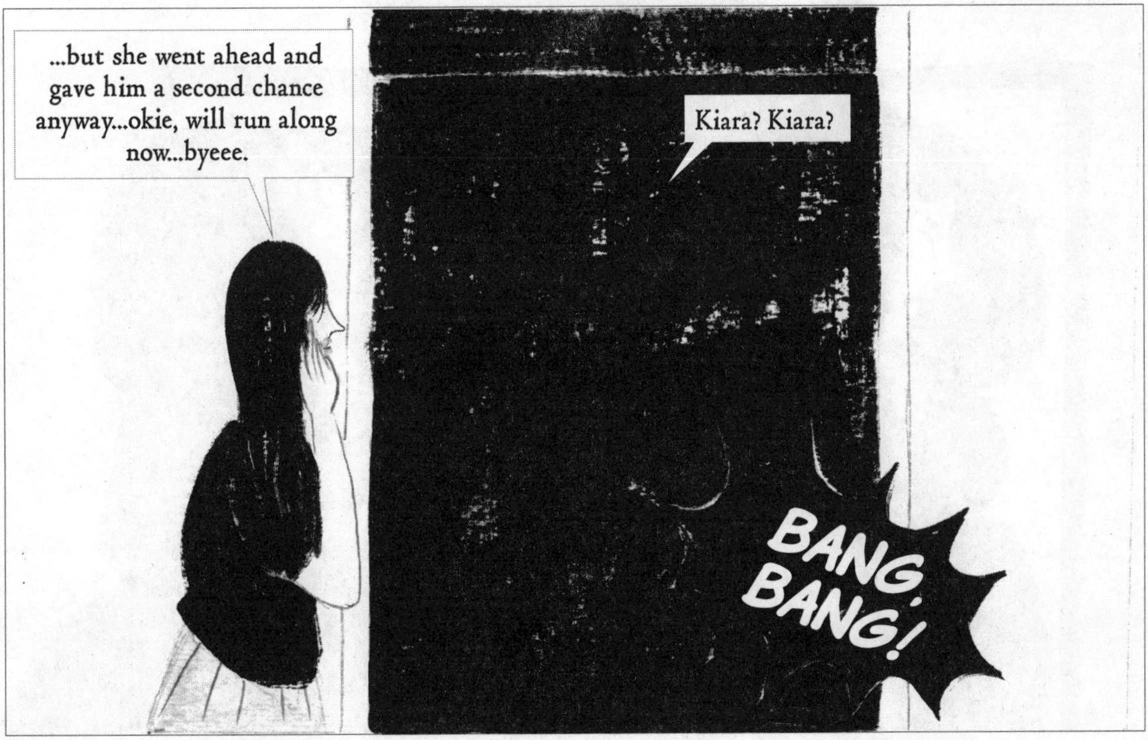
...but she went ahead and gave him a second chance anyway...okie, will run along now...byeee.
Kiara? Kiara?
BANG, BANG!

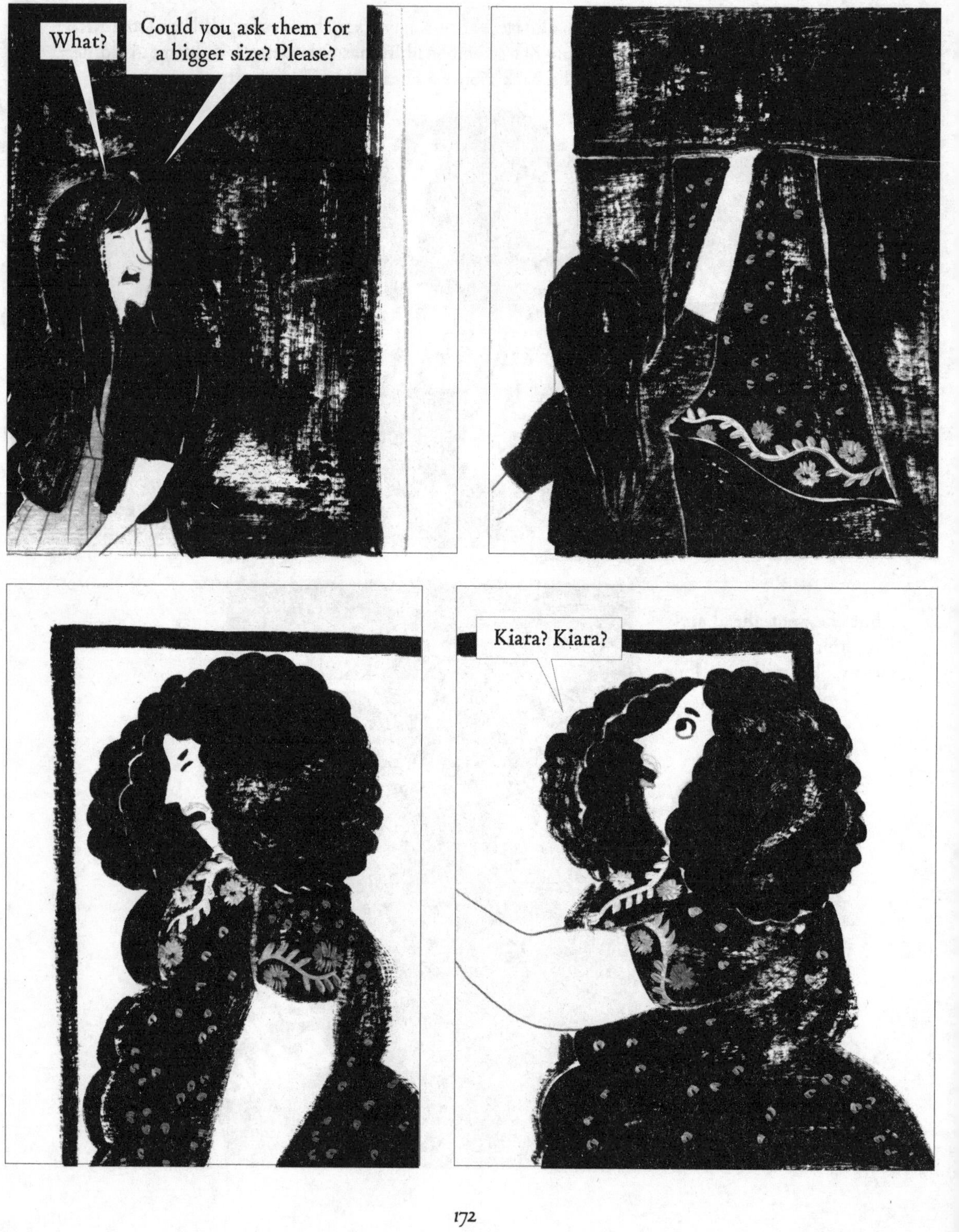
What?
Could you ask them for a bigger size? Please?
Kiara? Kiara?

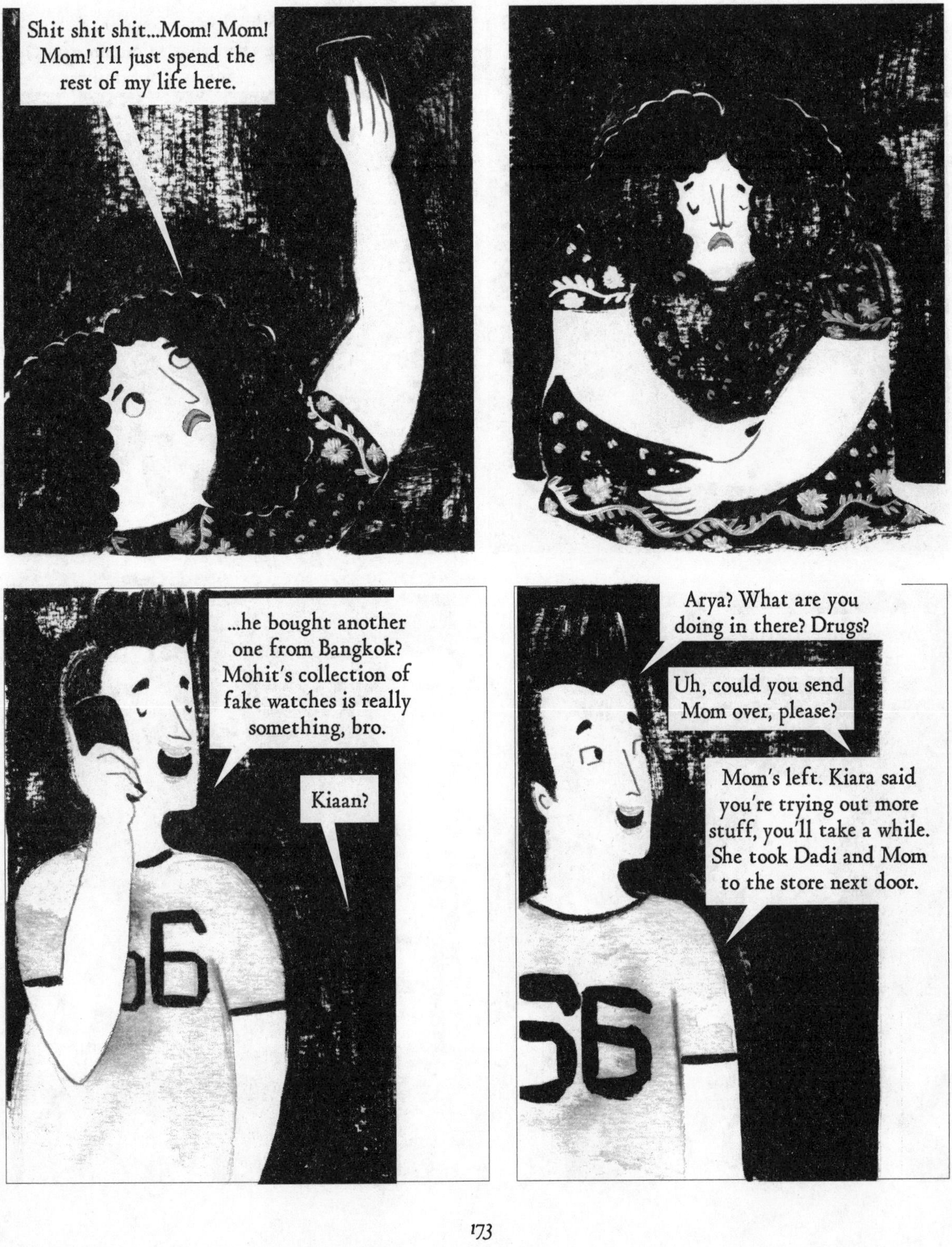
Shit shit shit...Mom! Mom! Mom! I'll just spend the rest of my life here.
...he bought another one from Bangkok? Mohit's collection of fake watches is really something, bro.
Kiaan?
Arya? What are you doing in there? Drugs?
Uh, could you send Mom over, please?
Mom's left. Kiara said you're trying out more stuff, you'll take a while. She took Dadi and Mom to the store next door.
66
66

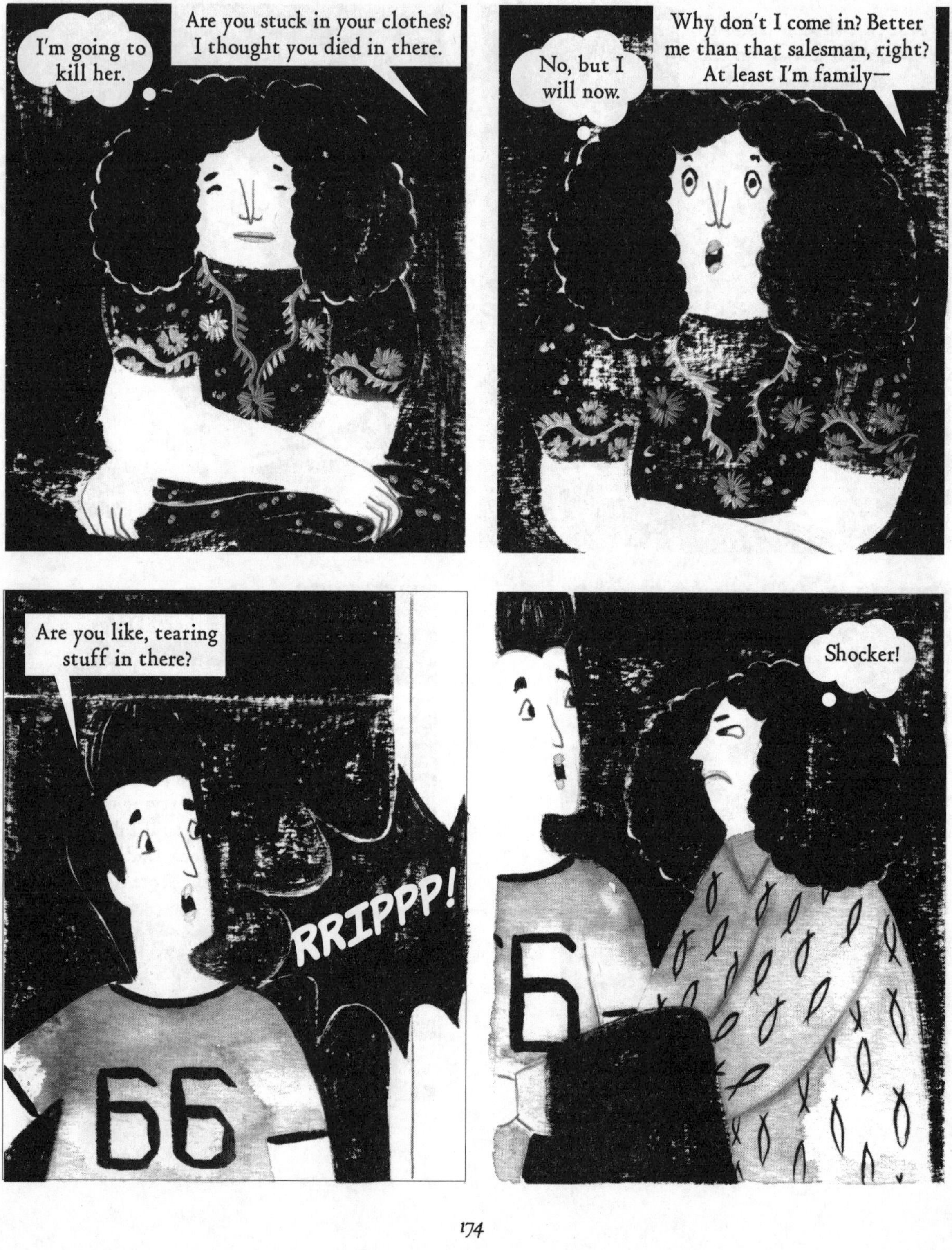
Are you stuck in your clothes? I thought you died in there.
I'm going to kill her.
Why don't I come in? Better me than that salesman, right? At least I'm family—
No, but I will now.
Are you like, tearing stuff in there?
RRIPPP!
Shocker!

21 Debbie G's debut got 300 likes. 300! I didn't have as many followers on my own Instagram, for god's sake. My real account hardly ever saw any action – a stray comment here or there, a handful of likes, followers who disappeared as quickly as they had appeared. (Explains the Unfollow = Unfollow bit on my profile).

Yet, I wasn't sure if I was going to keep at it. Was worried I'd run out of ammo or grow out of it or something. But the adulation! It blew me away. Fans—okay, followers— kept pouring in. Fan mail—okay, DMs—kept pouring in. I mean, people pay big bucks for that sort of stuff. Debbie G was well on her way to becoming an influencer. A public figure. Blue tick and all. And let's face it, online or offline, attention is attention. I didn't realise how much I'd missed it. If you ask me, fame is as dangerous as cocaine. It's as addictive (if not more), it gives the same high—oh, the rush, the euphoria, the confidence. And the withdrawal symptoms—shudder—they aren't worth thinking about. In case you're wondering, nope, I'm no Walter White. But I've watched enough movies and TV shows to know what happens to addicts.

Anyway, so, I started craving the high. I couldn't get enough of it. Sure enough, that month the crème de la crème got creamed. And not just XI graders, I cast the net wide, threw in our seniors for good measure. Dope courtesy—pun entirely unintended—Kiaan. Oh, I was on a hot streak...

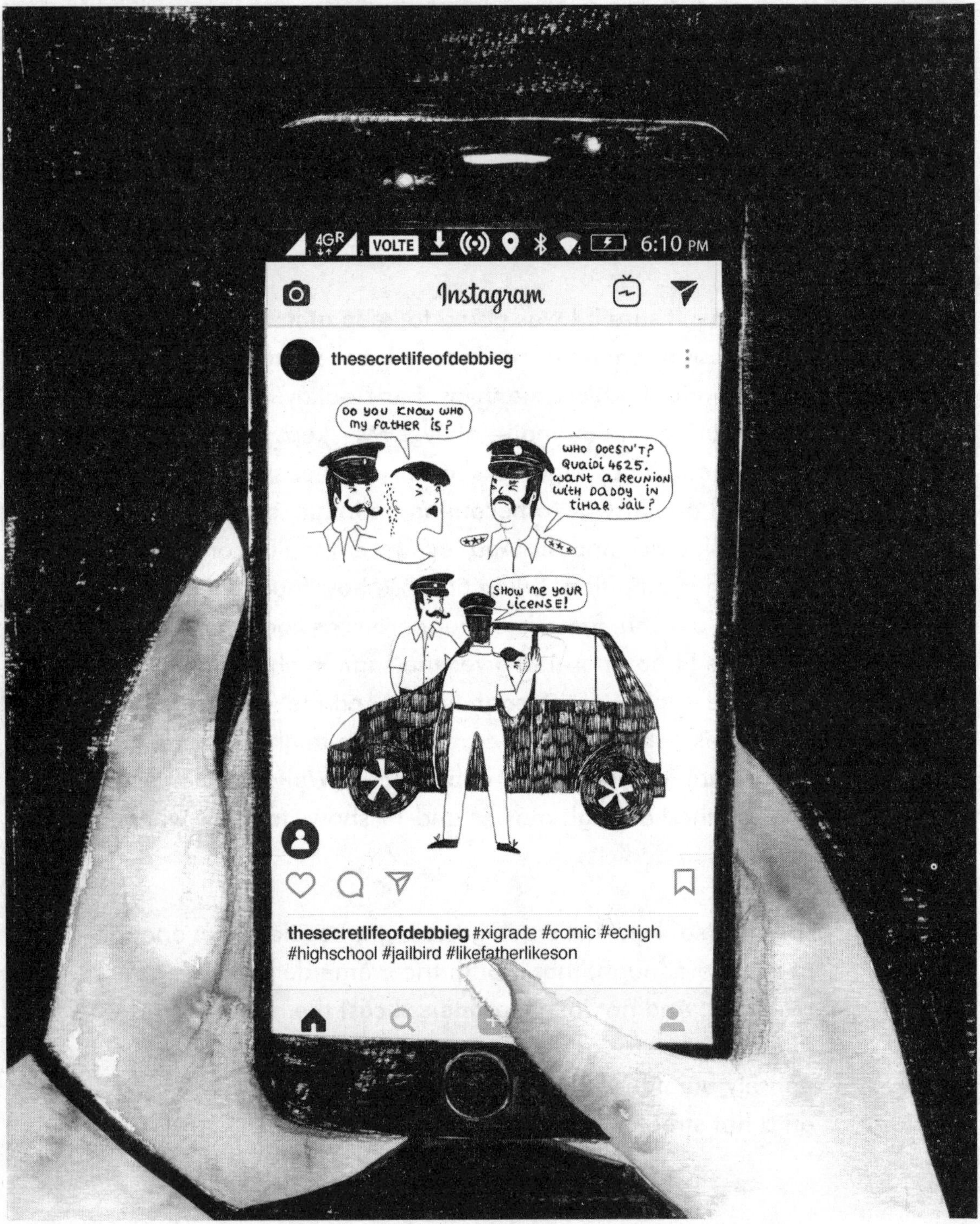
4GR
VOLTE
6:10 PM
Instagram
thesecretlifeofdebbieg
DO YOU KNOW WHO my FATHER IS?
WHO DOESN'T? QUAIDI 4625. WANT A REUNION WITH DADDY IN TIHAR JAIL?
SHOW ME YOUR LICENSE!
thesecretlifeofdebbieg #xigrade #comic #echigh #highschool #jailbird #likefatherlikeson

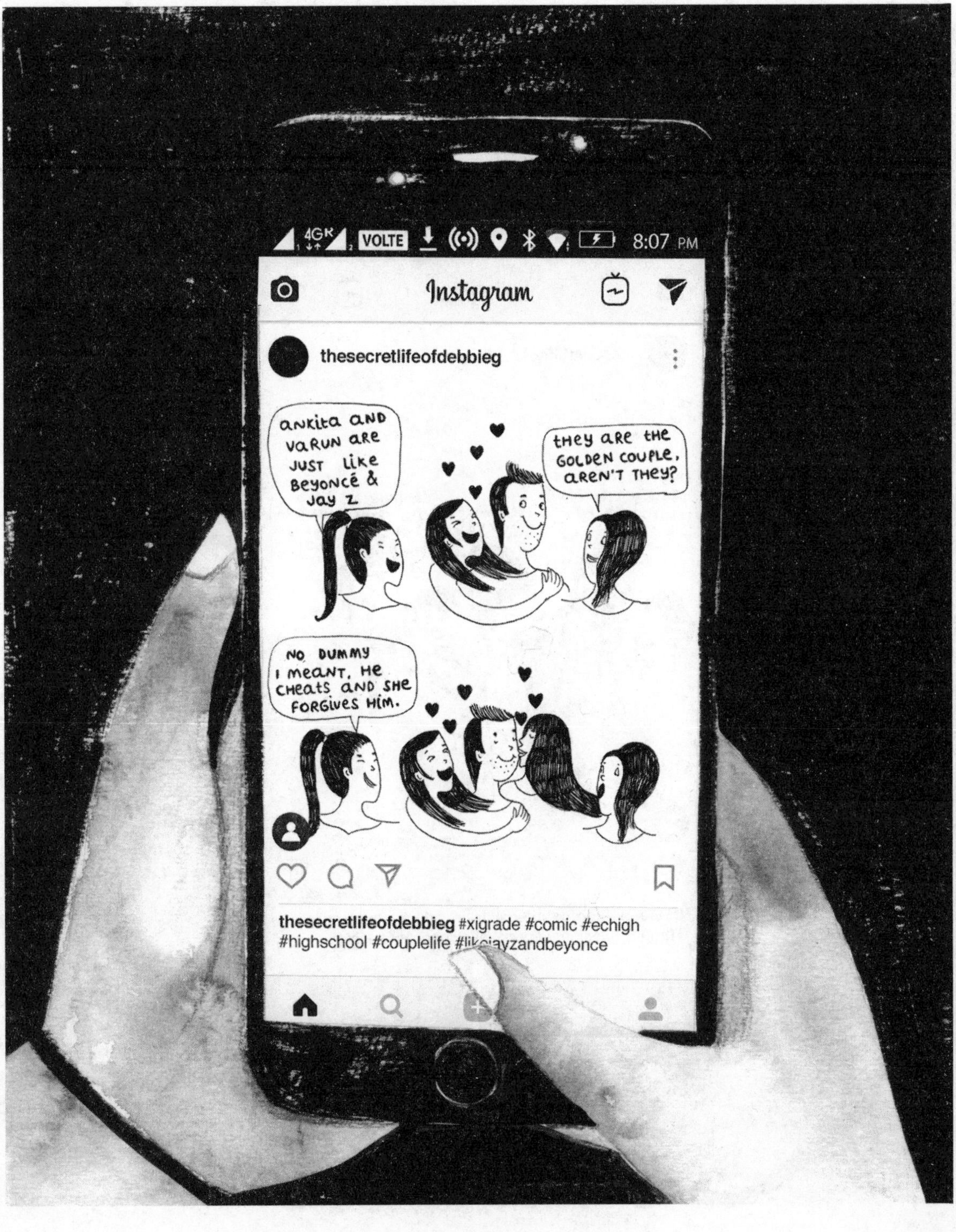
4G VOLTE 8:07 PM
Instagram
thesecretlifeofdebbieg
ankita and varun are just like Beyoncé & Jay Z
they are the golden couple, aren't they?
no dummy I meant, he cheats and she forgives him.
thesecretlifeofdebbieg #xigrade #comic #echigh #highschool #couplelife #likejayzandbeyonce

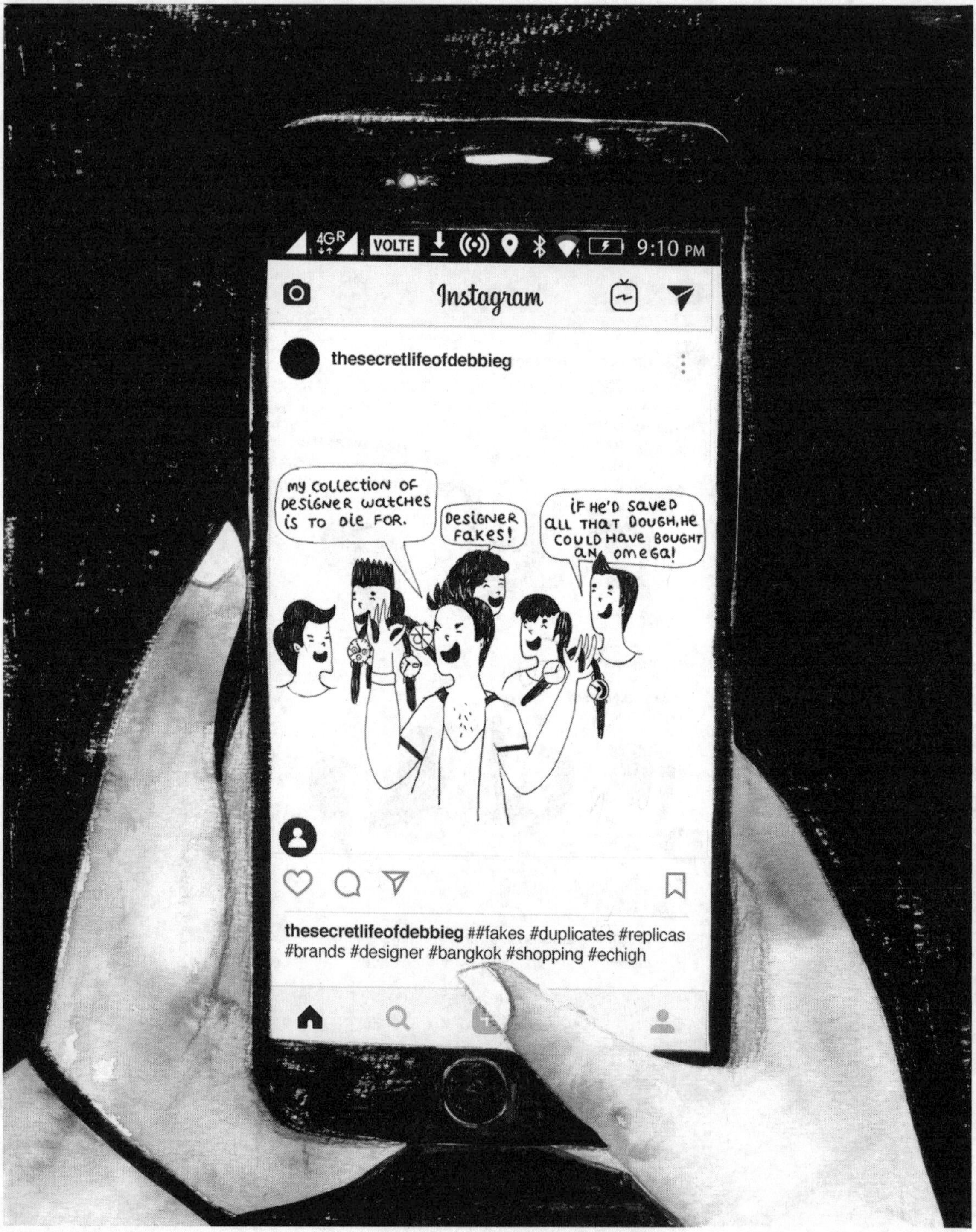
4GR VOLTE 9:10 PM
Instagram
thesecretlifeofdebbieg
MY COLLECTION OF DESIGNER WATCHES IS TO DIE FOR.
DESIGNER FAKES!
IF HE'D SAVED ALL THAT DOUGH, HE COULD HAVE BOUGHT AN OMEGA!
thesecretlifeofdebbieg ##fakes #duplicates #replicas #brands #designer #bangkok #shopping #echigh

You know, initially, I was worried, I'd get caught. Someone would figure it out, someone would out me. But I quickly realised that no one cared who was dishing out the dirt. So long as they got their quota of goss, they were totally fine. And suddenly, it started making sense. The breaking news culture. The need for instant gratification. The sense of schadenfreude. I started feeling invincible. Guilty? Yeah, maybe a little. But I convinced myself that I was doing a social service. Kinda like Robin Hood. You know, robbing the high and mighty of their pride and giving the hoi polloi something to laugh about. All through I was very, very careful. I mean, it had the potensch to blow up in my face. I had to watch out against minefields like posting the comic strips from my real IG ID, linking the fake account to my real accounts and such. Mercifully, no one suspected it was me. Though someone did come pretty close...

How was Day One at the football club?

It was all right, I guess.

Got a ride back home easily?

Yeah. Do you know Snehesh...in XII B...he dropped us back.

Someone's happily ditched their old carpooler pals, I see.

It's just once a week.

So major bonding with your new buds, huh?

Hardly. They kept talking about the scandal strip the whole time... Wonder who this Debbie G person is. An XI Grader? A senior?

If this were a slasher movie, I'd be coming over to your place, right now.

No clue. But obvs, it's one of the Invincibles. I mean, who else would have access to that kind of info?

Yeah, yeah. Unless...

There's no unless, dude.

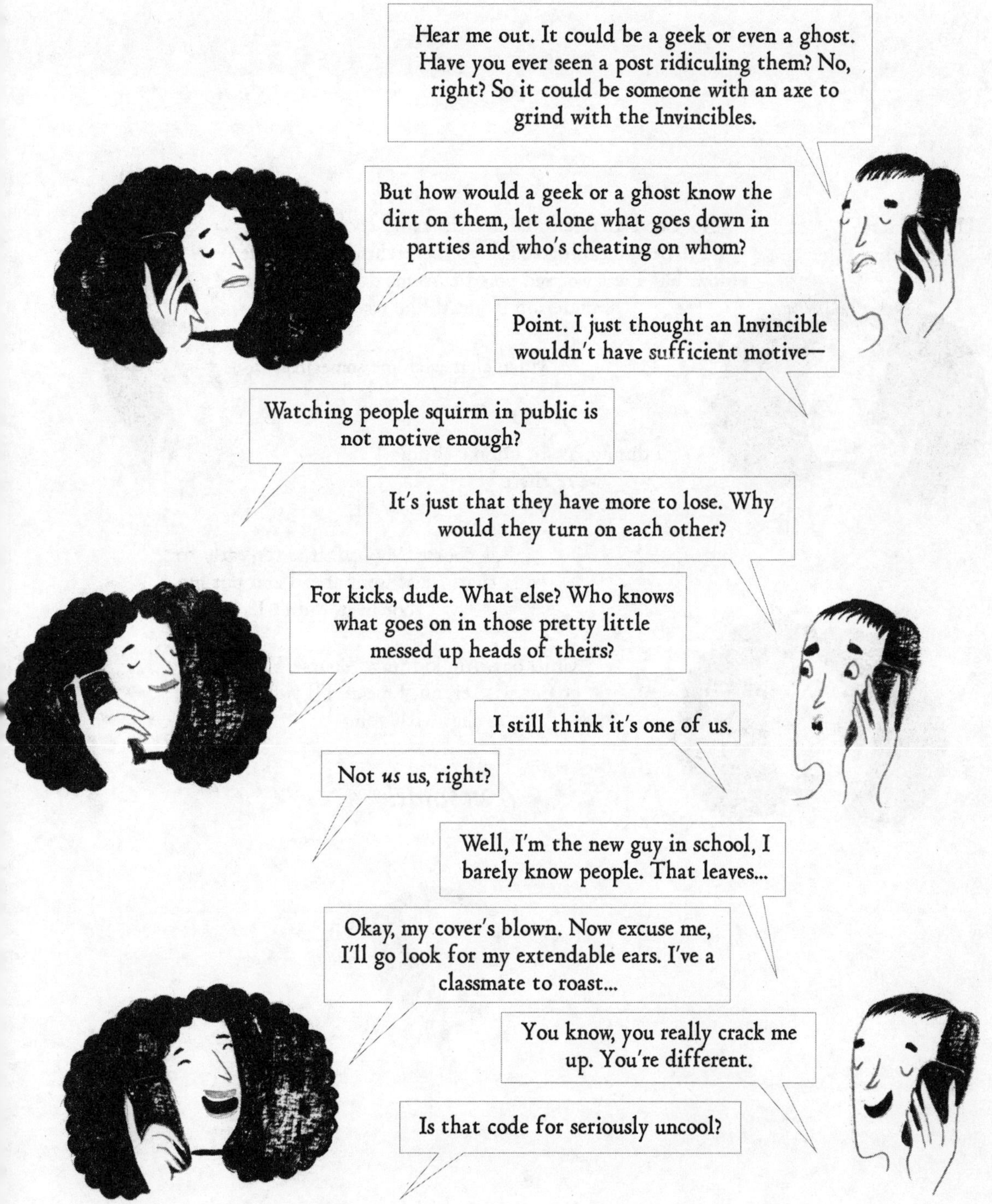
Hear me out. It could be a geek or even a ghost. Have you ever seen a post ridiculing them? No, right? So it could be someone with an axe to grind with the Invincibles.
But how would a geek or a ghost know the dirt on them, let alone what goes down in parties and who's cheating on whom?
Point. I just thought an Invincible wouldn't have sufficient motive—
Watching people squirm in public is not motive enough?
It's just that they have more to lose. Why would they turn on each other?
For kicks, dude. What else? Who knows what goes on in those pretty little messed up heads of theirs?
I still think it's one of us.
Not *us* us, right?
Well, I'm the new guy in school, I barely know people. That leaves...
Okay, my cover's blown. Now excuse me, I'll go look for my extendable ears. I've a classmate to roast...
You know, you really crack me up. You're different.
Is that code for seriously uncool?

Uh oh. Here it comes.

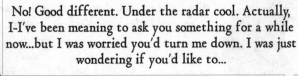

No! Good different. Under the radar cool. Actually, I-I've been meaning to ask you something for a while now...but I was worried you'd turn me down. I was just wondering if you'd like to...

...video chat with me sometime?

I dunno, Yash. I don't think we're there yet.

Of course. My bad. It is too early for that. I just went ahead and put my foot in it, didn't I?

Chill out. Am kidding. 'Course, I'll go out wit...er, uh, I mean, I'll video chat with you.

Awesome!

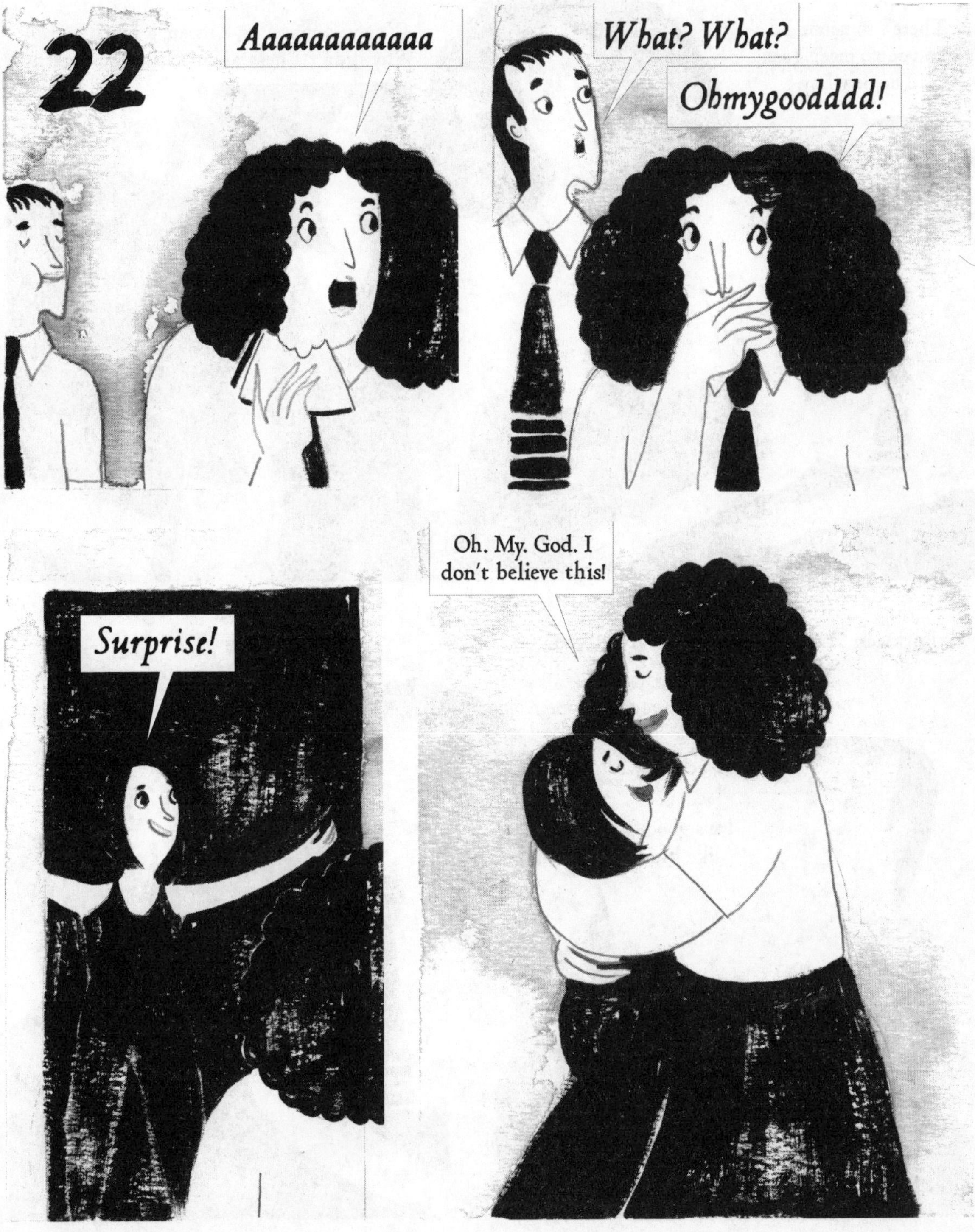
22
Aaaaaaaaaaa
What? What?
Ohmygoodddd!
Surprise!
Oh. My. God. I
don't believe this!

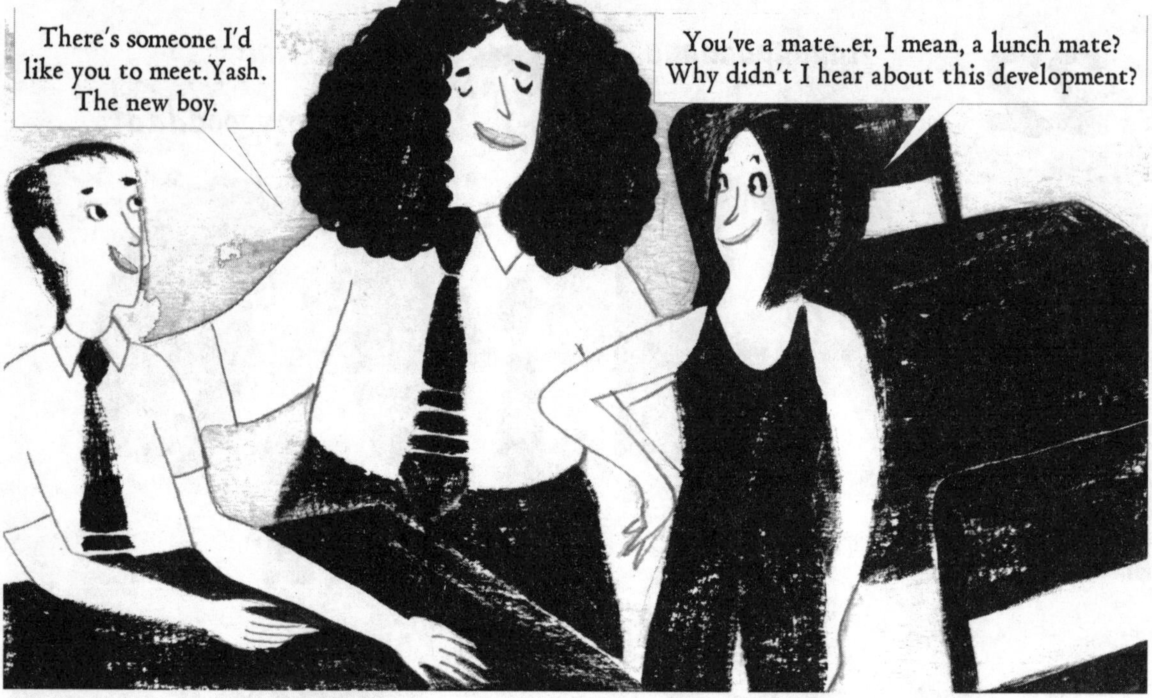
There's someone I'd like you to meet. Yash. The new boy.
You've a mate...er, I mean, a lunch mate? Why didn't I hear about this development?

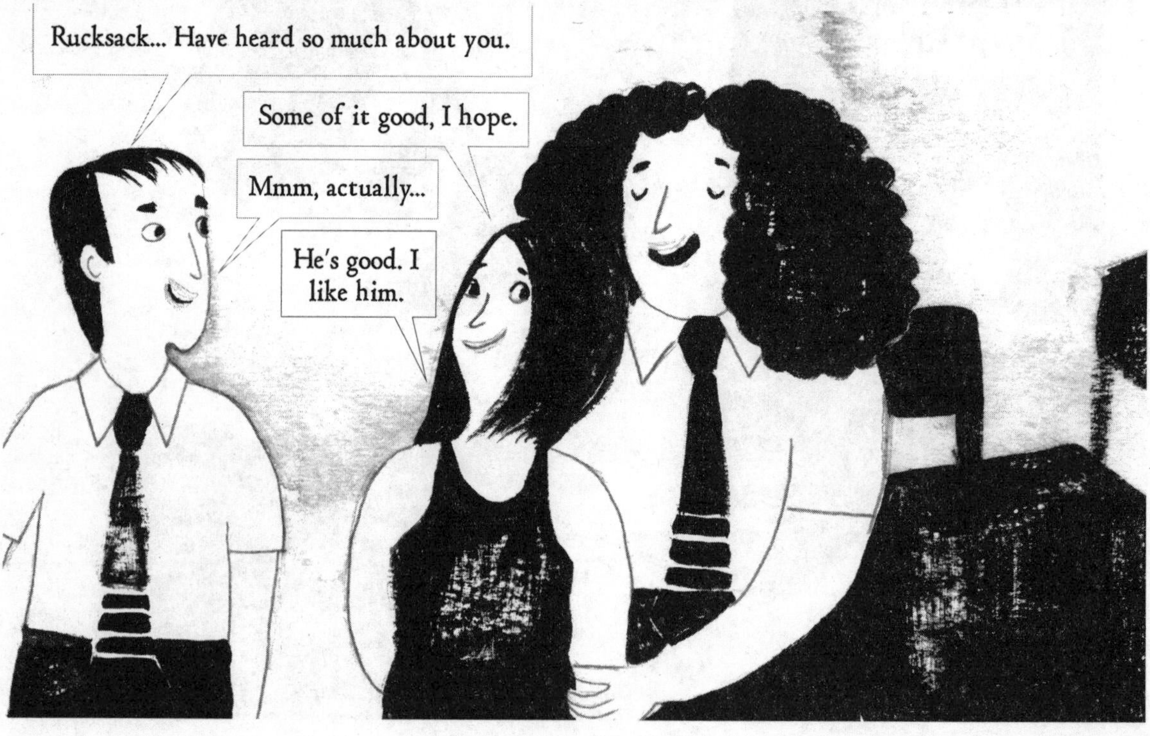
Rucksack... Have heard so much about you.
Some of it good, I hope.
Mmm, actually...
He's good. I like him.

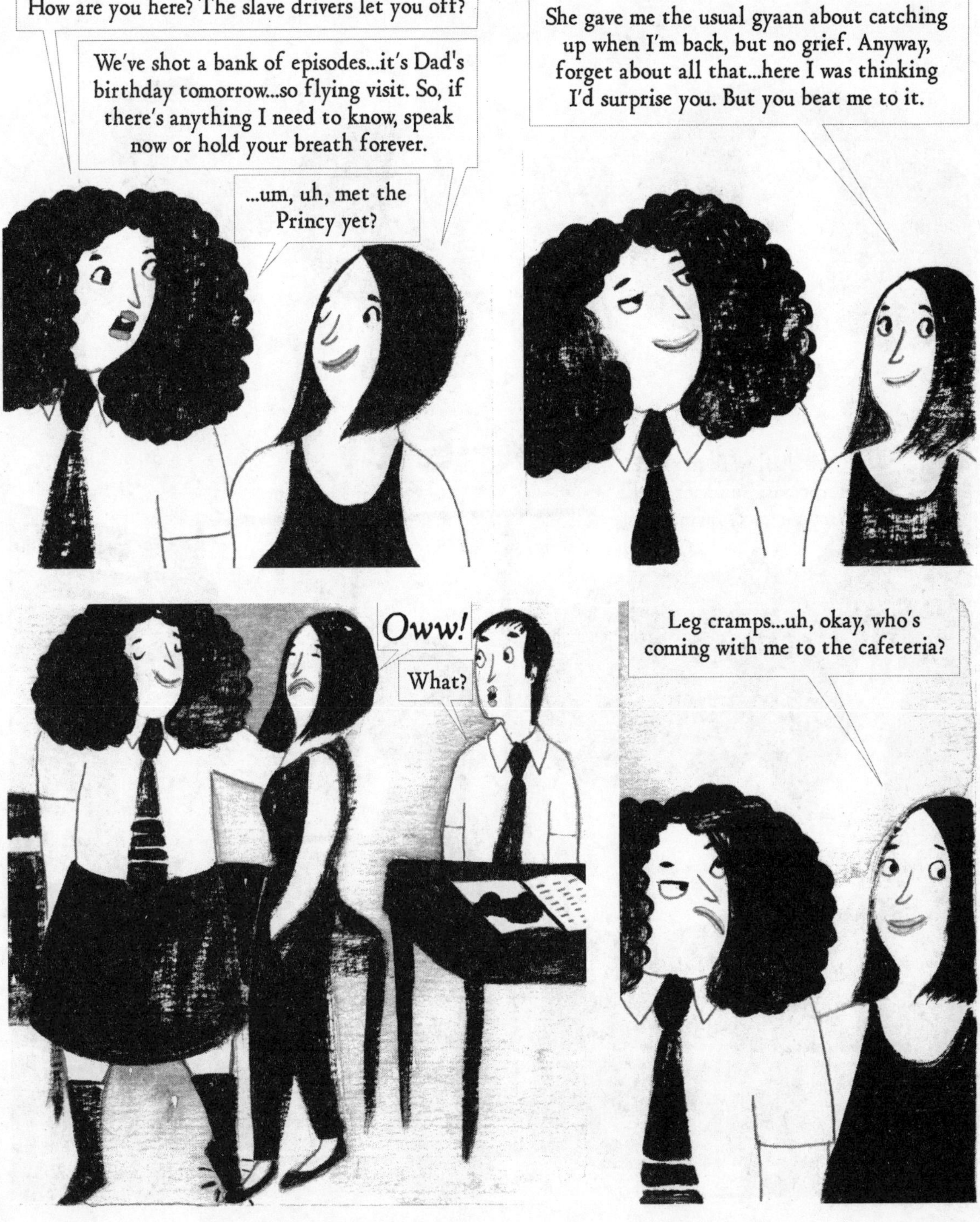
How are you here? The slave drivers let you off?
We've shot a bank of episodes...it's Dad's birthday tomorrow...so flying visit. So, if there's anything I need to know, speak now or hold your breath forever.
...um, uh, met the Princy yet?
She gave me the usual gyaan about catching up when I'm back, but no grief. Anyway, forget about all that...here I was thinking I'd surprise you. But you beat me to it.
Oww!
What?
Leg cramps...uh, okay, who's coming with me to the cafeteria?

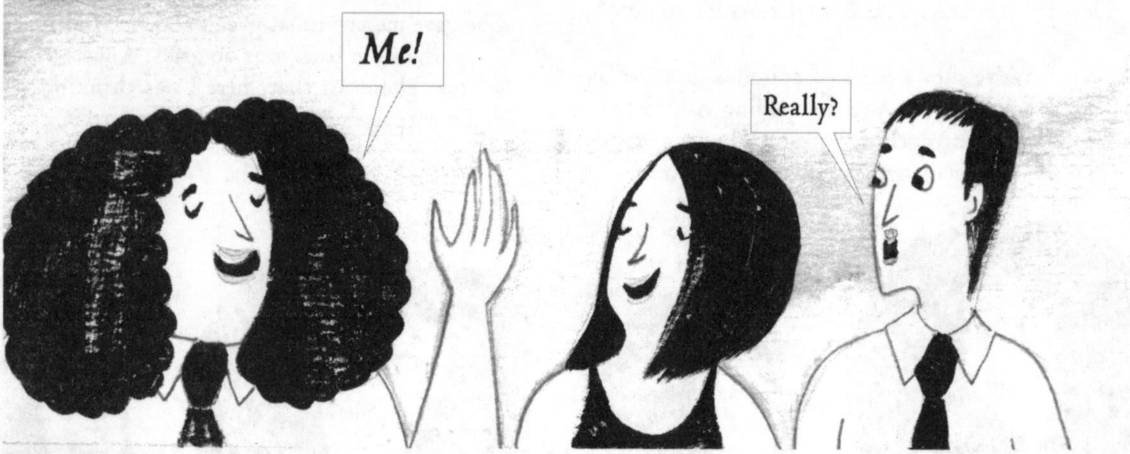
Me!
Really?

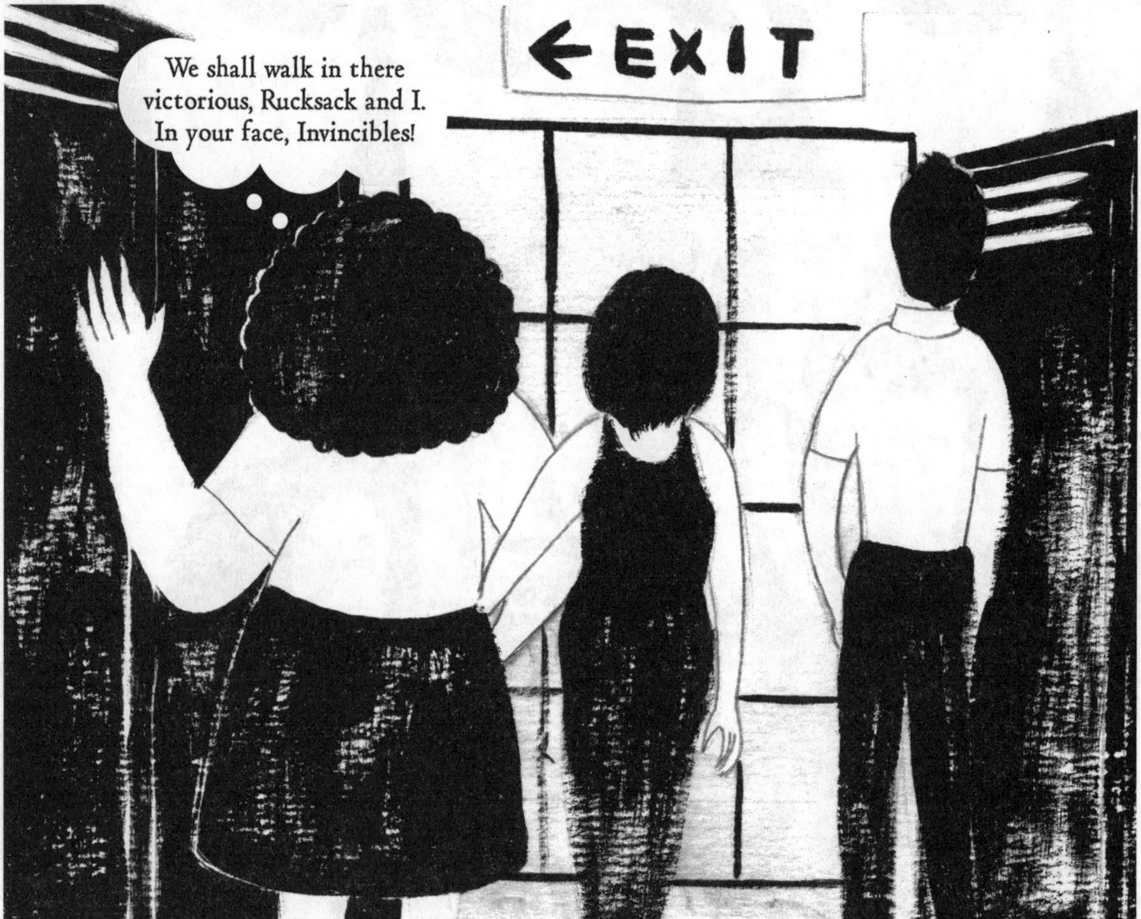
EXIT
We shall walk in there victorious, Rucksack and I. In your face, Invincibles!

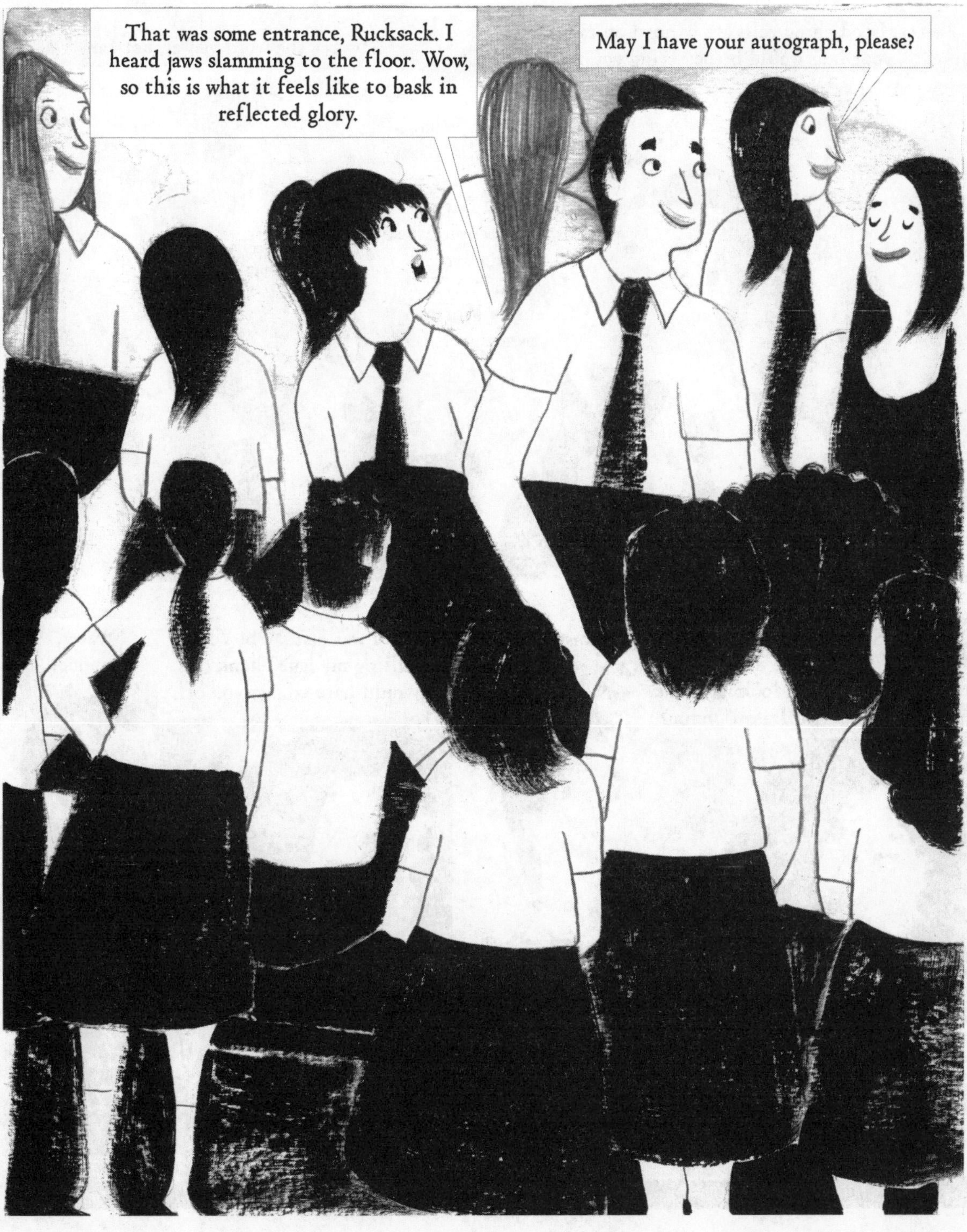
That was some entrance, Rucksack. I heard jaws slamming to the floor. Wow, so this is what it feels like to bask in reflected glory.
May I have your autograph, please?

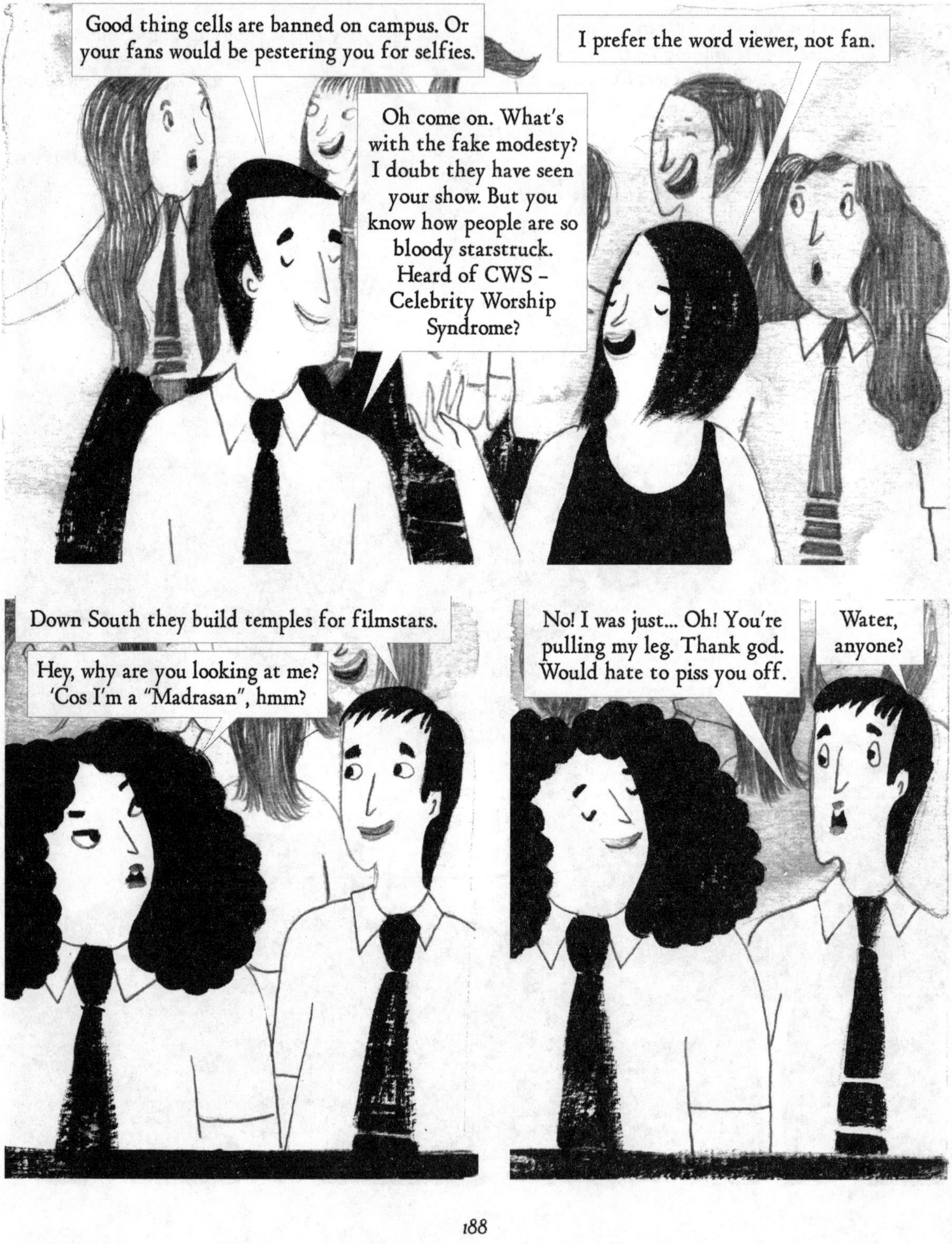
Good thing cells are banned on campus. Or your fans would be pestering you for selfies.
Oh come on. What's with the fake modesty? I doubt they have seen your show. But you know how people are so bloody starstruck. Heard of CWS – Celebrity Worship Syndrome?
I prefer the word viewer, not fan.
Down South they build temples for filmstars.
Hey, why are you looking at me? 'Cos I'm a "Madrasan", hmm?
No! I was just... Oh! You're pulling my leg. Thank god. Would hate to piss you off.
Water, anyone?

Nick, don't even.

What? I didn't say anything.

Nick, are you seeing what I'm seeing?

You mean, the chemistry between these two?

What chemistry? Don't be silly. Gawd, what's wrong with you guys? Grow up.

Oh, so it's a mature relationship.

What, only you and Fatal Attraction are capable of having one?

I thought we were taking Arya's trip.

Ooh. Can't wait to grill you about your GF. Let's catch up for coffee this evening?

I'm in!

You guys know I'm a budding doctor, right?

Get over yourself. You're just going to be a dentist. Not as if you're going to be saving lives.

Could you guys BE more insensitive? Arya, you're much nicer to Yash, but I guess he's your new boyfriend, so—

Shhh, here he comes...behave.

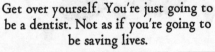

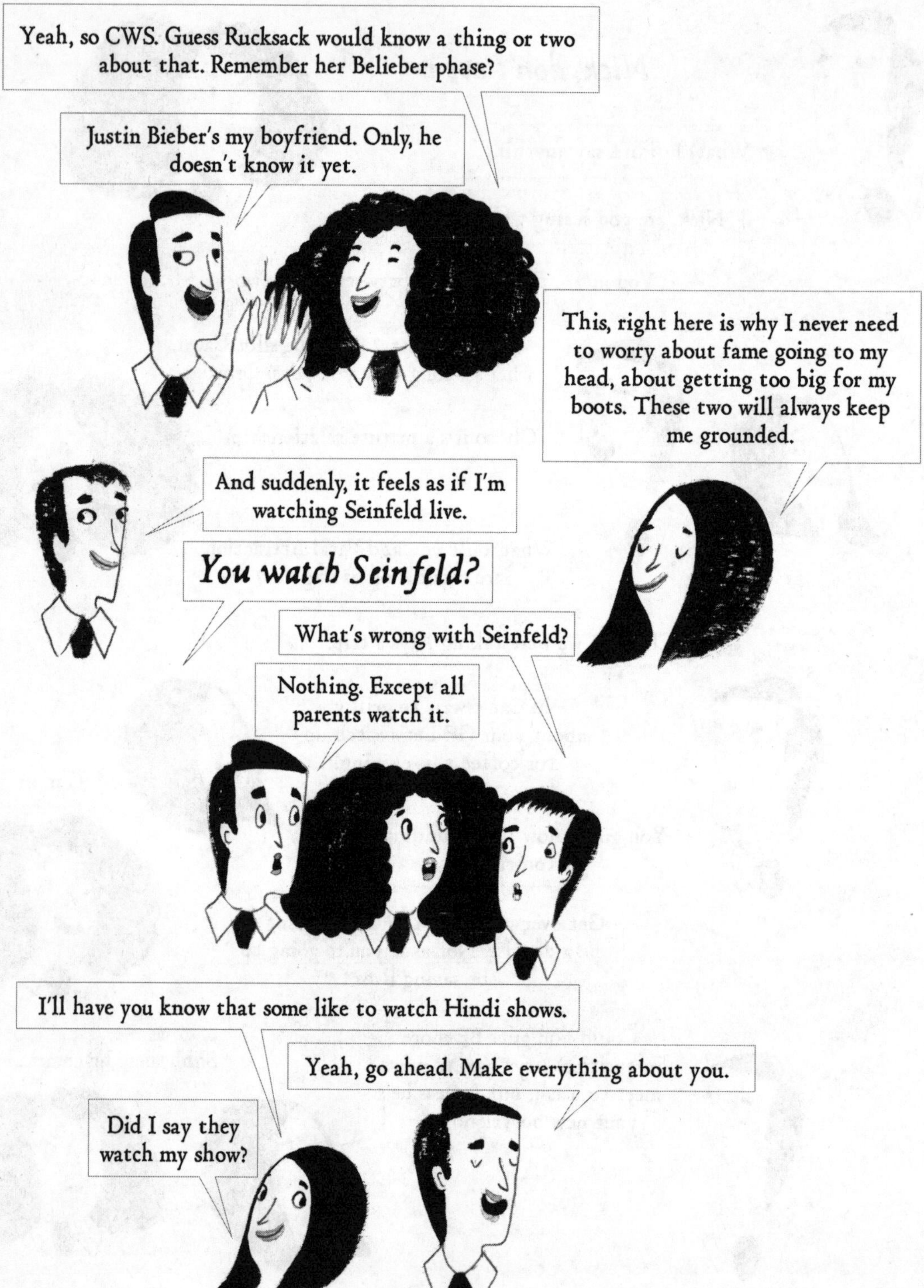
Yeah, so CWS. Guess Rucksack would know a thing or two about that. Remember her Belieber phase?
Justin Bieber's my boyfriend. Only, he doesn't know it yet.
This, right here is why I never need to worry about fame going to my head, about getting too big for my boots. These two will always keep me grounded.
And suddenly, it feels as if I'm watching Seinfeld live.
You watch Seinfeld?
What's wrong with Seinfeld?
Nothing. Except all parents watch it.
I'll have you know that some like to watch Hindi shows.
Yeah, go ahead. Make everything about you.
Did I say they watch my show?

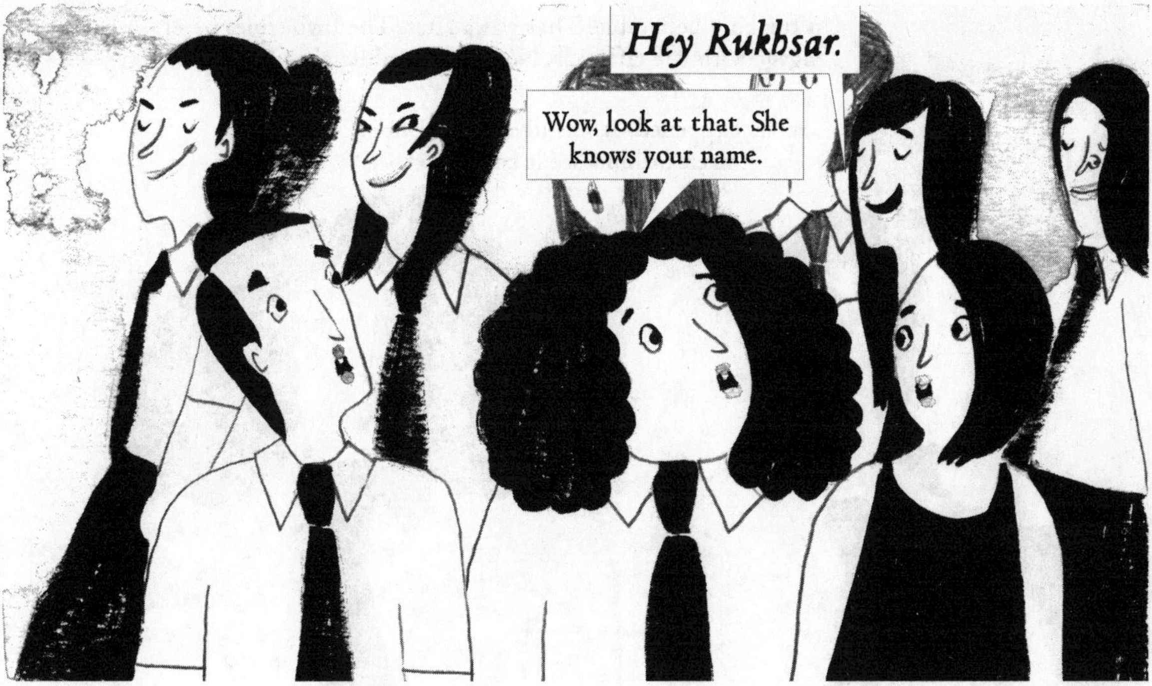
Hey Rukhsar.
Wow, look at that. She knows your name.

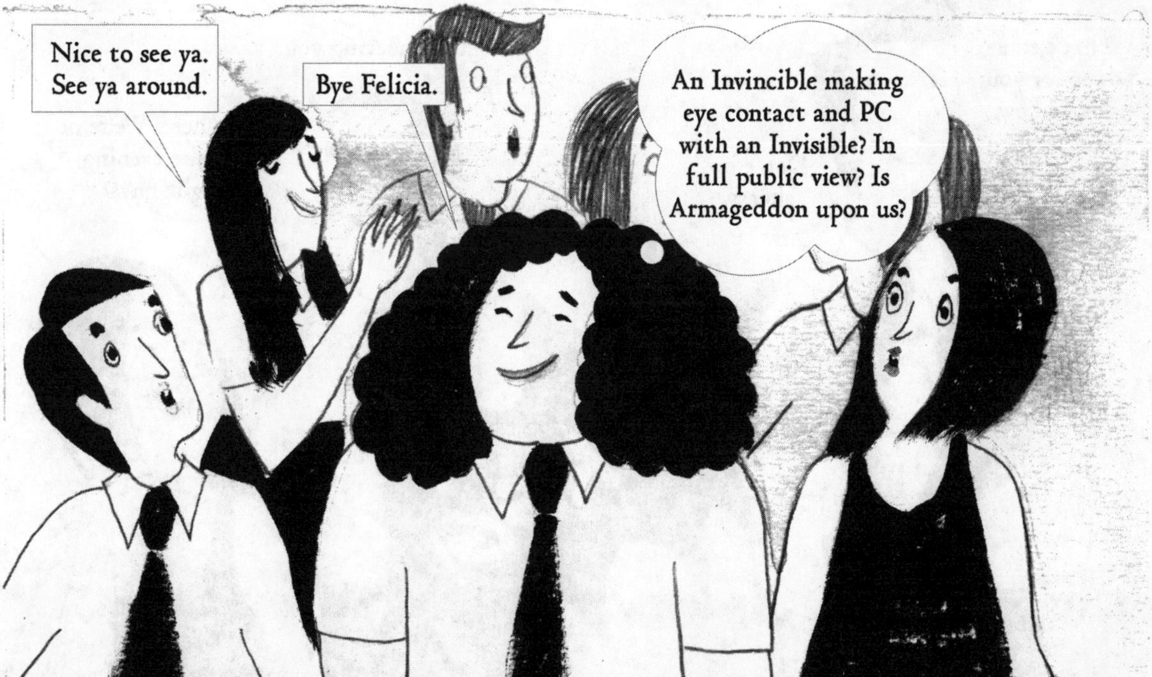
Nice to see ya. See ya around.
Bye Felicia.
An Invincible making eye contact and PC with an Invisible? In full public view? Is Armageddon upon us?

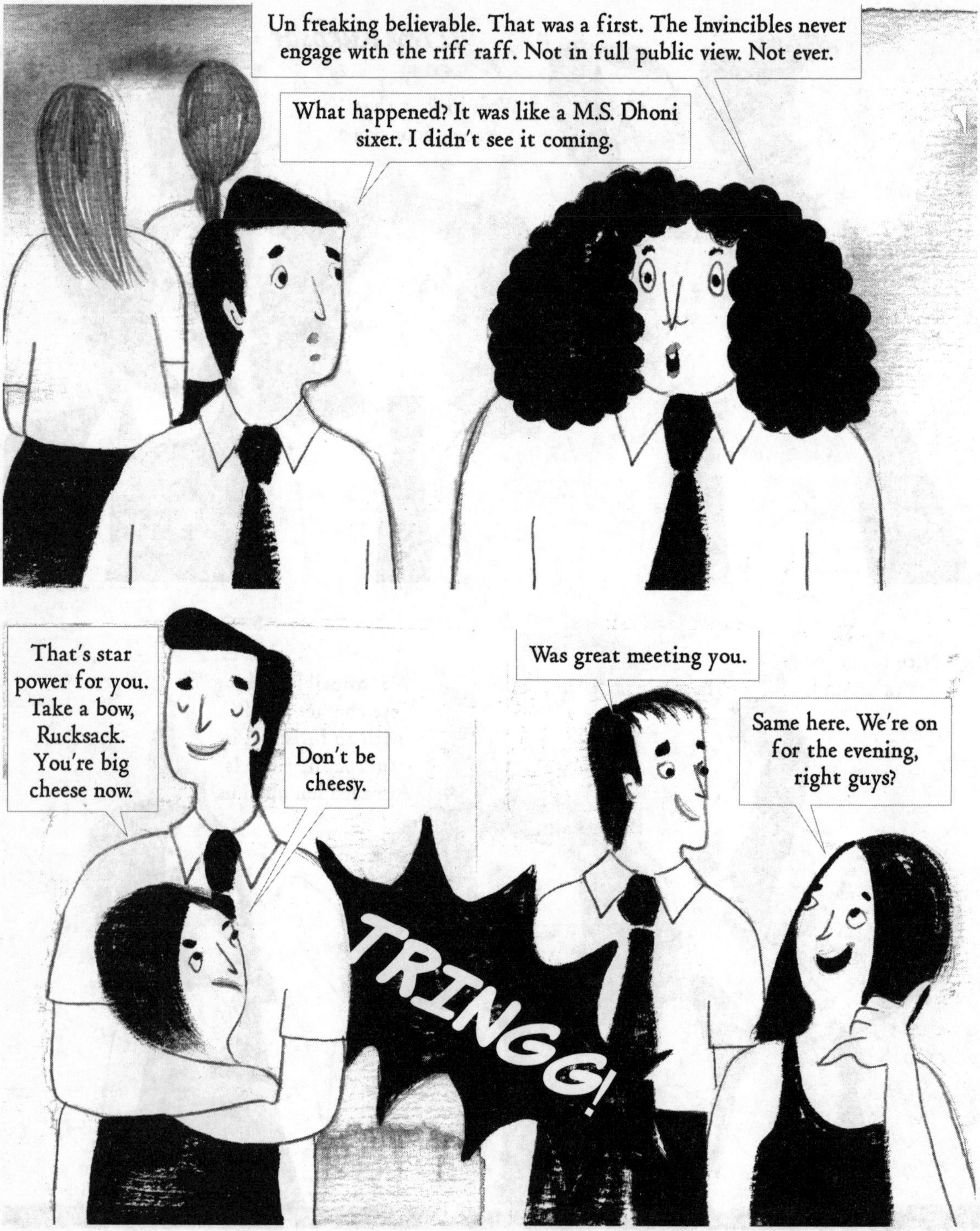

Un freaking believable. That was a first. The Invincibles never engage with the riff raff. Not in full public view. Not ever.
What happened? It was like a M.S. Dhoni sixer. I didn't see it coming.
That's star power for you. Take a bow, Rucksack. You're big cheese now.
Don't be cheesy.
TRINGG!
Was great meeting you.
Same here. We're on for the evening, right guys?

23

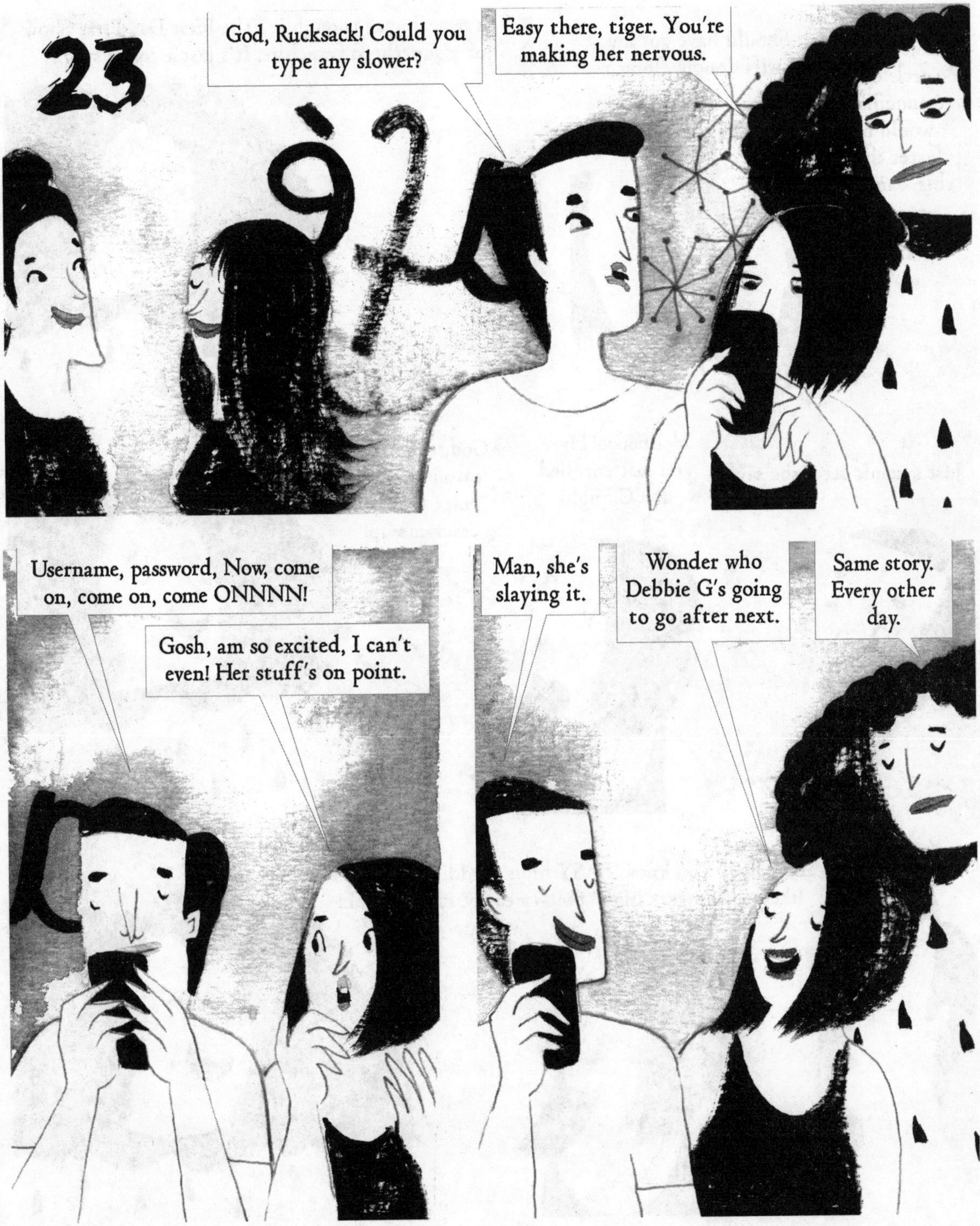
God, Rucksack! Could you type any slower?
Easy there, tiger. You're making her nervous.
Username, password, Now, come on, come on, come ONNNN!
Gosh, am so excited, I can't even! Her stuff's on point.
Man, she's slaying it.
Wonder who Debbie G's going to go after next.
Same story. Every other day.

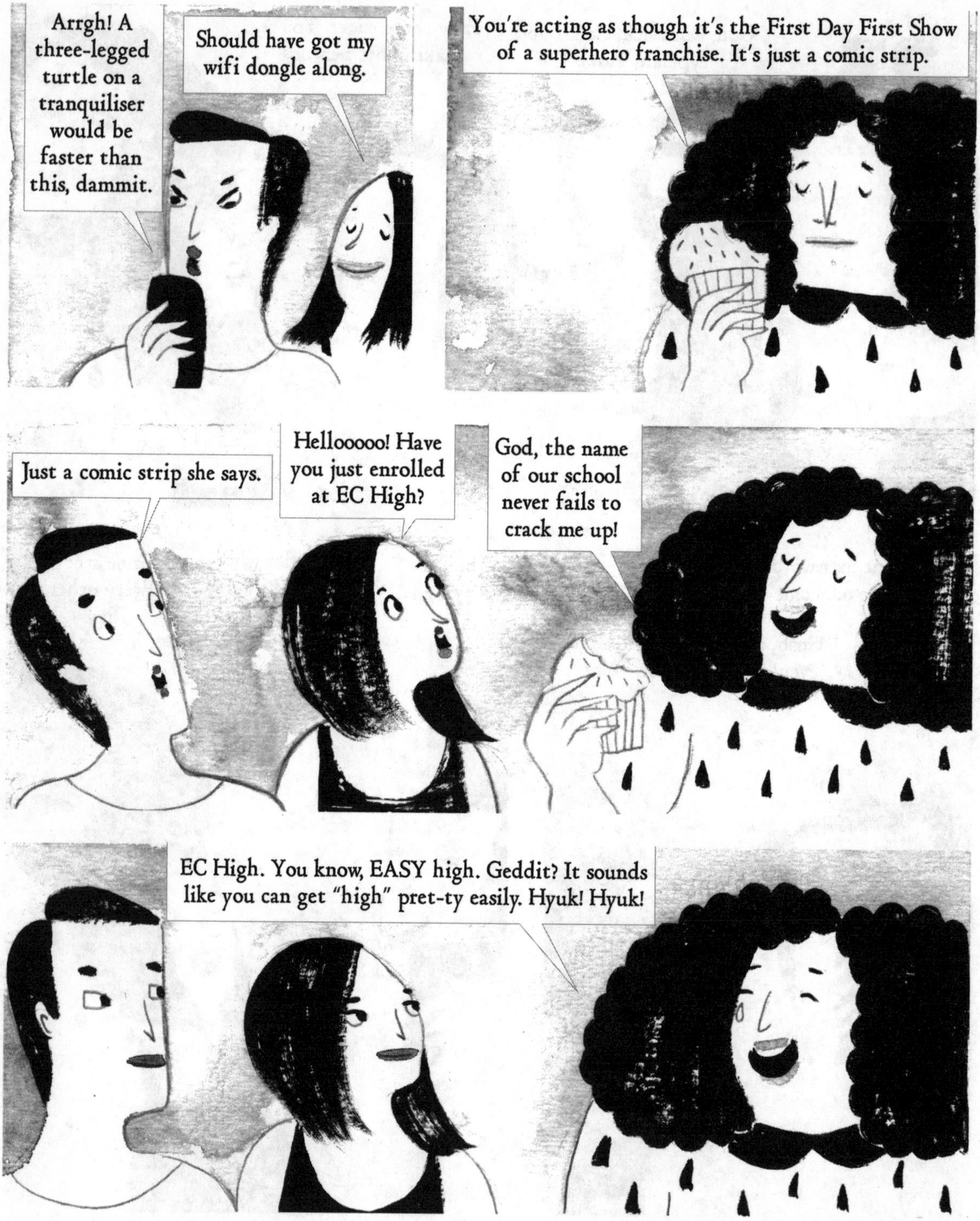
Arrgh! A three-legged turtle on a tranquiliser would be faster than this, dammit.
Should have got my wifi dongle along.
You're acting as though it's the First Day First Show of a superhero franchise. It's just a comic strip.
Just a comic strip she says.
Hellooooo! Have you just enrolled at EC High?
God, the name of our school never fails to crack me up!
EC High. You know, EASY high. Geddit? It sounds like you can get "high" pret-ty easily. Hyuk! Hyuk!

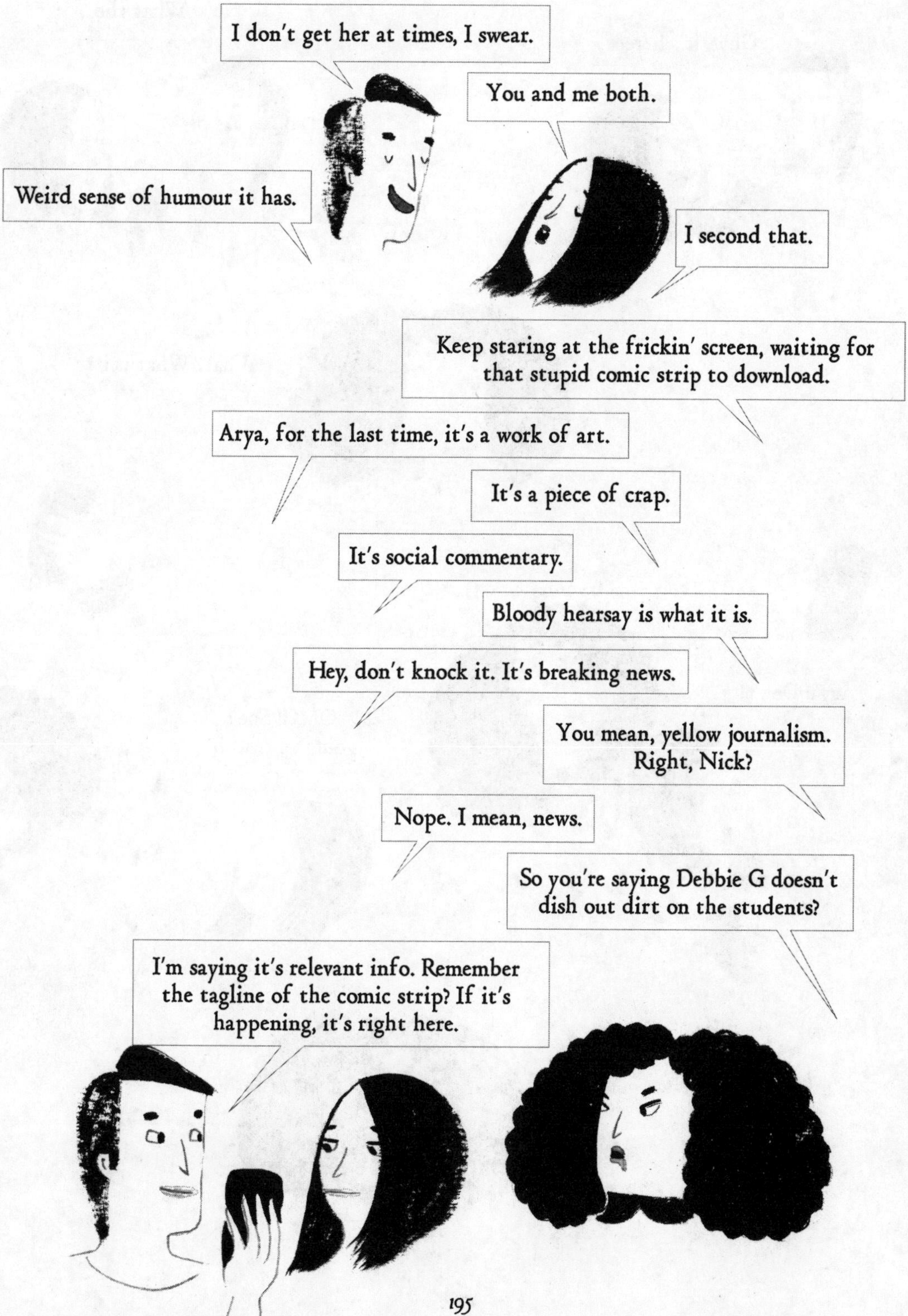
I don't get her at times, I swear.
You and me both.
Weird sense of humour it has.
I second that.
Keep staring at the frickin' screen, waiting for that stupid comic strip to download.
Arya, for the last time, it's a work of art.
It's a piece of crap.
It's social commentary.
Bloody hearsay is what it is.
Hey, don't knock it. It's breaking news.
You mean, yellow journalism. Right, Nick?
Nope. I mean, news.
So you're saying Debbie G doesn't dish out dirt on the students?
I'm saying it's relevant info. Remember the tagline of the comic strip? If it's happening, it's right here.

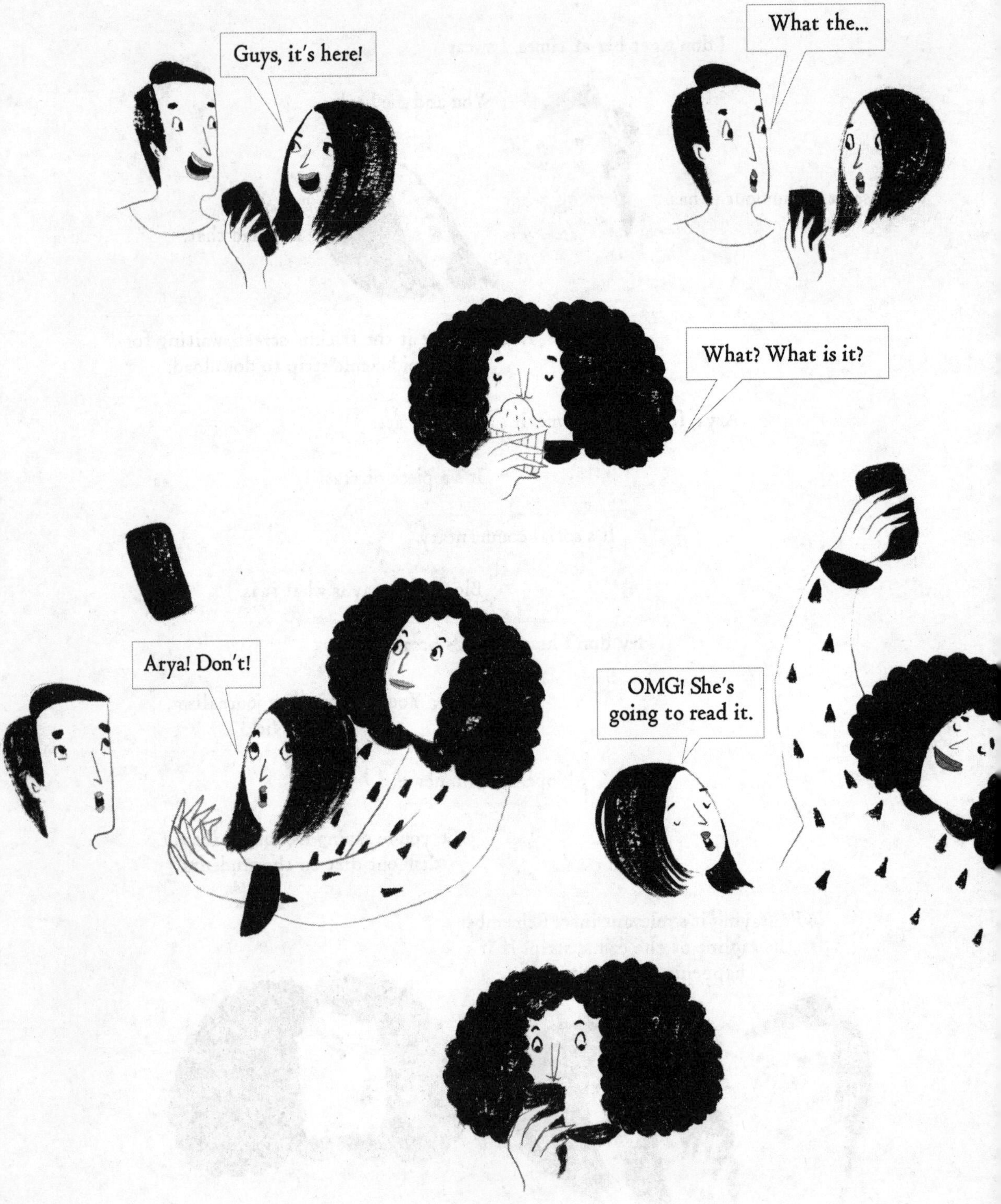

Guys, it's here!
What the...
What? What is it?
Arya! Don't!
OMG! She's going to read it.

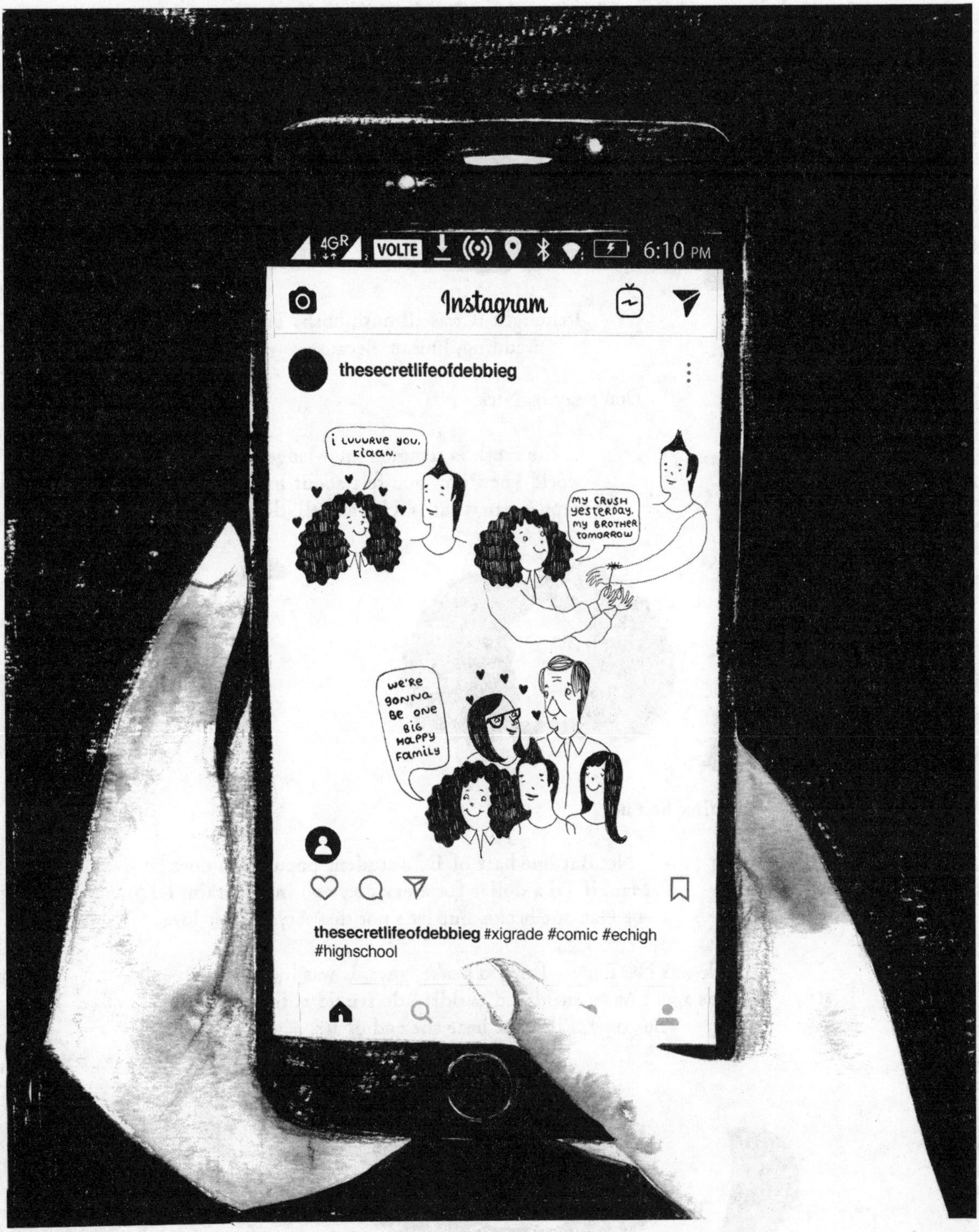
4G VOLTE 6:10 PM
Instagram
thesecretlifeofdebbieg
i luuurve you, kiaan.
my crush yesterday, my brother tomorrow
we're gonna be one big happy family
thesecretlifeofdebbieg #xigrade #comic #echigh #highschool

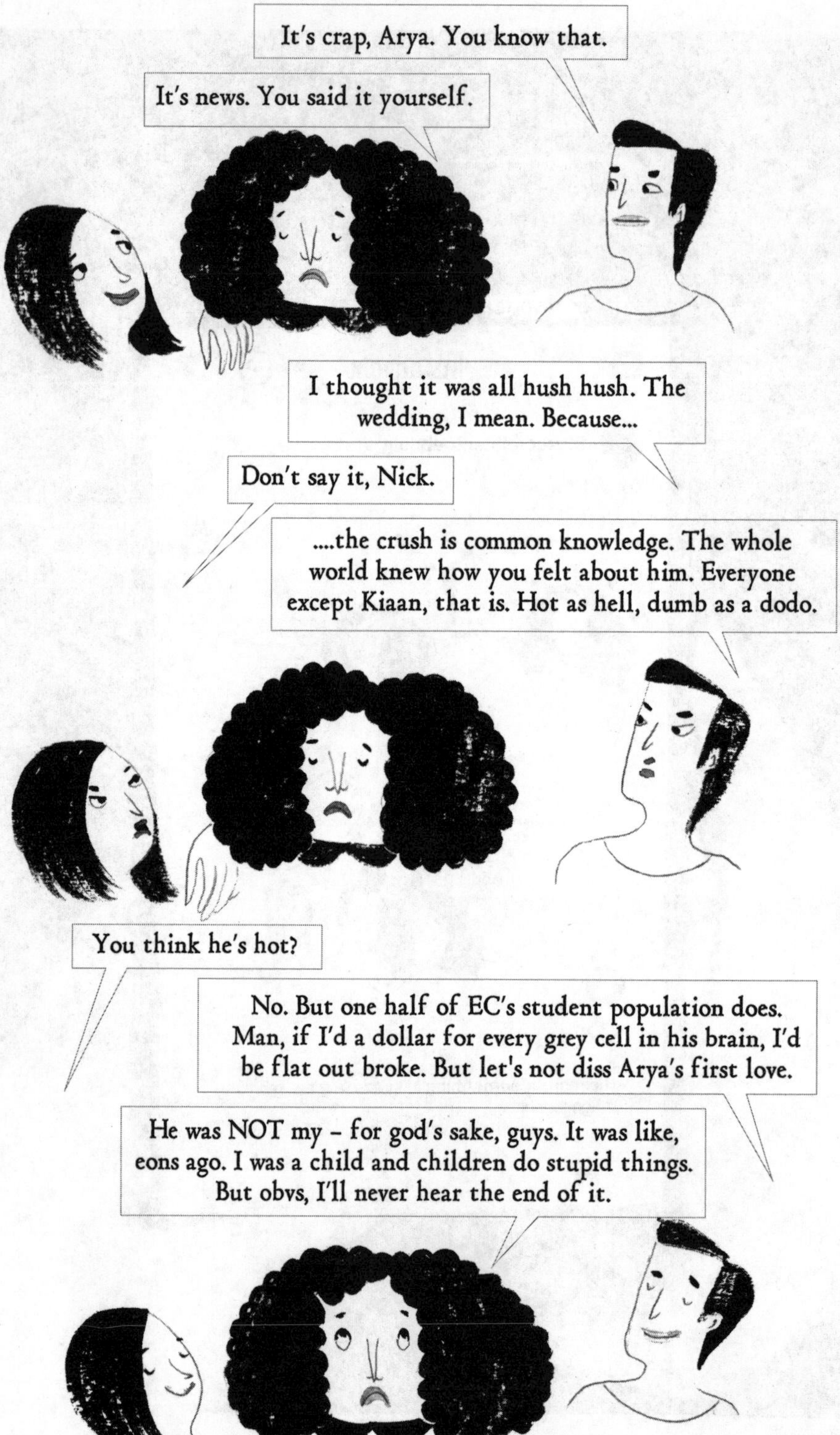
It's crap, Arya. You know that.
It's news. You said it yourself.
I thought it was all hush hush. The wedding, I mean. Because...
Don't say it, Nick.
....the crush is common knowledge. The whole world knew how you felt about him. Everyone except Kiaan, that is. Hot as hell, dumb as a dodo.
You think he's hot?
No. But one half of EC's student population does. Man, if I'd a dollar for every grey cell in his brain, I'd be flat out broke. But let's not diss Arya's first love.
He was NOT my – for god's sake, guys. It was like, eons ago. I was a child and children do stupid things. But obvs, I'll never hear the end of it.

I bet Kiaan's the source of the leak. He must have blabbed to someone in his group. The dingbat has trouble keeping his trap shut.

I wouldn't put it past Kiara either. That girl likes to yak and yak and yak.

They know better than that, guys. Mom and Tarun Uncle have made it very clear. They want to keep things low key. They don't want to end up inviting the whole bloody town.

I don't get it. How? How the hell did Debbie G find out?

She knows everything, don't you know that? Girls like to gossip.

Are you listening to yourself? Ever heard of harmful gender stereotypes? Bah! I mean, our pal Nick here gossips more than any girl we know. Mirror mirror on the wall, who's the bitchiest of 'em all? Nickster. Nickster.

I'm just thinking aloud. Wait, maybe, it's something like Alexa. Amazon's virtual assistant? Apparently, they chose a female voice 'cos it's easy on the ears and—

And some people prefer ordering females around.

Or maybe Debbie is someone's nickname. Do we have any Debyanis/Debens/Debus/ Debashrees in Grade XI/XII?

Who cares. Who takes this bullshit seriously anyway?

Um. Only everyone at EC High.

Forget it, dude.

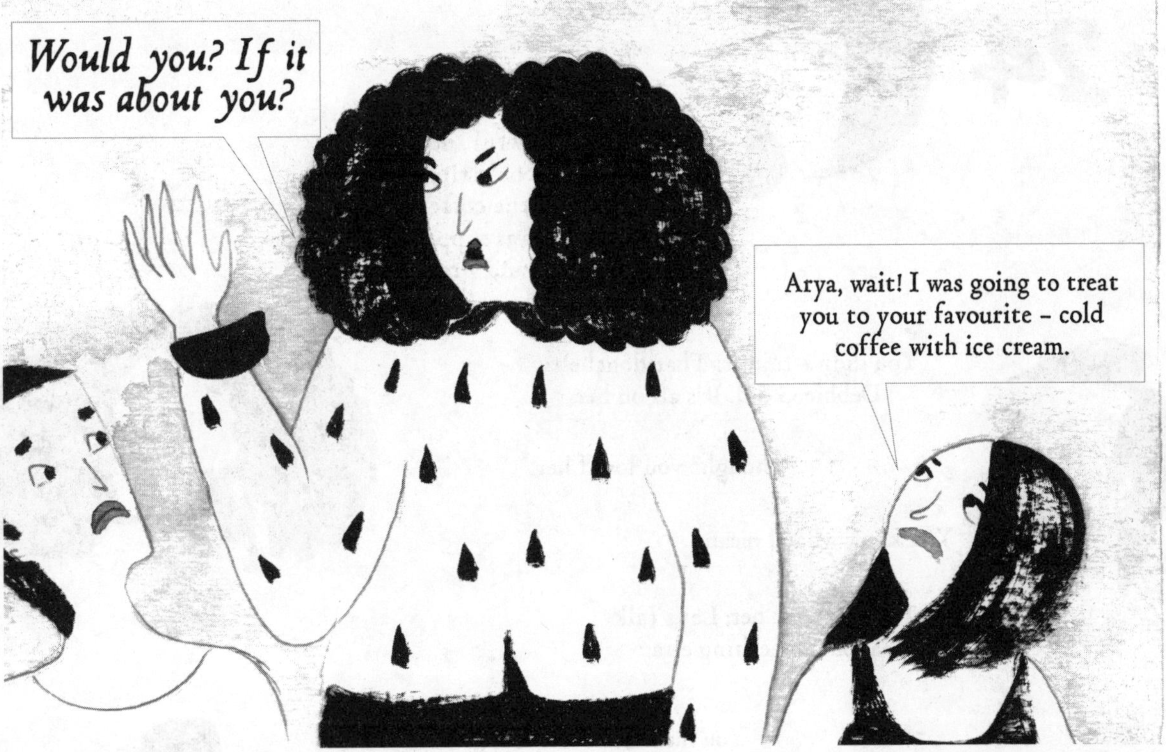
Would you? If it was about you?
Arya, wait! I was going to treat you to your favourite - cold coffee with ice cream.

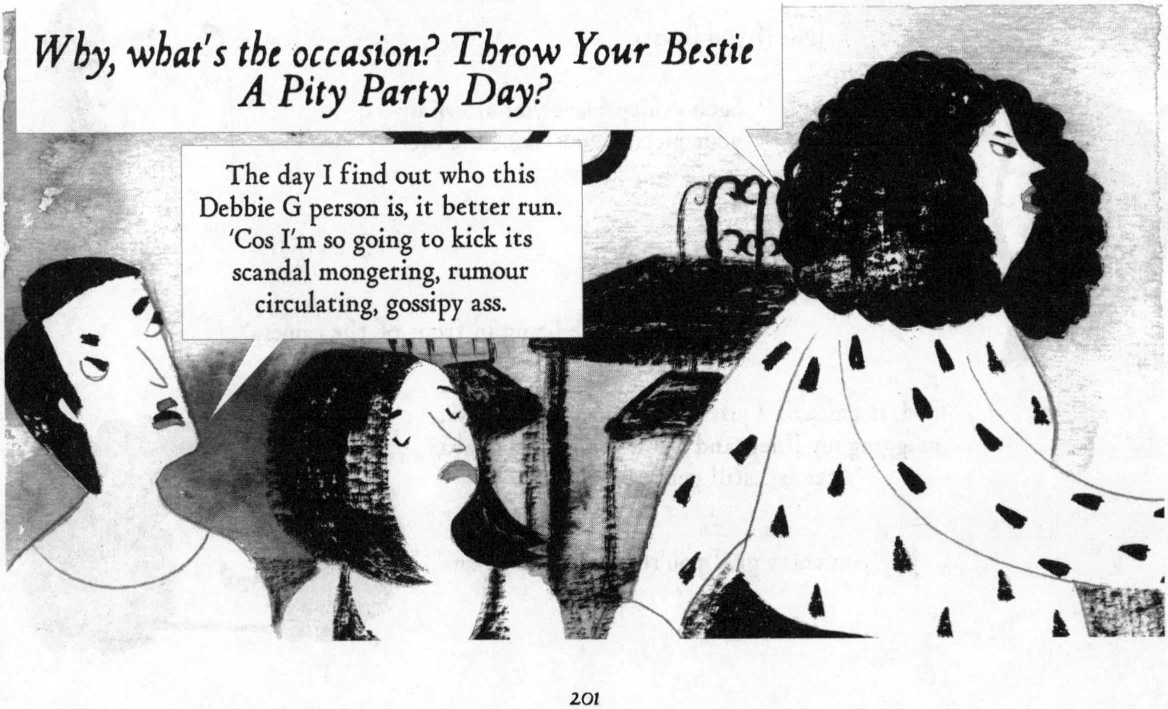
Why, what's the occasion? Throw Your Bestie A Pity Party Day?
The day I find out who this Debbie G person is, it better run. 'Cos I'm so going to kick its scandal mongering, rumour circulating, gossipy ass.

24

Hey, you okay?

Am feeling awful...nope, not about the cartoon strip, about my outburst at the coffee shop. Sorry, guys. It was supposed to be our reunion and I ruined it.

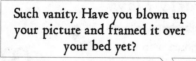

You didn't ruin it. That douchebag Debbie G did. It's all on her.

I thought you loved her.

You know what I mean.

Forget about her. Let's talk about something else.

You mean let's talk about you.

OK, if you insist.

Such vanity. Have you blown up your picture and framed it over your bed yet?

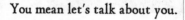

I'm thinking about it.

So. What's it like being in front of the camera?

God, it's amaze. I just luuurve being on the set, mugging my lines...and when the director says, "Action"...still get goosebumps...

Am crazy glad you're living your dream.

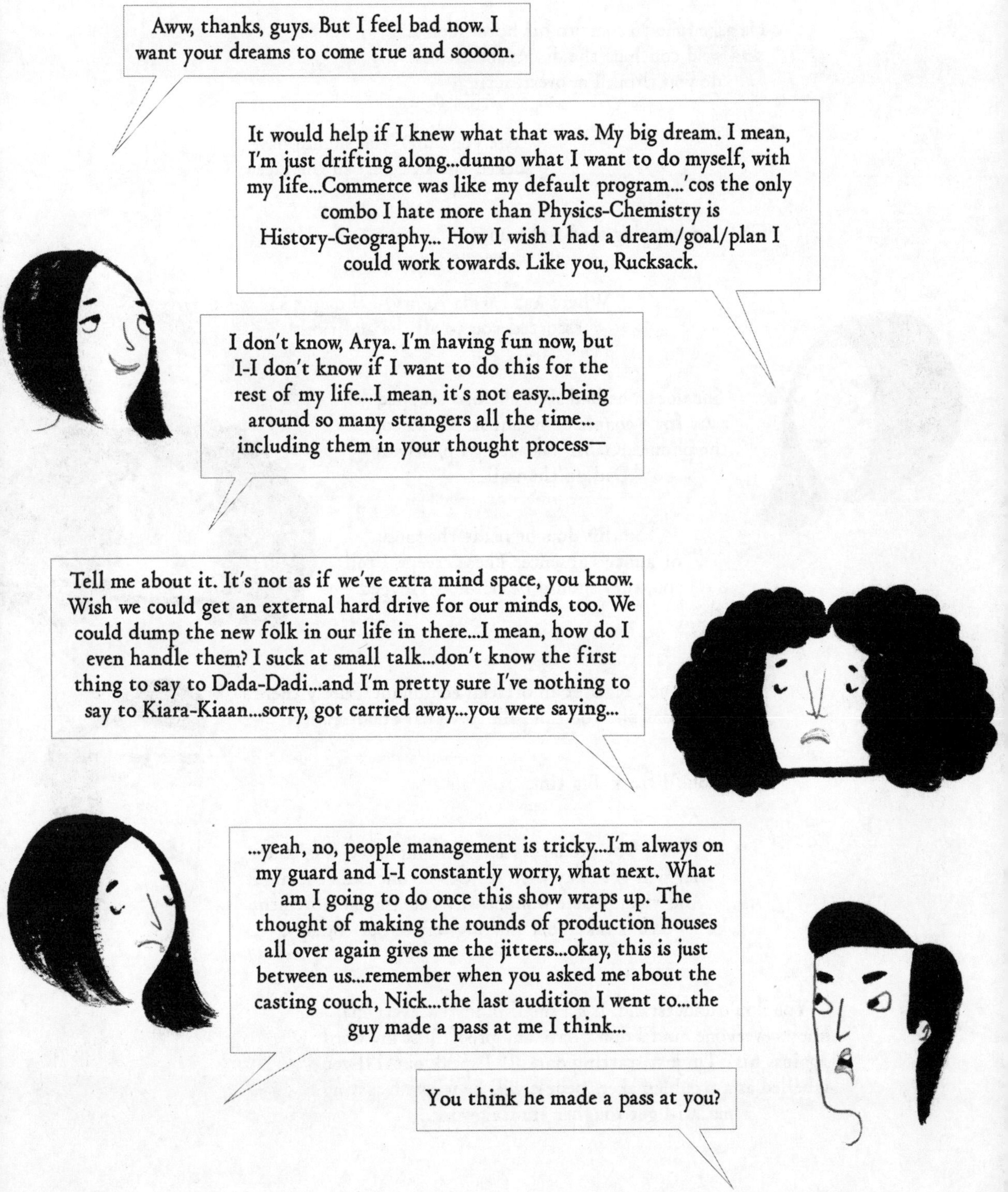
Aww, thanks, guys. But I feel bad now. I want your dreams to come true and soooon.
It would help if I knew what that was. My big dream. I mean, I'm just drifting along...dunno what I want to do myself, with my life...Commerce was like my default program...'cos the only combo I hate more than Physics-Chemistry is History-Geography... How I wish I had a dream/goal/plan I could work towards. Like you, Rucksack.
I don't know, Arya. I'm having fun now, but I-I don't know if I want to do this for the rest of my life...I mean, it's not easy...being around so many strangers all the time... including them in your thought process—
Tell me about it. It's not as if we've extra mind space, you know. Wish we could get an external hard drive for our minds, too. We could dump the new folk in our life in there...I mean, how do I even handle them? I suck at small talk...don't know the first thing to say to Dada-Dadi...and I'm pretty sure I've nothing to say to Kiara-Kiaan...sorry, got carried away...you were saying...
...yeah, no, people management is tricky...I'm always on my guard and I-I constantly worry, what next. What am I going to do once this show wraps up. The thought of making the rounds of production houses all over again gives me the jitters...okay, this is just between us...remember when you asked me about the casting couch, Nick...the last audition I went to...the guy made a pass at me I think...
You think he made a pass at you?

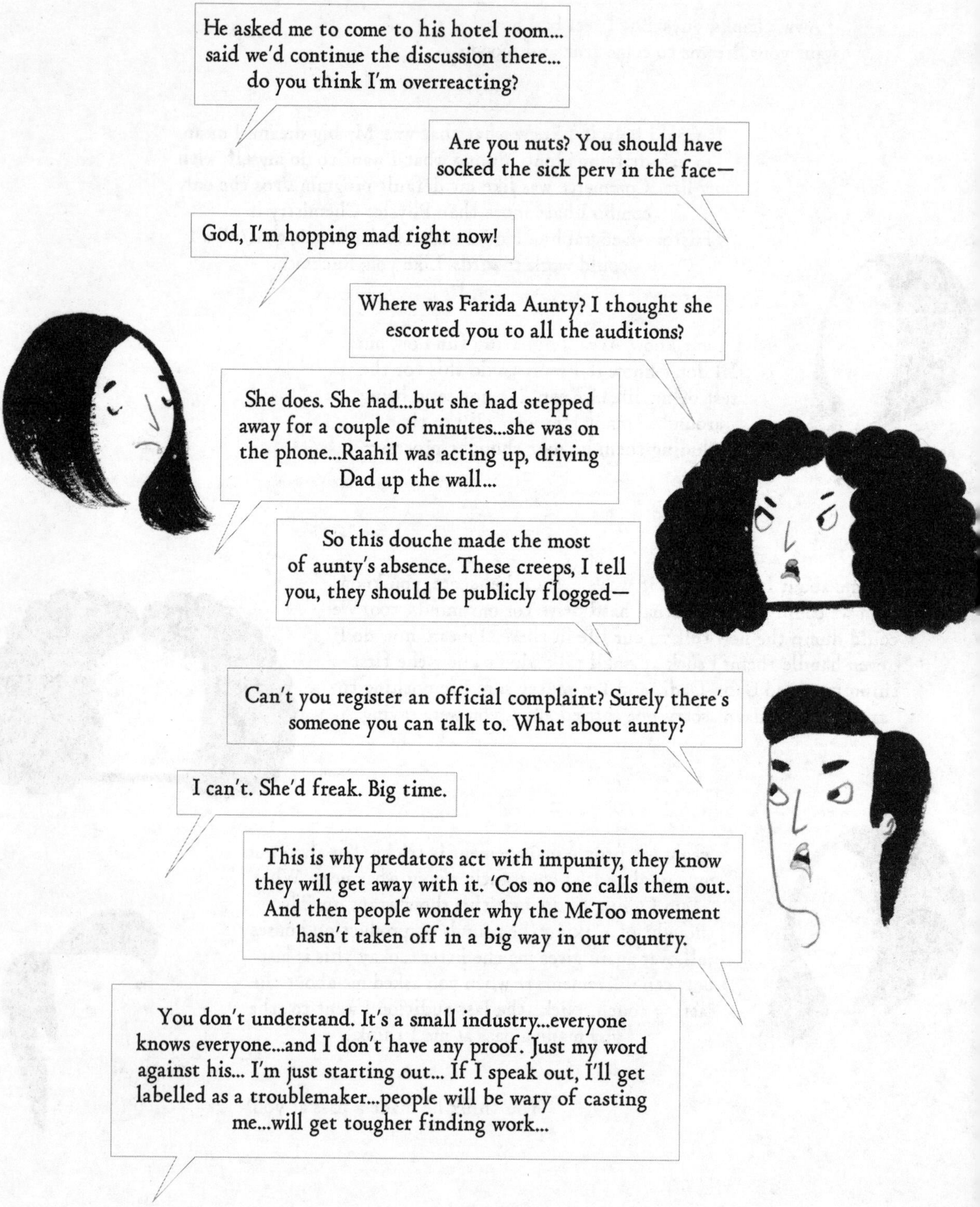
He asked me to come to his hotel room... said we'd continue the discussion there... do you think I'm overreacting?
Are you nuts? You should have socked the sick perv in the face—
God, I'm hopping mad right now!
Where was Farida Aunty? I thought she escorted you to all the auditions?
She does. She had...but she had stepped away for a couple of minutes...she was on the phone...Raahil was acting up, driving Dad up the wall...
So this douche made the most of aunty's absence. These creeps, I tell you, they should be publicly flogged—
Can't you register an official complaint? Surely there's someone you can talk to. What about aunty?
I can't. She'd freak. Big time.
This is why predators act with impunity, they know they will get away with it. 'Cos no one calls them out. And then people wonder why the MeToo movement hasn't taken off in a big way in our country.
You don't understand. It's a small industry...everyone knows everyone...and I don't have any proof. Just my word against his... I'm just starting out... If I speak out, I'll get labelled as a troublemaker...people will be wary of casting me...will get tougher finding work...

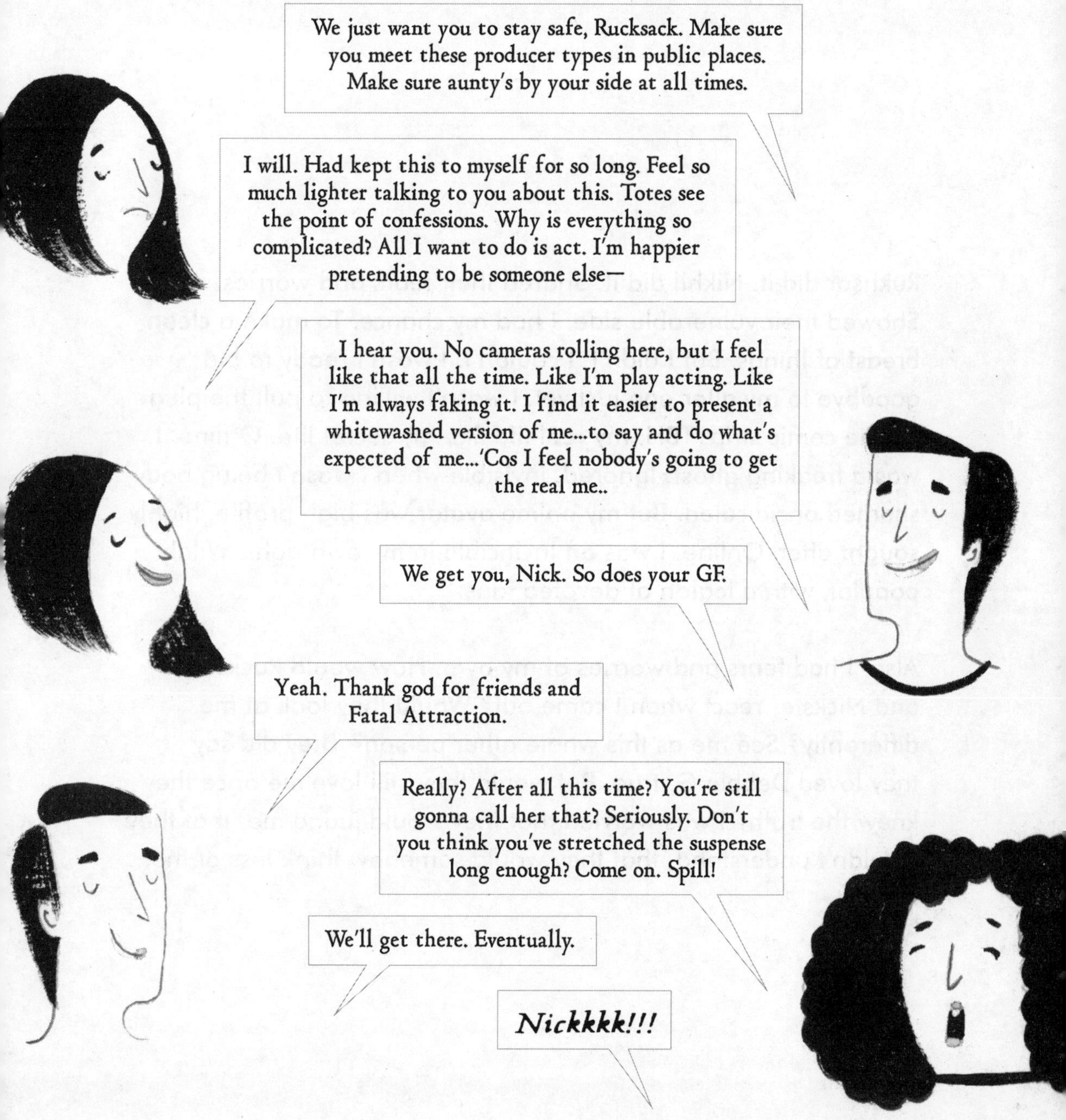
We just want you to stay safe, Rucksack. Make sure you meet these producer types in public places. Make sure aunty's by your side at all times.
I will. Had kept this to myself for so long. Feel so much lighter talking to you about this. Totes see the point of confessions. Why is everything so complicated? All I want to do is act. I'm happier pretending to be someone else—
I hear you. No cameras rolling here, but I feel like that all the time. Like I'm play acting. Like I'm always faking it. I find it easier to present a whitewashed version of me...to say and do what's expected of me...'Cos I feel nobody's going to get the real me..
We get you, Nick. So does your GF.
Yeah. Thank god for friends and Fatal Attraction.
Really? After all this time? You're still gonna call her that? Seriously. Don't you think you've stretched the suspense long enough? Come on. Spill!
We'll get there. Eventually.
Nickkkk!!!

Rukhsar did it. Nikhil did it. Shared their fears and worries. Showed their vulnerable side. I had my chance. To make a clean breast of things. But I didn't. I couldn't. I wasn't ready to bid goodbye to my alter ego just yet. I wasn't willing to pull the plug on the comic strip. TBH, my real life like my secret life. Offline, I was a freaking ghost. Ignored, invisible when I wasn't being body shamed or ridiculed. But my online avatar was high profile, highly sought after. Online, I was an Invincible in my own right. Wildly popular, with a legion of devoted fans.

Also, I had fears and worries of my own. How would Rucksack and Nickster react when I came out? Would they look at me differently? See me as this whole other person? They did say they loved Debbie G, true. But would they still love *me* once they knew the truth? I was worried that they would judge me, that they wouldn't understand, that they would somehow think less of me...

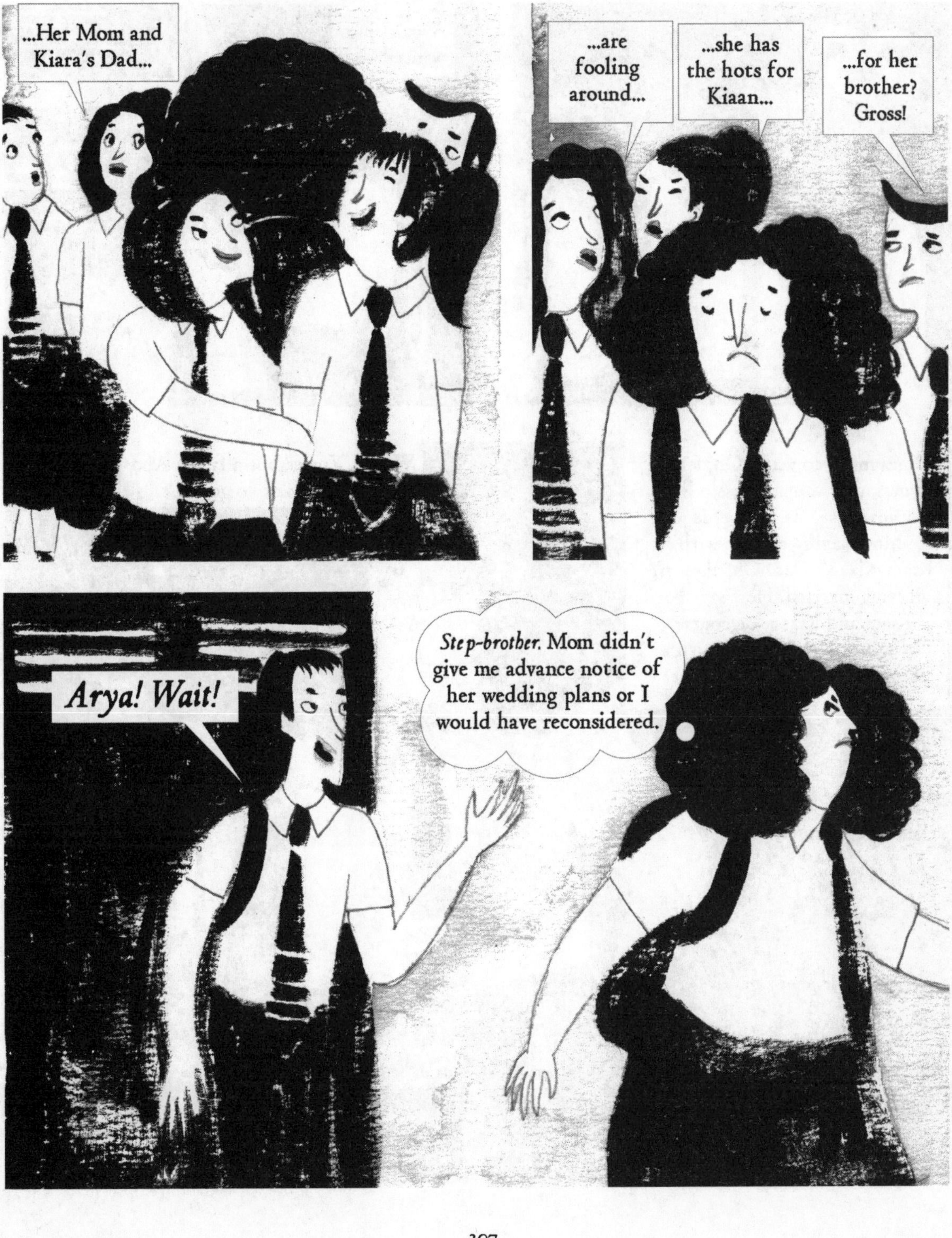
...Her Mom and Kiara's Dad...
...are fooling around...
...she has the hots for Kiaan...
...for her brother? Gross!
Arya! Wait!
Step-brother. Mom didn't give me advance notice of her wedding plans or I would have reconsidered.

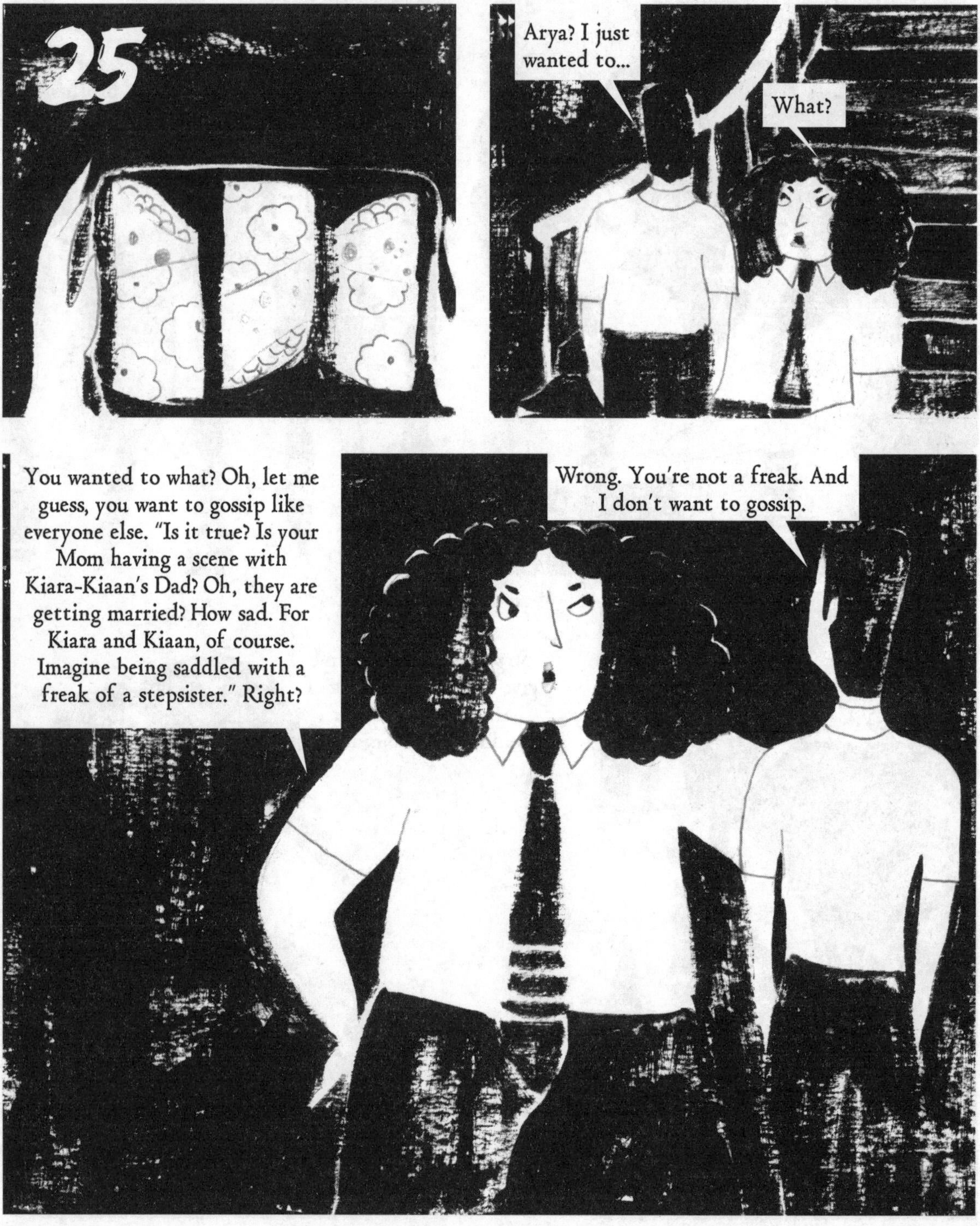
25
Arya? I just wanted to...
What?
You wanted to what? Oh, let me guess, you want to gossip like everyone else. "Is it true? Is your Mom having a scene with Kiara-Kiaan's Dad? Oh, they are getting married? How sad. For Kiara and Kiaan, of course. Imagine being saddled with a freak of a stepsister." Right?
Wrong. You're not a freak. And I don't want to gossip.

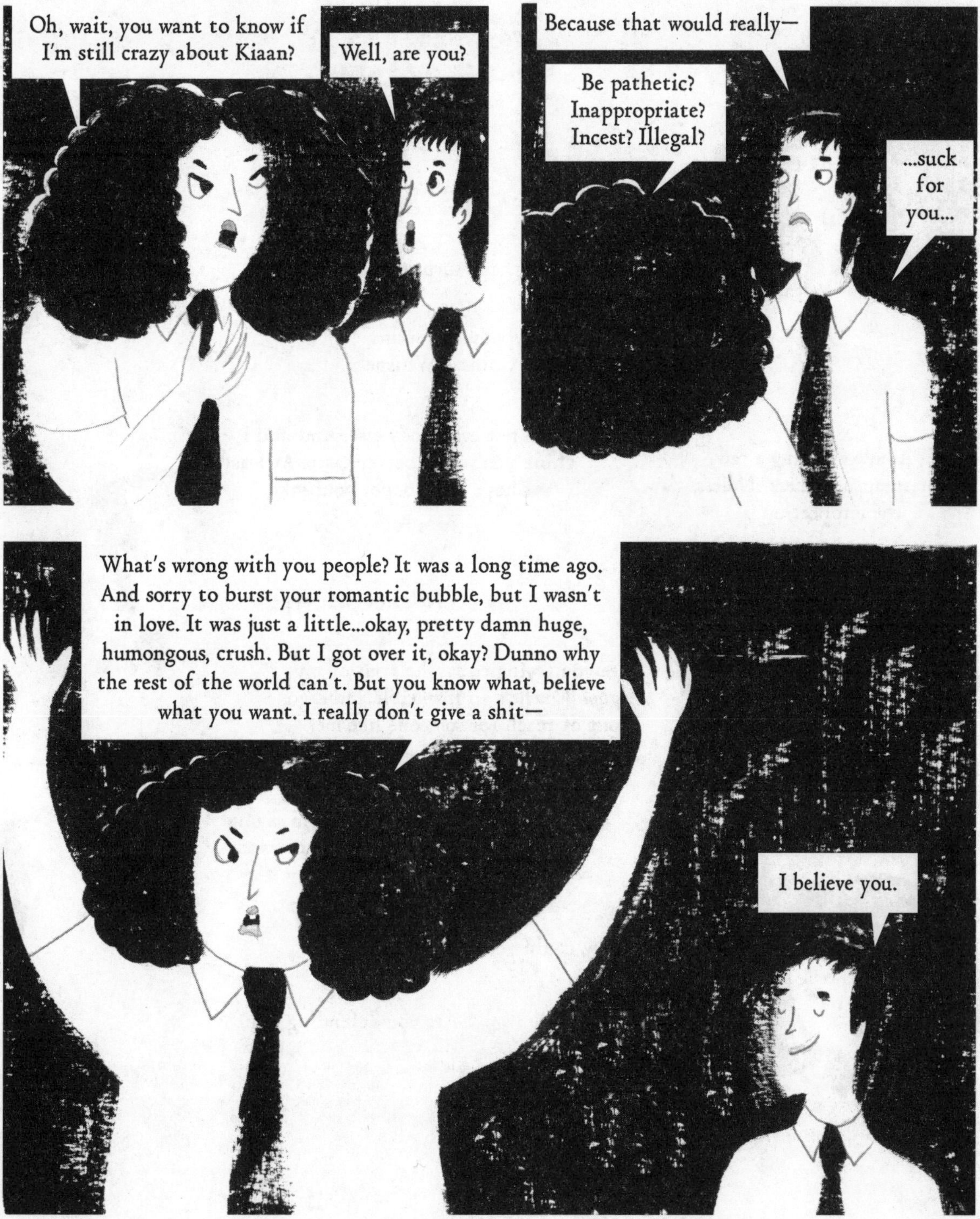
Oh, wait, you want to know if I'm still crazy about Kiaan?
Well, are you?
Because that would really—
Be pathetic? Inappropriate? Incest? Illegal?
...suck for you...
What's wrong with you people? It was a long time ago. And sorry to burst your romantic bubble, but I wasn't in love. It was just a little...okay, pretty damn huge, humongous, crush. But I got over it, okay? Dunno why the rest of the world can't. But you know what, believe what you want. I really don't give a shit—
I believe you.

You do?

And that's surprising because?

Because everybody else seems happier to play Chinese Whispers.

I'm not everybody else. And-and I think you've got better taste. At least I hope you do. For your sake.

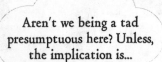

Aren't we being a tad presumptuous here? Unless, the implication is...

He's not your type.

Are you trying to say, he's out of my league? 'Cos he's an Invincible and ergo, out of reach for someone like me?

No! Of course not. All I'm saying is...he-he doesn't come across as particularly bright—

Wow, could you BE more judge-y.

Are you defending him?

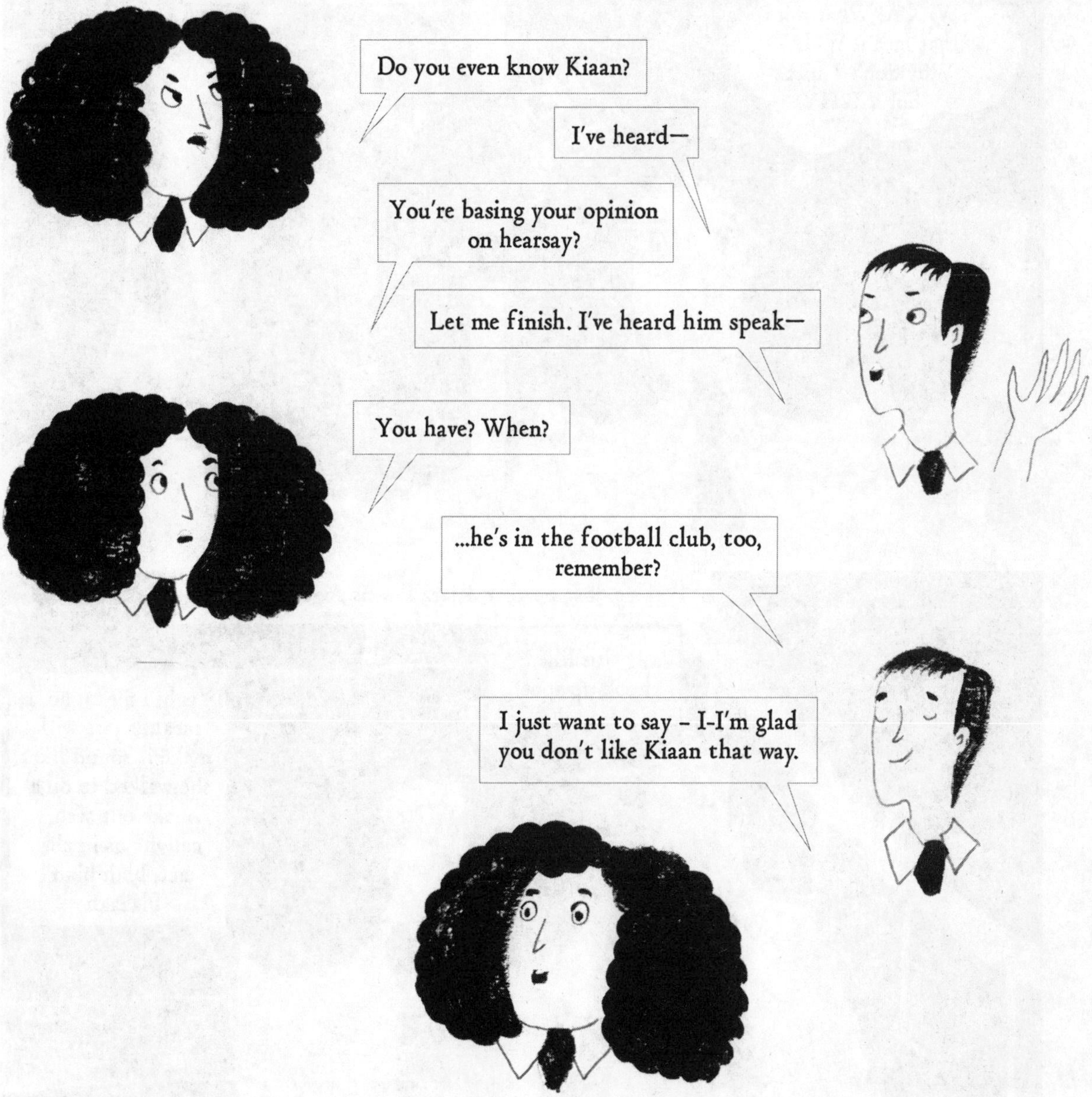
Do you even know Kiaan?
I've heard—
You're basing your opinion on hearsay?
Let me finish. I've heard him speak—
You have? When?
...he's in the football club, too, remember?
I just want to say – I-I'm glad you don't like Kiaan that way.

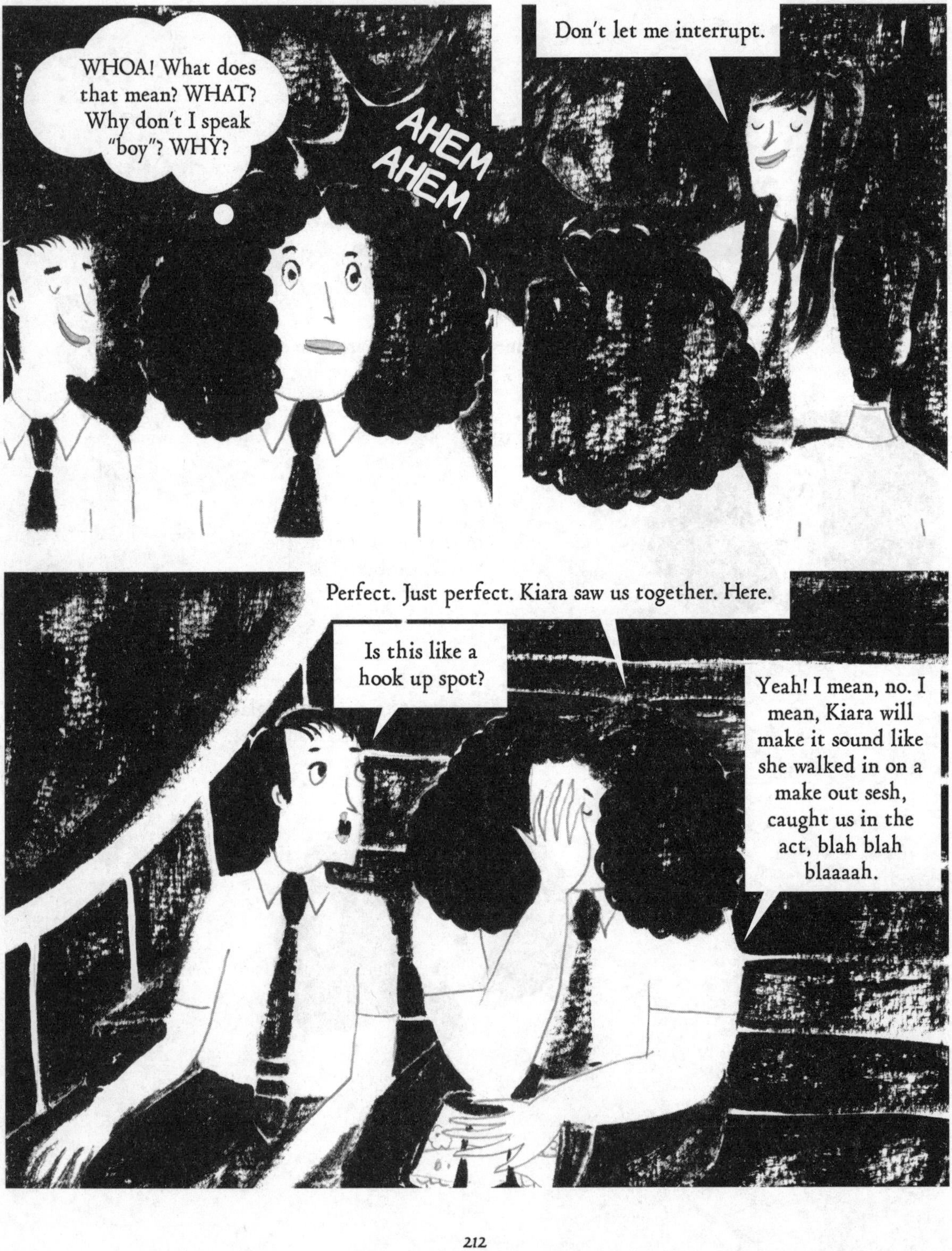
WHOA! What does that mean? WHAT? Why don't I speak "boy"? WHY?
AHEM AHEM
Don't let me interrupt.
Perfect. Just perfect. Kiara saw us together. Here.
Is this like a hook up spot?
Yeah! I mean, no. I mean, Kiara will make it sound like she walked in on a make out sesh, caught us in the act, blah blah blaaaah.

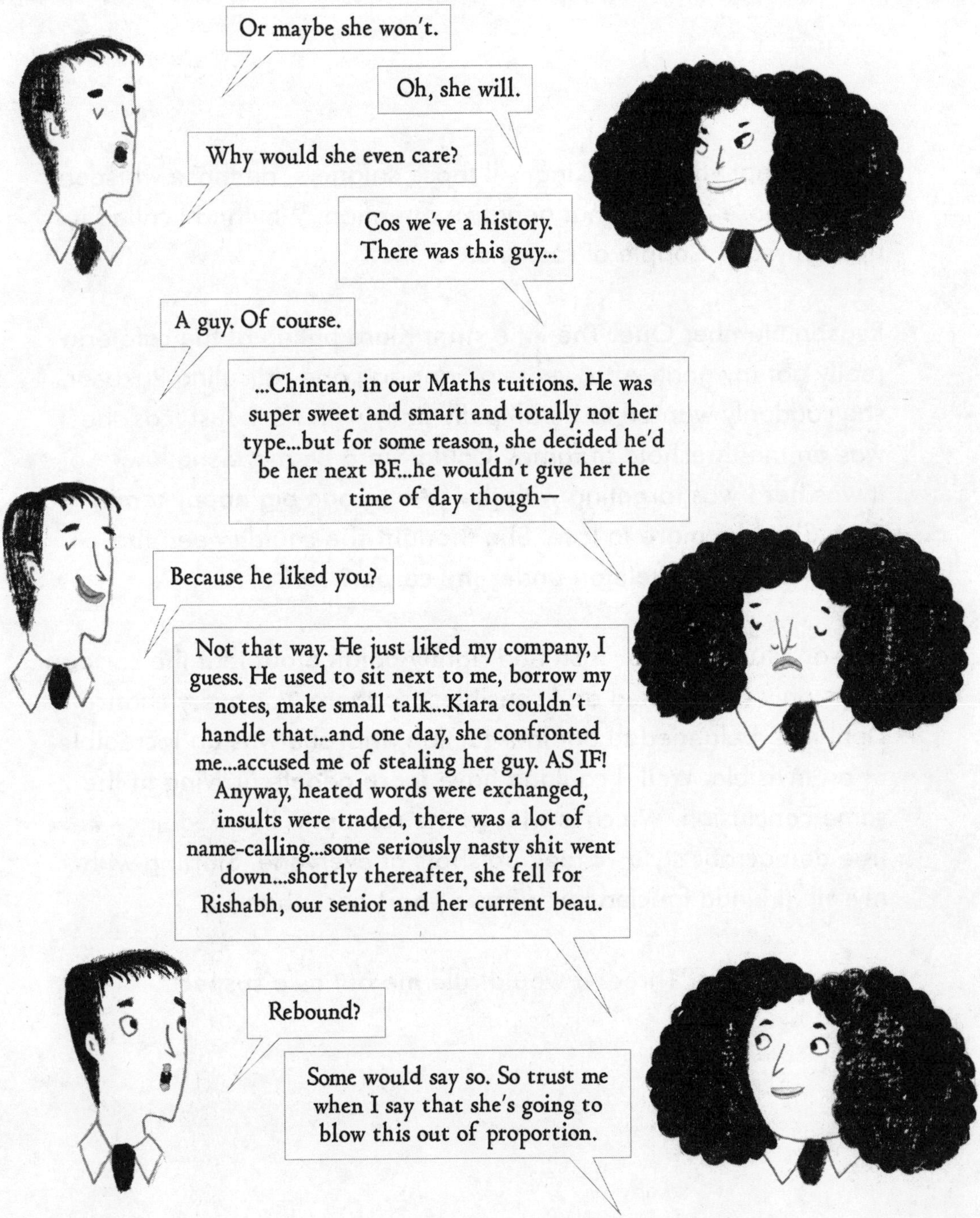
Or maybe she won't.
Oh, she will.
Why would she even care?
Cos we've a history. There was this guy...
A guy. Of course.
...Chintan, in our Maths tuitions. He was super sweet and smart and totally not her type...but for some reason, she decided he'd be her next BF...he wouldn't give her the time of day though—
Because he liked you?
Not that way. He just liked my company, I guess. He used to sit next to me, borrow my notes, make small talk...Kiara couldn't handle that...and one day, she confronted me...accused me of stealing her guy. AS IF! Anyway, heated words were exchanged, insults were traded, there was a lot of name-calling...some seriously nasty shit went down...shortly thereafter, she fell for Rishabh, our senior and her current beau.
Rebound?
Some would say so. So trust me when I say that she's going to blow this out of proportion.

I know what you're thinking. All those sniggers, all those whispers, all that loose talk, all that negative attention. Why had I called it upon myself? Couple of reasons.

Reason Number One. The little stunt Kiara pulled at the cafeteria really got my goat. After years of ignoring and ridiculing Rukhsar, she suddenly wanted to be all pally pally with her? Just 'cos she was on the threshold of fame? Could Kiara BE more shallow? So, it was her I was targeting with the "We're one big happy family" post. She had more to lose. She thought she could sweep the flakey-stepsister skeleton under the carpet? Ha!

Reason Number Two. Yash had rightly pointed out that the cartoon strips only ever picked on Invincibles, so there was every chance Debbie G belonged to another faction, that she was an Incredible or an Invisible. Well, I couldn't have more people arriving at the same conclusion. Which is why, in the run up to the wedding—in true democratic style—I took potshots at everyone. Starting with myself. (I kinda fancied myself as a sport back then.)

Reason Number Three: It would rule me out as a suspect.

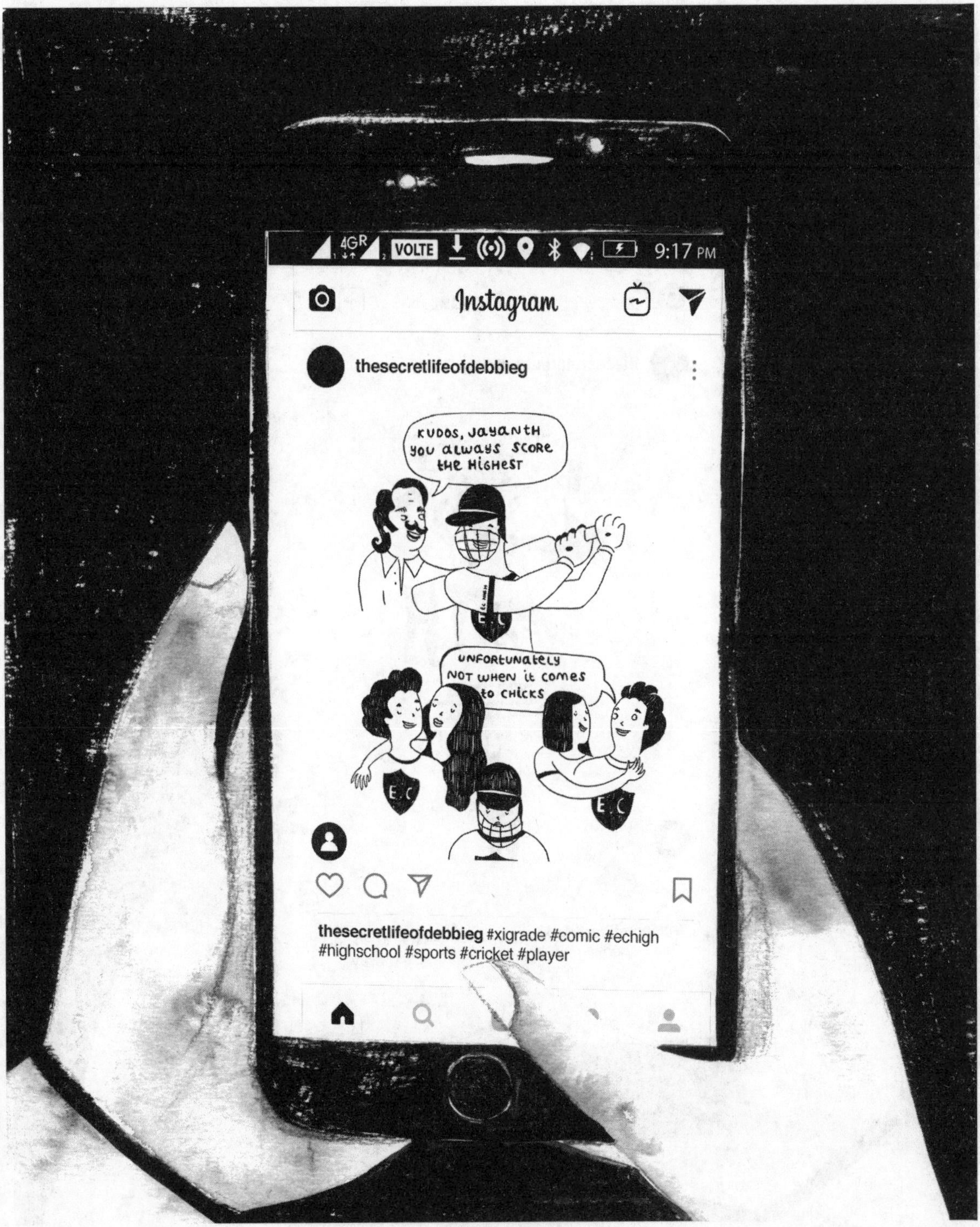
4GR
VOLTE
9:17 PM
Instagram
thesecretlifeofdebbieg
KUDOS, JAYANTH YOU ALWAYS SCORE THE HIGHEST
UNFORTUNATELY NOT WHEN IT COMES TO CHICKS
E.C
E.C
thesecretlifeofdebbieg #xigrade #comic #echigh
#highschool #sports #cricket #player

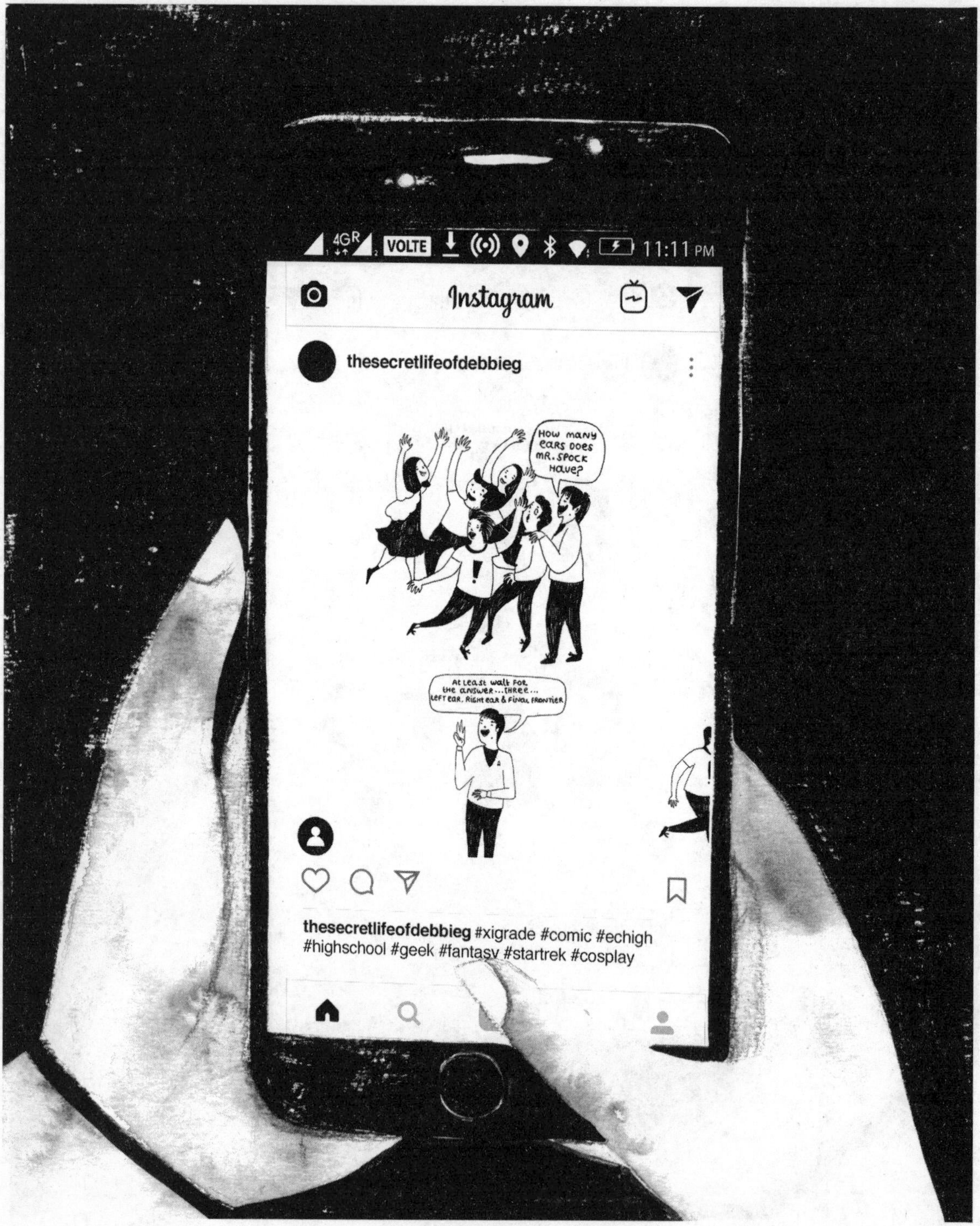
4GR
VOLTE
11:11 PM
Instagram
thesecretlifeofdebbieg
How many ears does Mr. Spock have?
At least wait for the answer...three... left ear, right ear & final frontier
thesecretlifeofdebbieg #xigrade #comic #echigh #highschool #geek #fantasy #startrek #cosplay

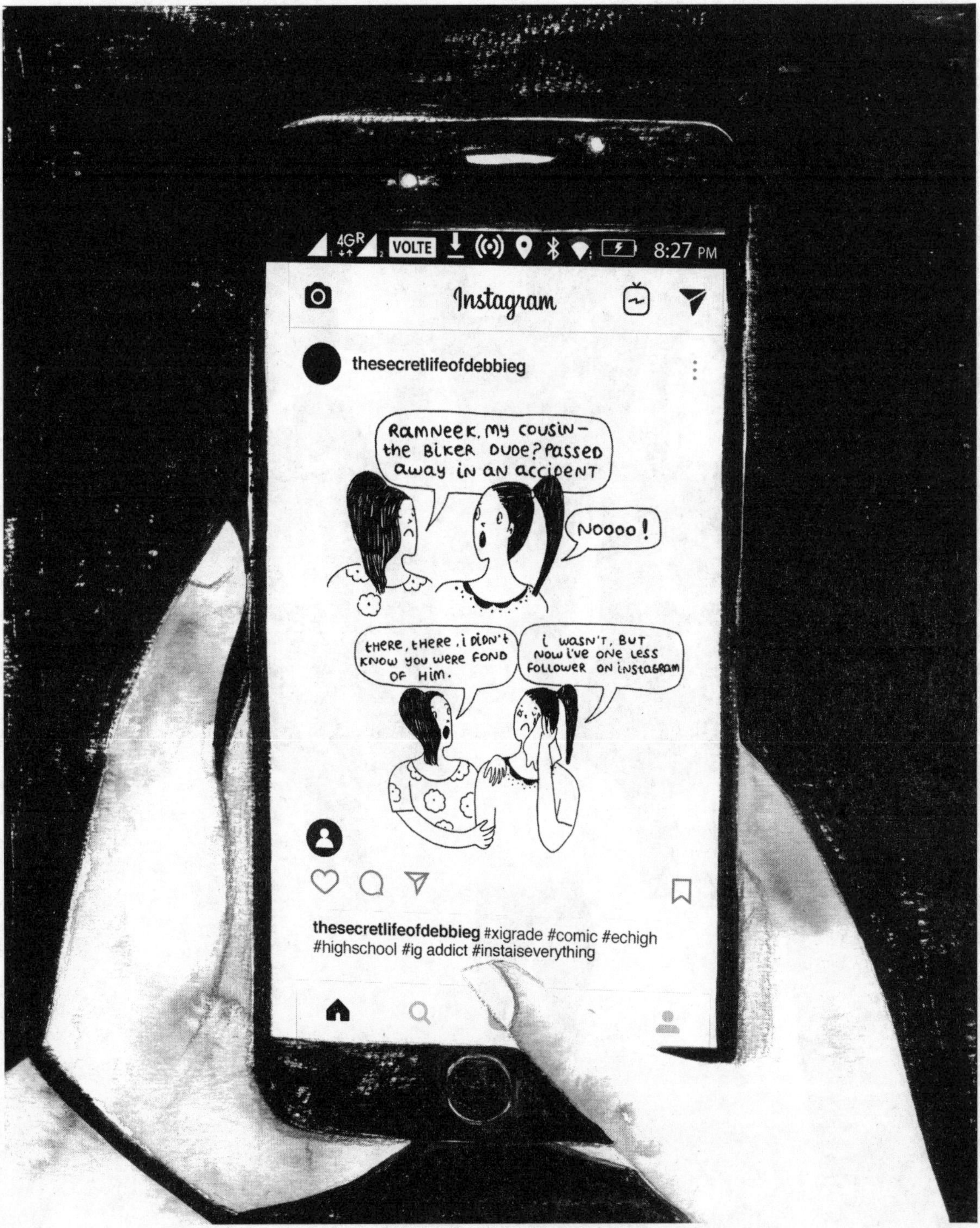
4GR VOLTE 8:27 PM
Instagram
thesecretlifeofdebbieg
RAMNEEK, MY COUSIN— THE BIKER DUDE? PASSED AWAY IN AN ACCIDENT
NOOOO!
THERE, THERE. I DIDN'T KNOW YOU WERE FOND OF HIM.
I WASN'T, BUT NOW I'VE ONE LESS FOLLOWER ON INSTAGRAM
thesecretlifeofdebbieg #xigrade #comic #echigh #highschool #ig addict #instaiseverything

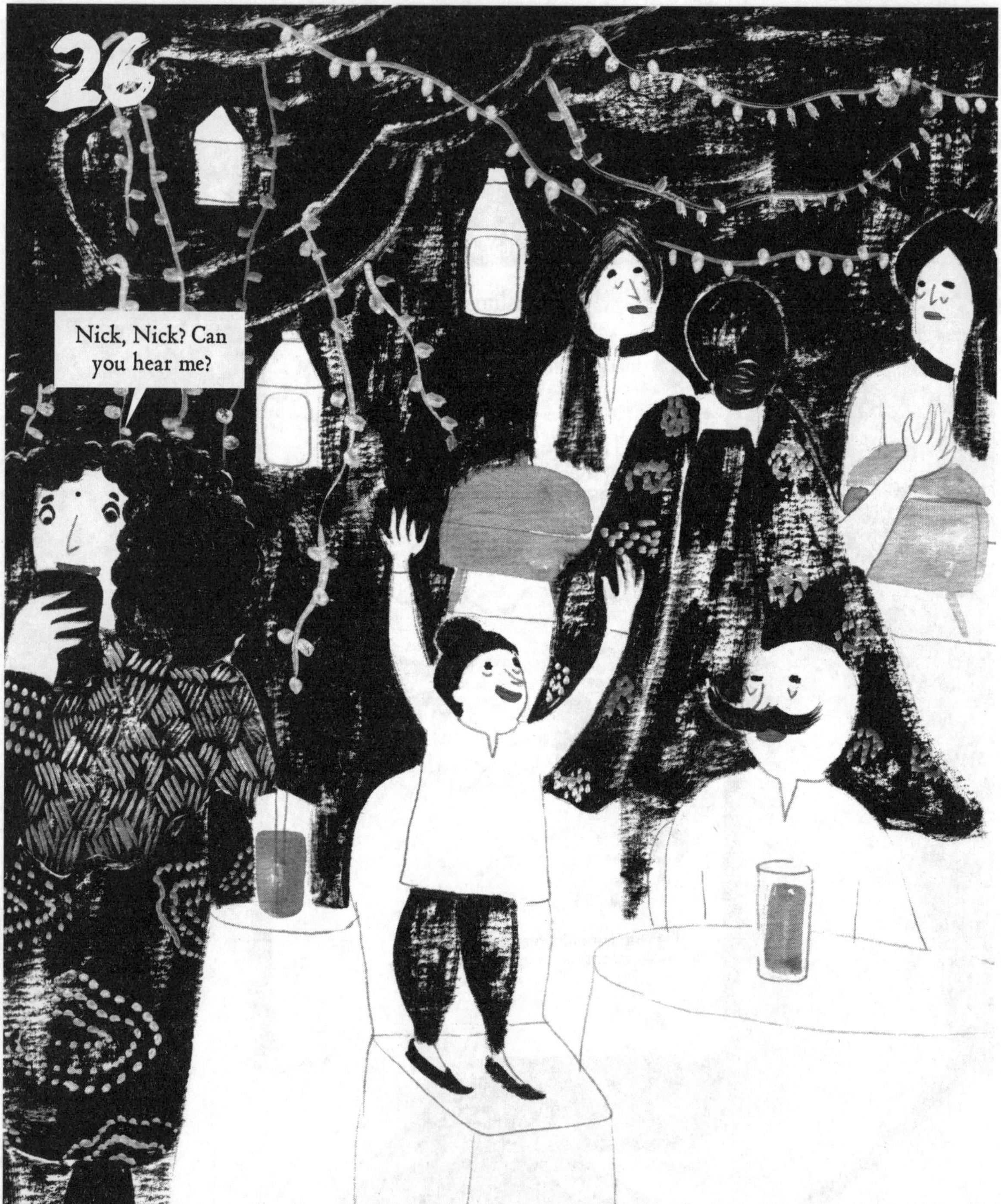
26
Nick, Nick? Can you hear me?

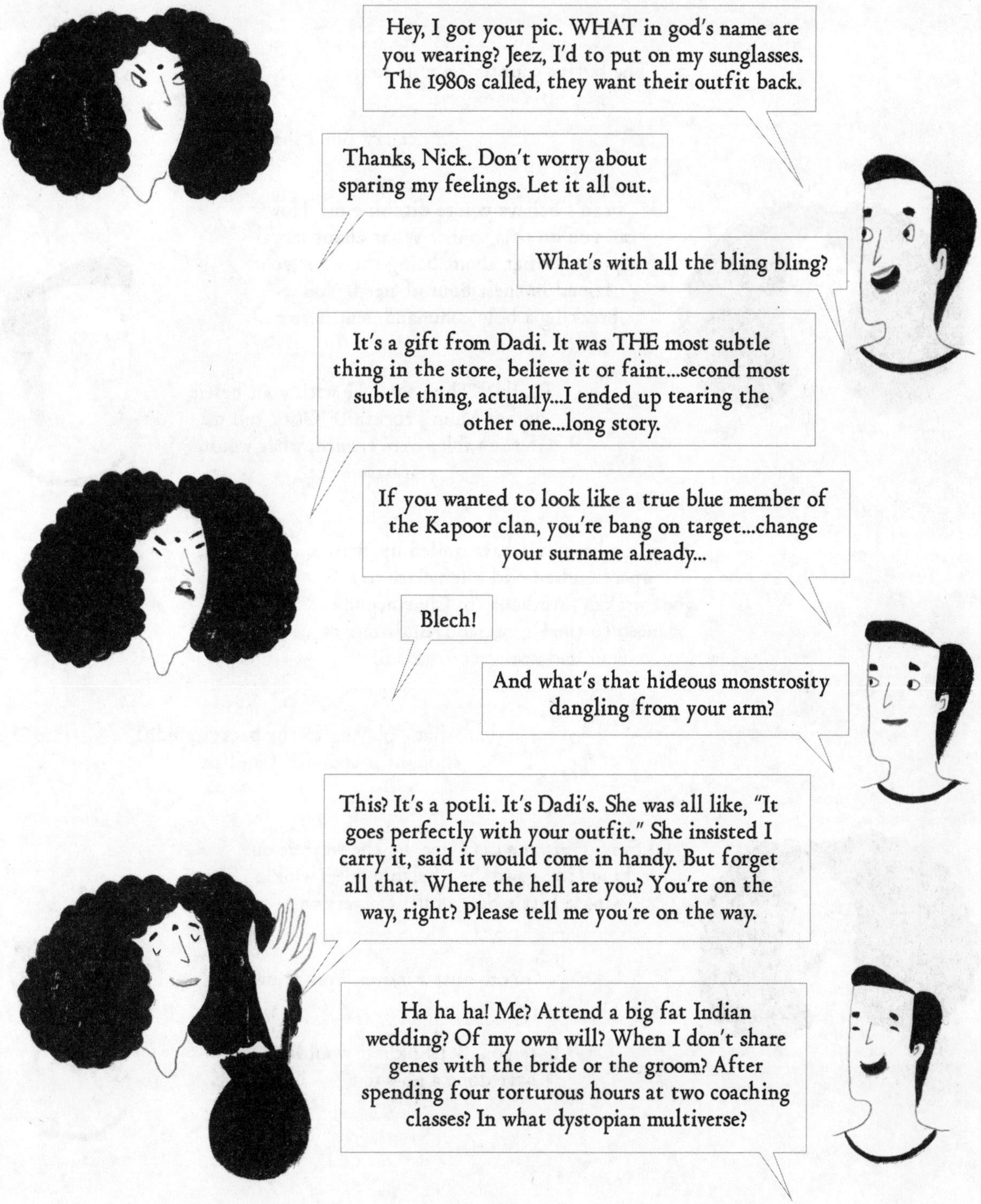
Hey, I got your pic. WHAT in god's name are you wearing? Jeez, I'd to put on my sunglasses. The 1980s called, they want their outfit back.
Thanks, Nick. Don't worry about sparing my feelings. Let it all out.
What's with all the bling bling?
It's a gift from Dadi. It was THE most subtle thing in the store, believe it or faint...second most subtle thing, actually...I ended up tearing the other one...long story.
If you wanted to look like a true blue member of the Kapoor clan, you're bang on target...change your surname already...
Blech!
And what's that hideous monstrosity dangling from your arm?
This? It's a potli. It's Dadi's. She was all like, "It goes perfectly with your outfit." She insisted I carry it, said it would come in handy. But forget all that. Where the hell are you? You're on the way, right? Please tell me you're on the way.
Ha ha ha! Me? Attend a big fat Indian wedding? Of my own will? When I don't share genes with the bride or the groom? After spending four torturous hours at two coaching classes? In what dystopian multiverse?

The buffet counter's a mile long.

Nice try. But I shall pass.

I can't believe you're ditching me. How can you do this to me? What about moral support? What about being there for your friend in their hour of need? You're breaking a holy commandment here—

Really? "Thou shalt be with your bestie on her Mum's cocktail?" Okay, tell me, if the tables were turned, what would you have done?

Hand on heart, I'd have dolled up, driven up a hundred odd kilometres to a godforsaken farmhouse in Chattarpur and danced to the Despacito Dandia mix at your dad's sangeet/cocktail.

Is that what's playing in the background? I thought it sounded familiar.

DJ Swiggy—that's his name, by the way—is on freaking fire...gawd, he's belting out Twinkle Twinkle Little Star's bhangra version...

Go on, bust a move. Work it, work it.

Oh, I hate you. Bet Rukhsar wouldn't have done a no-show.

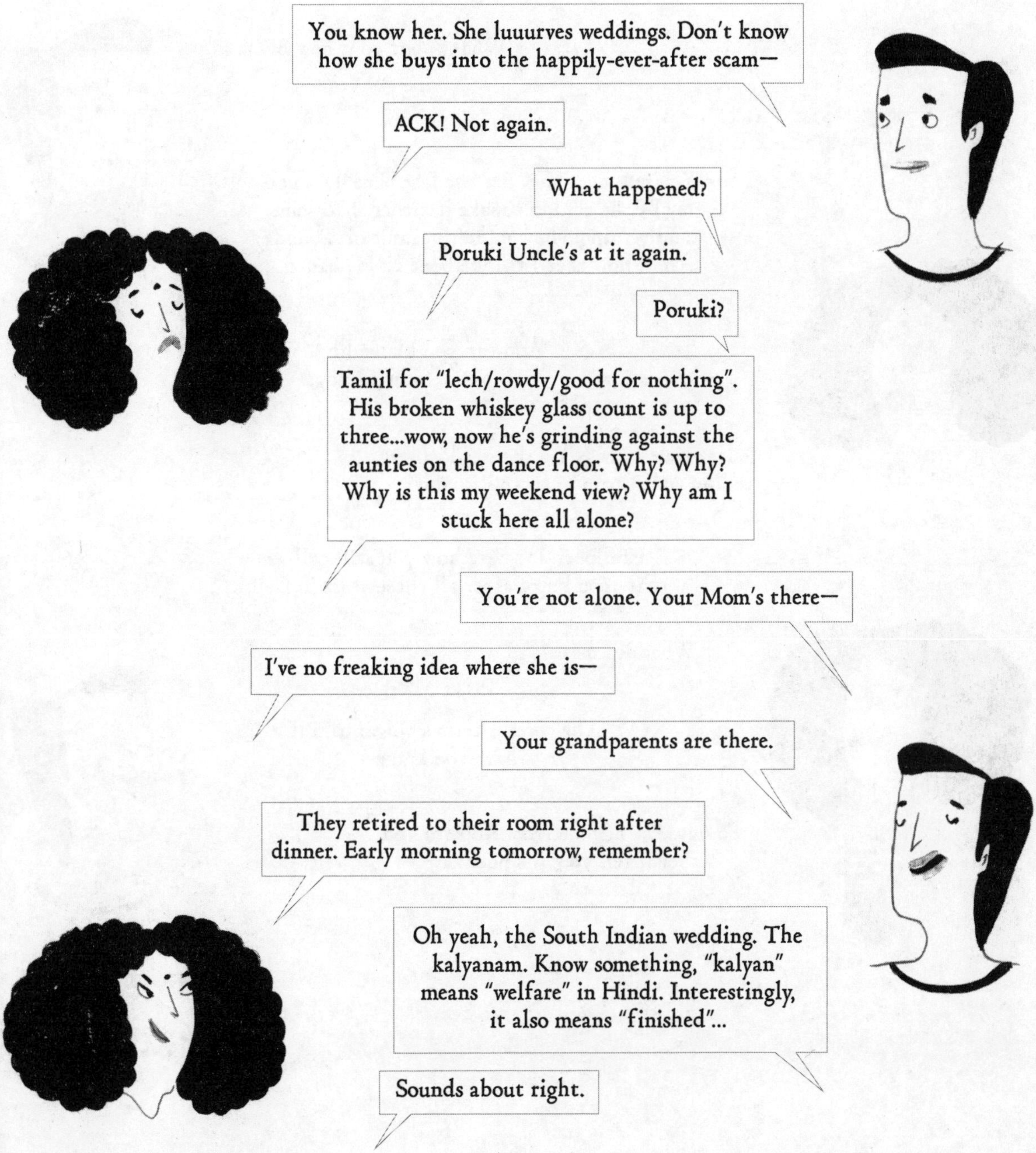
You know her. She luuurves weddings. Don't know how she buys into the happily-ever-after scam—
ACK! Not again.
What happened?
Poruki Uncle's at it again.
Poruki?
Tamil for "lech/rowdy/good for nothing". His broken whiskey glass count is up to three...wow, now he's grinding against the aunties on the dance floor. Why? Why? Why is this my weekend view? Why am I stuck here all alone?
You're not alone. Your Mom's there—
I've no freaking idea where she is—
Your grandparents are there.
They retired to their room right after dinner. Early morning tomorrow, remember?
Oh yeah, the South Indian wedding. The kalyanam. Know something, "kalyan" means "welfare" in Hindi. Interestingly, it also means "finished"...
Sounds about right.

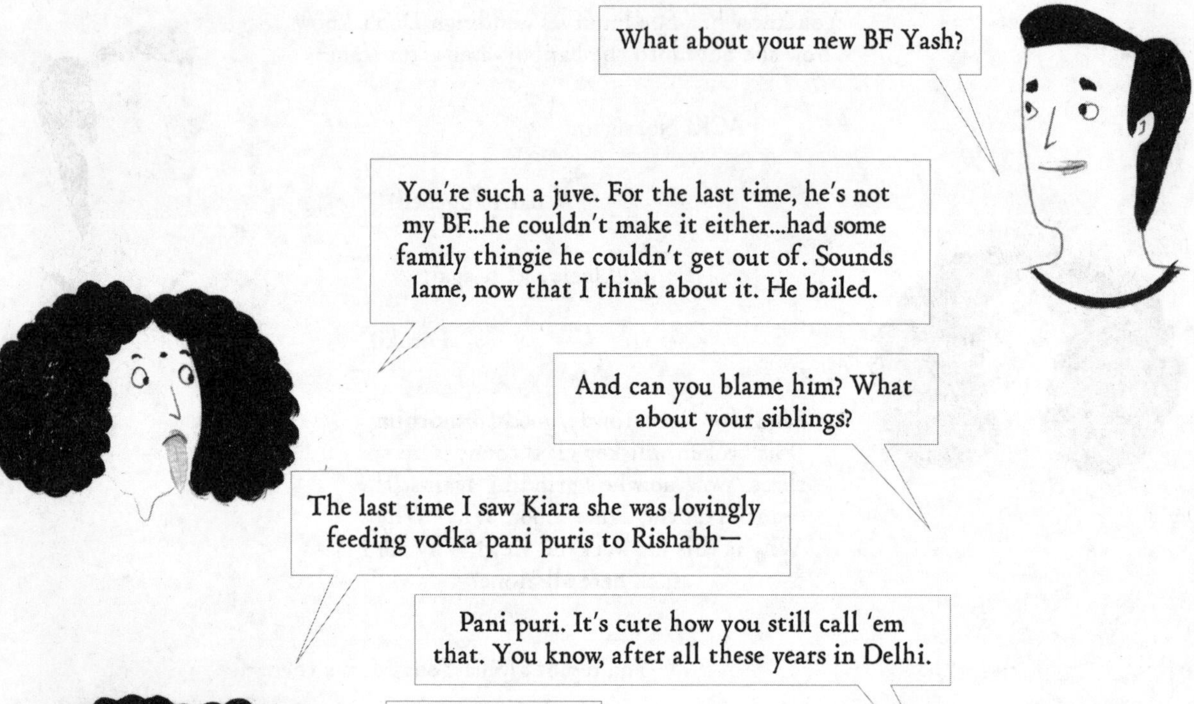

What about your new BF Yash?

You're such a juve. For the last time, he's not my BF...he couldn't make it either...had some family thingie he couldn't get out of. Sounds lame, now that I think about it. He bailed.

And can you blame him? What about your siblings?

The last time I saw Kiara she was lovingly feeding vodka pani puris to Rishabh—

Pani puri. It's cute how you still call 'em that. You know, after all these years in Delhi.

Whaddya mean?

The correct term's golgappa, I'll have you know.

So not. Ask anyone from Kolkata and they'll tell you, it's puchka—

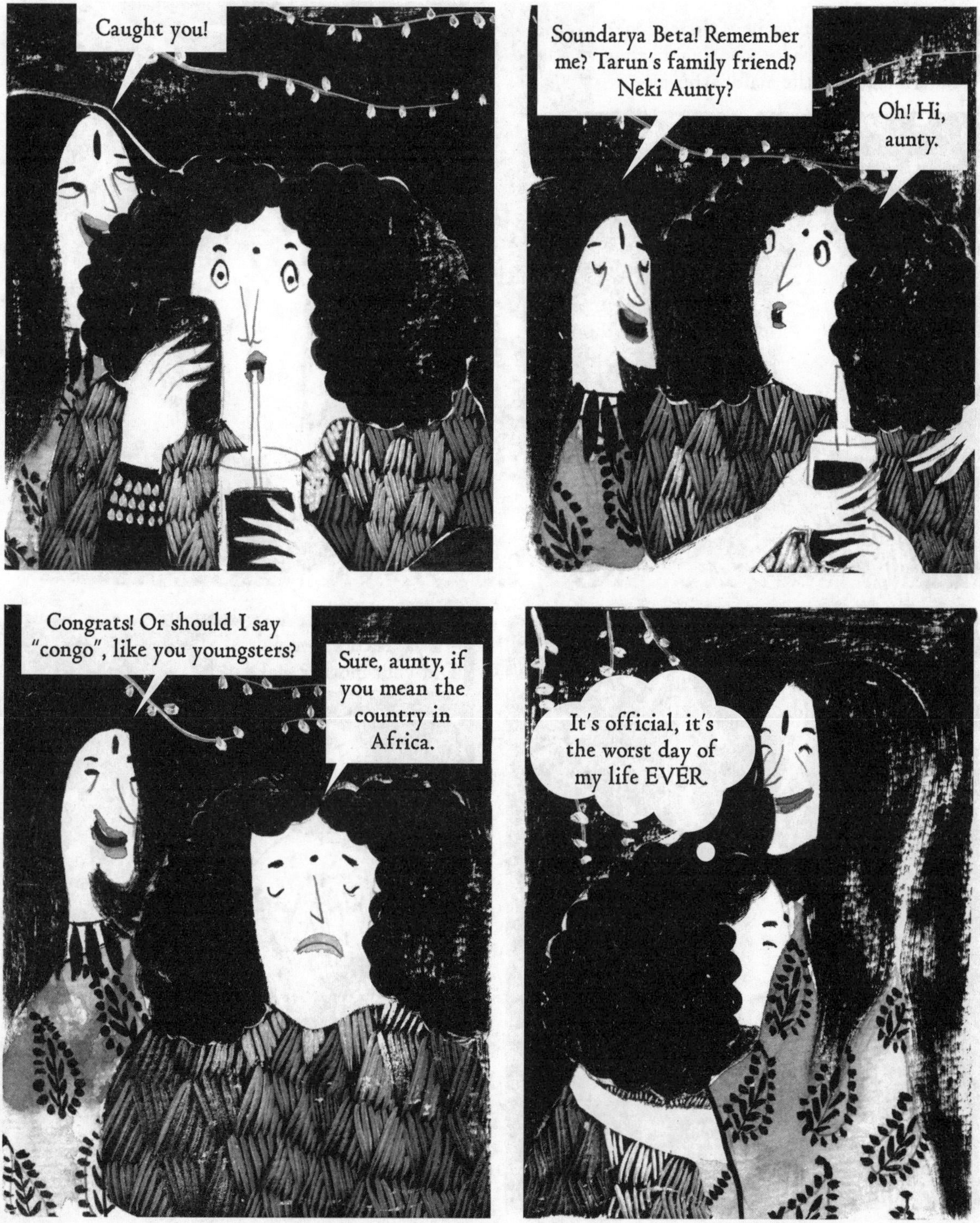
Caught you!
Soundarya Beta! Remember me? Tarun's family friend? Neki Aunty?
Oh! Hi, aunty.
Congrats! Or should I say "congo", like you youngsters?
Sure, aunty, if you mean the country in Africa.
It's official, it's the worst day of my life EVER.

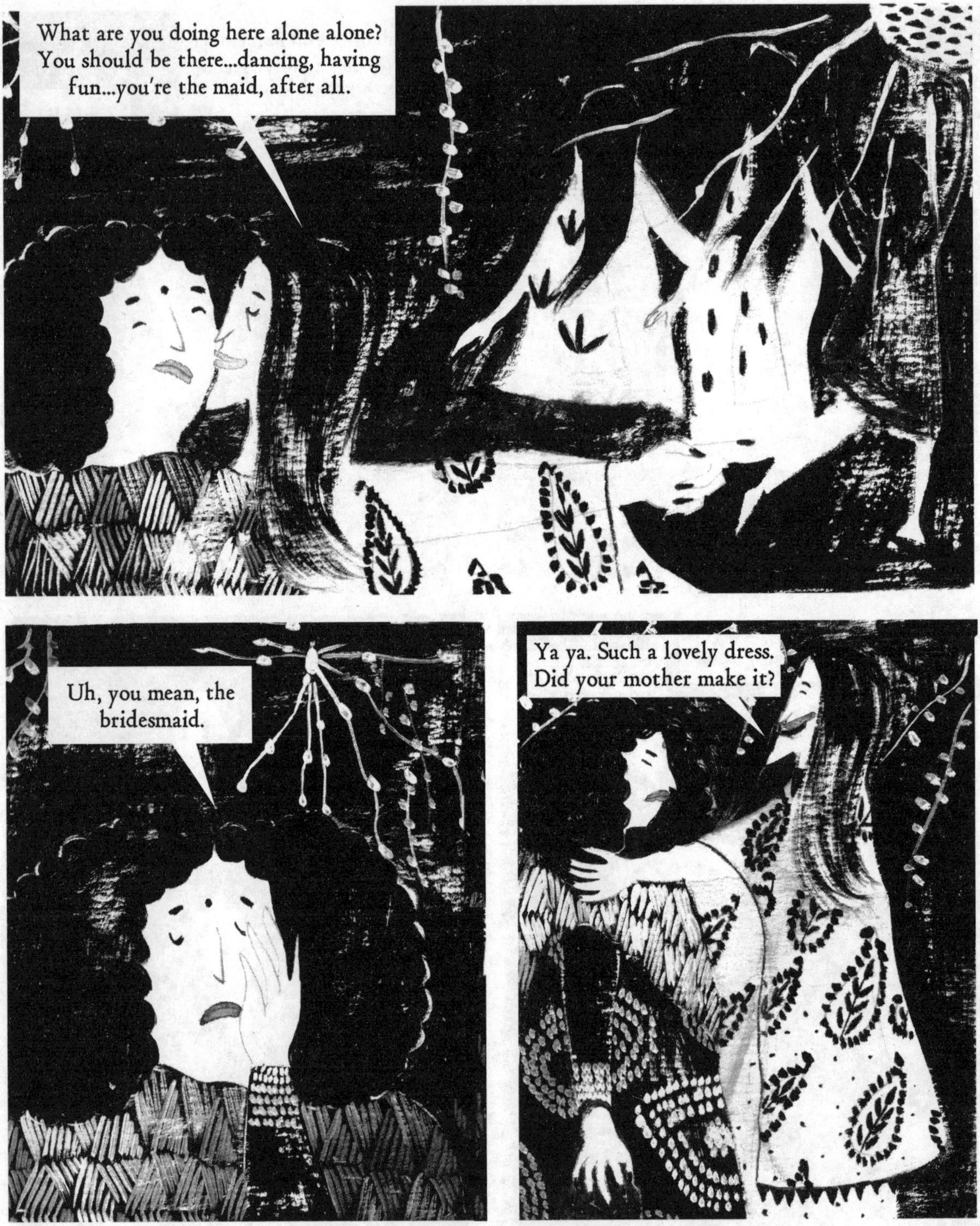
What are you doing here alone alone? You should be there...dancing, having fun...you're the maid, after all.
Uh, you mean, the bridesmaid.
Ya ya. Such a lovely dress. Did your mother make it?

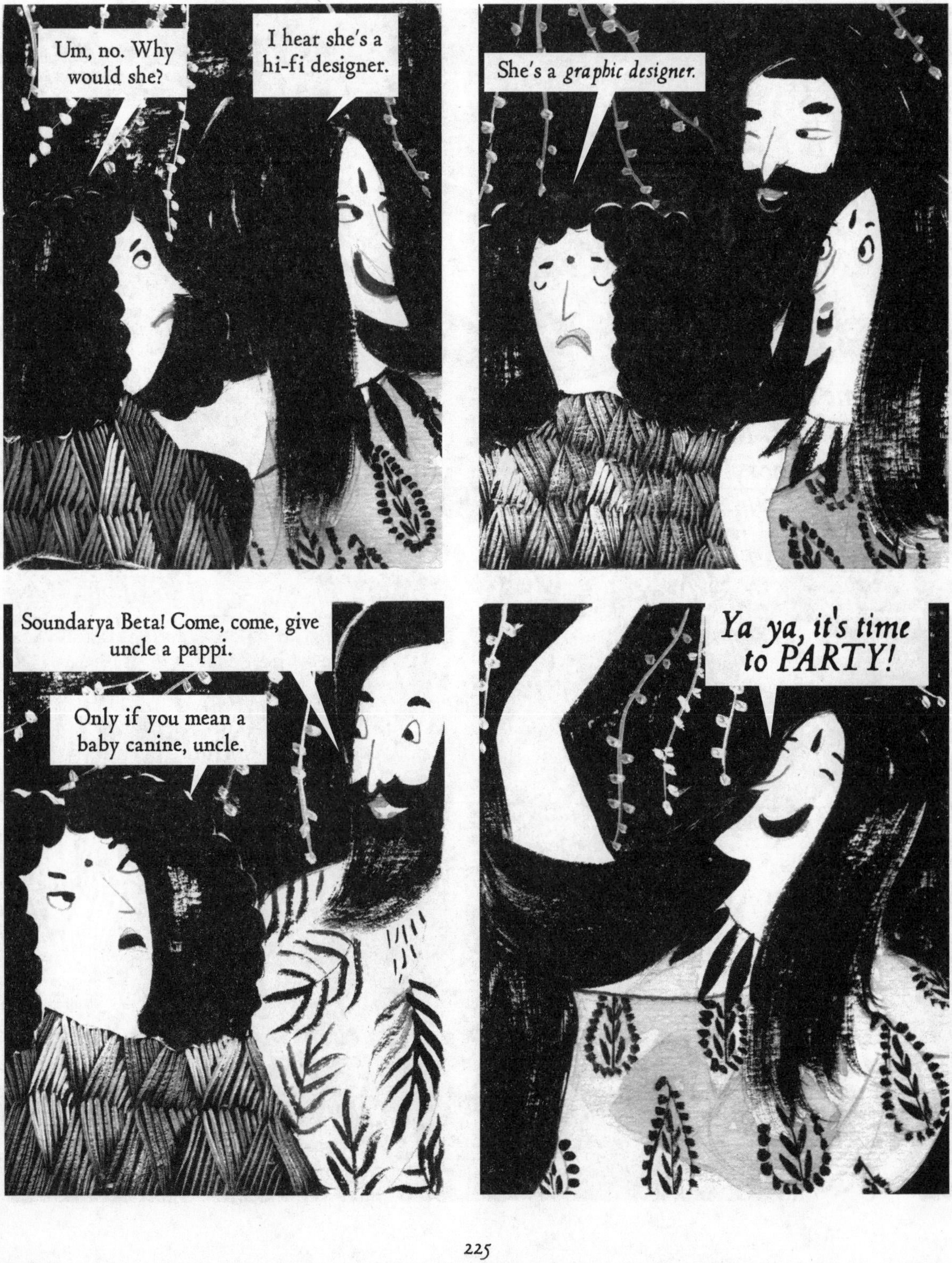
Um, no. Why would she?
I hear she's a hi-fi designer.
She's a *graphic designer.*
Soundarya Beta! Come, come, give uncle a pappi.
Only if you mean a baby canine, uncle.
Ya ya, it's time to PARTY!

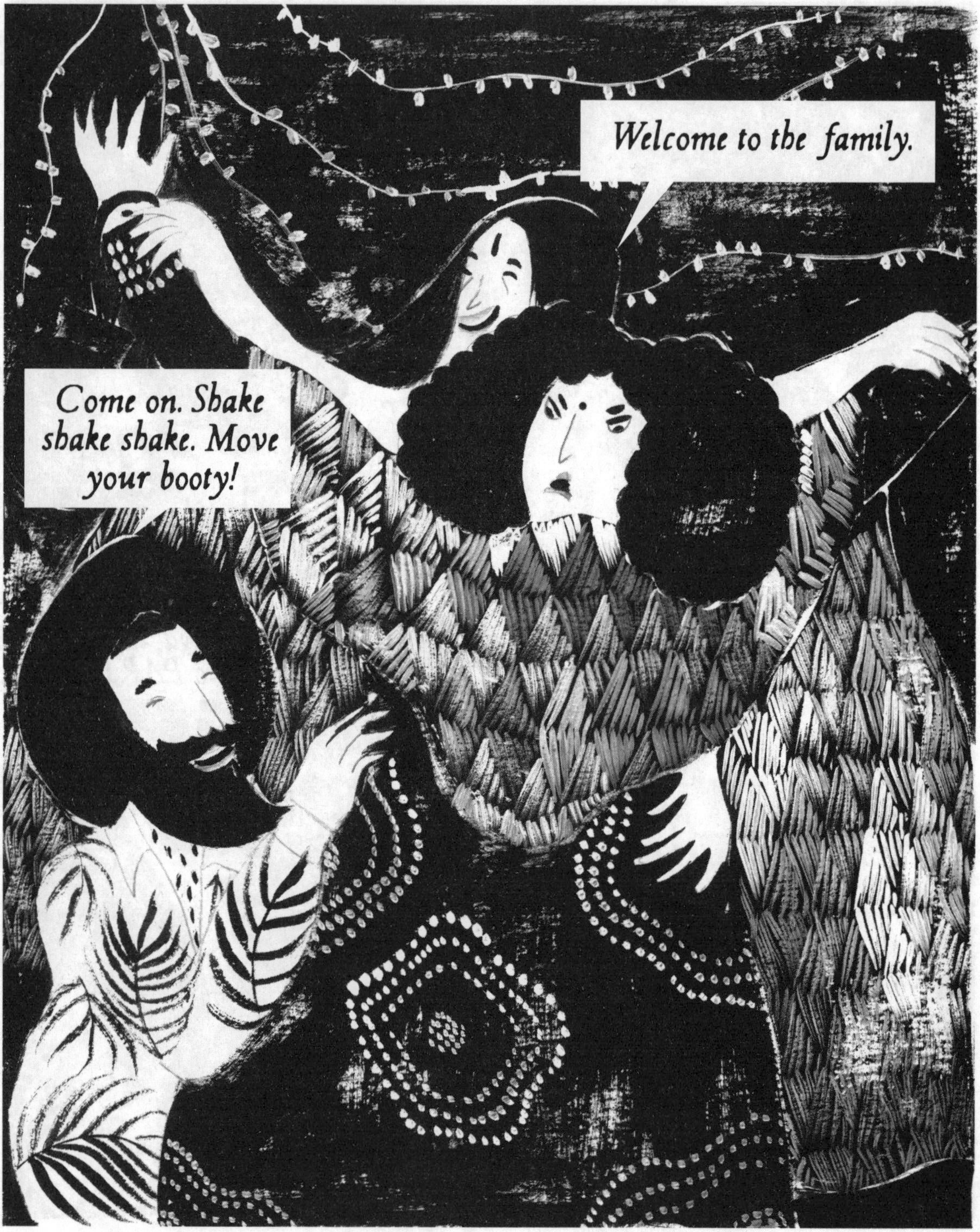
Welcome to the family.
Come on. Shake shake shake. Move your booty!

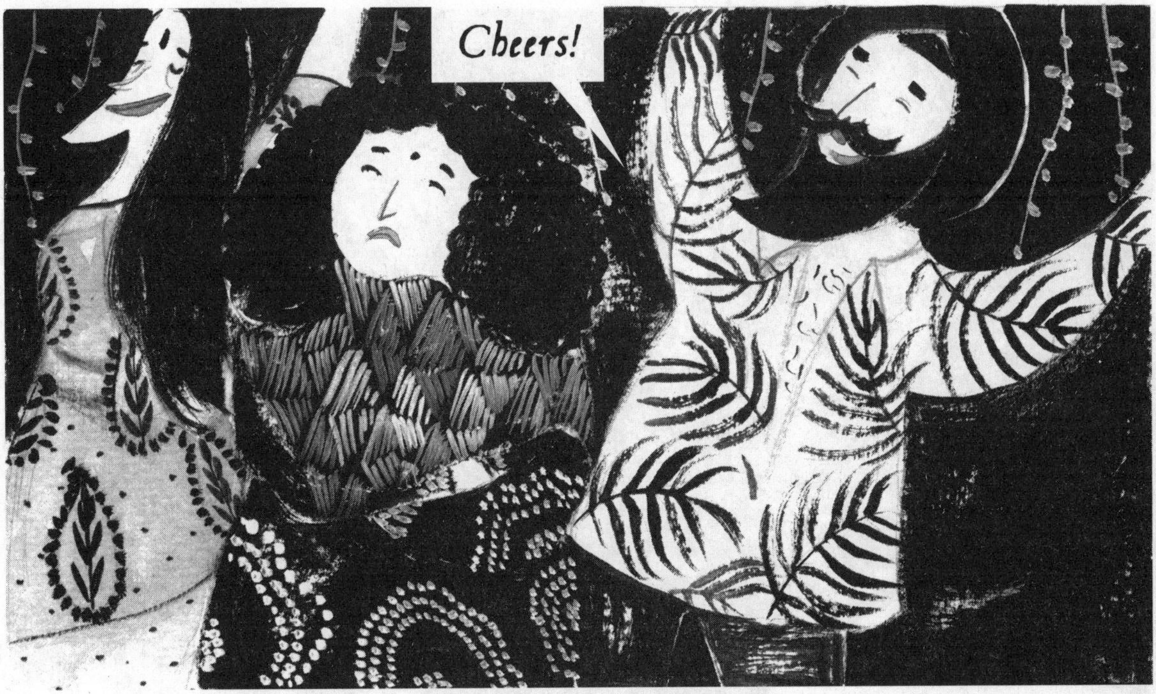
Cheers!

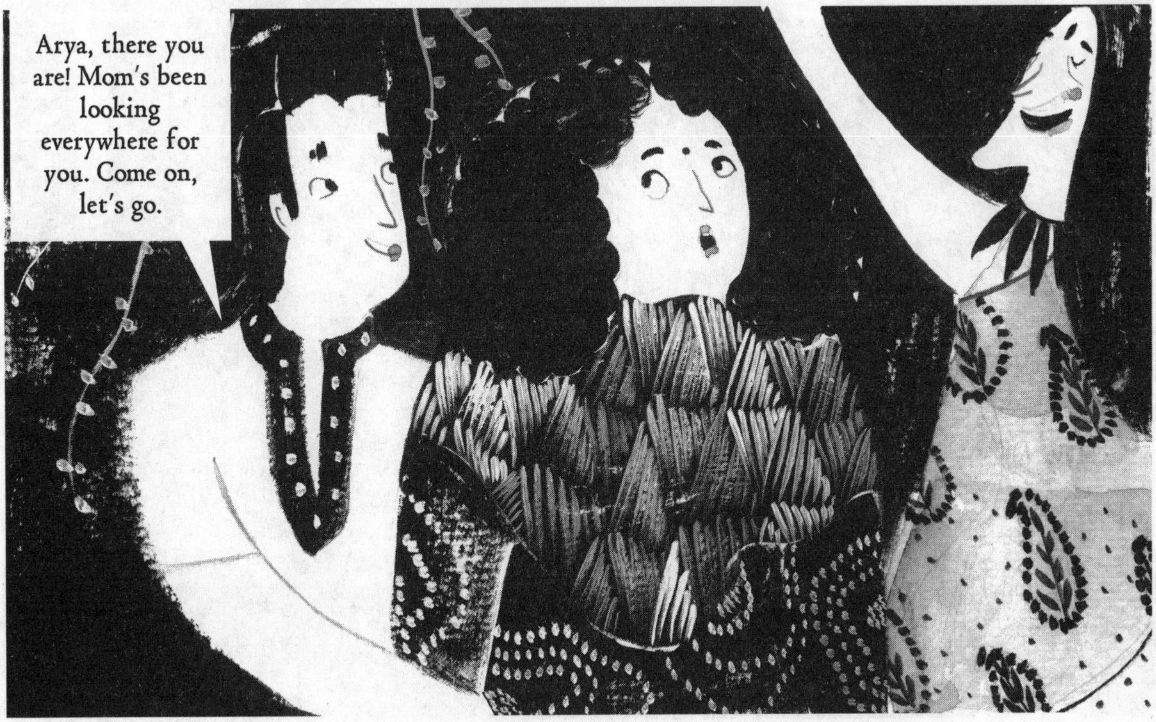
Arya, there you are! Mom's been looking everywhere for you. Come on, let's go.

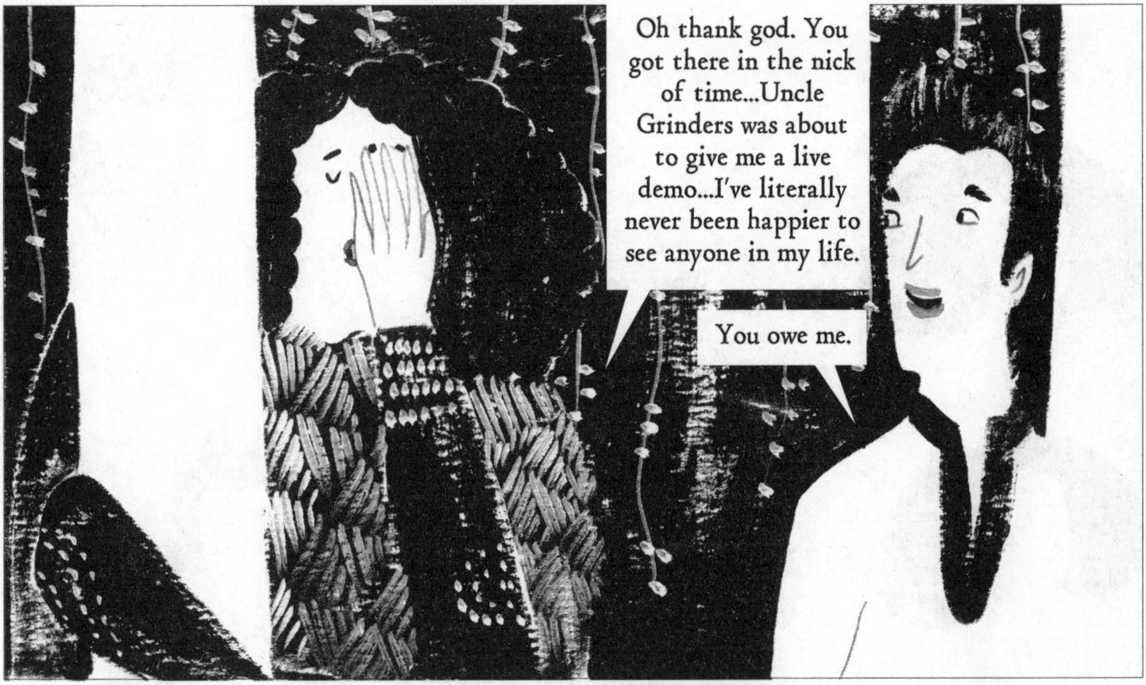
Oh thank god. You got there in the nick of time...Uncle Grinders was about to give me a live demo...I've literally never been happier to see anyone in my life.
You owe me.

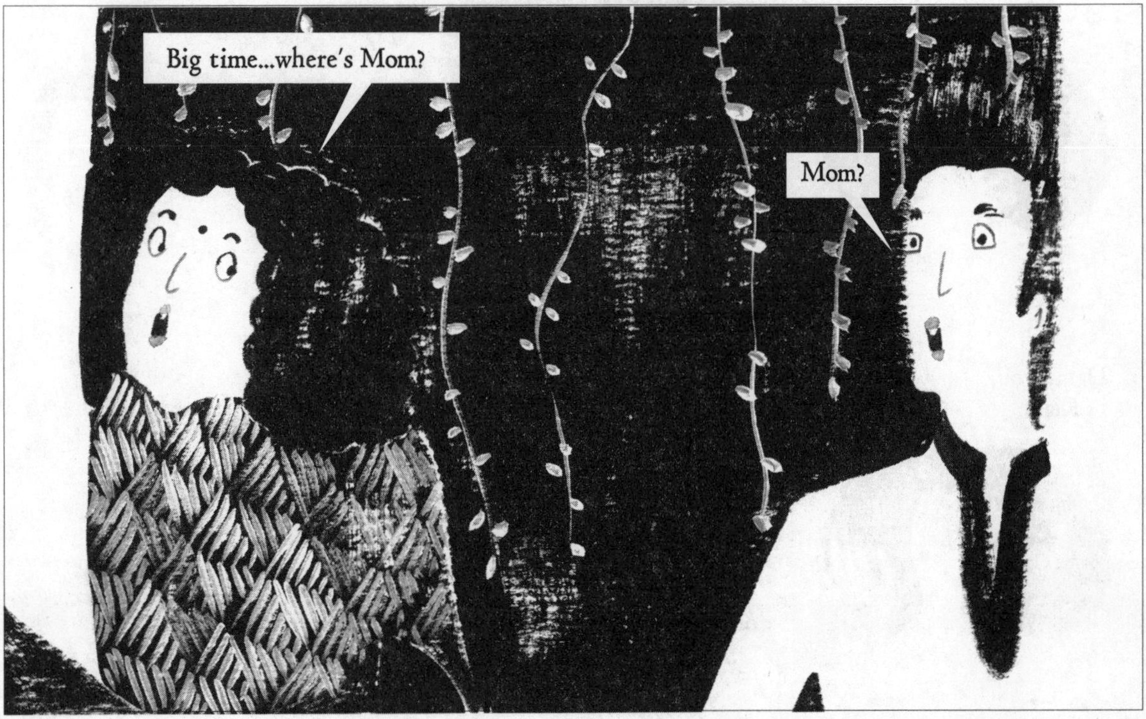
Big time...where's Mom?
Mom?

Please let it not be about the comic strip...

But you said—

Actually I wanted to talk to you. Alone...I saw the comic strip.

What comic strip?

You know, TSLODG.

Sounds like a sidey boarding lodge.

The Secret Life of Debbie G, yaar.

Who? What?

You don't know...haven't you heard...it's like the Hello/People of our school...an online gossip mag...it's rad...it's all everyone can talk about these days...I can't believe you haven't read it—

What about it?

So, according to it...it says...that you-you've a massive crush on me.

Heh! Heh! Very funny...no truth to it. Debbie G's full of shit. Don't believe everything you read online.

Damn you, Kiara.

But Kiara said you've been crushing on me for years.

You know what, I'll come clean with you. I did have a...uh, soft spot for you...for a bit...back in the day...but it's over and done with...I swear I'm over it, over you...

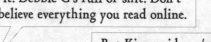

I'd no idea. None.

230

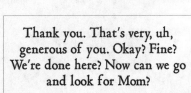

What wouldn't I have given to hear this two years ago.

It doesn't matter. It's all in the past. Ancient history. It's all good now.

I just want to say that I'm flattered. I really am.

Thank you. That's very, uh, generous of you. Okay? Fine? We're done here? Now can we go and look for Mom?

Wha—?!

Arya. Wait.

Are you seeing anyone right now?

Kiara says she's heard rumours. About you and the new guy...

If you must know, I'm not. Not seeing Yash or anyone else.

I'm not with anyone right now either...I'm single, you're single...but it's too late now... Unless you think it's not too late...I'm done chasing after hot girls...and it's not as if we're own brother and sister...

Are you freaking wasted?

It's a wedding. Everyone's wasted.

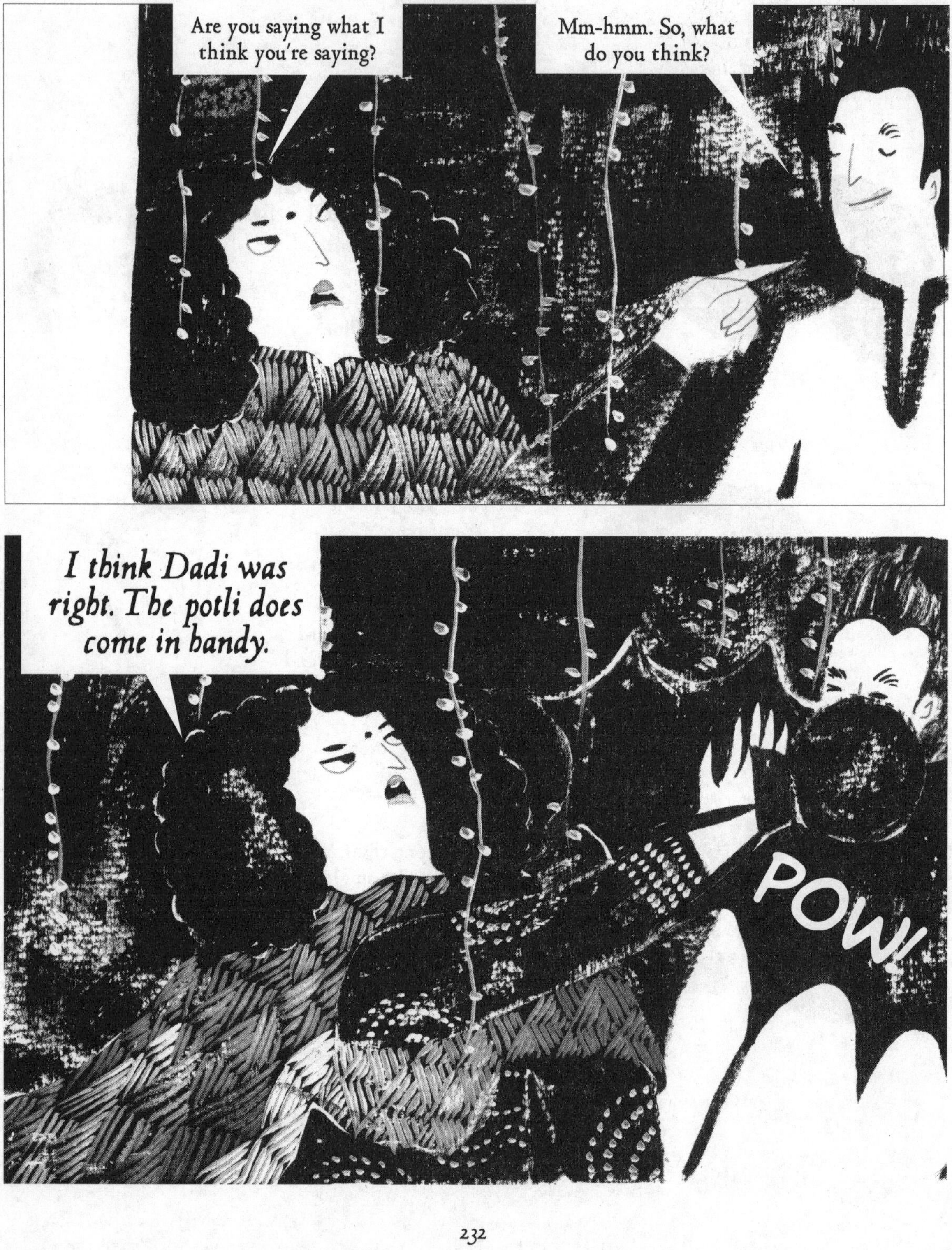
Are you saying what I think you're saying?
Mm-hmm. So, what do you think?
I think Dadi was right. The potli does come in handy.
POW!

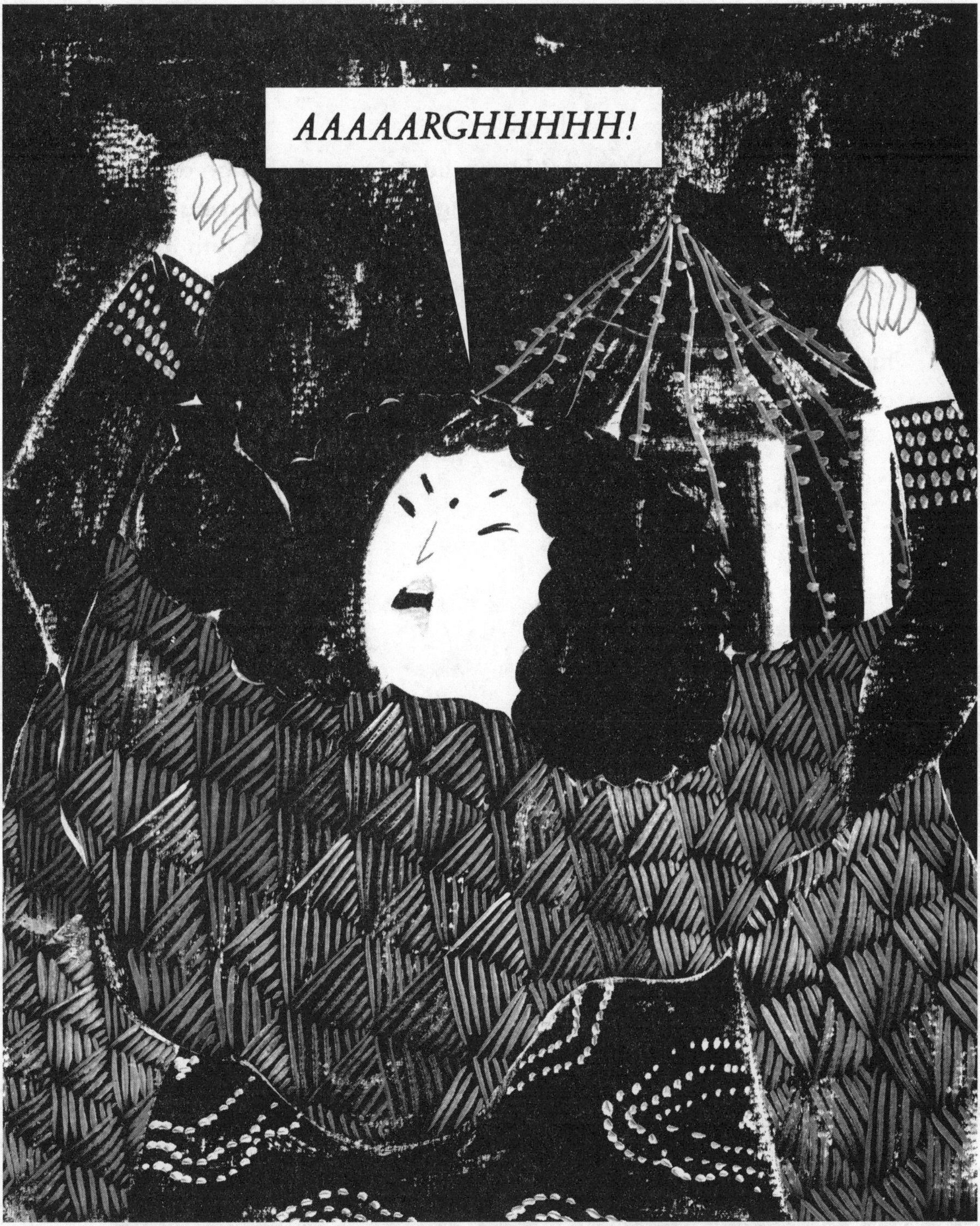
AAAAARGHHHHH!

Has it ever happened to you? Has a tidal wave of change ever swept over your life, taking everything away with it, leaving you with an empty feeling and not much else? One month into the wedding, all traces of my old life were gone. It was as if it had never been. As if I'd imagined the whole damn thing. I had a new family, a new room, a new roomie, a new car pool, a new lunch and dinner menu, even a new WhatsApp group....

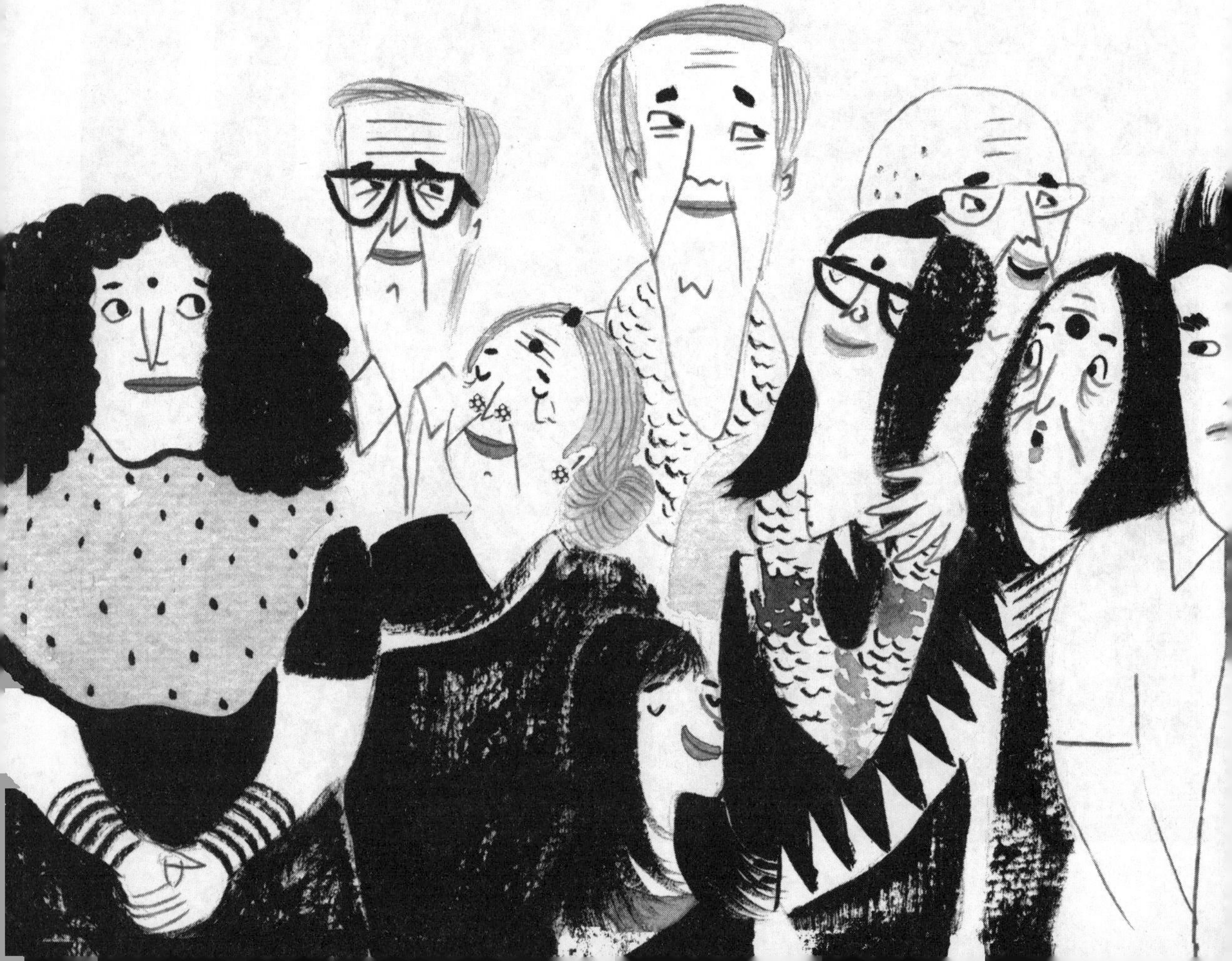

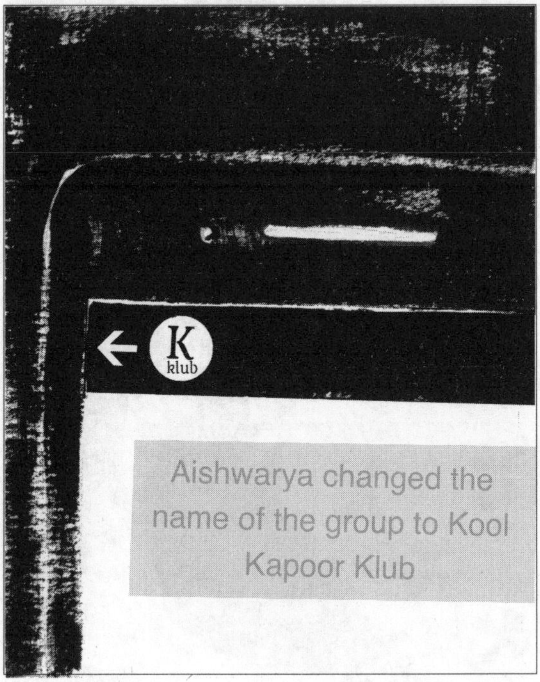
K klub
Aishwarya changed the name of the group to Kool Kapoor Klub

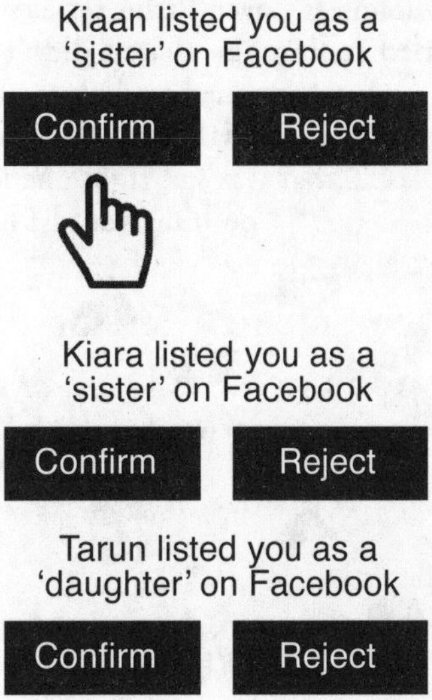
Kiaan listed you as a 'sister' on Facebook
Confirm
Reject
Kiara listed you as a 'sister' on Facebook
Confirm
Reject
Tarun listed you as a 'daughter' on Facebook
Confirm
Reject

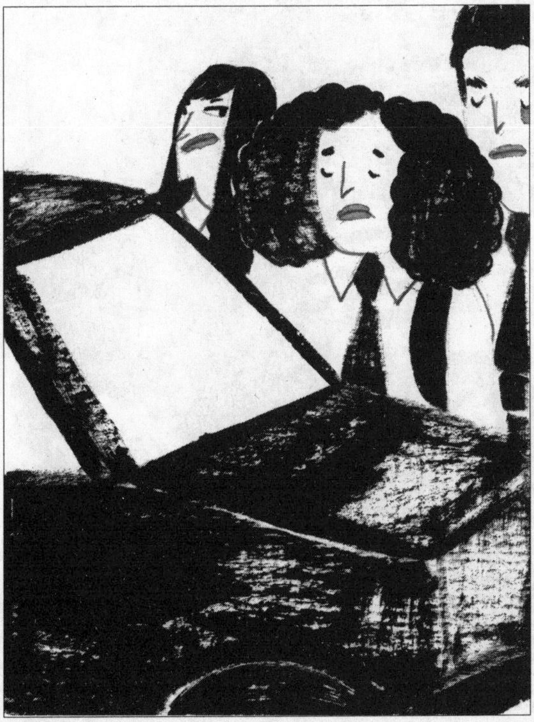

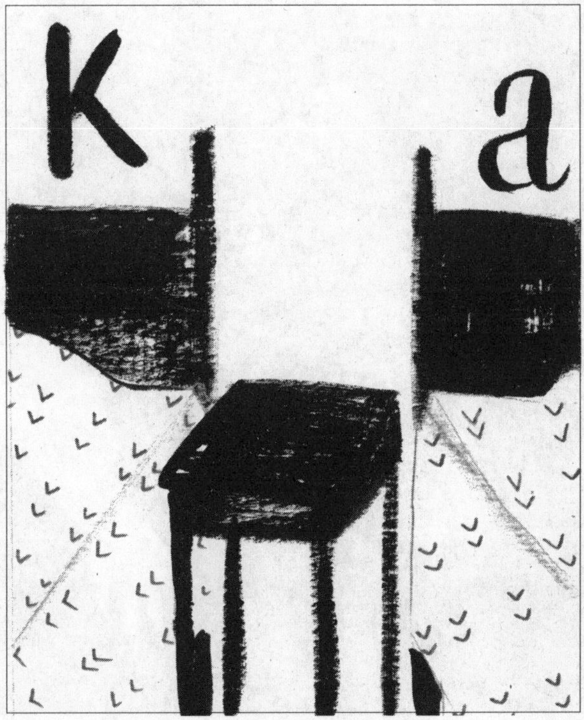
K
a

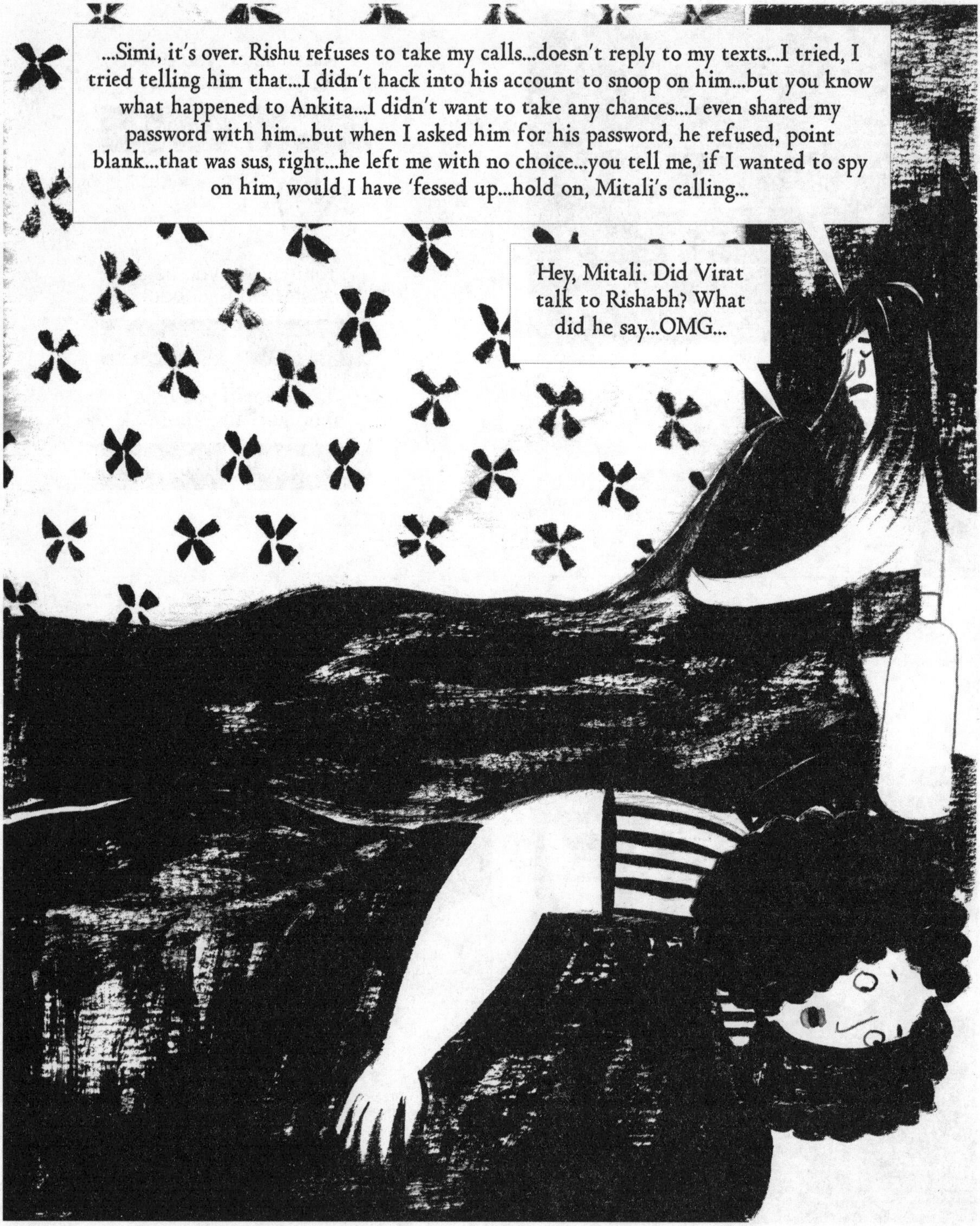
...Simi, it's over. Rishu refuses to take my calls...doesn't reply to my texts...I tried, I tried telling him that...I didn't hack into his account to snoop on him...but you know what happened to Ankita...I didn't want to take any chances...I even shared my password with him...but when I asked him for his password, he refused, point blank...that was sus, right...he left me with no choice...you tell me, if I wanted to spy on him, would I have 'fessed up...hold on, Mitali's calling...
Hey, Mitali. Did Virat talk to Rishabh? What did he say...OMG...

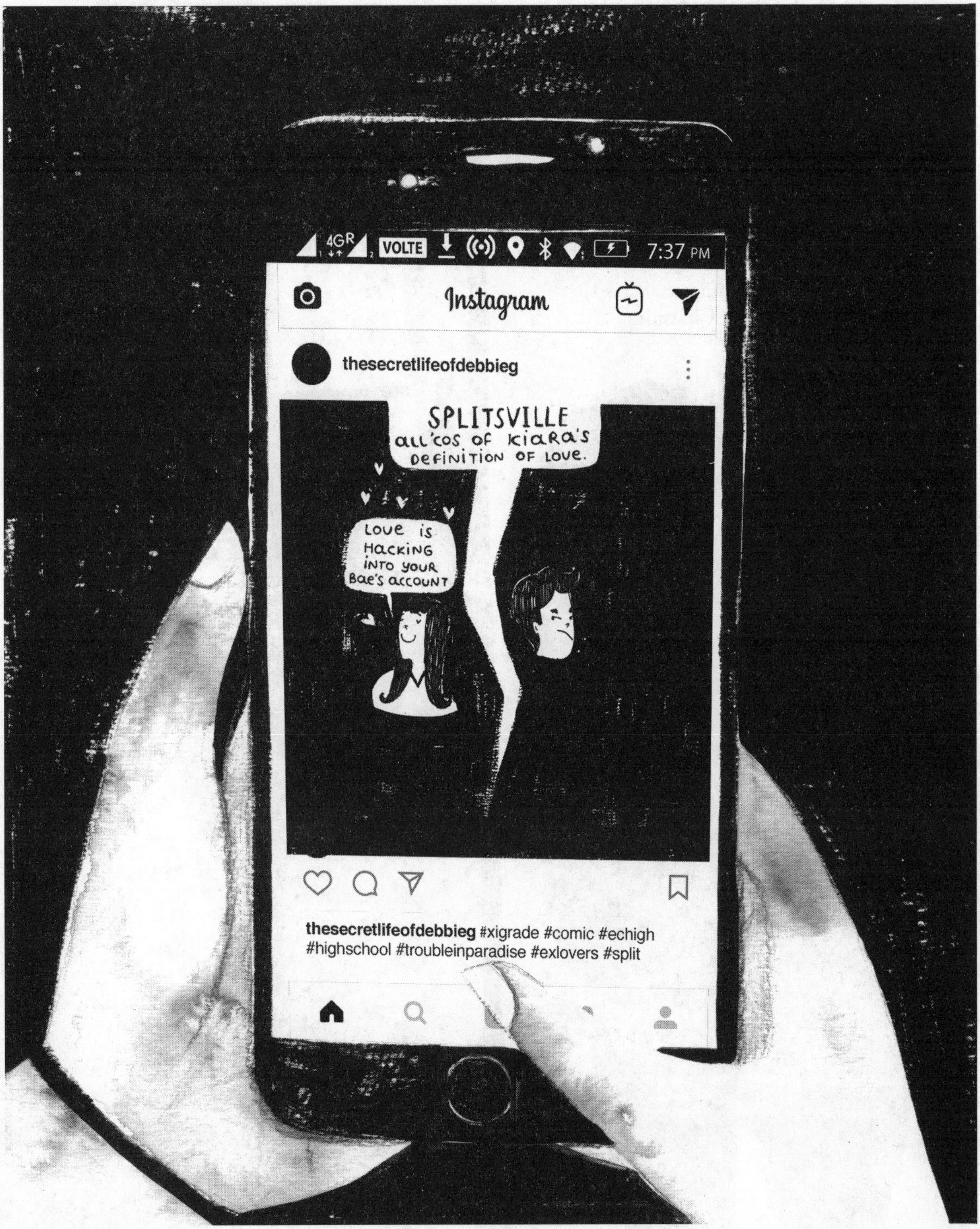
7:37 PM
Instagram
thesecretlifeofdebbieg
SPLITSVILLE
all 'cos of kiara's definition of love.
Love is hacking into your Bae's account
thesecretlifeofdebbieg #xigrade #comic #echigh #highschool #troubleinparadise #exlovers #split

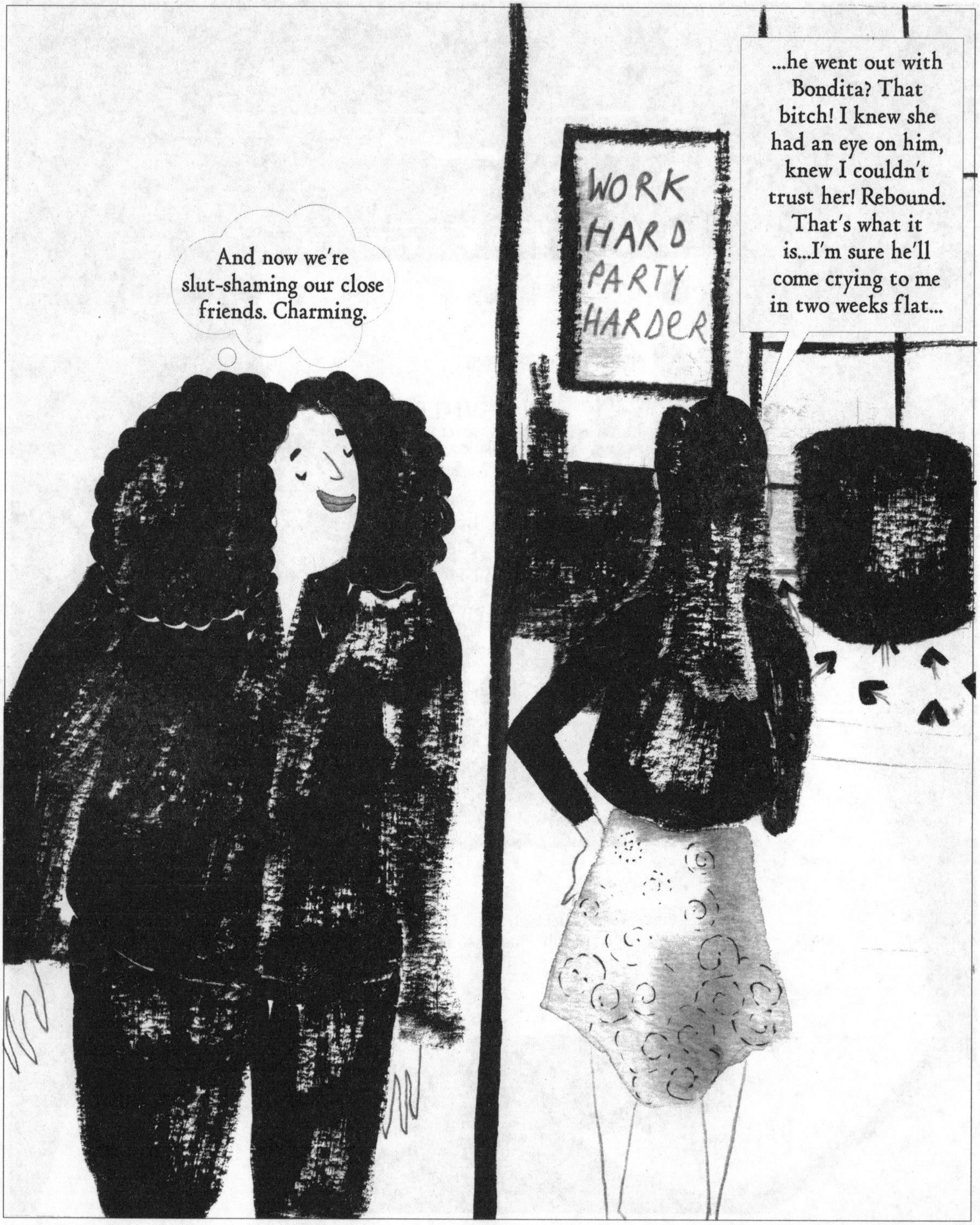
And now we're slut-shaming our close friends. Charming.
WORK HARD PARTY HARDER
...he went out with Bondita? That bitch! I knew she had an eye on him, knew I couldn't trust her! Rebound. That's what it is...I'm sure he'll come crying to me in two weeks flat...

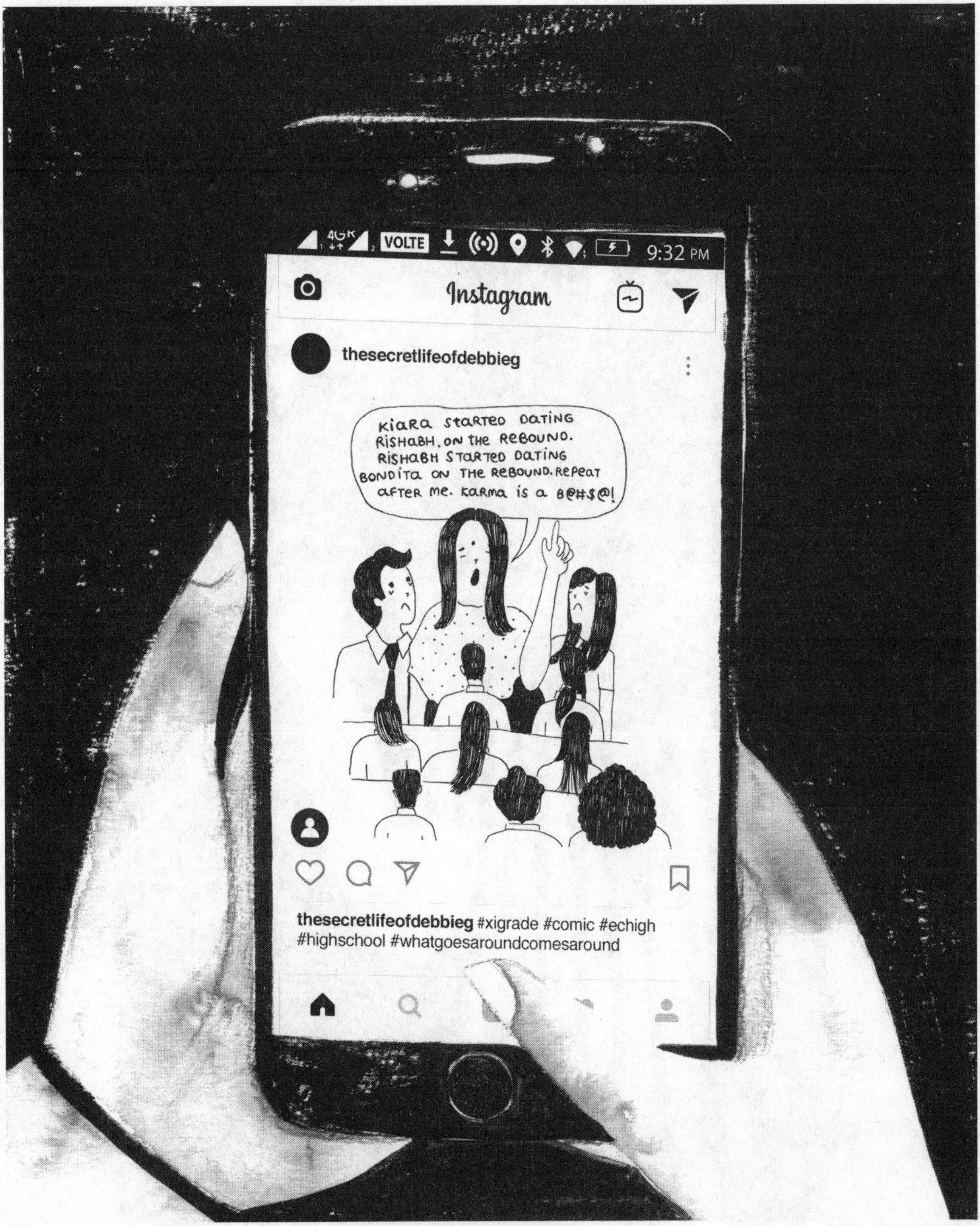
9:32 PM
Instagram
thesecretlifeofdebbieg
KIARA STARTED DATING RISHABH, ON THE REBOUND. RISHABH STARTED DATING BONDITA ON THE REBOUND. REPEAT AFTER ME. KARMA IS A B@#$@!
thesecretlifeofdebbieg #xigrade #comic #echigh #highschool #whatgoesaroundcomesaround

28

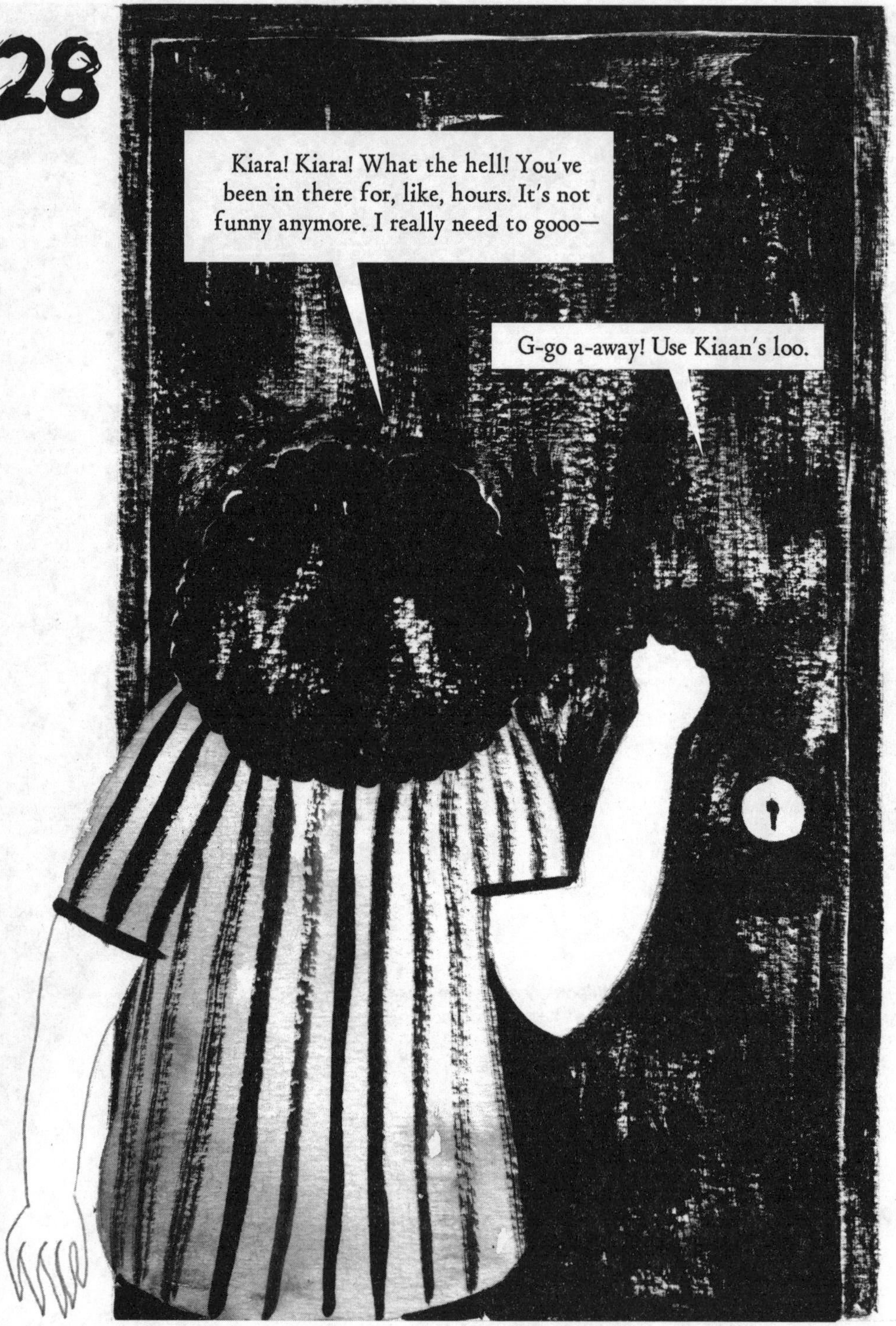
Kiara! Kiara! What the hell! You've been in there for, like, hours. It's not funny anymore. I really need to gooo—
G-go a-away! Use Kiaan's loo.

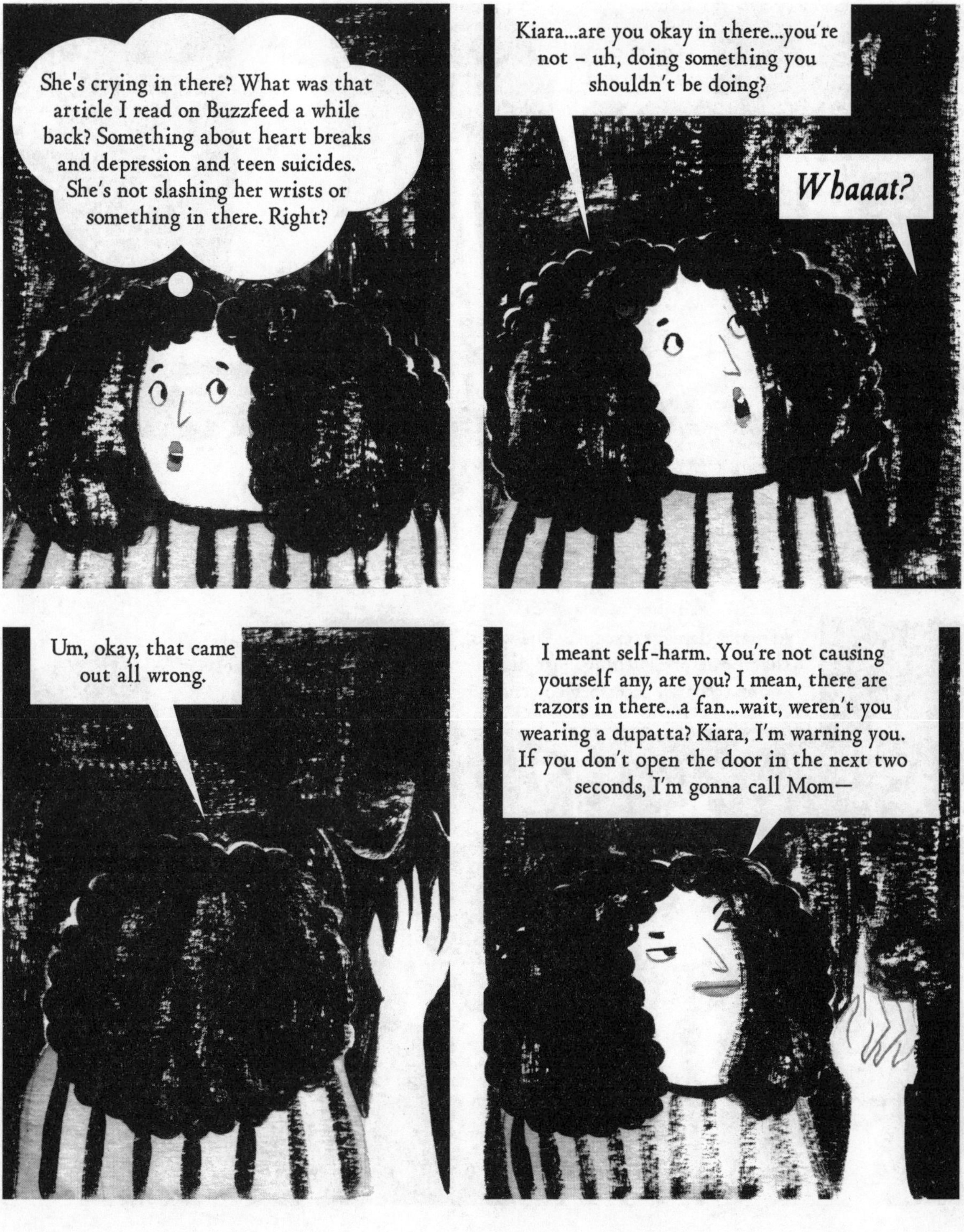
She's crying in there? What was that article I read on Buzzfeed a while back? Something about heart breaks and depression and teen suicides. She's not slashing her wrists or something in there. Right?
Kiara...are you okay in there...you're not – uh, doing something you shouldn't be doing?
Whaaat?
Um, okay, that came out all wrong.
I meant self-harm. You're not causing yourself any, are you? I mean, there are razors in there...a fan...wait, weren't you wearing a dupatta? Kiara, I'm warning you. If you don't open the door in the next two seconds, I'm gonna call Mom—

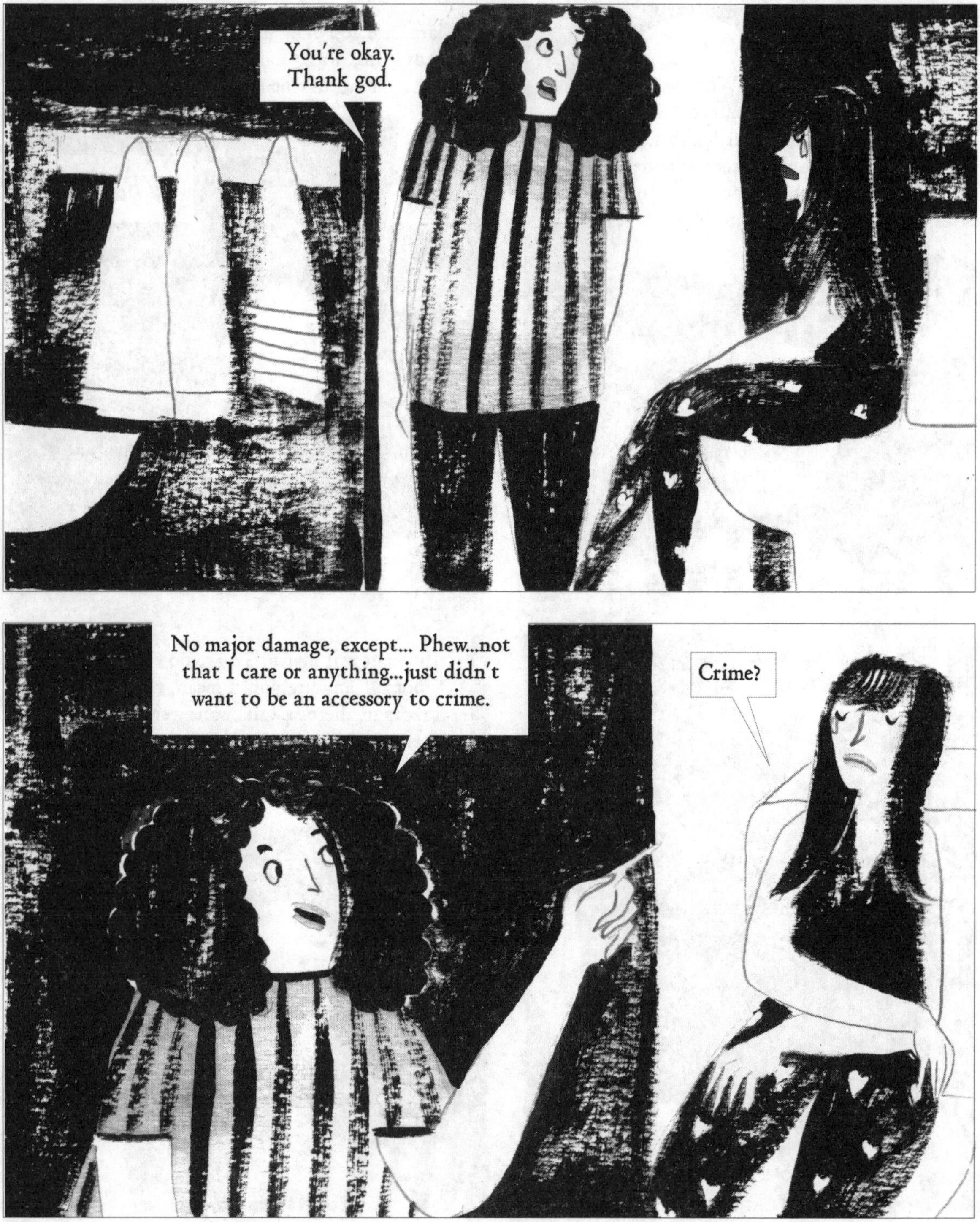
You're okay. Thank god.
No major damage, except... Phew...not that I care or anything...just didn't want to be an accessory to crime.
Crime?

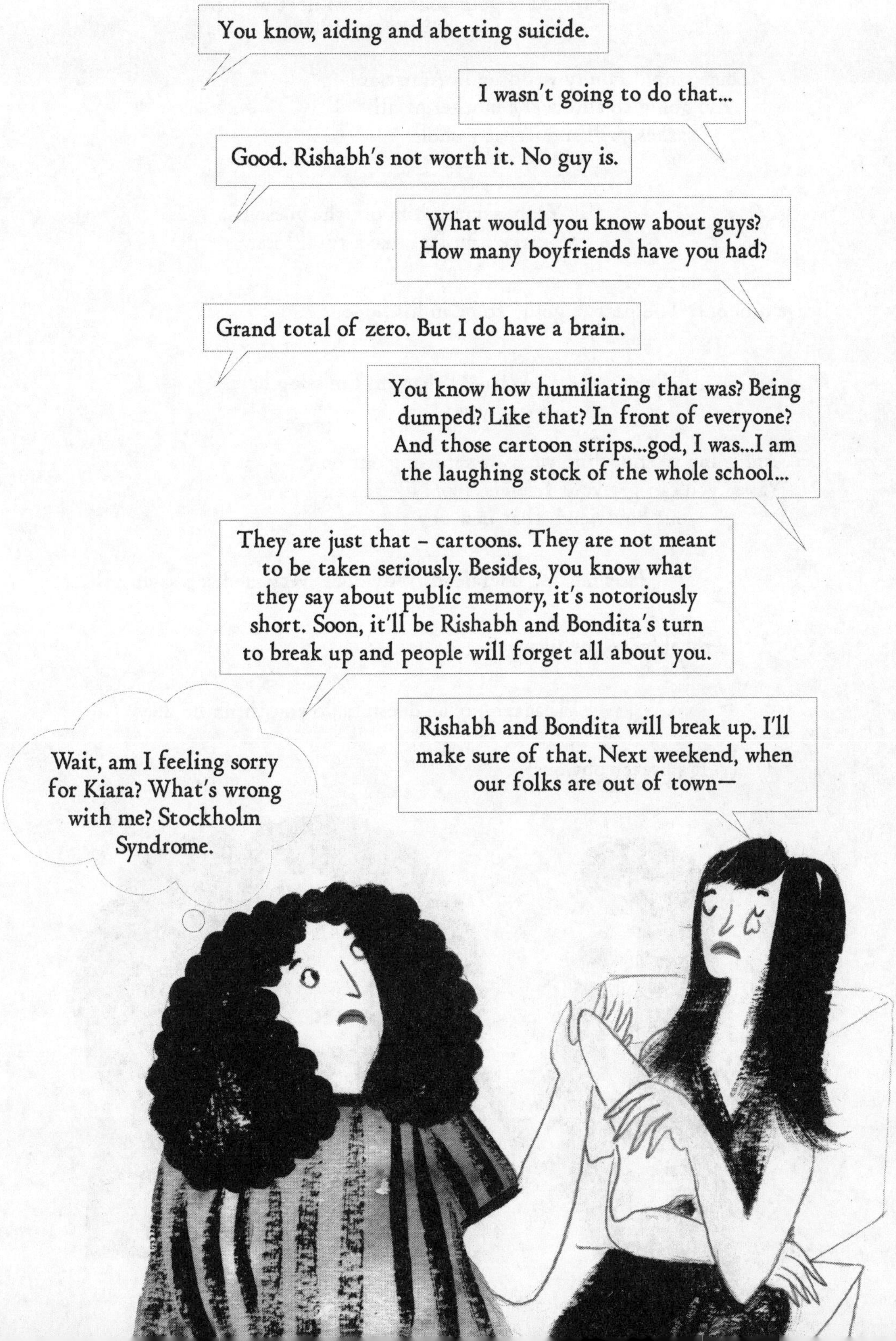

You know, aiding and abetting suicide.
I wasn't going to do that...
Good. Rishabh's not worth it. No guy is.
What would you know about guys? How many boyfriends have you had?
Grand total of zero. But I do have a brain.
You know how humiliating that was? Being dumped? Like that? In front of everyone? And those cartoon strips...god, I was...I am the laughing stock of the whole school...
They are just that – cartoons. They are not meant to be taken seriously. Besides, you know what they say about public memory, it's notoriously short. Soon, it'll be Rishabh and Bondita's turn to break up and people will forget all about you.
Wait, am I feeling sorry for Kiara? What's wrong with me? Stockholm Syndrome.
Rishabh and Bondita will break up. I'll make sure of that. Next weekend, when our folks are out of town—

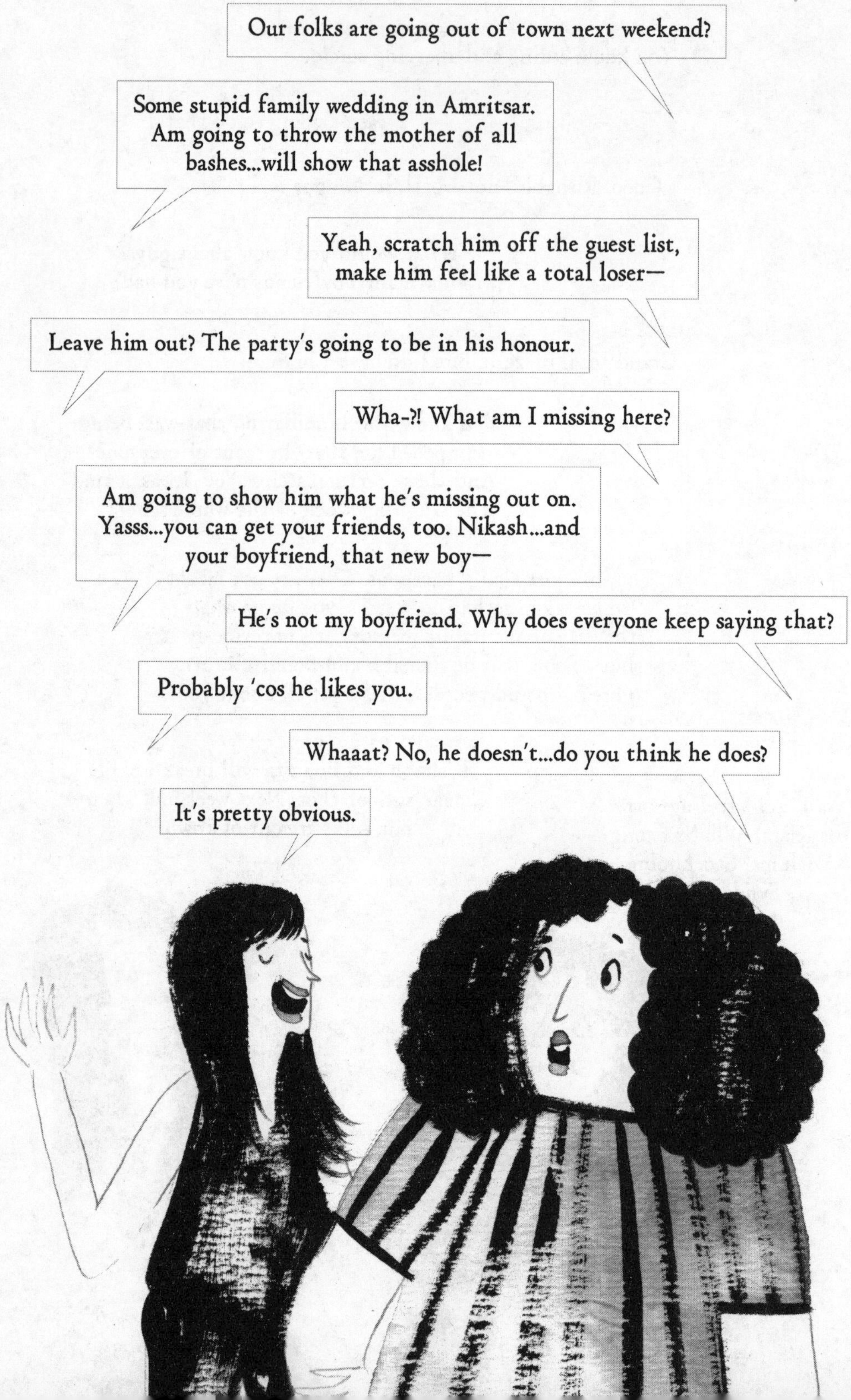
Our folks are going out of town next weekend?
Some stupid family wedding in Amritsar. Am going to throw the mother of all bashes...will show that asshole!
Yeah, scratch him off the guest list, make him feel like a total loser—
Leave him out? The party's going to be in his honour.
Wha-?! What am I missing here?
Am going to show him what he's missing out on. Yasss...you can get your friends, too. Nikash...and your boyfriend, that new boy—
He's not my boyfriend. Why does everyone keep saying that?
Probably 'cos he likes you.
Whaaat? No, he doesn't...do you think he does?
It's pretty obvious.

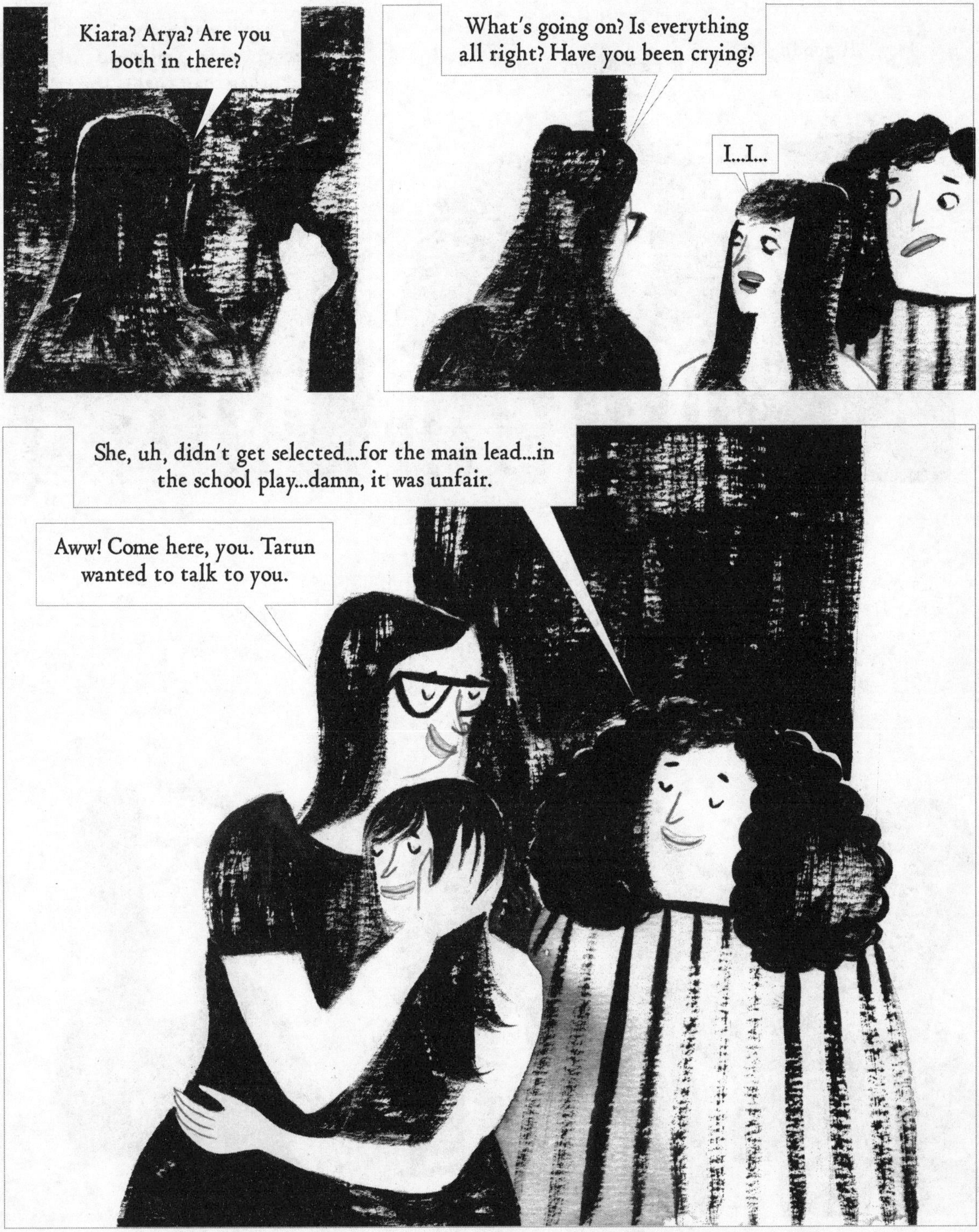
Kiara? Arya? Are you both in there?
What's going on? Is everything all right? Have you been crying?
I...I...
She, uh, didn't get selected...for the main lead...in the school play...damn, it was unfair.
Aww! Come here, you. Tarun wanted to talk to you.

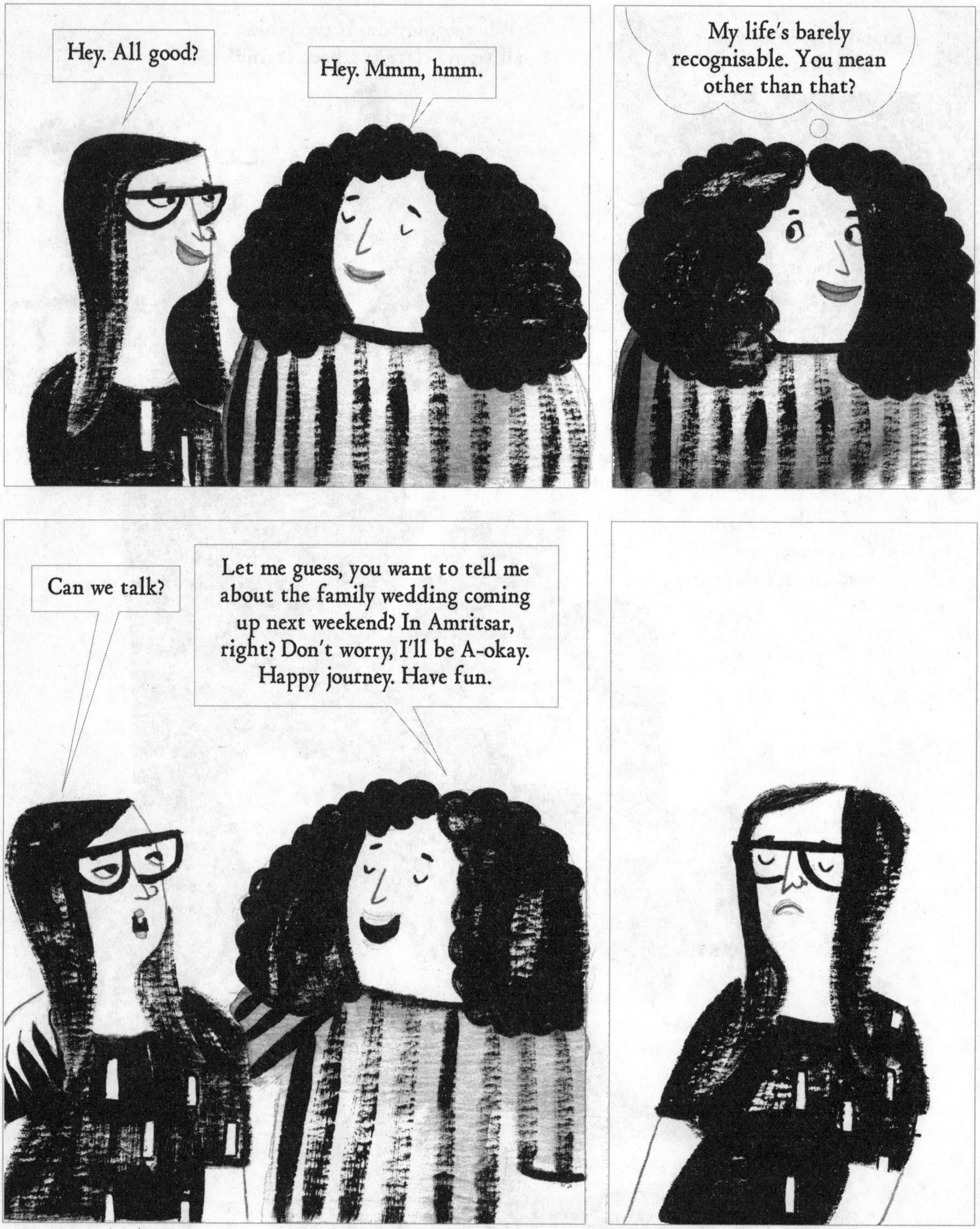
Hey. All good?
Hey. Mmm, hmm.
My life's barely recognisable. You mean other than that?
Can we talk?
Let me guess, you want to tell me about the family wedding coming up next weekend? In Amritsar, right? Don't worry, I'll be A-okay. Happy journey. Have fun.

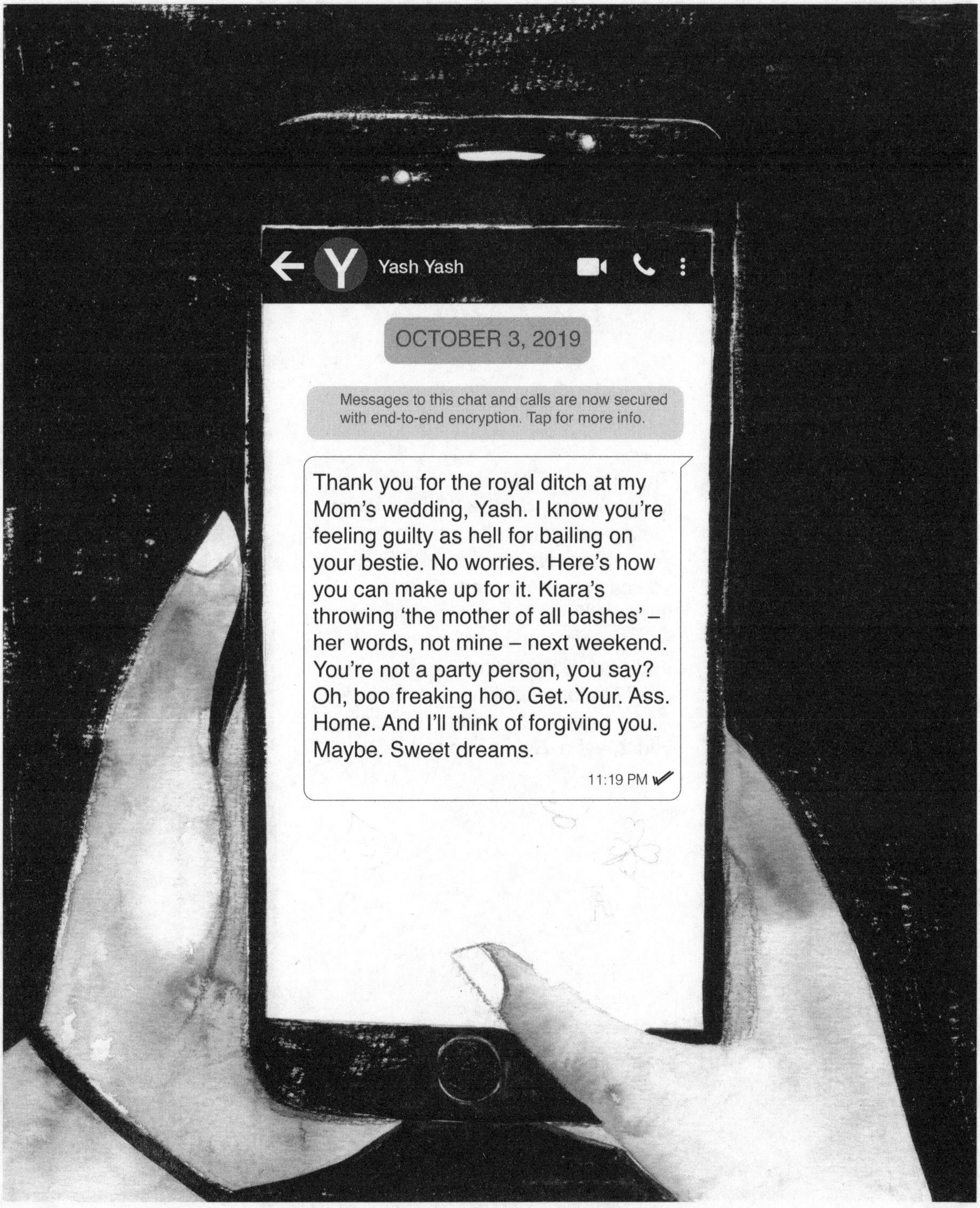
Yash Yash
OCTOBER 3, 2019
Messages to this chat and calls are now secured with end-to-end encryption. Tap for more info.
Thank you for the royal ditch at my Mom's wedding, Yash. I know you're feeling guilty as hell for bailing on your bestie. No worries. Here's how you can make up for it. Kiara's throwing 'the mother of all bashes' – her words, not mine – next weekend. You're not a party person, you say? Oh, boo freaking hoo. Get. Your. Ass. Home. And I'll think of forgiving you. Maybe. Sweet dreams.
11:19 PM

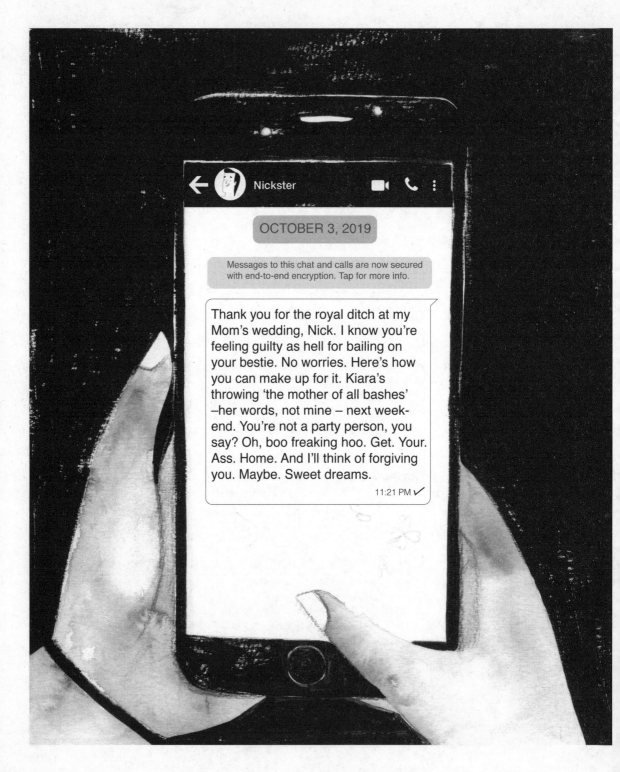

I was BEYOND excited about the party. Did I say "party" and "excited" in the same sentence? Yeah, you heard that right. Let's just say Debbie G couldn't wait for the next weekend. (sighs) Gawd, I don't know how celebs and social media influencers do it. How do they create engaging content? Day after day? Week after week? Month after month? Here I was killing myself thinking up ways to create something fresh/different/entertaining. It was getting tougher with each passing week. Maybe the novelty factor had worn off. (Hey, even the best viral content comes with an expiry date.) Or maybe I was getting repetitive. How could I not? All my "source" had done in the last few weeks was cry, crib, carp about Rishabh. In any case, there were only so many Invincibles at school. And I'd finished dissing them all. Not surprisingly, the posts were getting fewer and fewer likes, barely any comments, and I was getting zero DMs. Worse, the account was bleeding followers. I had to do something. And fast. And where else could I get hot goss except at a pardyyyy!

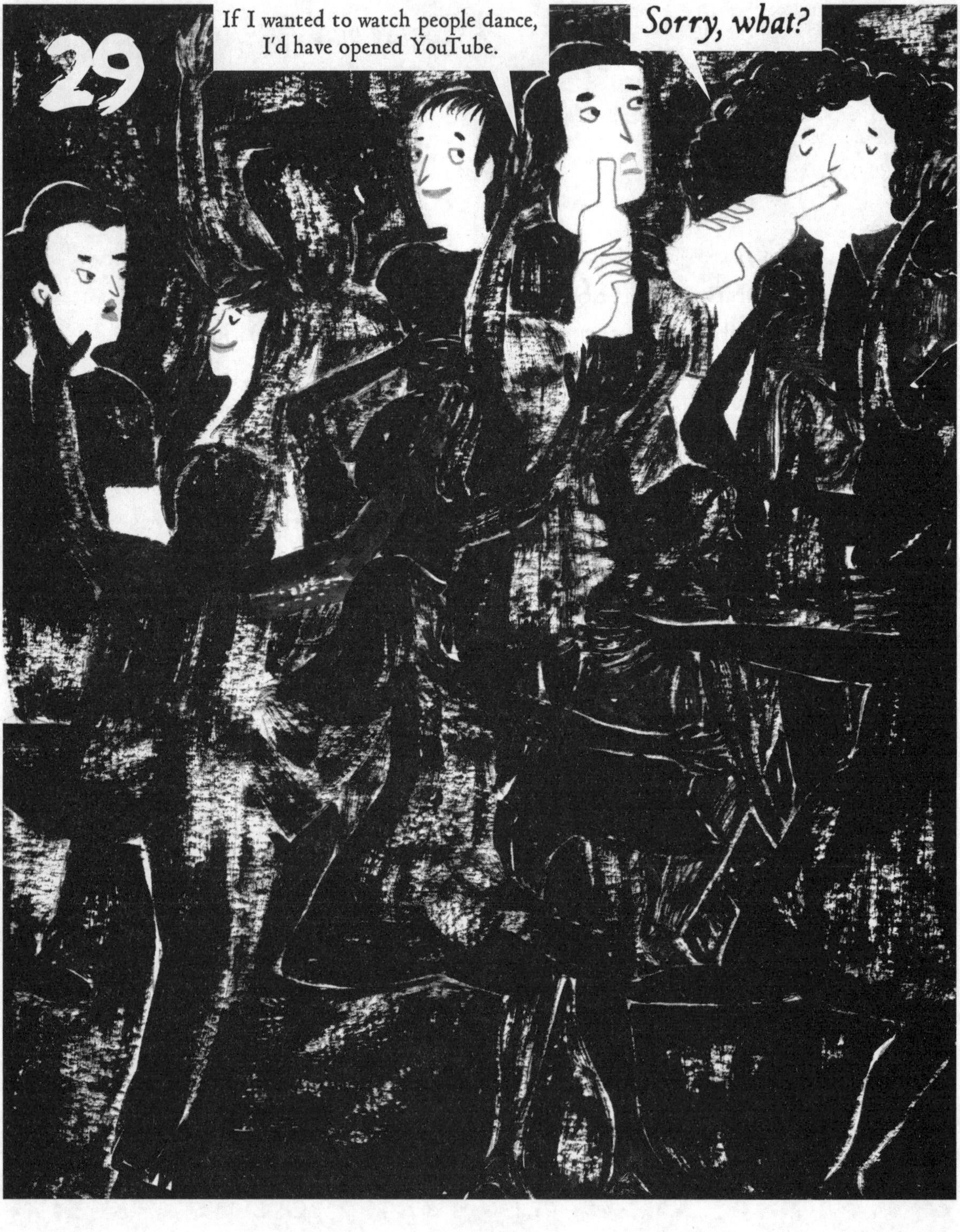
29
If I wanted to watch people dance, I'd have opened YouTube.
Sorry, what?

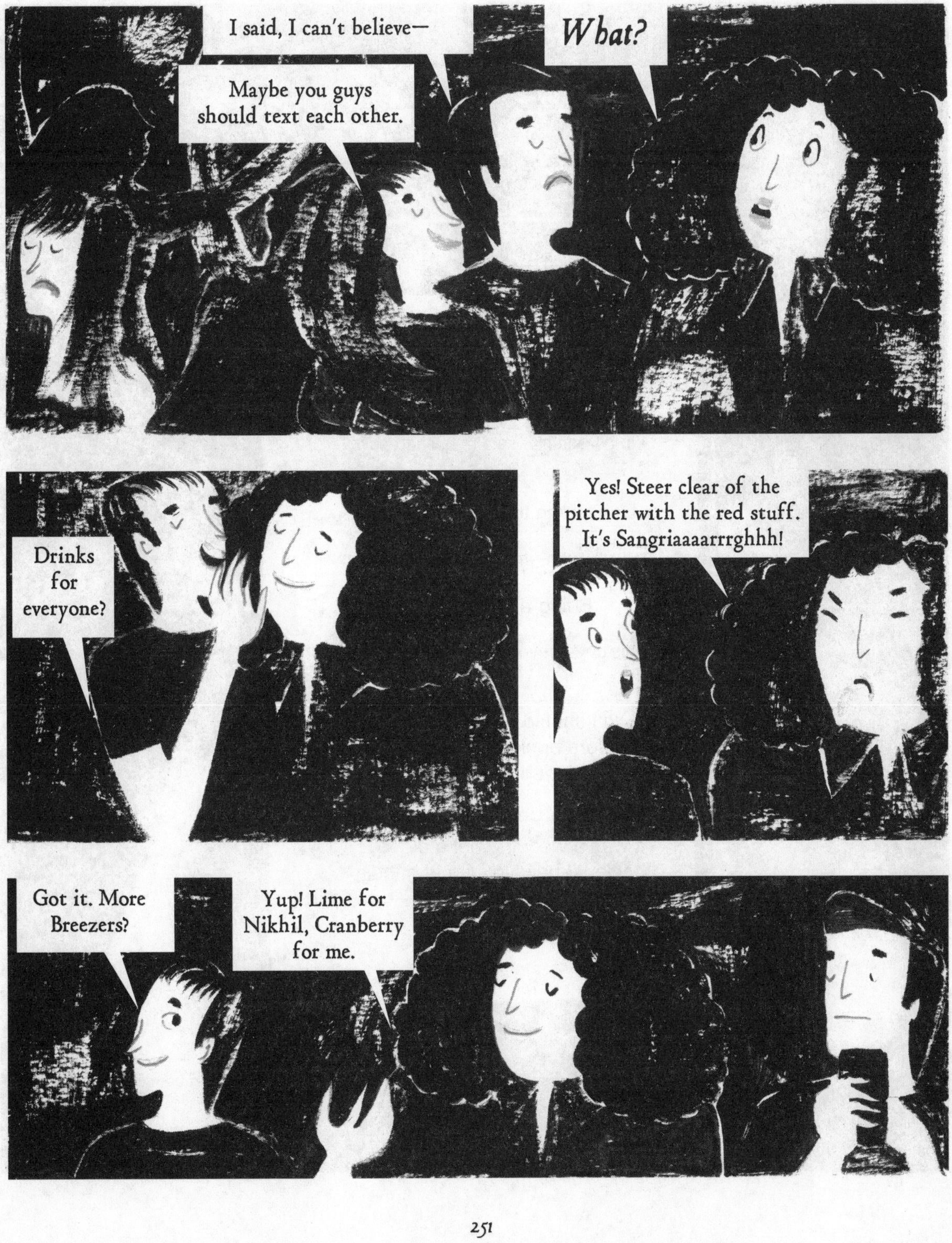
I said, I can't believe—
Maybe you guys should text each other.
What?
Drinks for everyone?
Yes! Steer clear of the pitcher with the red stuff. It's Sangriaaaarrrghhh!
Got it. More Breezers?
Yup! Lime for Nikhil, Cranberry for me.

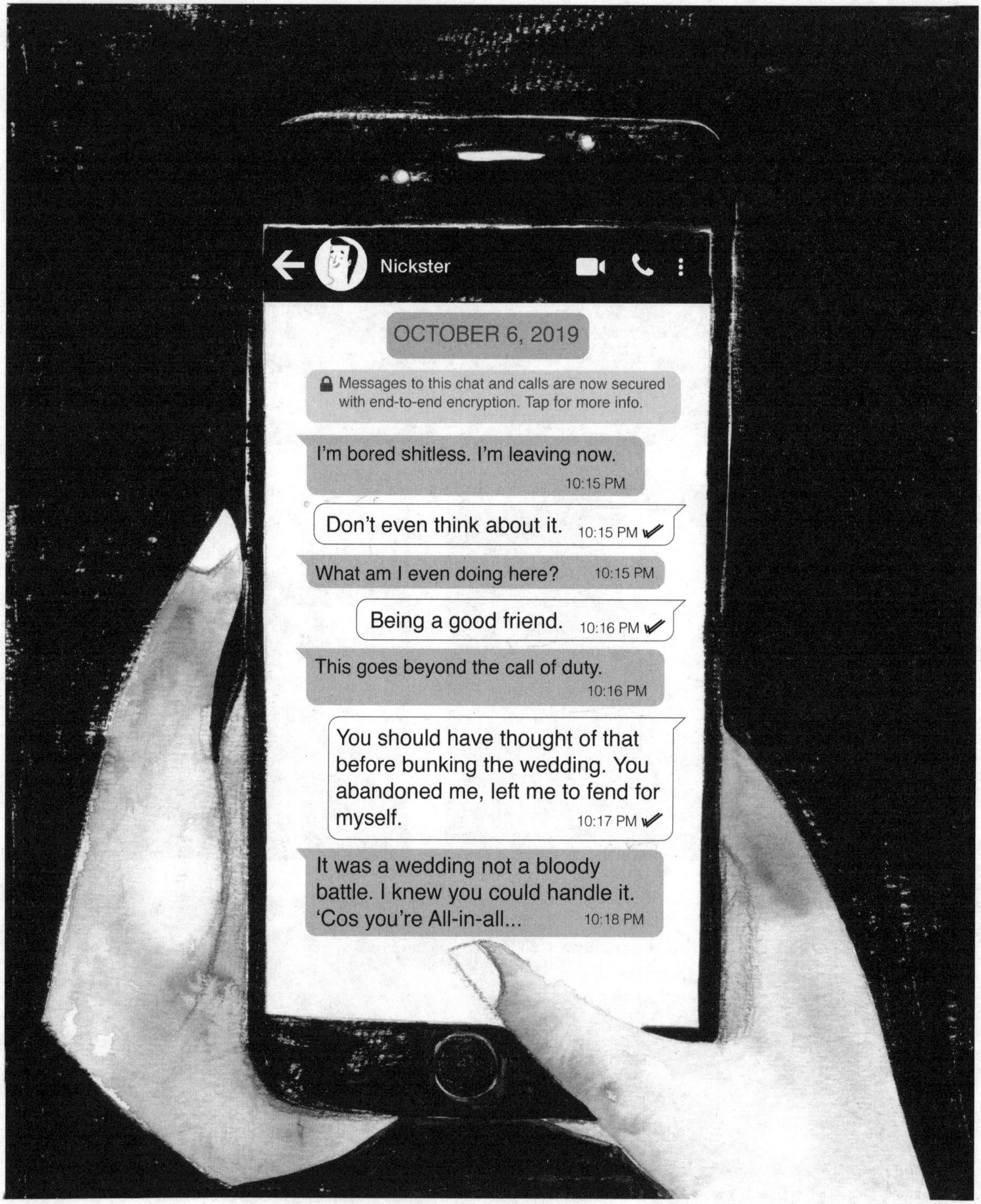
Nickster
OCTOBER 6, 2019
Messages to this chat and calls are now secured with end-to-end encryption. Tap for more info.
I'm bored shitless. I'm leaving now. 10:15 PM
Don't even think about it. 10:15 PM
What am I even doing here? 10:15 PM
Being a good friend. 10:16 PM
This goes beyond the call of duty. 10:16 PM
You should have thought of that before bunking the wedding. You abandoned me, left me to fend for myself. 10:17 PM
It was a wedding not a bloody battle. I knew you could handle it. 'Cos you're All-in-all... 10:18 PM

All-in-all Azhagaraj. 10:19 PM ✔

Yeah, that. 10:19 PM

Will scoot in thirty. Tops. 10:20 PM

Don't be such a party pooper! 10:21 PM ✔

Just giving you and Yash some alone time. 😉
Good choice of crush though. I approve. He seems like a stand up guy. Way better than the Kiaans and the Chintans of the world.
10:22 PM

Poor thing. And I'm talking about Chintan here. You haven't even met him. 10:23 PM ✔

Checked him out on FB. The hair on that guy's arms alone could fashion a wig. 10:23 PM

😊 What about Kiaan? What did he ever do to you? 10:23 PM ✔

I mean, just look at him. His vice like grip shoving tequila down his guest's throats! 10:24 PM

He probably thinks he's being a good host or something. 10:24 PM

I see what you mean. 10:25 PM ✔

What do you have against Yash? What, he's not cool enough for you? 10:25 PM

It's not like that. 10:25 PM ✔

But you do like him, right? Now don't say, 'Yeah, but not like that'. Either you like him or you don't. So which is it? 10:26 PM

253

Option 1. 😊 😊 😊 10:27 PM ✔

There we have it, a declaration. At long last. 10:27 PM

Please. 10:29 PM ✔

What's the problem? 10:29 PM

No problem. Don't know him nearly well enough. Don't know if he likes me back. 10:30 PM ✔

Even after all those long drives? 10:27 PM

What long drives... oh, you mean the carpool. 😊 Don't know if I'm reading too much into it, but he did say something the other day. And it got me thinking. 10:30 PM ✔

What? What did he say? 10:31 PM

Ha! Wouldn't you like to know? Let's start with you. What's Fatal Attraction's name? 10:31 PM ✔

Nice chatting with ya. 10:31 PM

What's taking Yash so long? 10:32 PM ✔

Maybe he went home. 10:33 PM

He wouldn't dare. Come on, let's go look for him. Hope Kiaan's not making him do shots. 10:35 PM ✔

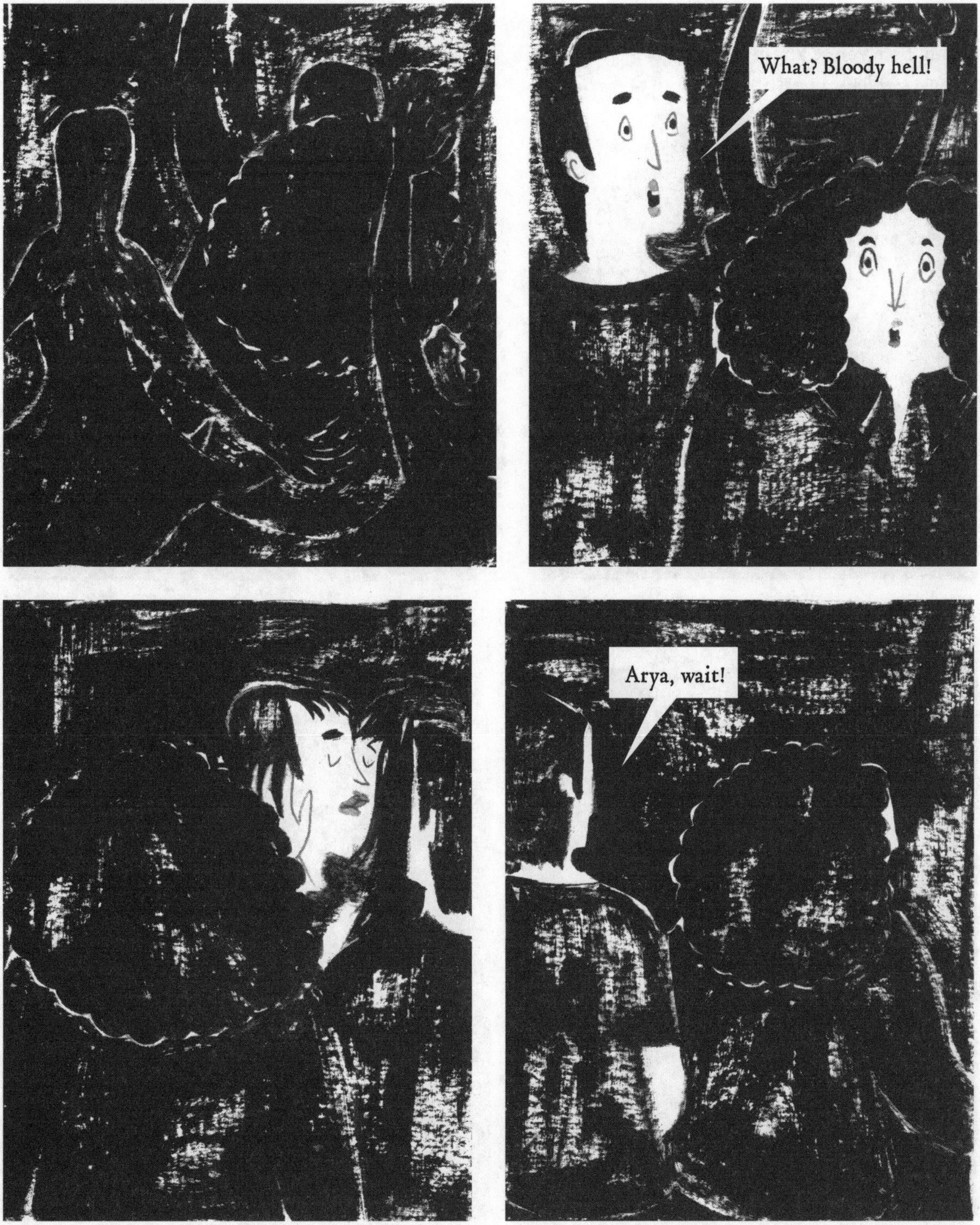
What? Bloody hell!
Arya, wait!

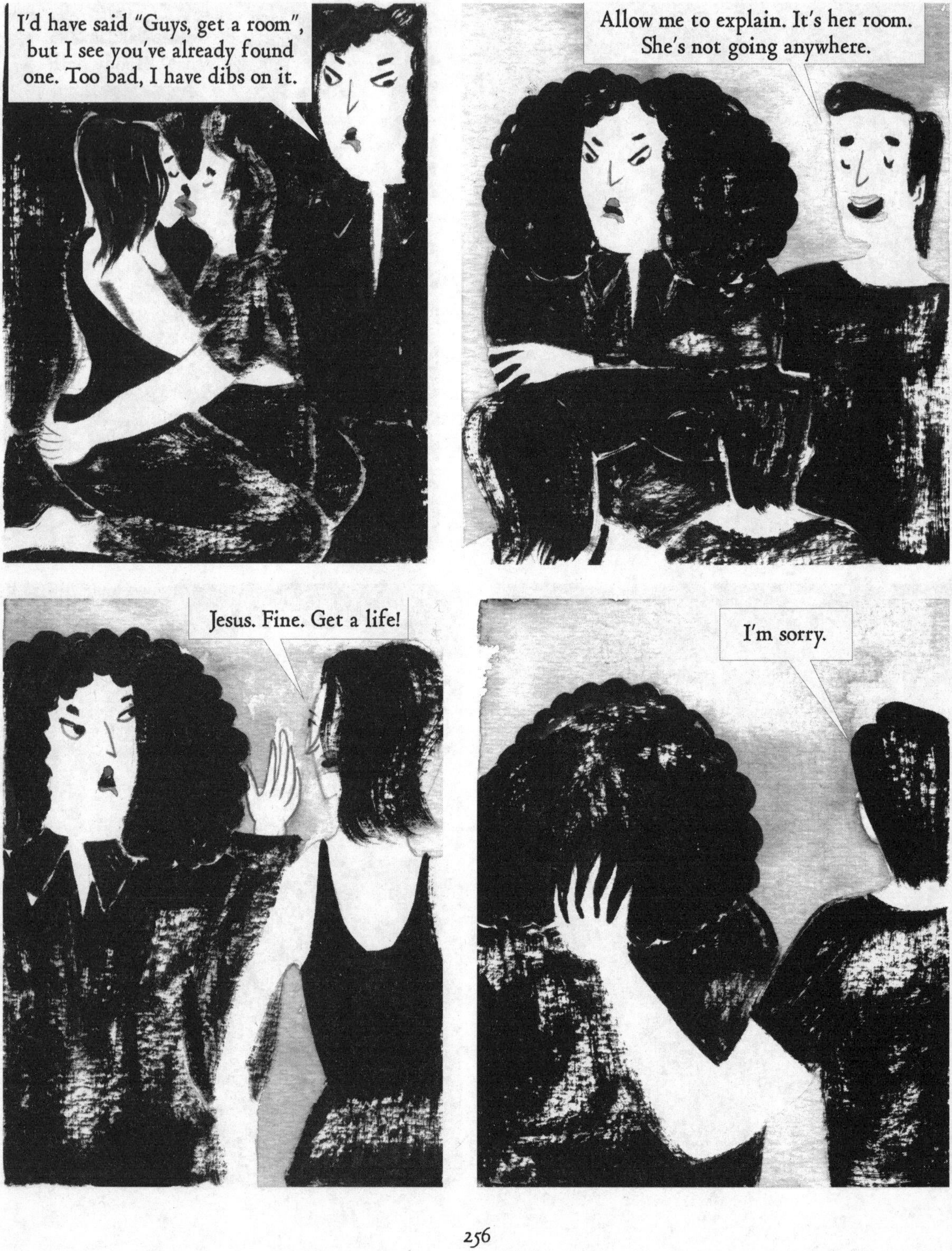
I'd have said "Guys, get a room", but I see you've already found one. Too bad, I have dibs on it.
Allow me to explain. It's her room. She's not going anywhere.
Jesus. Fine. Get a life!
I'm sorry.

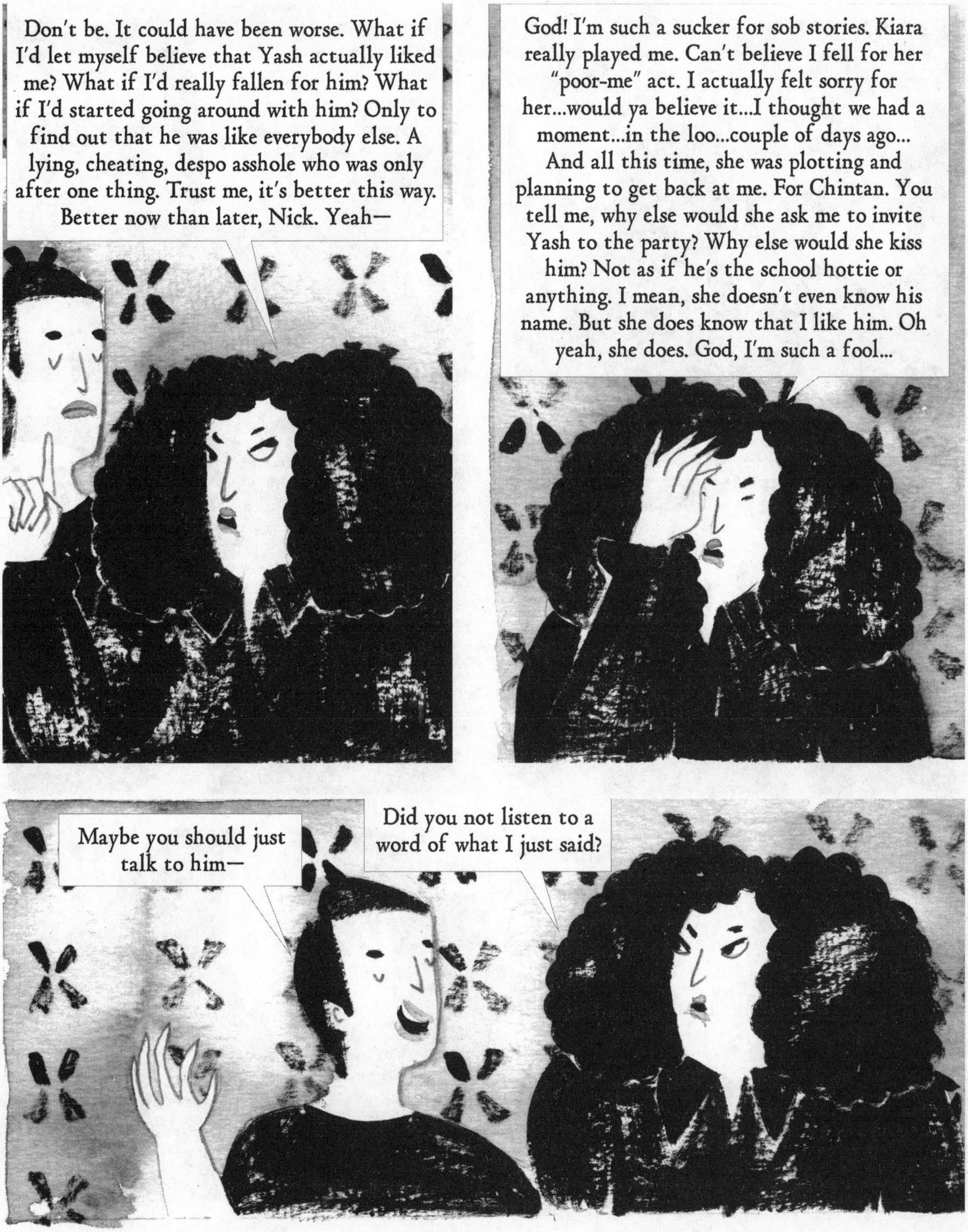
Don't be. It could have been worse. What if I'd let myself believe that Yash actually liked me? What if I'd really fallen for him? What if I'd started going around with him? Only to find out that he was like everybody else. A lying, cheating, despo asshole who was only after one thing. Trust me, it's better this way. Better now than later, Nick. Yeah—
God! I'm such a sucker for sob stories. Kiara really played me. Can't believe I fell for her "poor-me" act. I actually felt sorry for her...would ya believe it...I thought we had a moment...in the loo...couple of days ago... And all this time, she was plotting and planning to get back at me. For Chintan. You tell me, why else would she ask me to invite Yash to the party? Why else would she kiss him? Not as if he's the school hottie or anything. I mean, she doesn't even know his name. But she does know that I like him. Oh yeah, she does. God, I'm such a fool...
Maybe you should just talk to him—
Did you not listen to a word of what I just said?

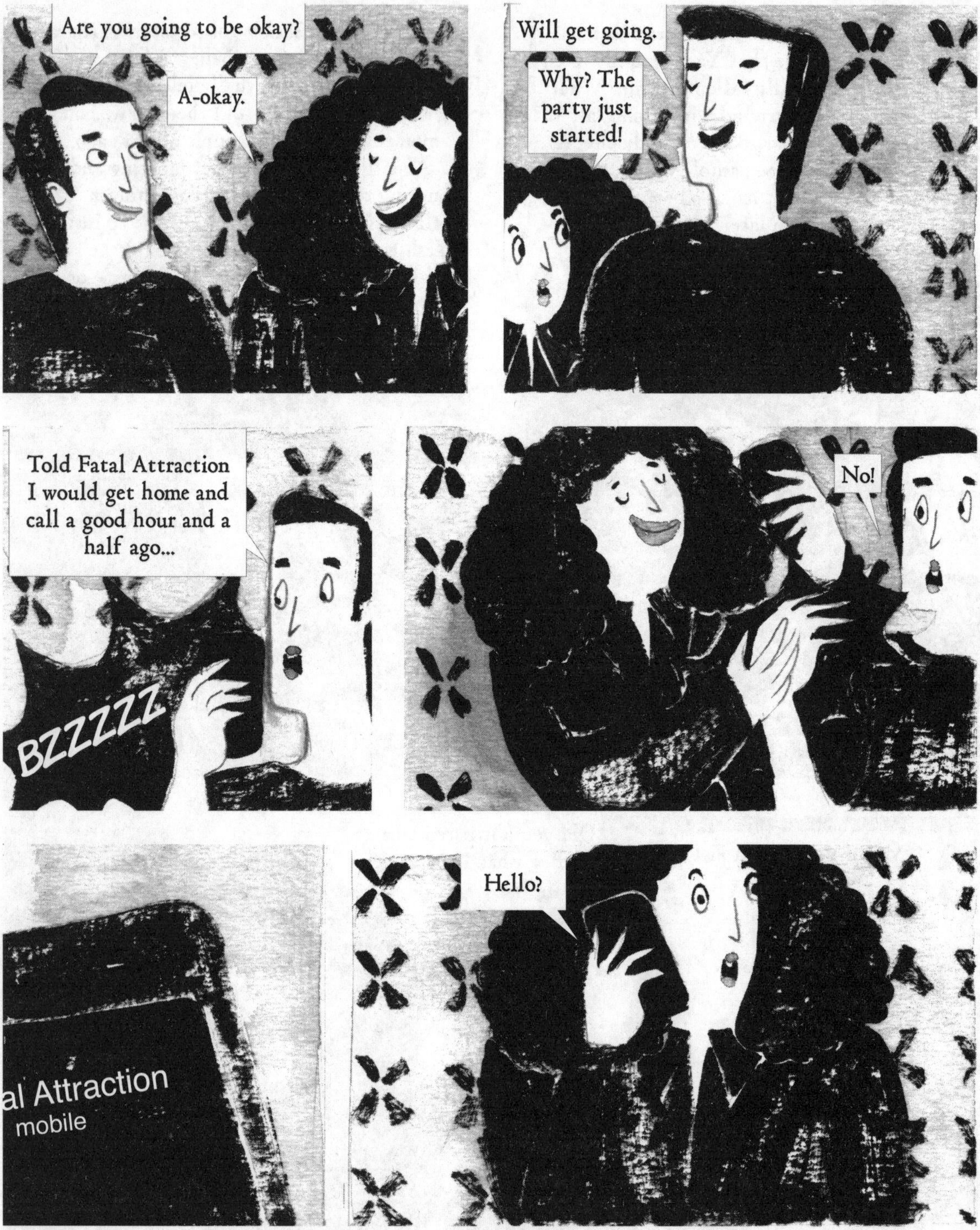
Are you going to be okay?
A-okay.
Will get going.
Why? The party just started!
Told Fatal Attraction I would get home and call a good hour and a half ago...
BZZZZZ
No!
al Attraction
mobile
Hello?

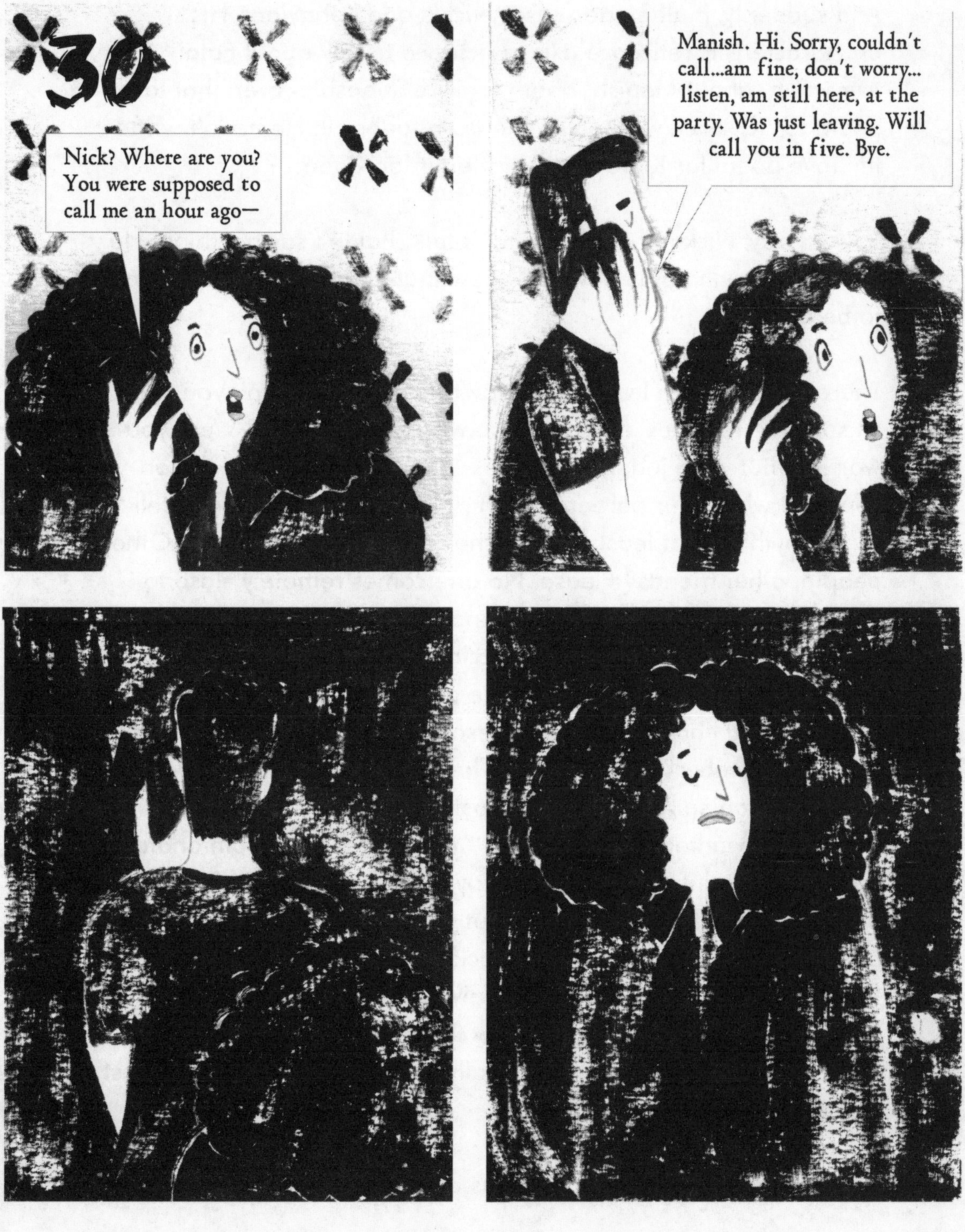
30
Nick? Where are you? You were supposed to call me an hour ago—
Manish. Hi. Sorry, couldn't call...am fine, don't worry... listen, am still here, at the party. Was just leaving. Will call you in five. Bye.

And suddenly, it all made sense: Nick's odd behaviour. His uncharacteristic reticence. His reluctance to talk about Fatal Attraction, about Manish, about their relationship. Even that love poem to "K". Nick was telling the truth, after all. He hadn't written the love poem for Kiara. He'd written it for Kiaan.

So, anyway, Nick left. No, we didn't talk. I didn't say anything. He didn't say anything. I knew. He knew that I knew. And that seemed to be enough.

There was so much I wanted to say to him. "Why didn't you tell us sooner? Your best friends in the whole wide world? Were you worried that we'd judge you? Were you afraid that we'd tell on you? Tell who? Our parents? Yeah right. You know we don't tell them anything – at least none of the stuff that truly matters. Other people, other friends? Please. No one comes remotely close to what we feel for each other. You know that better than anyone. Why then? Did you think we'd acccidentally let it slip? Give us more credit than that, will you? We guard our secrets as fiercely as we defend each other. The Awesome Threesome versus The World, remember? And now, it's The Awesome Threesome versus The Homosapien Agenda." But most of all, there was just one thing that I wanted to say to Nick. "You're stubborn, opinionated, brutally frank, infuriating and annoying as hell—more often than not, I just want to biff you one—but you're also kind and caring and thoughtful. And I love you. Rucksack and I both do. You know that, right? And even though you give us such a hard time and act like you don't really care, we know that you love us. We'll always have each other. That's all that really matters. To hell with the rest of the world."

I wish I'd said that to him. I've tons of regrets. But this one...

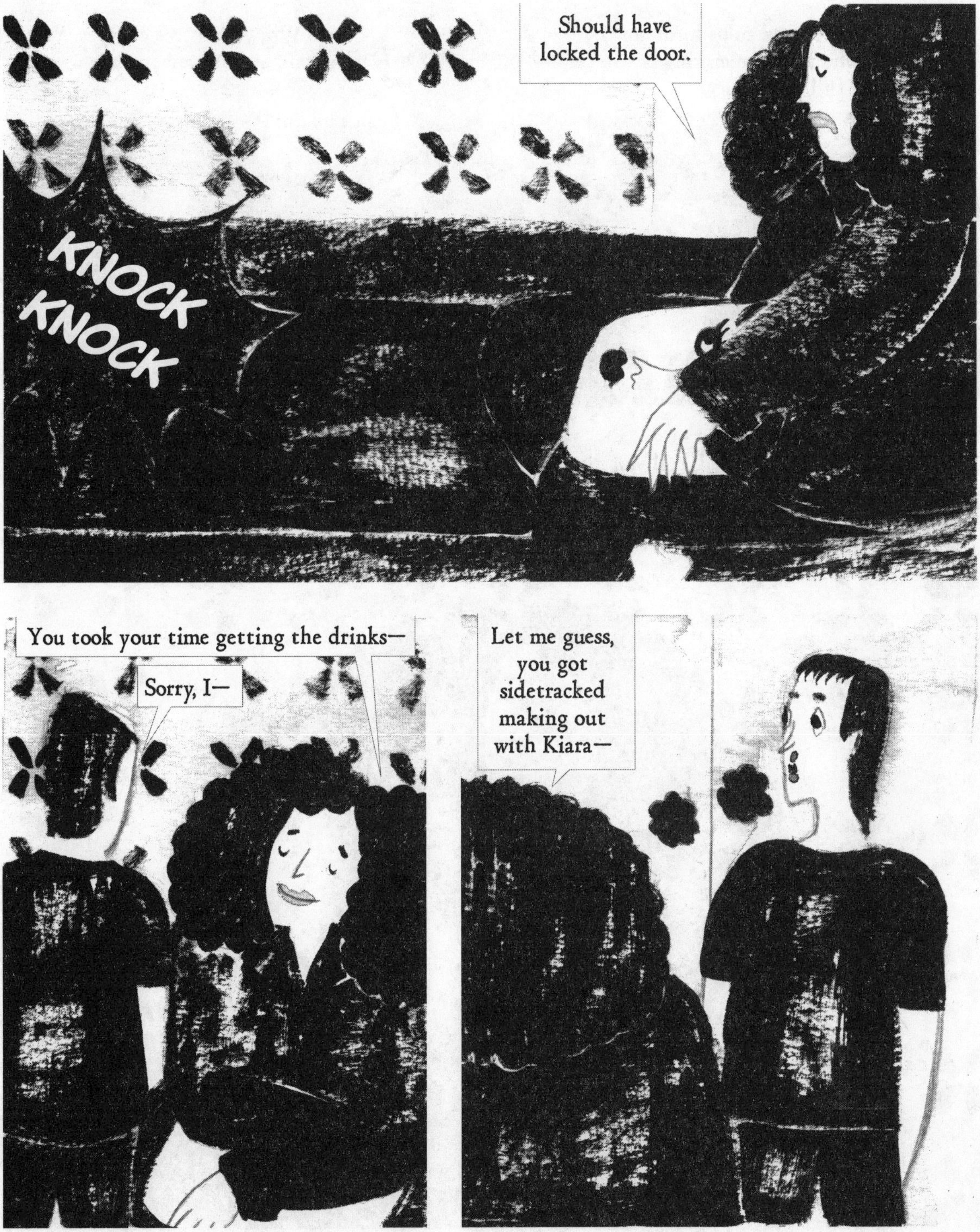
KNOCK KNOCK
Should have locked the door.
You took your time getting the drinks—
Sorry, I—
Let me guess, you got sidetracked making out with Kiara—

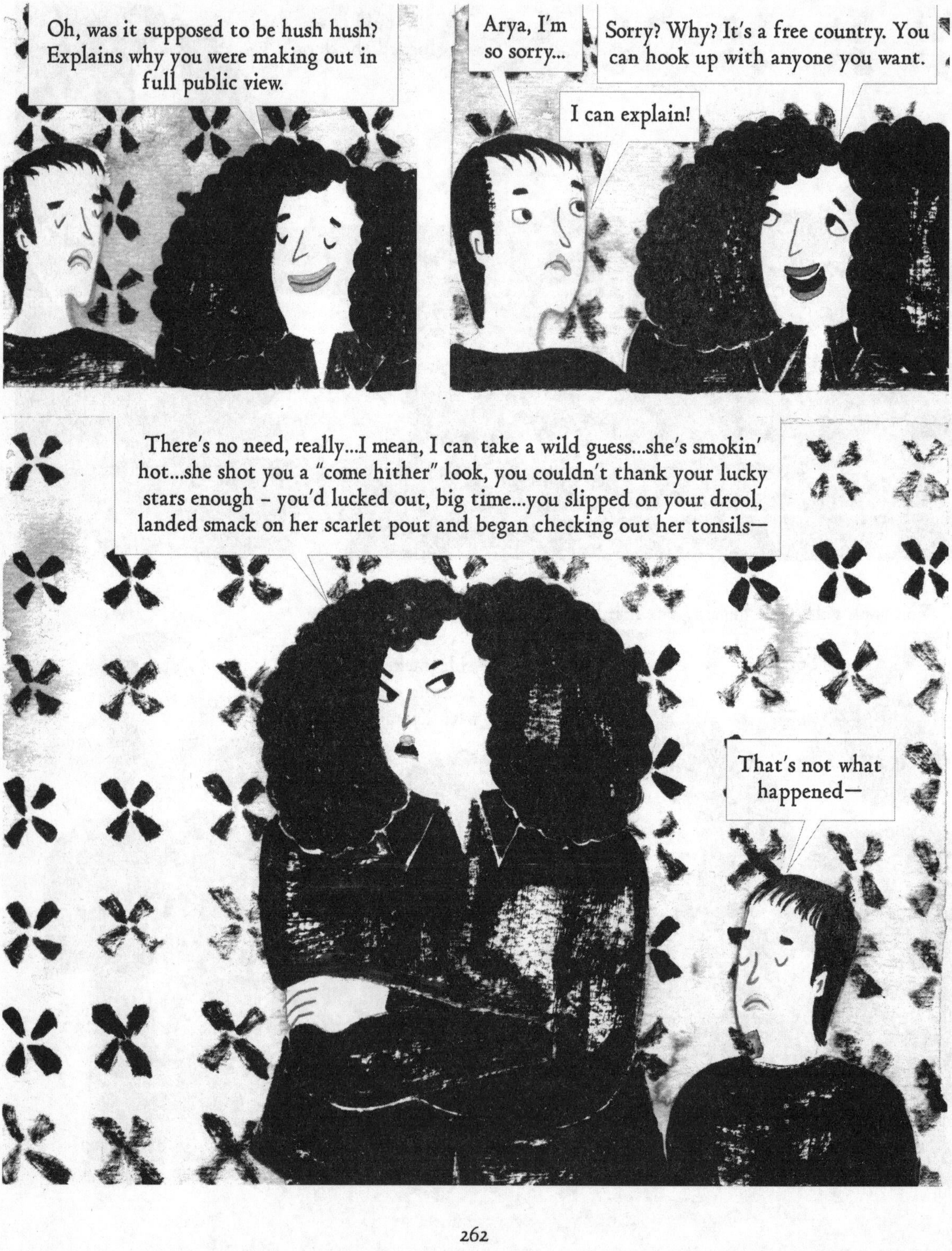
Oh, was it supposed to be hush hush? Explains why you were making out in full public view.
Arya, I'm so sorry...
Sorry? Why? It's a free country. You can hook up with anyone you want.
I can explain!
There's no need, really...I mean, I can take a wild guess...she's smokin' hot...she shot you a "come hither" look, you couldn't thank your lucky stars enough – you'd lucked out, big time...you slipped on your drool, landed smack on her scarlet pout and began checking out her tonsils—
That's not what happened—

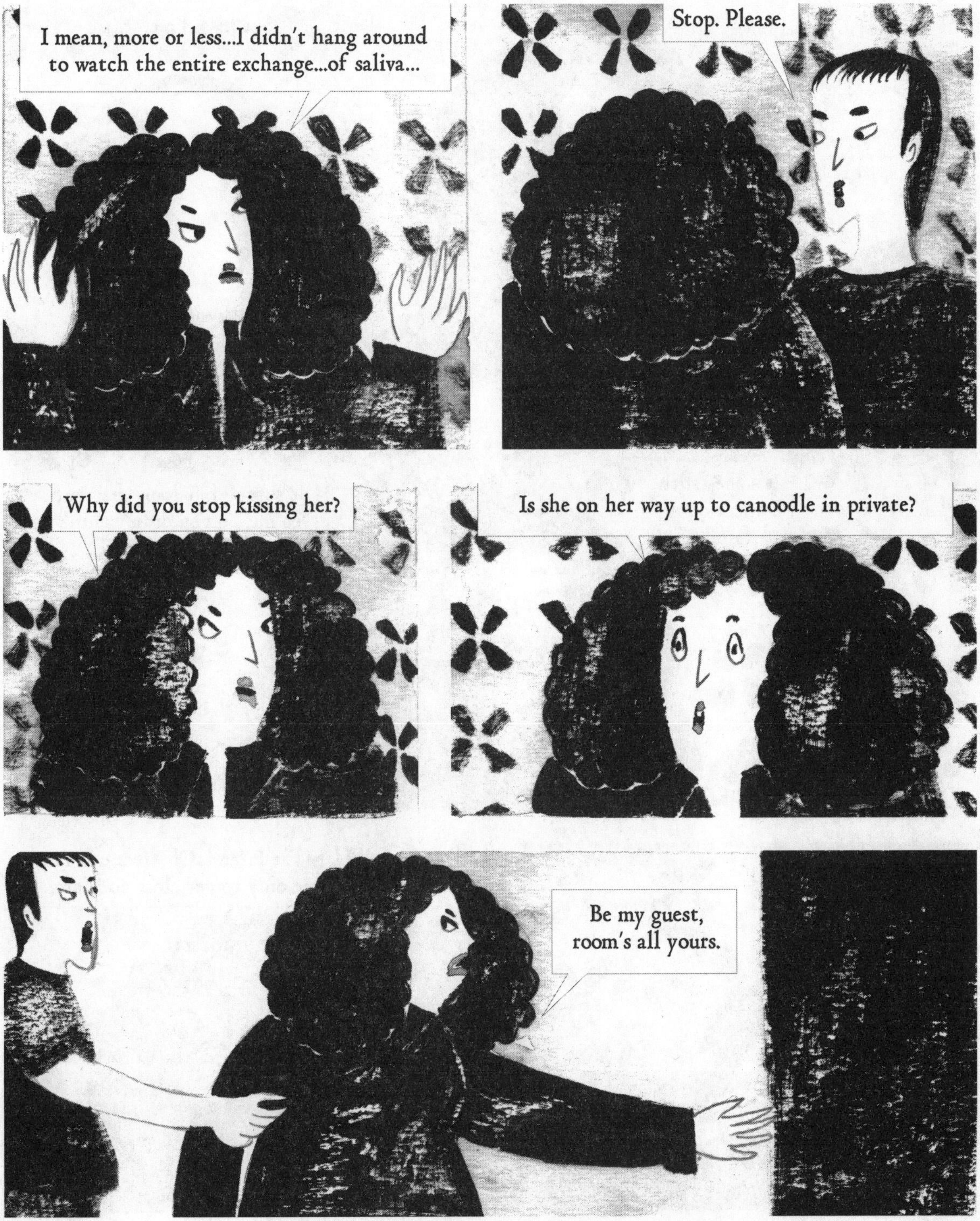
I mean, more or less...I didn't hang around to watch the entire exchange...of saliva...
Stop. Please.
Why did you stop kissing her?
Is she on her way up to canoodle in private?
Be my guest, room's all yours.

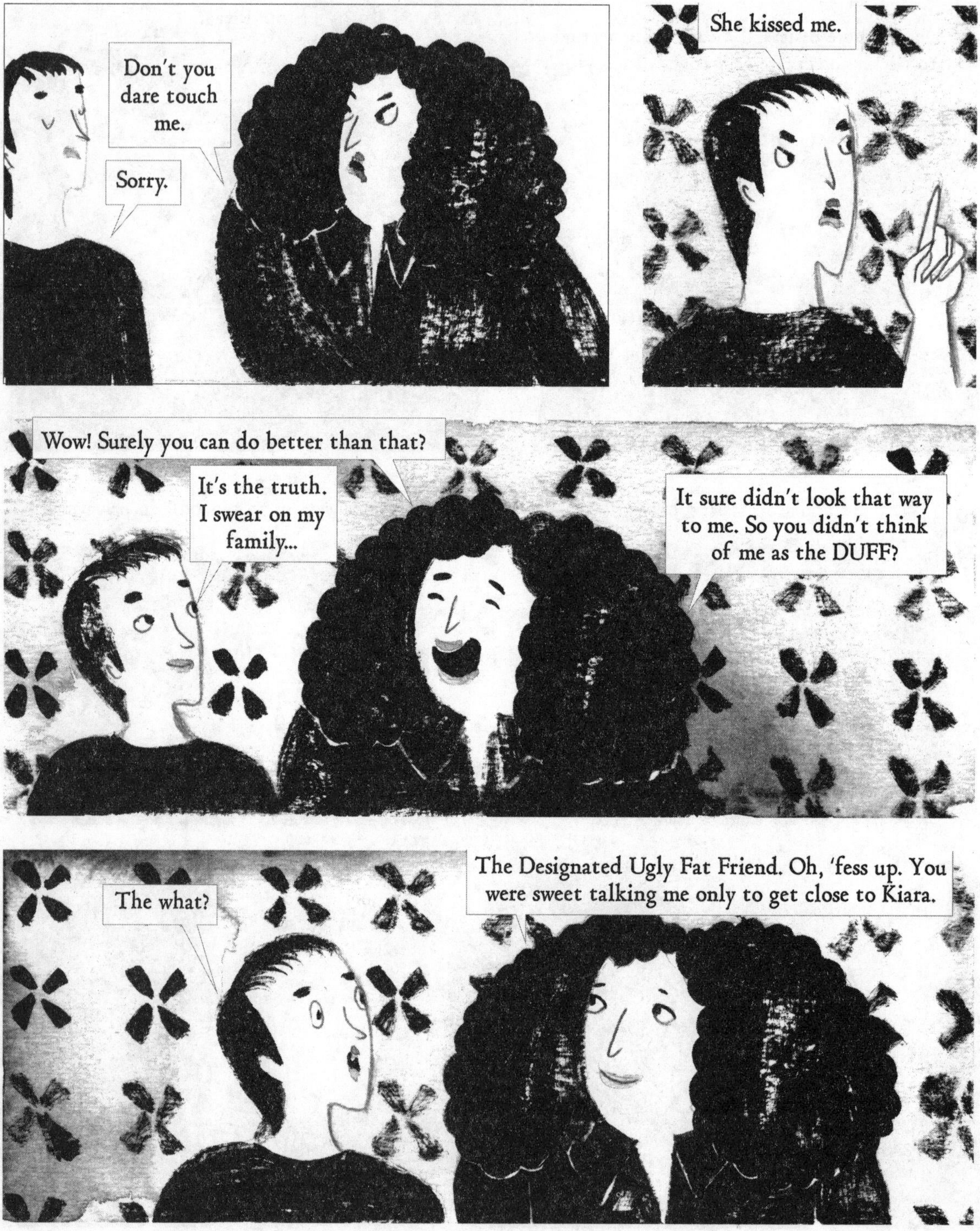

Don't you dare touch me.
Sorry.
She kissed me.
Wow! Surely you can do better than that?
It's the truth. I swear on my family...
It sure didn't look that way to me. So you didn't think of me as the DUFF?
The what?
The Designated Ugly Fat Friend. Oh, 'fess up. You were sweet talking me only to get close to Kiara.

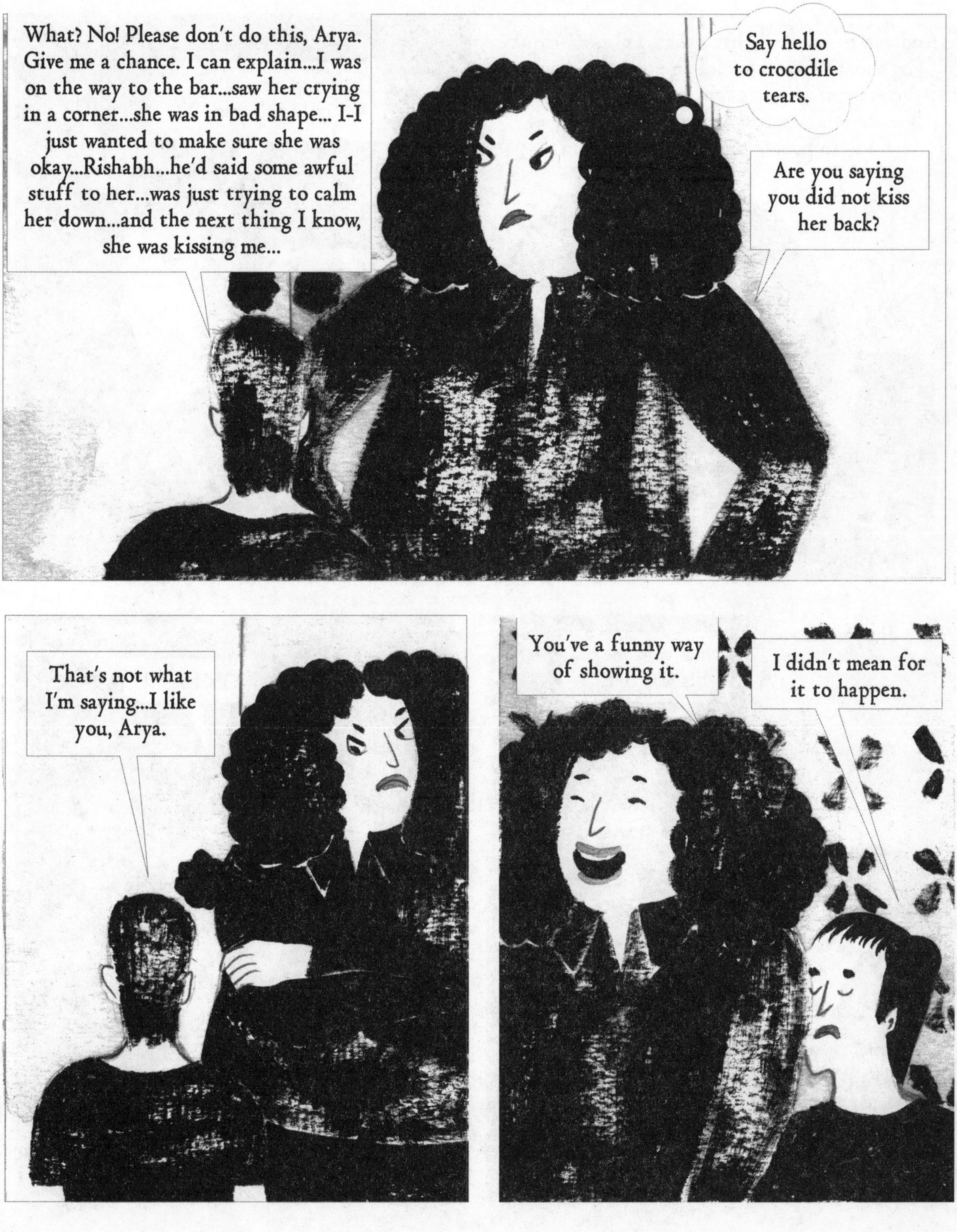
What? No! Please don't do this, Arya. Give me a chance. I can explain...I was on the way to the bar...saw her crying in a corner...she was in bad shape... I-I just wanted to make sure she was okay...Rishabh...he'd said some awful stuff to her...was just trying to calm her down...and the next thing I know, she was kissing me...
Say hello to crocodile tears.
Are you saying you did not kiss her back?
That's not what I'm saying...I like you, Arya.
You've a funny way of showing it.
I didn't mean for it to happen.

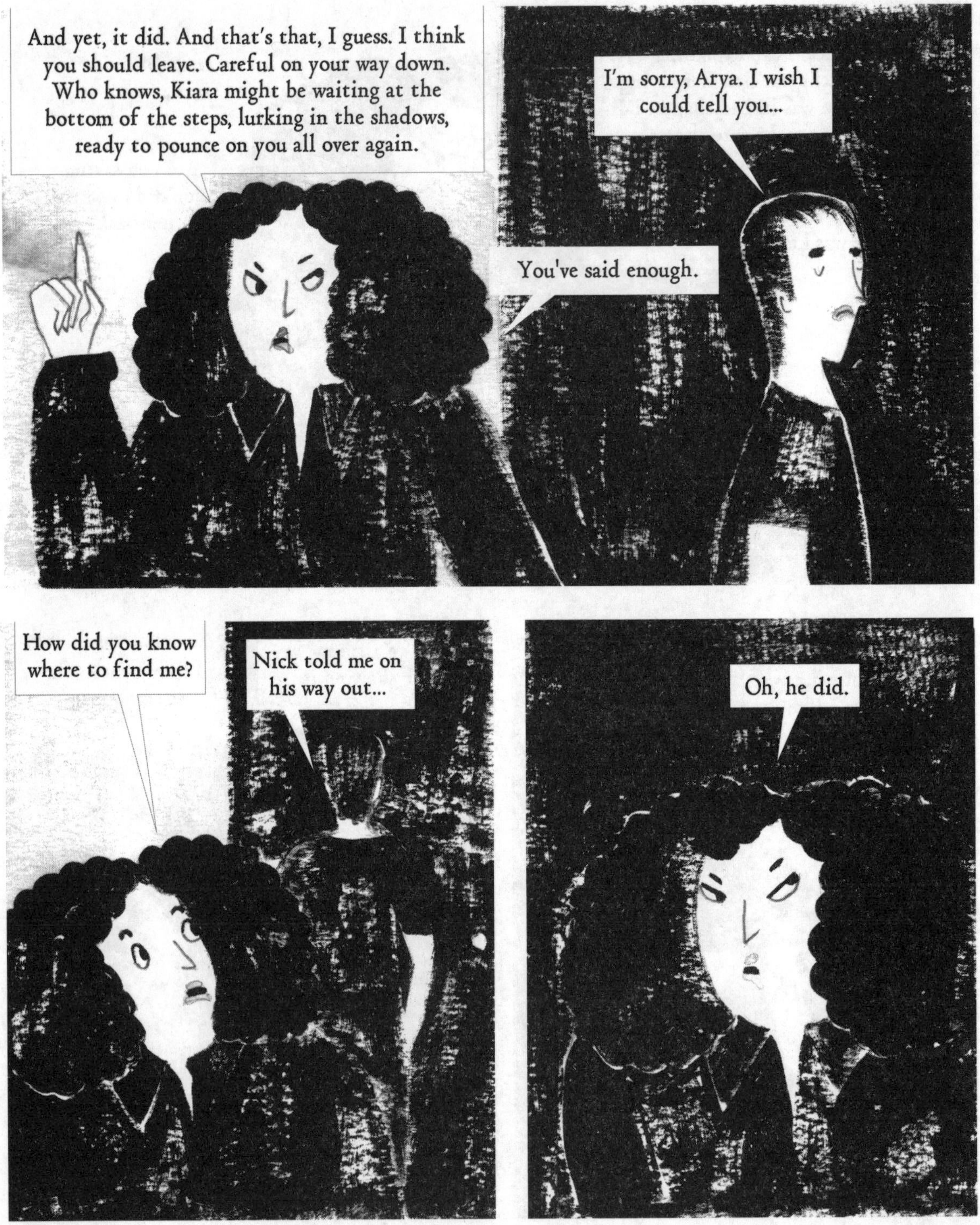
And yet, it did. And that's that, I guess. I think you should leave. Careful on your way down. Who knows, Kiara might be waiting at the bottom of the steps, lurking in the shadows, ready to pounce on you all over again.
I'm sorry, Arya. I wish I could tell you...
You've said enough.
How did you know where to find me?
Nick told me on his way out...
Oh, he did.

And suddenly, I was mad. At Nick. What was his problem? Why couldn't he leave things alone? Who the hell did he think he was? Freaking Agony Aunt? As if he didn't have issues in life. Was I poking my nose into them? So what business did he have meddling with my life? Acting like a go-between? Sending Yash up to my room? After I'd expressly stated I didn't want to have anything to do with him. God, I was livid.

I'd been angry a long time. At life in general. At my parents in particular. I'd held on to my anger for so long that it had become a part of me. That's the thing about rage, it consumes you from within, leaves you hollow. It's like a parasite that needs a host to live off. Once it infects you, it takes over your mind, impairs your judgement slowly but surely, until eventually you can't tell right from wrong, friend from foe.

But, I didn't know that then. All I knew was that I wanted to hit out at someone, everyone.

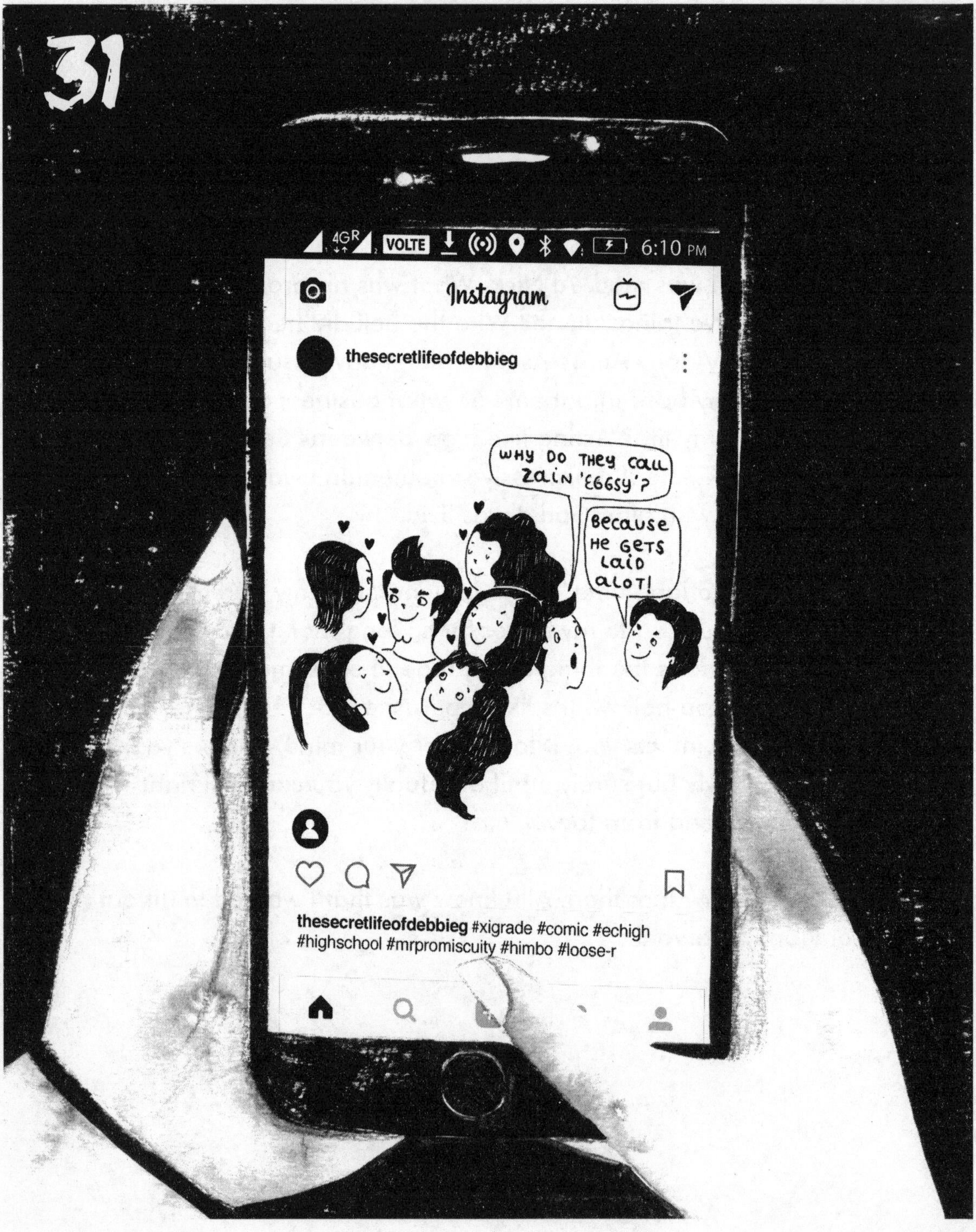
31
4GR
VOLTE
6:10 PM
Instagram
thesecretlifeofdebbieg
WHY DO THEY CALL ZAIN 'EGGSY'?
BECAUSE HE GETS LAID ALOT!
thesecretlifeofdebbieg #xigrade #comic #echigh #highschool #mrpromiscuity #himbo #loose-r

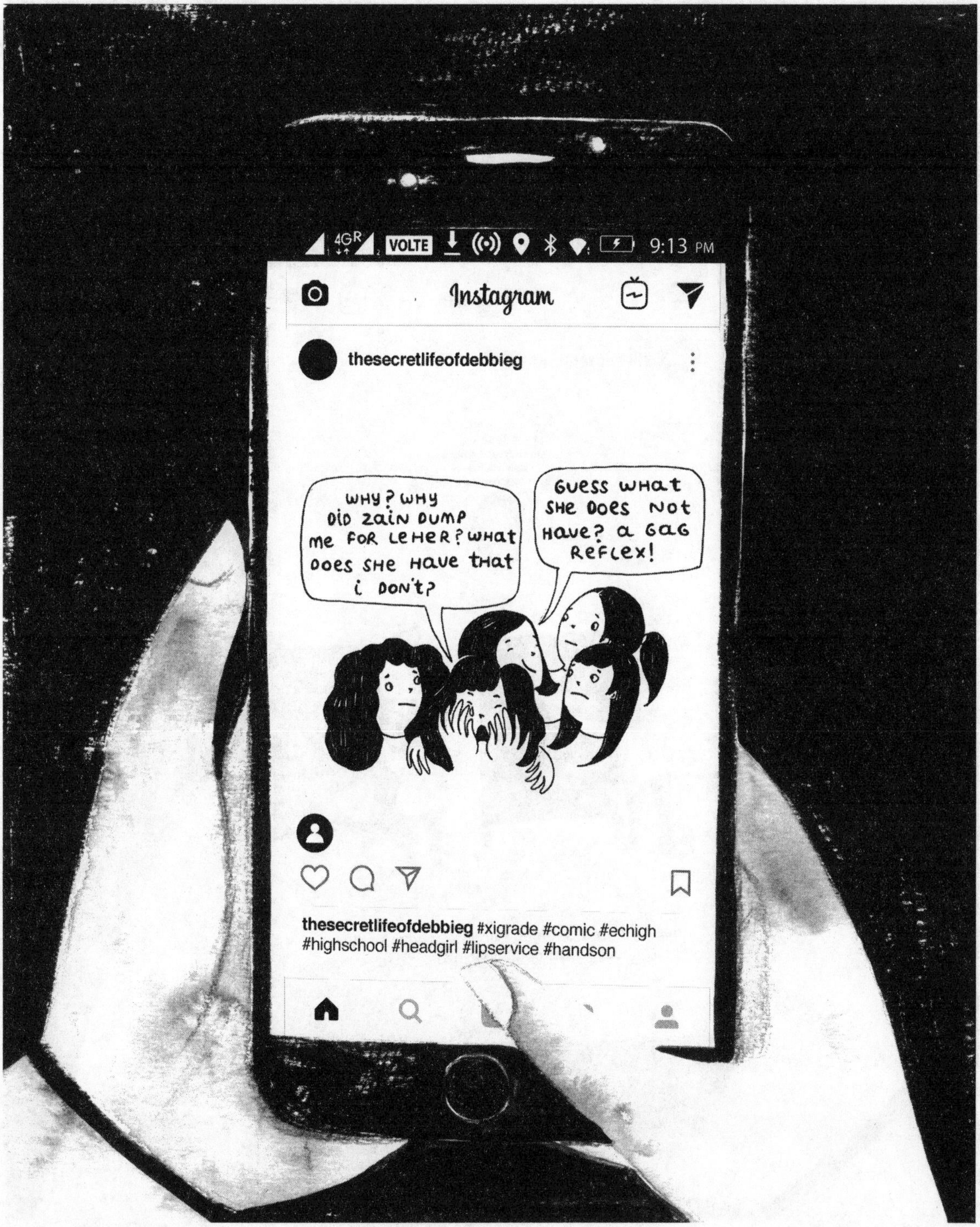
9:13 PM
Instagram
thesecretlifeofdebbieg
WHY? WHY DID ZAIN DUMP ME FOR LEHER? WHAT DOES SHE HAVE THAT I DON'T?
GUESS WHAT SHE DOES NOT HAVE? A GAG REFLEX!
thesecretlifeofdebbieg #xigrade #comic #echigh #highschool #headgirl #lipservice #handson

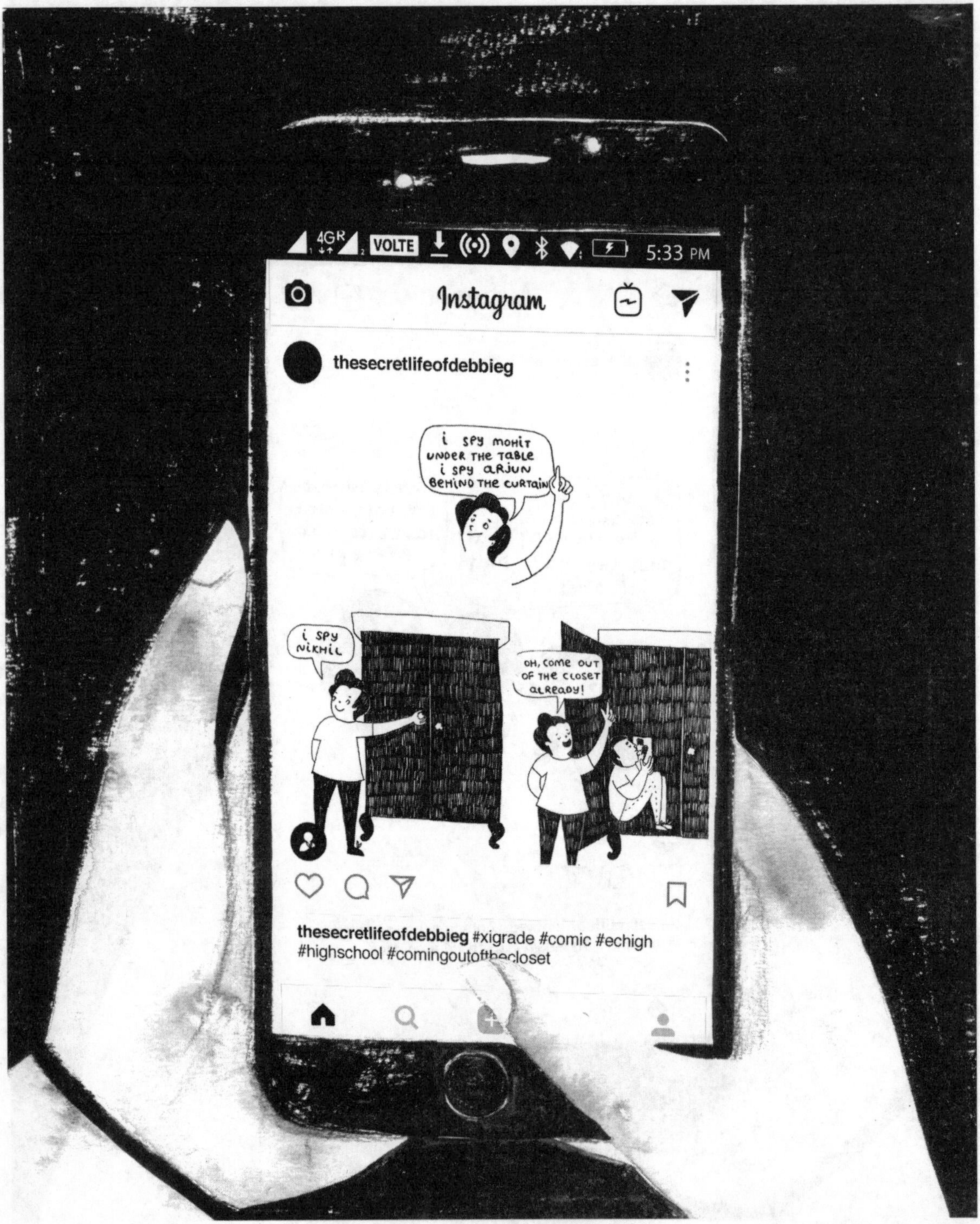
4GR VOLTE 5:33 PM
Instagram
thesecretlifeofdebbieg
i spy mohit under the table i spy arjun behind the curtain
i spy nikhil
oh, come out of the closet already!
thesecretlifeofdebbieg #xigrade #comic #echigh #highschool #comingoutofthecloset

Why did I do it? Why did I do that to my best friend? I wish I could say I don't know how it happened. Wish I could say I didn't mean to do it. Wish I could claim I was under the influence. Wish I could plead temporary insanity. Or blame it on Debbie G, on the desperate need to stay relevant. But I've promised to tell you the truth, the whole truth and nothing but the truth.

I was smarting from Yash's rejection. I was angry and unhappy and hurting inside.

It was only after I stared at my cell screen, at my post, at the little red heart and the rapidly escalating 'likes' below the comic strip that it hit me: the enormity of what I'd done. I was overcome with shame and guilt and remorse. Filled with self-loathing. Then, I wondered how Nick was feeling. Alone? Afraid? Abandoned? Betrayed? Devastated? All of the above? The way I'd felt when my folks split up? What was he thinking looking at the cartoon strip?

I felt sick to my stomach. Don't think I've ever hated myself more. I took the post down. Deleted the damn account. I was done, done with Debbie G, done proving a point to people, done settling scores with them. But it was too little, too late. The damage had been done. I reached for my cell, clicked on favourites, but my fingers refused to dial Nick. So I settled for having a tear-stained conversation with Nick – in my head. Where I—I'm ashamed to say—tried to justify my actions. "It was all done tongue-in-cheek. Don't think anyone will believe it. I deleted the post almost immediately. Don't think many people saw it. Are we good? Are we still friends? Can we please go back to being the way we were? I'm sorry, I'm sorry, I'm so sorry…"

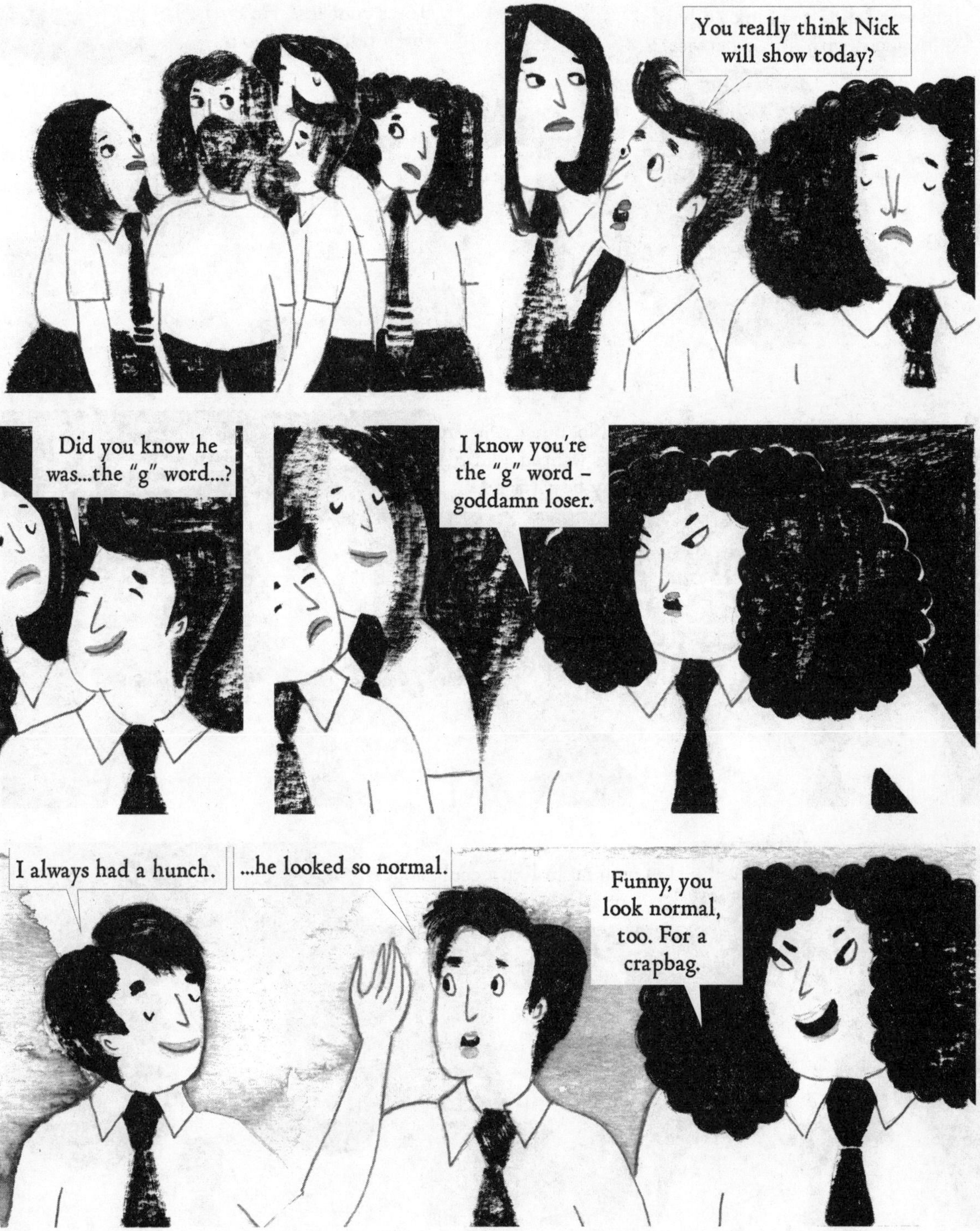
You really think Nick will show today?
Did you know he was...the "g" word...?
I know you're the "g" word – goddamn loser.
I always had a hunch.
...he looked so normal.
Funny, you look normal, too. For a crapbag.

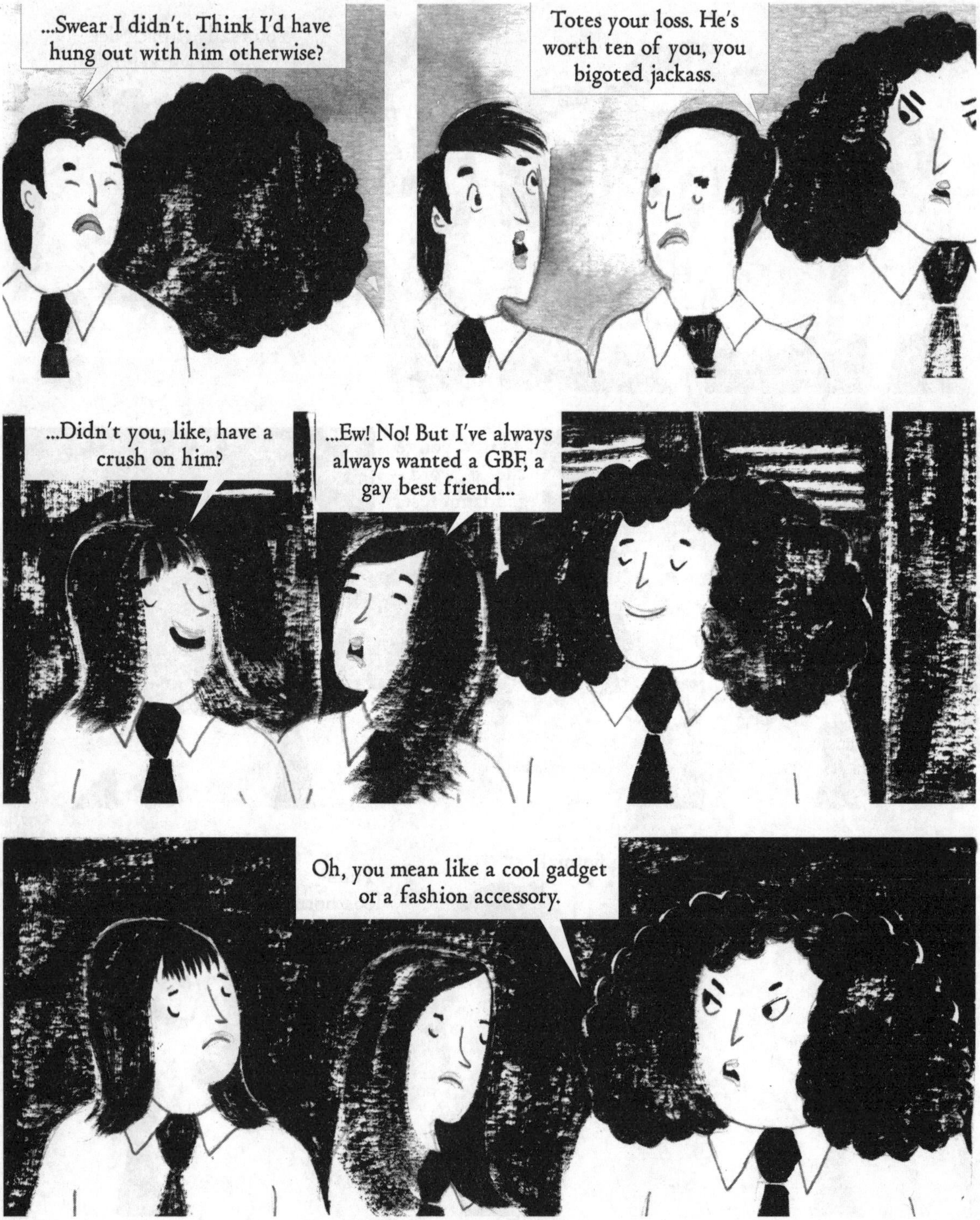
...Swear I didn't. Think I'd have hung out with him otherwise?
Totes your loss. He's worth ten of you, you bigoted jackass.
...Didn't you, like, have a crush on him?
...Ew! No! But I've always always wanted a GBF, a gay best friend...
Oh, you mean like a cool gadget or a fashion accessory.

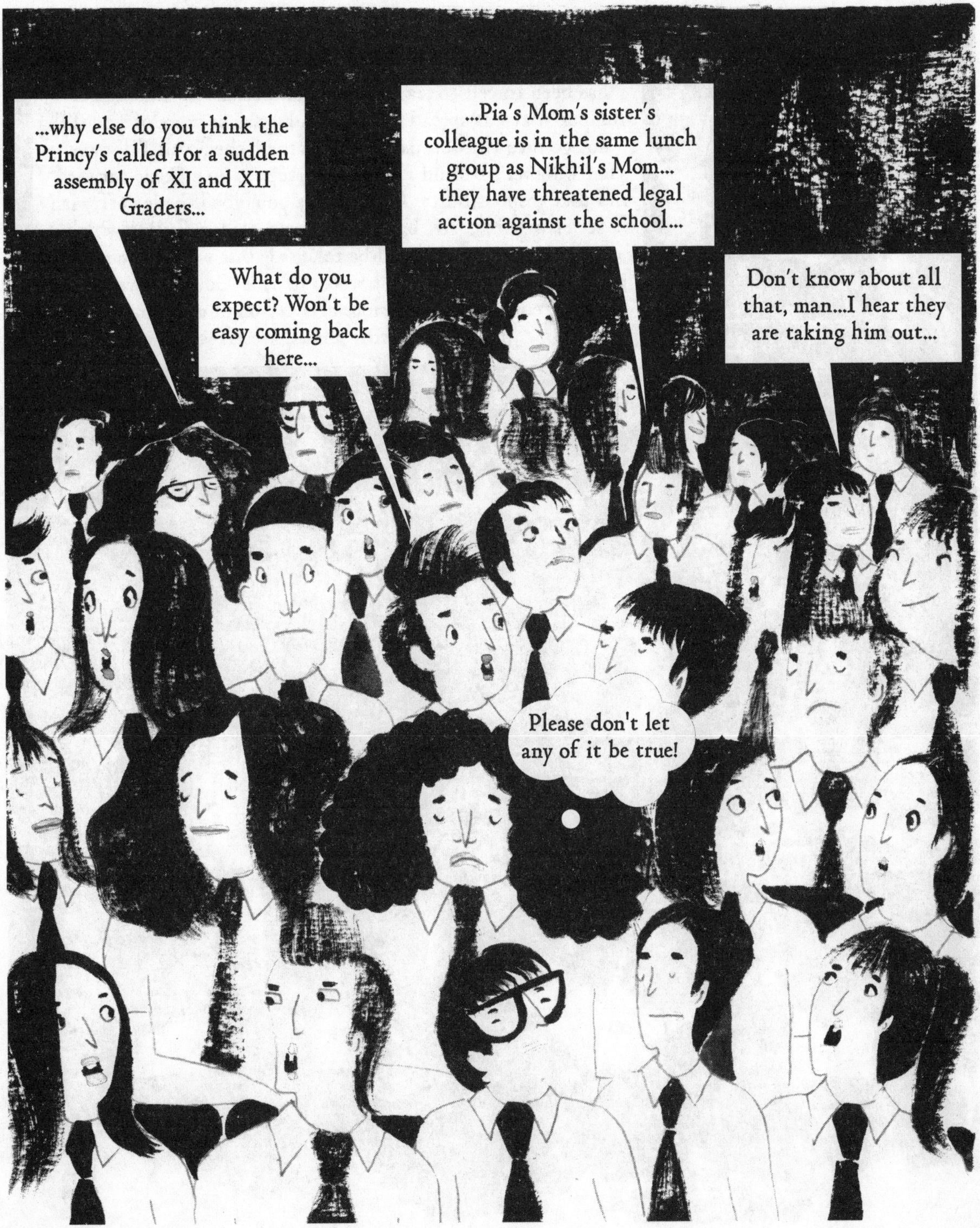
...why else do you think the Princy's called for a sudden assembly of XI and XII Graders...
What do you expect? Won't be easy coming back here...
...Pia's Mom's sister's colleague is in the same lunch group as Nikhil's Mom... they have threatened legal action against the school...
Don't know about all that, man...I hear they are taking him out...
Please don't let any of it be true!

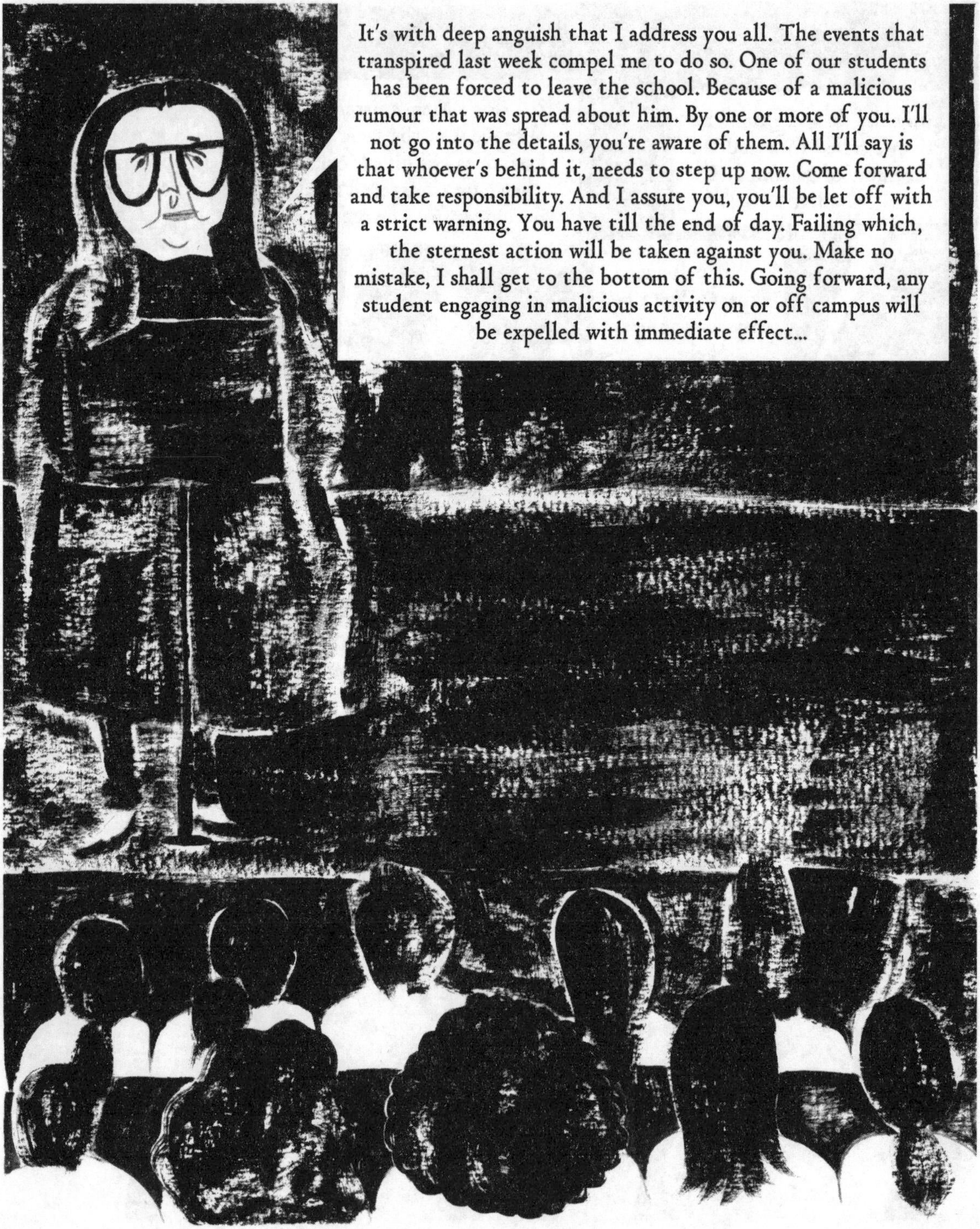
It's with deep anguish that I address you all. The events that transpired last week compel me to do so. One of our students has been forced to leave the school. Because of a malicious rumour that was spread about him. By one or more of you. I'll not go into the details, you're aware of them. All I'll say is that whoever's behind it, needs to step up now. Come forward and take responsibility. And I assure you, you'll be let off with a strict warning. You have till the end of day. Failing which, the sternest action will be taken against you. Make no mistake, I shall get to the bottom of this. Going forward, any student engaging in malicious activity on or off campus will be expelled with immediate effect...

EPILOGUE

If the Princy and the teachers and the students were hoping for a hand to go flying up in the air, they were sorely disappointed. Don't get me wrong. I wasn't worried about getting expelled. Nor was I scared of facing the backlash of the Invincibles. Or afraid of being the Person Most Hated in school. No one could hate me more than I hated myself. It's just that I didn't want to be let off that easily. I'd outed my best friend online. I was going to do the same to Debbie G.

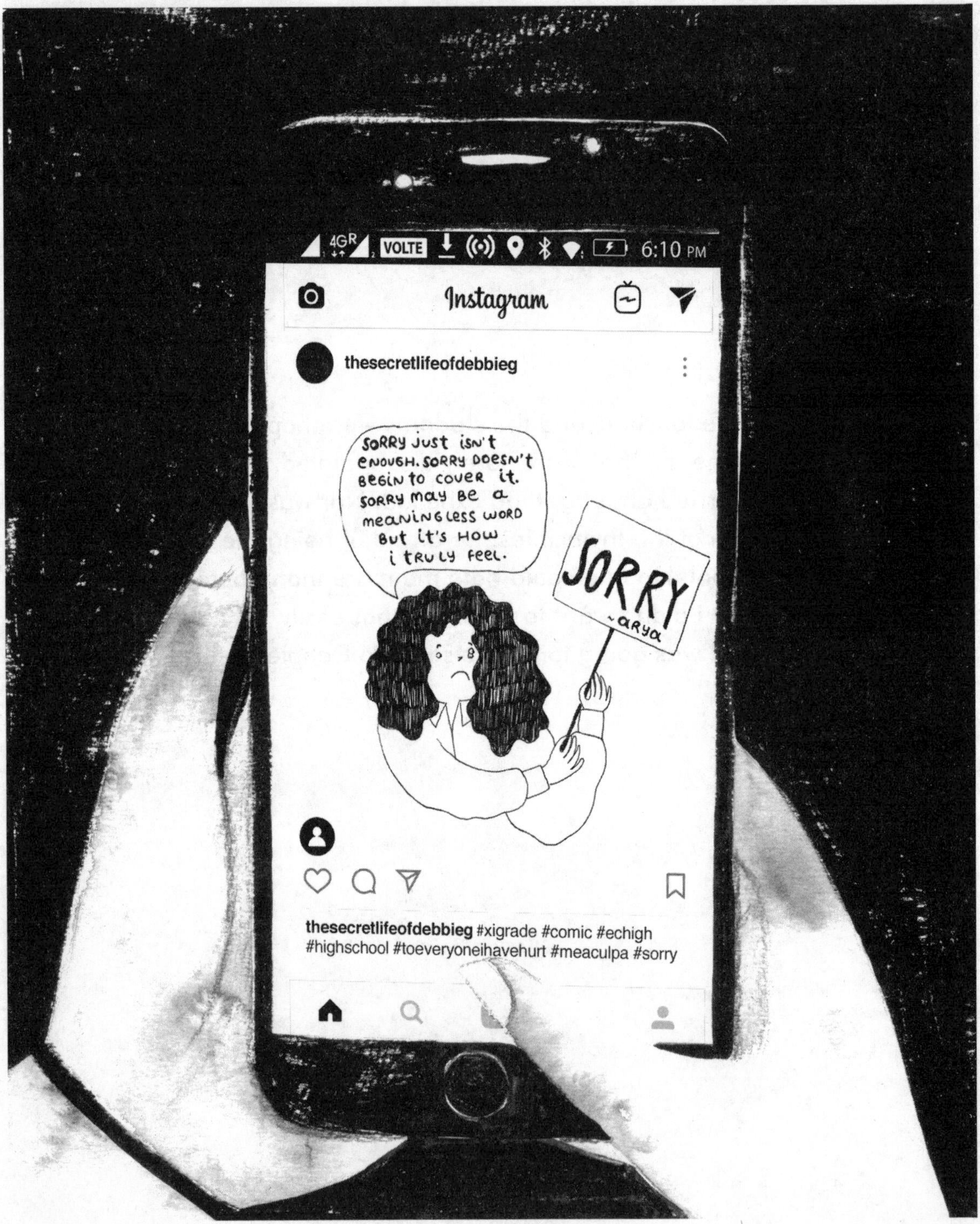
4GR VOLTE 6:10 PM
Instagram
thesecretlifeofdebbieg
SORRY JUST ISN'T ENOUGH. SORRY DOESN'T BEGIN TO COVER IT. SORRY MAY BE A MEANINGLESS WORD BUT IT'S HOW I TRULY FEEL.
SORRY ~ARYA
thesecretlifeofdebbieg #xigrade #comic #echigh #highschool #toeveryoneihavehurt #meaculpa #sorry

Told you she'd be here. You thought you could mess with us? WITH US?
We can drag your sorry ass to the Princy—

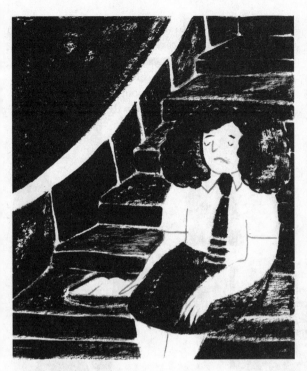

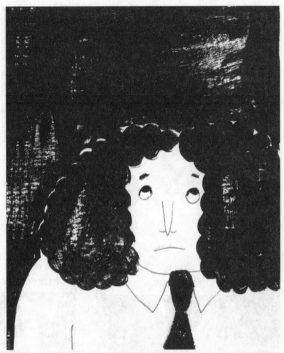

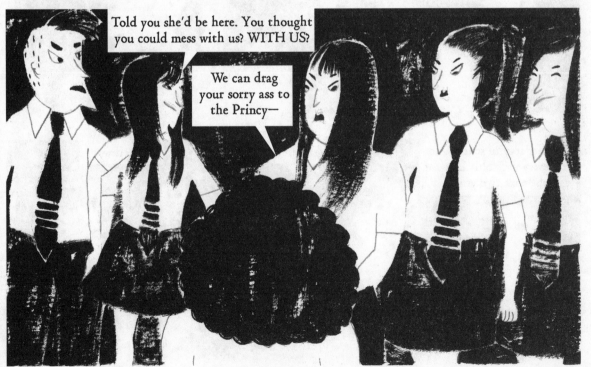

Do what you want. I don't care.
How could you do it? To me? Your family? Don't you have any feelings?
Shoo, your face will get blotchy...
I say we report her right away.
Yeah, let's get her kicked out of school.
What good would that be? She'll get away scot free.
Let her stay in school and top everyone's Shit List for the next two years.
Sounds good.
Shall we?

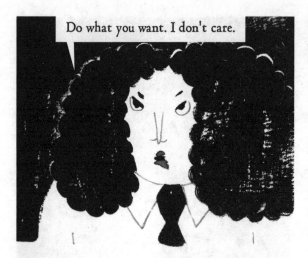

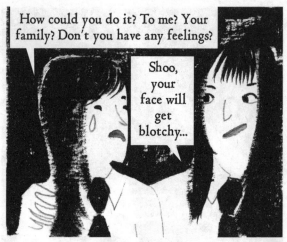

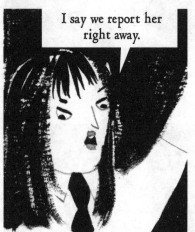

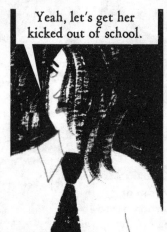

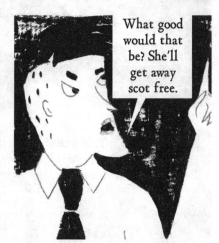

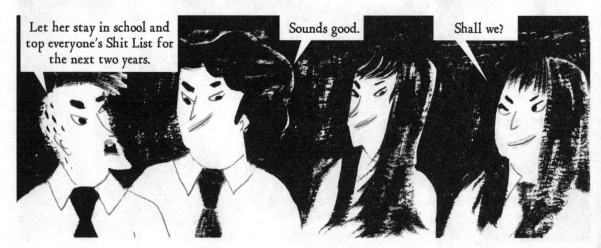

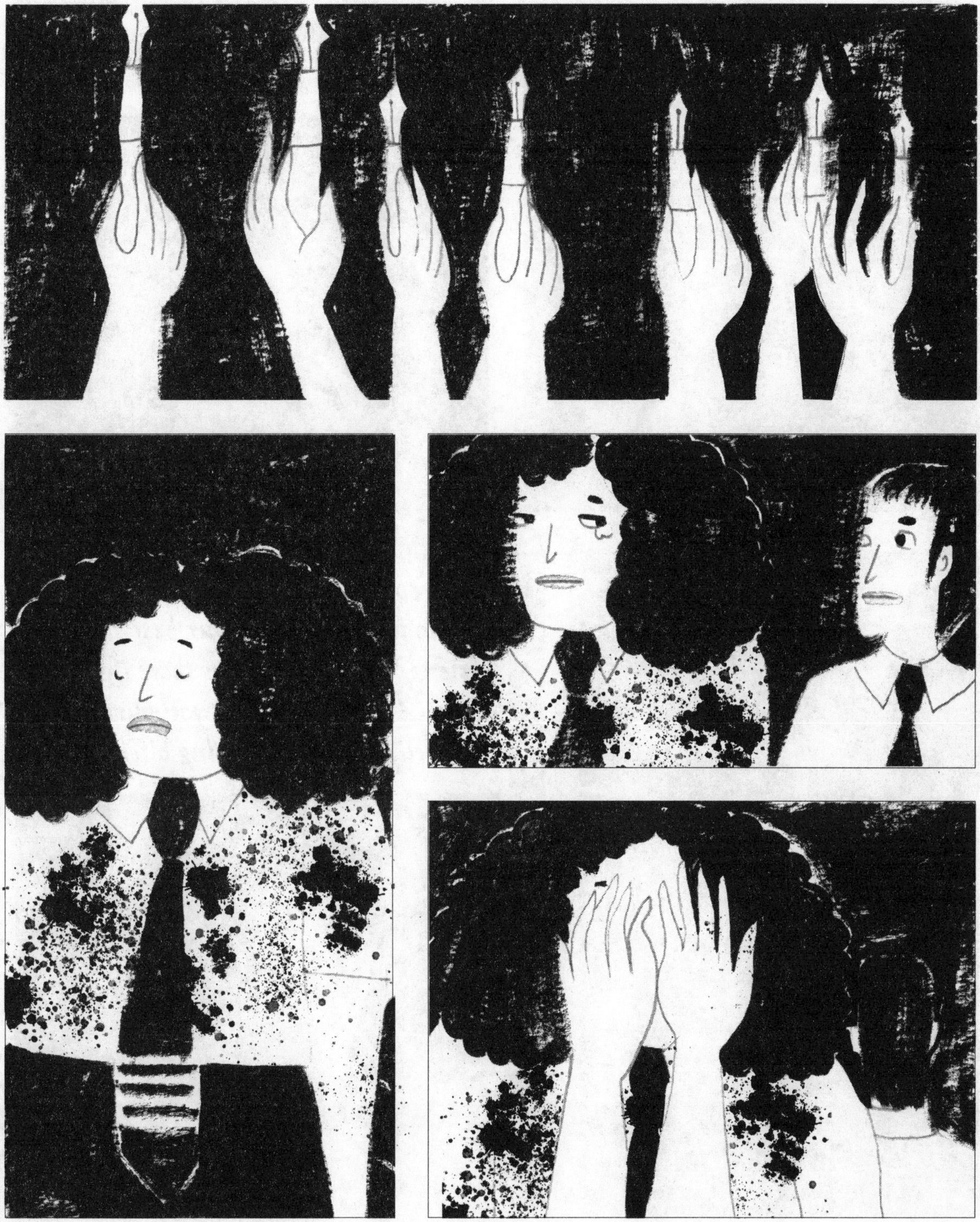

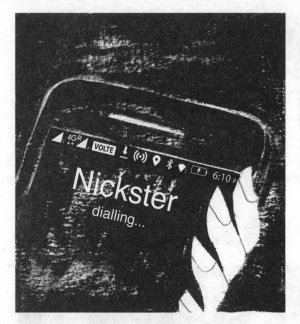

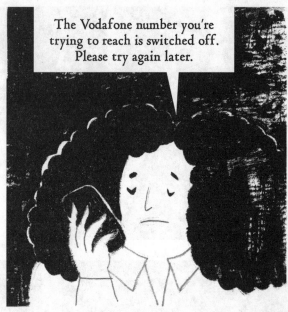

VOLTE
6:10
Nickster
dialling...
The Vodafone number you're trying to reach is switched off. Please try again later.
VOLTE
6:10
Rucksack
mobile
How could you? How could you do it to him? To your best friend? He was always there for you. And you...I hope you burn in hell, you backstabbing bitch!

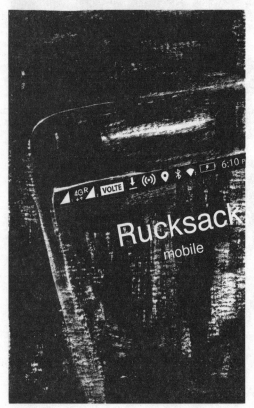

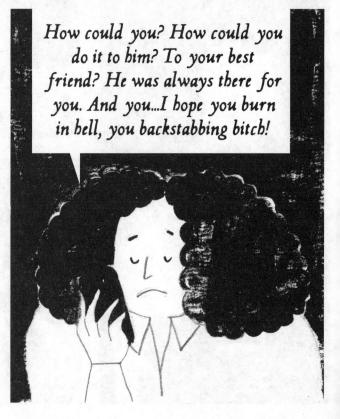

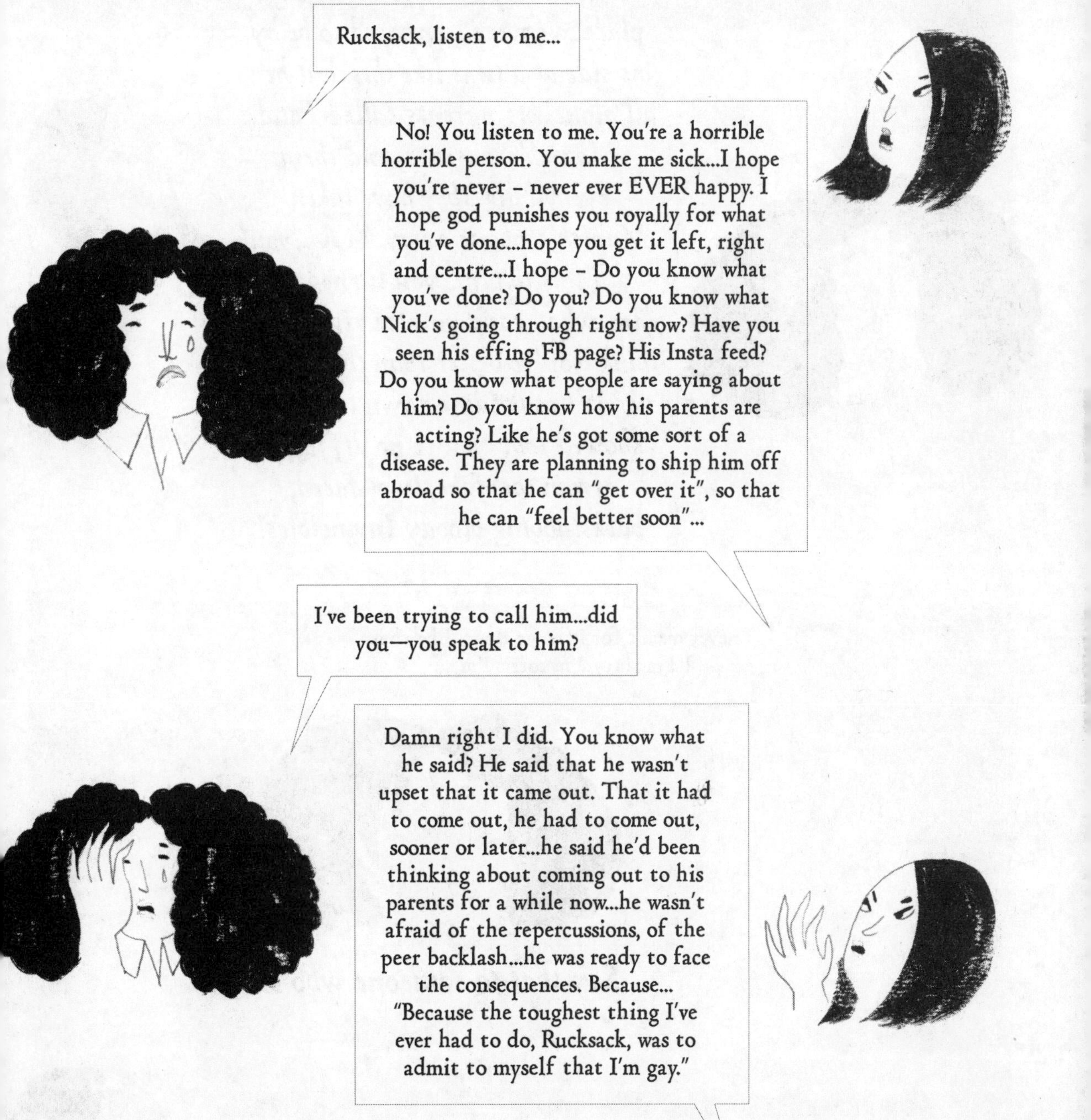
Rucksack, listen to me...
No! You listen to me. You're a horrible horrible person. You make me sick...I hope you're never – never ever EVER happy. I hope god punishes you royally for what you've done...hope you get it left, right and centre...I hope – Do you know what you've done? Do you? Do you know what Nick's going through right now? Have you seen his effing FB page? His Insta feed? Do you know what people are saying about him? Do you know how his parents are acting? Like he's got some sort of a disease. They are planning to ship him off abroad so that he can "get over it", so that he can "feel better soon"...
I've been trying to call him...did you—you speak to him?
Damn right I did. You know what he said? He said that he wasn't upset that it came out. That it had to come out, he had to come out, sooner or later...he said he'd been thinking about coming out to his parents for a while now...he wasn't afraid of the repercussions, of the peer backlash...he was ready to face the consequences. Because... "Because the toughest thing I've ever had to do, Rucksack, was to admit to myself that I'm gay."

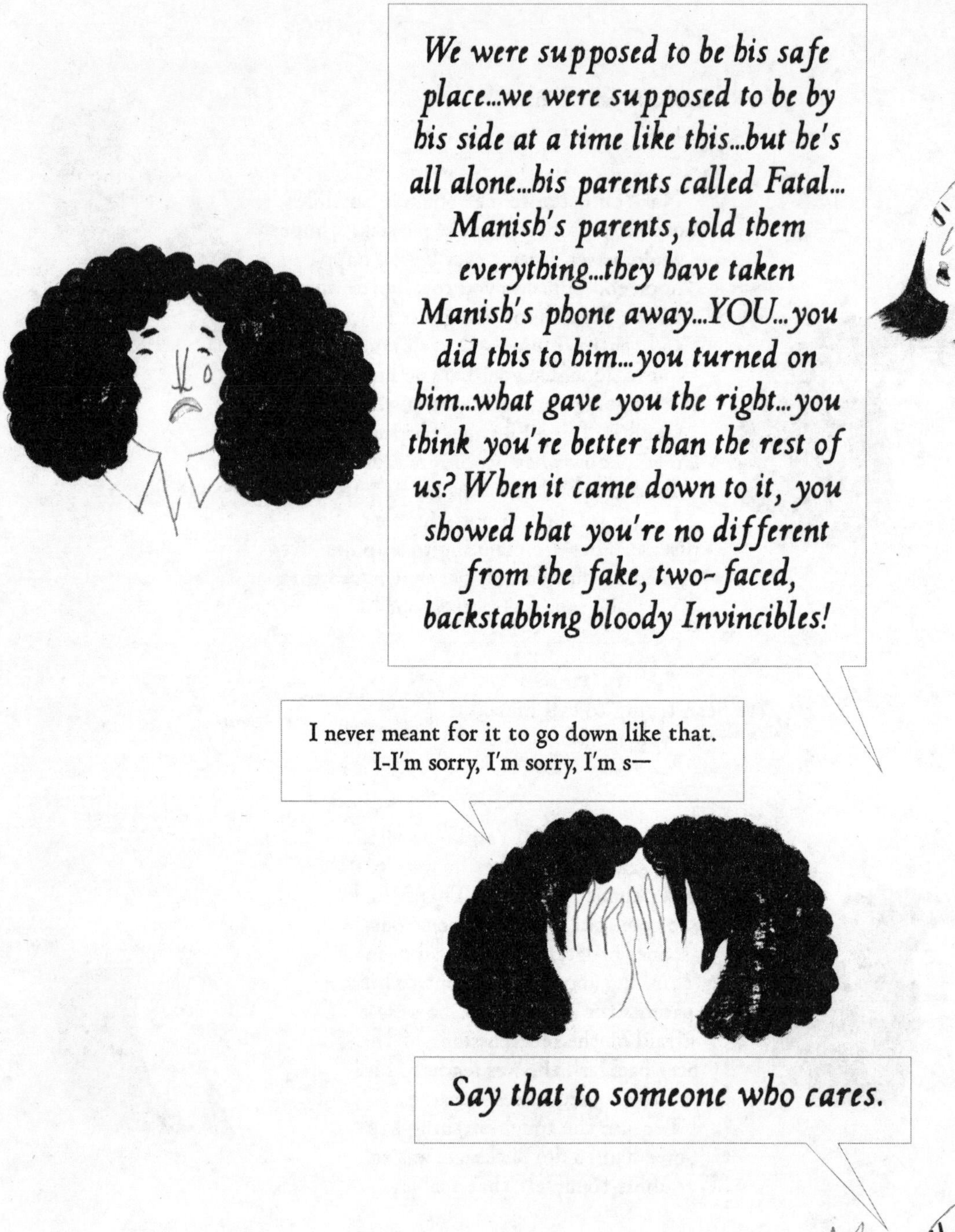
We were supposed to be his safe place...we were supposed to be by his side at a time like this...but he's all alone...his parents called Fatal... Manish's parents, told them everything...they have taken Manish's phone away...YOU...you did this to him...you turned on him...what gave you the right...you think you're better than the rest of us? When it came down to it, you showed that you're no different from the fake, two-faced, backstabbing bloody Invincibles!
I never meant for it to go down like that. I-I'm sorry, I'm sorry, I'm s—
Say that to someone who cares.

That was a year ago. The last time we spoke, Rucksack.

Things really went to shit after that. Not 'cos everyone at school hated me. Not 'cos I'd no one to talk to. Not 'cos Yash started seeing Kiara. I felt I deserved all that. And more. I felt I had to atone. I felt I had to do something to make up for what I'd done. And then I came across this article online. About a non-profit organisation. They believed in bringing about social change through art – perhaps you've heard of them? Art Heals Hearts. Their campaign on gender inclusivity had just gone viral... Well, I'd used my art to destroy everything I'd ever loved...I thought if I could use it to make a positive difference, if I could touch even one life... Volunteering for them's the best thing I've ever done. Second best thing, actually. The best was making friends with you and Nick.

So, anyway. I know you hate me. Guess what, I hate me more. I don't expect Nick to forgive me. 'Cos I'll never be able to forgive myself. But if I could just talk to him. Once. I'm not asking for a second chance. I know I don't deserve it. But if I could talk to him, tell him everything that I've just told you... It would mean a lot to me, Rucksack. I've tried reaching him, but he's changed his number, deleted all his social media accounts. I know you've moved base to Mumbai, but I'm sure you're in touch with him. I'm not asking you to tell me where he is or share his contact deets, but if I could just apologise to Nick—

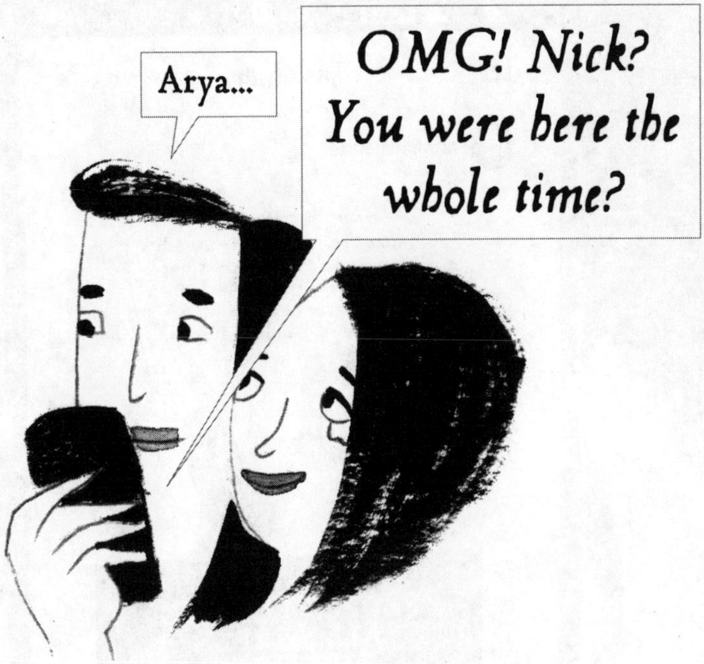
Arya...
OMG! Nick? You were here the whole time?

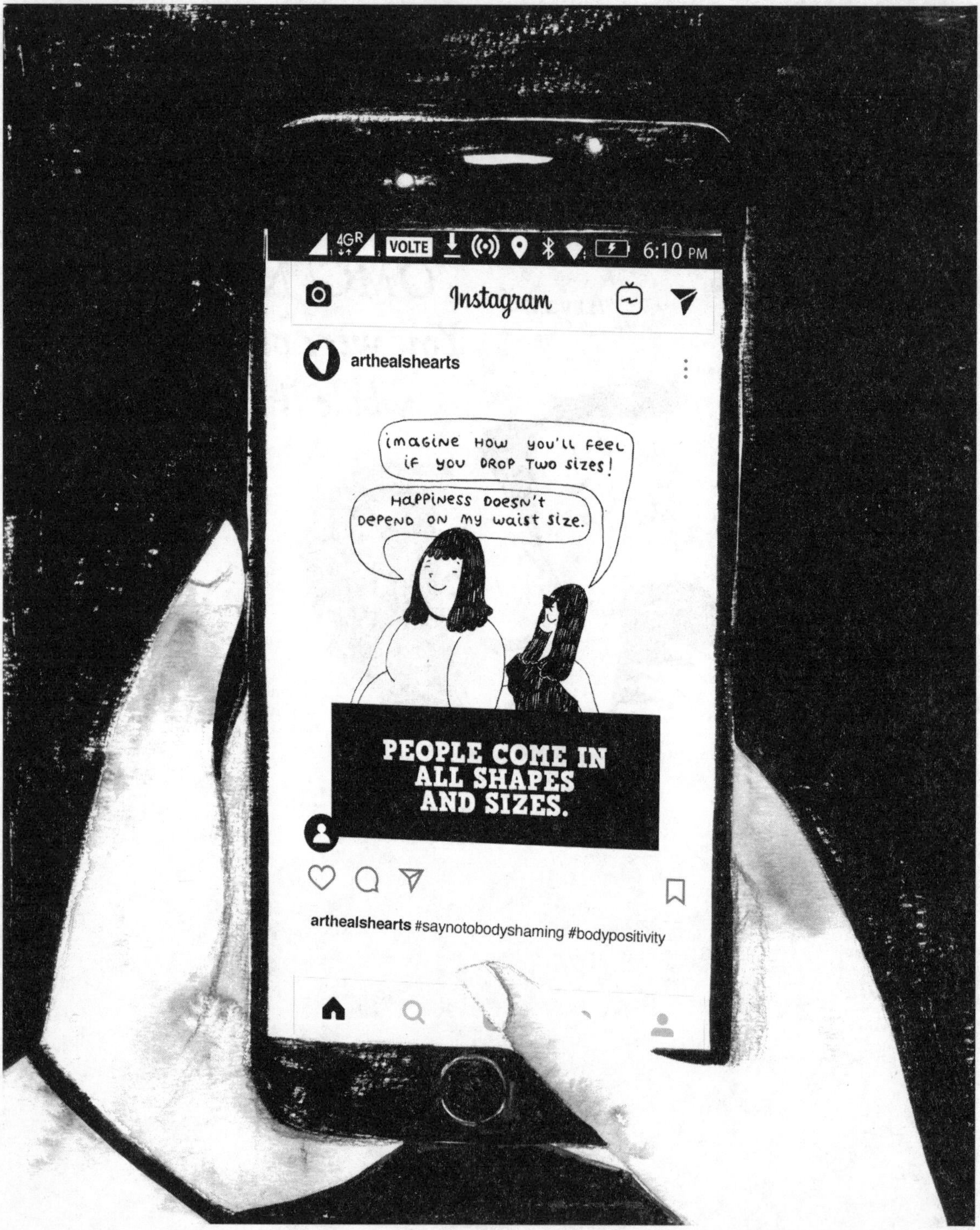
4GR VOLTE 6:10 PM
Instagram
arthealshearts
imagine how you'll feel if you drop two sizes!
Happiness doesn't depend on my waist size.
PEOPLE COME IN ALL SHAPES AND SIZES.
arthealshearts #saynotobodyshaming #bodypositivity

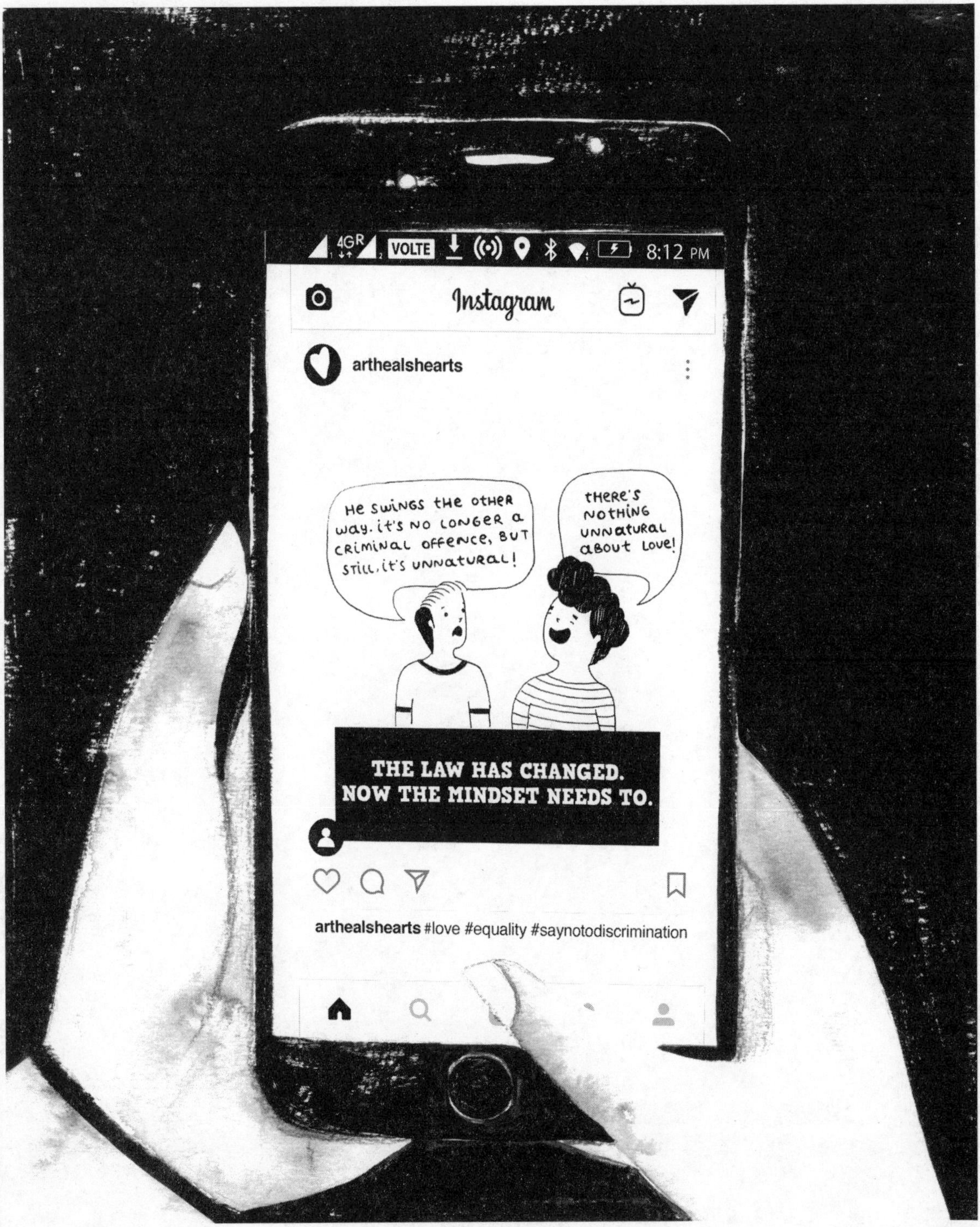
4GR VOLTE 8:12 PM
Instagram
arthealshearts
He swings the other way. it's no longer a criminal offence, but still, it's unnatural!
there's nothing unnatural about love!
THE LAW HAS CHANGED.
NOW THE MINDSET NEEDS TO.
arthealshearts #love #equality #saynotodiscrimination

Vibha Batra is an author, graphic novelist, advertising consultant, poet, lyricist, translator, playwright, travel writer, columnist and creative writing facilitator. She writes for toddlers, tweens, teens, adults, and senior citizens. She can be found in quaint cafes in Chennai, hunched over her laptop, writing away like a human possessed or on FB: facebook/vibhy.batra and Instagram: @vibhybatra. She just published her 16th book (but hey, who's counting).

Kalyani Ganapathy enjoys illustrating fiction and non-fiction picture books. When she's not making picture books she's busy planting in her garden or learning about holistic health. Her books include A is for Anaar, Hambreelmai's Loom, Janice goes to Chinatown, Amrita Sher-Gil - Rebel with a Paintbrush and The Song at the Heart of the River. You can follow her on Instagram @ganapathy_kalyani and see more of her work at www.kalyani-ganapathy.com.

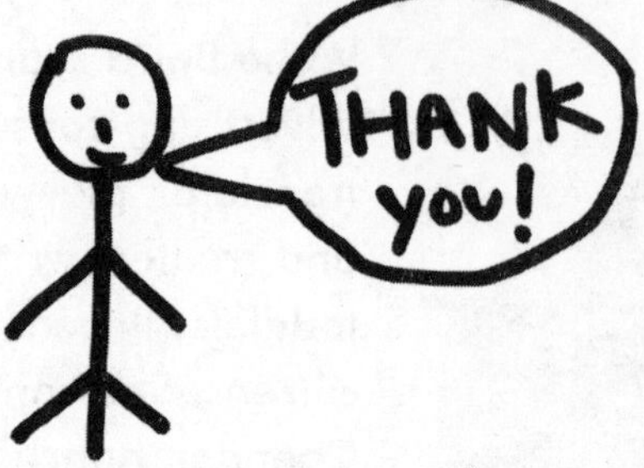
THANK you!

To my family: What's the first rule of Fight Club?

To Tina: Not to apportion blame or anything (okay, maybe a little), but merci beaucoup for getting me to write a graphic novel and cheering me on along the way.

To Kalyani: (Didn't mean to steal your thunder with this strip, you're the best.) Danke schon for making Debbie and Co. come alive with your magic.

To Nayantara: For catching everything I missed and culling every typo that was invisible to my naked eye. Grazie, Hawkeye.

To Team HarperCollins: For the brilliant cover, the fab marketing plan (there is a marketing plan, right?) and everything in between.

To my friends, well-wishers and readers: Gracias and lo siento. Another book review request coming your way.

To HP: Qathlo. Kirimvose. M'athchomaroon.